實戰新多益高分必備

狠準五回1000題黃金試題

作者 Eduwill 語學研究所　譯者 黃詩韻／劉嘉珮／莊曼淳

如何下載 **MP3** 音檔

❶ **寂天雲 APP 聆聽**：掃描書上 QR Code 下載「寂天雲－英日語學習隨身聽」APP。加入會員後，用 APP 內建掃描器再次掃描書上 QR Code，即可使用 APP 聆聽音檔。

❷ **官網下載音檔**：請上「寂天閱讀網」（www.icosmos.com.tw），註冊會員／登入後，搜尋本書，進入本書頁面，點選「MP3 下載」下載音檔，存於電腦等其他播放器聆聽使用。

實戰新多益高分必備

狠準五回1000題黃金試題

作者 Eduwill 語學研究所
譯者 黃詩韻／劉嘉珮／莊曼淳
編輯 林明佑
校對 郭軒安
主編 丁宥暄
內文排版 林書玉／蔡怡柔
封面設計 林書玉
製程管理 洪巧玲
出版者 寂天文化事業股份有限公司
發行人 黃朝萍
電話 +886-(0)2-2365-9739
傳真 +886-(0)2-2365-9835
網址 www.icosmos.com.tw
讀者服務 onlineservice@icosmos.com.tw
出版日期 2023 年 8 月 初版一刷

郵撥帳號 1998620-0 寂天文化事業股份有限公司
訂書金額未滿 1000 元，請外加運費 100 元。
〔若有破損，請寄回更換，謝謝。〕

國家圖書館出版品預行編目（CIP）資料

實戰新多益高分必備：狠準五回 1000 題黃金試題
(寂天雲隨身聽 APP 版)/Eduwill 語學研究所著；
黃詩韻，劉嘉珮，莊曼淳譯．-- 初版．--
[臺北市]：寂天文化事業股份有限公司，2023.07
面；公分
ISBN 978-626-300-196-1(平裝)
1.CST: 多益測驗
805.1895 112009498

目錄

前言

多益是結構和類型都很明確的考試，因此只要具備一定的基礎，並且持續練習模擬試題，提高對題目的熟悉感，就能獲得高分。所以，盡可能多練習模擬試題並複習錯誤的題目，藉此補強弱點是相當重要的。

然而，在練習模擬試題時，比起題海戰術，更重要的是解決「好的問題」。考生需要**練習難度適中並且和考古題相近的題型**，才能正確診斷自己的程度和弱點，並依此建立學習計畫。

本書詳細分析近年考題的出題趨勢，並經過資深多益研究員和母語人士團隊的反覆研究，透過多次審查和各種程度的考生試測後，才研發出此本絕佳的模擬試題。因此，本書值得各位考生信賴，相信使用本書能讓你應考過程事半功倍。

本實戰題庫不僅提供良好的練習題，還特別著重於測驗後的檢討與複習。在解題之後，可以使用附錄中提供的「核心字彙表」，確實熟悉重要字彙與常用片語。即使起初測驗分數不如預期，只要充分利用這些內容，逐漸掌握不熟悉的字彙和片語，很快就能成功考取目標分數。

聽力 & 閱讀金選戰略

聽力

第一大題	照片描述（6 題）	本大題是測驗看圖作答的能力，可藉由以下方式來練習：找一些照片來看，並思索針對這些照片，可能會問哪些問題。
第二大題	應答問題（25 題）	本大題是測驗對問句的理解，作答時請特別注意問句開頭的疑問詞（Who、What、Where、When、Why、How 為六大疑問詞），可提示需要什麼樣的答案。
第三大題	簡短對話（39 題）	本大題會先播放簡短的對話，再測驗你對於對話的理解程度。本大題訣竅是先看問題、答案選項和圖表，然後再聽對話內容，這樣你在聽的時候會比較知道要注意哪方面的資訊。
第四大題	獨白（30 題）	本大題是聽力測驗中最具挑戰性的部分，平時就需要多聽英文演講和廣播等來加強聽力。

Look at the example item below. Now listen to the four statements.

(A) They're pointing at the monitor.
(B) They're looking at the document.
(C) They're talking on the phone.
(D) They're sitting by the table.

Statement (B), They're "looking at the document," is the best description of the picture, so you should select answer (B) and mark it on your answer sheet.

Photographs I 第一大題：照片描述

第一大題

指示：本大題的每一小題，在測驗本上都會印有一張圖片，考生會聽到針對照片所做的四段描述，然後選出最符合照片內容的適當描述，接著在答案卡上找到題目編號，將對應的答案選項圓圈塗黑。描述的內容不會印在測驗本上，而且只會播放一次。

（A）他們正指著螢幕。
（B）他們正在看文件。
（C）他們正在講電話。
（D）他們正坐在桌子旁。

描述 (B)「他們正在看文件」是最符合本圖的描述，因此你應該選擇選項 (B)，並在答案卡上劃記。

高分戰略

❶ 如照片以人物為主，人物的動作特徵是答題關鍵。

照片題中有 7–8 成的題目是以人物為照片主角，這些照片時常會測驗人的動作特徵，因此要先預想相關的動作用語。舉例來說，如照片中有一個人在走路，就要立刻想到和走路有關的動詞，如 walking、strolling 等，聽題目的時候會更容易抓到線索。

❷ 如照片以事物為主，事物的狀態或位置是答題關鍵。

如照片以事物為中心，要特別注意其狀態或位置。須預先熟習表示「位置」時常用的介系詞，還有表現「狀態」的片語。舉例來說，如要表達「在⋯⋯旁邊」時，next to、by、beside、near 等用語可能會出現，最好一起背誦。另外，也須事先熟悉多益中常出現的事物名稱。

❸ 出人意料的問題時常出現。

與一般題型不同，題目的考點可能會靈活變化。舉例來說，照片是一個小孩用手指著掛在牆上的畫，按照常理，會想到是要考人物的動作，要回答 pointing 之類的動詞。但有時正確答案會是掛在牆上的畫（The picture has been hung on the wall.）。所以出現人的照片時，除了注意人的動作，周邊事物也必須稍微觀察。

II Response 第二大題：應答問題

第二大題

指示：考生會聽到一個問題句或敘述句，以及三句回應的英語。題目只會播放一次，而且不會印在測驗本上。請選出最符合擺放內容的答案，在答案卡上將 (A)、(B)、(C) 或 (D) 的答案選項塗黑。

高分戰略

❶ 新制加考推測語意的考題。

PART 2 少了五題，但命題方式變得更靈活，難度也隨之提升。新制多了推測語意的考題，考生必須根據全文判斷語意才能找出答案。聽完此類題目後，須迅速推敲並挑出正確的答案，才不會錯失下一題的解題機會。請務必勤加練習，熟悉此類題型的模式。

❷ 題目最前面的疑問詞至關重要。

Part 2 經常出現以疑問詞（Who、What、Where、When、Why、How）開頭的疑問句只要聽清楚句首的疑問詞，幾乎就能找到這類題型的正確答案，所以平常要培養對疑問詞的敏銳度。

❸ 善用消去法縮小選擇範圍。

Part 2 是最多陷阱的大題，所以事先統整陷阱題可以事半功倍。舉例來說，若疑問句題目以疑問詞開頭，那幾乎可以判斷用 yes 或 no 回答的選項不可選，可以先將其刪除。另外，若題目出現的單字在選項中再次出現，或出現與題目中字彙發音類似的單字，如 copy 與 coffee，也是常見陷阱題。在準備時可將具代表性的陷阱題整理好，以提升本大題的答對率。

❹ **常考片語**要熟背。

多益中常出現的用語或片語，最好整組背起來。舉例來說，疑問句「Why don't you . . . ?」是表達「做……好嗎？」的提議句型，而非詢問原因。

III Conversations 第三大題：簡短對話

第三大題

指示：考生會聽到一些兩個人或多人的對話，並根據對話所聽到的內容，回答三個問題。請選出最符合播放內容的答案，在答案卡上將 (A)、(B)、(C) 或 (D) 的答案選項塗黑。這些對話只會播放一次，而且不會印在測驗本上。

高分戰略

❶ **有策略地聽**比全部聽更高效。

Part 3 是兩到三人的對話，本大題作答時並非記下全部內容，而是事先快速瀏覽題目和圖表，判斷須注意哪些線索，在聽對話時重點記下與題目對應的資訊。

❷ **聽對話**與**找答案**要同步進行。

光是事先掃過題目，而沒有邊聽邊找答案，仍無法達到高答對率，因為有些細微末節聽過後很容易忘記。邊聽邊作答的能力於新制多益中更為重要，因為新增了角色性別及彼此關係更為複雜的三人對話題，所以避免聽完後混淆的方式則是立刻作答，須在平時就不斷積累。

❸ 對話**開頭**不可漏聽。

詢問職業、場所或主題的問題在 Part 3 中經常出現，這些問題的答案時常會出現在對話開頭。不僅如此，掌握對話開頭也可幫助推敲接下來會出現什麼內容，在解其他題目時更為順利。

IV Talks 第四大題：簡短獨白

第四大題

指示：考生會聽到好幾段單人獨白，並根據每一段話的內容，回答三個問題。請選出符合播放內容的答案，在答案卡上將 (A)、(B)、(C) 或 (D) 的答案選項塗黑。每一段話只會播放一次，而且不會印在測驗本上。

高分戰略

❶ 要事先整理好**常考的詢問內容**。

不同於 Part 3，本大題談話種類較固定，像是交通廣播、天氣預報、旅行導覽、電話留言等的題目經常出現，且內容大同小異。所以只需要按這些談話種類，整理出常考的問題類型即可。

❷ 具備**背景知識**可加快答題速度。

Part 4 的談話種類常依循固定模式。舉例來說，若是機場的情境談話，飛機誤點或取消是最典型的情境，最可能的原因則是天候不佳，這就是多益的背景知識——不一定要全部聽懂，光看題目也能找出最接近正確答案的選項。平時多累積背景知識很重要。

❸ 訓練找出**重點線索**的能力。

Part 4 和 Part 3 一樣，每個題組有三個問題，所以同樣要養成先掃描過題目和表格的習慣。由於 Part 4 的談話內容更長，聽完全部內容後再答題很容易會有所遺漏。因此可以先找出題目的要點，利用背景知識，在試題本上推敲正確答案。不像 Part 3，Part 4 的答案通常會按照題目的順序，一一出現在對話中，答案逐題出現的機率很高。

閱讀

第五大題	句子填空 （30 題）	本大題字彙和文法能力最重要。其所考的字彙大都跟職場或商業有關，平時就要多背誦單字。
第六大題	段落填空 （16 題）	除了單字，也需要將比較長的片語或子句，甚至是一整個句子填入空格中，掌握整篇文章來龍去脈才能找出答案。
第七大題	單篇文章理解 （29 題） 多篇文章理解 （25 題）	本大題比較困難，須熟習經常出現的商業文章，像是公告或備忘錄等。平時就要訓練自己能夠快速閱讀文章和圖表，並且能夠找出主要的內容。當然，在本大題字彙量越多，越可快速理解文意。

Incomplete Sentences 第五大題：單句填空

第五大題

指示：本測驗中的每一個句子皆缺少一個單字或詞組，在句子下方會列出四個答案選項，請選出最適合的答案來完成句子，並在答案卡上將 (A)、(B)、(C) 或 (D) 的答案選項塗黑。

高分戰略

❶ 要先看**選項**。

試題主要考句型、字彙、文法以及慣用語。要先看選項，掌握是上述的哪一個，便能更快速解題。所以要練習判斷題型，並正確掌握各題型的解題技巧。

❷ 找出**意思最接近**的單字。

Part 5 是填空選擇題，若能找出和空格關係最密切的關鍵字彙，便能快速又正確地解題。所以要練習分析句子的結構，並找出和空格關係最密切的字彙作為答題線索。一般來說，空格前後的單字就是線索。舉例來說，如果空格後有名詞，此名詞就是空格的線索單字，以此名詞可以猜想出空格可能是個形容詞。

❸ 擴大片語量。

多益會拿來出題的字彙，通常以片語形式出現。最具代表的是：動詞和受詞、形容詞和名詞、介系詞和名詞、動詞和副詞等。有些詞組中每個單字都懂，但合起來就並非所猜想的中文意思。因此，平日要將這些片語視為一個單位整個背下來。舉例來說，中文說「打電話」，但英文是「make a phone call」；而付錢打電話不能用「pay a phone call」，要用「pay for the phone call」。但是多益中 Part 5 考「pay for the phone call」的可能性很低，因為多益大多出常見用語，而這句不是。所以，常考片語要直接背起來，不要直接用中文去猜想，才能在本大題奪得高分。

VI Text Completion 第六大題：短文填空

第六大題

指示：閱讀本大題的文章，文章中的某些句子缺少單字、片語或句子，這些句子都會有四個答案選項，請選出最適合的答案來完成文章中的空格，並在答案卡上將 (A)、(B)、(C) 或 (D) 的答案選項塗黑。

高分戰略

❶ 掌握空格前後的文意。

Part 5 和 Part 6 不同的地方是，Part 5 只探究一個句子的結構，而 Part 6 要探究句子和句子間的關係，因此要練習觀察空格前後句子彼此的連結關係。如果有空格的句子是第一句，要看後一句來解題；如果有空格的句子是第二句，就要看前一句來解題。偶爾，也有要看整篇文章才能作答的題目。PART 6 最難處在於要從選項的四個句子中，選出適當的句子填入空格中。此為新制增加的題型，不僅要多費時解題，平時也得多花功夫訓練掌握上下文意。

❷ 掌握動詞時態

Part 5 的動詞時態問題，只要看該句子內的動詞是否符合時態即可，但 Part 6 的動詞時態，要看其他句子才能決定該句空格中的時態。大部分的時態題目都區分為：已發生的事或尚未發生的事。從上下文來看，已發生的事，要用現在完成式或過去式；尚未發生的事，就選包含 will 等與未來式相關的助動詞（will、shall、may 等）選項，或用「be going to . . .」。針對 Part 6 的時態問題，多練習區分已發生的事和尚未發生的事便能順利答題。

❸ 掌握連接副詞（轉折語）的功用

所謂的連接副詞，是指翻譯時要和前面的內容一起翻譯的副詞。一般來說，這不會出現在只考一句話的 Part 5，而會出現在有多個句子的 Part 6。舉例來說，副詞 therefore 是「因此」的意思，所以若前後句的內容有因果關係，多半會用它。若是轉折語氣，用有「然而」含意的 however。此外，連接副詞還有 otherwise（否則）、consequently（因此）、additionally（此外）、instead（反而）等。另外，連接詞用於連接句子，而連接副詞是單獨使用的，要將它們做清楚區分。

VII Single Passage / Multiple Passage 第七大題：單篇／多篇文章理解

第七大題

指示：這大題中會閱讀到不同種類的文章，如雜誌和新聞文章、電子郵件或通訊軟體的訊息等。每篇或每組文章之後會有數個題目，請選出最適合的答案，並在答案卡上將 (A)、(B)、(C) 或 (D) 的答案選項塗黑。

高分戰略

❶ 字彙量是答題關鍵。

字彙能力是在 Part 7 拿高分最重要的一環，它能幫助你正確且快速地理解整個篇章。平時就要將意思相似的字彙或用語一起熟記，以快速增加字彙量。

❷ 要將問題分類。

Part 7 的題目看似無規則可循，事實上可以分作幾種類型，如：

① **細節訊息類型：**詢問文章細節。
② **主題類型：**詢問文章主題。
③ **Not / True 類型：**詢問哪個選項是錯誤資訊。
④ **邏輯推演類型：**從文章提供的線索推知內容。
⑤ **文意填空類型：**將題目中的句子填入文意通順的地方。

在解題前先將題目分類，解題會更有頭緒。

❸ 複合式文章題要注意彼此關聯性。

從 176 題開始是複合式文章類型，每題組由兩到三篇文章組成，有許多問題出自多篇文章內容的相關性。解題關鍵在於找出相關或相同的地方，並注意篇章之間是以何種方式連接。

❹ 培養耐心。

Part 7 是整個聽力閱讀測驗的尾聲，注意力是否在前面的奮戰後仍高度集中是勝負的關鍵。平常要訓練至少要持續一個小時不休息地解題，養成習慣才能在正式考試時不被疲勞影響。

〔寂天編輯群整理製作〕

SELF CHECK 自我檢測表

請以參加實際測驗的心態作答每回試題，並於作答完畢後，記錄測驗結果。此作法將有助於提升學習動力與專注力。

		作答日期	作答時間	答對題數	答對總題數	下個目標
Actual Test 1	聽力					寫完所有題目！
	閱讀					
Actual Test 2	聽力					要有更遠大的夢想！
	閱讀					
Actual Test 3	聽力					我做得很好！
	閱讀					
Actual Test 4	聽力					離目標越來越近了！
	閱讀					
Actual Test 5	聽力					我做得到！
	閱讀					

Actual Test 1

LISTENING TEST

In the Listening test, you will be asked to demonstrate how well you understand spoken English. The entire Listening test will last approximately 45 minutes. There are four parts, and directions are given for each part. You must mark your answers on the separate answer sheet. Do not write your answers in your test book.

PART 1 01

Directions: For each question in this part, you will hear four statements about a picture in your test book. When you hear the statements, you must select the one statement that best describes what you see in the picture. Then find the number of the question on your answer sheet and mark your answer. The statements will not be printed in your test book and will be spoken only one time.

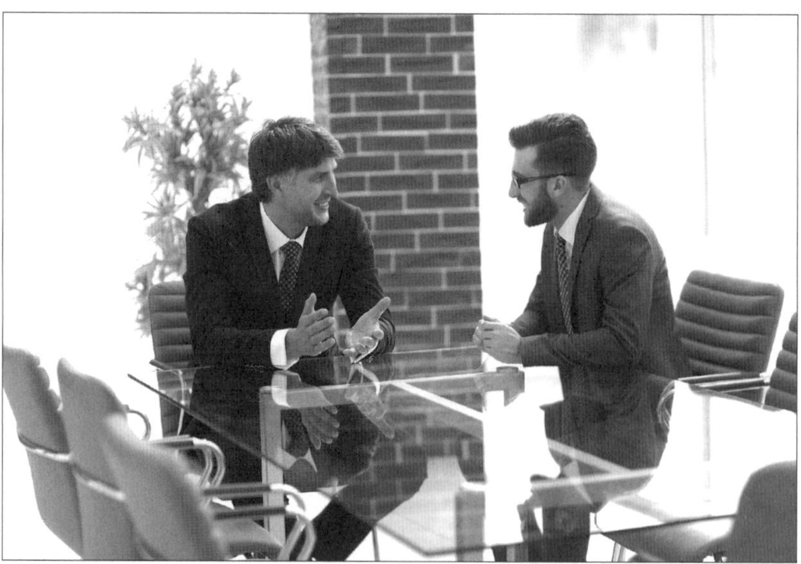

Statement (C), "They're sitting at the table," is the best description of the picture, so you should select answer (C) and mark it on your answer sheet.

1.

2.

GO ON TO THE NEXT PAGE

3.

4.

5.

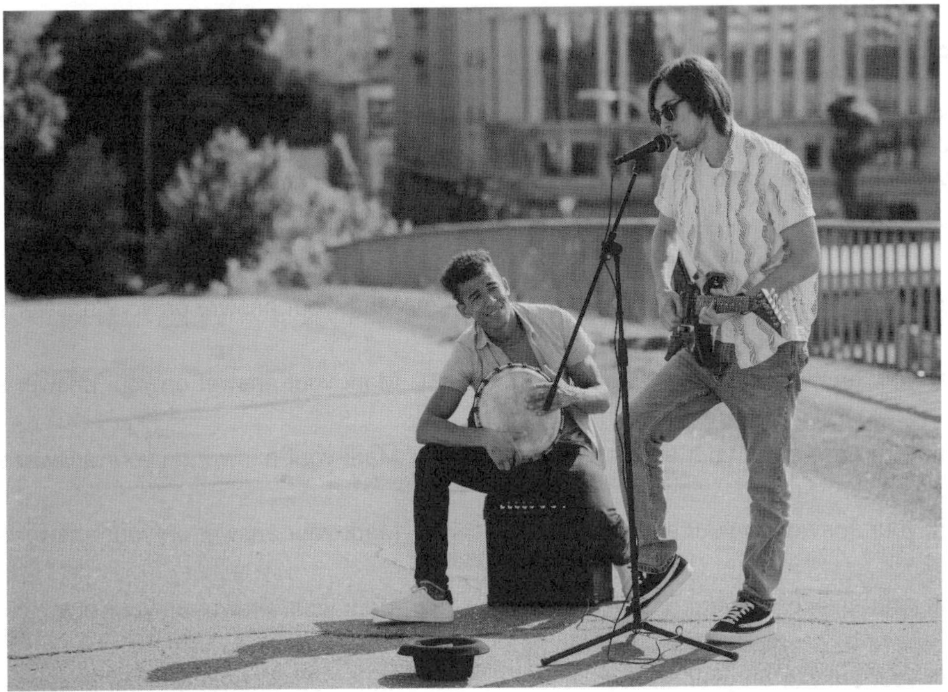

6.

GO ON TO THE NEXT PAGE

PART 2 02

Directions: You will hear a question or statement and three responses spoken in English. They will not be printed in your test book and will be spoken only one time. Select the best response to the question or statement and mark the letter (A), (B), or (C) on your answer sheet.

7. Mark your answer on your answer sheet.

8. Mark your answer on your answer sheet.

9. Mark your answer on your answer sheet.

10. Mark your answer on your answer sheet.

11. Mark your answer on your answer sheet.

12. Mark your answer on your answer sheet.

13. Mark your answer on your answer sheet.

14. Mark your answer on your answer sheet.

15. Mark your answer on your answer sheet.

16. Mark your answer on your answer sheet.

17. Mark your answer on your answer sheet.

18. Mark your answer on your answer sheet.

19. Mark your answer on your answer sheet.

20. Mark your answer on your answer sheet.

21. Mark your answer on your answer sheet.

22. Mark your answer on your answer sheet.

23. Mark your answer on your answer sheet.

24. Mark your answer on your answer sheet.

25. Mark your answer on your answer sheet.

26. Mark your answer on your answer sheet.

27. Mark your answer on your answer sheet.

28. Mark your answer on your answer sheet.

29. Mark your answer on your answer sheet.

30. Mark your answer on your answer sheet.

31. Mark your answer on your answer sheet.

PART 3 (03)

Directions: You will hear some conversations between two or more people. You will be asked to answer three questions about what the speakers say in each conversation. Select the best response to each question and mark the letter (A), (B), (C), or (D) on your answer sheet. The conversations will not be printed in your test book and will be spoken only one time.

32. Where is the conversation taking place?
(A) At a bookstore
(B) At a dry cleaner's
(C) At a department store
(D) At a post office

33. What does the man check?
(A) The available sizes
(B) The sale price
(C) The delivery fees
(D) The shipment date

34. What does the man recommend doing?
(A) Checking for an item online
(B) Placing a rush order
(C) Visiting another branch
(D) Purchasing a different brand

---

35. What most likely is the man's job?
(A) Head of marketing
(B) Graphic designer
(C) Repairperson
(D) Personnel manager

36. What has the woman ordered for the man?
(A) A uniform
(B) A desk
(C) A file cabinet
(D) A laptop computer

37. What does the woman remind the man to do?
(A) Sign up for a workshop
(B) Read a user manual
(C) Transport an item carefully
(D) Contact a customer

---

38. What does the man want his friend's opinion about?
(A) A payment method
(B) A reservation time
(C) A food order
(D) A seating option

39. Why does the man say, "That's more than I expected"?
(A) To make a complaint
(B) To turn down an offer
(C) To give an excuse
(D) To express excitement

40. What does the man inquire about?
(A) A discount offer
(B) A chef's recommendation
(C) The hours of operation
(D) The parking situation

---

41. Where do the speakers work?
(A) At a business institute
(B) At a library
(C) At a publishing company
(D) At a newspaper office

42. What was Jennifer surprised about?
(A) Attendance at an event
(B) Some negative reviews
(C) A proposed contract
(D) A coworker's transfer

43. What will happen this afternoon?
(A) Some customers will give feedback.
(B) A new shipment will arrive.
(C) The man will conduct an interview.
(D) Photos will be added to a Web site.

GO ON TO THE NEXT PAGE

44. Where most likely are the speakers?
(A) At a business school
(B) At an accounting firm
(C) At an insurance company
(D) At a government office

45. How did the woman learn about the job opening?
(A) By reading a magazine
(B) By receiving an e-mail
(C) By speaking to a colleague
(D) By attending a career fair

46. What accomplishment does the woman mention?
(A) Training other staff members
(B) Earning the highest employee rating
(C) Developing a new software program
(D) Bringing in the most new customers

---

47. What is the problem?
(A) Some equipment was damaged.
(B) A company is not reliable.
(C) Some new employees are inexperienced.
(D) A workspace is too small.

48. Why does the man say, "my friend Felix works in real estate"?
(A) To suggest getting a recommendation
(B) To reject a business proposal
(C) To correct a misunderstanding
(D) To explain the reason for a decision

49. What does the woman say she will do?
(A) Visit a neighborhood
(B) Read some reviews
(C) Make a phone call
(D) Prepare some documents

---

50. Where most likely does the man work?
(A) At a coffee shop
(B) At a bank
(C) At a car rental company
(D) At a shoe store

51. According to the man, what is the problem?
(A) Some products are sold out.
(B) A delivery did not arrive.
(C) Some software is malfunctioning.
(D) An employee has made an error.

52. What does the man offer to do for the woman?
(A) Call her later
(B) Get a supervisor
(C) Provide a refund
(D) Send a catalog

---

53. Who most likely is the woman?
(A) A travel agent
(B) A delivery driver
(C) A furniture salesperson
(D) A hotel manager

54. What will the man do next month?
(A) He will take a trip out of town.
(B) He will open a new business.
(C) He will give a talk at an event.
(D) He will move to a new home.

55. What does the woman suggest?
(A) Advertising on a Web site
(B) Viewing some images online
(C) Hiring a professional decorator
(D) Downloading a smartphone app

---

56. In which department do the speakers work?
(A) Human resources
(B) Finance
(C) Marketing
(D) Shipping

57. What does the woman offer to do?
(A) Review a company policy
(B) Call one of Ms. Lee's clients
(C) Organize a work schedule
(D) Make preparations for a meal

58. According to the woman, why should the man talk to Tina?
(A) To contribute to a gift
(B) To collect a prize
(C) To express a preference
(D) To check a report

---

59. What does the man want to talk about at the meeting?
(A) Some customer survey responses
(B) Some employee complaints
(C) A new supplier of ingredients
(D) An upcoming sales promotion

60. What problem does Claire mention?
(A) An ingredient is considered unhealthy.
(B) The product selection is not large enough.
(C) Some business hours are inconvenient.
(D) Some staff members are not fully trained.

61. What are the women asked to do?
(A) Oversee an ad campaign
(B) Work some additional shifts
(C) Create a summary report
(D) Hire a new employee

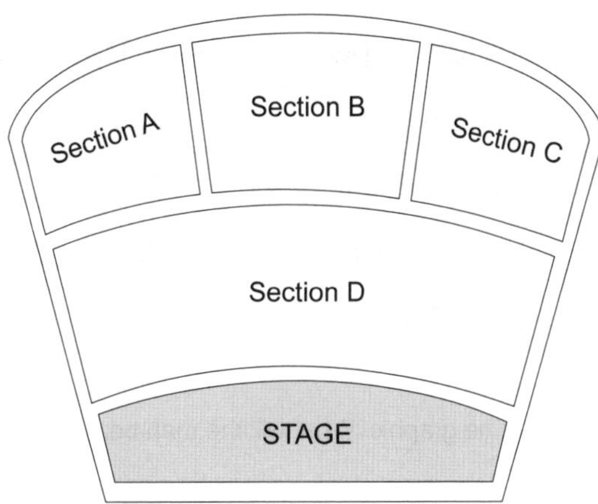

62. Why does the woman express surprise?
(A) The price of some tickets has increased.
(B) Some new performance dates have been added.
(C) A dance group has won an award.
(D) The man is interested in watching ballet.

63. Look at the graphic. For which section are the man's tickets?
(A) Section A
(B) Section B
(C) Section C
(D) Section D

64. What will the man's sister do on Friday?
(A) Go to a party
(B) Move out of town
(C) Attend an interview
(D) Teach a dance class

GO ON TO THE NEXT PAGE

Vehicle Type	Daily Rate
Standard Sedan	$65
Premium Sedan	$70
Luxury Sedan	$85
Elite Sedan	$110

65. Look at the graphic. What will the man be charged per day?

(A) $65
(B) $70
(C) $85
(D) $110

66. Why is the man visiting Atlanta?

(A) To sign a contract
(B) To lead a group discussion
(C) To attend a conference
(D) To tour a building

67. What does the woman recommend doing?

(A) Avoiding a busy road
(B) Keeping a receipt
(C) Downloading an app
(D) Visiting a popular restaurant

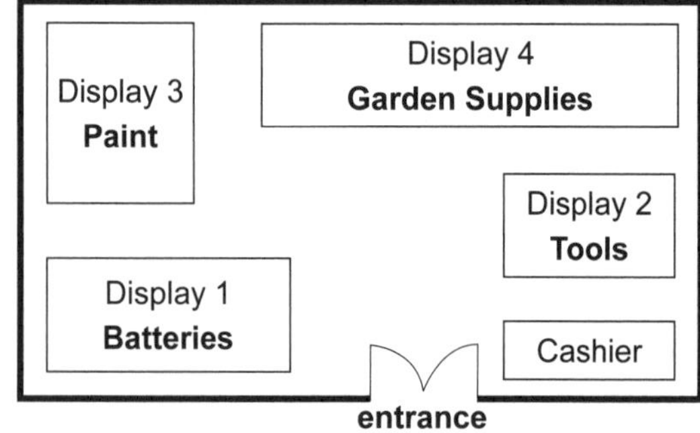

68. Where are the speakers?

(A) At an art institute
(B) At a repair shop
(C) At a hardware store
(D) At a toy store

69. According to the man, what did employees do yesterday?

(A) Recorded a video
(B) Completed some training
(C) Unloaded some new items
(D) Installed safety equipment

70. Look at the graphic. Where will some paint cans be moved?

(A) Display 1
(B) Display 2
(C) Display 3
(D) Display 4

PART 4 041

Directions: You will hear some talks given by a single speaker. You will be asked to answer three questions about what the speaker says in each talk. Select the best response to each question and mark the letter (A), (B), (C), or (D) on your answer sheet. The talks will not be printed in your test book and will be spoken only one time.

71. How does each workshop tour end?
(A) An employee answers questions.
(B) An informative video is shown.
(C) A group photo is taken.
(D) A piece of equipment is demonstrated.

72. What does each tour participant receive?
(A) A piece of jewelry
(B) A voucher
(C) A map of the site
(D) A beverage

73. What do the listeners receive a warning about?
(A) Which entrance to use
(B) Where to meet
(C) What clothing to bring
(D) How to book in advance

---

74. Who most likely is giving the speech?
(A) A factory worker
(B) A driving instructor
(C) A gym manager
(D) A bank employee

75. What have the listeners been given?
(A) A product sample
(B) An employee directory
(C) A daily pass
(D) A list of classes

76. What does the speaker mean when she says, "You won't see anything like it again"?
(A) A membership process can be confusing.
(B) A presentation is worth watching.
(C) The business is expected to succeed.
(D) Listeners should take advantage of an offer.

---

77. What kind of business do the listeners most likely work for?
(A) A construction company
(B) An international delivery service
(C) A newspaper publisher
(D) A medical facility

78. What does the speaker say she is reassured about?
(A) A worker's attention to detail
(B) An investor's future plan
(C) The responses from a customer survey
(D) The score on an inspection

79. What are the listeners encouraged to do?
(A) E-mail Ms. Arnold
(B) Ask for advice
(C) Attend a training event
(D) Sample a new product

---

80. Why is the bus's departure delayed?
(A) It is being cleaned.
(B) It is undergoing repairs.
(C) There is heavy traffic in the area.
(D) There was a scheduling error.

81. Why does the speaker say, "We do have some indirect routes"?
(A) To confirm a new schedule
(B) To explain a policy
(C) To suggest an alternative
(D) To make a complaint

82. What are the listeners asked to do?
(A) Talk to the speaker
(B) Show a ticket
(C) Come back later
(D) Present a receipt

GO ON TO THE NEXT PAGE

83. Where most likely is the speaker calling from?

(A) A real estate agency
(B) A dental clinic
(C) An architecture firm
(D) A manufacturing facility

84. What qualification does the speaker mention?

(A) A flexible schedule
(B) A university degree
(C) State certification
(D) Sales experience

85. What does the speaker say she plans to do?

(A) Send an employment contract
(B) Arrange an interview time
(C) Keep some documents
(D) Check the listener's references

---

86. Where most likely does the speaker work?

(A) At a marketing firm
(B) At a local newspaper
(C) At a cosmetics company
(D) At a fashion magazine

87. Why does the speaker say, "our photographer works full time"?

(A) To explain a problem
(B) To reject an offer
(C) To correct a misunderstanding
(D) To request some help

88. What does the speaker ask the listener to do?

(A) Inform him of her availability
(B) Send him some documents
(C) Confirm a final payment
(D) Select some photographs

---

89. What is the speaker mainly discussing?

(A) A customer complaint
(B) A staff promotion
(C) A payment system
(D) A company policy

90. What are the listeners asked to do?

(A) Complete an online form
(B) Work with a partner
(C) Read a handout
(D) Attend a training session

91. According to the speaker, what will Olivia do?

(A) Return some equipment
(B) Print some materials
(C) Answer questions
(D) Create a schedule

---

92. What will be discussed during the broadcast?

(A) Online deliveries
(B) Fruit picking
(C) Home gardening
(D) Farmer's markets

93. According to the speaker, why is an activity popular?

(A) It keeps people in shape.
(B) It is fun for all ages.
(C) It saves participants money.
(D) It is environmentally friendly.

94. Who is Stephanie Lutz?

(A) A reporter
(B) A city official
(C) A farmer
(D) A radio host

Room 201	Room 202	Room 204
Elevator		
Staff Room	Room 203	Storage Room

Project A	Corporate Sponsorship
Project B	Video Competition
Project C	Free Webinar
Project D	Annual Trade Expo

95. Who is the speaker addressing?
(A) Potential investors
(B) Company managers
(C) Job applicants
(D) Government inspectors

96. Look at the graphic. Which office will the listeners use for most of the day?
(A) Room 201
(B) Room 202
(C) Room 203
(D) Room 204

97. Where will listeners go at four-thirty?
(A) To a conference room
(B) To a computer lab
(C) To a cafeteria
(D) To a security office

98. Why does the speaker thank the team?
(A) They finished a project on short notice.
(B) They created a popular product.
(C) They found some new clients.
(D) They helped to train new employees.

99. Look at the graphic. Which project will start tomorrow?
(A) Project A
(B) Project B
(C) Project C
(D) Project D

100. What will Patrick do on Thursday?
(A) Receive an award
(B) Give a speech
(C) Visit a client
(D) Finalize a budget

This is the end of the Listening test. Turn to Part 5 in your test book.

GO ON TO THE NEXT PAGE

READING TEST

In the Reading test, you will read a variety of texts and answer several different types of reading comprehension questions. The entire Reading test will last 75 minutes. There are three parts, and directions are given for each part. You are encouraged to answer as many questions as possible within the time allowed.

You must mark your answers on the separate answer sheet. Do not write your answers in your test book.

PART 5

Directions: A word or phrase is missing in each of the sentences below. Four answer choices are given below each sentence. Select the best answer to complete the sentence. Then mark the letter (A), (B), (C), or (D) on your answer sheet.

101. Some officials ------- expressed concerns about the changes to the corporate tax structure.

(A) privacy
(B) privatize
(C) private
(D) privately

102. The new electric car from Baylor Motors is intended for ------- journeys within an urban environment.

(A) shortness
(B) short
(C) shortly
(D) shorten

103. Ames Manufacturing developed a packaging method that ------- much less cardboard.

(A) uses
(B) using
(C) to use
(D) use

104. The building's owner increased the fees ------- parking lot access.

(A) for
(B) about
(C) at
(D) among

105. Few market analysts ------- predicted the industry effects of the factory's closure.

(A) locally
(B) constantly
(C) kindly
(D) correctly

106. Customers who wish to ------- us a review on social media are encouraged to do so.

(A) explain
(B) say
(C) give
(D) have

107. Every weekend ------- the month of August, the hotel's restaurant features live musical performances.

(A) even
(B) during
(C) when
(D) while

108. Portland Insurance's employees should complete a form with ------- desired vacation days.

(A) their
(B) its
(C) themselves
(D) it

109. Many construction businesses are nervous about a new ------- on the importation of building materials.

(A) restrictively
(B) restrict
(C) restrictive
(D) restriction

110. Concert tickets have not been selling well, ------- the event has been advertised heavily for weeks.

(A) because
(B) unless
(C) in addition to
(D) even though

111. Prices were ------- reduced for the store's summer sale.

(A) significantly
(B) significance
(C) significant
(D) signify

112. People who are self-employed should keep ------- records of their business's profits and costs.

(A) accurate
(B) unfair
(C) visual
(D) spacious

113. Attendance at Saturday's community picnic was high ------- the cold weather.

(A) regarding
(B) opposite
(C) despite
(D) across

114. Soil samples were taken to carry out the ------- testing to check for pollution.

(A) narrow
(B) mandatory
(C) perishable
(D) obvious

115. Before ------- the air conditioner, Mr. Perkins ordered some replacement parts for the task.

(A) fixing
(B) fixed
(C) fix
(D) fixes

116. Product sales ------- a setback recently and may not improve without further action.

(A) to suffer
(B) have suffered
(C) suffering
(D) suffer

117. Business travelers tend to ------- hotel rooms with a large desk.

(A) apply
(B) involve
(C) prefer
(D) believe

118. Even though ------- than expected, the delivery service was not worth the high cost.

(A) quick
(B) quicker
(C) quickest
(D) quickly

119. The three tallest ------- in the city, luxury apartment complexes can be seen from most parts of town.

(A) communities
(B) streets
(C) residents
(D) structures

120. The garage was damaged ------- repair in the storm and had to be rebuilt.

(A) of
(B) under
(C) beyond
(D) onto

GO ON TO THE NEXT PAGE

121. Department managers ------- between June 4 and 8 to formally assess employees' work performance.

(A) will be meeting
(B) meeting
(C) having met
(D) to meet

122. The past few years' favorable market conditions have resulted in more business ------- across most industries.

(A) invested
(B) investment
(C) to invest
(D) investor

123. All meeting rooms at the VC Conference Hall are ------- with built-in speakers and a projector.

(A) conducted
(B) equipped
(C) activated
(D) revealed

124. The new shopping center will have a ------- effect on the local economy.

(A) benefits
(B) beneficially
(C) beneficial
(D) benefit

125. Employees are expected to complete all assigned tasks, ------- difficult they may seem.

(A) however
(B) likewise
(C) indeed
(D) rather

126. How ------- a candidate answers the questions is an important component of being considered for the role.

(A) create
(B) creation
(C) creative
(D) creatively

127. Visitors to the national park must be accompanied by a guide ------- the trails can be dangerous.

(A) than
(B) given that
(C) although
(D) much as

128. The purchase of the restaurant by a corporate chain led to a decline ------- food quality.

(A) below
(B) at
(C) in
(D) as

129. Mr. McCrae explained that ------- between the two companies has created innovative products.

(A) confirmation
(B) consequence
(C) competition
(D) commission

130. Southfield Fitness Center ------- closed its main swimming pool for a week while it was being cleaned.

(A) currently
(B) perfectly
(C) adamantly
(D) temporarily

PART 6

Directions: Read the texts that follow. A word, phrase, or sentence is missing in parts of each text. Four answer choices for each question are given below the text. Select the best answer to complete the text. Then mark the letter (A), (B), (C), or (D) on your answer sheet.

Questions 131-134 refer to the following e-mail.

Georgina Harrison
962 Warner Street
Cape Girardeau, MO 63703

Dear Ms. Harrison,

Thank you for your interest in making a group booking at Westside Hotel. I have attached a comprehensive ------- **131.** of our amenities for your convenience. We aim to personalize the guest experience. We are prepared to meet the needs of most guests on short notice. However, if you have ------- **132.** requests, we may need advance notice in order to fulfill them. Once your booking is made, you may be charged a fee according to our cancellation policy. ------- **133.**. Before confirming your booking, please download a copy of the payment details and ------- **134.** them carefully.

Warmest regards,

The Westside Hotel Team

131. (A) describe
(B) describes
(C) described
(D) description

132. (A) unusual
(B) absent
(C) plain
(D) flexible

133. (A) The front desk is open twenty-four hours a day.
(B) You should complete the form with honest feedback.
(C) We appreciate your ongoing patronage.
(D) The terms of this are included on our Web site.

134. (A) reviewing
(B) review
(C) to review
(D) reviewed

GO ON TO THE NEXT PAGE

Questions 135-138 refer to the following information.

Environmental Responsibility at the Kimball Museum

"Waves of Wonder" will be on display throughout the summer at the Kimball Museum. This -------(135.) features sculptures made from beach glass. The artwork focuses -------(136.) marine animals whose populations have been severely hurt due to ocean pollution. Interesting facts about each animal will be posted next to the work. Visitors -------(137.) advice on reducing their impact on the oceans, both locally and worldwide. -------(138.). "Waves of Wonder" will be available from June 10 to September 5.

135. (A) award
(B) manuscript
(C) exhibit
(D) film

136. (A) before
(B) to
(C) on
(D) by

137. (A) are also getting
(B) can also get
(C) have also gotten
(D) also got

138. (A) See how you can make a positive change.
(B) To become a member, visit our Web site.
(C) Fortunately, the hours have been extended.
(D) The glass can be recycled at most locations.

Questions 139-142 refer to the following advertisement.

Verdant Landscaping, founded by brothers John and Jeremy Robles, ------- (139.) top-quality landscaping services for residential properties. We can plant a garden from scratch, maintain existing lawns and flowerbeds, trim trees, and remove unwanted garden debris.

------- (140.), your outdoor area will be a beautiful and relaxing place for you to enjoy. ------- (141.). We can send a crew of any size, including just one person. If you're unsure whether hiring professionals would be within your budget, call us at 555-4433 for a free ------- (142.) of the costs. We look forward to serving you!

139. (A) will provide
(B) provides
(C) had provided
(D) providing

140. (A) For example
(B) On the contrary
(C) As a result
(D) In comparison

141. (A) Other businesses cannot compete with us.
(B) These techniques are environmentally friendly.
(C) We are willing to offer training.
(D) No job is too big or too small.

142. (A) vacation
(B) estimate
(C) installation
(D) pathway

Questions 143-146 refer to the following article.

As a small business owner, Kelly Spencer spends a lot of time researching the best way to improve -------. Her staff was not responding well to her previous methods, but then she
143.

found an interesting piece of software, Pause-Pro. "I was hesitant at first due to the high cost. However, the company was offering free use of the software for thirty days, so I thought I'd give ------- a try."
144.

Pause-Pro allows employers to block access to distracting Web sites, such as social media pages, so employees don't waste time. It wasn't ------- what Ms. Spencer was looking for,
145.

but she couldn't deny the results. She purchased the full version of the software for all of her employees' computers. -------. "With Pause-Pro's help," she said, "we can all focus on the most
146.

important tasks."

143. (A) wages
(B) efficiency
(C) competition
(D) education

144. (A) mine
(B) everyone
(C) these
(D) it

145. (A) more original
(B) originally
(C) original
(D) originality

146. (A) She also bought the program for her laptop.
(B) She has founded a few different businesses.
(C) She looks forward to meeting them.
(D) She could not understand the features.

PART 7

Directions: In this part you will read a selection of texts, such as magazine and newspaper articles, e-mails, and instant messages. Each text or set of texts is followed by several questions. Select the best answer for each question and mark the letter (A), (B), (C), or (D) on your answer sheet.

Questions 147-148 refer to the following article.

New Library Program Creates "Buzz"

April 30—This summer, Syracuse Library is launching a program to help local bees. The number of local bees has sharply declined, and the library aims to help these creatures. It will have a special section with books about bees and will host lectures about how they benefit the environment. Anyone who attends a lecture will be given a free pack of seeds for flowers that will attract bees.

147. What is the purpose of the program?
(A) To support the bee population
(B) To teach people a new skill
(C) To attract new library members
(D) To raise money for a charity

148. How can participants get a free gift?
(A) By completing a survey
(B) By attending a talk
(C) By making a donation
(D) By showing a library card

GO ON TO THE NEXT PAGE

Questions 149-150 refer to the following invitation.

Please join us for a meet-and-greet session with Adam Jackson, the new Public Relations Director of Watkins Bank.

Monday, December 12, 1 P.M.-2 P.M.
Conference Room A

Adam Jackson handled public relations for CHK Bank for nearly two decades. He will give a brief presentation on his plans for rebranding Watkins Bank and building closer connections with our customers. If you have a question for Mr. Jackson, please send it to the HR team prior to the event.

Coffee and hot tea will be served.

149. What is implied about Mr. Jackson?

(A) He currently works at CHK Bank.
(B) He recently changed his employer.
(C) He will receive an award on December 12.
(D) He founded his own business.

150. What can guests do in advance?

(A) Order hot beverages
(B) View some images
(C) Reserve a seat
(D) Submit their questions

Questions 151-152 refer to the following e-mail.

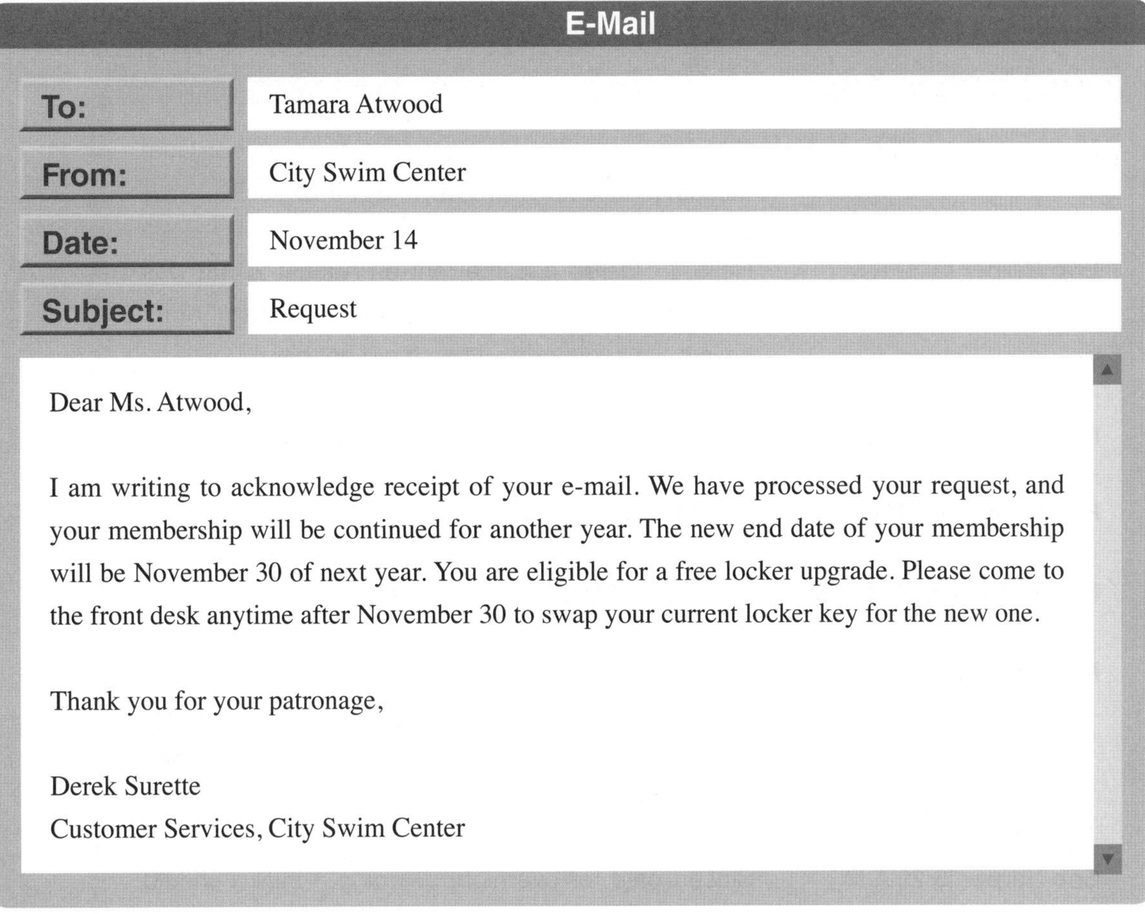

E-Mail

To:	Tamara Atwood
From:	City Swim Center
Date:	November 14
Subject:	Request

Dear Ms. Atwood,

I am writing to acknowledge receipt of your e-mail. We have processed your request, and your membership will be continued for another year. The new end date of your membership will be November 30 of next year. You are eligible for a free locker upgrade. Please come to the front desk anytime after November 30 to swap your current locker key for the new one.

Thank you for your patronage,

Derek Surette
Customer Services, City Swim Center

151. Why did Mr. Surette send the e-mail?
(A) To apologize for an error
(B) To introduce a new service
(C) To confirm a renewal
(D) To make a job offer

152. What can Ms. Atwood do after November 30?
(A) Contact Mr. Surette
(B) Receive a refund
(C) Attend a class
(D) Exchange a key

Questions 153-154 refer to the following text-message chain.

Monique Ross [9:21 A.M.]	Good morning. I'm Monique from the Outdoor Gear customer service team. How may I help you?
Eric Harper [9:22 A.M.]	Hello. I ordered a dome tent on August 2 that was supposed to arrive yesterday. However, I still don't have it. I'm wondering when it will get here.
Monique Ross [9:23 A.M.]	I can help with that. What is the order number?
Eric Harper [9:24 A.M.]	It's order #034587.
Monique Ross [9:25 A.M.]	Thank you. Please wait a moment.
Monique Ross [9:28 A.M.]	It looks like there was an issue at the warehouse, and the item is now scheduled to be sent tomorrow. So, it will arrive on Thursday, two days later than originally expected.
Eric Harper [9:29 A.M.]	Since I paid for overnight shipping, I think I should be refunded for the shipping fee.
Monique Ross [9:31 A.M.]	Absolutely. I'll take care of that right now, and it should appear on your account within a few hours. Do you need any other help?
Eric Harper [9:32 A.M.]	Not for now. Thanks.

153. Why did Mr. Harper send a message to Outdoor Gear?

(A) To report damage to a tent
(B) To request a product catalog
(C) To exchange an unwanted product
(D) To check when an item will arrive

154. At 9:31 a.m., what does Ms. Ross most likely mean when she writes, "Absolutely"?

(A) She understands the need for a fast service.
(B) She can open a new account for Mr. Harper.
(C) She enjoyed resolving a problem.
(D) She agrees to issue Mr. Harper a refund.

Questions 155-157 refer to the following Web page.

Posted: January 19

Cincinnati Encounter

Saturday, March 12, 9:00 A.M.-11:00 A.M.
Instructor: Diane Robinson

Are you new to Cincinnati? Learn about what the city has to offer, such as:

- Where and how to look for jobs with local businesses
- What bus and streetcar routes are available to commuters
- Volunteer opportunities with charities and how to participate

This class would be especially helpful to those who have moved to Cincinnati from overseas. Registration opens on January 25 and ends on March 5. Spots will be assigned on a first-come, first-served basis. The class is expected to fill up quickly, so early registration is recommended.

Thanks to a government grant, Cincinnati Encounter is provided for free to anyone living in Cincinnati, but registration is required.

155. When will Ms. Robinson teach a class?
(A) On January 19
(B) On January 25
(C) On March 5
(D) On March 12

156. What is NOT indicated as a topic in Cincinnati Encounter?
(A) Using public transportation
(B) Running for local government
(C) Seeking employment in the area
(D) Assisting nonprofit organizations

157. What is stated about Cincinnati Encounter?
(A) It is offered to residents at no cost.
(B) It will last for three hours.
(C) It was developed by a businessperson.
(D) It is part of an ongoing series.

GO ON TO THE NEXT PAGE

Questions 158-160 refer to the following e-mail.

E-Mail

To: Angela Klein <kleina@rtinternet.net>
From: José Damico <jose@sapphire-yoga.com>
Date: June 12
Subject: Level 3 Certification

Dear Ms. Klein,

We have received your deposit payment for Sapphire Yoga Studio's upcoming Yoga Teacher Training Course for the Level 3 certification course. —[1]—. This is a full-time intensive course that will last four weeks, beginning on June 29.

—[2]—. Please e-mail Veronica Clark at veronica@sapphire-yoga.com to submit health check records from your doctor showing that you are fit to take on the demands of the course. This is for your safety and is required by our insurance provider.

Yoga mats and blocks are available on site for every class. —[3]—. So, you can use them with confidence. However, we find that most students would rather bring personal items from home. You are free to do so, but please be aware that we cannot store anything for you overnight.

Please let me know if you have any questions about the course. —[4]—.

Warmest regards,

José Damico
Manager, Sapphire Yoga Studio

158. Why should Ms. Klein e-mail Ms. Clark?
(A) To get a doctor recommendation
(B) To sign up for insurance
(C) To confirm her physical health
(D) To get more course information

159. What does Mr. Damico suggest about students?
(A) They prefer to use their own equipment.
(B) They will do part of the course from home.
(C) They can participate in the class for free.
(D) They have the option of different start times.

160. In which of the positions marked [1], [2], [3], and [4] does the following sentence best belong?
"We implement sanitization practices between each use."
(A) [1]
(B) [2]
(C) [3]
(D) [4]

Questions 161-163 refer to the following contract.

Contract Agreement

This contract is entered into by Adrienne Sales and Oscar Rascon, a freelance graphic designer, on April 22. Mr. Rascon agrees to create an original logo for Adrienne Sales. Mr. Rascon will meet with representatives from Adrienne Sales at the company's headquarters to discuss the intended appearance of the logo. Adrienne Sales will reimburse Mr. Rascon for up to £25 in travel-related expenses for the meeting, provided Mr. Rascon presents receipts of the spending. Mr. Rascon will create and submit three versions of the logo by May 20. Adrienne Sales can ask for up to three additional rounds of revisions to the selected logo. Adrienne Sales agrees to pay Mr. Rascon £750 upon completion of the final image.

Agreed by:

Oscar Rascon	*April 22*
Graphic Designer	Date
Elizabeth Norris	*April 22*
Adrienne Sales	Date

161. What does the contract imply about Mr. Rascon?

(A) He will complete a project by April 22.
(B) He used to work with Ms. Norris.
(C) He is a salesperson at Adrienne Sales.
(D) He will be paid to create a design.

162. The word "presents" in paragraph 1, line 5, is closest in meaning to

(A) publishes
(B) submits
(C) gifts
(D) displays

163. According to the agreement, what is Mr. Rascon required to do?

(A) Give a presentation
(B) Research some industry trends
(C) Make some requested adjustments
(D) Provide professional references

GO ON TO THE NEXT PAGE

Questions 164-167 refer to the following e-mail.

From: Nicola Fallaci
To: All Briarhill Employees
Date: July 2
Subject: For your information

Dear Briarhill Employees,

To keep employees better informed, I'll be sending you regular updates about the company's progress. —[1]—. Compared to this quarter last year, our domestic sales have increased by 15%. Though it seems that having some of our goods as part of the *Family Fun* TV show set did not make much difference, it still provided some interesting photos for our Web site.

—[2]—. In Indonesia, we experienced an amazing 63% boost in sales following our participation in the Jakarta Housewares Trade Fair. Sales were steady in Australia, where we saw an increase of just 0.5%. —[3]—. This was not a surprise, as our new line of cotton curtains has been receiving mixed reviews. In Sweden and Norway, sales have been sluggish, down 8% and 6%, respectively. This is due to heavy competition from other businesses.

—[4]—. As you can see, there are some regions that need improvement and others that are doing well. I am sure that the proposal made by Pedro Reid, which targets hotels directly for sales across their entire chain, will yield promising results and grow our sales further.

Sincerely,

Nicola Fallaci

164. What type of company most likely is Briarhill?
(A) A chain of supermarkets
(B) A home furnishings retailer
(C) A book publisher
(D) An electronics manufacturer

165. According to Ms. Fallaci, where did people see Briarhill's merchandise in person?
(A) In Australia
(B) In Indonesia
(C) In Norway
(D) In Sweden

166. What does Ms. Fallaci expect will likely lead to increased business?
(A) A customer loyalty program
(B) Association with a TV show
(C) Contracts with hotel chains
(D) Online advertising campaigns

167. In which of the positions marked [1], [2], [3], and [4] does the following sentence best belong?
"Here is an overview of our international performance."
(A) [1]
(B) [2]
(C) [3]
(D) [4]

Questions 168-171 refer to the following article.

BERLIN (September 7)—The Historical Preservation Foundation (HPF) aims to make historical artifacts available to the public as well as provide support for ongoing research. The HPF plans to work on a collection of objects from a 1940s excavation in Western Asia. Fragments of vases and bowls dating back to the 2nd century were acquired by Aldeen University. These will be restored at HPF's main facility in Berlin. "We are honored to have these items under our care," said director Mathias Vogel. "Our track record for dealing with fragile artifacts is unmatched, and we have the resources to give them the attention they deserve."

HPF's staff members are proficient in working with metal objects such as tools, weapons, and jewelry, but they are somewhat new to working with clay items, especially molded ones. "We are forming a partnership with Aldeen University to ensure the work is carried out properly," Vogel said. "We're excited that Jamila Ahmed will travel to our site in Berlin to oversee operations. This project lines up perfectly with her specialized knowledge and extensive experience."

The artifacts are currently housed at Aldeen University. The university's team is starting to examine them to prepare them to be shipped to Berlin, which they are expecting to do on October 2. A date for a public display of the items has not yet been determined.

168. What is the main topic of the article?
(A) The grand opening of a museum
(B) A fundraiser for an excavation
(C) The new discovery of some artifacts
(D) A pottery restoration project

169. What position does Mr. Vogel have?
(A) Maintenance manager
(B) Assistant researcher
(C) Head of Aldeen University
(D) HPF director

170. What is most likely true about Ms. Ahmed?
(A) She is an expert in pottery.
(B) She graduated from Aldeen University.
(C) She grew up in Berlin.
(D) She plans to publish a book.

171. What is implied about the artifacts?
(A) They have been donated by private collectors.
(B) They will be examined for several weeks before transportation.
(C) They will go on display from October 2.
(D) They sustained some damage while being shipped.

GO ON TO THE NEXT PAGE

Questions 172-175 refer to the following online chat discussion.

Yuhan Gao [9:18 A.M.]	Hi, everyone. Since I canceled yesterday's team meeting, I wanted to check in with how things are going. Lisa, how is your trade show research coming along?
Lisa Timko [9:19 A.M.]	Even better than I expected! I have found one in August, the National Beauty Expo, that I think would be perfect for promoting our natural skincare products. The registration fee is only $1,500.
Yuhan Gao [9:21 A.M.]	Wonderful! Please go forward with that.
George Lainez [9:22 A.M.]	That's great! High-profile events are just what we need.
Ron Fulkerson [9:23 A.M.]	Good job, Lisa! If you send me the details, I can register our company for the event by the end of the day.
Lisa Timko [9:24 A.M.]	I guess we'll be busy preparing for this along with our extensive television campaign on the Mayfair Network.
Yuhan Gao [9:25 A.M.]	Unfortunately, that fell through. We can't afford the prices the station was charging, so we're going to have to promote the new line of lotions in another way.
Lisa Timko [9:27 A.M.]	I see. And I appreciate your dealing with this so quickly, Ron.
Ron Fulkerson [9:28 A.M.]	It's nothing.
Yuhan Gao [9:29 A.M.]	Keep up the good work, everyone!

SEND

172. In what industry do the writers most likely work?
(A) Travel
(B) Technology
(C) Clothing
(D) Cosmetics

173. What most likely is Ms. Gao's occupation?
(A) Security advisor
(B) Human resources director
(C) Marketing manager
(D) Research assistant

174. What is true about the Mayfair Network?
(A) It is hosting an annual event.
(B) It will form a partnership with the writers' company.
(C) Its employees have a lot of experience.
(D) Its fees are too high for the writers' company.

175. At 9:28 A.M., what does Mr. Fulkerson mean when he writes, "It's nothing"?
(A) He is pleased that Ms. Timko will resolve a problem.
(B) He is willing to complete a registration process quickly.
(C) He is surprised about the lack of information available.
(D) He is happy to have found an event for the team.

GO ON TO THE NEXT PAGE

Questions 176-180 refer to the following advertisement and e-mail.

Make your event magical and memorable with Edsel Gardens!

Edsel Gardens, located near Stockton and comprising 4 acres of botanical gardens, features a truly unique and romantic location. You'll love the peaceful backdrop, gorgeous views, and modern amenities offered at our site. We specialize in weddings and anniversary parties and have recently doubled the size of our parking lot to accommodate larger groups. You can hold your event completely outdoors or use our giant tent, which protects against rain and can be heated in cold weather. Our tent seats up to 180 guests, and we have a Food and Liquor License that permits us to serve food and/or drinks from 11 A.M. to midnight on weekdays and 10 A.M. to 1 A.M. on weekends.

Our team will work with you to make sure everything is exactly what you want. With our Premium Package, you can use our in-house photographer and caterer to make planning easy. If you want live music, we can provide a recommendation for bands or singers.

Call us today at 555-8790 to get started. And if you're not sure what kind of theme you'd like for your event, get inspired by visiting our photo gallery at www.edselgardens.com. We look forward to hosting your event!

E-Mail

To: Edsel Gardens <info@edselgardens.com>
From: Ramona Murphy <rmurphy@haven-mail.com>
Date: April 11
Subject: Thank you!

To Whom It May Concern:

I recently held an anniversary party for my parents at your site, and I wanted to thank you for a great experience. I got the Premium Package, which was convenient and affordably priced. I was really impressed with the photos taken by Fred Warren, the professional photographer. I also got a lot of compliments on the band I hired. The beautiful venue was a perfect fit for my parents' style. I plan to highly recommend Edsel Gardens to all my friends and family who are looking for a place to hold an event.

Warmest regards,

Ramona Murphy

176. What is NOT true about Edsel Gardens?

(A) It is now operating under new ownership.
(B) It recently expanded its parking area.
(C) It can provide recommendations for musicians.
(D) It can accommodate different types of weather.

177. When can food be served at Edsel Gardens?

(A) Monday at 10 A.M.
(B) Wednesday at 1 A.M.
(C) Saturday at 11 A.M.
(D) Sunday 9 A.M.

178. Why does the advertisement recommend visiting a Web site?

(A) To view a price list
(B) To read customer comments
(C) To get some inspiration
(D) To make a reservation

179. What is suggested about Fred Warren?

(A) He only took photos inside a tent.
(B) He had excellent reviews on a Web site.
(C) He is a friend of Ms. Murphy's parents.
(D) He is employed directly by Edsel Gardens.

180. In the e-mail, the word "fit" in paragraph 1, line 4, is closest in meaning to

(A) position
(B) match
(C) development
(D) adaptation

Questions 181-185 refer to the following letter and e-mail.

Wanda Milburn
Corbitt Enterprises
4443 Rardin Road
Nashville, TN 37210
January 5

Dear Ms. Milburn,

We are writing to inform you of an increase in the fees for the cleaning services we perform for Corbitt Enterprises at the above address. The current fees you pay will be valid until March 4. As you were one of our customers in the very first month we opened, we have kept the fees at a lower rate for as long as possible.

We are implementing this change to ensure that our workers are compensated fairly, as they always perform a complete and careful cleaning service. This is rare in our industry. Enclosed you will find a breakdown of the new fees.

The change will go into effect on March 5. If you wish to terminate the contract, please inform us of your desired final day of service. We hope to continue serving you for many years to come.

Sincerely,

Grant Berg
Grant Berg
Manager, Shinetime Commercial Cleaning

To:	Grant Berg <grant@shinetimecommcleaning.com>
From:	Wanda Milburn <w.milburn@corbittenterprises.com>
Date:	January 11
Subject:	Cleaning contract

Dear Mr. Berg,

Thanks for informing me about the upcoming changes. We've been satisfied with the level of care provided. I know many business owners have had trouble hiring reliable cleaners, so I feel very lucky. I can't believe it has already been four years since you started working for us. Everyone who has visited us to receive financial advice has been impressed by our office, and your company has played an important role in creating that positive first impression.

In spite of your excellence, we will soon no longer need your services, and we would like the last cleaning day to be February 28. We are moving to a new office building at 579 Ohio Avenue, and the building's maintenance team provides cleaning as part of the monthly fee. I'd be happy to recommend your business to others if the situation arises.

All the best,

Wanda Milburn

181. According to the letter, when will fees for a service increase?

(A) January 5
(B) January 31
(C) March 4
(D) March 5

182. On what point do Mr. Berg and Ms. Milburn agree?

(A) That cleaning should be done regularly
(B) That good cleaners are hard to find
(C) That regulations are becoming tighter
(D) That the cost of cleaning services has risen

183. What type of business does Ms. Milburn most likely work for?

(A) A graphic design firm
(B) A software development company
(C) A commercial construction company
(D) A financial consulting firm

184. What is suggested about Shinetime Commercial Cleaning?

(A) It has been in operation for four years.
(B) It will relocate its head office in March.
(C) It has recently been sold to a competitor.
(D) It plans to recruit more employees.

185. How does Ms. Milburn provide what Mr. Berg has requested?

(A) By giving feedback about a service
(B) By agreeing to some new contract terms
(C) By confirming the desired termination date
(D) By reporting a new business address

GO ON TO THE NEXT PAGE

Questions 186-190 refer to the following article and forms.

Oakdale (April 9)—Preparations are underway for Oakdale's 8th Annual Health and Well-Being Expo, which will take place on Sunday, June 19. The expo will feature businesses offering a variety of health-related goods and services. Additionally, local physicians and nurses will provide free screenings for blood pressure and cholesterol levels as well as a basic eye exam.

After many years at Juniper Hall, the expo has been moved to the Bayridge Convention Center this year. "Due to the growing popularity of the event, Juniper Hall could no longer contain the number of vendors interested in participating in the expo," said Ken Exley, one of the event planners. "Visitors can easily find what they're looking for, with vendors of vitamins and health supplements in the main hall, massage therapists and spa representatives in the east wing, and gym representatives and sports-related businesses in the west wing."

To register, visit www.oakdalehealthexpo.com. Members of the Oakdale Business Association can get a twenty percent discount.

Annual Health and Well-Being Expo
Vendor Feedback Survey

Name: Anna Pierson
Business/Company: Sunrise Spa

I was informed about the event through my membership in the Oakdale Business Association. This was my first time participating as a vendor, and I reached more people than I expected. However, I would have liked a larger booth to provide massages on-site, and I spoke to some other vendors that needed a smaller one. Not everyone has the same needs, so it would be a good idea to address this in the future.

http://www.rtgoakdale.com/reviews

Please let us know about your experience.

Reviewed by (optional):

Sheryl Baum

How did you first find out about RTG Oakdale?

By visiting the Oakdale Health and Well-Being Expo

How satisfied were you with your experience (0=Very Dissatisfied, 5=Very Satisfied)?

5

Comments:

I have recently become more interested in the vegetarian lifestyle due to its beneficial effects on the environment. I decided to transition to a completely vegetarian diet very soon but was concerned about getting enough protein, iron, and anything else that may be lacking. However, I wasn't sure what kind of vitamin supplements I would need. After speaking to Anthony Cress at his business's booth, I felt like I was fully informed. Mr. Cress was knowledgeable and made great recommendations for my specific circumstances. Overall, it was a very positive experience for me.

186. According to the article, why did the event planners use a different site this year?
(A) To ensure more space
(B) To minimize traffic problems
(C) To promote a new building
(D) To reduce travel times

187. What is suggested about Ms. Pierson?
(A) She qualified for early registration.
(B) She recently started her business.
(C) She has participated in past events.
(D) She was eligible for a discount.

188. What does Ms. Pierson recommend for the next expo?
(A) Addressing some noise complaints
(B) Providing more power outlets
(C) Offering booths in various sizes
(D) Advertising the event to more people

189. What is implied about Mr. Cress?
(A) He has lived in Oakdale for a long time.
(B) He worked at a booth in the main hall.
(C) He was an event planner for the expo.
(D) He is considering hiring Ms. Baum.

190. What does Ms. Baum plan to do?
(A) Undertake further research on a topic
(B) Write another online review
(C) Change her daily eating habits
(D) Start a health-related business

GO ON TO THE NEXT PAGE

Questions 191-195 refer to the following e-mail, article, and Web page.

E-Mail

To: Armina Giordano <a.giordano@conway-co.com>
From: Rashid Fadel <r.fadel@conway-co.com>
Date: August 21
Subject: Submission

Dear Ms. Giordano,

We appreciate your participation in the Conway Future Growth Initiative here at Conway Co. This is the first time we have requested suggestions for expanding the business, and we were pleased to see so many ideas shared by staff throughout the entire company.

Your submission regarding opening a small-scale version of our usual store in the Brighton Shopping Complex is intriguing. The committee members loved the idea of exposing customers to our most popular items, but we feel like we don't have the big picture. For example, we're wondering what kind of foot traffic could be expected at that site. I understand that the monthly lease fee is quite high, so we would have to make sure it's worth it. In addition, what other businesses are in operation there or plan to do business there? I know that Arcadia has advertised a grand opening at the Brighton Shopping Complex for October. This may be a major issue, as it is our main competitor and carries a very similar inventory to ours. We would like to explore this matter further before making a final decision.

Warmest regards,

Rashid Fadel
Committee Head, Conway Future Growth Initiative

LONGVIEW (October 3)—Later this month, Arcadia, the maker of high-end athletic shoes for basketball, running, and more, will hold a grand opening at its newest branch at the Brighton Shopping Complex. Customers who attend the event will have the opportunity to enter a prize drawing for $5,000 in Arcadia merchandise.

The store will be located next to Golden Apparel and is expected to become one of the company's highest-earning branches. With famous athletes such as basketball player Scott Atkinson and marathon runner Caroline Holmes wearing its products, it is no surprise that Arcadia has grown in popularity over the past few years.

http://www.brightonsc.com/floorplan

HOME	DIRECTORY	**FLOOR PLAN**	CONTACT

Site Map of Brighton Shopping Complex

Unit 101 (Vacant)	Officeland	Home Designs	Unit 107 (Vacant)
	Food Court		
Superb Gifts	Unit 104 (Vacant)	Unit 106 (Vacant)	Golden Apparel

191. What is suggested about the Conway Future Growth Initiative?

(A) It targets new staff members.
(B) It will last for one month.
(C) It was suggested by Mr. Fadel.
(D) It was open to all employees.

192. Why did Mr. Fadel send the e-mail?

(A) To suggest merging with a competitor
(B) To request further information about a proposal
(C) To explain the rules of a company program
(D) To recommend improvements to a department's operations

193. In what industry does Conway Co. work?

(A) Footwear manufacturing
(B) Property development
(C) Job recruitment
(D) Media services

194. In what unit of the Brighton Shopping Complex will Arcadia be located?

(A) Unit 101
(B) Unit 104
(C) Unit 106
(D) Unit 107

195. What aspect of Arcadia's products is emphasized in the article?

(A) Its wide range of options
(B) Its affordable price
(C) Its use by celebrities
(D) Its environmentally friendly design

GO ON TO THE NEXT PAGE

Questions 196-200 refer to the following article and e-mails.

FOR IMMEDIATE RELEASE

TORONTO (15 March)—A spokesperson for Millerbrook Enterprises has announced that Salvador Tolentino has been promoted to CEO to replace the outgoing CEO, Mary Gilhurst. He was unanimously selected by the Millerbrook Enterprises board and will take on his new role from May 25 after training with Ms. Gilhurst.

Millerbrook Enterprises provides cutting-edge software for artificial intelligence. Its products and research have led the industry for the past decade, and it has plans to open several international branches in the next few years. As Mr. Tolentino was formerly working as the company's CFO, the company is seeking to fill this position quickly. Duties include analyzing financial data and monitoring company expenditures. The role requires the ability to clearly communicate to the board and investors in both written and spoken form. Further details about the position and the hiring process are posted on www.millerbrook.com.

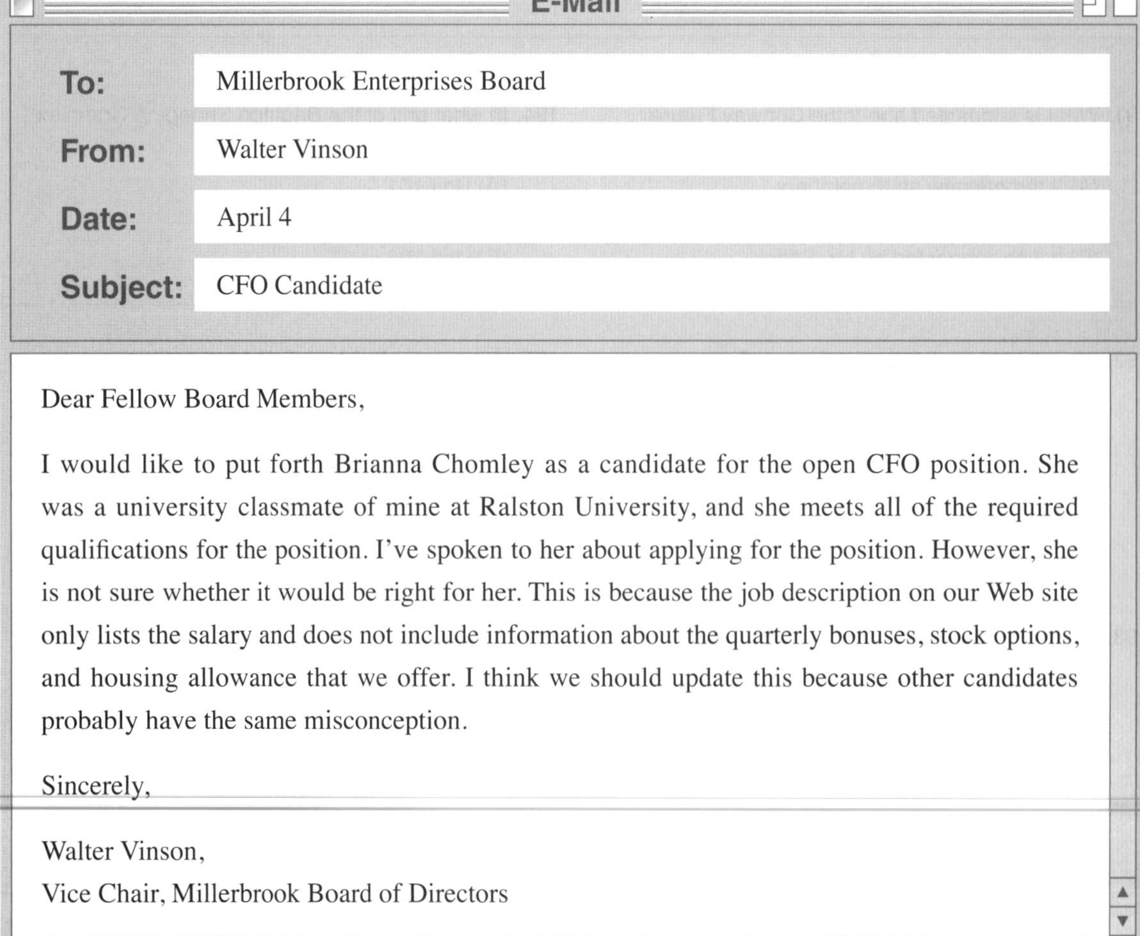

E-Mail

To: Millerbrook Enterprises Board

From: Walter Vinson

Date: April 4

Subject: CFO Candidate

Dear Fellow Board Members,

I would like to put forth Brianna Chomley as a candidate for the open CFO position. She was a university classmate of mine at Ralston University, and she meets all of the required qualifications for the position. I've spoken to her about applying for the position. However, she is not sure whether it would be right for her. This is because the job description on our Web site only lists the salary and does not include information about the quarterly bonuses, stock options, and housing allowance that we offer. I think we should update this because other candidates probably have the same misconception.

Sincerely,

Walter Vinson,
Vice Chair, Millerbrook Board of Directors

E-Mail

To:	Walter Vinson
From:	Erin Solberg
Date:	April 4
Subject:	Updated job description

Hi Walter,

Thank you for your advice on the job description for the CFO position. I've added the information you suggested. As we voted in the last meeting to add another member to our board, we need to start the search for that person as well. According to the bylaws, the selection process should be carried out by a committee of three people and must be headed by a high-ranking officer on the board—that is, the chair or vice chair. Please let me know what you think.

Sincerely,

Erin Solberg
Secretary, Millerbrook Board of Directors.

196. What is indicated about Mr. Tolentino in the press release?
(A) He will be given an award from the company.
(B) He is leaving to start his own business.
(C) He had the support of all board members.
(D) He plans to train his replacement.

197. What is suggested about Ms. Chomley?
(A) She plans to relocate to a new city.
(B) She has strong communication skills.
(C) She is Mr. Vinson's former coworker.
(D) She has designed software programs before.

198. According to Mr. Vinson, why is Ms. Chomley unsure about the position?
(A) The job responsibilities are too specialized.
(B) The expected working hours are too long.
(C) The compensation package is not fully described.
(D) The company has a lengthy interview process.

199. In the second e-mail, what is implied about the Millerbrook board?
(A) It will increase in size.
(B) It will meet more frequently.
(C) It will receive larger payments.
(D) It will update the bylaws.

200. What is suggested about Mr. Vinson?
(A) He is the newest member of the board.
(B) He opposed a proposed change.
(C) He will be supervising his friend.
(D) He is eligible to lead a committee.

Stop! This is the end of the test. If you finish before time is called, you may go back to Parts 5, 6, and 7 and check your work.

Actual Test 2

LISTENING TEST

In the Listening test, you will be asked to demonstrate how well you understand spoken English. The entire Listening test will last approximately 45 minutes. There are four parts, and directions are given for each part. You must mark your answers on the separate answer sheet. Do not write your answers in your test book.

PART 1 05

Directions: For each question in this part, you will hear four statements about a picture in your test book. When you hear the statements, you must select the one statement that best describes what you see in the picture. Then find the number of the question on your answer sheet and mark your answer. The statements will not be printed in your test book and will be spoken only one time.

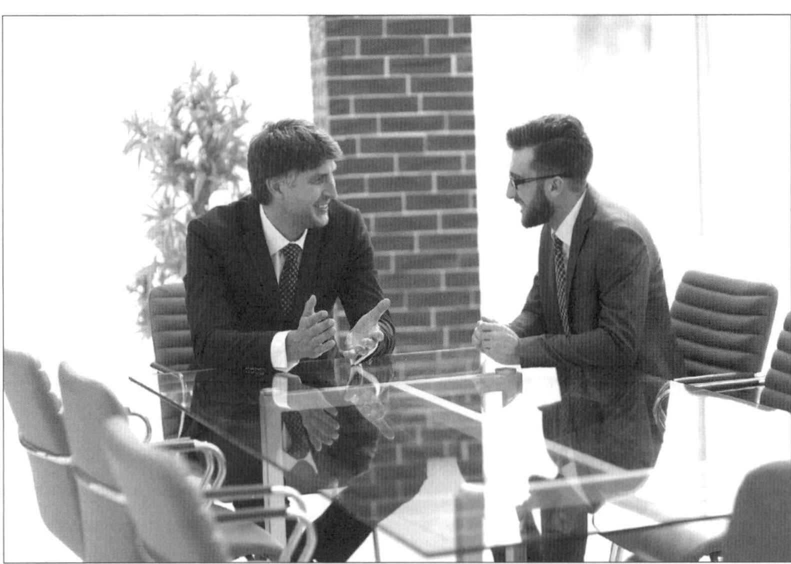

Statement (C), "They're sitting at the table," is the best description of the picture, so you should select answer (C) and mark it on your answer sheet.

1.

2.

3.

9.2

4.

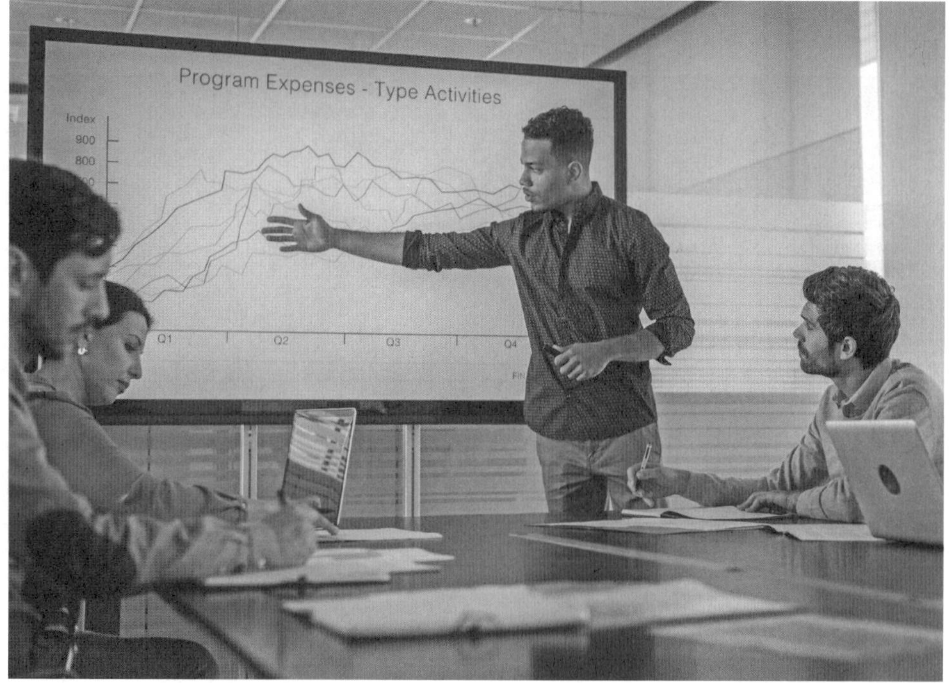
Program Expenses - Type Activities
Index
900
800
Q1
Q2
Q3
Q4

5.

6.

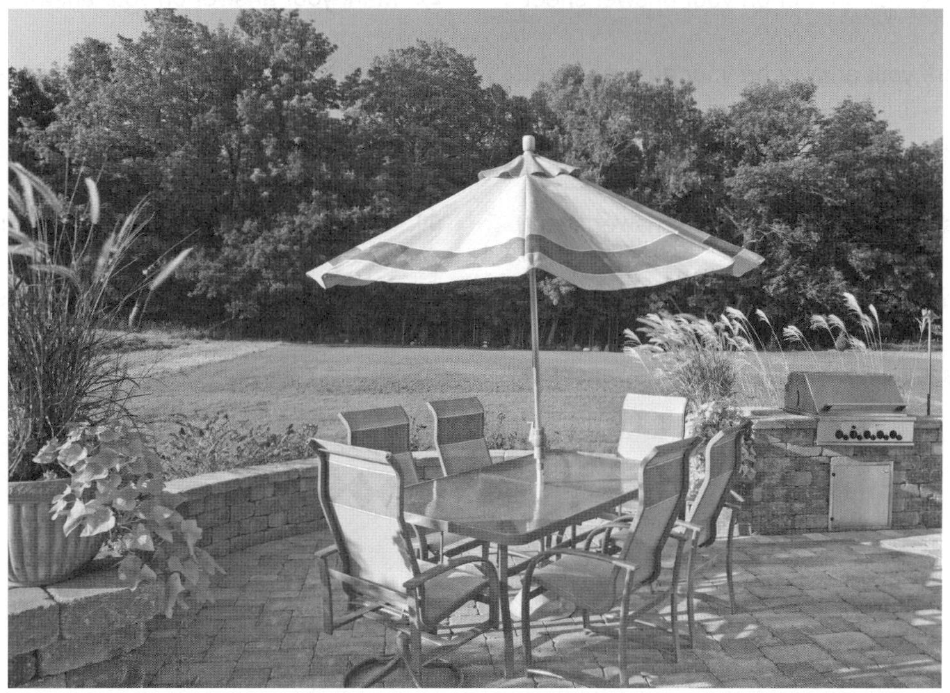

GO ON TO THE NEXT PAGE

PART 2 06

Directions: You will hear a question or statement and three responses spoken in English. They will not be printed in your test book and will be spoken only one time. Select the best response to the question or statement and mark the letter (A), (B), or (C) on your answer sheet.

7. Mark your answer on your answer sheet.
8. Mark your answer on your answer sheet.
9. Mark your answer on your answer sheet.
10. Mark your answer on your answer sheet.
11. Mark your answer on your answer sheet.
12. Mark your answer on your answer sheet.
13. Mark your answer on your answer sheet.
14. Mark your answer on your answer sheet.
15. Mark your answer on your answer sheet.
16. Mark your answer on your answer sheet.
17. Mark your answer on your answer sheet.
18. Mark your answer on your answer sheet.
19. Mark your answer on your answer sheet.
20. Mark your answer on your answer sheet.
21. Mark your answer on your answer sheet.
22. Mark your answer on your answer sheet.
23. Mark your answer on your answer sheet.
24. Mark your answer on your answer sheet.
25. Mark your answer on your answer sheet.
26. Mark your answer on your answer sheet.
27. Mark your answer on your answer sheet.
28. Mark your answer on your answer sheet.
29. Mark your answer on your answer sheet.
30. Mark your answer on your answer sheet.
31. Mark your answer on your answer sheet.

PART 3 07

Directions: You will hear some conversations between two or more people. You will be asked to answer three questions about what the speakers say in each conversation. Select the best response to each question and mark the letter (A), (B), (C), or (D) on your answer sheet. The conversations will not be printed in your test book and will be spoken only one time.

32. How did the woman find out about the sale?
(A) By reading a banner
(B) By performing an Internet search
(C) By receiving a flyer in the mail
(D) By seeing an ad in the newspaper

33. What does the man recommend buying?
(A) An electronic device
(B) Some cookware
(C) A piece of furniture
(D) Some clothing

34. Why does the woman want to make a phone call?
(A) To increase a budget
(B) To get an opinion
(C) To confirm an address
(D) To check another store

35. Where most likely are the speakers?
(A) At a conference hall
(B) At a vehicle rental agency
(C) At a computer repair shop
(D) At an airport

36. What does the man say he did yesterday?
(A) Traveled by airplane
(B) Opened a new business
(C) Ordered some components
(D) Gave a presentation

37. What does the woman offer to do for the man?
(A) Show him a catalog
(B) Provide a refund
(C) Consult an expert
(D) Work extra hours

38. What is the purpose of the man's visit?
(A) To make a delivery
(B) To inspect a building
(C) To introduce a company
(D) To install security equipment

39. What does the woman plan to do?
(A) Call the man back
(B) Keep an entrance locked
(C) Reschedule a visit
(D) Put up a sign

40. What does the man inquire about?
(A) A company invoice
(B) A parking situation
(C) An hourly fee
(D) A road closure

41. What are the men encouraged to do?
(A) Borrow a company car
(B) Sign up for a workshop
(C) Share rides to work
(D) Reserve a parking spot

42. What will the woman do in the afternoon?
(A) Meet with managers
(B) E-mail a plan
(C) Announce a change
(D) Launch a program

43. Why does the woman thank Aiden?
(A) He completed a task ahead of schedule.
(B) He agreed to attend a meeting for her.
(C) He volunteered to provide suggestions.
(D) He will help new employees get settled.

44. What does the man need assistance with?
(A) A film screening
(B) A retirement party
(C) A training session
(D) A recruiting process

45. Why is the woman unable to help the man?
(A) She has to meet with a client.
(B) She has interviews with candidates.
(C) She has to complete a coworker's tasks.
(D) She has a doctor's appointment.

46. What will the man probably discuss with Ms. Hendricks?
(A) Changing a due date
(B) Transferring to another office
(C) Hiring a temporary worker
(D) Updating a company policy

---

47. What has the man recently done?
(A) Accepted a promotion to a new position
(B) Introduced new products to a company
(C) Received negative feedback from employees
(D) Encouraged the business owner to buy more vans

48. What does the man mean when he says, "it's a lot to ask"?
(A) He believes a workload is unreasonable.
(B) He feels bad for needing a big favor.
(C) He is unable to meet a deadline.
(D) He needs some time to think about a decision.

49. What does the woman suggest doing?
(A) Expanding the hours of operation
(B) Recruiting some drivers
(C) Finding a new supplier
(D) Reducing a service fee

---

50. What is the conversation mainly about?
(A) Misprints in a catalog
(B) Images on a Web site
(C) A product launch
(D) A customer complaint

51. What does the woman mention about a project?
(A) It doesn't have enough workers.
(B) It has been canceled.
(C) It needs a budget adjustment.
(D) It is still in progress.

52. What does the man plan to do next week?
(A) Assess a service
(B) Replace some images
(C) Assign a new task
(D) Repair some equipment

---

53. Why is the man visiting the business?
(A) To have a dental checkup
(B) To get a receipt
(C) To pick up an item
(D) To schedule an appointment

54. What did Ms. Michaels do in the morning?
(A) Processed a credit card payment
(B) Noticed a billing error
(C) Filled out some paperwork
(D) Left a telephone message

55. What will the man most likely do next?
(A) Speak to a dentist
(B) Confirm a schedule
(C) Show an ID card
(D) Go to an exam room

---

56. What is the purpose of the call?
(A) To complain about a damaged item
(B) To apologize for a delay
(C) To check on the status of an order
(D) To inquire about a discount

57. According to the man, what has caused a problem?
(A) An engine malfunction
(B) A computer error
(C) An employee's absence
(D) A major storm

58. What does the man recommend doing?
(A) Checking information online
(B) Calling back later
(C) Waiting another day
(D) Providing a tracking number

---

59. Where most likely are the speakers?
(A) At an airport
(B) In a public library
(C) At a convention center
(D) In a hotel lobby

60. What does the woman mention about the parking lot?
(A) It is restricted to guests.
(B) It is currently full.
(C) It is under construction.
(D) It is closed in the evenings.

61. What does the woman imply when she says, "I can't help you"?
(A) She does not know the directions to a place.
(B) She is not allowed to make exceptions.
(C) She has trouble making recommendations.
(D) She cannot explain the policy's details.

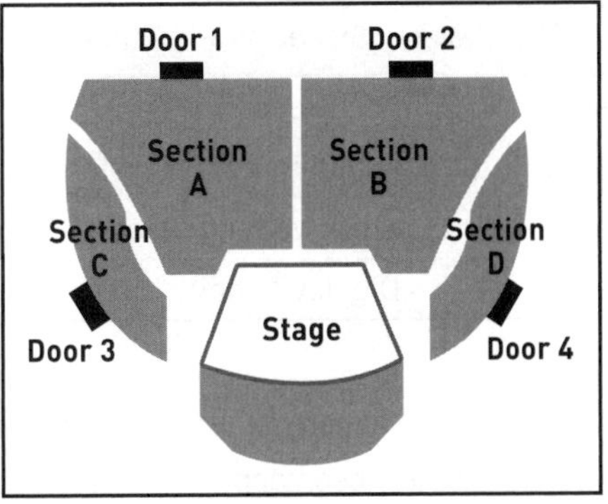

62. Who most likely is the woman?
(A) A theater employee
(B) A media critic
(C) A musical performer
(D) A stage manager

63. Look at the graphic. In which section will the man probably sit?
(A) Section A
(B) Section B
(C) Section C
(D) Section D

64. What will the man most likely do next?
(A) Send a message
(B) Give the woman his seat
(C) Exchange a ticket
(D) Wait for a friend outside

GO ON TO THE NEXT PAGE

778 Crowley Street: Work Schedule	
Week 1	Trim trees
Week 2	Install irrigation system
Week 3	Erect wooden fence
Week 4	Dig flower bed

65. What does the woman mention about the permit?
(A) It has already been approved by the city.
(B) It is required because of the fence's height.
(C) It will take several weeks to process.
(D) It will be valid for eight months.

66. Look at the graphic. What will the speakers do next week?
(A) Trim trees
(B) Install an irrigation system
(C) Erect a wooden fence
(D) Dig a flower bed

67. What will the woman send to Ms. Kenmore?
(A) A set of photographs
(B) An updated schedule
(C) A final bill
(D) A list of materials

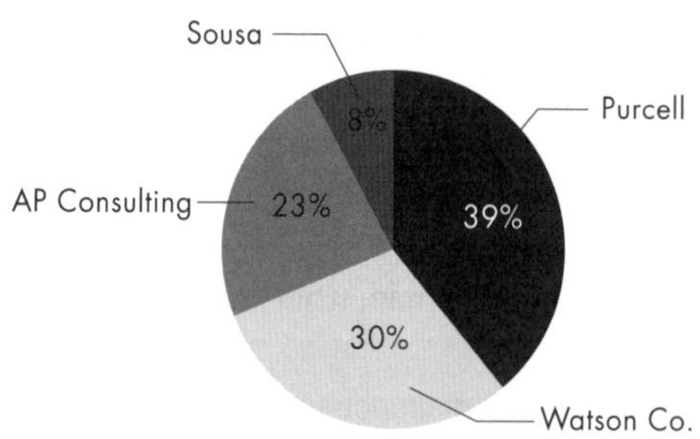

68. What does the man say happened yesterday?
(A) A budget proposal was submitted.
(B) A new branch opened.
(C) A marketing campaign was launched.
(D) An award was presented.

69. Look at the graphic. Which company recently changed its CEO?
(A) Purcell
(B) Watson Co.
(C) AP Consulting
(D) Sousa

70. What is the woman concerned about?
(A) Losing customers to a competitor
(B) Spending too much on marketing
(C) Failing to keep up with demand
(D) Having dissatisfied staff members

PART 4 08

Directions: You will hear some talks given by a single speaker. You will be asked to answer three questions about what the speaker says in each talk. Select the best response to each question and mark the letter (A), (B), (C), or (D) on your answer sheet. The talks will not be printed in your test book and will be spoken only one time.

71. What is the main topic of the broadcast?
(A) A museum tour
(B) An art contest
(C) A painting lesson
(D) A fundraiser

72. How can participants receive a free gift?
(A) By adding their names to a mailing list
(B) By making a regular donation
(C) By being one of the first fifty people to enroll
(D) By purchasing more than one ticket

73. What does the speaker encourage listeners to do?
(A) Call the radio station
(B) Contact Ms. Coleman
(C) Listen to a program
(D) Visit a Web site

---

74. Where most likely does the speaker work?
(A) At a taxi company
(B) At an airport
(C) At a train station
(D) At a travel agency

75. What will listeners be asked to do?
(A) Show a receipt
(B) Take their seats
(C) Wait for further instructions
(D) Present their tickets

76. What does the speaker say that employees will do?
(A) Issue new tickets
(B) Help to move luggage
(C) Update safety procedures
(D) Hang up some notices

---

77. Why is the speaker calling?
(A) To accept a task
(B) To handle a complaint
(C) To show appreciation
(D) To leave early

78. What does the speaker imply when he says, "Tourist season is starting soon"?
(A) He is concerned about being short-staffed.
(B) He doesn't understand why profits are low.
(C) He agrees with the listener's suggestion.
(D) He thinks the store should advertise more frequently.

79. What does the speaker ask for?
(A) An access code
(B) A floor plan
(C) An authorization form
(D) A colleague's phone number

---

80. Who most likely is the speaker?
(A) A librarian
(B) A personnel manager
(C) A marketer
(D) A teacher

81. Why does the speaker say, "It truly saddens me to say this"?
(A) To express his regret
(B) To emphasize his disagreement
(C) To reject an application
(D) To show his mood change

82. What does the speaker ask the listener to do?
(A) Volunteer for a charity
(B) Provide a document
(C) Recommend a worker
(D) Lead a new program

GO ON TO THE NEXT PAGE

83. What is the purpose of the meeting?

(A) To report on a competitor's plan
(B) To announce a leadership change
(C) To explain a new company policy
(D) To congratulate the listeners on an award

84. What kind of company do the listeners most likely work for?

(A) An energy plant
(B) A vehicle manufacturer
(C) A communications company
(D) A construction firm

85. According to the speaker, what has Ms. Melville done?

(A) Ordered replacement parts
(B) Received an award
(C) Analyzed a competitor
(D) Prepared an employee list

---

86. Where is the introduction taking place?

(A) At a manufacturing plant
(B) At an auto repair shop
(C) At a construction site
(D) At a convention center

87. Who is Gustav Palmer?

(A) A business owner
(B) An engineer
(C) A reporter
(D) A physician

88. What does the speaker ask the listeners to do?

(A) Suggest ideas for a design
(B) Wear protective gear
(C) Refrain from taking pictures
(D) Stay together as a group

---

89. What is the speaker mainly discussing?

(A) An educational program
(B) A registration fee
(C) A library fundraiser
(D) A community picnic

90. Why is the speaker concerned?

(A) There is a shortage of funding.
(B) A meeting space is not available.
(C) Bad weather is expected soon.
(D) Interest in a project has declined.

91. What does the speaker ask the listeners to do?

(A) Register for an event
(B) Send her property information
(C) Meet in front of a building
(D) Make a financial donation

---

92. Who most likely is the speaker?

(A) A security guard
(B) A college lecturer
(C) A tour guide
(D) A medical professional

93. What does the speaker mean when he says, "This is really valuable information"?

(A) He encourages the listeners to complete a survey.
(B) He is concerned that some documents will get lost.
(C) He wants some data to be carefully protected.
(D) He is pleased that so much information has been gathered.

94. What are the listeners reminded to do?

(A) Keep their personal items with them
(B) Call later for some test results
(C) Be ready to present an ID card
(D) Fill out a registration form in advance

Customer: Faye Segura
Order number: 1223389

Description	Quantity
Daffodil bulbs	35
Tulip bulbs	30
Rose bushes	15
Lavender bushes	6

95. What is the purpose of the call?

(A) To change an appointment
(B) To verify an order
(C) To notify of a delivery error
(D) To request a payment

96. Look at the graphic. Which quantity does the speaker refer to?

(A) 35
(B) 30
(C) 15
(D) 6

97. What does the speaker say about Phillip?

(A) He can issue a refund.
(B) He can take a message.
(C) He can design a garden.
(D) He can pick up some plants.

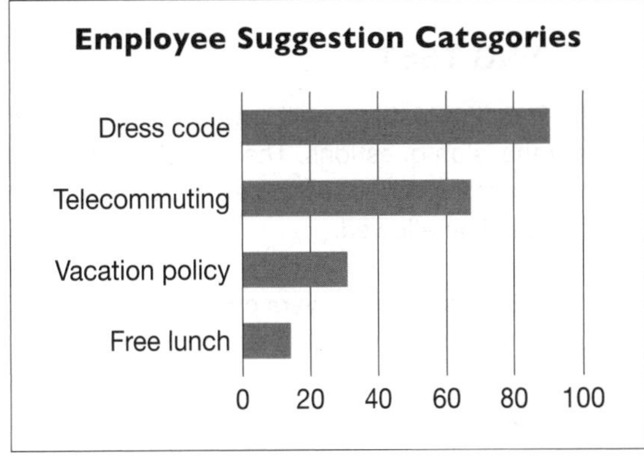

98. Where do the listeners most likely work?

(A) At an insurance company
(B) At a law firm
(C) At a magazine publisher
(D) At an environmental agency

99. Look at the graphic. What topic will the company address in June?

(A) Dress code
(B) Telecommuting
(C) Vacation policy
(D) Free lunch

100. According to the speaker, what is available in the staff lounge today?

(A) A policy explanation
(B) Some survey forms
(C) Some refreshments
(D) A customer list

This is the end of the Listening test. Turn to Part 5 in your test book.

GO ON TO THE NEXT PAGE

READING TEST

In the Reading test, you will read a variety of texts and answer several different types of reading comprehension questions. The entire Reading test will last 75 minutes. There are three parts, and directions are given for each part. You are encouraged to answer as many questions as possible within the time allowed.

You must mark your answers on the separate answer sheet. Do not write your answers in your test book.

PART 5

Directions: A word or phrase is missing in each of the sentences below. Four answer choices are given below each sentence. Select the best answer to complete the sentence. Then mark the letter (A), (B), (C), or (D) on your answer sheet.

101. Most attendees at the conference confirmed that ------- learned a lot of useful information.

(A) theirs
(B) their
(C) them
(D) they

102. ------- in meeting the delivery demands is an important part of any courier business.

(A) Relied
(B) Relying
(C) Reliable
(D) Reliability

103. Keller Automotive's mini hybrid is the most affordable ------- among mini hybrids sold in the country.

(A) such
(B) one
(C) what
(D) each

104. Emerson Railways is interested in ------- its insurance provider in order to save money.

(A) covering
(B) emerging
(C) changing
(D) obtaining

105. Participants in the marathon will run ------- the Ness River and finish the race at Willow Park.

(A) along
(B) onto
(C) apart
(D) except

106. The new dryer from Chipley Appliances is designed ------- when the clothes are dry.

(A) to sense
(B) senses
(C) sensing
(D) sensed

107. The caterer was surprised that the seafood appetizers seemed ------- touched by the guests.

(A) conveniently
(B) apparently
(C) barely
(D) lightly

108. The peak season for winter wear is coming up, so it is ------- that we find a new manager for the Berka branch soon.

(A) imperative
(B) responsive
(C) exclusive
(D) persuasive

109. The construction of an additional lane on Highway 27 was delayed ------- a shortage of materials.

(A) because of
(B) since
(C) in case
(D) as a result

110. Community center officials were pleased that course ------- has increased by fifteen percent.

(A) description
(B) enrollment
(C) inventory
(D) attitude

111. Patrons may take out reference books from the library ------- they have received special permission from the head librarian.

(A) or else
(B) so
(C) whereas
(D) provided that

112. After the ticketing machines were installed, it was ------- to handle more passengers at the station.

(A) possible
(B) possibility
(C) possibly
(D) possibilities

113. Dewitt Communications ------- provides customer service training for its employees, so it has built a reputation for excellence.

(A) regularly
(B) firmly
(C) recently
(D) promptly

114. In compliance with regulations, we will give updates to those who are ------- involved in the matter.

(A) more direct
(B) directly
(C) direct
(D) directness

115. The research database maintained by Gyron Pharmaceuticals provides a ------- of information for physicians.

(A) quality
(B) similarity
(C) wealth
(D) mention

116. Once the transaction is complete, the person who requested the transfer will receive a message ------- the deposit.

(A) confirming
(B) confirms
(C) confirmed
(D) confirmation

117. Mr. Lincoln always flies with the same airline ------- he has joined a frequent flyer program.

(A) so that
(B) even if
(C) unless
(D) now that

118. After washing the car, Mr. Howard ------- a thin coat of wax to make the surface shine.

(A) to apply
(B) applying
(C) was applied
(D) applied

119. Ms. Mason forgot to take the fluctuations ------- currency rates into account when making the projections.

(A) often
(B) in
(C) finally
(D) on

120. Many potential customers were discouraged by ------- similar cell phone plans at Fletcher Mobile.

(A) confusing
(B) confusingly
(C) confusion
(D) confused

121. Ms. Cheng added her ------- to the contract as a witness to the agreement.

(A) signed
(B) signs
(C) signature
(D) to sign

122. If you have lost or damaged your boarding pass, please speak to the gate agent, who can verify it and print -------.

(A) another
(B) each other
(C) others
(D) one another

123. Employees are asked to ------- the model number of the device that needs repairs.

(A) intensify
(B) specify
(C) unify
(D) testify

124. Lucy Berman has set a number of swimming records ------- her eight-year career as a professional swimmer.

(A) above
(B) regarding
(C) throughout
(D) of

125. Late for the meeting, Ms. Diaz took a seat in the back of the room to avoid -------.

(A) noticed
(B) being noticed
(C) to notice
(D) having noticed

126. The town's Independence Day Parade will commence with a brief speech by the newly ------- mayor.

(A) elected
(B) elects
(C) electing
(D) elect

127. Carla Stenton is an ------- entrepreneur who launched a start-up that expanded quickly across the nation.

(A) embarrassed
(B) acceptable
(C) ambitious
(D) alarmed

128. The sound quality of Vivico speakers is ------- superior compared to others on the market, but many people cannot afford them.

(A) markedly
(B) respectively
(C) adamantly
(D) permissibly

129. The first two rows in the auditorium are specially reserved for VIP guests, ------- are presenters.

(A) the reason why
(B) as a matter of fact
(C) most of whom
(D) on the contrary

130. Many participants in the tour were delighted to discover how ------- learning about the city's history could be.

(A) considerable
(B) accountable
(C) enjoyable
(D) transferable

PART 6

Directions: Read the texts that follow. A word, phrase, or sentence is missing in parts of each text. Four answer choices for each question are given below the text. Select the best answer to complete the text. Then mark the letter (A), (B), (C), or (D) on your answer sheet.

Questions 131-134 refer to the following advertisement.

During the first week of July, Twinkle Jewelry will hold a special event to celebrate its first anniversary. For one week only, get two items, and we ------- **131.** you for only one. For example, if you buy one necklace and one bracelet, you'll pay for the cheaper item only! You can choose any two items you like from our wide ------- **132.** of jewelry. This offer applies to all of our products! ------- **133.**, there is no limit to the number of times a person can benefit from it. However, jewelry will be given out on a first come, first served basis while supplies last. ------- **134.**. The event starts on July 1.

131. (A) will charge
(B) will be charged
(C) were charging
(D) have been charging

132. (A) select
(B) selects
(C) selection
(D) selected

133. (A) In addition
(B) As a result
(C) Therefore
(D) Accordingly

134. (A) That is why we have agreed to refund your purchase.
(B) So come early to make sure you don't miss out.
(C) We will set the items you request aside for you.
(D) Please complete your payment as soon as possible.

Questions 135-138 refer to the following notice.

Public Seminar with Nora Devons
Thursday, May 14, 7 P.M.

Nora Devons, a prominent ------- (135.) of eliminating homelessness in Fredrick City, will be presenting a two-hour seminar at the Renner Convention Center. Ms. Devons is the president of the Association of Social Workers, a group with over three hundred members. She ------- (136.) efforts to support the homeless community for the past eight years. During the seminar, she will tell the audience about the seriousness of the homeless problem. ------- (137.) .

The talk is open to audience members of all ages, and there is no entrance fee. ------- (138.) , donations will be collected at the door to support the Marigold Homeless Shelter. For more information, visit www.assocofsw.org.

135. (A) founder
(B) advocate
(C) candidate
(D) prosecutor

136. (A) had been leading
(B) has led
(C) is leading
(D) will lead

137. (A) She will also mention ways to help resolve it.
(B) The audience asked questions during the break.
(C) At that time, she served as a city council member.
(D) She plans to return to Grayson University to earn a master's degree.

138. (A) Accordingly
(B) Specifically
(C) Apparently
(D) However

Questions 139-142 refer to the following e-mail.

To: Natasha Seymour <nseymour@vicivenues.com>
From: Robert Thornton <r.thornton@hvelectronics.net>
Date: October 3
Subject: Event at Boulevard Hall

Dear Ms. Seymour,

I am part of a committee that is in charge of ------- (139.) a retirement dinner for one of my coworkers at HV Electronics. Several of your venues ------- (140.), but Boulevard Hall received the most support. This was due to ------- (141.) modern facilities and proximity to our office in Blakeley Towers.

This will be our first time holding an event at Boulevard Hall. Could you confirm which dates are available in November? We prefer November 20, so we hope that evening is still free. ------- (142.).

Sincerely,

Robert Thornton

139. (A) inspiring
(B) arranging
(C) contributing
(D) visiting

140. (A) will be considered
(B) had considered
(C) were considered
(D) were considering

141. (A) their
(B) it
(C) its
(D) them

142. (A) We think you will be impressed with the spacious room.
(B) Even so, many people can walk from the office.
(C) This fee is within our estimated budget.
(D) If not, we have a few other possibilities in mind.

Questions 143-146 refer to the following e-mail.

To: Travel Times <info@traveltimes-magazine.com>
From: Christopher Venn <c.venn@frequenx.com>
Subject: Subscription #28571
Date: September 3

To Whom It May Concern:

I currently have a subscription to *Travel Times* magazine which is valid until the end of February. I'm wondering ------- **143.** it is possible to change the mailing address before the next issue comes out. ------- **144.**. I'm currently receiving the magazine at work, but the new manager ------- **145.** that we no longer have personal mail delivered there. ------- **146.** residential address is 798 Trelawney Way, Phoenix, AZ 85010. If there is a fee associated with this change, please e-mail me.

Thank you,

Christopher Venn

143. (A) what
(B) if
(C) while
(D) for

144. (A) The information on Spain was particularly interesting.
(B) The monthly bill had charged me for two subscriptions.
(C) I couldn't find any information about doing this through your Web site.
(D) I appreciate your printing the article I submitted.

145. (A) requested
(B) facilitated
(C) acknowledged
(D) canceled

146. (A) Your
(B) Its
(C) Each
(D) My

PART 7

Directions: In this part you will read a selection of texts, such as magazine and newspaper articles, e-mails, and instant messages. Each text or set of texts is followed by several questions. Select the best answer for each question and mark the letter (A), (B), (C), or (D) on your answer sheet.

Questions 147-148 refer to the following notice.

Warm Hands Warm Hearts (WHWH) is seeking new members for Melville's local group, which knits mittens and gloves to donate to the homeless. Our next meeting will be on Saturday, November 2, from 1 P.M. to 4 P.M. at the Lindale Coffee Shop. To get there, take subway line 5 to Kingstown Arena Station and use exit 5.

Participants should bring their own yarn and knitting needles. In addition, we would like a variety of colors and yarn types, so please let us know what you plan to bring for your project by commenting in the forum at warmhandswh.org/forum.

147. Where most likely would the notice be found?
(A) In a product catalog
(B) On a public bulletin board
(C) On a subway ticket receipt
(D) In a craft instruction book

148. According to the notice, why should people visit the Web site?
(A) To view photos of past projects
(B) To confirm registration for an event
(C) To request instructions by e-mail
(D) To report their choices of materials

GO ON TO THE NEXT PAGE

Questions 149-150 refer to the following invoice.

Wallace Tools

Invoice Date: October 25
Invoice Number: 8395
Name: Dean Monette
Address: 805 Carriage Drive, Arlington Heights, IL 60005
Contact Number: 555-6950

One-week Rental: $49.99

[Contents]
Hadron-360 electric drill
Plastic carrying case
Charging device for unit battery
One-week insurance coverage (policy information printout)

Tax and Shipping: $8.95
Total: $58.94

Payment has been received in full for the above service. If you would like to keep the item longer, please call us at 555-2900. The device's user manual can be downloaded from our Web site at www.wallacetools.net.

149. What was NOT sent with the rental item?

(A) A user manual
(B) A battery charger
(C) Insurance details
(D) A portable container

150. Why should Mr. Monette call the number provided?

(A) To give feedback about a service
(B) To make a payment
(C) To request instructions
(D) To extend a rental period

Questions 151-152 refer to the following article.

BEIJING (July 5)—The price of raw silk is on the rise again after hitting a four-year low last quarter. This is in part due to trends in China and India, the world's largest producers of silk. Silk suppliers have been accumulating large quantities of the product at cheap prices and storing it rather than putting it on the market. This has led to an increase in price, which is expected to continue for the next few quarters. Clothing producers have enjoyed the low price of silk, but now that a higher cost of raw materials is projected, the fabric is much less attractive. As a result, many such producers are designing clothing made from man-made fabric, such as nylon and rayon, to avoid the unpredictability of the silk market.

151. According to the article, what has affected the price of silk?

(A) Some dealers are stocking up on the material.
(B) The currency value in China and India has dropped.
(C) Production has increased in efficiency.
(D) Customers are starting to prefer other fabrics.

152. How are clothing manufacturers dealing with a change?

(A) By negotiating directly with suppliers
(B) By developing products with alternative materials
(C) By purchasing supplies in bulk
(D) By changing the way goods are advertised

Questions 153-155 refer to the following e-mail.

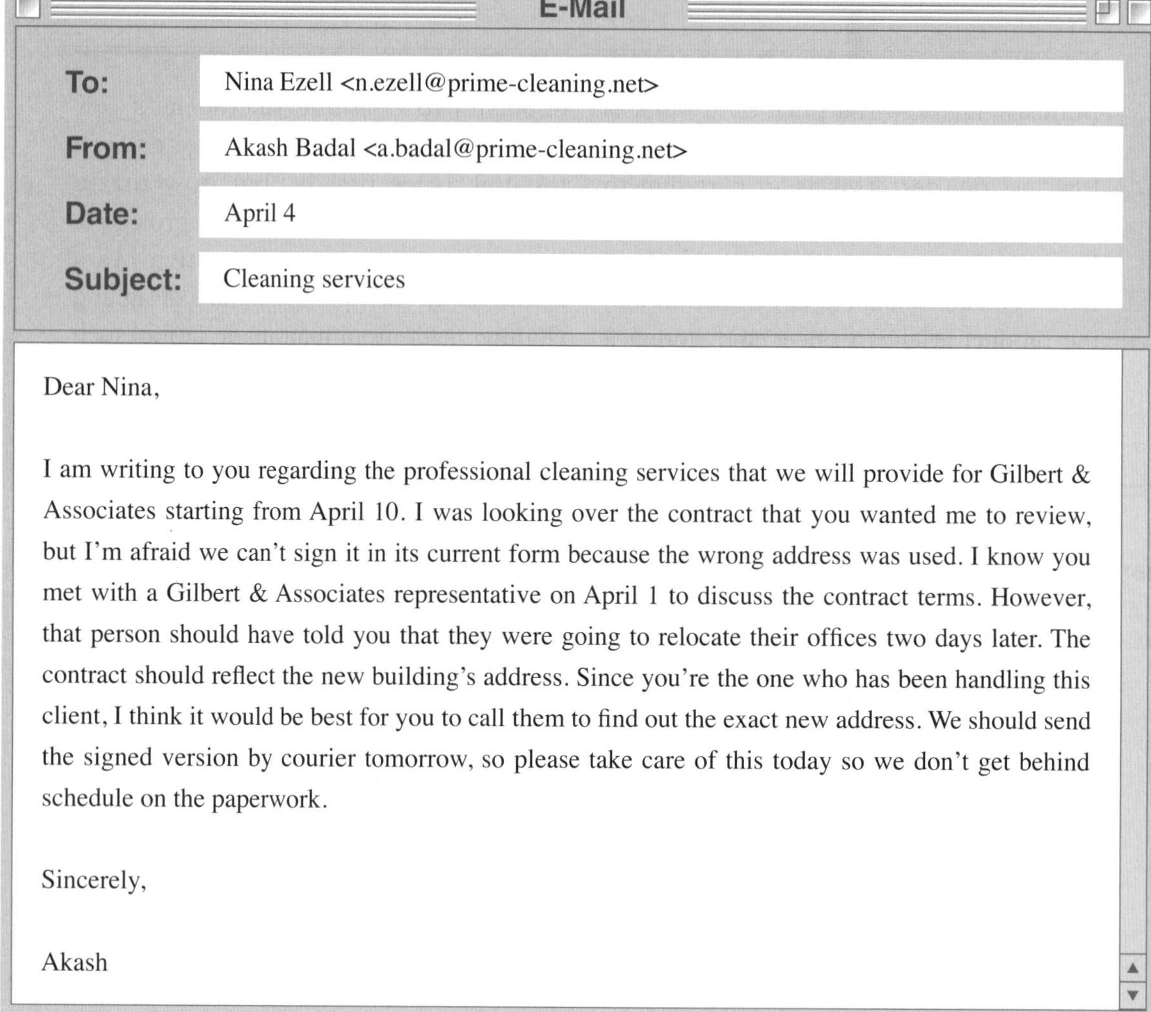

E-Mail

To: Nina Ezell <n.ezell@prime-cleaning.net>

From: Akash Badal <a.badal@prime-cleaning.net>

Date: April 4

Subject: Cleaning services

Dear Nina,

I am writing to you regarding the professional cleaning services that we will provide for Gilbert & Associates starting from April 10. I was looking over the contract that you wanted me to review, but I'm afraid we can't sign it in its current form because the wrong address was used. I know you met with a Gilbert & Associates representative on April 1 to discuss the contract terms. However, that person should have told you that they were going to relocate their offices two days later. The contract should reflect the new building's address. Since you're the one who has been handling this client, I think it would be best for you to call them to find out the exact new address. We should send the signed version by courier tomorrow, so please take care of this today so we don't get behind schedule on the paperwork.

Sincerely,

Akash

153. Why did Mr. Badal send the e-mail?
(A) To recommend a business
(B) To change a cleaning schedule
(C) To send an updated contract
(D) To point out an error

154. When did Gilbert & Associates move to a new building?
(A) March 28
(B) March 30
(C) April 1
(D) April 3

155. What should Ms. Ezell do by the end of the day?
(A) Negotiate some contract terms
(B) Contact the Gilbert & Associates office
(C) Send Mr. Badal a client recommendation
(D) Mail some documents to Prime Cleaning

Questions 156-157 refer to the following text-message chain.

Donald Graham [9:12 A.M.]
I've e-mailed you the estimate from the interior designer for remodeling our lobby.

Wei Lu [9:14 A.M.]
It's more expensive than I was expecting, especially since our lawyers don't even use that area much.

Donald Graham [9:15 A.M.]
Yes, it's slightly over budget, but I think it's worth it.

Wei Lu [9:16 A.M.]
Do you? It doesn't even include the cost of furniture.

Donald Graham [9:18 A.M.]
You have to understand that the lobby is the first thing people see when they arrive. It's essential that they have a good opinion of our business right from the start.

Wei Lu [9:19 A.M.]
You have a point. I guess it will give people more confidence in our services.

156. What are the writers mainly discussing?
- (A) Hotel accommodations
- (B) Budget limits
- (C) Renovation costs
- (D) Customer reviews

157. At 9:19 A.M., what does Ms. Lu most likely mean when she writes, "You have a point"?
- (A) Attracting new customers is not easy.
- (B) The business should be careful about spending.
- (C) Making a good impression is important.
- (D) The lobby needs to be expanded soon.

Questions 158-160 refer to the following article.

NEW YORK (September 10)–Paula Frederick is known for her trendy and sophisticated fashions both on and off the runway. In addition to her retail business, she has created award-winning costumes for a number of films, most recently the sci-fi blockbuster *Golden Galaxy*. Now Ms. Frederick is lending her talents to a new project–designing warm-up uniforms and performance outfits for the national ice skating team. The team will wear them at the International Ice Skating Tournament, which will take place from January 3 to January 16.

Ms. Frederick was offered the project after meeting the team's coach, Vince Oliero, at an anniversary event for Charlotte Reeves, whose fashion house was Ms. Frederick's first employer after she graduated from design school. When Mr. Oliero mentioned that the team needed to update its look, the idea for the project was born.

Industry insiders are interested to see how Ms. Frederick's elaborate style will translate to the sports world. "I'm looking forward to the challenge," Ms. Frederick said at the debut event for *Golden Galaxy* earlier this week. "With the film, I was able to work with over-the-top designs and lavish embellishments. With my new project, I'll have limited fabric options and will need to prioritize comfort and practicality." *Golden Galaxy* producer Liam Hart, who accompanied Ms. Frederick to the event, also commented on the project, saying that he was certain Ms. Frederick's limitless creativity would help to make it a success.

Fans of Ms. Frederick's work can see *Golden Galaxy* costumes on the big screen and on her Web site. However, to see the uniforms they'll have to watch the tournament in person or live on television.

158. What is true about the *Golden Galaxy* costumes?
(A) They were Ms. Frederick's first project.
(B) They are practical and comfortable.
(C) They received an award.
(D) They are available for sale online.

159. Who most likely is Ms. Reeves?
(A) An ice skating coach
(B) A fashion designer
(C) A film producer
(D) A professional athlete

160. What is suggested about Mr. Hart?
(A) He has worked with Ms. Frederick on several projects.
(B) He recently attended a movie premiere.
(C) He met Ms. Frederick at an anniversary party.
(D) He knows Ms. Reeves personally.

Questions 161-163 refer to the following letter.

March 8

Store Manager Shawn Boyd
Outdoors Plus, Soulard Branch
1009 Ash Avenue
Saint Louis, MO 63146

Dear Mr. Boyd,

As you know, Camping Sphere Inc. is introducing a new lightweight backpack to its product line. For the entire months of April and May, we will hold a special promotion, offering the product at 30% off its suggested retail price. We'll start advertising the sale two weeks in advance. The official launch date will be April 1, and there will be a special launch event at the McKinley Heights branch. I know you also applied to hold the event at the Soulard branch, but we decided to go with a store that had already been in charge of large-scale events such as this. I will visit your store next week to drop off the displays for the new backpacks. These stands should be placed in a prominent area, and I can advise you on the arrangement at that time.

Sincerely,

Justin Dawson
Justin Dawson

161. How long will the discount on the new product be offered?

(A) One week
(B) Two weeks
(C) One month
(D) Two months

162. According to the letter, why was the McKinley Heights branch selected for an event?

(A) It needs the most improvement in its sales figures.
(B) Its employees have hosted similar events.
(C) It is the company's largest store.
(D) Its customers voted to hold the event there.

163. What will happen next week?

(A) A branch manager will print out some promotional material.
(B) Mr. Dawson will recommend some display strategies.
(C) A store will start selling a new line of backpacks.
(D) Mr. Boyd will oversee a product launch event.

Questions 164-167 refer to the following online chat discussion.

Clara Starnes 1:09 P.M.	Hi. I'm going to write about the Lafayette Art Museum for my next exhibit review. I know you've all been there before. Do you have any advice for me?
Radha Pai 1:18 P.M.	The size of the collection is enormous, so you need to plan ahead to see everything.
Clara Starnes 1:42 P.M.	I've heard that visitors aren't allowed to take pictures in some sections of the museum.
Joyce Garza 1:46 P.M.	You're right, Clara. Photos are not permitted in some sections, but signs are prominently displayed to inform visitors.
Clara Starnes 1:59 P.M.	I assume it's really busy on weekends, so I think I'll go on a weekday. Which day is best?
Joyce Garza 2:16 P.M.	It's always packed. But in my experience, Tuesday is the best day to go if you don't want to be around a lot of tourists and school groups.
Clara Starnes 2:25 P.M.	Then I think I'll go there on Tuesday.
Alyssa Verdi 2:37 P.M.	You can get information about their regulations from the Web site, information desk, and signs posted throughout the museum.
Radha Pai 2:51 P.M.	Right. Lafayette is better than the place I visited last week, Timber Museum. Timber Museum should follow its example.
Alyssa Verdi 2:55 P.M.	If you plan on going more than once, it's worth signing up for a membership. It costs $20 for a one-year membership, but you save $7 each time you visit.
Clara Starnes 3:39 P.M.	I appreciate your advice, everyone.

164. What does Ms. Starnes ask for?

(A) Recommendations for tourist sites
(B) Tips for visiting a place
(C) Advice for opening an exhibit
(D) Explanation about a schedule

165. Why does Ms. Starnes decide to make a visit on Tuesday?

(A) Because she wants to avoid the crowds.
(B) Because she can listen to a special lecture.
(C) Because the entrance fee is discounted.
(D) Because a guided tour is being offered.

166. At 2:51 P.M., what does Ms. Pai most likely mean when she writes, "Timber Museum should follow its example"?

(A) The attendance at Timber Museum has gone down significantly.
(B) The entrance fee at Timber Museum is too expensive for tourists.
(C) The policies at Timber Museum are not clearly explained.
(D) The collection at Timber Museum is not very big.

167. What does Ms. Verdi imply about a membership?

(A) It should be purchased online.
(B) It should be renewed annually.
(C) It offers a $20 discount each year.
(D) It allows members to buy a two-day pass.

Questions 168-171 refer to the following e-mail.

E-Mail

To: Aida Mazzanti <a.mazzanti@smindustries.net>
From: Li Zhang <zhangli@metrorealty99.com>
Date: June 10
Subject: From Metro Realty

Dear Ms. Mazzanti,

Thank you for meeting with me last week to tour some of the apartments available through our firm. Please note that the apartments in Elliot Tower and the one in Geo Suites have been rented. —[1]—. The two-bedroom apartment in the HSW Building is still available. I know this is larger than what you wanted. —[2]—. However, it's in the Arleta neighborhood, so you'd be able to walk to your office. —[3]—. The current tenant is moving out on June 20, so you can move in on June 21. If you are interested, I can send you a lease agreement, which should be signed and returned no later than June 14. At that time, we will collect a $200 holding fee. —[4]—. This apartment is in a popular building, so I hope to hear from you soon so that you don't miss your chance.

Sincerely,

Li Zhang

168. Why did Mr. Zhang send the e-mail?
(A) To accept a suggestion
(B) To schedule a tour
(C) To send a housing contract
(D) To update property information

169. What is suggested in the e-mail?
(A) Ms. Mazzanti prefers a two-bedroom home.
(B) Mr. Zhang will meet Ms. Mazzanti at her office.
(C) Ms. Mazzanti's workplace is located in Arleta.
(D) Metro Realty is gathering survey information.

170. According to Mr. Zhang, by when should Ms. Mazzanti submit some paperwork?
(A) June 10
(B) June 14
(C) June 20
(D) June 21

171. In which of the positions marked [1], [2], [3], and [4] does the following sentence best belong?
"Additionally, you will be expected to pay a deposit equal to one month's rent when you move in."
(A) [1]
(B) [2]
(C) [3]
(D) [4]

GO ON TO THE NEXT PAGE

Questions 172-175 refer to the following article.

Cleanup Begins on Carriage Lake *By Jeremy Trigg*

September 9—Plans for an extensive cleanup project at Carriage Lake are finally underway after the city encountered several obstacles. — [1] —. Talks regarding the need to improve the lake's condition began earlier this year, and it didn't take long to gather the public support needed. The city opened the project up for bids from companies in late March. — [2] —. Fortunately, the second round of bids resulted in a suitable contract agreement with Morris Enterprises.

The work, which began last week, involves removing contaminated soil from the bottom of the lake. — [3] —. Crews from Morris Enterprises are using a Preston-680 hydraulic dredge to remove the sediment. This equipment has a pump that is 24 inches in diameter, and Morris Enterprises bought it to replace its Caramillo-55, which would not have been powerful enough for this project.

"While Carriage Lake used to be a major draw for boating and fishing enthusiasts, attendance figures have been on a downward trend for years," said city councilperson Jane Clifton. "This project is costing taxpayers tens of millions of dollars, but the finished result will attract tourists, and the revenue they bring along with them. When you take the environmental impact into account as well, it's a win-win situation for everyone."

Once the work is completed, mercury levels in the water are expected to be reduced by as much as 97%. — [4] —. Because of that, officials will once again permit swimming in the lake, which hasn't been the case for decades. The city will also build an outdoor stage at the site, which will host music concerts, awards ceremonies, and more. To follow the progress of the cleanup, visit www.carriagelakecleanup.org.

172. What is the article mainly about?

(A) A project's progress
(B) A machine's availability
(C) A change in policy
(D) A tourism trend

173. What does Ms. Clifton most likely think about the project?

(A) It should have been started earlier in the year.
(B) The people handling it do not have enough experience.
(C) It will benefit the community despite its high costs.
(D) The final cost should be paid by boaters and fishermen.

174. What is NOT true about Carriage Lake?

(A) It is currently unsuitable for swimming.
(B) Its number of visitors has been steadily declining.
(C) It is the main source of drinking water in the town.
(D) It will be the site of an outdoor performance area.

175. In which of the positions marked [1], [2], [3], and [4] does the following sentence best belong?

"None of the prospective businesses could complete the scope of the work within the proposed budget."

(A) [1]
(B) [2]
(C) [3]
(D) [4]

Questions 176-180 refer to the following letter and survey.

July 3

Anne Stein
414 Fulton Street
Winchester, KY 40391

Dear Ms. Stein,

You recently booked a vehicle rental through the Trivo Rentals mobile phone app. We appreciate your business and would like to get your feedback on the enclosed form about the rental in order to improve our services further. We conduct research such as this regularly because we find that it is the best way to understand our customers.

We hope you will also introduce us to a friend who might be interested in our service. If you do so, your friend will receive a voucher by e-mail for 10 percent off any rental, and you will be given a voucher for a free GPS rental for the next time you rent from us.

Thank you for your participation!

The Trivo Rentals Team

Trivo Rentals

Thank you for taking the time to complete this survey. Your opinion matters to us!

Name: Anne Stein | Most Recent Rental Date: June 25

Rental Location: Winchester | Duration of Rental: 1 week

1. How often do you use Trivo Rentals and why?
My personal vehicle is a van, so a few times a year I rent a fuel-efficient car to go on business trips out of state.

2. Why did you choose Trivo Rentals?
It's great that Trivo Rentals keeps costs down by using cars that are a few years old, rather than brand-new ones. What really sets the company apart is that it sends a representative to my home to give me a ride to the Trivo Rentals office.
This is very convenient because I can't drive there myself without creating a parking issue.

3. How can we improve our services?
I think the added charges for insurance and extra services should be explained more clearly up front.

4. Would you like to recommend our services to a friend or family member? (Y) / N
Name: Cliff Bower | E-mail Address: c.bower@ferrel.com

176. What is the purpose of the letter?

(A) To request information about a customer's experience

(B) To gather feedback about a new product

(C) To thank a customer for their opinion

(D) To ask for some research results

177. What is implied about Trivo Rentals?

(A) It provides special packages to business professionals.

(B) It operates branches across the country.

(C) It offers a wide variety of insurance options.

(D) It has a smartphone application for reservations.

178. In the letter, the word "find" in paragraph 1, line 3, is closest in meaning to

(A) suggest

(B) discover

(C) believe

(D) acquire

179. What is true about Ms. Stein?

(A) She can collect reward points for her rental.

(B) She will be e-mailed a coupon for 10% off.

(C) She will be entered into a drawing for a GPS device.

(D) She can receive a free equipment rental.

180. What is one thing that Ms. Stein likes about Trivo Rentals?

(A) Its convenient location

(B) Its brand-new vehicles

(C) Its cheap insurance

(D) Its pick-up service

GO ON TO THE NEXT PAGE

Questions 181-185 refer to the following memo and schedule.

To: Cervantes Incorporated Staff
From: Armando Dixon, General Manager
Subject: For your immediate attention
Attachment: Inventory Schedule

February 23

Following last year's merger, we are still downsizing our staff and looking for ways to cut overhead costs. As a result, we will be moving our offices next month from the Rinehart Building to the Werner Building, which has a lower rental fee. Those of you who drive will be pleased to know that the Werner Building has an underground parking lot for employees only, just like our current building does.

We have hired a professional moving company, Guerra Co., whose crew will visit our building on Friday, March 17. You do not need to report to work on that day. Prior to the move, employees will assist with taking inventory of the company's furniture, equipment, and supplies according to the attached schedule. The head of HR will supply boxes, tape, and labels for you to gather your personal belongings.

Inventory Schedule

DATE	LOCATION	DEPARTMENT	MANAGER
Monday, March 13	2nd Floor	Accounting	Naoto Kodama
Tuesday, March 14	3rd Floor	Sales	Troy Concord
		Marketing	Jesse Mateo *
Wednesday, March 15	4th Floor	Human Resources	Alana Templeton
		R&D	Kamal Bakshi
Thursday, March 16	1st Floor	Administration	Joan Pafford

* As Jesse Mateo will be absent that week, Joan Pafford from administration will fill in for him on his department's assigned day.

181. Why did Mr. Dixon send the memo?

(A) To announce a company merger
(B) To explain a relocation procedure
(C) To give an update on a construction project
(D) To ask employees to reduce spending

182. What is indicated about the Rinehart Building?

(A) It has a private parking area.
(B) It will become the Cervantes Incorporated headquarters.
(C) It will be torn down in March.
(D) It is larger than the Werner Building.

183. What is implied about Cervantes Incorporated's employees?

(A) They will be reassigned to different departments.
(B) They should work from home temporarily.
(C) They will be given a day off in March.
(D) They should report inventory problems to Mr. Dixon.

184. What is suggested about Ms. Templeton?

(A) She took a tour of the Werner Building.
(B) She works on the third floor.
(C) She made a suggestion to Mr. Dixon.
(D) She will distribute packing supplies.

185. What is scheduled to happen on March 14?

(A) A company will move to a new building.
(B) Ms. Pafford will assist a department that is not hers.
(C) Employees from Guerra Co. will visit the business.
(D) Mr. Concord will be absent from the office.

Questions 186-190 refer to the following flyer and e-mails.

Wednesday Night Documentary Screenings at Elsberry Hall

Elsberry Hall is pleased to bring you award-winning documentaries followed by a question-and-answer session with the special guests listed.

June 7: *Hourglass* / Running Time: 2 hrs 21 mins
Special Guest: Orlando Briggs (director)
This film explores how tourism has affected the small island of Kihoa over the past fifty years.

June 14: *Powering the North* / Running Time: 2 hrs 18 mins
Special Guest: Bruce Morrison (Can-Elec Vice President)
This film explores how Canadian energy company Can-Elec has adapted its business model since its inception decades ago.

June 21: *In the Game* / Running Time: 2 hrs 5 mins
Special Guest: Shamba Metha (director)
Watch the development of soccer from its humble beginnings in 19th-century England to becoming the world's most popular sport today.

June 28: *Not for Sale* / Running Time: 1 hr 48 mins
Special Guest: Erin Hanson (director)
See how politician Benjamin Tribble's career has unfolded from his first election in 1982 to the present day.

Book ahead for big savings! Buy your tickets within the month of May to get $5 off the entrance fee.

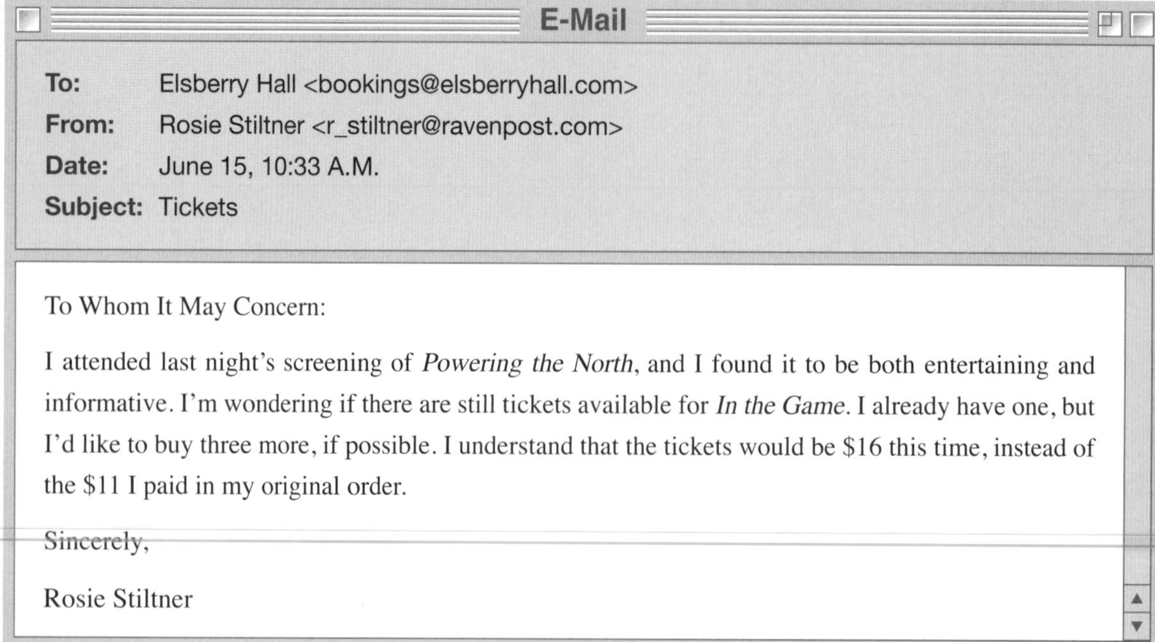

E-Mail

To: Elsberry Hall <bookings@elsberryhall.com>
From: Rosie Stiltner <r_stiltner@ravenpost.com>
Date: June 15, 10:33 A.M.
Subject: Tickets

To Whom It May Concern:

I attended last night's screening of *Powering the North*, and I found it to be both entertaining and informative. I'm wondering if there are still tickets available for *In the Game*. I already have one, but I'd like to buy three more, if possible. I understand that the tickets would be $16 this time, instead of the $11 I paid in my original order.

Sincerely,

Rosie Stiltner

To: Rosie Stiltner <r_stiltner@ravenpost.com>
From: Elsberry Hall <bookings@elsberryhall.com>
Date: June 15, 1:41 P.M.
Subject: RE: Tickets

Dear Ms. Stiltner,

Elsberry Hall enjoys a spacious seating area that can accommodate nearly five hundred people, so I'm pleased to inform you that we still have tickets available for the film you requested. However, you should note that the special guest for that date will be screenwriter Kevin Drummond, as the director cannot attend as planned. If you still want the tickets despite this change, you will have to call our box office at 555-3866 to give us your credit card details again, as we do not save information from previous transactions.

Sincerely,

Miles Rahn
Customer Service Agent, Elsberry Hall

186. What characteristic is shared by all of the films?

(A) They last longer than two hours.
(B) They explore a subject over time.
(C) They focus on business-related matters.
(D) They are made by well-known directors.

187. What is implied about Ms. Stiltner?

(A) She wants to exchange her tickets for a different film.
(B) She created a documentary film on her own.
(C) She booked her original ticket before June 1.
(D) She signed up for a theater membership program.

188. Which film's special guest has changed?

(A) Hourglass
(B) Powering the North
(C) In the Game
(D) Not for Sale

189. In the second e-mail, the word "enjoys" in paragraph 1, line 1, is closest in meaning to

(A) experiences
(B) possesses
(C) appreciates
(D) welcomes

190. According to Mr. Rahn, why should Ms. Stiltner call the box office?

(A) To verify a change
(B) To get an updated schedule
(C) To cancel a purchase
(D) To provide payment information

GO ON TO THE NEXT PAGE

Questions 191-195 refer to the following article, Web page, and online review.

McCabe Home Appliances to Trim Its Product Line

August 27—McCabe Home Appliances plans to halt production of its PrimeAir-60 air purifier sometime in September, and stores carrying the product will sell it until it is sold out. Consumers who currently have the PrimeAir-60 are encouraged to stock up on filters, as the filters made for other McCabe air purifiers are a different shape and cannot be accommodated by the device.

A spokesperson for McCabe Home Appliances commented that the decision was made in order to focus on better-selling products. The PrimeAir-60 accounts for less than two percent of the company's revenue, so decision-makers at McCabe believed it was time to start promoting other designs. In addition, the majority of customers who did purchase the device complained about its loud operation. For a complete listing of McCabe Home Appliances' products, visit www.mccabehomeapp.com.

www.mccabehomeapp.com

Home ≫ Catalog ≫ Sale Items ≫ Clearance

The following items are on sale until all items are sold. *Updated October 1*

PrimeAir-60 ADD TO CART

Regular Price: $169.99 **Clearance Price:** $75.99

PrimeAir-60 is an air purifier that can be used in rooms up to 1,500 cubic feet. It has low energy usage and operates more efficiently than most air purifiers on the market today. Regular use of the PrimeAir-60 can reduce the presence of bacteria, viruses, and allergens in your home. The device is highly recommended for allergy sufferers and those with respiratory problems. The filter can be cleaned by hand and reused up to ten times.

PrimeAir-60 Replacement Filters 3-Pack ADD TO CART

Regular Price: $59.99 **Clearance Price:** $39.99

PrimeAir-60 Replacement Filters 5-Pack ADD TO CART

Regular Price: $89.99 **Clearance Price:** $55.99

All orders, including those containing clearance items, qualify for free delivery from October 1 to October 31.

www.mccabehomeapp.com

Home ≫ Reviews ≫ PrimeAir-60

Written by: Olivia Densmore **Posted:** October 5

I will be sad to see this product go. I bought mine last year and have enjoyed using it constantly since then. I understand that the company has to take action on the most common complaint, but I've never experienced that problem. Even though the filters can be hand-washed and reused, I bought a 5-pack from the clearance sale today so I could ensure the use of the device for a long time.

191. What is the purpose of the article?
(A) To promote a new product in the line
(B) To notify consumers of a product recall
(C) To commemorate a company achievement
(D) To report the discontinuation of a product

192. In the article, the phrase "accounts for" in paragraph 2, line 2, is closest in meaning to
(A) uses
(B) represents
(C) happens
(D) explains

193. According to the Web page, what can customers receive in October?
(A) An extended warranty
(B) Free replacement filters
(C) An updated catalog
(D) Complimentary shipping

194. What does Ms. Densmore imply about the PrimeAir-60?
(A) She uses it during the daytime only.
(B) She will replace it with a newer model.
(C) She does not think it was too noisy.
(D) She made a complaint about it to the company.

195. What is most likely true about Ms. Densmore?
(A) She bought the PrimeAir-60 for $75.99.
(B) Her living room is less than 1,500 cubic feet.
(C) She spent $55.99 on replacement filters.
(D) Her purchase was delivered by express mail.

GO ON TO THE NEXT PAGE

Questions 196-200 refer to the following announcement, memo, and e-mail.

Volunteers Needed

Richmond Public Library provides essential educational services to the community, and we are looking for volunteers to assist us with our programs. You must be at least eighteen years old and be available for a minimum of four hours a week. To apply as a volunteer, fill out a form at the front desk by March 20. Please note that all volunteers must go to an orientation workshop at the library before they can begin volunteering. With help from members of the community, we can reach more people and help them to attain their literacy goals. We hope to get at least thirty new volunteers for our programs, so please encourage your family and friends to volunteer as well.

MEMO

To employees,

Thank you, everyone, for taking the time out of your busy schedules to train our new library volunteers. The training session will be held on April 7, starting at 1 P.M. There will be two hours of general library information followed by overviews of individual projects (30 minutes each) by the head of each program as below. At the end of the orientation, volunteers will be given a form on which they can indicate which programs they would like to assist with. I cannot guarantee that all volunteers will be matched with their first choice, but I will do my best.

Program Coordinators:

- Silvano Marchesi, Adult Literacy
- Walter Vance, Children's Storytime
- Elizabeth Lancaster, Homework Help
- Hariti Nayak, Early Readers

We didn't quite make our recruitment goal. However, I'm still pleased with the group's size. I will send a list of the volunteers later this week.

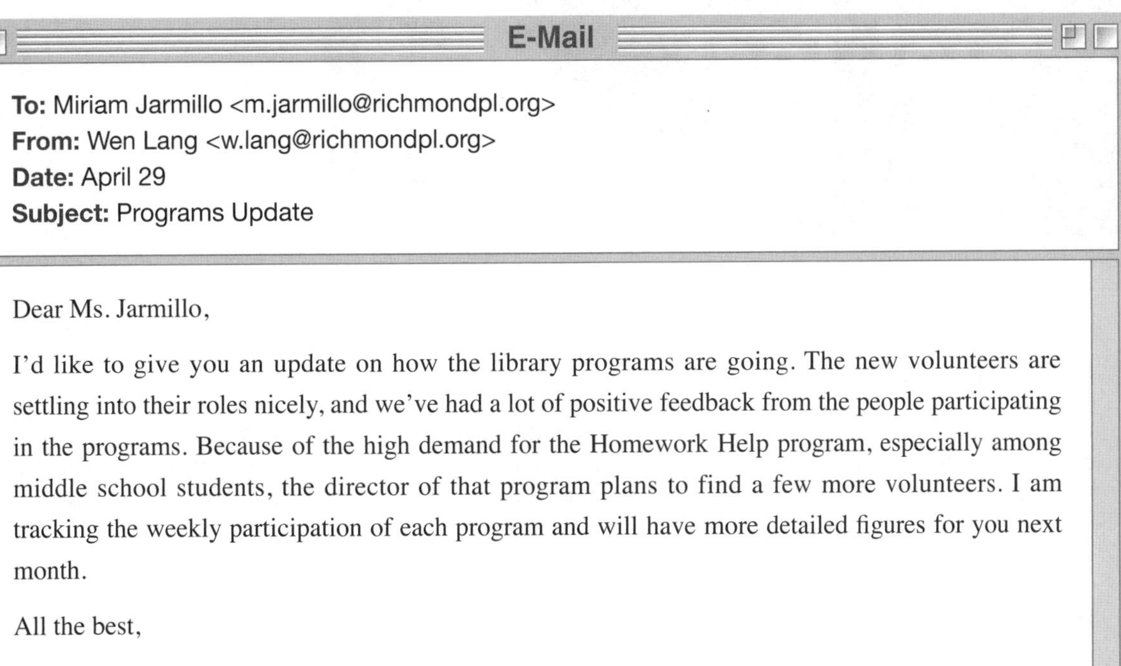

E-Mail

To: Miriam Jarmillo <m.jarmillo@richmondpl.org>
From: Wen Lang <w.lang@richmondpl.org>
Date: April 29
Subject: Programs Update

Dear Ms. Jarmillo,

I'd like to give you an update on how the library programs are going. The new volunteers are settling into their roles nicely, and we've had a lot of positive feedback from the people participating in the programs. Because of the high demand for the Homework Help program, especially among middle school students, the director of that program plans to find a few more volunteers. I am tracking the weekly participation of each program and will have more detailed figures for you next month.

All the best,

Wen Lang
Richmond Public Library Program Coordinator

196. What is NOT expected from volunteers?
(A) Working over a certain number of weekly hours
(B) Attending an on-site training session
(C) Meeting a minimum age requirement
(D) Submitting a letter of recommendation

197. In the announcement, the word "reach" in paragraph 1, line 5, is closest in meaning to
(A) equal
(B) stretch
(C) achieve
(D) approach

198. What is suggested about the April 7 training session?
(A) It lasted for two hours in total.
(B) It assessed the volunteers' literacy.
(C) It had fewer than thirty participants.
(D) It got positive feedback from the volunteers.

199. Why will volunteers fill out a form at the training session?
(A) To express their preferences
(B) To rate the speakers' performances
(C) To confirm their schedules
(D) To suggest new programs

200. Who plans to recruit more volunteers?
(A) Mr. Marchesi
(B) Mr. Vance
(C) Ms. Lancaster
(D) Ms. Nayak

Stop! This is the end of the test. If you finish before time is called, you may go back to Parts 5, 6, and 7 and check your work.

Actual Test 3

LISTENING TEST

In the Listening test, you will be asked to demonstrate how well you understand spoken English. The entire Listening test will last approximately 45 minutes. There are four parts, and directions are given for each part. You must mark your answers on the separate answer sheet. Do not write your answers in your test book.

PART 1 09

Directions: For each question in this part, you will hear four statements about a picture in your test book. When you hear the statements, you must select the one statement that best describes what you see in the picture. Then find the number of the question on your answer sheet and mark your answer. The statements will not be printed in your test book and will be spoken only one time.

Statement (C), "They're sitting at the table," is the best description of the picture, so you should select answer (C) and mark it on your answer sheet.

1.

2.

GO ON TO THE NEXT PAGE

3.

4.

5.

6.

GO ON TO THE NEXT PAGE

PART 2 (10)

Directions: You will hear a question or statement and three responses spoken in English. They will not be printed in your test book and will be spoken only one time. Select the best response to the question or statement and mark the letter (A), (B), or (C) on your answer sheet.

7. Mark your answer on your answer sheet.

8. Mark your answer on your answer sheet.

9. Mark your answer on your answer sheet.

10. Mark your answer on your answer sheet.

11. Mark your answer on your answer sheet.

12. Mark your answer on your answer sheet.

13. Mark your answer on your answer sheet.

14. Mark your answer on your answer sheet.

15. Mark your answer on your answer sheet.

16. Mark your answer on your answer sheet.

17. Mark your answer on your answer sheet.

18. Mark your answer on your answer sheet.

19. Mark your answer on your answer sheet.

20. Mark your answer on your answer sheet.

21. Mark your answer on your answer sheet.

22. Mark your answer on your answer sheet.

23. Mark your answer on your answer sheet.

24. Mark your answer on your answer sheet.

25. Mark your answer on your answer sheet.

26. Mark your answer on your answer sheet.

27. Mark your answer on your answer sheet.

28. Mark your answer on your answer sheet.

29. Mark your answer on your answer sheet.

30. Mark your answer on your answer sheet.

31. Mark your answer on your answer sheet.

PART 3

Directions: You will hear some conversations between two or more people. You will be asked to answer three questions about what the speakers say in each conversation. Select the best response to each question and mark the letter (A), (B), (C), or (D) on your answer sheet. The conversations will not be printed in your test book and will be spoken only one time.

32. Where most likely does the woman work?
(A) At a hospital
(B) At a university
(C) At a museum
(D) At a restaurant

33. What does the man ask about?
(A) How much a service costs
(B) What classes are being taught
(C) Which day is convenient
(D) How busy a location is

34. What information will the woman provide next week?
(A) A business's opening hours
(B) A detailed schedule
(C) The topic of a lecture
(D) The number of visitors

---

35. Who most likely is the man?
(A) A manager's assistant
(B) An applicant for a grant
(C) The director of a company
(D) The keynote speaker at a convention

36. What is the woman doing this week?
(A) Writing up a proposal
(B) Attending a conference
(C) Interviewing candidates
(D) Training at a new company

37. Why does the man want to meet the woman?
(A) To negotiate a deal
(B) To prepare a presentation
(C) To discuss a job opportunity
(D) To introduce a coworker

---

38. Where most likely are the speakers?
(A) At a clothing shop
(B) At a grocery store
(C) At a beauty salon
(D) At a paint retailer

39. What do first-time customers receive?
(A) A discount
(B) A free item
(C) A gift certificate
(D) A membership card

40. What will the man most likely do next?
(A) Make a purchase
(B) Wash some hair
(C) Choose a color
(D) Provide a refund

---

41. Why is the man calling?
(A) To complain about a rule
(B) To place an order
(C) To explain a service
(D) To ask about a price

42. What problem does the man mention about the lawn mower?
(A) It wasn't delivered on time.
(B) It doesn't work properly.
(C) It is the wrong model.
(D) It was incorrectly priced.

43. What does the woman say she will do?
(A) Contact a manager
(B) Issue a refund
(C) Organize a sales event
(D) Repair a device

GO ON TO THE NEXT PAGE

44. What does the woman say she plans to do?
(A) Go on a cruise
(B) Write a negative review
(C) Work some extra hours
(D) Resign from her position

45. What do the men imply about Gulliver Travel?
(A) It has poor customer service.
(B) It offers discounts to its employees.
(C) It has the cheapest cruises on the market.
(D) It is more expensive than Blue Green Travel.

46. According to the woman, what happened at the company while the men were away?
(A) A coworker left her job.
(B) A customer made a complaint.
(C) A new person was hired.
(D) A survey was conducted.

---

47. What are the speakers mainly discussing?
(A) An article's contents
(B) A course's difficulty
(C) A product's packaging
(D) A beverage's price

48. Why does the man say, "they went a little too far"?
(A) He finds a design childish.
(B) He thinks a product is expensive.
(C) He wants to relocate a branch.
(D) He disagrees with a policy.

49. What does the woman say she will do?
(A) Return an item
(B) Report a choice
(C) Create an advertisement
(D) Contact some customers

---

50. What are the speakers mainly discussing?
(A) A new opening
(B) A job change
(C) A customer complaint
(D) An office layout

51. What does the woman say she is looking forward to?
(A) Talking to people directly
(B) Working with the man
(C) Reading some reviews
(D) Joining a new company

52. What does the man suggest the woman do?
(A) File a complaint
(B) Consult a coworker
(C) Find a different job
(D) Provide some advice

---

53. What will happen on August 8?
(A) A business will be relocated.
(B) An author will be interviewed.
(C) A contract will be signed.
(D) A book signing will be held.

54. What does the woman suggest doing?
(A) Putting away some items
(B) Registering for an event
(C) Waiting in line
(D) Moving some furniture

55. What does the man say he will do?
(A) Prepare an advertisement
(B) Reserve some tickets
(C) Write a summary
(D) Visit a venue

---

56. What has the woman recently done?

(A) Attended a lecture series
(B) Registered for an event
(C) Reviewed a research study
(D) Given a presentation

57. What does the woman think the man should do?

(A) Meet a speaker
(B) Extend a deadline
(C) Submit a study
(D) Choose a topic

58. What does the woman imply about a review she wrote?

(A) It is outdated.
(B) It will be published soon.
(C) It took a long time to make.
(D) It was presented at a conference.

---

59. Who most likely is the man?

(A) A secretary
(B) A dentist
(C) A plumber
(D) A nutritionist

60. Why does the woman say, "Drinking cold water causes it"?

(A) To suggest a possible treatment
(B) To describe a healthy habit
(C) To give details about her diet
(D) To explain when a problem occurs

61. What does the man recommend the woman do?

(A) Follow a personal hygiene routine
(B) Make an appointment with a doctor
(C) Avoid drinking sweet beverages
(D) Take some time off from work

Interview Hours

Time Slot	Day	Time
1	Monday	3:00 P.M.
2	Wednesday	10:30 A.M.
3	Wednesday	5:00 P.M.
4	Friday	1:45 P.M.

62. What was announced in an e-mail?

(A) An employee has been promoted.
(B) A new branch is opening.
(C) A deadline has been extended.
(D) A company is relocating.

63. What is the man hesitating to do?

(A) Accept an offer
(B) Apply for a position
(C) Choose a candidate
(D) Talk to a supervisor

64. Look at the graphic. Which time slot is the man able to attend?

(A) Time Slot 1
(B) Time Slot 2
(C) Time Slot 3
(D) Time Slot 4

~ Special Menu ~

Each drink on the special menu
comes with a free pastry!

black coffee	⟶ croissant	$2.50
single latte	⟶ éclair	$3.00
mocha	⟶ Danish	$3.50
cappuccino	⟶ cinnamon roll	$3.50

65. What does the woman ask about?

(A) What food is available
(B) How much an item costs
(C) Which coffee is best
(D) Where a menu is located

66. Look at the graphic. Which pastry will the woman get?

(A) A croissant
(B) An éclair
(C) A Danish
(D) A cinnamon roll

67. Why is the woman surprised?

(A) The prices have been lowered.
(B) The shop closes late.
(C) The menu options have changed.
(D) The coffee is strong.

	Maximum passengers	Transmission
Vehicle 1	5	Manual
Vehicle 2	5	Automatic
Vehicle 3	8	Manual
Vehicle 4	8	Automatic

68. Why does the man prefer renting a car to taking the train?

(A) It is cheaper.
(B) It is more convenient.
(C) It is faster.
(D) It is more reliable.

69. Look at the graphic. Which vehicle will the woman most likely reserve?

(A) Vehicle 1
(B) Vehicle 2
(C) Vehicle 3
(D) Vehicle 4

70. What does the man ask the woman?

(A) Where they will park
(B) How many people will drive
(C) How much the rental will cost
(D) When they should leave

PART 4 (12)

Directions: You will hear some talks given by a single speaker. You will be asked to answer three questions about what the speaker says in each talk. Select the best response to each question and mark the letter (A), (B), (C), or (D) on your answer sheet. The talks will not be printed in your test book and will be spoken only one time.

71. What industry does the speaker work in?
(A) Entertainment
(B) Fashion
(C) Automobile
(D) Marketing

72. According to the speaker, what should the company focus on?
(A) More comfortable products
(B) Better customer service
(C) More competitive prices
(D) Safer designs

73. What will the listeners most likely do next?
(A) Look at some designs
(B) Test-drive some vehicles
(C) Try on some clothes
(D) Review some materials

---

74. What type of business does the speaker work for?
(A) An insurance company
(B) A real estate agency
(C) A law firm
(D) An accounting business

75. What does the speaker mention about the position?
(A) Its salary can be negotiated.
(B) Its location has been changed.
(C) Its start date is fixed.
(D) Its duties require advanced skills.

76. What is the listener asked to do?
(A) Come in for an interview
(B) Return a phone call
(C) Submit a job application
(D) Modify a schedule

---

77. What department do the listeners most likely work in?
(A) Human resources
(B) Marketing
(C) Accounting
(D) Customer service

78. What can listeners find in the document the speaker sent last week?
(A) Contract terms
(B) Benefit options
(C) Employee information
(D) Required qualifications

79. What should listeners do by Wednesday?
(A) Read about some occupations
(B) Review job applications
(C) Advertise a job opening
(D) Update a Web site

---

80. What is the speaker preparing for?
(A) Hosting an event
(B) Entering a contest
(C) Moving to a new location
(D) Installing new equipment

81. Why does the speaker say, "The total is fourteen"?
(A) To request a payment
(B) To report the number of participants
(C) To explain a policy
(D) To provide the number of lectures

82. What does the speaker offer to do?
(A) Apply a discount
(B) Arrange a pickup
(C) Postpone a meeting
(D) Send directions

GO ON TO THE NEXT PAGE

83. According to the speaker, what recently happened?
(A) A branch was opened.
(B) Two companies merged.
(C) A product was launched.
(D) A restaurant changed its menu.

84. What did Mr. Boyle study in graduate school?
(A) Cooking
(B) Business administration
(C) Italian
(D) Art

85. What is Mr. Boyle currently doing?
(A) Touring a restaurant
(B) Designing a menu
(C) Ordering some food
(D) Attending a class

---

86. What type of business has the caller reached?
(A) A communications provider
(B) An electronics manufacturer
(C) A Web design company
(D) A device repair shop

87. What problem does the speaker mention?
(A) A service is slow.
(B) A machine is defective.
(C) A delivery is delayed.
(D) A Web site is down.

88. Why should callers press 0?
(A) To upgrade a plan
(B) To report an issue
(C) To cancel an order
(D) To request a refund

---

89. Who most likely are the listeners?
(A) Visiting clients
(B) Retired employees
(C) Branch managers
(D) New workers

90. What is the purpose of the talk?
(A) To outline some rules
(B) To announce break times
(C) To introduce a new manager
(D) To assess a performance

91. Why does the speaker say, "We work in close proximity to one another"?
(A) To justify a policy
(B) To provide directions
(C) To explain a layout
(D) To demand respect

---

92. Who most likely will the speaker interview next week?
(A) Computer repair technicians
(B) Sales executives
(C) Graphic designers
(D) Laboratory researchers

93. What does the speaker mean when she says, "it was twice what we expected"?
(A) A job opening got many applicants.
(B) A company's market share grew significantly.
(C) A candidate requested a larger salary.
(D) A hiring process took longer than planned.

94. According to the speaker, what will Timothy do?
(A) Reserve a conference room for an interview
(B) Review the résumés of applicants
(C) Create a vacation schedule for the team
(D) Find volunteers to give up their workspaces

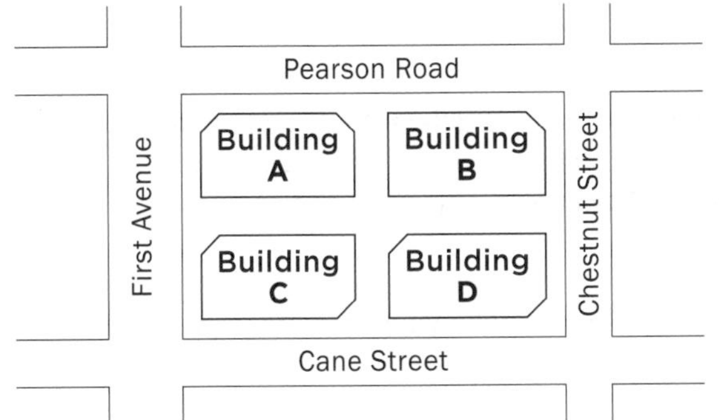

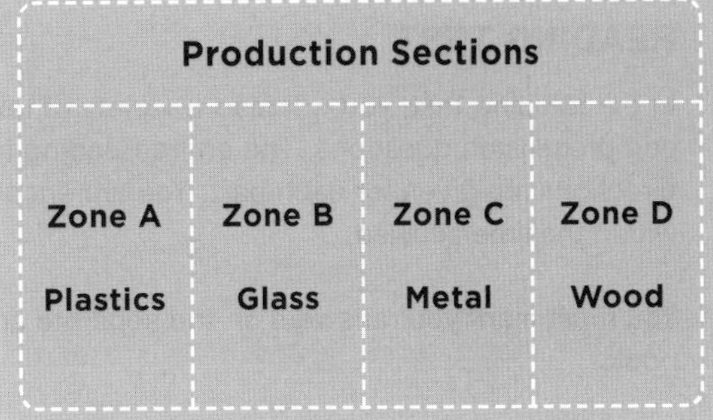

95. Look at the graphic. Which building is under construction?

(A) Building A
(B) Building B
(C) Building C
(D) Building D

96. What has caused a delay in the construction project?

(A) Insufficient materials
(B) A car accident
(C) Weather conditions
(D) Financial problems

97. What will take place this afternoon?

(A) A grand opening
(B) A sales event
(C) An anniversary party
(D) An artisan fair

98. What is the speaker in charge of doing?

(A) Assuring the quality of goods
(B) Overseeing the hiring process
(C) Promoting the company's products
(D) Repairing production equipment

99. Who most likely are the listeners?

(A) Safety inspectors
(B) New employees
(C) Potential investors
(D) Department managers

100. Look at the graphic. In which area will the listeners spend the shortest amount of time?

(A) Zone A
(B) Zone B
(C) Zone C
(D) Zone D

This is the end of the Listening test. Turn to Part 5 in your test book.

GO ON TO THE NEXT PAGE

READING TEST

In the Reading test, you will read a variety of texts and answer several different types of reading comprehension questions. The entire Reading test will last 75 minutes. There are three parts, and directions are given for each part. You are encouraged to answer as many questions as possible within the time allowed.

You must mark your answers on the separate answer sheet. Do not write your answers in your test book.

PART 5

Directions: A word or phrase is missing in each of the sentences below. Four answer choices are given below each sentence. Select the best answer to complete the sentence. Then mark the letter (A), (B), (C), or (D) on your answer sheet.

101. You may buy tickets for the May 11 concert in advance ------- at the door.

(A) for
(B) so
(C) or
(D) nor

102. For her lecture, Bridget Coleman provided ------- of foreign terms commonly used in court.

(A) translate
(B) translated
(C) translator
(D) translations

103. Most of Margos Electronics' devices are manufactured ------- factories overseas.

(A) by
(B) about
(C) past
(D) along

104. The team leader is too busy to pick up Colcott's CEO at the airport -------.

(A) her
(B) she
(C) hers
(D) herself

105. The ------- purpose of this meeting is to review our safety procedures.

(A) primary
(B) rigorous
(C) plentiful
(D) timely

106. Despite practicing, Peter Bertrand was not ------- prepared for the questions the interviewers asked him.

(A) suffice
(B) sufficiency
(C) sufficient
(D) sufficiently

107. Before his business trip to Mexico, Mr. Marcus studied Spanish so that he could ------- with the locals.

(A) state
(B) communicate
(C) reserve
(D) understand

108. ------- attendee will be given a folder with the program and notes about each presenter.

(A) Every
(B) Few
(C) Several
(D) All

109. Recent ------- in various scientific fields have caused a sudden increase in life expectancy.

(A) developments
(B) versions
(C) timelines
(D) ranges

110. Ms. Mander added six names to the ------- dinner guest list, bringing the number of expected diners up to twenty-three.

(A) origin
(B) originate
(C) original
(D) originally

111. The spring line of Vivi Fashion House's leather handbags was ------- at last week's runway show.

(A) consulted
(B) relieved
(C) attempted
(D) unveiled

112. Volunteers ------- in the lobby of the building at 11:00 A.M. next Saturday to prepare the fundraising event.

(A) gathered
(B) have gathered
(C) will be gathering
(D) will have been gathering

113. We can meet anytime that is convenient for you since my schedule is more flexible than -------.

(A) you
(B) yourself
(C) your
(D) yours

114. Gibson Department Store handed out small bags of free samples to customers to thank them for ------- its grand opening event.

(A) attend
(B) attending
(C) attendee
(D) attendance

115. Passengers traveling in first class are permitted to check in a maximum ------- three suitcases each.

(A) up
(B) beyond
(C) of
(D) to

116. Strict ------- with the company's policies is expected from employees at all times.

(A) application
(B) compliance
(C) management
(D) correction

117. Please enter the building through the north door, ------- is located on Sacramento Street.

(A) who
(B) what
(C) where
(D) which

118. According to the news anchor, the virus infected ------- ten thousand computers in just a few minutes.

(A) approximate
(B) approximately
(C) approximates
(D) approximation

119. Flucos Clothing plans on making a series of advertisements to appeal to a ------- clientele.

(A) diverse
(B) correct
(C) usual
(D) descriptive

120. This study indicates that customers would ------- shop online than try on items in a store.

(A) further
(B) probably
(C) rather
(D) mistakenly

GO ON TO THE NEXT PAGE

121. The new revelations about the emission of harmful gases by its factories has ------- as an issue for the company.

(A) become
(B) emerged
(C) resulted
(D) produced

122. Given the complex layout of the city, ------- the location of the Portville branch was difficult.

(A) choosing
(B) choice
(C) choose
(D) chosen

123. The restaurant manager reviewed food safety ------- with his staff to prepare for the monthly inspection.

(A) regulating
(B) regulated
(C) regulations
(D) regulates

124. To view a ------- explanation of presidential candidate Ann Lathrup's economic plans, visit her campaign Web site.

(A) repeated
(B) customized
(C) testified
(D) detailed

125. In order to receive a full refund for a returned item, the receipt ------- to the cashier.

(A) presented
(B) has presented
(C) would be presenting
(D) must be presented

126. By offering ------- prices, Ergo Supermarkets has become one of the most successful grocery stores in the area.

(A) competed
(B) competing
(C) competitive
(D) competitively

127. Abigail Hoskins was given a certificate of appreciation by the city ------- her efforts in improving educational standards.

(A) for
(B) into
(C) because
(D) when

128. Even though Maria's Grill is only ------- closer to the center of town, it gets a lot more customers than Primavera's.

(A) slightly
(B) overwhelmingly
(C) carefully
(D) popularly

129. The designer used a new type of software ------- the brochure advertising the convention.

(A) creates
(B) will create
(C) to create
(D) created

130. Management decided to hire Amy Volpert in spite of the ------- in her educational background because of her experience as an intern.

(A) attainments
(B) shortcomings
(C) submissions
(D) qualifications

PART 6

Directions: Read the texts that follow. A word, phrase, or sentence is missing in parts of each text. Four answer choices for each question are given below the text. Select the best answer to complete the text. Then mark the letter (A), (B), (C), or (D) on your answer sheet.

Questions 131-134 refer to the following e-mail.

To: Margaret Keeble <m_keeble@tysoncomm.com>
From: Juan Torres <j_torres@tysoncomm.com>
Date: November 18
Subject: Keep up the good work!

Dear Ms. Keeble,

I would like to thank you for handling the situation when Ms. Ferona came to our office upset because of a billing error. It is not always easy to know what to do in these situations, but the way you handled it was ------- **131.** . Pleasing our clients is an important part of the job. ------- **132.**, we can't give them everything they demand. This would have a detrimental effect on our finances. By explaining the reason for the error in a calm manner, you resolved the conflict quickly. ------- **133.** . The other managers and I agree that you deserve ------- **134.** from your hard work. Therefore, you will be given an extra day of paid vacation.

Congratulations!

Juan Torres
Office Manager, Tyson Communications

131. (A) feasible
(B) appropriate
(C) steady
(D) affordable

132. (A) In addition
(B) Even if
(C) Nonetheless
(D) For instance

133. (A) Ms. Ferona will oversee this area from now on.
(B) We have already reprinted your new bill showing the change.
(C) It was also a good example to set for our junior staff members.
(D) The company will upgrade its billing software soon.

134. (A) to benefit
(B) will benefit
(C) being benefits
(D) it benefitted

GO ON TO THE NEXT PAGE

Questions 135-138 refer to the following article.

March 16, Narton—A new library ------- (135.) in the center of the small town of Narton will be opening its doors next month. The Narton Library will hold a collection of books, magazines, and videos on all topics. In addition, it will offer free Internet access, host regular events, and provide various workshops to ------- (136.) the community. "I think this library will be extremely helpful," indicated ------- (137.) resident Samuel Prendy. "Narton is isolated in a remote location, and it is difficult for us to stay up-to-date on all the latest information." Mayor Brenkel is scheduled to give a speech at the opening ceremony on April 2. ------- (138.). For more information about it, check Narton's official Web site.

135. (A) will be located
(B) locating
(C) is located
(D) located

136. (A) serve
(B) organize
(C) request
(D) visit

137. (A) expert
(B) dependent
(C) local
(D) active

138. (A) All are invited to attend this event.
(B) It will be announced on that day.
(C) You can pick up your books at that time.
(D) He was elected with a large majority.

Questions 139-142 refer to the following notice.

As you know, the company donates to the F&Y homeless shelter every year. This year, instead of money, we have decided to donate various goods that the shelter is in need of. You'll see bins at the entrance of each department head's office. Employees are ------- (139.) to place items in good condition into these bins. When a bin is ------- (140.), it will be picked up by PR staff and taken to the shelter. A list of acceptable items will be posted in the staff lounge. ------- (141.). In particular, note that although clothing is welcome, certain ------- (142.) are not accepted due to common allergies and limited washing options. Thank you in advance for your donations.

139. (A) encouragement
(B) encourage
(C) encouraging
(D) encouraged

140. (A) open
(B) full
(C) finished
(D) consumed

141. (A) Please consult it carefully before placing anything in a bin.
(B) You may take anything that seems necessary to you.
(C) However, entrance is restricted to upper management only.
(D) If you agree with the terms, you may sign below.

142. (A) methods
(B) amounts
(C) materials
(D) payments

Questions 143-146 refer to the following letter.

September 14

Sterling Murray
25 Morocco Drive
Newtown, PA 18777

Dear Mr. Murray,

It is our pleasure to award you first place in the Graper Scientific Research Competition for your paper entitled "Quality Control in Pharmaceuticals: Testing Three Methods." The study you conducted and your findings were fascinating. ------- **143.** We trust that the rest of the readers in the scientific community will find your work ------- **144.**. In addition, you ------- **145.** $2,500 for further research. We hope that this will help in your future endeavors. Congratulations, and thank you for your ------- **146.** to the field of medicine.

Sincerely,

Richard Nelson
Director, Graper Science

143. (A) We highly recommend that you read this study.
(B) Many contestants have entered the competition.
(C) However, most of the information was already well-known.
(D) Your article will appear in next month's *Graper Science News*.

144. (A) inspires
(B) inspire
(C) inspirational
(D) inspiration

145. (A) will grant
(B) would have been granted
(C) would have granted
(D) will be granted

146. (A) distinction
(B) survey
(C) contribution
(D) knowledge

PART 7

Directions: In this part you will read a selection of texts, such as magazine and newspaper articles, e-mails, and instant messages. Each text or set of texts is followed by several questions. Select the best answer for each question and mark the letter (A), (B), (C), or (D) on your answer sheet.

Questions 147-148 refer to the following e-mail.

E-Mail

To: Veronica Tessier <v.tessier@greatinterior.com>
From: Lucy Bracker <l.bracker@memail.net>
Subject: Sample Pictures
Date: January 18

Dear Ms. Tessier,

Thank you for sending pictures of possible layouts for our living room. It is helpful to see pictures of various colors and textures put together to get an idea of how things would look. I am having trouble opening the last picture you sent, however. It seems to be in a different format from the others, and my computer doesn't seem to be able to read it. Could you send it again in the same format as the others?

Thank you very much.

Sincerely,

Lucy Bracker

147. Who most likely is Ms. Tessier?
(A) A professional photographer
(B) An interior designer
(C) An IT expert
(D) An art gallery owner

148. What problem is Ms. Bracker having?
(A) She doesn't have enough space.
(B) She doesn't like the color combinations.
(C) She is unable to view a file.
(D) She didn't receive an e-mail.

Questions 149-150 refer to the following calendar.

Mercer Real Estate New Employee Orientation Schedule

A

AUGUST						
Sunday	Monday	Tuesday	Wednesday	Thursday	Friday	Saturday
	1	2	3	4 **OR**	5	6
7	8	9	10	11	12	13
14	15	16	17	18	19	20
21	22	23	24 **DA**	25	26 **PRO**	27
28	29 **FFD**	30	31			

OR: First day of orientation. Walk-through of premises
DA: Individual department assignments announced
PRO: Pictures taken and creation of Web site profiles
FFD: First full day compensated as a full-time employee

149. On which day will employees tour the facilities?
(A) August 4
(B) August 24
(C) August 26
(D) August 29

150. What is indicated about the company's Web site pictures?
(A) They are required for finding one's department.
(B) They must be submitted on the first day of work.
(C) They are taken after departments have been assigned.
(D) They should be brought to work by employees on August 26.

Questions 151-152 refer to the following text-message chain.

Jimmie Kristof [3:08 P.M.]
Rebecca, have you made arrangements for going to the conference next Monday?

Rebecca Pauly [3:09 P.M.]
I thought the company was taking care of that. Aren't they providing a bus for us?

Jimmie Kristof [3:10 P.M.]
No. They decided not to after all. So most people are taking the subway or driving.

Rebecca Pauly [3:13 P.M.]
Then I guess I'll drive. There aren't any subway stations near my place. But I've never been to that venue. I have no idea how to get there.

Jimmie Kristof [3:14 P.M.]
Well, that's why I contacted you. I was wondering if you'd like me to pick you up.

Rebecca Pauly [3:15 P.M.]
That would be much easier for me. Are you sure you don't mind?

Jimmie Kristof [3:17 P.M.]
Of course not. Your house is on my way. And I've been to that hall many times before.

151. What is indicated about the writers' company?
(A) It is not handling transportation for employees.
(B) It has offices located near a subway station.
(C) It is organizing an event for its employees.
(D) It is moving to a new location.

152. At 3:15 P.M., what does Ms. Pauly mean when she writes, "That would be much easier for me"?
(A) She prefers to go by bus.
(B) She would like Mr. Kristof to drive her.
(C) She can pick up Mr. Kristof at the conference.
(D) She doesn't mind taking the subway.

Questions 153-155 refer to the following advertisement.

CLARENCE CO.

Clarence Co. provides the best service in the area for businesses that are relocating. We provide a variety of options so that your transition to the new location is as smooth as possible.

If you sign up for our deluxe package, we will provide the following services:
- Unlimited plastic crates for packing belongings
- Packing of large equipment and furniture
- Special packing by our IT experts for your computers and other electronics
- Loading and unloading of all items
- Special clean-up service from our sister company, Sparkly Clean

Call us today at 553-0295 to schedule a time for us to come take a look at your facilities. We will provide a free estimate for our services.

153. What kind of company is Clarence Co.?
(A) A machinery manufacturer
(B) A delivery service
(C) A moving company
(D) A marketing consultant

154. What is indicated about Clarence Co.?
(A) It partners with a cleaning company.
(B) It can fix broken devices.
(C) It has branches in several locations.
(D) It is currently offering free upgrades.

155. What can customers learn if they have a consultation?
(A) How to set up some equipment
(B) How much they will have to pay
(C) Where to relocate their business
(D) When a delivery will be made

Questions 156-158 refer to the following online review.

Hotel Review: Bashiva Hotel, 1882 Hummingbird Way

Rating: ★★★★☆
Name: Stella Manning
Date(s) of stay: January 18–20 **Room type:** Regular Single Room

I stayed at Bashiva Hotel for two nights. I was on a business trip to meet some clients. Bashiva Hotel was ideal for my purposes. The rooms are comfortable, and the breakfast buffet is nice and well worth the price. — [1] —. Most importantly, despite being in a busy area of the city, I didn't hear much noise at night.

I chose this hotel because of its proximity to the downtown area. It was convenient for finding restaurants and getting to my meetings. — [2] —. I was supposed to catch a train early in the afternoon. I asked the front desk to call a taxi. I had to wait about fifteen minutes for it to arrive. — [3] —. Then, although the hotel staff said it would take about twenty minutes to get to the train station, it took closer to forty-five minutes. — [4] —. Fortunately, I managed to make it on time for my train because I had left early. However, all of this hassle could have been avoided had there been a bus from the hotel. The hotel already offers rides to and from the airport, but I think many of its guests come by train. Offering rides to the station as well would be very helpful.

156. What does Ms. Manning indicate about the hotel?
(A) It provides free breakfast.
(B) It is very noisy during the night.
(C) It is located near the city center.
(D) It is twenty minutes away from an airport.

157. In which of the positions marked [1], [2], [3], and [4] does the following sentence best belong?
"The only issue I had was when I was leaving."
(A) [1]
(B) [2]
(C) [3]
(D) [4]

158. What does Ms. Manning want the hotel to do?
(A) Add a shuttle service
(B) Adjust a timetable
(C) Clean its facilities
(D) Hire more staff

Questions 159-160 refer to the following notice.

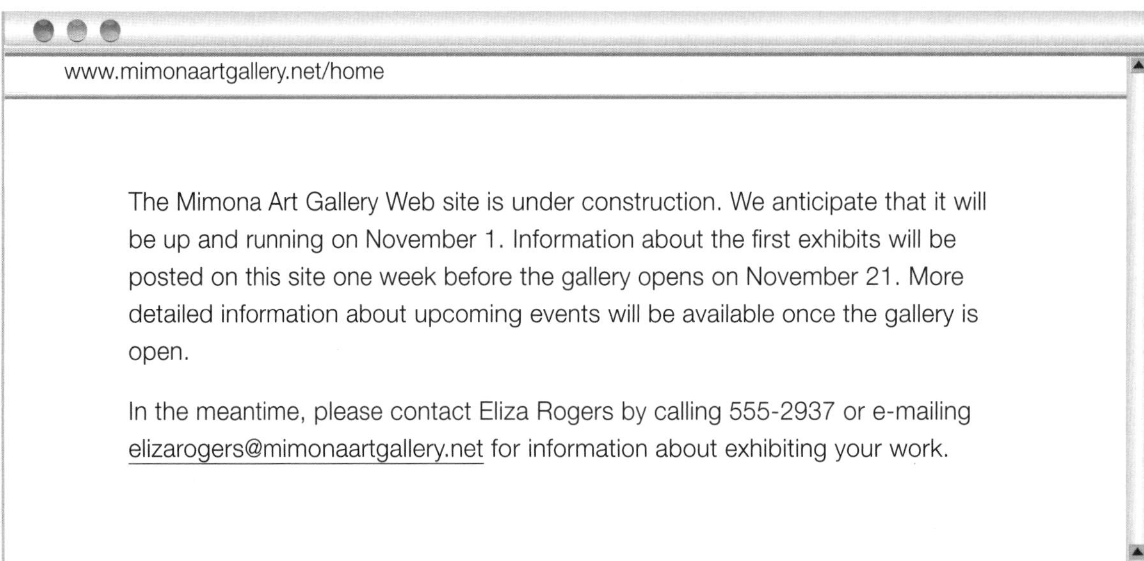

www.mimonaartgallery.net/home

The Mimona Art Gallery Web site is under construction. We anticipate that it will be up and running on November 1. Information about the first exhibits will be posted on this site one week before the gallery opens on November 21. More detailed information about upcoming events will be available once the gallery is open.

In the meantime, please contact Eliza Rogers by calling 555-2937 or e-mailing elizarogers@mimonaartgallery.net for information about exhibiting your work.

159. What is the purpose of the notice?

(A) To request reviews of an exhibit
(B) To announce the opening of a gallery
(C) To advertise artwork available for sale
(D) To provide a timeline for a new Web page

160. Why should Eliza Rogers be contacted?

(A) To make an appointment for a visit
(B) To purchase a work of art
(C) To ask about displaying artwork
(D) To register for an event

Questions 161-163 refer to the following e-mail.

E-Mail

To:	Brandon Mosher <bmosher@trupal.biz>
From:	Karen Pesco <kpesco@trupal.biz>
Date:	March 31
Subject:	Tax Forms

Dear Mr. Mosher,

I am currently going over your tax documents. However, it has come to my attention that you worked at another company for two months last year. Although this is just a short period of time, your previous income must be taken into account and stated when submitting tax forms. While companies submit the necessary declarations when the employee leaves, it appears that your previous place of employment has not. I would be happy to take care of this for you, but for that, I need information about your compensation at your last job. If you could provide the two pay stubs you received for those two months, I will gladly adjust your documents for the tax year.

Let me know if you have any questions.

Sincerely,

Karen Pesco

161. In what department does Ms. Pesco most likely work?
(A) Accounting
(B) Marketing
(C) Customer service
(D) Research and Development

162. What problem does Ms. Pesco mention?
(A) Some income must be declared.
(B) A payment has been rejected.
(C) A tax rate has increased.
(D) Lots of employees have quit.

163. What does Ms. Pesco ask Mr. Mosher for?
(A) A job description
(B) Salary records
(C) Proof of employment
(D) Tax schedules

Questions 164-167 refer to the following online chat discussion.

Clyde Mortensen [10:40 A.M.] Hi, Jennifer and Henry. I want to get started on the design for the April issue's cover. Do you know who we are interviewing for the main article?

Jennifer Sydnor [10:41 A.M.] It's going to be Jeff Blasio, a chef from an upcoming cooking show. I'll be writing that article, actually. I'm interviewing him next Tuesday.

Henry Tessor [10:42 A.M.] And I'm the photographer for this one. So I'll be there on Tuesday as well to do the photo shoot of Mr. Blasio.

Clyde Mortensen [10:44 A.M.] Oh, let me know when you're done. It would help to know what topics will be covered in the article and what the pictures will look like.

Jennifer Sydnor [10:45 A.M.] How about we all meet on Wednesday? Henry, you can show us your pictures, and I can tell you both about the interview.

Clyde Mortensen [10:47 A.M.] That works for me. I think the covers work best when the designers collaborate with the writers and photographers.

Henry Tessor [10:48 A.M.] I couldn't agree more. Wednesday works for me too. Morning or afternoon? I can meet at any time.

Clyde Mortensen [10:49 A.M.] The morning would be much better for me. Let's say at ten.

Jennifer Sydnor [10:50 A.M.] Ten is good. I'll see you two then.

164. Where do the writers most likely work?
(A) At a photo studio
(B) At a restaurant
(C) At a design firm
(D) At a magazine publisher

165. What is indicated about Mr. Blasio?
(A) He owns a popular restaurant.
(B) He will be on television.
(C) He writes for a magazine.
(D) He applied for a new job.

166. What will Mr. Tessor do on Tuesday?
(A) Create an advertisement
(B) Take some pictures
(C) Write an article
(D) Choose a menu

167. At 10:48 A.M., what does Mr. Tessor most likely mean when he writes, "I couldn't agree more"?
(A) He doesn't like the design of one of the projects.
(B) He believes pictures are the most important element.
(C) He thinks people from different departments should work together.
(D) He isn't sure what topics will be covered in the interview.

Questions 168-171 refer to the following article.

Broken Pearls to Be Performed at the Marina Theater

January 21—*Broken Pearls*, a play in three acts, will be performed at the Marina Theater in Dresdon on February 13, 14, and 15. The script was written by Maria Deluz, who also directed the play. It will be the Marina Theater's first modern-era play. — [1] —.

Because of a limited marketing budget and a rather low-profile cast, the premiere, which was at the Golden Volcano Theater in Henryville, did not attract a large audience. However, the performance received such good reviews that the troupe was encouraged to start a tour of the region and perform at various local venues. — [2] —. What sent the play's popularity skyrocketing was one review in particular, by notorious critic Joshua Corbett. Mr. Corbett, who is known for his strict and often scathing reviews, called *Broken Pearls* "a jewel of modern theater" in a long-form article. Thus, the play suddenly went from obscure piece to famous work. — [3] —.

"We never expected *Broken Pearls* to become such a hit," lead actor Jeremy Moriah explained. "It is all very exciting. I look forward to performing at new venues. I hope to even travel overseas for a show someday." — [4] —. Indeed, several venues around Europe have contacted production manager Isabelle Morton about possible future events.

168. What is implied about the Marina Theater?

(A) It usually shows performances of older works.
(B) It has already hosted *Broken Pearls* several times.
(C) It has become Dresdon's most popular theater.
(D) It received a lot of negative reviews in the past.

169. What is indicated about the play's troupe?

(A) It spent a lot of money on advertising.
(B) It is composed of little-known actors.
(C) It is used to performing in renowned venues.
(D) It has performed in a variety of countries.

170. According to the article, who contributed the most to the play's popularity?

(A) Maria Deluz
(B) Joshua Corbett
(C) Jeremy Moriah
(D) Isabelle Morton

171. In which of the positions marked [1], [2], [3], and [4] does the following sentence best belong?

"This dream might just become a reality."

(A) [1]
(B) [2]
(C) [3]
(D) [4]

Questions 172-175 refer to the following information.

Langda Goods Terms and Conditions

Thank you for choosing Langda Goods to carry your luggage on your next trip. All Langda luggage is covered by our one-year warranty. Please inspect your parcel carefully upon receiving it. If any part of the product is damaged, do not throw away any part of the product or its packaging. Immediately inform the delivery company. They will pick up the damaged goods and provide you with a claim form to fill out and a claim number. You may then follow the progress of your request on our Web site. It may take up to three weeks to review a claim.

A replacement will be sent to the customer if any of the following cases is reported within one year of purchase:
- Flaws in workmanship or material
- Tearing of the material
- Broken part
- Wearing of the wheels
- Color fading

Please note that in case of the following events, the customer is fully liable for the article and is entitled to no compensation:
- Unreasonable usage
- Staining
- Loss or theft

172. What is suggested about the recipients of the information?

(A) They have tried to return an item.
(B) They have recently purchased some luggage.
(C) They have just signed a contract with Langda Goods.
(D) They have posted a negative review of Langda Goods.

173. What does Langda Goods ask customers NOT to do if they receive a damaged item?

(A) Discard broken parts
(B) Notify the deliverer
(C) Complete a document
(D) Wait for a response

174. What can customers do on the Langda Goods Web site?

(A) Request faster delivery service
(B) Fill out a complaint form
(C) Check the status of a claim
(D) Extend the warranty of an item

175. In which case can a customer get a replacement?

(A) If the item is stolen.
(B) If the product has defects.
(C) If the material becomes stained.
(D) If the luggage is overused.

Questions 176-180 refer to the following flyer and form.

Arnett Co.

Arnett Co. has been providing high-quality services for the past five years. From May 1 to October 31, we're here to help you keep your yard and garden in excellent condition. We can provide mowing, tree-trimming, and weeding on a weekly or biweekly basis. If you are interested in having trees, flowers, or bushes planted, we can get you a discount with our partners at the Pineway Greenhouse, a reliable local business.

We have lots of returning customers every season, but slots are still available even if you've never used our services before. Please note that we do not serve corporate properties. If you'd like advice about the best way to care for your yard, we'll send one of our technicians to your home for a consultation at no charge. The monthly charge* for our basic service (mowing and cleanup only) is $425 for weekly visits or $250 for biweekly visits. There is also a premium service (the basic service plus weeding, bush trimming, and fertilizer treatments) for $675 for weekly visits or $450 for biweekly visits. Call us today at 555-5588.

*Applies to standard lots only. For oversized lots, please call to inquire about our rates.

Arnett Co. – New Customer Information

Customer: Vickie Warnick
Property: 226 Sunburst Drive, Portland, OR 97221
Lot Type: Standard
* **Equipment:** Lawnmower (model: Duncan-440)
Type of Service requested: [ ] Basic [X] Premium
[ ] Weekly [X] Biweekly
Start Date of Service: June 2

Consultation Date: May 26 **Property Assessed by:** Robert Cass

* If the customer prefers to use his/her own equipment, list the type and model name above.

176. What is the purpose of the flyer?
(A) To announce a change in ownership
(B) To promote a gardening care business
(C) To advertise a sales event
(D) To introduce a new service

177. What is indicated about Arnett Co.?
(A) It collaborates with a greenhouse.
(B) It accepts bookings by e-mail.
(C) It sells several varieties of plants and flowers.
(D) It offers services year-round.

178. What is NOT mentioned about Arnett Co.?
(A) It only caters to residential properties.
(B) It is not currently accepting new customers.
(C) It has different prices for standard and oversized lots.
(D) It offers a free consultation.

179. What is suggested about Ms. Warnick?
(A) She will receive a discount for the first month.
(B) She wants her own equipment to be used.
(C) She was referred to Arnett Co. by a friend.
(D) She has a property that is larger than average.

180. How much will Ms. Warnick be charged per month?
(A) $250
(B) $425
(C) $450
(D) $675

GO ON TO THE NEXT PAGE

Questions 181-185 refer to the following e-mails.

To: Gladwell Finance <info@gladwellfinance.com>
From: Keith Angulo <k.angulo@irvinemail.net>
Date: November 17
Subject: Transfer issue

To Whom It May Concern:

I tried to send money to my cousin in Vancouver using your online money transfer service. I applied a $5 credit toward the fees, which I got from signing up for your newsletter. He was able to pick up the cash at the Vancouver branch. However, after the transaction was completed, I noticed that I had been charged the full amount for the transfer fee. I looked over my account history to make sure I hadn't already used the credit, and I confirmed that I hadn't. However, the credit is no longer listed on my account. Please let me know why there was a problem with this transaction, request #45960, and what can be done to resolve it.

Thank you,

Keith Angulo

To: Keith Angulo <k.angulo@irvinemail.net>
From: Gladwell Finance <info@gladwellfinance.com>
Date: November 18
Subject: RE: Transfer issue

Dear Mr. Angulo,

On behalf of Gladwell Finance, I would like to apologize for the inconvenience you experienced. You did not mention the date that you sent the funds, but I was able to find it by using the number you provided. We were experiencing some problems when our internal server went down for a brief period on November 16, and this affected some customers. I have reissued you a credit of $5 to make up for the discount you should have gotten. My manager, Patrick Ogden, has also given me authorization to issue you a further $10 credit due to your inconvenience. This credit can be used toward our processing fees. You can verify that these amounts have been credited to you by clicking on the My Balance link after logging into your online account. You can use the credit anytime at your discretion. Should you have any further problems, you can call 555-3940, extension 31, rather than our customer service hotline. That way, you can get straight through to me.

Sincerely,

Brielle Stewart

181. What did Mr. Angulo do before contacting Gladwell Finance?

(A) He heard about the problem from his cousin.
(B) He received an invoice in the mail.
(C) He checked his past transactions.
(D) He reviewed his credit card bill.

182. What did Ms. Stewart use to look into Mr. Angulo's complaint?

(A) His transaction code
(B) His account number
(C) His request date
(D) His credit balance

183. In the second e-mail, the phrase "went down" in paragraph 1, line 3, is closest in meaning to

(A) deflated
(B) malfunctioned
(C) decreased
(D) lost

184. How can Mr. Angulo confirm that a credit was received?

(A) By reviewing an online page
(B) By checking a printed receipt
(C) By requesting a paper statement
(D) By e-mailing Ms. Stewart's manager

185. What is Mr. Angulo told to do if he has more issues?

(A) Call a customer service hotline
(B) Request a contract termination
(C) File a formal complaint online
(D) Contact Ms. Stewart directly

GO ON TO THE NEXT PAGE

Questions 186-190 refer to the following summary, flyer, and review.

Portrait Pro

Portrait Pro is a four-part series for people who have already mastered the basics of oil on canvas and want to move on to more advanced methods of painting. In these videos, renowned designer Gloria Hutton guides you through four steps to take your painting skills to the next level. In the first tutorial, you will learn how to choose the best brushes for various types of projects. The second video focuses on several advanced techniques. Third, you will create a portrait based on a provided model. Finally, you will learn how to paint your own ideas instead of using a model. The videos are available for download from all major Web sites.

Special Seminar at Hacksburg Museum of Arts and Crafts

On October 30, come to the Hacksburg Museum of Arts and Crafts for a special master class on painting. Artist Gloria Hutton will be giving a lecture based on the first video of her recently released four-part series, *Portrait Pro*.

Gloria Hutton is a prominent painter who created hundreds of breathtaking works that have been displayed in museums and festivals worldwide. Her natural talent has allowed Ms. Hutton to make a living off of her art early on, so money was not the motivation for making the videos. But she was receiving repeated requests for tips and private lessons and didn't have time to give regular classes. So she finally decided to release her tutorial series, which immediately became a bestseller.

Time: October 30, 3:00 P.M.
Place: Hacksburg Museum of Arts and Crafts, Shalandra Room
Fee: $35.00

Seating is limited for this event. Please register in advance by calling 555-8874.

Portrait Pro

Review by Margaret Jones

I highly recommend the *Portrait Pro* series to anyone passionate about art. I've been painting for several years now, and I thought all I could do to improve was to keep practicing. I never thought I'd learn so much simply by watching some videos. However, I've improved my skills tenfold by following Ms. Hutton's tutorials. She manages to explain complicated techniques in simple terms, and I was amazed by what I could accomplish by the time I finished watching these.

The only complaint I have is with the video about creating a project from scratch without referring to anything. I've watched that video dozens of times and still can't understand what Ms. Hutton is saying. However, because the three other videos were so helpful, I still think this series is worth the purchase.

186. According to the summary, who is the intended audience for the series?

(A) Professional artists with expert skills
(B) Beginners who never painted before
(C) People with experience in painting
(D) Collectors looking for artwork

187. What will attendants do at the seminar on October 30?

(A) Participate in filming a video
(B) Learn how to select utensils
(C) Create a portrait
(D) Practice some brushstrokes

188. According to the flyer, why did Ms. Hutton create the series?

(A) She needed more income.
(B) She wanted to advertise her classes.
(C) She was often asked for advice.
(D) She enjoyed her teaching experience.

189. In the review, the word "following" in paragraph 1, line 4, is closest in meaning to

(A) modifying
(B) coming after
(C) using
(D) testing

190. Which video of the *Portrait Pro* series does Ms. Jones say she watched many times?

(A) The first
(B) The second
(C) The third
(D) The fourth

GO ON TO THE NEXT PAGE

Questions 191-195 refer to the following advertisement, e-mail, and text message.

Divine Delights Caterer

For the best service in the area and the highest-quality food, choose Divine Delights Caterer! Summer is over, and our fall premium menus are here! See our Web site www.divinedelightscaterer.com for beverages and many other types of menus.

Premium Menu 1 ($50 per person)

Appetizer (choose one)
- ☐ Pumpkin soup
- ☐ Caesar salad

Main dish (choose one)
- ☐ Parmesan chicken
- ☐ Broccoli cream pasta

Dessert
Apple pie

Premium Menu 2 ($75 per person)
Includes one glass of wine

Appetizer (choose one)
- ☐ Onion soup
- ☐ Cobb salad

Main dish (choose one)
- ☐ Beef tenderloin
- ☐ Stuffed mushrooms

Dessert
Blueberry crumble

** Prices include service. Reservations for premium menus must be made at least one month in advance. A minimum of twenty people are required. Only one type of premium menu is possible per event. Please indicate each guest's dish preference at the time of reservation.*

From: Rooter, Phil <prooter@glypha.com>
To: Stacker, Lindsay <lstacker@glypha.com>
Date: September 15
Subject: Corporate Dinner

Hi. I think your suggestion of holding a corporate dinner to celebrate the merger of Glypha Corp. and Baller Inc. is an excellent idea. You mentioned October 20 as a possible date. I've checked with everyone, and it seems to be a good day to hold the event. As requested, I've attached a flyer for a catering company I told you about. I know we want to have a nice meal, so I think we should get a premium menu. But I'm not sure what our budget is. Let me know which one you think would be best. I will then pass the menu around the office so that everyone can select their dish choices.

From: Tracy Meloy
To: Phil Rooter

Since Stephanie is out on vacation this week, I chose her dish preferences for her for the corporate dinner. I told you that she and I would both be having the same thing. However, I just found out that she is a vegetarian, so could you switch her selection to the broccoli cream pasta? Sorry about the change.

191. What is suggested about Divine Delights Caterer?
(A) It is closed in the winter and spring.
(B) It adapts its menus to the seasons.
(C) It offers only two types of menus.
(D) It has an online reservation system.

192. What is the purpose of the planned event?
(A) To congratulate a colleague
(B) To celebrate a successful quarter
(C) To impress a potential client
(D) To mark a new partnership

193. When should Glypha Corp. make the catering reservation by?
(A) September 15
(B) September 20
(C) October 15
(D) October 20

194. What is Mr. Rooter asked to do?
(A) Postpone a vacation
(B) Modify a meal choice
(C) Reschedule an event
(D) Add a guest to an attendance list

195. What main dish will Ms. Meloy most likely have at the corporate dinner?
(A) Parmesan chicken
(B) Broccoli cream pasta
(C) Beef tenderloin
(D) Stuffed mushrooms

GO ON TO THE NEXT PAGE

Questions 196-200 refer to the following Web pages and e-mail.

www.kikilafabrics.com/about

HOME | **ABOUT** | PRODUCTS | CLEARANCE | CART

Kikila Fabrics is famous for having the widest selection of fabrics. You can find any texture and color you need for all of your projects right here on our site.

Make sure you check out the CLEARANCE page, where all items are 50 percent off. There, you'll find the best value for your money. In addition, if you order more than 10 meters of any fabric, you are eligible for free delivery.

Fabric is cut to the size indicated in the order form. Please check your measurements carefully as we do not grant returns or exchanges if you entered the wrong numbers.

www.kikilafabrics.com/clearance

HOME | ABOUT | PRODUCTS | **CLEARANCE** | CART

SEPTEMBER CLEARANCE ITEMS

Flannel – print

Available prints: owls, cats, bears
Description: This single layer flannel is wonderful for quilts and children's apparel.
Washing: machine wash/tumble dry
Price: $9.50 per meter

Wool Blend

Available colors: green, red
Description: This is the perfect material for coats, jackets, blankets, and other winter favorites.
Washing: machine wash cold/tumble dry low; Note: do NOT iron
Price: $12.00 per meter

Faux leather

Available colors: brown, black
Description: This heavyweight imitation leather is great for luxurious pillows and other home decor elements.
Washing: wipe down with damp rag
Price: $6.00 per meter

To: Frances Olsen <folsen@pozmail.net>
From: Kikila Fabrics <cs@kikilafabrics.com>
Subject: Order Number 201483
Date: September 21

Dear Mr. Olsen,

We have received your request to exchange the faux leather you purchased. Please accept our sincerest apologies for sending you the wrong color. We have verified your original order and confirmed that you had in fact requested black. Your order of 6 meters of faux leather in black has been shipped. You can expect to receive it by Friday afternoon. In addition, we've included 5 meters of red wool blend as an apology. It can be easily combined with the faux leather to create a variety of winter apparel.

As for the material we originally sent, we kindly request that you send it back to us and we will refund you for its shipping.

Thank you for your patience and understanding.

Sincerely,

Kikila Fabrics

196. According to the first Web page, what is Kikila Fabrics known for?

(A) Its low prices
(B) Its fast delivery
(C) Its variety of items
(D) Its return policy

197. How should the flannel material be washed?

(A) By wiping it with a wet piece of cloth
(B) By taking it to a dry cleaner
(C) By putting it in a washing machine
(D) By using cold water only

198. What color material did Mr. Olsen originally receive?

(A) Green
(B) Red
(C) Black
(D) Brown

199. What is implied about Mr. Olsen?

(A) He received a discount on his purchase.
(B) He provided the wrong measurements.
(C) He tried to exchange some apparel.
(D) He did not pay a delivery fee for his order.

200. What does Kikila Fabrics offer as an apology to Mr. Olsen?

(A) Complimentary fabric
(B) A refund for his purchase
(C) An article of winter clothing
(D) Free shipping on a future order

Stop! This is the end of the test. If you finish before time is called, you may go back to Parts 5, 6, and 7 and check your work.

Actual Test 4

LISTENING TEST

In the Listening test, you will be asked to demonstrate how well you understand spoken English. The entire Listening test will last approximately 45 minutes. There are four parts, and directions are given for each part. You must mark your answers on the separate answer sheet. Do not write your answers in your test book.

PART 1 13

Directions: For each question in this part, you will hear four statements about a picture in your test book. When you hear the statements, you must select the one statement that best describes what you see in the picture. Then find the number of the question on your answer sheet and mark your answer. The statements will not be printed in your test book and will be spoken only one time.

Statement (C), "They're sitting at the table," is the best description of the picture, so you should select answer (C) and mark it on your answer sheet.

1.

2.

Actual Test 4

GO ON TO THE NEXT PAGE

3.

4.

5.

6.

PART 2 14

Directions: You will hear a question or statement and three responses spoken in English. They will not be printed in your test book and will be spoken only one time. Select the best response to the question or statement and mark the letter (A), (B), or (C) on your answer sheet.

7. Mark your answer on your answer sheet.

8. Mark your answer on your answer sheet.

9. Mark your answer on your answer sheet.

10. Mark your answer on your answer sheet.

11. Mark your answer on your answer sheet.

12. Mark your answer on your answer sheet.

13. Mark your answer on your answer sheet.

14. Mark your answer on your answer sheet.

15. Mark your answer on your answer sheet.

16. Mark your answer on your answer sheet.

17. Mark your answer on your answer sheet.

18. Mark your answer on your answer sheet.

19. Mark your answer on your answer sheet.

20. Mark your answer on your answer sheet.

21. Mark your answer on your answer sheet.

22. Mark your answer on your answer sheet.

23. Mark your answer on your answer sheet.

24. Mark your answer on your answer sheet.

25. Mark your answer on your answer sheet.

26. Mark your answer on your answer sheet.

27. Mark your answer on your answer sheet.

28. Mark your answer on your answer sheet.

29. Mark your answer on your answer sheet.

30. Mark your answer on your answer sheet.

31. Mark your answer on your answer sheet.

PART 3 15

Directions: You will hear some conversations between two or more people. You will be asked to answer three questions about what the speakers say in each conversation. Select the best response to each question and mark the letter (A), (B), (C), or (D) on your answer sheet. The conversations will not be printed in your test book and will be spoken only one time.

32. What does the woman want to buy?
(A) A card
(B) A desk
(C) A computer
(D) A shelf

33. What does the man say about the items?
(A) Not all of them are discounted.
(B) Most of them are out of stock.
(C) Many of them are outdated.
(D) Some of them are mislabeled.

34. What will the man most likely do next?
(A) Verify a product's price
(B) Speak to a manager
(C) Check an account history
(D) Print out a coupon

35. What is the purpose of the woman's call?
(A) To make an appointment
(B) To extend a deadline
(C) To report some test results
(D) To change work hours

36. What does the man mention about the company?
(A) Its workers' shift schedules are flexible.
(B) Its major tasks are done before noon.
(C) Its medical office isn't open in the morning.
(D) Its productivity is particularly high this week.

37. What does the man say he will do?
(A) Inform a manager of a change
(B) Reduce the workload for employees
(C) Postpone a dental checkup
(D) Promote the woman to a higher position

38. Why is the man calling?
(A) To schedule the delivery of an item
(B) To notify of a document's availability
(C) To update his personal information
(D) To request directions to a location

39. What does the man say is required?
(A) Picture identification
(B) Contact information
(C) A local mailing address
(D) A payment receipt

40. Why can't the woman meet the man today?
(A) She forgot her passport.
(B) She didn't make an appointment.
(C) She is stuck in traffic.
(D) She lives too far away.

41. Where most likely is the conversation taking place?
(A) At a train station
(B) At a bookstore
(C) At a print shop
(D) At a library

42. What does the woman ask Mr. Clayton?
(A) Where a facility is located
(B) Whether an exception can be made
(C) How a process should be executed
(D) How much an item costs

43. What will need to be paid on Friday?
(A) An overdue fine
(B) A transportation fee
(C) A lost item charge
(D) A luggage delivery bill

GO ON TO THE NEXT PAGE

44. What are the speakers mainly talking about?

(A) An audience review
(B) A musician's performance
(C) An advertisement design
(D) An informational handout

45. What problem does the woman mention?

(A) A show's break time is too short.
(B) A piece of music was poorly interpreted.
(C) An entertainer is running late.
(D) A schedule printout is incomplete.

46. What does the man mean when he says, "How is that possible"?

(A) He doesn't understand how to do a task.
(B) He wants the woman to explain a change.
(C) He is surprised to notice an error.
(D) He disagrees with the woman's statement.

---

47. What most likely is the woman's job?

(A) Subway ticket vendor
(B) Interior designer
(C) Real estate agent
(D) Taxi driver

48. What does the man ask about?

(A) A meeting time
(B) A place's location
(C) Property values
(D) Ticket prices

49. What will the woman most likely do next?

(A) Find a property for the man
(B) Help the man locate a place
(C) Drive the man to a station
(D) Send a document to the man

---

50. Where most likely is the conversation taking place?

(A) At a fire station
(B) At a real estate agency
(C) At a jewelry store
(D) At an interior designer's

51. What characteristic do Maria and Clyde want?

(A) An old-fashioned appearance
(B) A contemporary look
(C) A traditional system
(D) A high energy production

52. What is mentioned about the Windsor Gold?

(A) It has sold out.
(B) It's a customer favorite.
(C) It has a gold finish.
(D) It's in a modern style.

---

53. Who most likely is the man?

(A) A hotel manager
(B) A restaurant worker
(C) A private caterer
(D) An event organizer

54. What does the woman plan on doing after work tomorrow?

(A) Going straight home
(B) Dining with colleagues
(C) Shopping for groceries
(D) Meeting her friends

55. What does the woman ask the man to do?

(A) Cancel her request
(B) Add items to her order
(C) Meet her at her office
(D) Make a reservation

---

56. What is the purpose of the woman's call?
(A) To ask for directions
(B) To schedule a meeting
(C) To inquire about a package
(D) To report a missing item

57. What does the man mean when he says, "I should have been clearer"?
(A) He needs to explain a new strategy.
(B) He thinks the woman went the wrong way.
(C) He is going to provide a status update.
(D) He is confused by the woman's statement.

58. What does the woman say about the intersection?
(A) She has already passed it.
(B) She used to work in an office near it.
(C) She doesn't know where it is.
(D) She has found a post office by it.

---

59. Who most likely is the man?
(A) A pastry chef
(B) A business consultant
(C) A newspaper reporter
(D) A fitness expert

60. What are the speakers mainly discussing?
(A) A business strategy
(B) A product launch
(C) A shortage of materials
(D) A training event

61. What does the woman say will happen next month?
(A) Free refreshments will be served.
(B) A new location will be opened.
(C) A class will be offered.
(D) More employees will be hired.

WEEKDAY TRAIN SCHEDULE

Train Number	Destination	Departure Time	Arrival Time
105	Atlanta	6:20 A.M.	7:40 A.M.
207	Atlanta	10:30 A.M.	11:50 A.M.
482	Atlanta	2:20 P.M.	3:40 P.M.
553	Atlanta	5:50 P.M.	7:10 P.M.

62. What type of company do the speakers most likely work at?
(A) A travel agency
(B) A clothing store
(C) A transportation company
(D) A food producer

63. What will the man do tomorrow?
(A) Depart for Atlanta
(B) Attend an event
(C) Search for a hotel
(D) Leave the office early

64. Look at the graphic. Which train will the man most likely take?
(A) Train 105
(B) Train 207
(C) Train 482
(D) Train 553

GO ON TO THE NEXT PAGE

Amateur Art Contest
Call for entries

Submission period: February 3-5
Awards Ceremony: February 7 at 6 P.M.
Show opens to the public: February 8
Show closes: February 20

Willow Art Museum

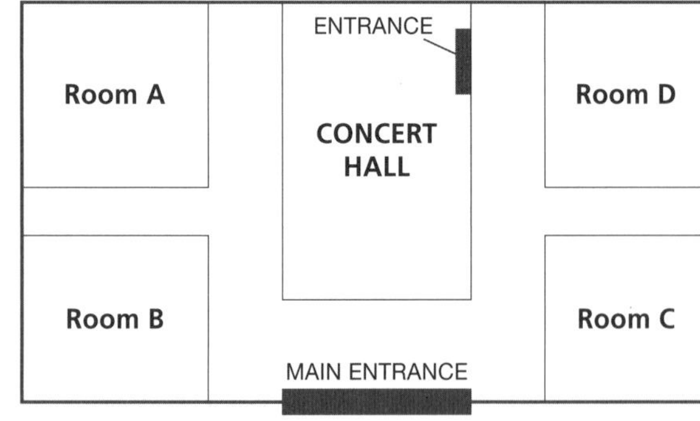

65. What will the man do tomorrow?
(A) Write an article
(B) Meet with a reporter
(C) Tour a museum
(D) Purchase some artwork

66. Look at the graphic. When does the man need extra help?
(A) February 3
(B) February 5
(C) February 7
(D) February 20

67. What does the woman say she will do?
(A) Move to a new home
(B) Submit an original painting
(C) Come to the museum early
(D) Create a registration form

68. Who most likely is the man?
(A) A conductor
(B) A musician
(C) A ticket agent
(D) An audience member

69. What does the man mention about the lecture?
(A) It costs extra to attend.
(B) It doesn't have any more seats available.
(C) It started a few minutes ago.
(D) It will be about tonight's music.

70. Look at the graphic. Where will the woman most likely go next?
(A) Room A
(B) Room B
(C) Room C
(D) Room D

PART 4 (16)

Directions: You will hear some talks given by a single speaker. You will be asked to answer three questions about what the speaker says in each talk. Select the best response to each question and mark the letter (A), (B), (C), or (D) on your answer sheet. The talks will not be printed in your test book and will be spoken only one time.

71. Where is this talk most likely being heard?
(A) At a museum
(B) At a department store
(C) At a concert hall
(D) At a souvenir shop

72. What will the speaker do at eleven thirty?
(A) Host an auction
(B) Play a song
(C) Explain a device
(D) Start a guided tour

73. What does the speaker recommend the listeners do at twelve o'clock?
(A) Meet with a specialist
(B) Attend a lecture
(C) Observe a specific item
(D) Exit the building

74. Why does the speaker apologize?
(A) There is a lack of seats.
(B) A machine malfunctioned.
(C) A meeting is starting late.
(D) A location has changed.

75. What is the purpose of the meeting?
(A) To introduce an employee
(B) To select group members
(C) To explain a new policy
(D) To review a project's goals

76. According to the speaker, why should the questions be written down?
(A) They should be reviewed by a supervisor.
(B) They will be read aloud for a recording.
(C) They need to be sorted by category.
(D) They are limited to one per person.

77. What kind of product does the report describe?
(A) Athletic shoes
(B) An electronic device
(C) Natural cosmetics
(D) A home appliance

78. According to the speaker, what is special about the product?
(A) Its safety features
(B) Its recyclable materials
(C) Its compact size
(D) Its lightweight design

79. What does the speaker recommend doing?
(A) Comparing prices
(B) Testing products
(C) Visiting a Web site
(D) Calling with questions

80. Who most likely are the listeners?
(A) Tour guides
(B) Job applicants
(C) Beach visitors
(D) Hotel guests

81. What are the listeners asked to do?
(A) Explain a problem
(B) Fill out a survey
(C) Find a partner
(D) Do a role-play activity

82. What will the listeners most likely do next?
(A) Pick up a handout
(B) Follow the speaker
(C) Take a break
(D) Sign up for a session

GO ON TO THE NEXT PAGE

83. Where is this announcement most likely being heard?

(A) At a grocery store
(B) At an airport
(C) At a daycare center
(D) At a zoo

84. Why does the speaker say, "This will only slow the process"?

(A) To prevent rude behavior
(B) To clarify an estimate
(C) To encourage purchases
(D) To announce a delay

85. What does the speaker offer some young visitors?

(A) Priority seating
(B) Free entry
(C) A toy animal
(D) Photographs of animals

---

86. What is the purpose of the message?

(A) To modify an order
(B) To make an apology
(C) To explain a process
(D) To request a payment

87. What is mentioned about *The Grand Hope*?

(A) It was written by a best-selling author.
(B) It is less expensive than *Agents and Foes*.
(C) It is currently out of stock.
(D) It was given as a birthday present.

88. What does the speaker ask the listener to do?

(A) Provide a refund
(B) Use a fast delivery service
(C) Update a Web site
(D) Return a phone call

---

89. What task are the listeners expected to do?

(A) Taste some beverage samples
(B) Record some music performances
(C) Review some advertisements
(D) Assess some job candidates

90. What does the speaker imply when he says, "Don't pay attention to them"?

(A) The company wants independent opinions.
(B) Some handouts contain an error.
(C) The listeners were given the wrong instructions.
(D) Some employees will be monitoring the activity.

91. What will the listeners most likely do next?

(A) Print some documents
(B) Write down questions
(C) Put on name tags
(D) Form small groups

---

92. What is the purpose of the talk?

(A) To introduce an author
(B) To advertise a book
(C) To criticize an idea
(D) To request nominations

93. What does the speaker imply when she says, "Trust me"?

(A) She has read the book.
(B) She will write a novel.
(C) She plans on answering questions.
(D) She has won several awards.

94. What will most likely happen next?

(A) A book will be signed.
(B) A passage will be read.
(C) Some questions will be asked.
(D) An award will be presented.

EMERALD PARK TOUR SCHEDULE

DEPARTURE TIME	GUIDE
11:00 A.M.	Cindy
12:30 P.M.	Sandra
2:00 P.M.	Josh
3:30 P.M.	Richard

95. Why has one of the tours been canceled?
(A) Weather conditions are unfavorable.
(B) An employee was injured.
(C) An area needs renovations.
(D) Not enough people registered.

96. Look at the graphic. At what time was the canceled tour supposed to leave?
(A) At 11:00 A.M.
(B) At 12:30 P.M.
(C) At 2:00 P.M.
(D) At 3:30 P.M.

97. What are the visitors prohibited from doing?
(A) Leaving children unattended
(B) Entering without a guide
(C) Running in the park
(D) Joining several tours

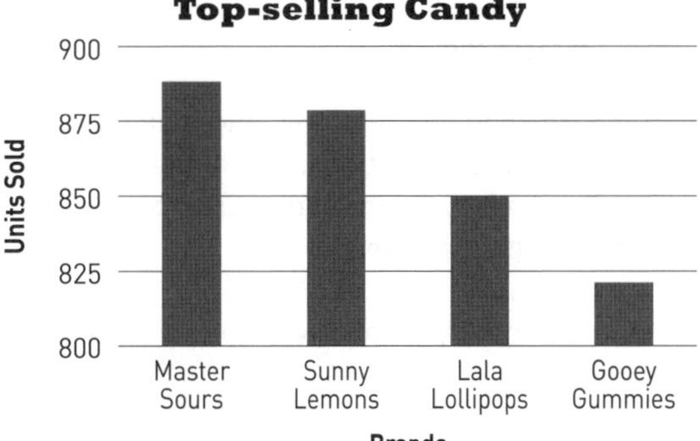

98. According to the speaker, how can the company increase profits?
(A) By selling a new product
(B) By changing suppliers
(C) By purchasing more goods
(D) By targeting different customers

99. Look at the graphic. What will the company buy less of?
(A) Master Sours
(B) Sunny Lemons
(C) Lala Lollipops
(D) Gooey Gummies

100. What will the speaker most likely do next?
(A) Place an order
(B) Finalize a plan
(C) Give out documents
(D) Negotiate a price

This is the end of the Listening test. Turn to Part 5 in your test book.

GO ON TO THE NEXT PAGE

READING TEST

In the Reading test, you will read a variety of texts and answer several different types of reading comprehension questions. The entire Reading test will last 75 minutes. There are three parts, and directions are given for each part. You are encouraged to answer as many questions as possible within the time allowed.

You must mark your answers on the separate answer sheet. Do not write your answers in your test book.

PART 5

Directions: A word or phrase is missing in each of the sentences below. Four answer choices are given below each sentence. Select the best answer to complete the sentence. Then mark the letter (A), (B), (C), or (D) on your answer sheet.

101. Ms. Anita always ------- participates in fundraisers by baking cookies and selling them.

(A) active
(B) acts
(C) actively
(D) activity

102. The parade for the town festival is ------- to start at 1 P.M. tomorrow.

(A) scheduled
(B) remained
(C) considered
(D) celebrated

103. Once the door opened, the usher showed the audience members to their ------- seats.

(A) respective
(B) respect
(C) respectful
(D) respecting

104. All of the furniture sold in our store comes with easy-to-follow ------- for fast assembly.

(A) estimates
(B) instructions
(C) comforts
(D) refunds

105. Mr. Crob had to wait fifteen minutes for an ------- when he called customer service.

(A) answer
(B) answering
(C) answered
(D) answers

106. Being fluent in at least two languages is a necessary qualification ------- working as a concierge at the Summertime Resort.

(A) about
(B) through
(C) by
(D) for

107. Technicians must turn off the power to the entire building when ------- the electrical system.

(A) repair
(B) repaired
(C) repairing
(D) repairs

108. The video ------- various ways in which the software can help a business to organize its data.

(A) inquires
(B) focuses
(C) terminates
(D) demonstrates

109. Recommend a friend of ------- to join our gym, and we will provide a discounted membership fee.

(A) you
(B) your
(C) yourself
(D) yours

110. The manager ------- asked that Ms. Nicola be the one to lead the negotiations with Cinta Corp.

(A) utterly
(B) specifically
(C) broadly
(D) gradually

111. Many candidates ------- applications for the sales associate position, so it will take time to go over all of them.

(A) to submit
(B) were submitted
(C) submission
(D) have submitted

112. It is impossible to get a shuttle bus from the airport to the hotel ------- any reservations.

(A) unless
(B) without
(C) except
(D) besides

113. Mr. Moss expressed interest in ------- a workshop to help improve his public speaking skills.

(A) joined
(B) join
(C) joining
(D) to join

114. The airline's new policy increases the baggage ------- from one suitcase per passenger to two for international flights.

(A) claim
(B) involvement
(C) allowance
(D) acquisition

115. Patrons of the Mencer Public Library can renew ------- checked-out books online and thus avoid overdue fines.

(A) their
(B) theirs
(C) they
(D) them

116. Not only senior staff members but also new employees will benefit ------- the revisions to the pay scale.

(A) of
(B) among
(C) from
(D) to

117. The branch supervisor decided to close the store early to let the staff go home ------- the snowstorm started.

(A) so as to
(B) before
(C) ahead of
(D) rather than

118. The date and venue for the convention have been chosen, but the program ------- needs to be finalized.

(A) still
(B) lately
(C) once
(D) exactly

119. Colleagues will offer to give money for gas to ------- who volunteer to drive them to the annual picnic.

(A) them
(B) those
(C) other
(D) anyone

120. The price of gold was rising steadily for a few months, but it started ------- at the end of June.

(A) to impede
(B) to decline
(C) to spend
(D) to eliminate

121. In response to severe ------- concerning its high pollution levels, the factory took measures to protect the surrounding environment.

(A) critical
(B) criticizes
(C) critically
(D) criticism

122. Now that the bookstore's Web site has been updated, regular customers can get reading recommendations ------- their purchase history.

(A) on behalf of
(B) such as
(C) based on
(D) in spite of

123. Pearly White Toothpaste, though ------- recommended by dentists nationwide, is not as popular among buyers as its main competitor.

(A) strong
(B) strength
(C) strongest
(D) strongly

124. Engineers must have a master's degree or ------- work experience to be considered for senior management openings.

(A) deliberate
(B) lucrative
(C) equivalent
(D) systematic

125. To alleviate traffic congestion in the downtown area, the city planner ------- some roadways to one-way streets.

(A) has been converted
(B) are converted
(C) is converting
(D) convert

126. While the final winners will be kept secret, the top ------- for the talent awards will be revealed two weeks before the ceremony.

(A) subscriptions
(B) confidences
(C) congratulations
(D) nominations

127. Denny Marlow became more and more ------- about his chances of getting the accounting job as the interview progressed.

(A) hope
(B) hopefully
(C) hopeful
(D) hoping

128. Guests are expected to reply to the invitation by the end of the month ------- they plan on attending the event or not.

(A) either
(B) whether
(C) since
(D) though

129. Chef Francis Gales opened a restaurant ------- menu changes daily depending on the best fish and produce available each morning.

(A) that
(B) when
(C) whose
(D) while

130. The directors of Hencer Inc. are very ------- about who they allow into the biannual meeting for setting the company's objectives.

(A) selective
(B) prominent
(C) accessible
(D) ambitious

PART 6

Directions: Read the texts that follow. A word, phrase, or sentence is missing in parts of each text. Four answer choices for each question are given below the text. Select the best answer to complete the text. Then mark the letter (A), (B), (C), or (D) on your answer sheet.

Questions 131-134 refer to the following e-mail.

To: All members <memberlist@bettermegym.com>
From: Dennis Primus <dprimus@bettermegym.com>
Subject: New Weekend Hours
Date: August 4

Dear members,

Thank you to all who ------- (**131.**) our survey to share ideas concerning Better Me Gym. We strive to keep our gym the most modern and convenient for our clients, so feedback such as yours is highly ------- (**132.**) to us. While we cannot reply to each of you individually, we are happy to make changes to address the most common ------- (**133.**). The first of these was about our closing times. Many of you complained about our short weekend hours. ------- (**134.**). We hope that you will enjoy these added hours.

See you at the gym!

Dennis Primus
Manager, Better Me Gym

131. (A) completing
(B) completes
(C) are completing
(D) completed

132. (A) values
(B) value
(C) valuable
(D) valuing

133. (A) demands
(B) schedules
(C) routines
(D) patrons

134. (A) Unfortunately, we cannot extend our hours of operation.
(B) In response, we have decided to stay open until 9 P.M. on Saturdays.
(C) Members are free to work out as many hours as they wish.
(D) These are described in detail in your gym membership contract.

Questions 135-138 refer to the following advertisement.

> Secure your house with Houseguard! Our -------(135.) security system has all the latest features you need to feel safe and comfortable in your own home. We will set up security cameras, motion sensors, and an alarm system that will cover all areas of your property. -------(136.), we will equip your home with our smart control robot, which constantly monitors your appliances to eliminate any danger. -------(131.). For example, should you leave the gas on when you leave, it will -------(138.) turn it off for you, thus preventing a potential fire. Make your home safer today! Visit www.houseguard.com today to schedule an installation.

135. (A) second-hand
(B) ill-equipped
(C) out-of-date
(D) state-of-the-art

136. (A) Therefore
(B) Nonetheless
(C) In addition
(D) On the other hand

137. (A) Indeed, burglaries have been on the rise lately.
(B) The Houseguard robot could save your house.
(C) There are many control systems to choose from.
(D) You can now cook amazing meals from your own kitchen.

138. (A) automatic
(B) automates
(C) automation
(D) automatically

Questions 139-142 refer to the following letter.

November 25

Eric Closter
2957 Marisol Avenue
Willows, PA 18765

Dear Mr. Closter,

We are writing to inform you that the latest payment for your subscription to *Monthly Talks* was declined. Thus, we were unable to process the transaction. -------. **139.** If you cannot determine the cause of the error after ------- **140.** all of your information, contact your bank.

Since your payment did not go through, we have ------- **141.** shipment of the latest issue to your address. In order to receive the December issue, you must ------- **142.** provide valid payment information as we will be sending out the last issues soon.

If you have any questions about your *Monthly Talks* subscription, please call us at 555-3548.

Sincerely,

The *Monthly Talks* Staff

139. (A) However, we do not have the correct credit card information.
(B) A cancelation fee of $12.99 will be deducted from your account.
(C) Attached is a form for renewing your subscription to our magazine.
(D) This problem may be due to an address change or card expiration.

140. (A) verifying
(B) verification
(C) verify
(D) verified

141. (A) timed
(B) refunded
(C) canceled
(D) measured

142. (A) incorrectly
(B) surely
(C) promptly
(D) temporarily

Questions 143-146 refer to the following article.

Local Companies Commit to Change

BETHOS (January 22)— -------. (143.) According to this potential contract, Frester Corp., Alphet Inc., and Proga Corp. would commit to limiting their factories' energy consumption and emission levels. Such changes could cost each company a large amount of money by slowing their production rates. -------, (144.) the directors agreed that focusing on environmentally friendly methods would be beneficial in the long run. "If all three companies ------- (145.) to the agreement, then no one will lose too much, and the environment will gain," argued a director of Frester Corp. ------- (146.) of the sixteen directors volunteered any details about the logistics of the plan, but they did confirm that an agreement was reached and will be made public soon.

143. (A) A recent study shows that pollution levels in Bethos are at an all-time high.
(B) Several local companies are currently seeking to hire entry-level workers.
(C) The directors of three large companies met yesterday to discuss an agreement.
(D) Solar energy is just one example of renewable energy that is easy to harvest.

144. (A) Furthermore
(B) Nevertheless
(C) Similarly
(D) Otherwise

145. (A) propose
(B) follow
(C) compare
(D) adhere

146. (A) Those
(B) Any
(C) None
(D) Neither

PART 7

Directions: In this part you will read a selection of texts, such as magazine and newspaper articles, e-mails, and instant messages. Each text or set of texts is followed by several questions. Select the best answer for each question and mark the letter (A), (B), (C), or (D) on your answer sheet.

Questions 147-148 refer to the following receipt.

Tina's Treasures

Date: 11/15
Member number: 194538838

Silk Tie	$22.99
Leather belt	$39.99
Linen shirt	$45.00
Subtotal	$107.98
Tax (6%)	$6.48
Total	**$114.46**
Cash	$120.00
Change	-$5.54

Member points earned	110
Total member points	1,005

Congratulations! You have reached more than one thousand member points and have earned this coupon:

Good for $5.00 at Tina's Treasures
Coupon Code: A2225SG56

Find us online at www.tinastreasures.com, where you can browse our merchandise, write product reviews, and place orders. You can also sign up for our newsletter to receive special promotions by e-mail.

147. What kind of store most likely is Tina's Treasures?
(A) A fabrics distributor
(B) A clothing outlet
(C) A hardware store
(D) A jewelry shop

148. According to the receipt, how did the buyer receive a coupon?
(A) By winning a contest
(B) By reviewing a product
(C) By being a loyal customer
(D) By subscribing to a newsletter

Questions 149-150 refer to the following text-message chain.

Laura Fisher [6:58 P.M.]
Thomas, are you still at the office by any chance?

Thomas Volpert [6:59 P.M.]
Yes, I'm still here, but I was just about to leave for Jarrod's retirement party.

Laura Fisher [7:00 P.M.]
I was supposed to bring Jarrod's gift to the restaurant, but I just noticed that I left it at the office. I'm almost at the restaurant already.

Thomas Volpert [7:01 P.M.]
No problem. Just tell me where it is, and I'll bring it.

Laura Fisher [7:02 P.M.]
Oh, that's such a relief. You'll see a box under my desk. It's blue and black. It has a label from Galinda's Collection Shop on it.

Thomas Volpert [7:03 P.M.]
Okay, hold on. Let me check.

Thomas Volpert [7:07 P.M.]
Got it. The invitation says seven thirty, right? I'd better get going.

Laura Fisher [7:08 P.M.]
Yes. Thank you so much! You're a lifesaver.

149. At 7:07 P.M., what does Mr. Volpert mean when he writes, "Got it"?

(A) He found the present.
(B) He understands the directions.
(C) He received a party invitation.
(D) He has a gift receipt.

150. Where is Mr. Volpert most likely going next?

(A) To the office
(B) To Ms. Fisher's home
(C) To a restaurant
(D) To a store

Questions 151-152 refer to the following e-mail.

E-mail

To: Sooyeon Baek <baeksooyeon@harligen.net>
From: Gerald Finn <finngerald@harligen.net>
Date: January 18
Subject: Urgent

Dear Ms. Baek,

I need your help. The foreman at the 171 Dutton Street property has informed me that his team has nearly run out of the gravel for the water barrier. They need more as soon as possible not to fall behind schedule. I'll be away from the office the rest of the day performing safety checks at our other sites, so I can't take care of this myself. Would you please call the supplier and ask for more gravel to be delivered? The type we're using is listed in the database under that property's name. It should be easy to find.

Thank you!

Gerald Finn

151. For what kind of business does Mr. Finn most likely work?
(A) A construction company
(B) A manufacturing facility
(C) A hardware store
(D) A real estate firm

152. What is Ms. Baek asked to do?
(A) Meet a potential customer
(B) Place an order
(C) Update a database
(D) Pick up a delivery

GO ON TO THE NEXT PAGE

Questions 153-154 refer to the following Web page.

To the Clouds was established over fifteen years ago and has continuously strived to create the most innovative climbing gear and apparel around. Contact us today to become an official To the Clouds distributor. We are one of the top-selling brands on the market, and you will want to have our products in your store to attract the climbing community. By selling To the Clouds equipment, you will gain a reputation as a trustworthy store that sells excellent gear and apparel. Moreover, all of our products come with lifetime warranties to reassure customers that they are buying superior equipment. And we supply high-quality posters, banners, and leaflets. Our merchandise is thus simple to market and always sells out quickly.

153. Who should contact To the Clouds?
(A) Sporting goods retailers
(B) Professional athletes
(C) Climbing club leaders
(D) Equipment manufacturers

154. What is NOT mentioned about To the Clouds products?
(A) Their warranty doesn't expire.
(B) They are sold at affordable prices.
(C) They are popular among climbers.
(D) They are easy to advertise.

Questions 155-157 refer to the following notice.

Employee Notice: Annual Juny Fundraising Gala

The annual fundraising gala for Juny Children's Organization will be held at the Sarcona Convention Center on Sunday, April 30, from 6 P.M. to 8:30 P.M. Attendance for Dream Voyages employees is optional but strongly encouraged. As usual, our company will be sponsoring the event. However, instead of donating money as we have every other year, we are donating prizes for the raffle. For those of you who have not been to this event before, please note the dress code.

Dress code

Men do not need to wear tuxedos but must wear dark-colored suits, with a white shirt and solid-color tie. Please avoid loud prints and patterns.

Acceptable attire for women includes long gowns and pantsuits. Please do not wear short-cut dresses. If you decide to wear high heels, make sure you can comfortably stand in the shoes for a long period of time.

Prize donations

Dream Voyages will be donating one all-inclusive tour package to Europe, three vacation packages to resorts in Mexico, and ten weekend spa packages. Please note that anyone affiliated with Dream Voyages is not eligible to win any of these prizes.

155. What has Dream Voyages changed?
(A) Its dress code for employees
(B) Its contribution to the organization
(C) Its policy on attendance to the event
(D) Its type of rewards for customers

156. What are women NOT allowed to wear?
(A) Dark-colored dresses
(B) High-heel shoes
(C) Long pants
(D) Short skirts

157. What is suggested about the prizes donated by Dream Voyages?
(A) They may not be won by Dream Voyages employees.
(B) They do not include expenses related to plane tickets.
(C) They will be awarded to the best-performing workers.
(D) They are the most expensive gifts at the fundraiser.

GO ON TO THE NEXT PAGE

Questions 158-160 refer to the following e-mail.

To: Garfield, Anna <annagarfield76@peoplesnet.com>
From: Customer Service <cs@featherflights.com>
Date: July 12
Subject: Flight reservation – Action needed

Dear Anna Garfield,

We are writing to inform you that payment for your flight to Los Angeles has not been processed. Please make a payment through our Web site in the amount of $636.88. — [1] —. Your reservation will not be complete until this amount has been received. If payment is not submitted within twenty-four hours after the request was made, the seats will be forfeited. — [2] —.

For your reference, you have requested two seats for a round-trip flight to Los Angeles departing from Austin on Saturday, August 7, at 3:20 P.M. and returning on Sunday, August 29, at 10:10 A.M. — [3] —.

Please note that the price you were originally quoted for the tickets may no longer be available after today. This is why we urge you to complete the reservation as soon as possible. If you require assistance, you may call our customer service line at 555-293-5892 between 9 A.M. and 5 P.M. on weekdays. — [4] —.

Thank you for choosing with Feather Flights. We look forward to serving you.

Regards,

The Feather Flights Customer Service Team

158. What is the purpose of the e-mail?
(A) To confirm a reservation
(B) To explain a flight change
(C) To acknowledge a cancelation
(D) To notify a customer of a due payment

159. In which of the positions marked [1], [2], [3], and [4] does the following sentence best belong?
"Thus, you will have to start the reservation process again."
(A) [1]
(B) [2]
(C) [3]
(D) [4]

160. What is indicated about the ticket price?
(A) It might change in the future.
(B) It is temporarily discounted.
(C) It includes only one way.
(D) It is payable only by phone.

Questions 161-164 refer to the following article.

January 30—After an unprecedented successful fourth quarter, it was rumored that Habbart Corp. would be giving large year-end bonuses to all of its employees. — [1] —. Habbart Corp. spokesperson Mr. Bryan Caster announced that the company would instead be making a large donation to Enviro First, an environmental foundation.

The revelation came as a surprise, as Habbart Corp. has a reputation for ignoring environmental issues. — [2] —. Controversy was especially intense after one of Habbart's plants had a small explosion that caused a chemical leak, contaminating a nearby river. Although the leak was quickly contained, local residents took to the streets to protest, denouncing the company's lack of care for ecological concerns. — [3] —.

Yet Habbart Corp.'s latest decision seems to contradict those claims. Mr. Caster emphasized that the company took matters related to sustainable production very seriously. "We want to support and work in collaboration with organizations that fight to protect the environment," Mr. Caster declared. — [4] —. The total amount of the donation has not been revealed, but it is expected to be the largest one Enviro First has yet received. Mr. Caster insisted that all of Habbart Corp.'s extra profits would go to the organization.

161. What is the purpose of the article?

(A) To criticize a corporation's approach to environmental issues
(B) To advocate stronger measures against natural disasters
(C) To announce a company's contribution to a nonprofit
(D) To report an accident that happened at a local factory

162. What is indicated about Habbart Corp.?

(A) It is known for its environment-friendly methods.
(B) It will be giving extra compensation to its employees.
(C) It had an exceptionally profitable fourth quarter.
(D) It is planning on building a new plant near a river.

163. According to the article, what caused people to protest against Habbart Corp.?

(A) Its neglect of the environment
(B) Its employee benefits packages
(C) Its frequent explosion accidents
(D) Its small charitable donations

164. In which of the positions marked [1], [2], [3], and [4] does the following sentence best belong?

"However, this was denied at a press conference held yesterday."

(A) [1]
(B) [2]
(C) [3]
(D) [4]

Questions 165-167 refer to the following advertisement.

Boca Chocolates is seventy-five years old, and to celebrate, the factory will be opening its doors to the public for one week, from May 6 to May 12. This is your chance to visit the premises and find out how Boca Chocolates makes its delicious sweets!

First, you will take a guided tour that will show you every step of the process from the bean to the box. You will see our workers operating the machinery, and our chocolate artists decorating the final products.

After you learn all about how chocolate is made, you can taste special samples of upcoming products, enjoy our magical chocolate fountain, and purchase gift baskets at a discount. In addition, every visitor will go home with a box of chocolates as a gift.

For security purposes, the number of visitors is limited, so make your reservation early! Tours are $45 for adults, $30 for students, and $20 for children under twelve. Call 555-9963 to schedule a time.

165. What is being advertised?

(A) A new kind of chocolate
(B) A special anniversary tour
(C) A sales event at a grocery store
(D) An innovative candy-making machine

166. What will be given out for free?

(A) Gift baskets
(B) Fountains
(C) Decorations
(D) Boxes of sweets

167. What are readers encouraged to do?

(A) Reserve a time slot
(B) Place an order
(C) Taste a product
(D) Try a piece of equipment

Questions 168-171 refer to the following online chat discussion.

Selam Habte [4:26 P.M.] I know you two had to miss my announcements at the end of the weekly staff meeting, so I wanted to fill you in.

Anna Morgan [4:28 P.M.] Thanks. What did we miss?

Selam Habte [4:29 P.M.] Our company is going to release a new long-lasting lipstick.

Kikuyo Tsuruta [4:30 P.M.] That's great news. I'm glad the R&D department took my advice about adding another product to the line.

Anna Morgan [4:31 P.M.] When will we start advertising the new lipstick?

Selam Habte [4:32 P.M.] Mr. Catteneo is putting together a marketing plan now.

Kikuyo Tsuruta [4:34 P.M.] Wouldn't this be a better job for a senior marketing executive?

Anna Morgan [4:35 P.M.] Yeah. Mr. Catteneo is new to our company and doesn't know much about our products.

Selam Habte [4:39 P.M.] I realize that, but he has a marketing background in cosmetics.

Anna Morgan [4:41 P.M.] I see. Well, it wouldn't hurt for him to see some of our previous work. I could send him a portfolio of previous projects.

Kikuyo Tsuruta [4:42 P.M.] And I'd be happy to review his work.

Selam Habte [4:43 P.M.] I don't think that'll be necessary, Kikuyo, but I like your idea, Anna.

Anna Morgan [4:44 P.M.] Okay. I'll do that now.

SEND

168. What is mainly being discussed?

(A) A policy update
(B) A new client
(C) A schedule change
(D) A product launch

169. What is implied about Ms. Tsuruta?

(A) She thinks the company needs to control spending.
(B) She made a suggestion about the company's goods.
(C) She asked Mr. Habte for some advice.
(D) She developed a new line of cosmetics.

170. At 4:41 P.M., what does Ms. Morgan most likely mean when she writes, "I see"?

(A) Mr. Catteneo is too busy to work on a project.
(B) Mr. Catteneo cannot help Ms. Morgan with a problem.
(C) Mr. Catteneo has already reviewed a portfolio.
(D) Mr. Catteneo may be qualified for a task.

171. What will Ms. Morgan most likely do next?

(A) Review documents prepared by Mr. Catteneo
(B) Send information about previous projects
(C) Set up a meeting with Mr. Catteneo
(D) Recommend a new marketing director

Questions 172-175 refer to the following e-mail.

E-Mail

To: Katrina Simon <ksimon@presslerlibrary.org>
From: Nora Yales <nyales@presslerlibrary.org>
Date: November 30
Subject: Opening tomorrow

Dear Ms. Simon,

I was told that you were willing to open the library in my place tomorrow morning and work my shift. I wanted to send you a quick reminder to help you out with the opening procedure. It's been a while since you last did this, and there are several steps, so I thought it would be helpful.

First, I wanted to make sure you know the code to disarm the alarm: 0358. Remember to pick up the mail, including the newspapers. You can leave the mail on my desk. Stamp the newspapers with the library stamp, and display them on the news shelf in the journals section. Make sure you take off yesterday's papers and classify them with the other past newspapers.

The key to the cash register is in the top drawer of my desk. Double check that there is $48 in it to start the day.

After you turn on the lights on every floor, you should be ready to unlock the front doors. The keys for that are in the key cabinet in my office.

The weather forecast says there will be a huge snowstorm, and since I live far away, I'd rather not drive in that weather, so I'm taking the whole day off and not leaving the house. But if you run into any trouble or have any questions, feel free to call me. I will also be available to chat online if you need my advice.

I am very thankful that you live close enough to be able to walk to the library. Thank you for being willing to do this.

Good luck!

Nora Yales
Library Assistant

172. What is the purpose of the e-mail?

(A) To warn of weather conditions

(B) To recommend a schedule change

(C) To offer a position

(D) To outline a procedure

173. What is suggested about Ms. Simon?

(A) She has opened the library before.

(B) She will drive to work tomorrow.

(C) She reads the newspaper every day.

(D) She usually closes the library.

174. What is NOT something Ms. Simon is expected to do?

(A) Disable a security system

(B) Open the front doors

(C) Read the mail

(D) Count money

175. What will Ms. Yales do tomorrow?

(A) Retire from her job

(B) Drive Ms. Simon to work

(C) Stay home for the day

(D) Handle customer questions

GO ON TO THE NEXT PAGE

Questions 176-180 refer to the following e-mail and voucher.

To: Cage, Peter <pcage@jaysmail.net>
From: Topher, Edward <etopher@sapphireflowers.com>
Date: May 8
Subject: Free Voucher

Dear Mr. Cage,

We are very sorry for the late delivery of your floral arrangement on May 5. We understand that because of this delay, the celebration of your daughter's acceptance into Boston University was not as special as it could have been.

Unfortunately, we ran out of roses on that day and had failed to set some aside for your afternoon delivery. We placed another order, but since our supplier is located in Stratton, it took time to get the flowers. We are in the process of switching to a more modern inventory management program, and we can assure you that this kind of mistake will not happen again. We hope that you will continue to choose Sapphire Flowers for your future special occasions.

To express our regret, we are offering you a voucher for a complimentary bouquet of your choice to be delivered at any address in the area. You will find it attached to this e-mail. Please print it and fill it out when you wish to order a delivery.

Sincerely,

Edward Topher
Sapphire Flowers

~ Sapphire Flowers ~

Voucher Code: XS564813

Good for one floral arrangement and its delivery within Jayville.

Choose from the following selection:

☐ Classic Roses ☐ Blue Bunch ☐ Dream Bouquet ☐ Spring Special

Delivery date: Monday, May 18 Delivery time: 10 A.M.
Address: Janice Richards
Frontier Corp. finance department
514 Enterprise Drive

Message(Optional):
Dear Janice,

I am sad to see you go. It was great working with you all these years. I hope you enjoy your new job in Bendertown!

Regards,
Peter Cage

176. What is the purpose of the e-mail?

(A) To notify of a delay

(B) To offer an apology

(C) To report a system error

(D) To congratulate a coworker

177. What does Mr. Topher indicate happened on May 5?

(A) His store's inventory was mismanaged.

(B) His daughter was accepted into college.

(C) His supplier was replaced.

(D) His flowers were all delivered late.

178. In the e-mail, the word "assure" in paragraph 2, line 4, is closest in meaning to

(A) convince

(B) remind

(C) guarantee

(D) compensate

179. Who most likely is Janice Richards?

(A) Mr. Cage's colleague

(B) Mr. Topher's supervisor

(C) Mr. Cage's customer

(D) Mr. Topher's supplier

180. Where most likely is Mr. Topher's store located?

(A) Boston

(B) Stratton

(C) Jayville

(D) Bendertown

GO ON TO THE NEXT PAGE

Questions 181-185 refer to the following letter and e-mail.

July 31

Jerome Madison
2675 Chenoweth Drive
Nashville, TN 37214

Dear Mr. Madison,

I heard that you are searching for a new assistant manager for the marketing team. As you know, I have been the manager of Gamma Motors' design team for eleven years. Ms. Skye Armand started working on my team six years ago and has proven to be a strong asset. She has informed me of her intention to apply for the position of assistant manager with the marketing team, and I offered to write a reference letter.

I believe that Ms. Armand's transfer could be beneficial to the company. Her understanding of design strategies and how to appeal to customers is evident in her work, and this talent would be of high value in the marketing team. Moreover, her experience within Gamma Motors and her intimate knowledge of its various models would contribute greatly to creating effective marketing campaigns. I know that you will soon be focusing on preparing for the launch of the new Gamma SUV 6. Ms. Armand has been involved in several aspects of the vehicle's design, and I think she will have some great ideas about how to present it in its best light.

If you have any questions about Ms. Armand's work, feel free to contact me.

Sincerely,

Melanie Yoder

Melanie Yoder, Design Manager

To: Marketing employees <marketingteam@gammamotors.com>
From: Jerome Madison <jmadison@gammamotors.com>
Date: September 2
Subject: Marketing Campaign

The campaign for our newest model has proven highly successful. Our teaser video has been shared all over social media and has reached millions of views. A reporter for a popular car magazine has even asked to interview one of our managers.

Congratulations to everyone, but especially to Ms. Armand. This was her first campaign, and we were able to come up with the best features to highlight in our advertisements thanks to her experience in developing its design. We already have a high number of test drive requests, and we expect the launch to be even more successful than our minivan's.

Regards,

Jerome Madison, Marketing Manager

181. Why did Ms. Yoder write to Mr. Madison?

(A) To recommend a worker
(B) To submit her résumé
(C) To offer him a position
(D) To advertise a product

182. In the letter, the word "intimate" in paragraph 2, line 4, is closest in meaning to

(A) private
(B) detailed
(C) objective
(D) faithful

183. What is mentioned about the teaser video?

(A) Many people have watched it.
(B) It features a talk with a Gamma employee.
(C) It became a top-rated movie.
(D) It was released by Gamma's competitor.

184. What is Mr. Madison congratulating his team about?

(A) A minivan's advertisement
(B) An SUV's marketing
(C) A member's promotion
(D) A magazine's popularity

185. What is suggested about Ms. Armand?

(A) She turned down a job offer.
(B) She has been promoted to manager.
(C) She recently switched teams.
(D) She wrote an article for a magazine.

GO ON TO THE NEXT PAGE

Questions 186-190 refer to the following Web page, log sheet, and e-mail.

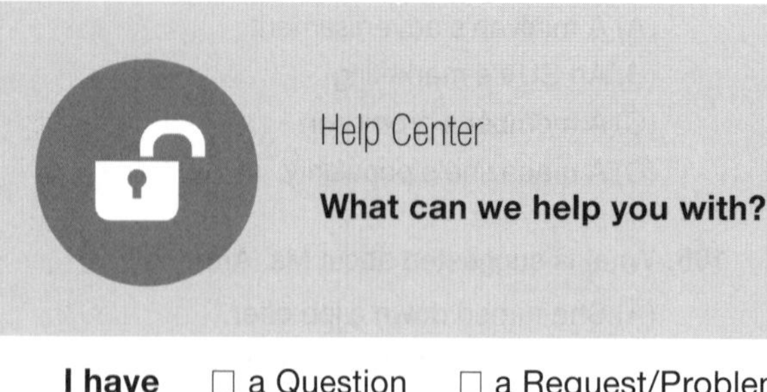

I have ☐ a Question ☐ a Request/Problem ☐ a Comment

My Message to Fuchsia Foods:

I've been receiving Fuchsia Foods' organic food delivery boxes for three months now. I really enjoy receiving my package each afternoon, so I wish to upgrade my plan to the next level. When you make the switch, please keep in mind that I am a vegetarian and continue to send me the packages that don't include meat or eggs. If this change is possible, please bill me accordingly.

Thank you very much.

Sebastian Palmer

Do you expect a reply?
☐ Yes ☐ No

If yes, please provide your e-mail address:
sebpalmer@yourmail.net

SUBMIT

Thank you for contacting us.
If you requested a reply, we will be in contact with you shortly regarding your inquiry.
If you have a question that requires immediate assistance, please call us at 352-555-2948.

March 15 Deliveries

	Basic	Deluxe	Basic vegetarian	Deluxe vegetarian	Delivery Time
86 Tassen Road			✓		11:35 A.M.
15 Jordan Drive				✓	11:50 A.M.
56 Preston Avenue		✓			2:12 P.M.
12 Mesca Street				✓	2:26 P.M.

To: Sebastian Palmer <sebpalmer@yourmail.net>
From: Customer Service <cservice@fuchsiafoods.com>
Date: March 15
Subject: About your upgrade request

Dear Mr. Palmer,

This is to confirm that we have switched your package delivery plan. Your first package of the new plan was delivered this afternoon. The credit card that we have on record for your account was billed accordingly.

Please note that we do not customarily allow plan switches before the end of a month since we preschedule our orders ahead of time. However, another member asked to change to your original plan, so we were able to simply switch your two deliveries. This was a lucky coincidence, but please note that if you wish to make future changes, you will have to wait until the end of a month to do so.

Thank you for your understanding, and enjoy your new food deliveries!

Sincerely,

Rebecca Lars
Customer Service Representative

186. Why did Mr. Palmer post on the Web page?
(A) To cancel an erroneous payment
(B) To ask for a non-vegetarian option
(C) To stop receiving packages
(D) To modify his current plan

187. What kind of package was Mr. Palmer originally receiving?
(A) Basic
(B) Deluxe
(C) Basic vegetarian
(D) Deluxe vegetarian

188. Where does Mr. Palmer most likely live?
(A) 86 Tassen Road
(B) 15 Jordan Drive
(C) 56 Preston Avenue
(D) 12 Mesca Street

189. In the e-mail, in paragraph 2, line 1, the word "customarily" is closest in meaning to
(A) normally
(B) fairly
(C) naturally
(D) rarely

190. According to the e-mail, why was Mr. Palmer's request granted?
(A) He waited until the end of the month.
(B) He asked to switch in advance.
(C) Another customer requested a plan switch.
(D) The desired plan is more expensive.

Questions 191-195 refer to the following invitation, article, and text message.

OFFICIAL INVITATION

Dear Mr. Pratt,

As a longtime investor of Barton Electronics, you are invited to Barton's Future and Progress Event on April 24. I will be making a major announcement that you do not want to miss.

Date: April 24
Time: From 2 P.M. to 4 P.M.
Location: Falcon Room (third floor), Hiver Hotel
Entrance: Free (must present this card)

Looking forward to seeing you,

Vin Vecino

Barton Electronics' Upcoming Announcement

Barton Electronics will be holding a special event on April 24. The company is to make what its CEO called a "major announcement" in the invitations that were sent out. It has since then been confirmed that Barton Electronics will be presenting a new device. Yet the type of device is still unconfirmed, and rumors have been flooding the Internet.

It all started when photos of a new laptop design were leaked on social media last week. However, the source of these leaks is unknown, and their authenticity has not been verified.

Mr. Vecino was also caught on camera meeting with Ms. Beatrix Starling, the famous fitness expert who created a popular series of training videos. Fitness trackers have recently seen a surge in popularity, so this meeting sparked rumors about a possible Barton fitness tracker. When asked about his reason for meeting with Ms. Starling, Mr. Vecino refused to comment.

Finally, it is likely that Barton Electronics will announce their new smartphone model. The company has released a new phone every year for the past four years, and their last model, the Barton 44, is close to a year old.

From: Vin Vecino
To: Steven Parker

Ms. Starling sent me a copy of the speech she intends to give. In it, she explains the advantages of the device's main features. Originally, we were going to have her present at the end, but I think it would be better if she went before we show the pictures of the device. So I've decided to save the pictures for last to build up anticipation. I'll e-mail her speech to you now. Take a look at it and tell me if you agree.

191. What is Mr. Pratt required to do for the event?
(A) Show the invitation
(B) Bring a device
(C) Reserve the room
(D) Prepare a presentation

192. Who is Vin Vecino?
(A) A special guest
(B) A company CEO
(C) A fitness expert
(D) A private investor

193. In the article, the word "caught" in paragraph 3, line 1, is closest in meaning to
(A) recorded
(B) scheduled
(C) arrested
(D) expected

194. What new device is Barton Electronics most likely launching?
(A) A smartphone
(B) A camera
(C) A laptop
(D) A fitness tracker

195. When will people see pictures of the new device?
(A) Before the event
(B) At the start of the event
(C) At the end of the event
(D) After the event

GO ON TO THE NEXT PAGE

Questions 196-200 refer to the following advertisement, online form, and review.

Yula School Programs

Yula School provides the most comprehensive programs for event decorators. Learn how to design a space to create the best customized environment. Our programs take just one year to complete! At Yula, you will take several core courses before moving on to your two specialty courses, which depend on the curriculum you choose. The specialty courses included in each curriculum are listed below.

Curriculum A: Weddings and Showers
- Draping and Fabrics
- Using Plants and Trees

Curriculum B: Private Holiday Celebrations
- Choosing a Color Scheme
- Mood Creation with Lighting

Curriculum C: Corporate Events
- Choosing a Color Scheme
- Creating a Stage

Curriculum D: Themed Children's Parties
- Balloon Sculptures
- Creating a Stage

* The deadlines for applying are August 15 for the fall semester and November 15 for the spring semester. Submit a résumé, motivation letter, and letter of recommendation to admissions@yula.com to apply.

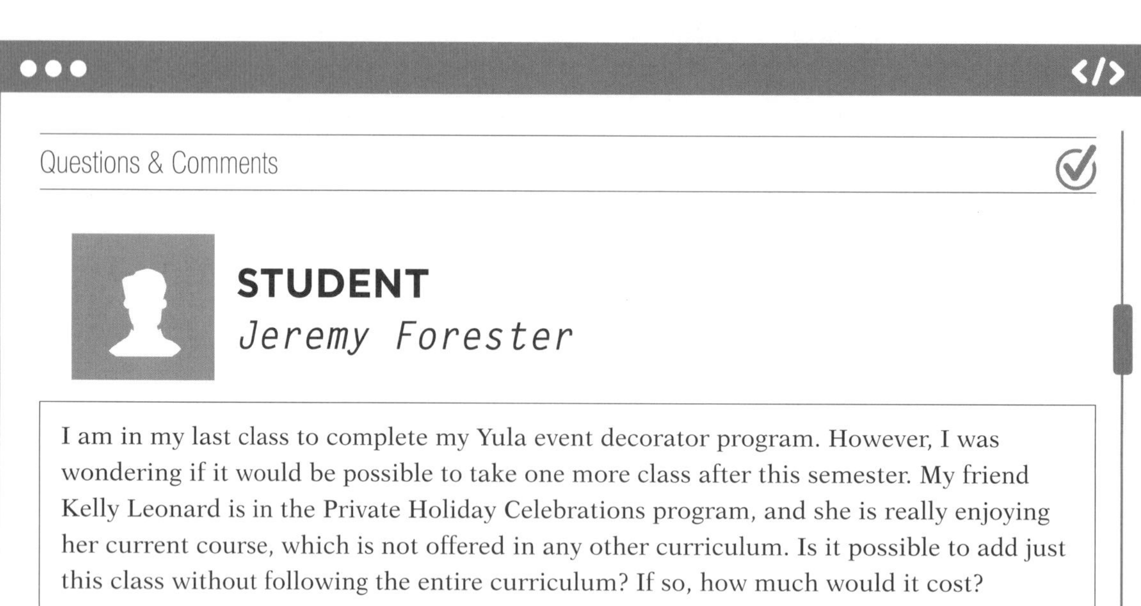

Questions & Comments

STUDENT
Jeremy Forester

I am in my last class to complete my Yula event decorator program. However, I was wondering if it would be possible to take one more class after this semester. My friend Kelly Leonard is in the Private Holiday Celebrations program, and she is really enjoying her current course, which is not offered in any other curriculum. Is it possible to add just this class without following the entire curriculum? If so, how much would it cost?

SUBMIT

Review: ★★★★★
Name: J. Forester

Shortly after I completed the curriculum, I was contacted by a company to decorate their venue for a new product launch party. Everyone was praising the decorations, and the company was so pleased with my work that they asked me to deal with their tenth anniversary celebration. I never expected to be so quickly hired for such a big event. Thanks to all the hands-on experience I received at Yula School, everyone thought I'd been in the business for years! Yula really prepares you well by giving you excellent tips and training you in everything you'll need for your decorating business. I highly recommend Yula to anyone who wants to become a professional decorator.

196. What is NOT mentioned about Yula School's programs?
(A) How to submit an application
(B) What the specialty courses are
(C) How long a program lasts
(D) When each semester begins

197. Which class is Ms. Leonard currently taking?
(A) Draping and Fabrics
(B) Choosing a Color Scheme
(C) Mood Creation with Lighting
(D) Creating a Stage

198. In the review, the phrase "deal with" in paragraph 1, line 3, is closest in meaning to
(A) handle
(B) touch
(C) inform
(D) compensate

199. What is suggested about Mr. Forester?
(A) He has not worked as a decorator for very long.
(B) He now teaches courses at Yula School.
(C) He recently designed a new product.
(D) He will start a new program at Yula School.

200. Which curriculum did Mr. Forester most likely study?
(A) Curriculum A
(B) Curriculum B
(C) Curriculum C
(D) Curriculum D

Stop! This is the end of the test. If you finish before time is called, you may go back to Parts 5, 6, and 7 and check your work.

Actual Test 5

LISTENING TEST

In the Listening test, you will be asked to demonstrate how well you understand spoken English. The entire Listening test will last approximately 45 minutes. There are four parts, and directions are given for each part. You must mark your answers on the separate answer sheet. Do not write your answers in your test book.

PART 1 17

Directions: For each question in this part, you will hear four statements about a picture in your test book. When you hear the statements, you must select the one statement that best describes what you see in the picture. Then find the number of the question on your answer sheet and mark your answer. The statements will not be printed in your test book and will be spoken only one time.

Statement (C), "They're sitting at the table," is the best description of the picture, so you should select answer (C) and mark it on your answer sheet.

1.

2.

GO ON TO THE NEXT PAGE

3.

4

5.

6

GO ON TO THE NEXT PAGE

PART 2 18

Directions: You will hear a question or statement and three responses spoken in English. They will not be printed in your test book and will be spoken only one time. Select the best response to the question or statement and mark the letter (A), (B), or (C) on your answer sheet.

7. Mark your answer on your answer sheet.
8. Mark your answer on your answer sheet.
9. Mark your answer on your answer sheet.
10. Mark your answer on your answer sheet.
11. Mark your answer on your answer sheet.
12. Mark your answer on your answer sheet.
13. Mark your answer on your answer sheet.
14. Mark your answer on your answer sheet.
15. Mark your answer on your answer sheet.
16. Mark your answer on your answer sheet.
17. Mark your answer on your answer sheet.
18. Mark your answer on your answer sheet.
19. Mark your answer on your answer sheet.
20. Mark your answer on your answer sheet.
21. Mark your answer on your answer sheet.
22. Mark your answer on your answer sheet.
23. Mark your answer on your answer sheet.
24. Mark your answer on your answer sheet.
25. Mark your answer on your answer sheet.
26. Mark your answer on your answer sheet.
27. Mark your answer on your answer sheet.
28. Mark your answer on your answer sheet.
29. Mark your answer on your answer sheet.
30. Mark your answer on your answer sheet.
31. Mark your answer on your answer sheet.

PART 3 (19)

Directions: You will hear some conversations between two or more people. You will be asked to answer three questions about what the speakers say in each conversation. Select the best response to each question and mark the letter (A), (B), (C), or (D) on your answer sheet. The conversations will not be printed in your test book and will be spoken only one time.

32. What are the speakers discussing?
(A) A product description
(B) A seating chart
(C) An entrance code
(D) A supplies order

33. What does the man give the woman?
(A) A product catalog
(B) An ID badge
(C) A new form
(D) A training manual

34. What does the man recommend doing?
(A) Canceling an order
(B) Directing questions to a coworker
(C) Viewing an example online
(D) Getting approval in advance

---

35. Who most likely are the speakers?
(A) Salespeople
(B) Researchers
(C) Lecturers
(D) Photographers

36. What does the man ask the woman to do?
(A) Contact a supplier right away
(B) Put some information on display
(C) Finish a project ahead of schedule
(D) Make some suggestions for improvements

37. What does the woman say she wants to do?
(A) Check the inventory
(B) Adjust a fee
(C) Arrange a meeting
(D) Confirm the attendance

---

38. What problem does the man mention?
(A) A board member hasn't arrived yet.
(B) A sales promotion didn't go well.
(C) A document is missing some information.
(D) A branch is performing more poorly than expected.

39. What does the woman ask about?
(A) The topic of a report
(B) The cost of a service
(C) The number of board members
(D) The start time of a meeting

40. What does the woman suggest doing?
(A) Hiring a different printing service
(B) Contacting the Fletcher branch
(C) Changing the meeting date
(D) Completing a task on site

---

41. What is the woman interested in buying?
(A) A refrigerator
(B) A television
(C) A smartphone
(D) A software program

42. Why does Barrett recommend the Stinson brand?
(A) It has the widest selection.
(B) It is currently on sale.
(C) It is the most popular brand.
(D) It has long-lasting products.

43. What will the woman probably do next?
(A) Watch a demonstration
(B) Ask for a discount
(C) Extend a warranty
(D) Fill out a registration form

GO ON TO THE NEXT PAGE

44. What are the speakers mainly discussing?

(A) A hiring decision
(B) An employee evaluation
(C) A registration process
(D) A business trip

45. Why was the man unable to read some materials?

(A) He had a problem with his computer.
(B) He recently returned from a vacation.
(C) He had to visit an important client.
(D) He was working on a coworker's task.

46. What does the woman imply when she says, "You shouldn't have to do that alone"?

(A) She will help train the new employees.
(B) She can assign an extra task to Liam.
(C) She can help the man finish a report.
(D) She will speak to the man's supervisor.

---

47. What kind of business do the speakers probably work for?

(A) A delivery service
(B) A printing company
(C) A clothing outlet
(D) An insurance agency

48. According to the man, what is the problem?

(A) There is a shortage of supplies.
(B) An order form contained an error.
(C) There are not enough workers.
(D) A client has made a complaint.

49. What do the speakers decide to do?

(A) Work additional hours
(B) Purchase some equipment
(C) Cancel a project
(D) Request a deadline extension

---

50. What does the man say he likes about the store?

(A) Its wide selection
(B) Its friendly employees
(C) Its convenient hours
(D) Its member rewards

51. Why is the man unable to use his coupon?

(A) It has already expired.
(B) It has a minimum purchase amount.
(C) It is for a different store.
(D) It cannot be used with other offers.

52. What does the woman mean when she says, "I'll go there shortly"?

(A) She can drop off some paperwork for the man.
(B) She will help the man carry his items.
(C) She plans to take a break soon.
(D) She will try to find some merchandise for the man.

---

53. What field does the man most likely work in?

(A) Tourism
(B) Ecology
(C) Construction
(D) Agriculture

54. What kind of project will the man explain?

(A) A local cleanup
(B) A building renovation
(C) A marketing campaign
(D) A company picnic

55. What is the woman concerned about?

(A) Staying within a budget
(B) Getting official approval
(C) Finding enough volunteers
(D) Starting a study on time

---

56. Where most likely is the conversation taking place?
(A) At a bus terminal
(B) At an airport
(C) At a hotel
(D) At a theater

57. According to the man, what is the additional fee for?
(A) A transportation service
(B) A room upgrade
(C) A cancellation fee
(D) A deposit

58. What will Alexandra most likely give Ms. Brooks next?
(A) A ticket
(B) A receipt
(C) A schedule
(D) A business card

---

59. What are the speakers mainly discussing?
(A) Vacation plans
(B) An opening celebration
(C) An end-of-year event
(D) A catering service

60. What will the woman ask her coworkers?
(A) What type of venue they want
(B) When their vacations are
(C) Who they plan to invite
(D) Which date they prefer

61. What does the man say he will do?
(A) Select menu items
(B) Reserve a restaurant
(C) Prepare a meal
(D) Contact guests

Dark Tan Shades

Brand	Product Code
Bridgeport	147
Lancaster	295
Reiser	466
Saldana	803

62. Why did the man change his mind?
(A) He asked a colleague's opinion.
(B) He tested some free samples.
(C) He found a cheaper item.
(D) He reviewed a product catalog.

63. Look at the graphic. Which product will the man purchase?
(A) Product 147
(B) Product 295
(C) Product 466
(D) Product 803

64. What is the man asked to do?
(A) Call back again later
(B) Provide room measurements
(C) Update an order form online
(D) Return some unused goods

GO ON TO THE NEXT PAGE

INTERPRETATION RATES	
Number of Hours	Price per Hour
1 hour	$80
2-4 hours	$75
5-6 hours	$70
More than 6 hours	$65

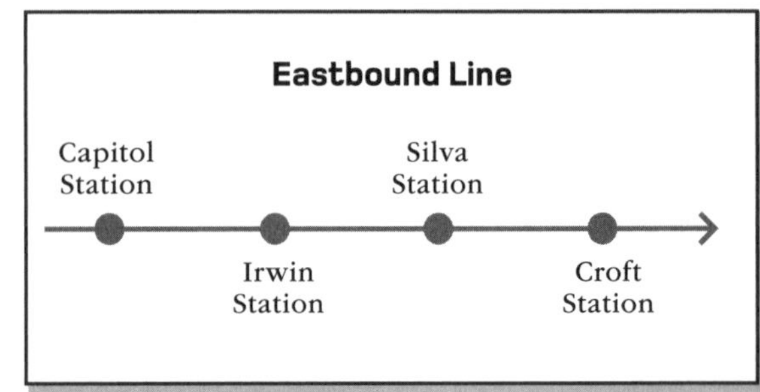

65. Who most likely is the man?
(A) An event organizer
(B) A language specialist
(C) An information technology expert
(D) A chemistry professor

66. What information does the woman ask for?
(A) The date of the event
(B) The address of a venue
(C) The languages needed
(D) The registration fee

67. Look at the graphic. How much will the man most likely pay per hour?
(A) $80
(B) $75
(C) $70
(D) $65

68. What does the man want to do?
(A) Find a sports facility
(B) Pick up a map
(C) Change a train ticket
(D) Get to a theater

69. Look at the graphic. To which stop is the man told to go?
(A) Capitol Station
(B) Irwin Station
(C) Silva Station
(D) Croft Station

70. What is the man concerned about?
(A) Having to buy another ticket
(B) Moving his luggage by himself
(C) Missing the next train
(D) Walking through a crowded station

PART 4 (20)

Directions: You will hear some talks given by a single speaker. You will be asked to answer three questions about what the speaker says in each talk. Select the best response to each question and mark the letter (A), (B), (C), or (D) on your answer sheet. The talks will not be printed in your test book and will be spoken only one time.

71. Where most likely are the listeners?
(A) At a fashion show
(B) At an art institute
(C) At a hardware store
(D) At a community center

72. According to the speaker, what can be found in the west wing?
(A) A promotional video
(B) A demonstration
(C) Some free samples
(D) Some paintings

73. What does the speaker encourage listeners to do?
(A) Enroll in a rewards program
(B) Share their feedback
(C) Make some suggestions
(D) Sign up for a workshop

74. Where most likely does the speaker work?
(A) At a construction company
(B) At a property management firm
(C) At an insurance agency
(D) At a plumbing company

75. What is the call mainly about?
(A) Arranging a repair
(B) Scheduling a tour
(C) Announcing renovations
(D) Signing a lease

76. Why should the listener call the speaker back?
(A) To pay for a service
(B) To register a complaint
(C) To approve a charge
(D) To change an appointment

77. Who is Jackie Galvani?
(A) A radio host
(B) A researcher
(C) A painter
(D) An art critic

78. What did Ms. Galvani recently do?
(A) Started a school
(B) Gave a lecture
(C) Opened a gallery
(D) Reviewed a sculpture

79. What does the speaker ask listeners to do?
(A) Register for a class
(B) Buy a painting
(C) Speak with the guest
(D) Submit questions

80. Who is this advertisement intended for?
(A) Job seekers
(B) Business owners
(C) New employees
(D) Interns

81. What field does the speaker's company specialize in?
(A) Pharmaceuticals
(B) Journalism
(C) Fashion
(D) Computer science

82. What are listeners asked to send?
(A) A description of their facilities
(B) A selection of preferred candidates
(C) An explanation of their needs
(D) A list of interview questions

GO ON TO THE NEXT PAGE

83. Why is the business closed?
(A) An emergency happened.
(B) Renovations are being made.
(C) A dentist recently retired.
(D) Workers are on vacation.

84. What does the speaker imply when he says, "Otherwise, tell us if you have a preferred dentist"?
(A) New customers may choose a dentist.
(B) A new dentist will be hired.
(C) Patients can write reviews of their dentists.
(D) Regulars may select a new dentist.

85. When will the clinic reopen?
(A) On July 30
(B) On July 31
(C) On August 8
(D) On August 9

---

86. Why did the speaker schedule the meeting?
(A) To give a demonstration of a product
(B) To make corrections to a sales report
(C) To provide information about an industry event
(D) To request volunteers for a trade fair booth

87. What recently changed about the Kenosha-50?
(A) Its battery weight was reduced.
(B) Its warranty period was extended.
(C) Its processing speed was improved.
(D) Its screen size was increased.

88. What does the speaker mean when she says, "it's currently just under five hundred grams"?
(A) The price is too high for the weight.
(B) A device does not meet the industry standard.
(C) Supplies are running out faster than expected.
(D) The product is inconvenient to carry around.

---

89. Who does the speaker introduce?
(A) An author
(B) A history professor
(C) A director
(D) A movie producer

90. What does the speaker apologize for?
(A) A leaflet has an error.
(B) A presentation is delayed.
(C) A movie screening is canceled.
(D) A guest cannot come.

91. What does the speaker imply when he says, "I hope you brought your own"?
(A) Items will not be available on site.
(B) Listeners need an entrance ticket for the talk.
(C) Mr. Stroud will answer some prepared questions.
(D) Listeners may suggest their own ideas.

---

92. Why does the speaker congratulate the listeners?
(A) They improved their work efficiency.
(B) They exceeded a sales goal.
(C) They hired a hard-working employee.
(D) They attracted a new client.

93. According to the speaker, what was the most impressive part of a presentation?
(A) Its simple explanations
(B) Its variety of photographs
(C) Its accompanying handout
(D) Its helpful charts

94. What will the speaker probably do next?
(A) Introduce a coworker
(B) Present some awards
(C) Write a list of companies
(D) Assign the listeners to teams

Elliot Bay Ferries
Seattle → Bainbridge Island
Departure: 9:20 A.M. **Arrival:** 10:10 A.M.
Ticket Type: Walk-on Passenger
Ticket Fee: $8.20

95. What does the speaker remind listeners to do?
(A) Direct questions to terminal employees
(B) Keep their belongings with them
(C) Check the departure dock
(D) Have their tickets ready

96. Look at the graphic. When should the ticket holder board the ferry?
(A) At 8:50 A.M.
(B) At 9:00 A.M.
(C) At 9:20 A.M.
(D)At 10:10 A.M.

97. What will be given to listeners soon?
(A) A ticket receipt
(B) A safety briefing
(C) A terminal map
(D) A seat assignment

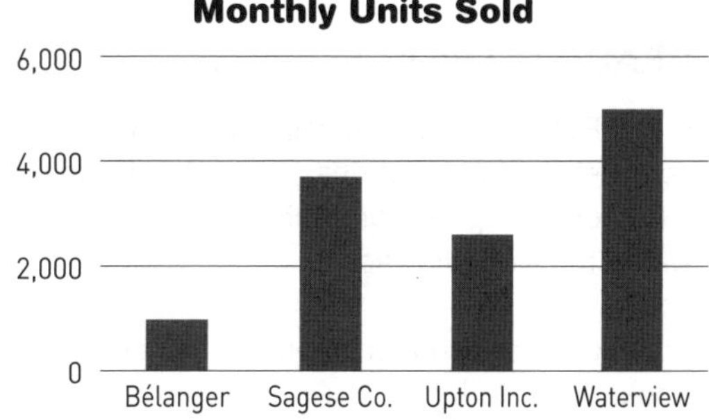

98. What did the speaker do on Tuesday?
(A) Met with a consultant
(B) Tested product samples
(C) Checked the inventory
(D) Processed an order

99. What is causing a change in product supplies?
(A) A building expansion
(B) A business closure
(C) An inventory error
(D) A training event

100. Look at the graphic. Which brand will have more items added?
(A) Bélanger
(B) Sagese Co.
(C) Upton Inc.
(D) Waterview

This is the end of the Listening test. Turn to Part 5 in your test book.

READING TEST

In the Reading test, you will read a variety of texts and answer several different types of reading comprehension questions. The entire Reading test will last 75 minutes. There are three parts, and directions are given for each part. You are encouraged to answer as many questions as possible within the time allowed.

You must mark your answers on the separate answer sheet. Do not write your answers in your test book.

PART 5

Directions: A word or phrase is missing in each of the sentences below. Four answer choices are given below each sentence. Select the best answer to complete the sentence. Then mark the letter (A), (B), (C), or (D) on your answer sheet.

101. Mr. Wexler bought lunch for ------- team as a way of showing appreciation.

(A) he
(B) him
(C) his
(D) himself

102. ------- the past three months, the number of members at Slate Gym has doubled.

(A) Under
(B) While
(C) At
(D) Over

103. The letter to the editor was written by Janice Reeves, a ------- to *National Gardening Magazine*.

(A) subscribed
(B) subscribes
(C) subscriber
(D) subscription

104. Bothell Manufacturing will ------- be streamlining its production line with modern equipment.

(A) quite
(B) soon
(C) else
(D) ever

105. Now that the bakery has brought in a long-term investor, it is in good shape -------.

(A) finances
(B) finance
(C) financial
(D) financially

106. Benz Athletics was able to increase sales thanks to the ------- of a new line of clothing designed for children.

(A) delivery
(B) suggestion
(C) content
(D) addition

107. Consumers can save a lot of money on furniture if the components ------- at home.

(A) assembling
(B) to be assembled
(C) have assembled
(D) are assembled

108. Nature enthusiasts enjoy taking hikes ------- the woods located at the northern section of Derby National Park.

(A) through
(B) onto
(C) regarding
(D) except

109. The guests seated at the VIP table at the company's banquet include ------- for the annual employee awards.

(A) nominated
(B) nominations
(C) nominees
(D) nominate

110. Security guards at Mayfair International Airport need to be ------- of the rules and regulations for travelers.

(A) alert
(B) precise
(C) aware
(D) strict

111. Since the director was not available that day, the members of the sales team gave the product presentation to the buyers by -------.

(A) themselves
(B) them
(C) they
(D) theirs

112. Shobe Utilities ------- the information on its Web site to Spanish and Chinese so that it can be understood by more customers.

(A) is translated
(B) have translated
(C) has translated
(D) be translated

113. The current IT department is indeed the most ------- group in the company's history.

(A) diversely
(B) diversification
(C) diverse
(D) diversify

114. The manuscript for Ms. Colby's award-winning bestseller was ------- rejected by the publisher.

(A) rather
(B) nearby
(C) yet
(D) almost

115. Ms. Simpson, who is the Carolina branch's top salesperson, requested that ------- be promoted to team leader.

(A) herself
(B) she
(C) her
(D) hers

116. EZ Couriers will purchase three more vans for its fleet in an effort to ------- the rise in demand for its services.

(A) predict
(B) accommodate
(C) attribute
(D) generate

117. Tourists and locals alike visit the farmers' market because the produce there is very ------- priced.

(A) reason
(B) reasoned
(C) reasonably
(D) reasonable

118. ------- arriving at their final destination, the airline passengers waited for their belongings at the luggage carousel.

(A) Along
(B) Upon
(C) Unlike
(D) During

119. The newly trained cook forgot two of the ------- ingredients in the soup, so it did not turn out right.

(A) essential
(B) inherent
(C) equal
(D) reliable

120. The company's image is built on trust, ------- employees are expected to be open and honest with customers at all times.

(A) never
(B) so
(C) what
(D) then

121. Mr. Vaughn wants to prepare a working model of the prototype ------- collaborating on the details with others.

(A) even so
(B) before
(C) so that
(D) instead

122. Lavola Restaurant is almost always filled to capacity and has earned a ------- for excellent food and service.

(A) clarification
(B) statement
(C) commitment
(D) reputation

123. The department store provided sample bottles of perfume ------- allow customers to try them.

(A) by far
(B) as a result of
(C) in order to
(D) above all

124. As its expansion project is completed, Lintz Hotel will ------- more staff members to handle the higher volume of guests.

(A) forfeit
(B) recruit
(C) dedicate
(D) delegate

125. The quality of the first draft of the report was not -------, so the manager asked for it to be rewritten.

(A) accepting
(B) acceptably
(C) acceptable
(D) acceptability

126. Event planners selected the Ingram Center for the software convention due to its ------- to major highways.

(A) publicity
(B) proximity
(C) regularity
(D) locality

127. Dr. Kapadia, who has conducted ------- research in the field of genetic engineering, is a highly respected biologist.

(A) furnished
(B) extensive
(C) perishable
(D) punctual

128. ------- gently the criticism of a staff member is made, it could still cause offense to a sensitive person.

(A) Somewhat
(B) However
(C) Entirely
(D) Seldom

129. Gabriel Falcone created a fully automated system that allowed the pharmaceutical company to more ------ evaluate a medical test's accuracy.

(A) narrowly
(B) increasingly
(C) partially
(D) efficiently

130. A number of board members questioned ------- Mr. Woodworth had the right qualifications for the position.

(A) both
(B) unless
(C) because
(D) whether

PART 6

Directions: Read the texts that follow. A word, phrase, or sentence is missing in parts of each text. Four answer choices for each question are given below the text. Select the best answer to complete the text. Then mark the letter (A), (B), (C), or (D) on your answer sheet.

Questions 131-134 refer to the following advertisement.

Jacobs Interiors

Why move when you can just upgrade for a fraction of the cost? Our experienced designers have ------- **131.** homes, offices, and even television studios! They will help you every step of the way, starting with the selection of materials. ------- **132.**. Nevertheless, we are willing to get items imported or shipped to get you exactly what you want. We will also keep your safety in mind, as we have engineers inspect structures ------- **133.** to the building's support system before making any changes. Visit our Web site at www.jacobsint.com to see photos of past projects and read testimonials about how we fulfilled customers' ------- **134.**.

131. (A) related
(B) transformed
(C) invested
(D) toured

132. (A) The business offers a money-back guarantee on the work.
(B) Don't hesitate to share your project ideas with the designer.
(C) Some colors remain popular from year to year.
(D) We try to use locally sourced supplies as often as we can.

133. (A) vitally
(B) vital
(C) vitalize
(D) vitality

134. (A) orders
(B) relations
(C) behaviors
(D) forms

Questions 135-138 refer to the following memo.

To: All Haynes Airlines Ticket and Gate Agents
From: Crystal Lecuyer
Date: October 25

In preparation for the busy holiday travel season, we will be ------- (135.) two extra lines in our check-in area. We believe this will help us to reduce the long wait times for check-in.

Under this new plan, part-time workers will have additional shifts ------- (136.) January 5. You may also ------- (137.) to work at the gate, as boarding is an important factor in on-time departures. Your supervisors plan to set a schedule soon. ------- (138.).

Thank you for your hard work and cooperation.

135. (A) opening
(B) relocating
(C) decorating
(D) suspending

136. (A) within
(B) until
(C) during
(D) following

137. (A) assigning
(B) be assigned
(C) assigned
(D) having assigned

138. (A) Gate numbers should be posted as soon as possible.
(B) A copy of it is attached to this memo.
(C) Travelers are expected to request this service.
(D) Please notify them of any potential scheduling conflicts.

Questions 139-142 refer to the following article.

Golf Club to Raise Funds for Local Museum

HOLTONVILLE, August 7—The Holtonville Golf Club will hold its first-ever tournament at Greenway Golf Course to raise money for the Contemporary Art Museum. -------. **139.** Winners will take home a trophy as well as gift cards. The club hopes that participants will not only have a good time but will also become ------- **140.** informed about the importance of art in the community. ------- **141.**, the event provides a great opportunity for young golfers to play in a friendly competition. All ------- **142.** from the event will go toward making urgent roof repairs at the museum.

139. (A) The city's mayor praised organizers for their focus on the environment.
(B) Golf lessons are offered at the site throughout the summer months.
(C) The prizes for the competition will be announced at a later date.
(D) The competition will grant participants prizes donated by local businesses.

140. (A) full
(B) fullness
(C) fuller
(D) fully

141. (A) Otherwise
(B) Thus
(C) Furthermore
(D) In fact

142. (A) interest
(B) proceeds
(C) materials
(D) separation

GO ON TO THE NEXT PAGE

Questions 143-146 refer to the following e-mail.

To: Pamela Rardin <p.rardin@montoyainc.net>
From: Aarom Communications <info@aaromcomm.com>
Date: September 4
Subject: Aarom-6 Phone

Dear Ms. Rardin,

Our records show that you recently made a ------- (143.) of an Aarom-6 smartphone from Aarom Communications. We are delighted to offer you our noise-canceling wireless headphones for just $89.99. ------- (144.). These headphones provide premium sound quality, a comfortable fit, and a long battery life.

If you are interested, please ------- (145.) to this e-mail no later than September 10 with your preferred mailing address. We will then make a charge to your Aarom customer account. ------- (146.) will appear on your monthly statement as "Aarom Headphones." We hope you will take advantage of this great deal, and we look forward to serving you.

Sincerely,

Sharon Kearney

Customer Service Agent, Aarom Communications

143. (A) review
(B) repair
(C) purchase
(D) profit

144. (A) This special price reflects a thirty percent discount.
(B) They come as a standard accessory at no extra charge.
(C) You can read more about this in your product warranty.
(D) We appreciate your notifying us of the issue promptly.

145. (A) respond
(B) subscribe
(C) disregard
(D) feel free

146. (A) Those
(B) Few
(C) Another
(D) It

PART 7

Directions: In this part you will read a selection of texts, such as magazine and newspaper articles, e-mails, and instant messages. Each text or set of texts is followed by several questions. Select the best answer for each question and mark the letter (A), (B), (C), or (D) on your answer sheet.

Questions 147-148 refer to the following notice.

Crestar Maintenance Project

From June 3 to July 18, we will be working on several maintenance projects on our network. This work may affect your departure time and/or journey duration. Signs are posted throughout the station to inform you of the changes to the timetable for each day. Please be sure to view this posted information to ensure that you know what to expect. Thank you for your patience.

147. For whom is the notice most likely intended?
(A) Safety inspectors
(B) Travel agents
(C) Construction workers
(D) Train passengers

148. What does the notice instruct people to do?
(A) Check an adjusted schedule
(B) Provide feedback about a service
(C) Report problems to the company
(D) Make a payment in advance

GO ON TO THE NEXT PAGE

Questions 149-150 refer to the following invoice.

Barrington Roofing
305 Acres Lane, Brentwood, TN 37027
(615) 555-8483

Customer: Leonard Harper
Property Site: 4651 Guevara Street, Brentwood, TN 37027
Description of Work: Replace roof on residential property

Original Quote	$7,500	**Issue Date**	May 3
Updated Quote	$6,300	**Issue Date**	May 7

Notes: The original quote included the entire roof replacement process. Now the client will remove the old shingles before the project begins and handle their disposal separately.

Start Date	May 15	**End Date**	May 16
Deposit and first payment received			$300 on May 7

* Half of the balance ($3,000) is due as a second payment on the first day of work. The final payment is due one week after the completion of the work. Please note that payments must be made in accordance with this schedule regardless of weather delays.

149. Why has a charge on the invoice been changed?
(A) The price of materials has increased.
(B) The customer presented a coupon.
(C) The permit had to be paid for separately.
(D) The customer will take care of some of the work.

150. When should Mr. Harper make his second payment?
(A) On May 15
(B) On May 16
(C) On May 22
(D) On May 23

Questions 151-152 refer to the following text-message chain.

Cynthia Spencer [11:13 A.M.]
Hi, Ralph. You're away from the office today, right?

Ralph Wallace [11:16 A.M.]
Yes. I'll be attending meetings with representatives from one of our largest accounts. Why?

Cynthia Spencer [11:17 A.M.]
I'm wondering if I could borrow your laptop just for today. Mine isn't working, and the IT team doesn't have a replacement.

Ralph Wallace [11:18 A.M.]
Of course. Just return it when you're done.

Cynthia Spencer [11:19 A.M.]
I will. Thanks a lot! It's in the common department locker, right?

Ralph Wallace [11:20 A.M.]
Yes, it should be. And there isn't a password, so you should be fine.

151. What is Mr. Wallace doing today?

(A) Meeting some clients off-site
(B) Training some IT workers
(C) Setting up a meeting room
(D) Giving some customers a tour

152. At 11:18 A.M., what does Mr. Wallace mean when he writes, "Of course"?

(A) He will call the IT team to make a request.
(B) He does not mind lending some equipment to Ms. Spencer.
(C) He can help repair Ms. Spencer's malfunctioning laptop.
(D) He will order a replacement item for Ms. Spencer.

Questions 153-154 refer to the following memo.

To: All Osage Consulting Employees
From: Carla Watson, Branch Supervisor
Date: October 17
Subject: Employee break room

Now that the employee break room is open again following the renovations, we want to make sure that this area is kept clean and tidy for all who use it. Therefore, from now on, we are changing the policy on the usage of the refrigerator. Whenever you put something in the refrigerator, it must have your name and the date marked on it clearly. Every Friday afternoon, the refrigerator will be cleaned out, and items that have expired and those that do not have names on them will be thrown out. This will ensure that the refrigerator does not get too full and does not have any spoiled food in it. Thank you in advance for your cooperation.

153. Why did Ms. Watson write the memo?
(A) To notify staff of a renovation
(B) To explain a break schedule
(C) To report a room closure
(D) To announce a new rule

154. What are readers of the memo asked to do?
(A) Refrain from eating food in the office
(B) Empty the refrigerator every Friday
(C) Label their food and drink items
(D) Volunteer for a weekly cleanup job

Questions 155-157 refer to the following Web page.

The Bloomfield Public Library is proud to be one of the venues for the city's first-ever Spring Literary Festival, which runs from April 16 to 20. The event will feature talks all over the city from professional writers who have had their works published recently, including Jiang Li, Linda Atchison, Yamuna Bose, and Patrick Corona. Ms. Atchison's talk, which will be held at our library, is expected to be a particularly big draw, as her latest mystery novel, *Onward North*, has spent thirty weeks on the bestseller list. The book also took home the prestigious Larochelle Prize last month.

Tickets for the event can be purchased at the Bloomfield Community Center.

155. What is NOT true about the Spring Literary Festival?

(A) It has never been held before.
(B) It will last for less than a week.
(C) It includes an author awards ceremony.
(D) It will take place in several locations.

156. Who has recently won an award?

(A) Jiang Li
(B) Linda Atchison
(C) Yamuna Bose
(D) Patrick Corona

157. What is mentioned about Bloomfield Public Library?

(A) It will be closed in preparation for the festival.
(B) It organizes the literary festival every year.
(C) It will host a lecture by a professional writer.
(D) It is seeking volunteers to assist with the festival.

GO ON TO THE NEXT PAGE

Questions 158-160 refer to the following e-mail.

To: Gwen Landry <gwenlandry@milagrosinc.com>
From: Amanda Morgan <amanda@nsrmembers.org>
Date: July 29
Subject: Important Notice

Dear Ms. Landry,

According to our records, you have been a member of the National Society of Realtors for the past three years. —[1]—. Thank you for your patronage, and we hope you are enjoying the benefits of being a part of this group.

We are currently holding our annual membership drive and would like to ask for your assistance. —[2]—. If you have friends or colleagues who would be suitable for our group, please have them complete the attached application form. This form has a special number so we can determine that the referral came from you. —[3]—.

For each member you refer, you will receive $10 off your monthly dues. In addition, you will have a seat reserved for you in the VIP section at our annual conference. —[4]—. We will also enter your name into a prize drawing for a five-day vacation in the Bahamas.

If you have inquiries about recruitment, please feel free to e-mail me anytime.

Sincerely,

Amanda Morgan
Membership Services

158. Who most likely is Ms. Landry?

(A) A group founder
(B) A real estate agent
(C) A homeowner
(D) A bank teller

159. What is NOT an advantage of referring members?

(A) A chance to win a trip
(B) Priority seating at an event
(C) A reduction in membership fees
(D) Discounted tickets to a conference

160. In which of the positions marked [1], [2], [3], and [4] does the following sentence best belong?

"It can be found at the bottom of the page."

(A) [1]
(B) [2]
(C) [3]
(D) [4]

Questions 161-163 refer to the following letter.

Aiden Holt
739 Kessler Way
Syracuse, NY 13202

Dear Mr. Holt,

We hope you have enjoyed the free one-month trial of our Premium Sports Package. Your access to the four international football channels, two basketball channels, and two mixed sports channels will end on April 30 if you take no further action. To make sure you don't miss any of the sports coverage you love, sign up for a one-year subscription to the Premium Sports Package, which will add just $7.95 to your monthly bill. You can do so by changing the settings on your online account with Chapman Cable through our Web site. There you can also check your user agreement for details about how to add or discontinue premium packages.

Enclosed you will also find a postage-paid postcard, on which you can share your suggestions, ideas, and complaints. We'd love to hear how you are finding your Chapman Cable experience so far.

Warmest regards,

The Chapman Cable Accounts Team

161. What is the purpose of the letter?
(A) To encourage a customer to continue a service
(B) To announce which channels will be added next month
(C) To introduce a new package of sports channels
(D) To remind a customer to make a payment on his account

162. What will happen on April 30?
(A) A free trial will expire.
(B) A sports event will take place.
(C) A discount will be applied.
(D) An online account will be disabled.

163. What is enclosed with the letter?
(A) A discount coupon
(B) A broadcast schedule
(C) An updated user agreement
(D) A comment card

GO ON TO THE NEXT PAGE

Questions 164-167 refer to the following online chat discussion.

Latika Nair 1:23 P.M.	Renovations on our office will not start next week as planned.
Chet Matthews 1:25 P.M.	I heard that the company we were supposed to use went out of business unexpectedly.
Latika Nair 1:26 P.M.	Right. So I'm looking for another construction firm, preferably one endorsed by someone I know. Any ideas?
Diane Perdue 1:27 P.M.	I was very pleased with the work done by Norris Construction at my house last year.
Chet Matthews 1:28 P.M.	But that business was sold to another person last month, so the quality might not be the same.
Diane Perdue 1:29 P.M.	I didn't know that. We'd better not take any chances.
Chet Matthews 1:30 P.M.	The dental clinic across the street recently had its interior redesigned, and it looks great.
Latika Nair 1:31 P.M.	We should try to find out the address and contact number of their contractor.
Motoshi Tenno 1:32 P.M.	I actually have an appointment there on Friday, so I'll do that during my visit.

164. Why did Ms. Nair start the online chat?
(A) To get a business recommendation
(B) To introduce a new contractor
(C) To review some contract terms
(D) To approve a renovation schedule

165. What is indicated about Norris Construction?
(A) It was endorsed by a dental clinic.
(B) It canceled a contract unexpectedly.
(C) It is under new ownership.
(D) It has lower prices than its competitors.

166. At 1:29 P.M., what does Ms. Perdue most likely mean when she writes, "We'd better not take any chances"?
(A) She wants to retract her suggestion.
(B) She thinks they should do a safety check.
(C) She plans to do further research.
(D) She needs more time for a decision.

167. What will Mr. Tenno do on Friday?
(A) Contact Norris Construction
(B) Gather information about a business
(C) Reschedule an appointment
(D) Visit a new contractor

Questions 168-171 refer to the following e-mail.

To: Gregory Pearlman <g.pearlman@oakway.com>
From: Tibbs Inc. <inquiries@tibbsinc.com>
Date: August 26
Subject: RE: Inquiry

Dear Mr. Pearlman,

I received your message about your recent participation in our sightseeing boat ride around Nieves Bay. I've checked our lost-and-found box, and there are indeed a few men's watches in there, one of which might be yours. Unfortunately, I cannot provide you with a photograph of these items as requested, as our company regulations do not allow it. To claim a lost item, you should come to our office at the harbor and give a description of the item. If possible, showing the ticket from your boat ride will make the process faster. That's because we will be able to determine exactly which boat you were on, and our found items are cataloged by date and boat.

There is no need to book an appointment in advance. Simply stop by during our office hours, which are 9 A.M. to 6 P.M. daily. Please note that we are a seasonal business, and the season is wrapping up at the end of the month. Therefore, you only have a few days to visit us before the office closes for the low season, so please do so if you can, as returning your item will become a lot more complicated after that.

Sincerely,

Lucy Wooldridge

Administrative Assistant, Tibbs Inc.

168. What kind of service does Tibbs Inc. most likely provide?
(A) Event photography
(B) Swimming lessons
(C) Group tours
(D) Hotel bookings

169. Why was Ms. Wooldridge unable to send Mr. Pearlman a picture?
(A) A Web site is not working.
(B) It is against company policy.
(C) Some equipment is missing.
(D) The image needs to be edited.

170. According to the e-mail, how can Mr. Pearlman expedite a process?
(A) By avoiding the peak times
(B) By paying an additional fee
(C) By booking an appointment
(D) By presenting a ticket

171. What does Ms. Wooldridge recommend doing?
(A) Purchasing a season pass
(B) Contacting her manager
(C) E-mailing a description
(D) Taking action quickly

GO ON TO THE NEXT PAGE

Questions 172-175 refer to the following article.

Investment at GT Communications

March 3—GT Communications has confirmed its plans to invest heavily in technology for its facilities. Customers have shifted away from landlines, which previously made up GT Communications' entire business, and started using mobile phone networks and the Internet. Therefore, the company is adapting its business model by changing its infrastructure. — [1] —.

The smallest of the company's facilities—located in Nashville—already received the new machines so that the plan could be tried out on a small scale before rolling out the changes companywide. — [2] —. GT Communications is taking measures to ensure that its staff members are not negatively affected by the upgrades. "During the transition at Nashville, we looked for areas where we could retrain our people instead of laying them off," said company spokesperson Katherine Coyle. "— [3] —. We expect similar figures at the rest of our facilities."

GT Communications is now ready for Phase 2 of its transition, which is installing the state-of-the-art equipment at all sites. — [4] —. The work will begin with the Detroit site later this year, followed by the Kansas City branch early next year, and the Houston branch late next year. Once all of the upgrades have been completed, the final site will be open for public tours so that people can see the operations for themselves.

172. According to the article, what caused GT Communications to transform its business plan?

(A) A new government regulation
(B) A complaint from the workforce
(C) A change in consumer behavior
(D) An increase in shareholders

173. What is mentioned about the company's facility in Nashville?

(A) It was used as a testing site.
(B) It received a technology award.
(C) It is the first factory opened by GT Communications.
(D) It was the meeting place of investors.

174. Where does GT Communications plan to offer public tours of a site?

(A) Nashville
(B) Detroit
(C) Kansas City
(D) Houston

175. In which of the positions marked [1], [2], [3], and [4] does the following sentence best belong?

"We were thus able to keep ninety percent of staff members at that location."

(A) [1]
(B) [2]
(C) [3]
(D) [4]

GO ON TO THE NEXT PAGE

Questions 176-180 refer to the following information and e-mail.

Four intense workshops are being made available to employees of HTT Corp. Employees must choose one of the four courses below. Each course comprises three three-hour sessions unless otherwise specified. The sessions will be held on Fridays (March 14, 21, and 28) from 2 P.M. to 5 P.M.

Exchange Rates Risk Management

❑ Instructor: Frederic Masker

This course will look closely at how exchange rates affect markets, explain how predictions are made, and go over the best strategies for investing in an international context. This course has one additional two-hour session on April 4.

International Capital Flows

❑ Instructor: Lydia Benson

This course will explain how capital flows globally, introduce a few key relationships among countries, and go over the major effects of these flows on the global economy.

Multinational Corporations

❑ Instructor: Sylvia Glazkova

This course will introduce three major multinational corporations and give an in-depth analysis of their functioning and budget management.

Case Studies

❑ Instructor: Trenton Blair

This hands-on course will have students work in groups to analyze a case and determine the best strategy for the sample corporation to take. Each group will present their findings in the last session.

To: Linda Kay <lindakay@httcorp.com>
From: Peter Moreno <petermoreno@httcorp.com>
Subject: Friday Afternoon
Date: Thursday, March 27

Dear Ms. Kay,

Ms. Benson has changed the last session for the workshop from tomorrow to next Tuesday. I am thus free to work tomorrow afternoon. However, I was wondering if it would be acceptable for me to watch the presentations from Mr. Blair's class. Several coworkers taking that course have told me about their work, and I am highly interested in seeing the results. Of course, if I am needed in the office at that time, I will be available to work.

Thank you for your consideration.

Sincerely,

Peter Moreno
Budget Analyst, HTT Corp.

176. Where will the information most likely appear?

(A) In a brochure
(B) On a bulletin board
(C) In a magazine
(D) On a flyer

177. When will Ms. Glazkova's last class be held?

(A) March 14
(B) March 21
(C) March 28
(D) April 4

178. Which instructor will have students collaborate on a project?

(A) Frederic Masker
(B) Lydia Benson
(C) Sylvia Glazkova
(D) Trenton Blair

179. Which course has Mr. Moreno been attending?

(A) Exchange Rates Risk Management
(B) International Capital Flows
(C) Multinational Corporations
(D) Case Studies

180. What is NOT true about Mr. Moreno?

(A) He has already attended several classes.
(B) He wants to see his coworkers' projects.
(C) He is scheduled to give a presentation.
(D) He is able to come to the office on Friday.

GO ON TO THE NEXT PAGE

Questions 181-185 refer to the following memo and schedule.

To: MMH Law Firm Employees
From: Tamara Caudill, Attorney
Subject: Re: Building for Sale

April 16

As discussed in the weekly meeting, the owner of Midland Tower will put the building up for sale next month, and we will relocate our offices. Aldridge Co., the realtor handling the sale of the building, would like professionals to take photos for the property listing on its Web site. This photo shoot will take place on April 24 and will be carried out in all parts of the building. I have attached a schedule with the offices that are going to be photographed. In preparation for the photographers' visit, all items must be cleared from your desk except your computer and phone. We will provide plastic bins for you, and you should put your items in them for the short duration of the shoot. A maintenance worker will visit you ten minutes before your appointed time to collect these bins with a cart. Furniture might be rearranged in your office, but it will be returned to its original placement before you get back. The entire process will take about twenty minutes maximum, during which time you can take a break in the staff lounge. This does not count toward your usual daily break time.

Thank you for your cooperation, and we apologize for any inconvenience this may cause.

[Attachment: Final Schedule]

Aldridge Co. Schedule: April 24

TIME	OFFICE	OCCUPANT(S)
9:00 A.M.	201	Harriet Duncan
9:20 A.M.	202	Ranjan Singh
9:40 A.M.	203	Dale Mumford, Michael Bellamy
10:00 A.M.	204	Shirley Swain
10:20 A.M.	205	Brandon Parra, Huan Ren

Brandon Parra will handle room 202 because the occupant won't be in the office that day.

181. What is the purpose of the memo?

(A) To introduce a new building owner to employees

(B) To explain how an office relocation will occur

(C) To distribute a schedule for a renovation project

(D) To announce a plan for photographing a building

182. What does Ms. Caudill advise the memo recipients to do?

(A) Direct their questions to Aldridge Co.

(B) Use containers to temporarily move items

(C) Contact her regarding their availability on April 24

(D) Leave their personal belongings at home

183. What can the memo recipients do on April 24?

(A) Take an additional break

(B) Work part of the day from home

(C) Leave work early

(D) Have an extended lunchtime

184. At what time will a maintenance worker arrive at Ms. Swain's office on April 24?

(A) 9:40 A.M.

(B) 9:50 A.M.

(C) 10:00 A.M.

(D) 10:10 A.M.

185. What is implied about Mr. Singh?

(A) He will move to office 203.

(B) He shares an office with Mr. Parra.

(C) He will be absent on April 24.

(D) He requested a change in the schedule.

GO ON TO THE NEXT PAGE

Questions 186-190 refer to the following product description, online review, and online response.

The Bag of the Future: Zimmer-40

The Zimmer-40 will revolutionize the way you think about backpacks. It features a fold-out solar panel that can be used to charge your personal electronics. The advanced battery ensures that you always have the power you need on the go. The outer section is fully resistant to water, so your devices are always protected. In addition, all plastic parts on the backpack come from recycled plastic.

The Zimmer is sold at department stores and sporting goods outlets. Sign up for our monthly newsletter at the time of purchase to get a free second battery.

www.ucanreview.net/customer_reviews/accessories

Brand: Zimmer
Reviewer: Tyson Quintero
Item: Zimmer-40
Post Type: New

After researching several technology-enabled backpacks on the market, I selected the Zimmer-40 because of Zimmer's solid reputation. The color of the bag was darker than it appeared in the catalog, but that wasn't a problem for me. I'm impressed with how long the battery holds its charge, and I'm glad to have the second free one. The only thing that disappointed me was that my 15-inch laptop does not fit inside the bag. Despite this, I highly recommend this product, and I intend to buy it as a gift for several friends.

www.ucanreview.net/customer_reviews/accessories

Brand: Zimmer
Commenter: Phillip Sandoval
Item: Zimmer-40
Post Type: Reply

As a Zimmer customer service agent, I'm sorry you were not completely satisfied with your purchase. Based on your needs, you might want to consider the Zimmer-40B. It has a special charging compartment on the inside that can accommodate up to a 17-inch laptop. It has the same gel-filled shoulder straps as the Zimmer-40, so you can still wear it comfortably even if it is loaded with heavy items. Since you already have the Zimmer-40, there isn't any point in buying a new battery because the same one can be used in all of our bags. I hope this resolves your issue.

186. What is NOT indicated about the Zimmer-40?
(A) It has a waterproof exterior.
(B) It makes use of renewable energy.
(C) It is partially made from recycled materials.
(D) It is light enough to use during sports.

187. What can be inferred about Mr. Quintero?
(A) He will receive monthly updates from Zimmer.
(B) He purchased the bag at a department store.
(C) He doesn't like the color of the bag.
(D) He mainly uses the bag for outdoor activities.

188. What is suggested in the online review?
(A) Zimmer is a relatively new company.
(B) Mr. Quintero plans to purchase more bags.
(C) Zimmer sells a line of laptop computers.
(D) Mr. Quintero noticed some damage on his bag.

189. Why does Mr. Sandoval recommend the Zimmer-40B to Mr. Quintero?
(A) It is the only bag with gel-filled straps.
(B) It can charge items more quickly.
(C) It has a larger carrying capacity.
(D) It is more durable than the Zimmer-40.

190. In the online response, the word "point" in paragraph 1, line 6, is closest in meaning to
(A) opinion
(B) reason
(C) aspect
(D) spot

Questions 191-195 refer to the following e-mails and information.

E-Mail

To: Kimberly Garrett <kgarrett@saezinc.net>
From: Marietta Convention Center <info@mariettacc.com>
Date: February 19
Subject: Information

Dear Ms. Garrett,

Thank you for taking a tour of the Marietta Convention Center on February 18. I hope you enjoyed viewing our technology-enabled facilities, including the expansion of the west wing. Based on your description of the banquet your company plans to hold, I believe we would be the perfect site. Each room comes equipped with a stage, which could be used to present awards to your art instructors and give speeches, and there are a variety of amenities to suit your needs. Furthermore, I can confirm that we currently have no reservations booked for your desired date of March 31. Attached, please find the detailed information you requested about each room. If you would like to make a booking, or if you have any further questions, do not hesitate to contact me at 555-6677, extension 21. I hope to hear from you soon.

Sincerely,

Ralph Shelby
Guest Services Representative, Marietta Convention Center

Marietta Convention Center Room Descriptions

Daisy Room—Maximum Capacity: 50 / Rental Fee: $2,600
4 x 8 m stage, podium, projector, pull-down video screen

Sunflower Room—Maximum Capacity: 50 / Rental Fee: $2,900
4 x 8 m stage, podium, projector, pull-down video screen, exterior doorway to garden

Peony Room—Maximum Capacity: 100 / Rental Fee: $3,500
6 x 10 m stage, podium, projector, flat-screen built-in television, full-service bar

Orchid Room—Maximum Capacity: 100 / Rental Fee: $4,800
6 x 12 m stage, podium, projector, flat-screen built-in television, full-service bar, view of Lochmere Bay

Various seating arrangements are available. Guests may use south or west parking lot for a nominal fee.

E-MAIL MESSAGE

To: Amina Jeffries, Dean McGraw, Kimberly Garrett, Bai Tan
From: Amil Rao
Date: February 20
Subject: Banquet plans

Hi Everyone,

It seems like we are making progress on our committee's plans for the upcoming banquet for our staff and their families. Thank you, Kimberly, for taking over the Marietta Convention Center visit for me, since I had to fly to Toronto that day for an unexpected business matter. I'm still waiting for the reports from the rest of you regarding the caterers you were assigned to research. Please e-mail that information to me by Thursday afternoon.

As for the venue options, I'd love our ninety guests to be able to overlook Lochmere Bay as they dine, but I don't think this will be feasible, given our limited budget. Instead, I think it would be best to rent the cheaper room that fits our size needs. We can discuss this further at Friday's meeting. See you then!

Amil

191. Where does Ms. Garrett most likely work?
(A) At a technology company
(B) At a fitness center
(C) At an art institute
(D) At a performance venue

192. Which room amenity is indicated in the information?
(A) Special lighting for the stage area
(B) A view of the city skyline
(C) Complimentary parking for guests
(D) Access to an outdoor space

193. What is implied about Mr. Rao?
(A) He joined the committee at the last minute.
(B) He visited several meeting venues.
(C) He wrote a review of a caterer.
(D) He took a business trip on February 18.

194. What can be inferred about Mr. McGraw?
(A) He is in charge of the committee's budget.
(B) He is gathering information about caterers.
(C) He is unable to attend Friday's meeting.
(D) He visited the Marietta Convention Center.

195. Which room would Mr. Rao most likely want to rent?
(A) Daisy Room
(B) Sunflower Room
(C) Peony Room
(D) Orchid Room

Questions 196-200 refer to the following article, Web page, and review.

Theater Fundraiser a Success

Last night's charity banquet to raise funds for the Gilcrest Theater was deemed a remarkable success by event planners, who reported proceeds of nearly $12,000, approximately $2,000 over the goal. The money will be used for the installation of a cutting-edge sound system in the theater, which will serve as a much-needed replacement for the outdated system currently being used.

The work will be completed just in time for the Regional Film Festival, of which the Gilcrest Theater is a hosting site. While the facility usually presents live theater performances, it is equipped with a large projection screen for movies. Other theaters across the region will also participate, but Gilcrest Theater has the highest seating capacity among them, more than double that of the second-largest one, Corinth Theater.

Tickets for the film festival go on sale next week. Movie fans can take in intense dramas by critically acclaimed directors. Or for those looking for something light, there are plenty of films with comedic writing.

---

www.regionalfilmfestival.com/schedule

| HOME | ABOUT | **SCHEDULE** | SEATING | DIRECTION |

Regional Film Festival

Thursday, September 6	Friday, September 7	**Saturday, September 8**	Sunday, September 9

Venue / Phone Number	Film	Start Time	
24th Street Theater / 555-4102	*Underground*	7:00 P.M.	[More Info]
Corinth Theater / 555-0578	*A Summer's Day*	7:30 P.M.	[More Info]
Gilcrest Theater / 555-5855	*The Tale of Marco*	7:05 P.M.	[More Info]
Palacios Theater / 555-9360	*Wilson's Army*	8:10 P.M.	[More Info]

Customers should select the seat number and row when purchasing tickets, so please review the map of the venue's seating sections, downloadable at www.regionalfilmfestival.com/seating, before calling to order tickets. This will speed up the ordering process.

Underground: Best Thriller of the Year

****

By Casey Ashton

If you're looking for a thriller that will keep you guessing until the very end, look no further than *Underground*, the latest masterpiece by director Mia Camacho. I recently saw it at the Regional Film Festival, and I was extremely impressed with the character development, intriguing plot, and fantastic acting. This film is a must-see!

196. In the article, the word "deemed" in paragraph 1, line 2, is closest in meaning to

(A) considered
(B) expected
(C) admired
(D) caused

197. How will the raised funds be used at Gilcrest Theater?

(A) To launch an advertising campaign
(B) To purchase a projection screen
(C) To upgrade an outdated Web site
(D) To install new audio equipment

198. When will the largest theater start its screening event on September 8?

(A) At 7:00 P.M.
(B) At 7:05 P.M.
(C) At 7:30 P.M.
(D) At 8:10 P.M.

199. What are ticket purchasers advised to do?

(A) Download a digital receipt
(B) Check a seating chart in advance
(C) Read some online movie reviews
(D) Receive tickets by express mail

200. Where did Mr. Ashton watch a film?

(A) 24th Street Theater
(B) Corinth Theater
(C) Gilcrest Theater
(D) Palacios Theater

Stop! This is the end of the test. If you finish before time is called, you may go back to Parts 5, 6, and 7 and check your work.

聽力內容 & 中譯

Actual Test 1

PART 1 01

1 (A) He's staring at a vase.
美M **(B) He's pouring a beverage.**
(C) He's spreading out a tablecloth.
(D) He's sipping from a coffee cup.

(A) 他正凝視著花瓶。
(B) 他正在倒飲料。
(C) 他正在鋪桌布。
(D) 他正拿起咖啡杯啜飲。

字彙 stare at 凝視 pour 傾倒 beverage 飲料 spread out 鋪開 sip 啜飲

2 **(A) The woman is wearing glasses.**
美W (B) The woman is watering some potted plants.
(C) Some books are being piled on a shelf.
(D) A laptop computer is being put away.

(A) 此女子正戴著眼鏡。
(B) 此女子在幫盆栽澆水。
(C) 有些書正被堆在書架上。
(D) 有人正把筆記型電腦收起來。

字彙 potted plant 盆栽 pile 堆放 put away 收拾

3 (A) They're folding a piece of paper.
英W (B) One of the men is cutting some wood.
(C) A toolbox has been set on the floor.
(D) A brick wall is being painted.

(A) 他們在折紙。
(B) 其中一個男子在砍柴。
(C) 地上放著一個工具箱。
(D) 有人在粉刷磚牆。

字彙 fold 折疊 toolbox 工具箱

4 (A) A piano has been positioned under a window.
澳M (B) Some cushions have been stacked in the corner.
(C) A seating area has been arranged on a rug.
(D) A carpet is being installed.

(A) 窗戶下有擺一架鋼琴。
(B) 角落有疊放一些抱枕。
(C) 座位區底下有鋪地毯。
(D) 有人正在鋪地毯。

字彙 position 放置 stack 疊放 arrange 整理；布置 rug 地毯

5 (A) One of the men is entering a music store.
英W (B) One of the men is repairing a guitar.
(C) The men are waiting in line at a bus stop.
(D) The men are playing instruments.

(A) 其中一名男子正進入一家樂器行。
(B) 其中一名男子正在修吉他。
(C) 男子們在公車站排隊等車。
(D) 男子們在演奏樂器。

字彙 music store 樂器行 repair 維修 wait in line 排隊 instrument 樂器

6 (A) A woman is signing copies of a book.
美W (B) A ladder is being stored in a closet.
(C) Some documents have fallen on the floor.
(D) Some books have been placed on shelves.

(A) 女子正在簽書。
(B) 有人把梯子放在壁櫥裡。
(C) 有些文件掉在地上。
(D) 有人把一些書放在書架上。

字彙 copy 一本、一冊 store 存放 closet 壁櫥 document 文件

PART 2 02

7 When will the landlord inspect the property?
澳M (A) No, it failed the inspection.
美W **(B) I'll e-mail him about it.**
(C) Do you like the apartment?

房東什麼時候會來視察此房產？
(A) 不，房產沒通過審察。
(B) 我會寫電子郵件告訴他。
(C) 你喜歡這間公寓嗎？

字彙 landlord 房東　inspect 視察　property 房產
inspection 視察

8 Who's giving the new employees a tour tomorrow?
美W 澳M
(A) I'll be at another branch.
(B) Let's visit the most famous sites.
(C) Our team has reached the goal.
明天是由誰帶新員工參觀公司？
(A) 我會在另一家分公司。
(B) 我們來參觀最有名的據點。
(C) 我們的團隊已經達標。

字彙 new employee 新員工
give a tour 負責帶領參觀　branch 分公司

9 Would you prefer coffee or a soft drink with your lunch set?
美M 英W
(A) A cup of black coffee, please.
(B) I'll show you our menu.
(C) He said he was thirsty.
您的午餐套餐想要搭配咖啡還是汽水？
(A) 請給我一杯黑咖啡。
(B) 我給您看一下菜單。
(C) 他說他口渴。

字彙 prefer 偏好　soft drink 汽水、無酒精飲料

10 Isn't this leather jacket on sale?
美M 澳M
(A) No, I like the other one.
(B) Yes, it's half off today.
(C) Some cold weather.
這件皮夾克不是在打折嗎？
(A) 不是，我喜歡另一件。
(B) 是啊，今天是半價。
(C) 天氣有點冷。

字彙 leather 皮革　half off 半價

11 How many people will attend the lecture?
英W 澳M
(A) A talk on sustainable energy.
(B) Professor Franklin starts at seven o'clock.
(C) Nearly fifty have signed up.
會有多少人來聽演講？
(A) 演說內容和永續能源有關。
(B) 富蘭克林教授會在七點開始演說。
(C) 已經有將近 50 個人報名。

字彙 lecture 演講　sustainable 永續的
sign up 報名

12 I appreciate your giving me a ride to the airport.
澳M 英W
(A) A direct flight, if possible.
(B) It's my pleasure.
(C) I went on a business trip.
我很感激你載我到機場。
(A) 如果可以的話，希望是直飛班機。
(B) 這是我的榮幸。
(C) 我去出差。

字彙 direct flight 直飛班機
go on a business trip 出差

13 Do you need me to check the copy machine?
美
(A) Press the green button on the front.
(B) The quarterly report for investors.
(C) Oh, I got it working again.
你需要我檢查一下影印機嗎？
(A) 按下前面的綠色按鈕。
(B) 這是給投資人的季度報告。
(C) 喔，我讓它正常運作了。

字彙 quarterly 每季　investor 投資人
get it working 正常運作

14 When will the crew finish trimming the bushes?
澳M 英W
(A) Probably around noon.
(B) In the front yard.
(C) Pink and white roses.
工班什麼時候會修剪好灌木叢？
(A) 大概中午左右。
(B) 在前院。
(C) 粉紅色和白色的玫瑰。

字彙 crew 工班　trim 修剪　bush 灌木叢

15 Is there a fee to park in this lot?
美
(A) I appreciate the help.
(B) Yes, according to the sign.
(C) To get to the Bennington Building.
這個停車場要收費嗎？
(A) 我感激你的幫忙。
(B) 要喔，告示牌有寫。
(C) 我們要去班寧頓大樓。

字彙 fee 費用　lot （某種）場地

16 I can arrive late to the presentation, right?
澳M (A) No, the presents have not arrived.
美W (B) Please feel free to use mine.
(C) Yes, but you'll have to stand at the back.

我可以晚點到簡報會，對嗎？
(A) 不行，禮物還沒送達。
(B) 用我的，別客氣。
(C) 對，但你就要站在後面。

字彙 presentation 簡報會
feel free to V 隨意去做某事

17 What can I do with the leftover promotional posters?
美M 英W
(A) Congratulations on your promotion!
(B) By five o'clock.
(C) Just recycle them.

剩下的促銷海報要怎麼辦？
(A) 恭喜你升遷！
(B) 五點以前。
(C) 拿去回收就好。

字彙 leftover 剩餘的 promotional 促銷的
congratulations 恭喜 promotion 升遷

18 I forgot the code to enter the laboratory.
英W (A) She'll show you some experiments.
美W **(B) It's five-seven-seven-one.**
(C) He is our top scientist.

我忘了進去實驗室的密碼。
(A) 她會做些實驗給你看。
(B) 是 5771。
(C) 他是我們最棒的科學家。

字彙 code 密碼、代碼 laboratory 實驗室
experiment 實驗

19 Would you like me to e-mail you a summary of the meeting?
美W 澳M
(A) Thanks, but I took notes.
(B) The entire management team.
(C) Approximately two hours.

你要我把會議摘要透過電子信箱寄給你嗎？
(A) 謝謝你，不過我有記筆記了。
(B) 整個管理團隊。
(C) 大約兩小時。

字彙 summary 摘要 entire 整個的
management 管理 approximately 大約

20 Where do I send the completed application?
美M (A) A full-time position, I think.
英W **(B) Details are on the Web site.**
(C) No later than July 1.

我要將填好的申請表寄到哪裡？
(A) 我想這是全職職位。
(B) 網站上有詳細說明。
(C) 要在 7 月 1 日以前送出。

字彙 completed 完成的 application 申請表
position 職位 no later than ……以前

21 I can bring two bags onto the plane, can't I?
英W **(A) No, you'll have to check one.**
美M (B) The flight will depart shortly.
(C) Yes, I've put them in a bag.

我可以帶兩個包包上飛機，對嗎？
(A) 不行，你必須託運一個包包。
(B) 此班機將很快起飛。
(C) 是的，我已經把它們放到包包裡。

字彙 check 託運 depart 起飛 shortly 很快地

22 I'll let the manufacturer know about this safety issue.
美
(A) I work at a manufacturing facility.
(B) We can save some for later.
(C) That's the right move. Thanks.

我會讓製造商知道這起安全議題。
(A) 我在製造廠工作。
(B) 我們可以留一些下來，等以後再用。
(C) 這個做法是對的，謝謝你。

字彙 manufacturer 製造商
manufacturing facility 製造廠 move 做法

23 Why don't we make comment cards for our customers?
美W 澳M
(A) Yes, I think she's a new customer.
(B) That would streamline our feedback process.
(C) Did you drive to work by yourself?

我們何不為顧客製作意見卡？
(A) 是的，我想她是新顧客。
(B) 這樣可以簡化我們的意見反饋程序。
(C) 你自己開車上班嗎？

字彙 comment 意見 streamline 簡化

24 Where can I get this month's copy of the magazine?
英W
美M
(A) No, I haven't had much time.
(B) There's a newsstand around the corner.
(C) Because of an interesting article.

我可以到哪裡取得這個月的雜誌？
(A) 沒有，我沒那麼多時間。
(B) 附近有一家書報攤。
(C) 因為一篇有趣的文章。

字彙 copy 一本、一份（副本） newsstand 書報攤

25 Doesn't the office seem extra quiet today?
美M
英W
(A) Yes, a lot of employees took the day off.
(B) Sorry, I'll try to keep it down.
(C) I think tomorrow is fine.

今天辦公室也太安靜了吧？
(A) 是啊，今天很多員工請假。
(B) 抱歉，我會盡量小聲一點。
(C) 我想明天可以。

字彙 extra 分外、過於 take a day off 請假
keep down 小聲一點

26 Can we meet by video conference, or do we need to do it in person?
美
(A) Yes, I enjoyed the conference.
(B) Face-to-face would be better.
(C) To discuss employee performance.

我們可以開視訊會議嗎？還是需要親自去開會？
(A) 是的，我開會時很開心。
(B) 當面開會比較好。
(C) 要討論員工績效。

字彙 video conference 視訊會議
in person 親自 face-to-face 當面
performance 績效

27 Why is the door to the side entrance locked?
美W
澳M
(A) No, you can leave it open.
(B) For a few more hours.
(C) I heard it was being repaired.

為什麼側門鎖上了？
(A) 不用，你可以讓門開著。
(B) 再幾個小時。
(C) 我聽說側門正在整修。

字彙 side entrance 側門

28 Where do you keep your lightweight backpacks?
美M
英W
(A) Mainly for hikers.
(B) Yes, I decided to bring one.
(C) They're next to the tents.

你把輕便的背包放在哪裡？
(A) 主要是給登山客使用。
(B) 對，我決定帶一個。
(C) 放在帳篷旁。

字彙 lightweight 輕便 hiker 登山客

29 Don't you have to turn in your portfolio today?
澳M
美W
(A) I'm putting the finishing touches on it.
(B) Please turn left at the corner.
(C) Yes, it is a portable device.

你今天不用交出作品集嗎？
(A) 我還在做最後的修飾。
(B) 請在街角左轉。
(C) 是的，這是一個攜帶式的裝置。

字彙 turn in 繳交
put the finishing touches (on)
對……做最後的修飾
portable 攜帶式的 device 裝置

30 Who was selected to give the opening speech at the awards ceremony?
美M
澳M
(A) At the end of the year.
(B) She did a wonderful job.
(C) It hasn't been announced yet.

誰獲選在頒獎典禮做開場致詞？
(A) 在年底。
(B) 她的表現很棒。
(C) 還沒有宣布。

字彙 select 遴選 give a speech 致詞
awards ceremony 頒獎典禮
announce 宣布

31 Which item can I use this coupon for?
澳M
英W
(A) It expired last month.
(B) Yes, I shop here often.
(C) Three would be enough.

這張折價券可以用在哪些品項？
(A) 這張上個月就過期了。
(B) 是的，我常在這裡購物。
(C) 三個應該就夠了。

字彙 expire 過期

PART 3 03

Questions 32-34 refer to the following conversation. 美M 英W 對話

M ㉜ **Welcome to Madison Department Store.** Can I help you find anything today?	男：㉜ **歡迎光臨麥迪遜百貨公司。**您需要我幫忙找什麼嗎？
W ㉝ **I'm wondering if these jeans come in a size fourteen.** I didn't see any on the shelf.	女：㉝ **我在想這些牛仔褲有沒有 14 號的尺寸。**我在架上都沒看到。
M ㉝ **I think twelve is the largest size we carry, but let me look it up on the computer.**	男：㉝ **我想我們這邊最大只有到 12 號，但我可以在電腦上查一下。**
W Thanks. I really like this style.	女：謝謝。我真的很喜歡這個款式。
M Hmm . . . yes, twelve is the largest size here, though the brand does make other sizes.	男：嗯……我們這邊最大尺寸真的只有 12 號，不過這個牌子確實有出其他尺寸。
W Could I buy one at another branch?	女：我可以在其他分店買到嗎？
M ㉞ **If you visit our company's Web site, you should be able to see if you can get it there.**	男：㉞ **如果你上我們公司的網站，可以看看能不能在官網買到。**

字彙 shelf 貨架　carry 販售　look up 查找　branch 分店

32 Where is the conversation taking place?
(A) At a bookstore
(B) At a dry cleaner's
(C) At a department store
(D) At a post office

中譯 此對話發生在什麼地方？
(A) 書店
(B) 乾洗店
(C) 百貨公司
(D) 郵局

33 What does the man check?
(A) The available sizes
(B) The sale price
(C) The delivery fees
(D) The shipment date

中譯 男子查找了什麼？
(A) 有賣的尺寸
(B) 售價
(C) 運費
(D) 出貨日期

34 What does the man recommend doing?
(A) Checking for an item online
(B) Placing a rush order
(C) Visiting another branch
(D) Purchasing a different brand

中譯 男子建議做什麼事？
(A) 到網路上查找某品項
(B) 下訂緊急訂單
(C) 前往另一家分店
(D) 購買不同的品牌

Questions 35-37 refer to the following conversation. 美W 澳M 對話

W I'm glad you got my message about stopping by, Rick.	女：瑞克，我很高興你有收到我請你過來一下的訊息。
M I came as soon as I read it. Is anything the matter?	男：我一收到訊息就儘快過來了。有什麼事嗎？
W Not at all. ㉟ **The head of marketing is very pleased with the designs you've made for us so far.** And since you said	女：沒事。㉟ **行銷部主管對你目前幫我們做的設計很滿意。**既然你說過偶爾也想在家工作，㊱ **我已經幫你訂了一台公司專用的筆記型電腦，**在這裡。

you'd like to work from home some days, ❸❻ **I've ordered you a company laptop.** Here it is.

M Oh, that's great. Thanks! Now I won't have to keep any company files on my personal computer anymore.

W Right. But you will be responsible for any damage to this device. So, ❸❼ **don't forget to use a protective case when moving it from place to place.**

男：喔，太好了。謝謝！我再也不用把公司檔案存在我的個人電腦了。

女：對啊。但你要對這台設備的任何損壞負責。所以，❸❼ **帶著筆電移動時，記得要用電腦包保護它。**

字彙 stop by 停留一下　work from home 在家工作　device 裝置　protective 保護的
from place to place 到處去

35 What most likely is the man's job?
(A) Head of marketing
(B) Graphic designer
(C) Repairperson
(D) Personnel manager

中譯 此男子最有可能擔任什麼職務？
(A) 行銷部主管
(B) 平面設計師
(C) 維修人員
(D) 人事部經理

36 What has the woman ordered for the man?
(A) A uniform
(B) A desk
(C) A file cabinet
(D) A laptop computer

中譯 女子已經幫男子下訂什麼物品？
(A) 制服
(B) 辦公桌
(C) 檔案櫃
(D) 筆記型電腦

37 What does the woman remind the man to do?
(A) Sign up for a workshop
(B) Read a user manual
(C) Transport an item carefully
(D) Contact a customer

中譯 女子提醒男子做什麼事？
(A) 報名工作坊
(B) 閱讀使用手冊
(C) 小心攜帶某物品
(D) 聯絡顧客

Questions 38-40 refer to the following conversation. 英W 美M 對話

W Welcome to the Seabreeze Café. ❸❽ **Would you like a table in our dining room or on our patio?**

M ❸❽ **I'm not sure what my friend would like. He'll be here in a minute, so I'll wait and ask him.**

W That's no problem. You can see here on our specials board that ❸❾ **we have six different fresh soups to choose from today.**

M That's more than I expected.

W Well, we try to make sure there's something for everyone.

M ❸❾ **That's great.** Oh, and ❹⓿ **are you still accepting this coupon from the newspaper for ten percent off any meal?**

W Yes, that's valid until the end of the month.

女：歡迎光臨海洋微風咖啡館。❸❽ **您想坐在室內用餐區還是露臺區呢？**

男：❸❽ **我不確定我朋友喜歡坐哪裡。他待會就到了，我等他來再問他。**

女：沒問題。您可以先看一下我們的特餐公告欄，❸❾ **今天有六種不同的新鮮湯品可以選。**

男：比我想的還要多。

女：嗯，我們想盡量滿足大家的胃口。

男：❸❾ **太好了。**喔，❹⓿ **你們現在還收這個報紙上的任意餐點九折券嗎？**

女：是的，到月底都還可以用。

字彙 patio 露臺　in a minute 等一下　valid 有效的

38 What does the man want his friend's opinion about?
(A) A payment method
(B) A reservation time
(C) A food order
(D) A seating option

中譯 男子想知道他朋友的什麼意見?
(A) 付款方式
(B) 訂位時間
(C) 點餐
(D) 座位選擇

39 Why does the man say, "That's more than I expected"?
(A) To make a complaint
(B) To turn down an offer
(C) To give an excuse
(D) To express excitement

中譯 男子為什麼說:「比我想的還要多」?
(A) 想抱怨
(B) 想拒絕提議
(C) 想找理由
(D) 想表達興奮之情

40 What does the man inquire about?
(A) A discount offer
(B) A chef's recommendation
(C) The hours of operation
(D) The parking situation

中譯 男子詢問什麼事?
(A) 某折扣優惠
(B) 主廚推薦餐點
(C) 營業時段
(D) 停車狀況

Questions 41-43 refer to the following conversation with three speakers. 美W 英W 澳M 三人對話

W1 Tommy and Jennifer, the two of you have been so much help in promoting Ruth Taylor's new novel. ❹❶ **I think it's going to be one of our publishing firm's best sellers.** I appreciate your taking charge of the book launch event. Jennifer, how did it go?
W2 It was great! ❹❷ **I didn't expect so many people to be there.** There was a line outside the store just to get in.
W1 I'm so glad to hear that! I guess the advertisements we made really worked. Tommy, ❹❸ **did you take a lot of pictures at the launch?**
M Yes, and ❹❸ **I'll upload them to the Web site this afternoon.**

女 1: 湯米和珍妮佛,你們兩位在推廣茹絲・泰勒的新小說方面不遺餘力。❹❶ **我想這會是我們出版社的暢銷書之一。**我很感激你們承辦新書發表會。珍妮佛,活動辦得怎麼樣呢?
女 2: 非常好!❹❷ **我沒料到會有這麼多人參加。**書店外有人排隊等著進來。
女 1: 真是令人高興的消息!我猜我們打的廣告有效。湯米,❹❸ **你有在發表會上拍很多照片嗎?**
男: 有的,❹❸ **我今天下午會上傳到網站。**

字彙 **promote** 推廣 **publishing firm** 出版社 **take charge of** 負責某件事 **launch** 發表會

41 Where do the speakers work?
(A) At a business institute
(B) At a library
(C) At a publishing company
(D) At a newspaper office

中譯 談話者在哪裡工作?
(A) 商業機構
(B) 圖書館
(C) 出版公司
(D) 報社

42 What was Jennifer surprised about?
(A) Attendance at an event
(B) Some negative reviews
(C) A proposed contract
(D) A coworker's transfer

中譯 珍妮佛對什麼情況感到驚訝?
(A) 活動的參加人數
(B) 某些負評
(C) 已提議的合約
(D) 同事調職的事

43 What will happen this afternoon?
(A) Some customers will give feedback.
(B) A new shipment will arrive.
(C) The man will conduct an interview.
(D) Photos will be added to a Web site.

中譯 下午會發生什麼事？
(A) 有的顧客會提出意見反饋。
(B) 會有一批新的貨物送達。
(C) 男子要進行面談。
(D) 會有人把照片放到網站上。

Questions 44-46 refer to the following conversation. 美 對話

03

M ㊹ **Welcome to Marshall Accounting,** Ms. Weston, and thanks for coming to this interview. ㊺ **How did you find out about this job opening?**	男：韋斯頓小姐，㊹ **歡迎來到馬歇爾會計事務所**，也感謝你參加這次的面試。㊺ **你如何得知這個職缺呢？**
W ㊺ **I signed up for e-mail alerts on a job Web site. When I got the message about this position,** I knew it'd be a great fit for me.	女：㊺ **我有到求職網站上訂閱電子通知信。我收到此職位的訊息時**，就知道這工作非常適合我。
M What makes you say that?	男：怎麼說呢？
W Your firm mainly serves corporate clients, rather than individuals. I worked at a multinational corporation for eight years, so I'm quite comfortable with that kind of client.	女：貴公司主要服務企業客戶，而非個體戶。我曾在跨國企業工作八年，因此我應對這類客戶相當游刃有餘。
M That's great to hear. And your résumé says you won an Employee of the Year Award. What was that for?	男：很高興聽你這麼說。你的履歷上提到曾獲得年度最佳員工，可以請你說說獲獎原因嗎？
W We were focused on building our customer base, and ㊻ **I registered the most new clients.**	女：我們的目標是累積客群，㊻ **而我這邊登記到的新客戶最多。**
M Fantastic!	男：了不起！

字彙 job opening 職缺 sign up for 登記、報名 alert 通知 position 職位 firm 事務所 corporate 企業的 rather than 而非…… individual 散戶、個體戶 multinational 跨國的 corporation 企業 résumé 履歷 focus A on B 將 A 著重在 B base 基礎 register 登記

44 Where most likely are the speakers?
(A) At a business school
(B) At an accounting firm
(C) At an insurance company
(D) At a government office

中譯 談話者最有可能在哪裡？
(A) 商學院
(B) 會計事務所
(C) 保險公司
(D) 政府辦事處

45 How did the woman learn about the job opening?
(A) By reading a magazine
(B) By receiving an e-mail
(C) By speaking to a colleague
(D) By attending a career fair

中譯 女子如何得知此職缺？
(A) 從雜誌上看到
(B) 收到電子郵件
(C) 和同事聊天
(D) 參加就業博覽會

46 What accomplishment does the woman mention?
(A) Training other staff members
(B) Earning the highest employee rating
(C) Developing a new software program
(D) Bringing in the most new customers

中譯 女子提到哪項成就？
(A) 訓練其他職員
(B) 獲得最高員工評等
(C) 開發新的軟體程式
(D) 招攬最多新顧客

Questions 47-49 refer to the following conversation. 英W 澳M 對話

W	We have three new employees starting here next month. ㊼ **I have no idea where we're going to put them.**	女：下個月會有三名新員工開始來這邊上班。㊼ **我實在不知道要把他們安置在哪裡。**
M	Oh, ㊼ **we're out of office space?**	男：喔，㊼ **我們辦公室空間不足了嗎？**
W	Yes, ㊼ **our current unit just isn't enough anymore.** Fortunately, our lease is up soon, so we could move to another site. But ㊽ **I have no idea which neighborhood would be best.**	女：對，㊼ **我們目前的空間就是不夠了。** 幸好，租約快到期了，我們可以搬到另一個地點。但是㊽ **我不知道哪一區會比較好。**
M	Well, my friend Felix works in real estate.	男：我朋友菲立克斯在房仲業工作。
W	Perfect! Would you mind calling him? While you're doing that, ㊾ **I can print the handouts we need for this afternoon's meeting.**	女：太好了！你可以打給他嗎？你打電話的時候，㊾ **我可以邊印出下午開會要發的資料。**
M	Of course. I'll try him now.	男：當然可以，我現在就打看看。

字彙 current 目前　unit 辦公空間　lease 租約　site 地點　real estate 房地產業　handout 資料

47 What is the problem?
(A) Some equipment was damaged.
(B) A company is not reliable.
(C) Some new employees are inexperienced.
(D) A workspace is too small.

中譯 出了什麼問題？
(A) 有些設備受損了。
(B) 某公司不可靠。
(C) 有些新員工沒有經驗。
(D) 辦公空間太小。

48 Why does the man say, "my friend Felix works in real estate"?
(A) To suggest getting a recommendation
(B) To reject a business proposal
(C) To correct a misunderstanding
(D) To explain the reason for a decision

中譯 男子為何說：「我朋友菲立克斯在房仲業工作」？
(A) 提議可以詢問朋友建議
(B) 因為要拒絕某商業提案
(C) 因為要釐清誤會
(D) 因為要說明做某決策的原因

49 What does the woman say she will do?
(A) Visit a neighborhood
(B) Read some reviews
(C) Make a phone call
(D) Prepare some documents

中譯 女子說她要做什麼？
(A) 參觀某鄰近社區
(B) 閱讀一些評價
(C) 打電話
(D) 準備一些文件

Questions 50-52 refer to the following conversation. 美 對話

M	Okay, ㊿ **the total for these hiking boots and high heels is ninety-seven fifty.**	男：好，㊿ **這些登山靴和高跟鞋的總價是 97.50 美元。**
W	Alright. And do you know when you're getting the new line of Cartright products?	女：好的。那你知道什麼時候會進卡特雷特的新系列產品嗎？
M	I'm very sorry, but 51 **our inventory program on the computer is not working at the moment.**	男：不好意思，51 **我們電腦上的庫存程式目前有點問題。**
W	Oh, that's too bad. I wanted to get those as soon as they were in stock.	女：喔，好可惜。我想在它們到貨的時候就趕快拿到。
M	We should have the system working again soon. 52 **If you give me your phone number, I can give you a call this afternoon.**	男：我們的系統應該很快就修好了。52 **您可以給我您的電話，我今天下午再打給您。**

字彙 hiking boots 登山靴　line 系列　inventory 存貨　work 運作良好　in stock 有存貨

50 Where most likely does the man work?
(A) At a coffee shop
(B) At a bank
(C) At a car rental company
(D) At a shoe store

中譯 男子最有可能在哪裡工作？
(A) 咖啡店
(B) 銀行
(C) 租車公司
(D) 鞋店

51 According to the man, what is the problem?
(A) Some products are sold out.
(B) A delivery did not arrive.
(C) Some software is malfunctioning.
(D) An employee has made an error.

中譯 根據男子的說法，出了什麼問題？
(A) 有些商品賣完了。
(B) 商品尚未送達。
(C) 某軟體故障。
(D) 員工出錯。

52 What does the man offer to do for the woman?
(A) Call her later
(B) Get a supervisor
(C) Provide a refund
(D) Send a catalog

中譯 男子向女子提議何事？
(A) 晚一點會打給她
(B) 請主管過來
(C) 退款
(D) 寄送型錄

Questions 53-55 refer to the following conversation. 美W 澳M 對話

W ㊸ **Thank you for visiting Augusta Furniture. How may I help you?**
M Hello. ㊹ **I will open a small hotel next month,** and I need some items for the lobby. There's room for two sofas and a few armchairs.
W What kind of style did you have in mind?
M I've renovated a historic building, so I'd like items that have a classic style. But as for the color combinations, I have no idea.
W Well, ㊺ **you might find it helpful to check out the photo gallery on our Web site.**
M Wouldn't that just be pictures of the merchandise I can see here in the store?
W Yes, but it shows the items in different settings, so it can help you to get some decorating ideas.

女：㊸ **歡迎光臨奧古斯塔家具行，我能幫您什麼忙？**
男：哈囉，㊹ **我下個月要開一家小旅館**，我的大廳需要一些家具。空間上可以擺放兩張沙發，和幾張扶手椅。
女：您有考慮哪一種風格嗎？
男：我已經整修了一個歷史悠久的大樓，所以我希望家具是典雅風格。但是我對配色沒有頭緒。
女：這樣的話，㊺ **也許您可以先到我們網站的照片區瀏覽一下，應該會有幫助。**
男：那些不就是店裡家具的照片嗎？
女：是的，不過照片區會展示各家具的不同擺設方式，因此能給您一些布置的靈感。

字彙 room 空間　armchair 扶手椅　renovate 整修　combination 搭配、組合　check out 看一下
merchandise 商品　setting 擺設方式

53 Who most likely is the woman?
(A) A travel agent
(B) A delivery driver
(C) A furniture salesperson
(D) A hotel manager

中譯 女子最有可能是什麼身分？
(A) 旅行社人員
(B) 快遞司機
(C) 家具行業務員
(D) 飯店經理

54 What will the man do next month?
(A) He will take a trip out of town.
(B) He will open a new business.
(C) He will give a talk at an event.
(D) He will move to a new home.

中譯 男子下個月要做什麼？
(A) 他會到外地旅遊。
(B) 他要開張新事業。
(C) 他要去某活動演講。
(D) 他會搬到新家。

55 What does the woman suggest?
(A) Advertising on a Web site
(B) Viewing some images online
(C) Hiring a professional decorator
(D) Downloading a smartphone app

中譯 女子有什麼建議？
(A) 到網站打廣告
(B) 線上瀏覽一些圖片
(C) 僱用專業的布置人員
(D) 下載某智慧型手機應用程式

Questions 56-58 refer to the following conversation. 英W 澳M 對話

W I'm thrilled that Ms. Lee has been promoted to the head of our department.

M Me, too. 56 **Everyone here on the finance team is excited about it.** She'll do a fantastic job. You know, we should have a team lunch to celebrate this accomplishment.

W How about we do it here at the office? 57 **I can call a caterer to provide the food for us.**

M Perfect! 58 **Maybe we should get her a gift as well.**

W Actually, Tina had the same idea. 58 **She's collecting money from each team member, so talk to her if you're willing to chip in.**

女：我很開心李小姐被提拔為我們的部門主管。

男：我也很開心。56 **財務部的每個人都很興奮。**她可以勝任這份職務。我們應該辦個團隊午餐聚會，來慶祝這項成就。

女：我們就辦在辦公室如何？57 **我可以請外燴人員來供餐。**

男：太好了！58 **或許我們也可以送她一份禮物。**

女：其實蒂娜也這麼想。58 **她正在向每位團隊人員募資，如果你也願意分攤，可以去找她。**

字彙 thrilled 雀躍、開心　be promoted to . . . 被提拔為……　finance 財務　accomplishment 成就
caterer 外燴人員　chip in 分攤

56 In which department do the speakers work?
(A) Human resources
(B) Finance
(C) Marketing
(D) Shipping

中譯 談話者在哪一個部門工作？
(A) 人資部
(B) 財務部
(C) 行銷部
(D) 貨運部

57 What does the woman offer to do?
(A) Review a company policy
(B) Call one of Ms. Lee's clients
(C) Organize a work schedule
(D) Make preparations for a meal

中譯 女子主動提議做什麼事？
(A) 審視公司政策
(B) 聯絡李小姐的其中一位客戶
(C) 籌備工作行程表
(D) 準備餐會

58 According to the woman, why should the man talk to Tina?
(A) To contribute to a gift
(B) To collect a prize
(C) To express a preference
(D) To check a report

中譯 根據女子的說法，男子為何要去找蒂娜？
(A) 為送禮出一份心力
(B) 收取某獎品
(C) 表達喜好
(D) 檢查報告

Questions 59-61 refer to the following conversation with three speakers. 美M 英W 美W 三人對話

M Thanks for coming to this meeting, Claire and Eleanor. I scheduled it because 59 **I want to talk about the answers we got on our latest survey of customers.**	男： 克萊兒與伊琳諾，感謝你們來開會。我安排會議是 59 **想談一下最新的顧客問卷調查結果。**
W1 We've both looked over your summary report. Overall, it seems that people are pleased with the new breads and cakes we're offering at our bakery. 60 **Right, Claire?**	女1： 我們都有看過你的摘要報告。整體而言，大家似乎都滿喜歡我們烘焙坊新推出的麵包和蛋糕。60 **對嗎，克萊兒？**
W2 Yes. Especially the low-sugar options. However, 60 **a lot of people complained about how inconvenient our short business hours are.**	女2： 對的。尤其是低糖的品項。不過，60 **許多人抱怨我們營業時間短所造成的不便。**
M Right, so we should extend them. 61 **But to do so, we'll need another employee. Could you two please take care of hiring someone?**	男： 好的，那我們應該延長營業時間。61 **但這麼做的話，我們會需要再請一名員工。可以請你們兩位負責招募新人嗎？**

03

字彙 schedule 安排　look over 瀏覽、查看　overall 整體而言　business hours 營業時間　extend 延長

59 What does the man want to talk about at the meeting?
(A) Some customer survey responses
(B) Some employee complaints
(C) A new supplier of ingredients
(D) An upcoming sales promotion

中譯 男子想在會議中討論什麼事？
(A) 顧客問卷調查的某些回應
(B) 員工抱怨的某些事
(C) 食材的 新供應商
(D) 即將舉辦的促銷活動

60 What problem does Claire mention?
(A) An ingredient is considered unhealthy.
(B) The product selection is not large enough.
(C) Some business hours are inconvenient.
(D) Some staff members are not fully trained.

中譯 克萊兒提到什麼問題？
(A) 有人認為某食材不健康。
(B) 產品選擇不夠多。
(C) 不夠便利的營業時間。
(D) 有些職員未完整訓練。

61 What are the women asked to do?
(A) Oversee an ad campaign
(B) Work some additional shifts
(C) Create a summary report
(D) Hire a new employee

中譯 女子們被要求做什麼事？
(A) 監督某廣告活動
(B) 多上一些班
(C) 製作摘要報告
(D) 招募新員工

Questions 62-64 refer to the following conversation and map. 澳M 美W 對話和地圖

M Allison, are you doing anything on Friday night? I've got an extra ticket to the 7 P.M. show for the Vancouver Ballet Company. 62 **The group added Friday and Sunday shows because tickets for the original date sold out.**	男： 艾莉森，你這週五晚上有事嗎？我有多一張票，可以看晚上 7 點的溫哥華芭蕾舞團演出。62 **舞團加開週五和週日的場次，因為原日期的票已經賣完了。**
W 62 **Oh, really? I didn't know they were offering more shows.** I'd love to go!	女： 62 **喔，真的嗎？我不曉得他們加開場次。**我想去！
M Great! 63 **The seats are near the back, but they're in the center,** so I think the view will be fine.	男： 太好了！63 **座位靠近後面，但它們位於中央，**所以我想視野會不錯。

M Great! ⓺③ **The seats are near the back, but they're in the center,** so I think the view will be fine.
W That sounds good to me. Why do you have an extra ticket?
M ⓺④ **I was planning on taking my sister, but she now has an out-of-town job interview on Friday.**

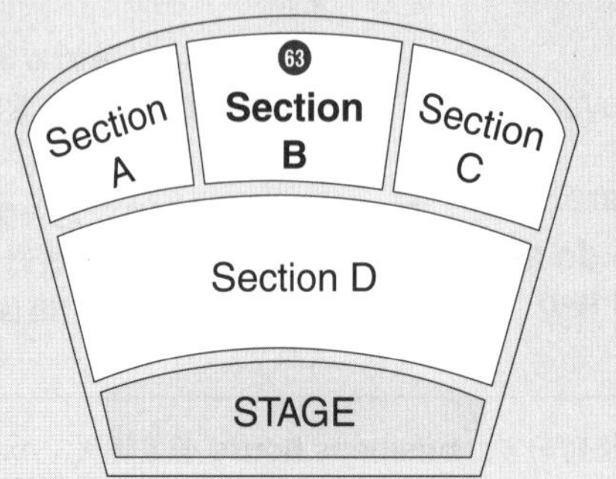

男： 太好了！63 **座位靠近後面，但它們位於中央**，所以我想視野會不錯。
女： 我都可以。你怎麼會有多的門票？
男： 64 **我原本打算帶我妹去，但她週五要去外地面試工作。**

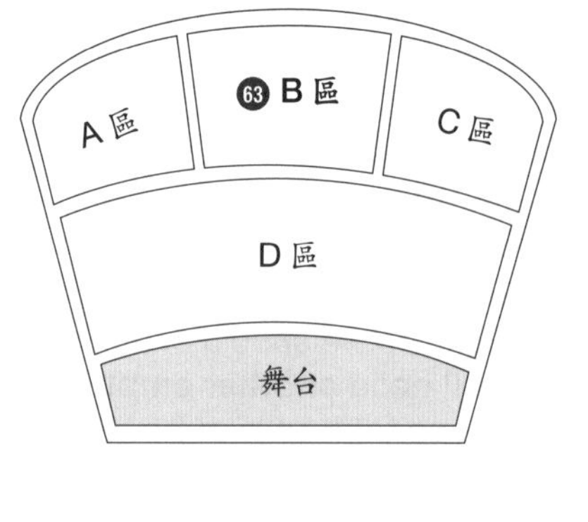

字彙 out-of-town 外地的 job interview 工作面試

62 Why does the woman express surprise?
(A) The price of some tickets has increased.
(B) Some new performance dates have been added.
(C) A dance group has won an award.
(D) The man is interested in watching ballet.

中譯 女子為何表現出驚訝的樣子？
(A) 有些票價調漲了。
(B) 表演日期有新增。
(C) 某舞團已獲獎。
(D) 男子有興趣看芭蕾舞表演。

63 Look at the graphic. For which section are the man's tickets?
(A) Section A
(B) Section B
(C) Section C
(D) Section D

中譯 請看圖示。男子的座位在哪一區？
(A) A 區
(B) B 區
(C) C 區
(D) D 區

64 What will the man's sister do on Friday?
(A) Go to a party
(B) Move out of town
(C) Attend an interview
(D) Teach a dance class

中譯 男子的妹妹週五要做什麼事？
(A) 參加派對
(B) 搬到外地
(C) 參加面試
(D) 教舞蹈課

Questions 65-67 refer to the following conversation and price list. 美 對話和價目表

M Hello. I reserved a vehicle online. My name is Doug Lambert.
W Let me just find your information, Mr. Lambert. Yes, 65 **you selected a standard sedan.**
M That's right. 66 **I'm here in Atlanta to be shown around the new Hamilton Apartment Tower.**

男： 哈囉，我有在網路上預約租車。我叫道格・蘭伯特。
女： 蘭伯特先生，我找一下您的資料。有的，65 **您選的是標準房車。**
男： 是的。66 **我來亞特蘭大這邊，想到新的漢彌敦公寓大樓附近看看。**

W That sounds great. Oh, and you have earned enough loyalty points for a free upgrade. So, ⑮ **I can give you a luxury sedan at the standard sedan price.** Would you like to do that this time?

M ⑮ **Sure!** Thank you.

W It's our pleasure. And, ⑰ **if you're not familiar with the city, there's a great driving app you can get for your smartphone. Downloading it is free.**

Vehicle Type	Daily Rate
⑮Standard Sedan	**$65**
Premium Sedan	$70
Luxury Sedan	$85
Elite Sedan	$110

女： 太好了。喔，您已經累積足夠的忠誠會員點數，可以免費升級。⑮ **我可以用標準房車價格幫您升等豪華房車。**您這次想要升級嗎？

男： ⑮ **好啊！**謝謝妳。

女： 這是我們的榮幸。⑰ **如果您不太熟悉本市，您可以在智慧型手機上下載一個很棒的行車 app。而且是免費的。**

汽車類型	日租費用
⑮標準房車	**$65**
頂級房車	$70
豪華房車	$85
尊榮房車	$110

字彙 **reserve** 預訂 **vehicle** 汽車 **select** 選擇 **standard** 標準的 **sedan** 房車 **loyalty point** 忠誠會員點數 **luxury** 豪華 **be familiar with** 熟悉某事

65 Look at the graphic. What will the man be charged per day?
(A) $65
(B) $70
(C) $85
(D) $110

中譯 請看圖表。男子每天會被收取多少費用？
(A) $65
(B) $70
(C) $85
(D) $110

66 Why is the man visiting Atlanta?
(A) To sign a contract
(B) To lead a group discussion
(C) To attend a conference
(D) To tour a building

中譯 男子為什麼要造訪亞特蘭大？
(A) 簽合約
(B) 主導某團隊討論事宜
(C) 參加會議
(D) 參觀某大樓

67 What does the woman recommend doing?
(A) Avoiding a busy road
(B) Keeping a receipt
(C) Downloading an app
(D) Visiting a popular restaurant

中譯 女子推薦男子做什麼事？
(A) 避開車多的道路
(B) 保留收據
(C) 下載某 app
(D) 造訪熱門的餐廳

Questions 68-70 refer to the following conversation and display plan. 美M 英W 對話與展示區平面圖

M ⑱ **We're glad you had time to visit the Westchester branch of our hardware store, Ms. Abrams.**

W I'm glad to be here. As regional manager, I like to make sure operations are running smoothly at all branches. How are things going?

男： ⑱ **亞伯拉姆斯小姐，我們很高興您撥冗來參觀我們五金百貨行的威斯徹斯特分店。**

女： 我很開心來到這裡。身為地區經理，我想確保所有分店都順利營運。一切都好嗎？

M We've been consistently meeting our sales quotas, and ⑥⑨ **our staff just finished their quarterly safety training yesterday.**

W Wonderful! Now, summer is the time when most people work on home projects. Did you get the display plan I e-mailed you?

M Yes, but ⑦⓪ **I'm wondering if we could move the paints closer to the entrance.** I'd like people to see them right when they enter the store.

W Sure. ⑦⓪ **You can swap those with the batteries.**

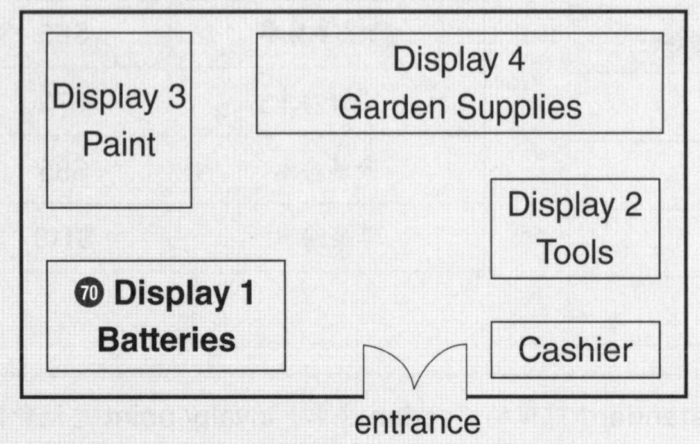

男：我們一直都有達到業績目標，⑥⑨ **職員昨天剛完成每季的安全性訓練。**

女：太棒了！夏天是多數人會開始進行居家改造計畫的時候。你有收到我用電子郵件傳給你的展示區平面圖嗎？

男：有的，但 ⑦⓪ **我在想我們是否能將油漆移到靠近大門一點的地方。**我想讓客人一進到店裡就會看見油漆。

女：好啊。⑦⓪ **你可以將油漆區跟電池區互換。**

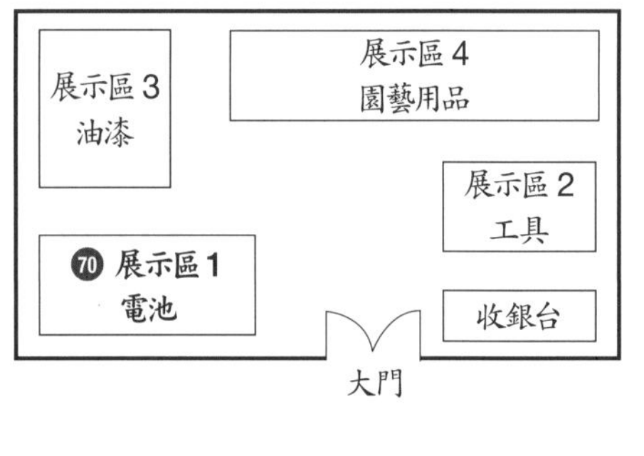

字彙 **branch** 分店　**hardware store** 五金行　**regional** 地區的　**operation** 營運　**smoothly** 順利地　**consistently** 持續地　**meet** 達到　**quota** 目標　**quarterly** 每季的　**swap** 交換

68 Where are the speakers?
(A) At an art institute
(B) At a repair shop
(C) At a hardware store
(D) At a toy store

中譯 談話者位於哪裡？
(A) 某藝術機構
(B) 修理廠
(C) 五金行
(D) 玩具店

69 According to the man, what did employees do yesterday?
(A) Recorded a video
(B) Completed some training
(C) Unloaded some new items
(D) Installed safety equipment

中譯 根據男子所說，員工昨天做了什麼事？
(A) 錄影片
(B) 完成某種訓練
(C) 將新品項卸貨
(D) 裝設安全設備

70 Look at the graphic. Where will some paint cans be moved?
(A) Display 1
(B) Display 2
(C) Display 3
(D) Display 4

中譯 請看圖示。油漆罐會被移到哪裡？
(A) 1 號展示區
(B) 2 號展示區
(C) 3 號展示區
(D) 4 號展示區

PART 4 04

Questions 71-73 refer to the following advertisement. 美M 廣告

Are you tired of the same old tourist sites? Try something new and tour the Lodgevile Jewelry Workshop. You'll get to see each step of the jewelry-making process. And, ⑪ **at the end, you'll have the chance to get your questions addressed by one of our talented jewelry makers.** ⑫ **Each participant is given a beautiful bracelet to identify their tour group,** and this gift is yours to keep. We're open daily. Please note there are big temperature differences inside the workshop, so ⑬ **be sure to bring an extra jacket or sweater that can easily be put on and taken off.**

對一成不變的觀光景點感到厭倦嗎?歡迎來洛吉維爾珠寶工作坊嘗鮮。您可以目睹珠寶製作程序的每一步,⑪ **最後還有機會向我們才華洋溢的珠寶工匠問問題。** ⑫ **我們會給每位參加者一條美麗的手鍊,做為所屬參觀團體的識別證,**並可當禮物帶回家。我們每天都開放參觀。請注意,工作坊內部的溫差極大,因此 ⑬ **請務必多帶一件方便穿脫的外套或毛衣。**

字彙 tourist site 觀光景點 workshop 工作坊 process 程序 address 處理;解決 talented 才華洋溢的 participant 參加者 bracelet 手鍊

71 How does each workshop tour end?
(A) An employee answers questions.
(B) An informative video is shown.
(C) A group photo is taken.
(D) A piece of equipment is demonstrated.

中譯 每一次的工作坊導覽都會以何種方式結束?
(A) 由某員工回答問題。
(B) 播放資訊量豐富的影片。
(C) 拍團體照。
(D) 展示某設備。

72 What does each tour participant receive?
(A) A piece of jewelry
(B) A voucher
(C) A map of the site
(D) A beverage

中譯 參加導覽的每個人會收到什麼?
(A) 一件珠寶
(B) 一張優惠券
(C) 一份場地地圖
(D) 一杯飲料

73 What do the listeners receive a warning about?
(A) Which entrance to use
(B) Where to meet
(C) What clothing to bring
(D) How to book in advance

中譯 聽者被提醒什麼事?
(A) 該從哪一個入口進出
(B) 會合的地點
(C) 該攜帶的衣物
(D) 事先預約的方式

Questions 74-76 refer to the following speech. 美W 演說

⑭ **I'm delighted to see so many people here for Herold Gym's membership drive.** We have a variety of exercise equipment to help you reach your fitness goals. ⑮ **You'll see from the class list you received when you arrived that there's something for everyone.** ⑯ **You don't have to sign up today, but if you do, we're offering a special deal—a one-year membership for just fifteen dollars a month.** You won't see anything like it again.

⑭ **我很開心見到這麼多人來參加哈洛德健身房的會員招募活動。**我們擁有各種運動器材,可協助大家達到健身目標。⑮ **大家可從今天到場時拿到的課程表中,找到適合每個人的課程。** ⑯ **不一定要今天報名,但如果今天報名,就能享有特殊優惠,一年會員只需每月15美元,**機會千載難逢喔。

字彙 delighted 開心的 membership 會員資格 drive 招募活動 reach a goal 達到目標 fitness 健身 sign up 報名 special deal 特殊優惠

74 Who most likely is giving the speech?
(A) A factory worker
(B) A driving instructor
(C) A gym manager
(D) A bank employee

中譯 演說的人最有可能是什麼身分?
(A) 工廠工人
(B) 駕訓班老師
(C) 健身房經理
(D) 銀行行員

75 What have the listeners been given?
(A) A product sample
(B) An employee directory
(C) A daily pass
(D) A list of classes

中譯 聽者已拿到什麼物品?
(A) 產品樣品
(B) 員工通訊錄
(C) 一日通行證
(D) 課程表

76 What does the speaker mean when she says, "You won't see anything like it again"?
(A) A membership process can be confusing.
(B) A presentation is worth watching.
(C) The business is expected to succeed.
(D) Listeners should take advantage of an offer.

中譯 說話者說:「機會千載難逢」的意思是什麼?
(A) 會員登記程序有點難懂。
(B) 某簡報值得觀賞。
(C) 此事業預計會成功。
(D) 聽者應利用此優惠機會。

Questions 77-79 refer to the following speech. 英W 演說

Good morning, everyone. 77 **I know it is a challenge to keep up with the demands of the medical industry while still providing the proper care to your patients, and you've done that beautifully.** As you may know, we've hired Judy Arnold as a consultant to inspect our site and help make improvements. 78 **I feel reassured that she will be the one carrying out this task because I know how thorough and meticulous she is.** As she is doing her work, 79 **please feel free to ask her for guidance on how to do things efficiently.** You'll see that she's very knowledgeable.

大家早。77 **我知道要跟上醫藥業的需求、同時為患者提供妥善照護,是一大挑戰,而你們都做得非常好。**大家應該都知道,我們已經聘僱茱蒂・阿諾擔任顧問,來視察我們的設施並協助改善。78 **有她來執行這項任務,我感到非常安心,因為我知道她是一個心思周全縝密的人。**她在的時候,79 **請大家儘管詢問她如何讓做事更有效率。**大家會發現她真的學識淵博。

字彙 keep up with 跟上……的腳步 demand 需求(量) consultant 顧問 inspect 視察 feel reassured 感到安心的 carry out 進行 thorough 周全的 meticulous 縝密的 feel free to V 自在地做某事 guidance 指引 efficiently 有效率地 knowledgeable 學識淵博的

77 What kind of business do the listeners most likely work for?
(A) A construction company
(B) An international delivery service
(C) A newspaper publisher
(D) A medical facility

中譯 聽者最有可能在哪一種公司工作?
(A) 建設公司
(B) 國際貨運服務公司
(C) 報社
(D) 醫療機構

78 What does the speaker say she is reassured about?
(A) A worker's attention to detail
(B) An investor's future plan
(C) The responses from a customer survey
(D) The score on an inspection

中譯 說話者表示對什麼事感到安心？
(A) 某工作者對細節的注重
(B) 某投資人的未來計畫
(C) 顧客問卷調查中的回應
(D) 考核分數

79 What are the listeners encouraged to do?
(A) E-mail Ms. Arnold
(B) Ask for advice
(C) Attend a training event
(D) Sample a new product

中譯 說話者鼓勵聽者做什麼事？
(A) 寫電子郵件給阿諾小姐
(B) 詢問建議
(C) 參加訓練活動
(D) 索取新產品的樣品

Questions 80-82 refer to the following announcement. 澳M 宣告

041

May I have your attention, please? ⑧⓪ **The departure of the 1:35 bus to Englewood has been delayed to approximately 3:20. There is a broken window that is being fixed now,** and we cannot operate the bus in its current condition. Due to this delay, ⑧① **the direct bus to Englewood may no longer be the faster option.** We do have some indirect routes. ⑧①⑧② **You can use any of those simply by presenting your valid ticket to the driver.**

請大家注意，⑧⓪ **1 點 35 分發車前往英格伍德的公車，已經誤點至約 3 點 20 分。因為目前正在修理破掉的窗戶，**公車在目前的狀態下無法行駛。由於此延誤事件，⑧① **前往英格伍德的直達公車可能不再是最快抵達目的地的選擇。**我們還是有非直達的公車路線。⑧①⑧② **您只要將出示有效的公車票給司機，即可搭乘任何一班非直達的公車。**

字彙 **attention** 注意　**departure** 發車　**delay** 延誤　**approximately** 大約　**operate** 運作　**current** 目前的　**condition** 狀態　**direct** 直達的　**indirect route** 非直達路線　**present** 出示　**valid** 有效的

80 Why is the bus's departure delayed?
(A) It is being cleaned.
(B) It is undergoing repairs.
(C) There is heavy traffic in the area.
(D) There was a scheduling error.

中譯 公車為何延誤發車？
(A) 有人在清洗公車。
(B) 公車正在進行維修。
(C) 該地區嚴重塞車。
(D) 時間表的安排出錯。

81 Why does the speaker say, "We do have some indirect routes"?
(A) To confirm a new schedule
(B) To explain a policy
(C) To suggest an alternative
(D) To make a complaint

中譯 說話者為什麼說：「我們還是有非直達的公車路線」？
(A) 確認新的時間表
(B) 說明某政策
(C) 提出替代方案
(D) 抱怨一下

82 What are the listeners asked to do?
(A) Talk to the speaker
(B) Show a ticket
(C) Come back later
(D) Present a receipt

中譯 說話者希望聽者可以怎麼做？
(A) 來找說話者談談
(B) 出示車票
(C) 晚點再過來
(D) 出示收據

Questions 83-85 refer to the following telephone message. 英W 電話留言

Good afternoon. This message is for Victor Henshaw. My name is Tessa Baxter, and ⓼⓷ **I'm calling from Duncan Realty.** We've received your application for our realtor position. ⓼⓸ **We were impressed that you have so much experience in a sales role. That is an essential skill to have in this field.** Unfortunately, we did not receive your application until after the deadline, and we had already selected another candidate. However, ⓼⓹ **I'll keep your cover letter and résumé on file in case a similar job becomes available in the future,** as I think you'd be a good fit for our company's needs. I hope we get a chance to work together in the future.

午安，⓼⓷ **我是鄧肯房地產公司**的泰莎・巴斯特，我想留言給維克多・亨肖。我們已經收到您應徵房仲人員的履歷。⓼⓸ **我們對於您豐富的業務員經驗印象深刻，而房仲業十分講究這樣的技能。**可惜的是，我們是在徵才截止之後才收到您的求職信，我們已經錄用另一名應徵者。不過，⓼⓹ **我想留存您的求職信和履歷，將來如果有類似職缺的時候，可以聯絡您。**因為我認為您很符合我們公司需求。希望我們將來能有機會共事。

字彙 realty 房地產　application 申請　realtor 房仲人員　position 職位　impressed 印象深刻的　essential 必需的　unfortunately 可惜的是　deadline 截止日期　candidate 求職應徵者　cover letter 求職信　résumé 履歷　in case 以防萬一　fit 適合

83 Where most likely is the speaker calling from?

(A) A real estate agency
(B) A dental clinic
(C) An architecture firm
(D) A manufacturing facility

中譯 說話者最有可能從哪裡打過來？

(A) 房地產公司
(B) 牙醫診所
(C) 建築事務所
(D) 製造廠

84 What qualification does the speaker mention?

(A) A flexible schedule
(B) A university degree
(C) State certification
(D) Sales experience

中譯 說話者提到什麼資歷？

(A) 彈性的工作時間
(B) 大學學歷
(C) 州立證照
(D) 業務經驗

85 What does the speaker say she plans to do?

(A) Send an employment contract
(B) Arrange an interview time
(C) Keep some documents
(D) Check the listener's references

中譯 說話者計劃怎麼做？

(A) 寄送聘僱合約
(B) 安排面試時間
(C) 保留某些文件
(D) 核實聽者的推薦人

Questions 86-88 refer to the following telephone message. 澳M 電話留言

Hi, Jessica. It's Luis Garza. ⓼⓺ **Thank you so much for agreeing to be interviewed for *World Fashions Magazine*.** I'm sure our readers will love getting a behind-the-scenes look at your studio and how you develop your lovely dresses. ⓼⓻ **I appreciate that you volunteered to have someone from your office take photos.**

嗨，潔西卡，我是路易・迦薩。⓼⓺ **很感謝您答應接受《世界時尚雜誌》的訪問。**我想我們的讀者一定會很想一窺您的工作室與催生可愛洋裝的幕後祕辛。⓼⓻ **我很感激您主動提議讓您公司的人負責。**不過，我們有全職攝影師。接下來想透過電話會議，跟您討論我此趟拜訪的細節。⓼⓼ **請讓我知道您何時方便，**我很樂意配合您的行程。

However, our photographer works full time. The next step would be a phone meeting so we can discuss the details of my visit. ⑱ **Please let me know when you are available.** I am happy to work around your schedule.

字彙 behind-the-scenes 不公開的　photographer 攝影師　work full time 全職工作

86 Where most likely does the speaker work?
(A) At a marketing firm
(B) At a local newspaper
(C) At a cosmetics company
(D) At a fashion magazine

中譯 說話者最有可能在哪裡工作？
(A) 行銷公司
(B) 當地報社
(C) 彩妝公司
(D) 時尚雜誌

87 Why does the speaker say, "our photographer works full time"?
(A) To explain a problem
(B) To reject an offer
(C) To correct a misunderstanding
(D) To request some help

中譯 說話者為什麼說：「我們有全職攝影師」？
(A) 為了說明某問題
(B) 為了婉拒某提議
(C) 為了釐清某誤會
(D) 為了尋求協助

88 What does the speaker ask the listener to do?
(A) Inform him of her availability
(B) Send him some documents
(C) Confirm a final payment
(D) Select some photographs

中譯 說話者請聽者做什麼事？
(A) 通知他有空的時間
(B) 寄送一些文件給他
(C) 確認尾款
(D) 選些照片

Questions 89-91 refer to the following excerpt from a meeting. 美M 會議節錄

Good morning, everyone. First on today's agenda, ⑲ **I'd like to explain our new vacation policy.** Last year, too many people took time off in the busy summer months. This meant we were short-staffed, so we were very busy serving customers. Unfortunately, this negatively affected the level of service we could provide. So, from now on, we will have a new system for making vacation requests. ⑳ **You'll need to fill out the form on our company's Web site.** We will try to give you at least some of your preferred dates, but this is not guaranteed. ㉑ **If you have any questions about the change, please e-mail Olivia. She will address them promptly.**

大家早。今天第一個議程，⑲ **我想說明我們新的休假政策。**去年有太多人在夏天的旺季月分請假，人手短缺使得服務顧客時忙不過來。不幸的是，這對我們的服務品質造成了負面影響。因此，從現在開始，我們將實施新的請假制度。⑳ **大家必須到公司網站填寫假單。**我們會盡量滿足大家指定休假的部分日期，但沒辦法保證一定能如你所願。㉑ **如果對於此變動有任何疑問，請傳電子郵件給奧莉維亞，她會即時處理。**

字彙 agenda 議程　policy 政策　take time off 請假　short-staffed 人手短缺的　request 請求
fill out 填寫　form 表單　preferred 更合意的　guarantee 保證　address 處理　promptly 及時地

89 What is the speaker mainly discussing?
(A) A customer complaint
(B) A staff promotion
(C) A payment system
(D) A company policy

中譯 說話者主要在討論什麼事?
(A) 客訴
(B) 職員升遷
(C) 付款系統
(D) 公司政策

90 What are the listeners asked to do?
(A) Complete an online form
(B) Work with a partner
(C) Read a handout
(D) Attend a training session

中譯 說話者要求聽者做什麼事?
(A) 填寫線上表單
(B) 與夥伴合作
(C) 閱讀講義資料
(D) 參加教育訓練

91 According to the speaker, what will Olivia do?
(A) Return some equipment
(B) Print some materials
(C) Answer questions
(D) Create a schedule

中譯 根據說話者的說法,奧莉維亞會做什麼事?
(A) 送回某設備
(B) 印出某些素材
(C) 回答問題
(D) 建置行程表

Questions 92-94 refer to the following broadcast. 美M 廣播

You're listening to *Time for the Town*, the show that keeps you up to date on local activities that may interest you. ㉒ **Today we're looking at a fairly new trend, picking fresh fruit.** Many farms and orchards are opening their sites to tourists to harvest their own fruits and vegetables. ㉓ **It's becoming popular because getting food locally is good for the environment.** Our guest today is ㉔ **Stephanie Lutz, whose strawberry farm has recently added this activity.** She's here to tell us how it works.

您現在收聽的是《本鎮關鍵時刻》,本節目會分享您可能感興趣的當地最新活動。㉒ **我們今天要探討一個相對新潮的趨勢——採摘新鮮水果。**許多農地和果園現正向觀光客開放,可自行採收蔬果。㉓ **取用在地食材對環境有益,使得此活動開始受歡迎。**今天的來賓是 ㉔ **史蒂芬妮・盧茲,她的草莓園最近也加入此活動行列。**請她來分享活動方式。

字彙 keep . . . up to date 讓(某人)得知最新消息 fairly 相當、十分 trend 趨勢 pick 採摘 orchard 果園 harvest 收割 locally 在本地

92 What will be discussed during the broadcast?
(A) Online deliveries
(B) Fruit picking
(C) Home gardening
(D) Farmer's markets

中譯 此廣播節目將討論什麼話題?
(A) 網路宅配
(B) 水果採摘活動
(C) 居家園藝
(D) 農夫市集

93 According to the speaker, why is an activity popular?
(A) It keeps people in shape.
(B) It is fun for all ages.
(C) It saves participants money.
(D) It is environmentally friendly.

中譯 根據說話者的說法,某活動為何變得受歡迎?
(A) 能讓人維持良好體態。
(B) 不分老小都能樂在其中。
(C) 能幫參加者省錢。
(D) 對環境有益。

94 Who is Stephanie Lutz?
(A) A reporter
(B) A city official
(C) A farmer
(D) A radio host

中譯 史蒂芬妮・盧茲是誰？
(A) 記者
(B) 市府官員
(C) 農民
(D) 電台主持人

Questions 95-97 refer to the following talk and map. 英W 談話和地圖

95 **Welcome, applicants. We're pleased that you are interested in working here at Collins International.** Today will be the group interview, and those of you who pass that stage will be invited back. We're here in the staff room now, but 96 **most of your time today will be spent in the HR office. It's at the end of the hallway, across from the storage room.** 97 **And at four-thirty, I'll show you how to get to the computer lab, where you'll be taking a series of personality tests.**

Room 201	Room 202	96 **Room 204**
Elevator		
Staff Room	Room 203	Storage Room

95 歡迎各位應徵者。很開心大家有意願在柯林斯國際公司工作。今天是團體面試，通過本階段的人會再次受邀。雖然我們現在位於員工休息室，但 96 各位今天多數時間都將待在人資辦公室，也就是走廊走到底、儲藏室對面的那間辦公室。97 4 點 30 分時，我會告訴大家如何前往電腦室，各位需要在那做一系列的性向測驗。

201 室	202 室	96 204 室
電梯		
員工休息室	203 室	儲藏室

字彙 **applicant** 應試者 **hallway** 走廊 **storage room** 儲藏室 **personality** 性向、性格

95 Who is the speaker addressing?
(A) Potential investors
(B) Company managers
(C) Job applicants
(D) Government inspectors

中譯 說話者在對誰說話？
(A) 潛在投資人
(B) 公司經理
(C) 應徵者
(D) 政府視察人員

96 Look at the graphic. Which office will the listeners use for most of the day?
(A) Room 201
(B) Room 202
(C) Room 203
(D) Room 204

中譯 請看圖表。聽者當日待最久的是哪一間辦公室？
(A) 201 室
(B) 202 室
(C) 203 室
(D) 204 室

97 Where will listeners go at four-thirty?
(A) To a conference room
(B) To a computer lab
(C) To a cafeteria
(D) To a security office

中譯 4 點 30 分的時候，聽者會去哪裡？
(A) 會議室
(B) 電腦室
(C) 自助餐廳
(D) 警衛室

Questions 98-100 refer to the following excerpt from a meeting and list. 美W 會議節錄和清單

Before we move on to the next agenda item, 98 **I'd like to give you all a big thank you. I know it was difficult to finish the contents for the webinar with little warning because of our schedule change.** We couldn't have done it without your hard work. 99 **Our new project, the annual trade expo, starts tomorrow.** There are quite a few components to consider, so I'd like to start planning for this. However, 100 **we won't be able to do much until we have our final budget. Patrick is doing that on Thursday,** so please do what you can in the meantime. At the next meeting, we'll cover the main tasks in more detail.

Project A	Corporate Sponsorship
Project B	Video Competition
Project C	Free Webinar
99 Project D	**Annual Trade Expo**

在進行下一個議程之前，98 **我想先好好的感謝大家。我知道因為行程異動，在沒什麼預警的情況下，要完成網路研討會的內容是很困難的。**如果沒有大家的努力，我們是沒法做到的。99 **而我們的新專案「年度貿易博覽會」，將於明天開始。**要考量的要素滿多的，所以我想開始籌備。不過，100 **我們在拿到最終確認的預算前，也無法有太多進展。派翠克星期四會給出預算，**所以在此期間，大家就盡力而為。我們下次開會，就會說明主要任務的更多細節。

專案 A	企業贊助
專案 B	影片競賽
專案 C	免費網路研討會
99 專案 D	**年度貿易博覽會**

字彙 move on to 進行下一個…… webinar 網路研討會 warning 預警 annual 年度的 trade expo 貿易博覽會 component 要素 budget 預算 task 任務

98 Why does the speaker thank the team?
(A) They finished a project on short notice.
(B) They created a popular product.
(C) They found some new clients.
(D) They helped to train new employees.

中譯 說話者為何要感謝團隊？
(A) 他們在臨時通知的狀態下完成一項專案。
(B) 他們創造了熱門的產品。
(C) 他們找到了新客戶。
(D) 他們協助訓練新進員工。

99 Look at the graphic. Which project will start tomorrow?
(A) Project A
(B) Project B
(C) Project C
(D) Project D

中譯 請看圖示。明天會開始哪一項專案？
(A) 專案 A
(B) 專案 B
(C) 專案 C
(D) 專案 D

100 What will Patrick do on Thursday?
(A) Receive an award
(B) Give a speech
(C) Visit a client
(D) Finalize a budget

中譯 派翠克星期四會做什麼？
(A) 獲頒獎項
(B) 演講
(C) 拜訪客戶
(D) 定好預算

PART 5

填入副詞

101 有些政府官員私下對企業稅制的改變表示擔憂。
(A) 隱私 (B) 私有化 (C) 私人的 **(D) 私下地**
字彙 official 政府官員 corporate 企業的
structure 制度 privately 私下地

填入形容詞

102 貝勒汽車公司新推出的電動車是專為都會區裡短程代步所設計。
(A) 短缺 **(B) 短的** (C) 很快地 (D) 縮短
字彙 electric car 電動車
be intended for 為……而設計的
journey 旅程

填入動詞＋單複數一致性

103 愛姆斯製造廠研發的包裝方法，使用的厚紙板可以大量減少。
(A) 使用 (B) 使用 (C) 使用 (D) 使用
字彙 manufacturing 製造 cardboard 厚紙板

介系詞 for

104 此大樓業主調高了停車場通行費。
(A) 為了…… (B) 關於……
(C) 在……某處 (D) ……之間
字彙 access 進出

副詞 correctly

105 幾乎沒有市場分析師正確預測到此工廠歇業造成的產業效應。
(A) 當地的 (B) 持續地 (C) 友好地 **(D) 正確地**
字彙 analyst 分析師 predict 預測 industry 產業
closure 歇業

動詞 give

106 我們非常歡迎顧客在社群媒體給我們評價。
(A) 說明 (B) 說 **(C) 給予** (D) 擁有

介系詞 during

107 八月的每個週末，此飯店的餐廳都會推出現場音樂演奏活動。
(A) 甚至 **(B) 期間** (C) 當時 (D) 一邊……
字彙 feature 推出特色活動 performance 表演

所有格

108 波特蘭保險公司的員工應於表單上填寫他們想要休假的日期。
(A) 他們的 (B) 它的 (C) 他們自己 (D) 它
字彙 form 表單 desired 想要的

填入名詞

109 許多營造公司對於進口建材的新限制感到緊張。
(A) 限制地 (B) 限制 (C) 限制的 **(D) 限制**
字彙 construction 營造工程 business 事業、商業
restriction 限制 importation 進口

連接詞 even though

110 儘管已經大力宣傳演唱會好幾週，門票銷售量還是不佳。
(A) 因為 (B) 除非 (C) 除了…… **(D) 儘管**
字彙 advertise 廣告 heavily 大量地

填入副詞

111 此商店因為夏季特賣而大幅降價。
(A) 大幅度地 (B) 重要性
(C) 顯著的 (D) 意味著
字彙 significantly 大幅度地 reduce 降低

形容詞 accurate

112 自僱工作者應該好好保留營業利潤與成本的正確記錄。
(A) 正確的 (B) 不公平的
(C) 視覺的 (D) 寬敞的
字彙 self-employed 自僱工作者
keep a record 保留紀錄 profit 利潤

介系詞 despite

113 儘管天氣寒冷，週六的社區野餐活動出席人數還是很多。
(A) 關於 (B) 相反的
(C) 儘管 (D) 在……對面
字彙 attendance 出席人數

形容詞 mandatory

114 土壤已採樣，以便進行是否被汙染的必要檢驗。
(A) 狹窄的 **(B) 必要的**
(C) 易腐敗的 (D) 明顯的
字彙 soil 土壤 sample 樣本 carry out 進行

現在分詞

115 柏金斯先生在修理冷氣前已訂購好替換零件。
(A) 修理 (B) 已修理 (C) 修理 (D) 修理
字彙 replacement 替換 part 零件

填入動詞＋現在完成式

116 產品銷售最近遭遇阻礙，若不採取進一步行動，可能不會改善。
(A) 經歷（不好的事）
(B) 已經歷（不好的事）
(C) 經歷（不好的事）
(D) 經歷（不好的事）

字彙 suffer 經歷（不好的事） setback 阻礙

動詞 prefer

117 商務旅客偏好有大型書桌的飯店房型。
(A) 申請 (B) 涉及 **(C) 偏好** (D) 相信

比較級

118 雖然比預期中更快，但這個寄送服務仍不值得這麼高的費用。
(A) 快速 **(B) 比較快的**
(C) 最快速的 (D) 快速地

字彙 delivery 宅配、外送 worth 值得

名詞 structure

119 此豪華公寓建築群是本市最高聳的三棟建築結構，在市鎮範圍內大多數地區都能看見。
(A) 社區 (B) 街道 (C) 居民 **(D) 建築物**

字彙 luxury 豪華的 complex 建築群；綜合大樓

介系詞 beyond

120 車庫在暴風雨中嚴重受損，必須重建才行。
(A) ……的 (B) ……之下
(C) 難以……的 (D) 到……之上

字彙 rebuild 重建

填入動詞

121 各部門經理將於 6 月 4 日至 8 日開會，以正式評估員工的工作表現。
(A) 將開會 (B) 開會 (C) 已會面 (D) 會面

字彙 formally 正式地 assess 評估

填入名詞

122 過去幾年有利的市場條件促成大多數產業更多的商業投資。
(A) 已投資 **(B) 投資**
(C) 投資 (D) 投資人

字彙 favorable 有利的 condition 條件
result in 導致 industry 產業

動詞 equip

123 VC 會議中心的所有會議室均配備內建喇叭和投影機。
(A) 進行 **(B) 配備** (C) 啟動 (D) 揭露

字彙 built-in 內建的 projector 投影機

填入形容詞

124 新的購物中心將會對當地經濟帶來益處。
(A) 益處 (B) 有益地 **(C) 有益的** (D) 益處

字彙 have an effect on 對……產生影響

複合關係副詞 however

125 無論交付的任務有多艱難，我們期許員工都能悉數完成。
(A) 無論…… (B) 同樣的 (C) 確實 (D) 相當

字彙 assign 指派 task 事務

填入副詞

126 求職者回答問題的創意度是能否勝任該職務的重要因素。
(A) 創造 (B) 創作 (C) 有創意的 **(D) 創意地**

字彙 candidate 求職者 component 因素、要件

連接詞 given that

127 有鑑於步道的危險性，國家公園的訪客必須由導覽員陪同。
(A) 比…… **(B) 有鑑於** (C) 雖然 (D) 即使

字彙 accompany 陪同 trail 步道

介系詞 in

128 這間餐廳被連鎖企業收購後導致餐點品質下降。
(A) 以下 (B) 在……某處
(C) 在……方面 (D) 作為

字彙 purchase 買下

名詞 competition

129 麥克雷先生解釋道，兩家公司間的競爭創造出創新的產品。
(A) 確認 (B) 後果 **(C) 競爭** (D) 佣金

字彙 create 創造 innovative 創新的

副詞 temporarily

130 南菲爾德健身中心暫時關閉主要游泳池一週，因其需要清理。
(A) 目前 (B) 完美地 (C) 固執地 **(D) 暫時地**

PART 6

Questions 131-134 refer to the following letter. 信函

Georgina Harrison
962 Warner Street
Cape Girardeau, MO 63703

Dear Ms. Harrison,

Thank you for your interest in making a group booking at Westside Hotel. I have attached a comprehensive ------- (131.) of our amenities for your convenience. We aim to personalize the guest experience. We are prepared to meet the needs of most guests on short notice. However, if you have ------- (132.) requests, we may need advance notice in order to fulfill them. Once your booking is made, you may be charged a fee according to our cancellation policy. ------- (133.). Before confirming your booking, please download a copy of the payment details and ------- (134.) them carefully.

Warmest regards,

The Westside Hotel Team

喬琪娜・哈里森 啟
63703 密蘇里州 開普吉拉多
華納街 962 號

親愛的哈里森小姐：

感謝您有意在西街飯店預訂團體住宿。我已經隨附完善的設施 ⑬① **說明**以便您參考。我們致力於提供個人化的住客體驗，並且準備好滿足多數房客的臨時需求。不過，若您有 ⑬② **特殊**需求，我們可能需要事前通知才能達成。一旦訂房完成，我們可能會依據取消政策向您收費，⑬③ **我們網站上亦列出相關條款。**您在確認訂房前，請先下載並仔細 ⑬④ **檢視**詳細的付款資訊副本。

誠摯感謝您
西街飯店團隊

字彙 comprehensive 完善的　amenity 設施　personalize 使個人化　meet the needs 滿足需求　short notice 臨時通知　advance notice 事先通知　charge 收取費用　cancellation 取消

填入名詞

131 (A) describe　(B) describes　(C) described　**(D) description**

中譯 (A) 說明　(B) 說明　(C) 說明　**(D) 說明**

形容詞 unusual

132 **(A) unusual**　(B) absent　(C) plain　(D) flexible

中譯 **(A) 特殊的**　(B) 缺席的　(C) 樸素的　(D) 彈性的

選出合適的句子

133 (A) The front desk is open twenty-four hours a day.
(B) You should complete the form with honest feedback.
(C) We appreciate your ongoing patronage.
(D) The terms of this are included on our Web site.

中譯 (A) 櫃檯 24 小時開放。
(B) 您應於表單填寫真實的意見。
(C) 我們感激您持續光臨。
(D) 我們的網站已列出此條款。

填入動詞

134 (A) reviewing **(B) review**
(C) to review (D) reviewed

中譯 (A) 正檢視 **(B) 檢視**
(C) 檢視 (D) 檢視了

Questions 135-138 refer to the following information. 資訊

Environmental Responsibility at the Kimball Museum

"Waves of Wonder" will be on display throughout the summer at the Kimball Museum. This ------- (135.) features sculptures made from beach glass. The artwork focuses ------- (136.) marine animals whose populations have been severely hurt due to ocean pollution. Interesting facts about each animal will be posted next to the work. Visitors ------- (137.) advice on reducing their impact on the oceans, both locally and worldwide. ------- (138.). "Waves of Wonder" will be available from June 10 to September 5.

金球博物館的環境責任

金球博物館將於夏季期間展出「驚奇之浪」。此 135 **展覽**的主展品為海灘玻璃所製成的雕像。藝術品聚焦 136 在因海洋汙染而嚴重減少的海洋動物。作品旁邊亦會張貼每種動物的有趣知識。訪客 137 **亦可獲得**降低當地與全球海洋衝擊的建議。大家可以藉此了解 138 **自己能帶來多少正面改變**。「驚奇之浪」的展出時間為6月10日至9月5日。

字彙 on display 展出　feature 特別推出　sculpture 雕像　marine 海洋的　population （動物）數量　severely 嚴重地　impact 衝擊

名詞 exhibit

135 (A) award (B) manuscript
(C) exhibit (D) film

中譯 (A) 獎項 (B) 手稿
(C) 展覽 (D) 電影

介系詞 on

136 (A) before (B) to
(C) on (D) by

中譯 (A) 之前 (B) 至……
(C) 在……上 (D) 在……附近

填入動詞

137 (A) are also getting
(B) can also get
(C) have also gotten
(D) also got

中譯 (A) 亦正在獲得
(B) 亦可獲得
(C) 也已經獲得
(D) 也獲得了

選出合適的句子

138 **(A) See how you can make a positive change.**
(B) To become a member, visit our Web site.
(C) Fortunately, the hours have been extended.
(D) The glass can be recycled at most locations.

中譯 **(A) 來看看自己能帶來多少正面改變吧。**
(B) 如欲加入會員，請前往我們的網站。
(C) 幸好，開放時間已延長。
(D) 玻璃可在多數地點回收。

Questions 139-142 refer to the following advertisement. 廣告

Verdant Landscaping, founded by brothers John and Jeremy Robles, -------(139.) top-quality landscaping services for residential properties. We can plant a garden from scratch, maintain existing lawns and flowerbeds, trim trees, and remove unwanted garden debris.

-------(140.), your outdoor area will be a beautiful and relaxing place for you to enjoy. -------(141.). We can send a crew of any size, including just one person. If you're unsure whether hiring professionals would be within your budget, call us at 555-4433 for a free -------(142.) of the costs. We look forward to serving you!

由約翰和傑瑞米・羅布斯兄弟所成立的「蓊鬱造景公司」，為住宅 139 **提供**頂級的造景服務。我們可從無到有栽植花園、養護現有草皮與花壇、修剪樹木與移除不要的花園廢棄物。

140 **因此**，您的戶外區域將會是讓您放鬆的優美一隅。141 **作業規模可大可小**。任何人數的工班都可派遣，即使只需一人亦可。如果您不確定僱用專業人員的費用是否在您的預算內，請撥 555-4433 以取得免費 142 **估價**。期待能為您提供服務！

字彙 **landscaping** 造景 **residential** 居住的 **property** 房產 **from scratch** 從零開始 **flowerbed** 花壇 **trim** 修剪 **debris** 垃圾、殘骸 **crew** 團隊 **budget** 預算 **look forward to V-ing** 期待做某事

填入動詞＋現在式

139 (A) will provide **(B) provides** (C) had provided (D) providing

中譯 (A) 將提供 **(B) 提供** (C) 已提供 (D) 提供

連接副詞 as a result

140 (A) For example (B) On the contrary **(C) As a result** (D) In comparison

中譯 (A) 舉例來說 (B) 相反的 **(C) 因此** (D) 相比之下

選出合適的句子

141 (A) Other businesses cannot compete with us.
(B) These techniques are environmentally friendly.
(C) We are willing to offer training.
(D) No job is too big or too small.

中譯 (A) 其他公司比不上我們。
(B) 這些技術均為環境友善。
(C) 我們願意提供訓練。
(D) 作業規模可大可小。

名詞 estimate

142 (A) vacation **(B) estimate** (C) installation (D) pathway

中譯 (A) 假期 **(B) 預估** (C) 裝設 (D) 小徑

Questions 143-146 refer to the following article. 文章

As a small business owner, Kelly Spencer spends a lot of time researching the best way to improve -------. (143.) Her staff was not responding well to her previous methods, but then she found an interesting piece of software, Pause-Pro. "I was hesitant at first due to the high cost. However, the company was offering free use of the software for thirty days, so I thought I'd give ------- (144.) a try."

Pause-Pro allows employers to block access to distracting Web sites, such as social media pages, so employees don't waste time. It wasn't ------- (145.) what Ms. Spencer was looking for, but she couldn't deny the results. She purchased the full version of the software for all of her employees' computers. -------. (146.) "With Pause-Pro's help," she said, "we can all focus on the most important tasks."

凱莉・史賓塞身為小型企業老闆，她投入許多時間研究改善 143 效率的最佳辦法。雖然她的職員對她之前的方法反應不佳，但後來她找到一個有趣的軟體「暫停專家」。「我一開始因為高額費用而猶豫。不過，這家公司有提供30天免費使用軟體的機會，所以我就試用 144 它看看。」

「暫停專家」能讓雇主封鎖令人分心的網站，例如社群媒體網頁，員工就不會浪費時間。雖然這不是史賓塞小姐 145 原本想找的工具，但其成效令她非常滿意。她為所有員工的電腦購買此軟體的完整版，146 **她也為自己的筆記型電腦購買此程式**。她表示：「在『暫停專家』的協助下，我們都可以專注於最重要的事務。」

字彙 respond to 對……有所反應　previous 之前的　hesitant 猶豫的　block 封鎖　distracting 令人分心的　waste 浪費　deny 否認　focus on 專注於

名詞 efficiency

143 (A) wages　**(B) efficiency**　(C) competition　(D) education

中譯 (A) 薪資　**(B) 效率**　(C) 競爭　(D) 教育

代名詞受格

144 (A) mine　(B) everyone　(C) these　**(D) it**

中譯 (A) 我的　(B) 每個人　(C) 這些　**(D) 它**

填入副詞

145 (A) more original　**(B) originally**　(C) original　(D) originality

中譯 (A) 更原創的　**(B) 原本地**　(C) 原本的　(D) 獨創性

選出合適的句子

146 **(A) She also bought the program for her laptop.**
(B) She has founded a few different businesses.
(C) She looks forward to meeting them.
(D) She could not understand the features.

中譯 **(A) 她也為自己的筆記型電腦購買此程式。**
(B) 她已成立一些不同的事業。
(C) 她期待見到他們。
(D) 她無法了解這些功能。

PART 7

Questions 147-148 refer to the following article. 文章

New Library Program Creates "Buzz"

April 30—This summer, ⑭⑦ **Syracuse Library is launching a program to help local bees. The number of local bees has sharply declined, and the library aims to help these creatures.** It will have a special section with books about bees and will host lectures about how they benefit the environment. ⑭⑧ **Anyone who attends a lecture will be given a free pack of seeds for flowers that will attract bees.**

圖書館的新計畫掀起一股「蜂」潮

4 月 30 日——今年夏季 ⑭⑦ **雪城圖書館將推出計畫協助當地蜜蜂。當地蜜蜂的數量已銳減，因此圖書館的目標在於協助這些生物。**館內將特別隔出蜜蜂相關的圖書區，並且舉辦講座來讓大家了解蜜蜂對環境的益處。⑭⑧ **參加講座的人都能免費獲得一包種子，其開花後能吸引蜜蜂前來。**

字彙 buzz 蜂鳴聲；風潮　launch 推出　local 當地的　sharply 疾速地　decline 減少　creature 生物

目的問題

147 What is the purpose of the program?
(A) To support the bee population
(B) To teach people a new skill
(C) To attract new library members
(D) To raise money for a charity

中譯 此計畫的目的是什麼？
(A) 幫助蜜蜂復育
(B) 教大家新技能
(C) 吸引新的圖書館會員
(D) 幫慈善機構募款

特定訊息確認問題

148 How can participants get a free gift?
(A) By completing a survey
(B) By attending a talk
(C) By making a donation
(D) By showing a library card

中譯 參加者如何獲得免費禮物？
(A) 完成問卷調查
(B) 參加演講
(C) 捐款
(D) 出示借閱證

Questions 149-150 refer to the following invitation. 邀請函

Please join us for a meet-and-greet session with
⑭⑨ **Adam Jackson, the new Public Relations Director of Watkins Bank.**

Monday, December 12, 1 P.M.–2 P.M.
Conference Room A

⑭⑨ **Adam Jackson handled public relations for CHK Bank for nearly two decades.** He will give a brief presentation on his plans for rebranding Watkins Bank and building closer connections with our customers. ⑮⓪ **If you have a question for Mr. Jackson, please send it to the HR team prior to the event.**

Coffee and hot tea will be served.

請與我們一同參加 ⑭⑨ **沃金斯銀行新任公關部總監**——亞當・傑克森見面會。

12 月 12 日週一，下午 1 點至 2 點
會議室 A

⑭⑨ **亞當・傑克森負責處理 CHK 銀行的公關事務已有將近 20 年的時間。**他將簡報他如何重塑沃金斯銀行品牌、建立更密切的顧客關係等方面的計畫。⑮⓪ **如果您有問題想問傑克森先生，請於活動前傳送至人資部。**

活動當天將供應咖啡與熱茶。

字彙 meet-and-greet 見面會　public relations 公關　rebrand 品牌重塑　connection 連結、關係
prior to 在……之前

推理問題

149 What is implied about Mr. Jackson?
(A) He currently works at CHK Bank.
(B) He recently changed his employer.
(C) He will receive an award on December 12.
(D) He founded his own business.

中譯 可從文中得知傑克森先生的何項資訊？
(A) 他目前在 CHK 銀行工作。
(B) 他最近剛換雇主。
(C) 他將於 12 月 12 日獲頒獎項。
(D) 他自行創業。

特定訊息確認問題

150 What can guests do in advance?
(A) Order hot beverages
(B) View some images
(C) Reserve a seat
(D) Submit their questions

中譯 參加者可以事先做什麼事？
(A) 訂熱飲
(B) 瀏覽一些圖片
(C) 預訂座位
(D) 提交問題

Questions 151-152 refer to the following e-mail. 電子郵件

To: Tamara Atwood
From: City Swim Center
Date: November 14
Subject: Request

Dear Ms. Atwood,

I am writing to acknowledge receipt of your e-mail. ⑮¹ **We have processed your request, and your membership will be continued for another year.** The new end date of your membership will be November 30 of next year. You are eligible for a free locker upgrade. ⑮² **Please come to the front desk anytime after November 30 to swap your current locker key for the new one.**

Thank you for your patronage,

Derek Surette
Customer Services, City Swim Center

收件人： 塔瑪拉・亞伍德
寄件人： 市立游泳中心
日期： 11 月 14 日
主旨： 請求

親愛的亞伍德女士：

我收到您的來信了。⑮¹ **我們已經處理您的申請，您的會員將可展延一年。**您新的會員資格將於明年 11 月 30 日到期，您亦符合免費升級置物櫃的資格。⑮² **請您在 11 月 30 日後，隨時攜帶您目前的置物櫃鑰匙來櫃檯更換新的鑰匙。**

謝謝您的惠顧，

德瑞克・蘇瑞特
市立游泳中心 客服部

字彙 request 請求　acknowledge 確認知悉　receipt 收到　process 處理　be eligible for 符合……資格的　swap 交換　patronage 惠顧

目的問題

151 Why did Mr. Surette send the e-mail?
(A) To apologize for an error
(B) To introduce a new service
(C) To confirm a renewal
(D) To make a job offer

中譯 蘇瑞特先生為什麼會傳送這封電子郵件？
(A) 為某錯誤道歉
(B) 介紹新服務
(C) 確認某更新事務
(D) 提出工作邀請

特定訊息確認問題

152 What can Ms. Atwood do after November 30?
(A) Contact Mr. Surette
(B) Receive a refund
(C) Attend a class
(D) Exchange a key

中譯 亞伍德女士可以在 11 月 30 日之後做什麼？
(A) 聯絡蘇瑞特先生
(B) 收到退款
(C) 參加課程
(D) 更換鑰匙

Questions 153-154 refer to the following text-message chain. 訊息串

Monique Ross [9:21 A.M.]
Good morning. I'm Monique from the Outdoor Gear customer service team. How may I help you?

Eric Harper [9:22 A.M.]
Hello. ⓯ **I ordered a dome tent on August 2 that was supposed to arrive yesterday. However, I still don't have it. I'm wondering when it will get here.**

Monique Ross [9:23 A.M.]
I can help with that. What is the order number?

Eric Harper [9:24 A.M.]
It's order #034587.

Monique Ross [9:25 A.M.]
Thank you. Please wait a moment.

Monique Ross [9:28 A.M.]
It looks like there was an issue at the warehouse, and the item is now scheduled to be sent tomorrow. So, it will arrive on Thursday, two days later than originally expected.

Eric Harper [9:29 A.M.]
Since I paid for overnight shipping, 154 **I think I should be refunded for the shipping fee.**

Monique Ross [9:31 A.M.]
Absolutely. 154 **I'll take care of that right now,** and it should appear on your account within a few hours. Do you need any other help?

Eric Harper [9:32 A.M.]
Not for now. Thanks.

莫妮克・羅斯 [早上 9:21]
早安，我是戶外用品客服部的莫妮克。我能幫您什麼忙？

艾瑞克・哈伯 [早上 9:22]
哈囉，153 **我在 8 月 2 日訂了一個圓頂帳篷，應該昨天就要到貨。但我還沒收到，我想問一下什麼時候會送達。**

莫妮克・羅斯 [早上 9:23]
我可以幫忙處理。請問訂單編號是多少？

艾瑞克・哈伯 [早上 9:24]
訂單是 #034587。

莫妮克・羅斯 [早上 9:25]
謝謝您，請稍等。

莫妮克・羅斯 [早上 9:28]
看來倉庫那邊出了問題，商品現在會安排明天寄出。所以，會在星期四送達，比原本預計的時間慢兩天。

艾瑞克・哈伯 [早上 9:29]
既然我支付的是貨物隔日送達的費用，
154 **我想應該要退運費給我。**

莫妮克・羅斯 [早上 9:31]
當然沒問題。154 **我現在會馬上處理**，幾個小時內就會退到您帳上。您還需要其他協助嗎？

艾瑞克・哈伯 [早上 9:32]
目前不用，謝謝你。

字彙 gear 用品　dome 圓頂　warehouse 倉庫　originally 原本　overnight shipping 隔日送達　refund 退款

目的問題

153 Why did Mr. Harper send a message to Outdoor Gear?
(A) To report damage to a tent
(B) To request a product catalog
(C) To exchange an unwanted product
(D) To check when an item will arrive

中譯 哈伯先生為什麼要傳訊息給戶外用品公司？
(A) 回報帳篷受損
(B) 索取產品型錄
(C) 更換不要的產品
(D) 確認某商品何時會送達

掌握意圖問題

154 At 9:31 a.m., what does Ms. Ross most likely mean when she writes, "Absolutely"?
(A) She understands the need for a fast service.
(B) She can open a new account for Mr. Harper.
(C) She enjoyed resolving a problem.
(D) She agrees to issue Mr. Harper a refund.

中譯 早上 9 點 31 分時，羅斯小姐的訊息「當然沒問題」最有可能是什麼意思？
(A) 她理解快速服務的需求。
(B) 她可以幫哈伯先生開新帳戶。
(C) 她樂於解決問題。
(D) 她同意幫哈伯先生退款。

Questions 155-157 refer to the following Web page. 網頁

www.cincinnaticommunitycenter.com

Home	Photo Gallery	Events	Contact Us

Posted: January 19
Cincinnati Encounter
155 **Saturday, March 12, 9:00 A.M.-11:00 A.M.**
155 **Instructor: Diane Robinson**

Are you new to Cincinnati? Learn about what the city has to offer, such as:

- 156C **Where and how to look for jobs with local businesses**
- 156A **What bus and streetcar routes are available to commuters**
- 156D **Volunteer opportunities with charities and how to participate**

This class would be especially helpful to those who have moved to Cincinnati from overseas. Registration opens on January 25 and ends on March 5. Spots will be assigned on a first-come, first-served basis. The class is expected to fill up quickly, so early registration is recommended.

Thanks to a government grant, 157 **Cincinnati Encounter is provided for free to anyone living in Cincinnati,** but registration is required.

www.cincinnaticommunitycenter.com

首頁	照片集錦	活動資訊	聯絡我們

發文時間：1 月 19 日
邂逅辛辛那提
155 **3 月 12 日星期六 早上 9 點至 11 點**
155 **講師：黛安・羅賓森**

您新來乍到辛辛那提嗎？一起來了解本市的資源吧：

- 156C **應徵當地工作的地點與方法**
- 156A **通勤族可參考的公車和電車路線**
- 156D **到慈善團體當志工的機會與參加辦法**

此課程對於從海外搬遷至辛辛那提的人格外有幫助。報名時間自 1 月 25 日開始，3 月 5 日截止。先搶先贏。此課程可能很快就額滿，因此建議大家儘早報名。

多虧政府補助金，157 **辛辛那提居民均可免費參加「邂逅辛辛那提」課程**，不過請務必報名。

字彙 encounter 邂逅 instructor 講師 streetcar 單軌電車 route 路線 commuter 通勤族 participate (in) 參加 registration 報名 assign 分配 on a first-come, first-served basis 依據先來後到的順序 fill up 額滿 grant 補助金

特定訊息確認問題

155 When will Ms. Robinson teach a class?
(A) On January 19
(B) On January 25
(C) On March 5
(D) On March 12

中譯 羅賓森小姐將於何時教課？
(A) 1 月 19 日
(B) 1 月 25 日
(C) 3 月 5 日
(D) 3 月 12 日

Not / True 問題

156 What is NOT indicated as a topic in Cincinnati Encounter?
(A) Using public transportation
(B) Running for local government
(C) Seeking employment in the area
(D) Assisting nonprofit organizations

中譯 「邂逅辛辛那提」不包括哪一個主題？
(A) 使用大眾運輸工具
(B) 參選當地政府官員
(C) 在該地區的求職
(D) 協助非營利組織

Not / True 問題

157 What is stated about Cincinnati Encounter?
(A) It is offered to residents at no cost.
(B) It will last for three hours.
(C) It was developed by a businessperson.
(D) It is part of an ongoing series.

中譯 文中提到「邂逅辛辛那提」的何項資訊？
(A) 居民可免費參加。
(B) 課程時間為三小時。
(C) 由商務人士所設計。
(D) 屬於進行中系列課程的一部分。

Questions 158-160 refer to the following e-mail. 電子郵件

To: Angela Klein <kleina@rtinternet.net>
From: José Damico <jose@sapphire-yoga.com>
Date: June 12
Subject: Level 3 Certification

Dear Ms. Klein,

We have received your deposit payment for Sapphire Yoga Studio's upcoming Yoga Teacher Training Course for the Level 3 certification course. —[1]—. This is a full-time intensive course that will last four weeks, beginning on June 29.

—[2]—. ⑮⑧ **Please e-mail Veronica Clark at veronica@sapphire-yoga.com to submit health check records from your doctor showing that you are fit to take on the demands of the course.** This is for your safety and is required by our insurance provider. ⑮⑨ ⑯⓪ **Yoga mats and blocks are available on site for every class.** —[3]—. ⑯⓪ **So, you can use them with confidence.** However, ⑮⑨ **we find that most students would rather bring personal items from home.** You are free to do so, but please be aware that we cannot store anything for you overnight.

Please let me know if you have any questions about the course. —[4]—.

Warmest regards,

José Damico
Manager, Sapphire Yoga Studio.

收件人： 安琪拉・克萊 <kleina@rtinternet.net>
寄件人： 荷西・戴米柯 <jose@sapphire-yoga.com>
日期： 6月12日
主旨： 第3級證照

親愛的克萊小姐：

我們已經收到您報名「藍寶石瑜珈工作室」即將開課的「瑜珈教師培訓課程第3級證照班」訂金。此密集課程從6月29日開始，為全時課程且持續四週。

⑮⑧ **請將您的健康檢查報告以電子郵件寄給維若妮卡・克拉克(veronica@sapphire-yoga.com)，以茲證明您的身體狀態能承受此課程的要求。**此做法不僅是為您的安全著想，我們的保險公司亦如此要求。⑮⑨ ⑯⓪ **每堂課現場均提供瑜珈墊和瑜珈磚。**每次用畢我們都會進行消毒。⑯⓪ **因此您能安心使用。**不過，⑮⑨ **我們發現多數學員會比較喜歡帶自己的用品。**您也可以這麼做，但請留意我們無法讓您放過夜。

如果您對課程有任何疑問，請跟我說。

祝一切順心

荷西・戴米柯
藍寶石瑜珈工作室經理

字彙 **certification** 證照 **deposit** 訂金 **payment** 付款 **intensive** 密集的 **submit** 提交 **fit** 適合 **take on** 承受 **provider** 供應商、公司 **on site** 現場

特定訊息確認問題

158 Why should Ms. Klein e-mail Ms. Clark?
(A) To get a doctor recommendation
(B) To sign up for insurance
(C) To confirm her physical health
(D) To get more course information

中譯 克萊小姐為什麼得寄電子郵件給克拉克小姐？
(A) 詢問有無推薦的醫生
(B) 以便投保保險
(C) 以便確認身體健康狀態
(D) 以便了解更多課程資訊

推理問題

159 What does Mr. Damico suggest about students?
(A) They prefer to use their own equipment.
(B) They will do part of the course from home.
(C) They can participate in the class for free.
(D) They have the option of different start times.

中譯 戴米柯先生暗示學生的什麼習慣？
(A) 他們偏好使用自己的器材。
(B) 他們會在家上部分課程。
(C) 他們可以免費上課。
(D) 他們可選擇不同的上課時間。

句子位置尋找問題

160 In which of the positions marked [1], [2], [3], and [4] does the following sentence best belong?
"We implement sanitization practices between each use."
(A) [1] (B) [2]
(C) [3] (D) [4]

中譯 此句子「每次用畢我們都會進行消毒。」最適合放在 [1]、[2]、[3]、[4] 哪一個位置？
(A) [1] (B) [2]
(C) [3] (D) [4]

Questions 161-163 refer to the following contract. 合約

Contract Agreement

This contract is entered into by Adrienne Sales and Oscar Rascon, a freelance graphic designer, on April 22. **161 Mr. Rascon agrees to create an original logo for Adrienne Sales.** Mr. Rascon will meet with representatives from Adrienne Sales at the company's headquarters to discuss the intended appearance of the logo. **162 Adrienne Sales will reimburse Mr. Rascon for up to £25 in travel-related expenses for the meeting, provided Mr. Rascon presents receipts of the spending.** Mr. Rascon will create and submit three versions of the logo by May 20. **163 Adrienne Sales can ask for up to three additional rounds of revisions to the selected logo. 161 Adrienne Sales agrees to pay Mr. Rascon £750 upon completion of the final image.**

合約同意書

此合約是由艾德里安銷售公司與自由接案的平面設計師奧斯卡・雷斯康，於 4 月 22 日共同簽訂。**161 雷斯康先生同意為艾德里安銷售公司設計原創標誌，並與艾德里安銷售公司的代表人員，在總公司開會討論想要的標誌外觀。162 艾德里安銷售公司將補貼雷斯康先生至多 25 英鎊的開會車馬費，前提是雷斯康先生須出具開銷收據。**雷斯康先生將於 5 月 20 日前設計與提交三種標誌版本。**163 艾德里安銷售公司可針對所選定的標誌，提出至多三次的修改要求。161 而艾德里安銷售公司同意於完成定稿圖像後，向雷斯康先生支付 750 英鎊。**

Agreed by:		立同意書人:	
Oscar Rascon	April 22	奧斯卡・雷斯康	4 月 22 日
Graphic Designer	Date	平面設計師	日期
Elizabeth Norris	April 22	伊莉莎白・諾麗斯	4 月 22 日
Adrienne Sales	Date	艾德里安銷售公司	日期

字彙 agreement 同意書　enter into a contract 簽訂合約　representative 代表人員　headquarters 總公司　intended 想要的　reimburse 補貼　expense 開銷　provided 前提是……　revision 修改

推理問題

161 What does the contract imply about Mr. Rascon?
(A) He will complete a project by April 22.
(B) He used to work with Ms. Norris.
(C) He is a salesperson at Adrienne Sales.
(D) He will be paid to create a design.

中譯 可從合約裡了解雷斯康先生的何項資訊?
(A) 他會在 4 月 22 日完成某專案。
(B) 他曾和諾麗斯小姐共事。
(C) 他是艾德里安銷售公司的業務人員。
(D) 他會因為創作某設計而獲得報酬。

同義詞問題

162 The word "presents" in paragraph 1, line 5, is closest in meaning to
(A) publishes
(B) submits
(C) gifts
(D) displays

中譯 第 1 段第 5 行的「presents」一字,意義最接近以下何者?
(A) 出版
(B) 提交
(C) 禮物
(D) 展示

特定訊息確認問題

163 According to the agreement, what is Mr. Rascon required to do?
(A) Give a presentation
(B) Research some industry trends
(C) Make some requested adjustments
(D) Provide professional references

中譯 根據同意書內容,雷斯康先生需要做什麼事?
(A) 發表簡報
(B) 研究某些產業趨勢
(C) 依據要求進行調整
(D) 提供專業推薦人

Questions 164-167 refer to the following e-mail. 電子郵件

From: Nicola Fallaci
To: All Briarhill Employees
Date: July 2
Subject: For your information

Dear Briarhill Employees,

To keep employees better informed, I'll be sending you regular updates about the company's progress. —[1]—. Compared to this quarter last year, our domestic sales

寄件人: 妮可拉・佛拉奇
收件人: 布萊爾丘全體員工
日期: 7 月 2 日
主旨: 通知大家一下

親愛的布萊爾丘員工:

為了讓員工更清楚知道公司概況,我將定期寄送公司進展的最新資訊。這一季與去年同期相較下,我們的國內業績已增加 15%。雖然我

have increased by 15%. Though it seems that having some of our goods as part of the *Family Fun* TV show set did not make much difference, it still provided some interesting photos for our Web site.

—[2]—. 164 165 **In Indonesia, we experienced an amazing 63% boost in sales following our participation in the Jakarta Housewares Trade Fair.** Sales were steady in Australia, where we saw an increase of just 0.5%. —[3]—. 164 **This was not a surprise, as our new line of cotton curtains has been receiving mixed reviews.** In Sweden and Norway, sales have been sluggish, down 8% and 6%, respectively. This is due to heavy competition from other businesses.

—[4]—. As you can see, there are some regions that need improvement and others that are doing well. 166 **I am sure that the proposal made by Pedro Reid, which targets hotels directly for sales across their entire chain, will yield promising results and grow our sales further.**

Sincerely,

Nicola Fallaci

們在電視節目《趣味家庭》置入部分商品，並沒有產生太大效益，但仍為我們的網站提供了一些有趣的照片。

以下是我們國際業績的概況。164 165 **以印尼來說，在我們參加了雅加達家用品商展後，業績激增了驚人的63%。**澳洲的業績穩定，只有增加0.5%。164 **這樣的情況並不讓人驚訝，因為我們新推出的純棉窗簾系列評價一直褒貶不一。**以瑞典和挪威而言，業績一直遲滯，分別下滑8%和6%。這是因為與其他公司產生激烈競爭的關係。

如大家所見，某些區域需要改進，某些區域則表現良好。166 **我確信佩德羅・瑞德的提案，也就是直接針對整個連鎖飯店業來銷售，將會有不錯的成果，也會帶動我們業績的成長。**

誠摯祝福大家

妮可拉・佛拉奇

字彙 quarter 季　domestic 國內的　boost 激增　houseware 傢飾　steady 穩定的　mixed 摻雜的　sluggish 遲緩的　respectively 分別地　yield 產出　promising 有前景的

推理問題

164 What type of company most likely is Briarhill?

(A) A chain of supermarkets
(B) A home furnishings retailer
(C) A book publisher
(D) An electronics manufacturer

中譯 布萊爾丘最有可能是哪一種公司？

(A) 連鎖超市
(B) 家飾零售商
(C) 書籍出版社
(D) 電子設備製造商

特定訊息確認問題

165 According to Ms. Fallaci, where did people see Briarhill's merchandise in person?

(A) In Australia
(B) In Indonesia
(C) In Norway
(D) In Sweden

中譯 根據佛拉奇小姐的說法，民眾曾在哪裡親眼看過布萊爾丘的商品？

(A) 澳洲
(B) 印尼
(C) 挪威
(D) 瑞典

特定訊息確認問題

166 What does Ms. Fallaci expect will likely lead to increased business?
(A) A customer loyalty program
(B) Association with a TV show
(C) Contracts with hotel chains
(D) Online advertising campaigns

中譯 佛拉奇小姐期待哪件事能增加業績？
(A) 顧客忠誠度計畫
(B) 與電視節目的關聯
(C) 與連鎖飯店簽合約
(D) 網路廣告活動

句子位置尋找問題

167 In which of the positions marked [1], [2], [3], and [4] does the following sentence best belong?
"Here is an overview of our international performance."
(A) [1] **(B) [2]**
(C) [3] (D) [4]

中譯 此句子「以下是我們國際業績的概況」最適合放在 [1]、[2]、[3]、[4] 哪一個位置？
(A) [1] **(B) [2]**
(C) [3] (D) [4]

Questions 168-171 refer to the following article. 文章

BERLIN (171 **September 7**)—The Historical Preservation Foundation (HPF) aims to make historical artifacts available to the public as well as provide support for ongoing research. The HPF plans to work on a collection of objects from a 1940s excavation in Western Asia. 168 170 **Fragments of vases and bowls dating back to the 2nd century were acquired by Aldeen University.** 168 169 **These will be restored at HPF's main facility in Berlin.** "We are honored to have these items under our care," said 169 **director Mathias Vogel.** "Our track record for dealing with fragile artifacts is unmatched, and we have the resources to give them the attention they deserve."

HPF's staff members are proficient in working with metal objects such as tools, weapons, and jewelry, but they are somewhat new to working with clay items, especially molded ones. "We are forming a partnership with Aldeen University to ensure the work is carried out properly," Vogel said. 170 **"We're excited that Jamila Ahmed will travel to our site in Berlin to oversee operations. This project lines up perfectly with her specialized knowledge and extensive experience."**

The artifacts are currently housed at Aldeen University. 171 **The university's team is starting to examine them to prepare them to be shipped to Berlin, which they are expecting to do on October 2.** A date for a public display of the items has not yet been determined.

柏林訊（171 **9 月 7 日**）—歷史文物保存基金會（HPF）的目標，在於讓大眾得以一睹歷史文物的風采，同時提供持續研究的支援。HPF 預計處理一系列 1940 年代從西亞挖掘出來的物品。168 170 **而艾爾丁大學已取得可追溯至西元二世紀的花瓶與碗缽碎片。** 168 169 **這些文物將於 HPF 位於柏林的主要機構進行修復。** 169 **馬提亞斯・沃格爾主任**表示：「我們很榮幸能照護這些物品。我們過去處理脆弱文物的紀錄無人能比，我們亦擁有可妥善照顧這些文物的資源。」

雖然 HPF 的職員均熟稔處理工具、武器和珠寶等金屬物品，但是比較不知道如何處理陶器，尤其是翻模物品。沃格爾表示：「我們與艾爾丁大學合作，以確保妥善執行修復工作。170 **我們很興奮賈米拉・阿曼德將前往我們柏林的據點來監督工作流程。此專案完全契合她的專業知識和豐富經驗。**」

文物目前置放於艾爾丁大學。171 **該大學團隊已開始檢查文物，並準備運往柏林，預計 10 月 2 日送出。**目前尚未決定文物公開展示的日期。

字彙 excavation 挖掘　fragment 碎片　acquire 取得　restore 修復　unmatched 無人能比的　resource 資源　proficient 有能力的　oversee 監督　line up 契合　specialized 專業的　extensive 廣泛的

主題問題

168 What is the main topic of the article?
(A) The grand opening of a museum
(B) A fundraiser for an excavation
(C) The new discovery of some artifacts
(D) A pottery restoration project

中譯 此文章的主題是什麼？
(A) 博物館盛大開幕
(B) 針對文物挖掘的募資活動
(C) 新發現的文物
(D) 陶器修復專案

特定訊息確認問題

169 What position does Mr. Vogel have?
(A) Maintenance manager
(B) Assistant researcher
(C) Head of Aldeen University
(D) HPF director

中譯 沃格爾先生是什麼職位？
(A) 養護部經理
(B) 助理研究員
(C) 艾爾丁大學校長
(D) HPF 主任

推理問題

170 What is most likely true about Ms. Ahmed?
(A) She is an expert in pottery.
(B) She graduated from Aldeen University.
(C) She grew up in Berlin.
(D) She plans to publish a book.

中譯 哪一項描述符合阿曼德小姐？
(A) 她是陶器專家。
(B) 她從艾爾丁大學畢業。
(C) 她在柏林長大。
(D) 她打算出版一本書。

推理問題

171 What is implied about the artifacts?
(A) They have been donated by private collectors.
(B) They will be examined for several weeks before transportation.
(C) They will go on display from October 2.
(D) They sustained some damage while being shipped.

中譯 可從文中得知文物的何項資訊？
(A) 是由私人收藏家所捐贈。
(B) 將於運送前進行數週檢查。
(C) 將於 10 月 2 日展出。
(D) 在運送途中部分受損。

Questions 172-175 refer to the following online chat discussion. 網路聊天

Yuhan Gao [9:18 A.M.]
Hi, everyone. Since I canceled yesterday's team meeting, ⓱⓷ **I wanted to check in with how things are going.** Lisa, how is your trade show research coming along?

Lisa Timko [9:19 A.M.]
Even better than I expected! ⓱⓶ **I have found one in August, the National Beauty Expo, that I think would be perfect for promoting our natural skincare products.** The registration fee is only $1,500.

高雨涵 [早上 9:18]
嗨，大家好。既然我取消了昨天的小組會議，⓱⓷ **我想了解一下進度。**麗莎，你的商展研究任務進展得怎麼樣？

麗莎・提姆科 [早上 9:19]
比我想的還要好！⓱⓶ **我找到在八月舉辦的一個「全國美容博覽會」，我覺得很適合推廣我們的天然護膚產品。**報名費只要 1500 美元。

Yuhan Gao [9:21 A.M.]
Wonderful! Please go forward with that.

George Lainez [9:22 A.M.]
That's great! High-profile events are just what we need.

Ron Fulkerson [9:23 A.M.]
Good job, Lisa! ⑮ **If you send me the details, I can register our company for the event by the end of the day.**

Lisa Timko [9:24 A.M.]
⑭ **I guess we'll be busy preparing for this along with our extensive television campaign on the Mayfair Network.**

Yuhan Gao [9:25 A.M.]
Unfortunately, that fell through. ⑭ **We can't afford the prices the station was charging,** ⑫ **so we're going to have to promote the new line of lotions in another way.**

Lisa Timko [9:27 A.M.]
I see. ⑮ **And I appreciate your dealing with this so quickly, Ron.**

Ron Fulkerson [9:28 A.M.]
It's nothing.

Yuhan Gao [9:29 A.M.]
⑬ **Keep up the good work, everyone!**

高雨涵 [早上 9:21]
太好了！請繼續推進這個部分。

喬治・賴內茲 [早上 9:22]
太好了！我們需要的就是能見度高的活動。

朗・福克森 [早上 9:23]
做得好，麗莎！⑮ **如果你傳詳細資料給我，我下班前就可以幫我們公司報名參加這個活動。**

麗莎・提姆科 [早上 9:24]
⑭ **我想我們會忙著準備這件事，還有在梅菲爾電視網大量打電視廣告的部分。**

高雨涵 [早上 9:25]
可惜的是，這件事泡湯了。⑭ **我們負擔不起電視台的收費，** ⑫ **因此我們必須另外想方法來推廣新的乳液系列。**

麗莎・提姆科 [早上 9:27]
原來如此。⑮ **還有朗，我很感激你這麼快就接手處理。**

朗・福克森 [早上 9:28]
小事情。

高雨涵 [早上 9:29]
⑬ **大家做得很好，繼續保持！**

字彙 check in with 了解一下　come along 進展　promote 推廣　registration 登記
high-profile 曝光度高的　register for 報名某活動　along with 一邊進行某事　extensive 廣泛的
fall through 泡湯了　Keep up the good work. 繼續良好的表現。

推理問題

172 In what industry do the writers most likely work?
(A) Travel　(B) Technology
(C) Clothing　**(D) Cosmetics**

中譯 傳訊息者最有可能在哪種產業工作？
(A) 旅遊業　(B) 科技業
(C) 服飾業　**(D) 美妝業**

推理問題

173 What most likely is Ms. Gao's occupation?
(A) Security advisor
(B) Human resources director
(C) Marketing manager
(D) Research assistant

中譯 高小姐最有可能從事什麼職業？
(A) 保全顧問　(B) 人資部總監
(C) 行銷部經理　(D) 研究助理

Not / True 問題

174 What is true about the Mayfair Network?
(A) It is hosting an annual event.
(B) It will form a partnership with the writers' company.
(C) Its employees have a lot of experience.
(D) Its fees are too high for the writers' company.

中譯 關於梅菲爾電視網的說明，何者為真？
(A) 電視台要舉辦年度活動。
(B) 將與傳訊息者的公司建立合作關係。
(C) 旗下員工經驗豐富。
(D) 對傳訊息者的公司來說，費用過高。

掌握意圖問題

175 At 9:28 A.M., what does Mr. Fulkerson mean when he writes, "It's nothing"?

(A) He is pleased that Ms. Timko will resolve a problem.

(B) He is willing to complete a registration process quickly.

(C) He is surprised about the lack of information available.

(D) He is happy to have found an event for the team.

中譯 早上9點28分的時候，福克森先生的訊息「小事情」是什麼意思？

(A) 他對於提姆科小姐解決某問題感到開心。

(B) 他願意快速完成報名程序。

(C) 他對於沒有可用資訊感到驚訝。

(D) 他很開心為團隊找到某活動。

Questions 176-180 refer to the following advertisement and e-mail. 廣告與電子郵件

Make your event magical and memorable with Edsel Gardens!

Edsel Gardens, located near Stockton and comprising 4 acres of botanical gardens, features a truly unique and romantic location. You'll love the peaceful backdrop, gorgeous views, and modern amenities offered at our site. We specialize in weddings and anniversary parties and 176B **have recently doubled the size of our parking lot to accommodate larger groups.** 176D **You can hold your event completely outdoors or use our giant tent, which protects against rain and can be heated in cold weather.** Our tent seats up to 180 guests, and we have a Food and Liquor License that permits us to 177 **serve food and/or drinks from 11 A.M. to midnight on weekdays and 10 A.M. to 1 A.M. on weekends.**

Our team will work with you to make sure everything is exactly what you want. 179-1 **With our Premium Package, you can use our in-house photographer and caterer to make planning easy.** If you want live music, 176C **we can provide a recommendation for bands or singers.**

Call us today at 555-8790 to get started. 178 **And if you're not sure what kind of theme you'd like for your event, get inspired by visiting our photo gallery at www.edselgardens.com.** We look forward to hosting your event!

「艾德塞爾花園」能讓您的活動既夢幻又令人印象深刻！

位於史塔克頓附近的「艾德塞爾花園」，擁有四英畝的植物園，堪稱獨特又浪漫的景點。您一定會愛上寧靜如畫般的優美景緻，以及本場所現代化的設施。我們專門為婚禮與周年慶典派對提供服務，176B **近期更將停車場拓寬兩倍以便容納規模更大的團體。** 176D **您可舉辦完全位於戶外的活動，或使用可避雨、天氣寒冷時可供應暖氣的巨大帳篷。**我們的帳篷可容納至多180名賓客，我們亦持有餐飲酒水執照。177 **平日可從早上11點至午夜、週末可從早上10點至凌晨1點供應食物及飲品。**

我們的團隊會與您合作，確保完全符合您的需求。179-1 **我們的「頂級方案」能提供您我們駐點的攝影師和外燴人員，讓您易於規劃活動。**如果您想要現場演奏音樂，176C **我們可推薦樂團或歌手。**

請馬上撥打555-8790與我們聯絡。178 **如果您不確定您的活動應選用何種主題，請至www.edselgardens.com網站參考我們的相片集來獲得靈感。**我們期待為您籌辦活動！

字彙 memorable 令人難忘的　comprise 構成　botanical garden 植物園　gorgeous 絕美的　amenity 設施　specialize in 專精於　accommodate 容納　in-house 駐點的　caterer 外燴人員

To: Edsel Gardens <info@edselgardens.com>
From: Ramona Murphy <rmurphy@haven-mail.com>
Date: April 11
Subject: Thank you!

To Whom It May Concern:

I recently held an anniversary party for my parents at your site, and I wanted to thank you for a great experience. 179-2 **I got the Premium Package, which was convenient and affordably priced. I was really impressed with the photos taken by Fred Warren, the professional photographer.** I also got a lot of compliments on the band I hired. The beautiful venue was a perfect 180 **fit** for my parents' style. I plan to highly recommend Edsel Gardens to all my friends and family who are looking for a place to hold an event.

Warmest regards,

Ramona Murphy

收件人： 艾德塞爾花園 <info@edselgardens.com>
寄件人： 雷夢娜・墨菲 <rmurphy@haven-mail.com>
日期： 4月11日
主旨： 謝謝你們！

敬啟者：

我最近在你們場地幫我爸媽舉辦結婚週年派對，我想感謝你們帶給我們很棒的體驗。179-2 **我選購的是「頂級方案」，服務方便且平價。專業攝影師佛瑞德・華倫拍的照片著實讓我印象深刻。**大家也對我僱用的樂團讚不絕口。漂亮的場地非常 180 **適合**我爸媽的風格。我打算向想要找場地舉辦活動的所有親友大力推薦「艾德塞爾花園」。

敬祝一切順心
雷夢娜・墨菲

字彙 affordably priced 平價　be impressed with 對……印象深刻　compliment 讚賞　venue 場地

Not / True 問題

176 What is NOT true about Edsel Gardens?
(A) It is now operating under new ownership.
(B) It recently expanded its parking area.
(C) It can provide recommendations for musicians.
(D) It can accommodate different types of weather.

中譯 關於艾德塞爾花園的描述，以下何者為非？
(A) 目前是由新的負責人營運。
(B) 近期拓展了停車場。
(C) 可推薦音樂表演人士。
(D) 可因應不同氣候。

特定訊息確認問題

177 When can food be served at Edsel Gardens?
(A) Monday at 10 A.M.
(B) Wednesday at 1 A.M.
(C) Saturday at 11 A.M.
(D) Sunday 9 A.M.

中譯 艾德塞爾花園何時可供餐？
(A) 星期一早上10點
(B) 星期三凌晨1點
(C) 星期六早上11點
(D) 星期天早上9點

特定訊息確認問題

178 Why does the advertisement recommend visiting a Web site?
(A) To view a price list
(B) To read customer comments
(C) To get some inspiration
(D) To make a reservation

中譯 廣告為何推薦大家造訪網站？
(A) 可查看價目表
(B) 可閱覽顧客評價
(C) 可獲得一些靈感
(D) 可預訂

兩則引文連結問題＿推理問題

179 What is suggested about Fred Warren?
(A) He only took photos inside a tent.
(B) He had excellent reviews on a Web site.
(C) He is a friend of Ms. Murphy's parents.
(D) He is employed directly by Edsel Gardens.

中譯 文中提到佛瑞德・華倫的何項資訊？
(A) 他只在帳篷裡拍照片。
(B) 他在某網站上的評價非常好。
(C) 他是墨菲小姐爸媽的朋友。
(D) 他直接受僱於艾德塞爾花園。

同義詞問題

180 In the e-mail, the word "fit" in paragraph 1, line 4, is closest in meaning to
(A) position
(B) match
(C) development
(D) adaptation

中譯 電子郵件第 1 段第 4 行的「fit」一字，意思最接近以下何者？
(A) 位置
(B) 相配的事物
(C) 發展
(D) 調適

Questions 181-185 refer to the following letter and e-mail. 信函與電子郵件

Wanda Milburn
Corbitt Enterprises
4443 Rardin Road
Nashville, TN 37210
January 5

Dear Ms. Milburn,

We are writing to inform you of an increase in the fees for the cleaning services we perform for Corbitt Enterprises at the above address. 181 **The current fees you pay will be valid until March 4.** 184-1 **As you were one of our customers in the very first month we opened, we have kept the fees at a lower rate for as long as possible.**

182-1 **We are implementing this change to ensure that our workers are compensated fairly, as they always perform a complete and careful cleaning service. This is rare in our industry.** Enclosed you will find a breakdown of the new fees.

181 **The change will go into effect on March 5.** 185-1 **If you wish to terminate the contract, please inform us of your desired final day of service.** We hope to continue serving you for many years to come.

Sincerely,

Grant Berg
Grant Berg
Manager, Shinetime Commercial Cleaning

汪達・米爾本 啟
柯比特企業
37210 田納西州納什維爾市
拉爾丁路 4443 號
1 月 5 日

親愛的米爾本小姐：

我們來函通知您，我們為上述地址的柯比特企業所進行的清潔服務，將調漲費用。181 **您目前支付的費用效期至 3 月 4 日。** 184-1 **由於您是本公司開幕第一個月就合作的顧客之一，我們已經盡可能的延長原費用使用期限。**

182-1 **有此異動的原因在於確保清掃人員能獲取合理的薪酬，因為他們一直都從事著徹底且謹慎的清掃服務。這樣的服務態度在業界實為罕見。**我們亦隨函附上新費用的明細表。

181 **此異動將於 3 月 5 日生效。** 185-1 **如果您想終止合約，請通知我們您希望服務的最後日期。**我們希望未來能持續為您服務。

誠摯敬祝一切順心

亮潔商業清潔公司 經理
葛蘭特・伯格

字彙 valid 有效的　rate 費率　implement 施行　ensure that 確保　compensate 薪資報酬　rare 罕見的　enclosed 隨函附上　breakdown 明細表　terminate 終止

To: Grant Berg <grant@shinetimecommcleaning.com>
From: Wanda Milburn <w.milburn@corbittenterprises.com>
Date: January 11
Subject: Cleaning contract

Dear Mr. Berg,

Thanks for informing me about the upcoming changes. We've been satisfied with the level of care provided. 182-2 **I know many business owners have had trouble hiring reliable cleaners, so I feel very lucky.** 184-2 **I can't believe it has already been four years since you started working for us.** 183 **Everyone who has visited us to receive financial advice** has been impressed by our office, and your company has played an important role in creating that positive first impression.

In spite of your excellence, we will soon no longer need your services, and 185-2 **we would like the last cleaning day to be February 28.** We are moving to a new office building at 579 Ohio Avenue, and the building's maintenance team provides cleaning as part of the monthly fee. I'd be happy to recommend your business to others if the situation arises.

All the best,
Wanda Milburn

收件人：葛蘭特・伯格 <grant@shinetimecommcleaning.com>
寄件人：汪達・米爾本 <w.milburn@corbittenterprises.com>
日期：1 月 11 日
主旨：清潔合約

親愛的伯格先生：

感謝您通知我即將生效的異動。我們一直對於貴公司的細心服務感到滿意。182-2 **我知道許多公司老闆很難僱用到可靠的清潔人員，因此我覺得自己非常幸運。** 184-2 **我不敢相信貴公司為我們提供服務至今已四年。** 183 **到我們公司諮詢財務建議的每個人，**都對我們公司印象深刻，有了你們協助，才有門面良好的第一印象。

儘管貴公司表現卓越，我們很快不再需要您的服務，185-2 **我們希望最後一天的清潔日期是 2 月 28 日。**因為我們即將搬遷至俄亥俄大道 579 號的新辦公大樓，而月費已經包含大樓養護團隊所提供的清潔服務。如果有人需要，我會很樂意推薦貴公司。

祝福一切安好
汪達・米爾本

字彙 reliable 可靠的　financial 財務的　impressed 印象深刻的　impression 印象　excellence 卓越　maintenance 養護　arise （有某情況）出現

特定訊息確認問題

181 According to the letter, when will fees for a service increase?
(A) January 5
(B) January 31
(C) March 4
(D) March 5

中譯 根據信函內容，服務費用何時會調漲？
(A) 1 月 5 日
(B) 1 月 31 日
(C) 3 月 4 日
(D) 3 月 5 日

兩則引文連結問題__特定訊息確認問題

182 On what point do Mr. Berg and Ms. Milburn agree?
(A) That cleaning should be done regularly
(B) That good cleaners are hard to find
(C) That regulations are becoming tighter
(D) That the cost of cleaning services has risen

中譯 伯格先生和米爾本小姐都同意哪一件事？
(A) 應定期進行打掃
(B) 好的清潔人員很難找
(C) 法規變得更嚴格
(D) 清潔費用已提高

推理問題

183 What type of business does Ms. Milburn most likely work for?
(A) A graphic design firm
(B) A software development company
(C) A commercial construction company
(D) A financial consulting firm

中譯 米爾本小姐最有可能在何種公司工作？
(A) 平面設計公司
(B) 軟體開發公司
(C) 商業建設公司
(D) 財務諮詢公司

兩則引文連結問題__Not / True問題

184 What is suggested about Shinetime Commercial Cleaning?
(A) It has been in operation for four years.
(B) It will relocate its head office in March.
(C) It has recently been sold to a competitor.
(D) It plans to recruit more employees.

中譯 可從文中得知亮潔商業清潔公司的何項資訊？
(A) 已經營業四年。
(B) 總公司將於三月搬遷。
(C) 近期剛賣給競爭對手。
(D) 預計招募更多員工。

兩則引文連結問題__特定訊息確認問題

185 How does Ms. Milburn provide what Mr. Berg has requested?
(A) By giving feedback about a service
(B) By agreeing to some new contract terms
(C) By confirming the desired termination date
(D) By reporting a new business address

中譯 米爾本小姐如何提供伯格先生要求的資訊？
(A) 針對某服務提出意見反饋
(B) 同意新合約的條款
(C) 確認想要終止服務的日期
(D) 回報新的公司地址

Questions 186-190 refer to the following article and forms. 文章與表單

Oakdale (April 9)—Preparations are underway for Oakdale's 8th Annual Health and Well-Being Expo, which will take place on Sunday, June 19. The expo will feature businesses offering a variety of health-related goods and services. Additionally, local physicians and nurses will provide free screenings for blood pressure and cholesterol levels as well as a basic eye exam.

奧克代爾訊（4 月 9 日）——奧克代爾第八屆年度身心健康博覽會已在籌備中，時間為 6 月 19 日星期天。博覽會將網羅各種提供健康相關商品與服務的公司。此外，當地醫師與護理人員將提供免費的血壓和膽固醇檢查服務，以及基本的視力檢查。

After many years at Juniper Hall, the expo has been moved to the Bayridge Convention Center this year. 186 **"Due to the growing popularity of the event, Juniper Hall could no longer contain the number of vendors interested in participating in the expo,"** said Ken Exley, one of the event planners. "Visitors can easily find what they're looking for, 189-1 **with vendors of vitamins and health supplements in the main hall,** massage therapists and spa representatives in the east wing, and gym representatives and sports-related businesses in the west wing."

To register, visit www.oakdalehealthexpo.com. 187-1 **Members of the Oakdale Business Association can get a twenty percent discount.**

在杜松廳舉辦多年之後，此博覽會今年移師到灣脊區會議中心。身為策展人員之一的肯・艾克力表示：「186 **由於此活動愈來愈受歡迎，杜松廳已無法容納有意參展的廠商。**觀展民眾可輕易找到自己想要的產品服務。189-1 **主展場有維他命和保健食品廠商，**東側有按摩療法與 SPA 業者代表人員駐點，西側則有健身房代表人員和運動相關的廠商。」

如欲報名，請至 www.oakdalehealthexpo.com。187-1 **奧克代爾商會會員則可獲得八折優惠。**

字彙 underway 進行中的　expo 博覽會　screening 篩檢　vendor 廠商　supplement 保健補充品　therapist 治療師　representative 代表人員　wing 側廳

Annual Health and Well-Being Expo
Vendor Feedback Survey

Name: Anna Pierson
Business/Company: Sunrise Spa

187-2 **I was informed about the event through my membership in the Oakdale Business Association.** This was my first time participating as a vendor, and I reached more people than I expected. 188 **However, I would have liked a larger booth to provide massages on-site, and I spoke to some other vendors that needed a smaller one. Not everyone has the same needs, so it would be a good idea to address this in the future.**

年度身心健康博覽會
廠商意見反饋問卷調查

姓名：安娜・皮爾森
事業／公司：日出 SPA

187-2 **我因為加入奧克代爾商會而得知此活動。**這是我第一次以廠商身分參展，我接觸到的人比我預期的還多。188 **不過，我希望現場能有更大的攤位來提供按摩服務會更好，但有些和我交談的廠商則需要小一點的攤位。由於每個人的需求不同，所以我想提出來讓貴單位參考將來的處理方式也好。**

字彙 association 協會　on-site 現場的；在現場　address 處理

http://www.rtgoakdale.com/reviews

Please let us know about your experience.

Reviewed by (optional):
Sheryl Baum

How did you first find out about RTG Oakdale?
By visiting the Oakdale Health and Well-Being Expo

How satisfied were you with your experience (0=Very Dissatisfied, 5=Very Satisfied)?

5

http://www.rtgoakdale.com/reviews

請告訴我們您的參展體驗。

評價人（可選填）：
雪若・波姆

您如何得知 RTG 奧克代爾？
參加奧克代爾身心健康博覽會

您參觀博覽會的滿意度為何？
（0= 非常不滿，5= 非常滿意）

5

Comments:
I have recently become more interested in the vegetarian lifestyle due to its beneficial effects on the environment. 190 **I decided to transition to a completely vegetarian diet very soon** but was concerned about getting enough protein, iron, and anything else that may be lacking. However, I wasn't sure what kind of vitamin supplements I would need. 189-2 **After speaking to Anthony Cress at his business's booth, I felt like I was fully informed. Mr. Cress was knowledgeable and made great recommendations for my specific circumstances.** Overall, it was a very positive experience for me.

評語：
我最近開始對吃素感興趣，因為素食生活習慣對環境有益。190 **我決定盡快轉換為全素的飲食習慣**，但會擔心要如何攝取吃素而可能缺乏的足夠蛋白質、鐵質等營養素。然而，我不太確定自己需要哪種維他命補充品。189-2 **我在安東尼・克瑞斯的公司攤位洽談後，我覺得獲益良多。克瑞斯先生擁有豐富知識，並能針對我的個別情況給予很棒的建議。**整體而言，我覺得是很正向的體驗。

字彙 beneficial 有益的　transition 轉換　knowledgeable 知識豐富的　circumstance 情況　overall 整體而言

特定訊息確認問題

186 According to the article, why did the event planners use a different site this year?
(A) To ensure more space
(B) To minimize traffic problems
(C) To promote a new building
(D) To reduce travel times

中譯 根據文章內容，策展人員今年為何選擇不同場地？
(A) 確保有更多空間
(B) 將交通問題降至最低
(C) 為了推廣新大樓
(D) 以便縮短車程

三則引文連結問題＿特定訊息確認問題

187 What is suggested about Ms. Pierson?
(A) She qualified for early registration.
(B) She recently started her business.
(C) She has participated in past events.
(D) She was eligible for a discount.

中譯 可從文中得知皮爾森小姐的何項資訊？
(A) 她符合優先報名的資格。
(B) 她最近剛創業。
(C) 她過去參加過此活動。
(D) 她享有打折的資格。

特定訊息確認問題

188 What does Ms. Pierson recommend for the next expo?
(A) Addressing some noise complaints
(B) Providing more power outlets
(C) Offering booths in various sizes
(D) Advertising the event to more people

中譯 皮爾森小姐針對下次博覽會提出何種建議？
(A) 處理對噪音的投訴
(B) 提供更多插座
(C) 提供各種大小的攤位
(D) 向更多人打廣告宣傳此活動

三則引文連結問題＿推理問題

189 What is implied about Mr. Cress?
(A) He has lived in Oakdale for a long time.
(B) He worked at a booth in the main hall.
(C) He was an event planner for the expo.
(D) He is considering hiring Ms. Baum.

中譯 可從文中得知克瑞斯先生的何項資訊？
(A) 他已經住在奧克代爾很久。
(B) 他的攤位在主展場。
(C) 他是此博覽會的策展人。
(D) 他在考慮僱用波姆小姐。

特定訊息確認問題

190 What does Ms. Baum plan to do?
(A) Undertake further research on a topic
(B) Write another online review
(C) Change her daily eating habits
(D) Start a health-related business

中譯 波姆小姐打算做什麼？
(A) 進一步研究某主題
(B) 寫下另一則網路評價
(C) 改變她的日常飲食習慣
(D) 創立健康相關的公司

Questions 191-195 refer to the following e-mail, article, and Web page. 電子郵件、文章和網頁

To: Armina Giordano <a.giordano@conway-co.com>
From: Rashid Fadel <r.fadel@conway-co.com>
Date: August 21
Subject: Submission

Dear Ms. Giordano,

We appreciate your participation in the Conway Future Growth Initiative here at Conway Co. 191 **This is the first time we have requested suggestions for expanding the business, and we were pleased to see so many ideas shared by staff throughout the entire company.** 192 **Your submission regarding opening a small-scale version of our usual store in the Brighton Shopping Complex is intriguing.** The committee members loved the idea of exposing customers to our most popular items, but we feel like we don't have the big picture. For example, we're wondering what kind of foot traffic could be expected at that site. I understand that the monthly lease fee is quite high, so we would have to make sure it's worth it. In addition, what other businesses are in operation there or plan to do business there? 193-1 **I know that Arcadia has advertised a grand opening at the Brighton Shopping Complex for October. This may be a major issue, as it is our main competitor and carries a very similar inventory to ours.** 192 **We would like to explore this matter further before making a final decision.**

Warmest regards,

Rashid Fadel
Committee Head, Conway Future Growth Initiative

收件人： 亞米娜・佐丹奴 <a.giordano@conway-co.com>
寄件人： 雷希德・費德爾 <r.fadel@conway-co.com>
日期： 8月21日
主旨： 提交的建議

親愛的佐丹奴小姐：

我們很感謝您參加康威公司的「康威未來成長計畫」。191 **這是我們首次請大家針對業務拓展一事提出建議，很開心看到全體職員所分享的眾多構想。** 192 **你所提交的建議很有吸引力，你提到在布萊敦複合購物中心設立一間規模比較小的門市。**委員會成員很喜歡這個點子，讓顧客能接觸我們熱賣品項，但我們覺得不太能掌握整體情況。例如不確定那個地點會有多少客流量。我理解那裡的每月租金相當高，因此我們得確保這麼做是值得的。此外，有哪些店家已經在那裡駐點或打算在那裡營業？193-1 **我知道阿卡迪亞已經打廣告宣傳，十月會在布萊敦複合購物中心盛大開幕。這可能會是個大問題，因為他們是我們的主要競爭對手，商品存貨和我們非常相似。** 192 **在做最後決定之前，我們想再多進一步研究。**

祝一切順心

雷希德・費德爾
康威未來成長計畫 委員會主委

字彙 **submission** 提交的資料 **initiative** 計畫 **expand** 拓展 **complex** 綜合大樓 **intriguing** 有趣的 **committee** 委員會 **expose** 使接觸到 **big picture** 整體情況 **foot traffic** 客流量 **lease fee** 租金 **in operation** 營業中 **carry** 出售 **inventory** 存貨

LONGVIEW (October 3)— 193-2 **Later this month, Arcadia, the maker of high-end athletic shoes for basketball, running, and more, will hold a grand opening at its newest branch at the Brighton Shopping Complex.** Customers who attend the event will have the opportunity to enter a prize drawing for $5,000 in Arcadia merchandise.

194-1 **The store will be located next to Golden Apparel** and is expected to become one of the company's highest-earning branches. 195 **With famous athletes such as basketball player Scott Atkinson and marathon runner Caroline Holmes wearing its products, it is no surprise that Arcadia has grown in popularity over the past few years.**

長景市訊(10 月 3 日)—— 193-2 **專門製造高級籃球鞋、慢跑鞋等運動鞋款的阿卡迪亞，將於本月底在布萊敦複合購物中心的最新分店舉辦盛大開幕活動。**參加活動的顧客，將有機會抽中價值 5000 美元的阿卡迪亞商品。

194-1 **門市將位於黃金服飾店隔壁，**預計此據點將成為該公司營業額最高的分店之一。195 **在籃球員史考特・艾金森與馬拉松跑者凱洛琳・荷姆斯等知名運動員均穿著其產品的情況下，難怪阿卡迪亞在過去幾年的知名度大增。**

字彙 **high-end** 高級的　**athletic** 運動的　**drawing** 抽獎　**merchandise** 商品　**earn** 賺取(金錢)　**popularity** 知名度

http://www.brightonsc.com/floorplan

HOME	DIRECTORY	FLOOR PLAN	CONTACT

Site Map of Brighton Shopping Complex

Unit 101 (Vacant)	Officeland	Home Designs	Unit 107 (Vacant)
Superb Gifts	Unit 104 (Vacant)	194-2 **Unit 106 (Vacant)**	**Golden Apparel**

Food Court

http://www.brightonsc.com/floorplan

首頁	樓層導覽	平面圖	聯絡窗口

布萊敦複合購物中心地圖

櫃位 101 (待出租)	辦公園地	傢飾設計	櫃位 107 (待出租)
絕讚禮品店	櫃位 104 (待出租)	194-2 **櫃位 106 (待出租)**	**黃金服飾店**

美食街

推理問題

191 What is suggested about the Conway Future Growth Initiative?

(A) It targets new staff members.

(B) It will last for one month.

(C) It was suggested by Mr. Fadel.

(D) It was open to all employees.

中譯 可從文中得知「康威未來成長計畫」的何項資訊？

(A) 以新職員為目標。

(B) 會持續一個月。

(C) 由費德爾先生所提議。

(D) 開放給所有員工參加。

目的問題

192 Why did Mr. Fadel send the e-mail?
(A) To suggest merging with a competitor
(B) To request further information about a proposal
(C) To explain the rules of a company program
(D) To recommend improvements to a department's operations

中譯 費德爾先生為什麼要寄送此電子郵件？
(A) 提議與競爭對手合併
(B) 要求某提案能提供更多資訊
(C) 說明某公司計畫的規則
(D) 建議某部門營運有所改進

三則引文連結問題＿特定訊息確認問題

193 In what industry does Conway Co. work?
(A) Footwear manufacturing
(B) Property development
(C) Job recruitment
(D) Media services

中譯 康威公司經營何種產業？
(A) 製鞋業
(B) 房地產開發業
(C) 人力銀行業
(D) 媒體服務業

三則引文連結問題＿特定訊息確認問題

194 In what unit of the Brighton Shopping Complex will Arcadia be located?
(A) Unit 101 (B) Unit 104
(C) Unit 106 (D) Unit 107

中譯 阿卡迪亞在布萊敦複合購物中心的櫃位會在哪裡？
(A) 櫃位 101 (B) 櫃位 104
(C) 櫃位 106 (D) 櫃位 107

特定訊息確認問題

195 What aspect of Arcadia's products is emphasized in the article?
(A) Its wide range of options
(B) Its affordable price
(C) Its use by celebrities
(D) Its environmentally friendly design

中譯 此文章強調了阿卡迪亞產品的哪個面向？
(A) 廣泛的產品選擇
(B) 平價
(C) 名人愛用
(D) 對環境友善的設計

Questions 196-200 refer to the following article and e-mails. 文章和電子郵件

FOR IMMEDIATE RELEASE

TORONTO (15 March)—A spokesperson for Millerbrook Enterprises has announced that Salvador Tolentino has been promoted to CEO to replace the outgoing CEO, Mary Gilhurst. 196 **He was unanimously selected by the Millerbrook Enterprises board** and will take on his new role from May 25 after training with Ms. Gilhurst.

Millerbrook Enterprises provides cutting-edge software for artificial intelligence. Its products and research have led the industry for the past decade, and it has plans to

立即發布

多倫多訊（3 月 15 日）——米勒布魯克企業的發言人宣布，塞爾瓦多．托倫提諾已升遷為執行長，來接替即將離職的執行長瑪莉．吉爾赫斯特。196 **他獲得米勒布魯克企業董事會全體支持**，並將於接受吉爾赫斯特小姐訓練後，在 5 月 25 日接任新職務。

米勒布魯克企業提供先進的人工智慧軟體。其產品和研究已於過去十年引領業界，並預計於未來幾年開拓若干國際分公司。197-1 **由於托倫提諾先生曾任該公司的財務長，因此該公**

open several international branches in the next few years. 197-1 **As Mr. Tolentino was formerly working as the company's CFO, the company is seeking to fill this position quickly. Duties include analyzing financial data and monitoring company expenditures. The role requires the ability to clearly communicate to the board and investors in both written and spoken form.** Further details about the position and the hiring process are posted on www.millerbrook.com.

司須迅速找人遞補此職位。職務包括分析財務數據與監督公司開銷。此職位還需具備能與董事會和投資人以書面或口頭方式清楚溝通的能力。關於此職位的進一步詳情以及招聘程序，均張貼於 www.millerbrook.com。

字彙 immediate 立即的　release 發布　spokesperson 發言人　outgoing 即將離職的　unanimously 全體一致地　board 董事會　take on 接下　cutting-edge 先進的　artificial intelligence 人工智慧　CFO 財務長　monitor 監督　expenditure 開銷

To: Millerbrook Enterprises Board
From: Walter Vinson
Date: April 4
Subject: CFO Candidate

Dear Fellow Board Members,

I would like to put forth Brianna Chomley as a candidate for the open CFO position. She was a university classmate of mine at Ralston University, and 197-2 **she meets all of the required qualifications for the position.** I've spoken to her about applying for the position. However, 198 **she is not sure whether it would be right for her. This is because the job description on our Web site only lists the salary and does not include information about the quarterly bonuses, stock options, and housing allowance that we offer.** I think we should update this because other candidates probably have the same misconception.

200-1 **Sincerely,**

Walter Vinson,
Vice Chair, Millerbrook Board of Directors

收件人： 米勒布魯克企業董事會
寄件人： 華特・文森
日期： 4月4日
主旨： 財務長人選

親愛的董事會同仁：

我想推薦布里安娜・喬姆利做為空缺的財務長人選。她是我在雷爾斯頓大學的同學，197-2 **她符合此職位的所有必要資格。**我已經跟她談過應徵此職位的事。不過，198 **她不太確定適不適合她。因為我們網站上的徵才說明只有列出薪資，沒有包含我們提供的每季獎金、員工認股權與住房津貼。**我想我們應該更新這些資訊，因為其他應徵者可能也會有相同的誤解。

200-1 **敬祝一切順心**

華特・文森
米勒布魯克董事會 副董事長

字彙 put forth 推薦　candidate 應徵者、人選　meet 符合　qualification 資格　job description 徵才說明　quarterly 每季的　housing allowance 住房津貼　misconception 誤解

To: Walter Vinson
From: Erin Solberg
Date: April 4
Subject: Updated job description

Hi Walter,

Thank you for your advice on the job description for the CFO position. I've added the information you suggested. 199 **As we voted in the last meeting to add another member to our board, we need to start the search for that person as well.** According to the bylaws, 200-2 **the selection process should be carried out by a committee of three people and must be headed by a high-ranking officer on the board—that is, the chair or vice chair. Please let me know what you think.**

Sincerely,

Erin Solberg
Secretary, Millerbrook Board of Directors.

收件人:華特・文森
寄件人:艾琳・索伯格
日期:4月4日
主旨:更新過的徵才說明

嗨,華特,

謝謝您對財務長職位徵才說明提出建議。我已經新增您建議的資訊。199 **由於我們上次開會表決要新增一位董事會成員,我們亦需要開始找尋人選。**根據公司制度,200-2 **應由三位委員會成員執行遴選程序,且務必由一位董事會的高階主管帶領,也就是董事長或副董事長。請再告訴我您的想法。**

敬祝一切順心

艾琳・索伯格
米勒布魯克董事會 祕書

字彙 bylaw 制度　carry out 執行　committee 委員會　head 帶領　high-ranking 高階的　chair 主席　vice chair 副主席

推理問題

196 What is indicated about Mr. Tolentino in the press release?
(A) He will be given an award from the company.
(B) He is leaving to start his own business.
(C) He had the support of all board members.
(D) He plans to train his replacement.

中譯 可從新聞稿裡得知托倫提諾先生的何項資訊?
(A) 公司將頒獎給他。
(B) 他即將離職去創業。
(C) 他獲得所有董事會成員的支持。
(D) 他預計訓練自己的接替人選。

三則引文連結問題_推理問題

197 What is suggested about Ms. Chomley?
(A) She plans to relocate to a new city.
(B) She has strong communication skills.
(C) She is Mr. Vinson's former coworker.
(D) She has designed software programs before.

中譯 可從文中得知喬姆利小姐的何項資訊?
(A) 她打算搬遷至新城市。
(B) 她有優秀的溝通技巧。
(C) 她是文森先生以前的同事。
(D) 她曾設計過軟體程式。

特定訊息確認問題

198 According to Mr. Vinson, why is Ms. Chomley unsure about the position?

(A) The job responsibilities are too specialized.

(B) The expected working hours are too long.

(C) The compensation package is not fully described.

(D) The company has a lengthy interview process.

中譯 根據文森先生的說法，喬姆利小姐為何對於此職位有所疑慮？

(A) 職務內容過於專業。

(B) 預計工時過長。

(C) 未完全說明薪資報酬的結構。

(D) 該公司的面試程序冗長。

推理問題

199 In the second e-mail, what is implied about the Millerbrook board?

(A) It will increase in size.

(B) It will meet more frequently.

(C) It will receive larger payments.

(D) It will update the bylaws.

中譯 可從第二封電子郵件裡，得知米勒布魯克董事會的何項資訊？

(A) 即將增加人數。

(B) 即將更頻繁開會。

(C) 即將收到更大筆的款項。

(D) 即將更新公司章程。

三則引文連結問題__推理問題

200 What is suggested about Mr. Vinson?

(A) He is the newest member of the board.

(B) He opposed a proposed change.

(C) He will be supervising his friend.

(D) He is eligible to lead a committee.

中譯 可從文中得知文森先生的何項資訊？

(A) 他是最晚加入董事會的成員。

(B) 他反對某項異動提議。

(C) 他會監督自己的朋友。

(D) 他符合領導某委員會的資格。

Actual Test 2

PART 1

1 (A) She is putting fruit into a basket.
美W **(B) She is standing behind a counter.**
(C) She is placing products on a shelf.
(D) She is buying some groceries.

(A) 她正把水果放到籃子裡。
(B) 她站在櫃檯後面。
(C) 她在把產品上架
(D) 她在買生活雜貨。

字彙 groceries 生活雜貨

2 (A) One of the men is strolling past a bench.
美M (B) One of the men is jogging along the water.
(C) One of the men is riding a bicycle in the park.
(D) One of the men is pushing a stroller.

(A) 其中一個男子漫步經過長椅。
(B) 其中一個男子沿著水岸慢跑。
(C) 其中一個男子在公園裡騎腳踏車。
(D) 其中一個男子在推嬰兒車。

字彙 stroll 漫步 stroller 嬰兒車

3 (A) A customer is reaching for an item.
美W **(B) Some plants are on display.**
(C) A woman is arranging a bouquet.
(D) Flowers are being watered.

(A) 顧客正伸手拿一項物品。
(B) 有些植物正在展示中。
(C) 女子在整理花束。
(D) 有人在澆花。

字彙 reach for 伸手取得某物 on display 陳列展示

4 **(A) Some people are attending a presentation.**
澳M (B) Some people are raising their hands.
(C) A man is drawing a graph.
(D) A woman is writing on a whiteboard.

(A) 有些人在參加簡報會。
(B) 有些人在舉手。
(C) 男子在畫圖表。
(D) 女子在白板寫字。

5 (A) He's repairing some safety glasses.
美M (B) He's putting away some equipment.
(C) He's operating a machine.
(D) He's removing a hard hat from his head.

(A) 他在維修護目鏡。
(B) 他在收拾某設備。
(C) 他在操作機器。
(D) 他在脫掉頭上的工程帽。

字彙 safety glasses 護目鏡 put away 收拾
hard hat 工程帽

6 (A) Several chairs are lined up in a row.
英W (B) Furniture has been left on the lawn.
(C) A barbecue is being installed on a terrace.
(D) A sitting area is unoccupied.

(A) 有幾張椅子排成一排。
(B) 家具被留在草皮上。
(C) 有人正在陽臺裝設烤肉架。
(D) 座位區沒人坐。

字彙 be lined up 排列(成排) in a row 一排
unoccupied 閒置的

PART 2

06

7 Where is the nearest gas station?
美 (A) Yes, for my new car.
(B) On the other side of the park.
(C) The train is departing soon.

離這裡最近的加油站在哪裡?
(A) 是的,為了我的新車。
(B) 在公園的另一側。
(C) 火車即將發車。

8 This hotel is more spacious than the last one we stayed in, isn't it?
美W
英W (A) I'd be happy to recommend one.
(B) It's booked for the next three nights.
(C) Yes, we've got plenty of room this time.

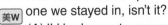

這家飯店比我們上次住的那家還寬敞，對嗎？
(A) 我很樂意推薦一家。
(B) 接下來的三個晚上都被訂走了。
(C) 是啊，我們這次有蠻多空間。

字彙 spacious 寬敞的　recommend 推薦

---

9 Isn't this sweater twenty-five percent off?
美 **(A) No, the sale has ended.**
(B) This is the only size we have.
(C) I think it fits you perfectly.

這件毛衣不是打七五折嗎？
(A) 不是喔，優惠已經結束了。
(B) 我們只有這個尺寸。
(C) 我覺得你穿起來很合身。

字彙 fit 合身

---

10 Who does the manager plan to promote to assistant marketing director?
澳M 美W
(A) It's our sales promotion.
(B) Yes, it happened quite suddenly.
(C) Rachel, from the Westland branch.

經理打算升遷誰當行銷部副理？
(A) 是我們的優惠促銷。
(B) 是的，發生得很突然。
(C) 是西岸分公司的瑞秋。

字彙 promote 升遷　assistant director 副理
promotion 促銷　branch 分公司

---

11 Why is the vending machine in the break room unplugged?
美
(A) Let's take a break.
(B) It was having electrical problems.
(C) Can I get you something to drink?

休息室的販賣機為什麼沒插插頭？
(A) 我們休息一下。
(B) 因為有電路問題。
(C) 我可以幫你拿什麼喝的嗎？

字彙 vending machine 販賣機　unplug 拔掉(插頭)
electrical 電路的

---

12 We reached our fundraising goal at the charity event, right?
英W 澳M
(A) No, we're a few hundred dollars short.
(B) Yes, it'll be a lot of fun.
(C) To help restore the museum.

我們已經在慈善活動達到募款目標了，對嗎？
(A) 沒有，我們還差幾百美元。
(B) 是的，會很好玩喔。
(C) 為了幫忙修復博物館。

字彙 fundraising 募款　charity 慈善　short 短缺的
restore 修復

---

13 These sales figures need to be accurate.
美M 英W
(A) I'll be sure to double-check them.
(B) The past quarter, I think.
(C) They need the sales report for a meeting.

這些銷售數據必須準確無誤。
(A) 我一定會再確認一次。
(B) 我想是上一季。
(C) 他們需要開會用的業績報告。

字彙 sales figure 銷售數據　accurate 準確的

---

14 When will we have the monthly fire evacuation drill?
美
(A) For everyone's safety.
(B) No, I finished my evaluation.
(C) The alarm will sound at three.

我們什麼時候舉行每月消防避難演習？
(A) 為了大家的安全著想。
(B) 不對，我已經完成我的評鑑。
(C) 警報會在三點響起。

字彙 monthly 每月的　evacuation drill 避難演習
evaluation 評鑑

---

15 Do you mind ending the meeting a bit early?
美M 澳M
(A) I'm sending it right now.
(B) But we have a lot to cover.
(C) Do you want me to come in early?

你介意早一點結束會議嗎？
(A) 我現在就寄出。
(B) 但我們還有很多內容要討論。
(C) 你要我早點進公司嗎？

字彙 cover 探討；涵蓋　come in 進 (公司)

---

16 Will you be ready in time for the speech?
澳M 美W
(A) I just need to practice a few more times.
(B) It started at two o'clock.
(C) She's a very good public speaker.

你來得及準備好演講嗎？
(A) 我只需要再多練習幾次就好。
(B) 兩點就開始了。
(C) 她是很優秀的公開演說家。

字彙 public speaker 公開演說家

17 Which pharmacy do you use to fill your prescriptions?
美
(A) I'm taking one pill a day.
(B) No, I'm not a pharmacist.
(C) The one across the street.

你去哪家藥局拿處方箋的藥？
(A) 我每天吃一顆藥。
(B) 不是，我不是藥劑師。
(C) 這條街對面那家。

字彙 pharmacy 藥局
fill a prescription 領處方箋的藥
pharmacist 藥劑師

18 Did you see the new laboratory equipment?
美
(A) What should we order?
(B) I've been out of town.
(C) A chemical experiment.

你有看到新的實驗器材嗎？
(A) 我們應該訂什麼？
(B) 我一直在外地。
(C) 是化學實驗。

字彙 laboratory 實驗室 be out of town 在外地
chemical experiment 化學實驗

19 Would you prefer a seminar on marketing techniques or budget management?
澳M 美W
(A) It depends on who is presenting.
(B) No, I haven't given any lectures lately.
(C) I didn't know the budget proposal was due today.

你偏好行銷技巧還是預算管理的研討會呢？
(A) 要看是誰主講。
(B) 不是，我最近沒有教任何課。
(C) 我不曉得預算提案今天就要交了。

字彙 management 管理 present 主講
give a lecture 教課 due 到期的

20 What was Dale's reaction to the news of his raise?
英W 美M
(A) Yesterday morning.
(B) He got a bonus.
(C) He couldn't believe it.

戴爾對他加薪的消息有何反應？
(A) 昨天早上。
(B) 他得到獎金。
(C) 他不敢相信。

字彙 reaction 反應

21 How often does the lawn need to be mowed?
美
(A) About twice a month.
(B) With a gas-powered device.
(C) No, a landscaping company.

草皮多久需要除草一次？
(A) 大約一個月兩次。
(B) 需使用以汽油驅動的裝置。
(C) 不是，一家造景公司。

字彙 mow 除草 gas-powered 汽油驅動的
device 裝置 landscaping 造景

22 Are you moving to a new apartment or renewing your current lease?
澳M 英W
(A) I haven't seen that movie.
(B) It was released last month.
(C) I'm planning to stay here.

你想搬到新公寓或續簽現在的租約？
(A) 我還沒看過那部電影。
(B) 上個月發行的。
(C) 我打算留在這邊。

字彙 renew 延長……的期限 lease 租約
release 發行

23 Do you know who will translate these documents for our German partners?
美
(A) By Thursday afternoon.
(B) Mainly the trade agreement.
(C) Let me check with my supervisor.

你知道誰會幫我們的德國合作夥伴翻譯這些文件嗎？
(A) 星期四下午之前。
(B) 主要是貿易協議書。
(C) 我問一下我主管。

字彙 translate 翻譯 trade agreement 貿易協議書

24 The bed frame is easy to assemble without any special tools.
美
(A) Let's take it apart.
(B) That's a relief.
(C) The instructions are on the table.

此床架不須使用任何特殊工具，也能輕鬆組裝。
(A) 我們來拆卸它。
(B) 我放心了。
(C) 說明書在桌子上。

字彙 frame 框架 assemble 組裝
take apart 拆卸 relief 安心
instructions 說明書

25 Where can I get a charger for my phone?

澳M (A) Probably around 7 P.M.

美W **(B) Why don't you just borrow mine?**

(C) Its battery is completely dead.

我可以在哪裡買到我手機的充電器？

(A) 大概晚上七點左右。

(B) 你何不跟我借就好？

(C) 它的電池完全沒電了。

字彙 **charger** 充電器 **dead** （機械或裝置等）沒電的

---

26 The manager approved my vacation request, didn't she?

美

(A) Yes, a few days ago.

(B) We need her approval to conduct the study.

(C) I hope you had fun.

經理已經核准我的假單，對嗎？

(A) 是的，幾天前就准假了。

(B) 我們需要她核准以進行此研究。

(C) 希望你們玩得開心。

字彙 **approve** 核准 **request** 請求 **approval** 核准 **conduct** 進行

---

27 Did the package arrive without any broken contents?

英W (A) I checked the arrival time.

美M (B) Glasses and flower vases.

(C) It's still in transit.

包裹送達時，內容物是否完好無損？

(A) 我檢查過抵達時間。

(B) 玻璃杯和花瓶。

(C) 還在運輸途中。

解析 本題詢問包裹的內容物送達時是否完好無損，回答說「還在運送中」的 **(C)** 為正解。**(B)** 是利用可以從 **broken** 聯想到的 **glasses** 和 **vases** 構成之錯誤答案。

字彙 **contents** 內容物 **in transit** 運輸途中

---

28 Who requested repairs to the air conditioner?

澳M (A) Half an hour, probably.

美W **(B) Mr. Lambert should know.**

(C) It will be repaired tomorrow.

是誰要求維修冷氣？

(A) 大概要半小時。

(B) 蘭伯特先生應該知道。

(C) 明天會維修。

---

29 Doesn't Curtis teach the advanced yoga class?

英W

澳M (A) No, I strongly recommend jogging.

(B) If you think it's not too difficult.

(C) Usually, but he has a minor injury.

柯提斯不是有教進階的瑜伽課？

(A) 沒有，我大力推薦慢跑。

(B) 如果你不會覺得太難的話。

(C) 通常是，但他受了點小傷。

字彙 **advanced** 進階的

---

30 Can you calculate the departmental spending for the past week?

美

(A) I'll try to cut back, if possible.

(B) Adam has all the figures.

(C) When will we get corporate cards?

你可以計算一下上週的部門開支嗎？

(A) 如果有可能，我會盡量縮減。

(B) 亞當那邊有所有的數字。

(C) 我們什麼時候會拿到公司卡？

字彙 **calculate** 計算 **departmental** 部門的 **cut back** 縮減 **figure** 數字

---

31 I can proofread the document by Wednesday.

英W

美M (A) So did I. It's a great article.

(B) I didn't notice any big mistakes.

(C) Is it possible to have it done sooner?

我可以在星期三以前校對好文件。

(A) 我也是，這篇文章好棒。

(B) 我沒注意到任何嚴重錯誤。

(C) 有可能早一點做完嗎？

字彙 **proofread** 校對

PART 3

07

Questions 32-34 refer to the following conversation. 美 對話

W Good morning. ㉜ **Your store sent me a flyer a few days ago saying that you were having a sale in some of your departments.** I'd like to buy a microwave for my apartment.

M All right. We have plenty of models to choose from. ㉝ **I also suggest getting some pots and pans if you need any.** The Warner brand is seventy-five percent off because the products will be discontinued.

W Really? I don't need any, but my sister does. ㉞ **Let me call her to see if there's a certain color she prefers.** Just a moment.

女： 早安。㉜ **你們店幾天前寄傳單給我，說某些櫃位在促銷。**我想幫我的公寓買微波爐。

男： 好的。我們有很多機型可選。㉝ **我也建議如果有需要，可以添購鍋具。**華納牌因為即將停產，折扣為二五折。

女： 真的嗎？我雖然不需要，但我妹妹需要。㉞ **我打電話給她看看她是否有想要的顏色。**等我一下。

字彙 flyer 傳單　pots and pans 鍋具　discontinue 停產

32 How did the woman find out about the sale?
(A) By reading a banner
(B) By performing an Internet search
(C) By receiving a flyer in the mail
(D) By seeing an ad in the newspaper

中譯 女子如何得知此促銷活動？
(A) 看到廣告橫幅
(B) 上網搜尋到的
(C) 收到購物中心傳單
(D) 看到報紙上的廣告

33 What does the man recommend buying?
(A) An electronic device
(B) Some cookware
(C) A piece of furniture
(D) Some clothing

中譯 男子推薦購買什麼物品？
(A) 電子裝置
(B) 烹飪器具
(C) 家具
(D) 服飾

34 Why does the woman want to make a phone call?
(A) To increase a budget
(B) To get an opinion
(C) To confirm an address
(D) To check another store

中譯 女子為什麼要打電話？
(A) 想增加預算
(B) 想詢問意見
(C) 要確認地址
(D) 要查看另一家商店

Questions 35-37 refer to the following conversation. 美 對話

M Hi. ㉟ **I need to have my laptop fixed, and my friend recommended you.** How long does it usually take? I need it for a presentation tomorrow.

男： 嗨，㉟ **我的筆記型電腦需要維修，我朋友推薦我來這裡。**通常多久會修好？我明天的簡報會要用。

W Well, that depends on the kind of problem you're having and whether or not we need to order additional components. What seems to be the issue?

M **㊱ I was coming home from a business trip yesterday, and during the flight, the entire screen suddenly went black.**

W That could be caused by a number of factors. Actually, we're supposed to close in about fifteen minutes. **㊲ However, since you're in a hurry, I can work overtime to make sure it's ready as soon as possible.**

女：要看是什麼樣的問題，以及我們是否需要訂其他的零件。是什麼問題呢？

男：**㊱ 我昨天剛出差回來，搭機的時候，整個螢幕突然黑掉。**

女：造成這個問題的原因很多。其實我們再 15 分鐘就要打烊了。**㊲ 不過，既然你急著要，我會加班以確保你能儘快拿到筆電。**

字彙 component 零件　work overtime 加班

35 Where most likely are the speakers?
(A) At a conference hall
(B) At a vehicle rental agency
(C) At a computer repair shop
(D) At an airport

中譯 談話者最有可能在哪裡交談？
(A) 會議廳
(B) 租車公司
(C) 電腦維修商家
(D) 機場

36 What does the man say he did yesterday?
(A) Traveled by airplane
(B) Opened a new business
(C) Ordered some components
(D) Gave a presentation

中譯 男子說他昨天做了什麼事？
(A) 搭機旅行
(B) 新創立一間公司
(C) 訂購一些零件
(D) 發表簡報

37 What does the woman offer to do for the man?
(A) Show him a catalog
(B) Provide a refund
(C) Consult an expert
(D) Work extra hours

中譯 女子提議要幫男子做什麼事？
(A) 給他看型錄
(B) 退款
(C) 諮詢專家
(D) 加班處理

Questions 38-40 refer to the following conversation. 美M 英W 對話

M Hello. I'm calling from Oshea Inc. My name is Gregory, and **㊳ I'm scheduled to visit your building at 1 P.M. to install a security camera and a monitoring system.** I just wanted to let you know that I'm still on schedule.

W All right. You'll be working at our main entrance, so **㊴ I'll post a notice** letting customers know that they should use our side entrance on Franklin Street.

男：您好，我從奧希亞公司打電話過來。我是葛雷格瑞，**㊳ 公司安排我下午一點前往您的大樓，裝設監視攝影機和監控系統。**我只是想通知您一聲，我會準時到達。

女：好的。請你在我們的大門施作，**㊴ 我會張貼告示**，讓顧客知道從法蘭克林街的側門進出。

男：好的，謝謝幫忙。還有，**㊵ 我是否需要特殊許可證才能停在你們的停車場？**

女：**㊵ 不用，你可以停在任一車位。**停車場是給一般大眾使用的，所以都可以停。

M Good. That would be helpful. Also, ㊵ **do I need a special permit to use your lot?**

W ㊵ **No. You can park in any spot.** They're all for the general public, so you can take your pick.

字彙 **security camera** 監視器 **monitoring system** 監控系統 **permit** 許可證 **general public** 一般大眾 **take one's pick** 任……挑選

38 What is the purpose of the man's visit?
(A) To make a delivery
(B) To inspect a building
(C) To introduce a company
(D) To install security equipment

中譯 男子拜訪的目的是什麼？
(A) 送貨
(B) 檢查大樓
(C) 介紹某公司
(D) 裝設保全設備

39 What does the woman plan to do?
(A) Call the man back
(B) Keep an entrance locked
(C) Reschedule a visit
(D) Put up a sign

中譯 女子打算做什麼？
(A) 回撥電話給男子
(B) 鎖上某入口
(C) 重新安排拜訪時間
(D) 設立告示

40 What does the man inquire about?
(A) A company invoice
(B) A parking situation
(C) An hourly fee
(D) A road closure

中譯 男子詢問什麼事情？
(A) 公司帳單
(B) 停車的情況
(C) 每小時的費用
(D) 道路封閉情況

Questions 41-43 refer to the following conversation with three speakers. 美W 澳M 美M 三人對話

W Aiden, Bernard, you both usually drive to work, right? ㊶ **We're starting a carpool program at our office. Why don't you join?**

M1 That's a good idea. The parking lot here is so small.

M2 Yeah, and about half of the spots are reserved for customers.

W I hope this plan will help. We're also going to offer some kind of benefit to employees who take part in the program.

M1 Oh, really? Like what?

W I'm not sure yet. ㊷ **I'm going to get together with the department heads after lunch to discuss it.**

M2 Let us know what you come up with.

M1 You know, ㊸ **I'd be happy to brainstorm a few ideas that I think the staff might like.**

W ㊸ **Thanks, Aiden.** That would be helpful.

女： 艾登、伯納德，你們兩個通常都開車上班，對嗎？㊶ **我們公司要開始共乘計畫，你們何不加入？**

男 1： 這個點子不錯。這裡的停車場很小。

男 2： 對啊，而且有一半的停車位都保留給顧客。

女： 我希望這個計畫能有幫助。我們也會為參加此計畫的員工，提供一些福利。

男 1： 喔，真的嗎？有什麼福利？

女： 我還不確定。㊷ **我午餐後會跟各部門主管一起討論。**

男 2： 再跟我們說討論的結果。

男 1： 你知道嗎，㊸ **我很樂意腦力激盪一些我覺得職員可能會喜歡的構想。**

女： ㊸ **艾登，謝謝你**。你幫了大忙。

字彙 reserve 保留　take part in 參加　head 負責人

41 What are the men encouraged to do?
(A) Borrow a company car
(B) Sign up for a workshop
(C) Share rides to work
(D) Reserve a parking spot

中譯 男子們被鼓勵做什麼事？
(A) 借公司車
(B) 報名工作坊
(C) 共乘上班
(D) 預約停車位

42 What will the woman do in the afternoon?
(A) Meet with managers
(B) E-mail a plan
(C) Announce a change
(D) Launch a program

中譯 女子下午要做什麼？
(A) 和經理們開會
(B) 用電子郵件寄送某計畫
(C) 宣布某異動
(D) 推出某計畫

43 Why does the woman thank Aiden?
(A) He completed a task ahead of schedule.
(B) He agreed to attend a meeting for her.
(C) He volunteered to provide suggestions.
(D) He will help new employees get settled.

中譯 女子為何感謝艾登？
(A) 他提早完成某事務。
(B) 他同意替女子參加某會議。
(C) 他主動提出建議。
(D) 他會協助安頓新員工。

Questions 44-46 refer to the following conversation. 美 對話

M Amy, could you help me with something this afternoon? 44 **I'm overseeing the company's efforts to hire new employees, and I need help screening the résumés that we've received.**

W I would love to help, but 45 **Anthony, who works in my department, is out sick today. So I have to finish some of his assignments.** I'm already on a tight schedule, and 45 **I'm worried I won't even be able to handle that.**

M I understand. 46 **I can take care of it myself as long as Ms. Hendricks extends the deadline for my other project.**

W I'm sure she will, but 46 **you'd better talk to her soon.**

男：艾咪，你今天下午可以幫忙我嗎？44 **我負責公司僱用新人事宜，我需有人幫忙篩選收到的履歷。**

女：我很想幫忙，但 45 **我部門的安東尼今天請病假，所以我得完成一些他的工作。**我時間已經有點緊迫，45 **我擔心連原本的事情都忙不過來了。**

男：我了解。46 **我能自己處理，只要亨德瑞克小姐延長我其他專案的交期就好。**

女：我確定她會延長，但 46 **你還是要盡快找她談談。**

字彙 oversee 監督　screen 篩選　be out sick 請病假　assignment 工作　extend 延長　deadline 截止期限

44 What does the man need assistance with?
(A) A film screening
(B) A retirement party
(C) A training session
(D) A recruiting process

中譯 男子什麼事需要協助？
(A) 電影放映
(B) 辦退休派對
(C) 教育訓練課程
(D) 徵才程序

45 Why is the woman unable to help the man?
(A) She has to meet with a client.
(B) She has interviews with candidates.
(C) She has to complete a coworker's tasks.
(D) She has a doctor's appointment.

中譯 女子為什麼無法幫忙男子?
(A) 她必須和客戶會面。
(B) 她要面試應徵者。
(C) 她必須完成同事的工作。
(D) 她有跟醫師約診。

46 What will the man probably discuss with Ms. Hendricks?
(A) Changing a due date
(B) Transferring to another office
(C) Hiring a temporary worker
(D) Updating a company policy

中譯 男子大概會跟亨德瑞克小姐討論什麼事?
(A) 更改截止日期
(B) 調到另一個部門
(C) 僱用臨時工
(D) 更新公司政策

Questions 47-49 refer to the following conversation. 英W 美M 對話

07

W Hi, Mr. Ritter. You wanted to speak to me?
M Yes. Ever since we released the new delivery schedule last week, ㊼ **a lot of the delivery drivers have been telling me how upset they are.**
W Oh, really? What's causing them to feel that way?
M ㊽ **Previously, drivers were expected to make ten deliveries in a day, and now that number has been changed to fifteen. Since they have to install the items too,** it's a lot to ask.
W I see what you mean. Hmm... ㊾ **we could buy more vans and hire more people,** and then start charging a higher installation fee.

女: 嗨,瑞特先生,你要和我談談嗎?
男: 是的。自從我們上週發布新的配送行程表後,㊼ **很多物流司機一直跟我說他們很不爽。**
女: 喔,真的嗎?他們為什麼會這樣覺得?
男: ㊽ **以前司機一天只要配送 10 趟,現在變成 15 趟。由於他們還需要安裝物品,** 這樣的要求太多了。
女: 我懂你的意思。嗯…… ㊾ **我們可以買更多貨車與僱用更多人,** 然後開始收取較高的安裝費。

字彙 **previously** 以前地 **make a delivery** 配送 **installation** 裝設

47 What has the man recently done?
(A) Accepted a promotion to a new position
(B) Introduced new products to a company
(C) Received negative feedback from employees
(D) Encouraged the business owner to buy more vans

中譯 男子最近做了什麼事?
(A) 接受升遷至新職位
(B) 向某公司介紹新產品
(C) 收到員工的負面回饋
(D) 鼓勵老闆買更多貨車

48 What does the man mean when he says, "it's a lot to ask"?
(A) He believes a workload is unreasonable.
(B) He feels bad for needing a big favor.
(C) He is unable to meet a deadline.
(D) He needs some time to think about a decision.

中譯 男子說:「這樣的要求太多了」是什麼意思?
(A) 他認為工作量不合理。
(B) 他因需要別人幫自己大忙而感到慚愧。
(C) 他無法如期交出東西。
(D) 他需要時間來思考某決策。

49 What does the woman suggest doing?
(A) Expanding the hours of operation
(B) Recruiting some drivers
(C) Finding a new supplier
(D) Reducing a service fee

中譯 女子提議做什麼事？
(A) 延長營業時間
(B) 招募司機
(C) 找新的供應商
(D) 降低服務費

Questions 50-52 refer to the following conversation. 

M Melissa, (50) **I was looking at our online store's catalog, and there seems to be a problem when it's viewed on a mobile device. The photographs are too big,** so I think that's going to make it difficult for customers to make purchases.

W (51) **My team is still running the tests and making adjustments,** so you're not looking at the final version. (51) **We have three more days to complete the work.**

M I see. In that case, (52) **I'll hold off my evaluation of the service until next week.** I'm sure you've got everything under control.

男：梅麗莎，(50) **我在看我們網路商店的型錄。用手機瀏覽的時候，好像會有點問題。照片會變得太大，**我覺得會讓顧客很難下訂單。

女：(51) **我的團隊還在執行測試和做出調整，**所以你現在看到的不是最終版本。(51) **我們還需要三天才能完工。**

男：我知道了。這樣的話，(52) **我會保留到下週再評鑑該項服務。**我確定一切都在你們的掌控之中。

字彙 make a purchase 下訂單　make an adjustment 調整　hold off 保留

50 What is the conversation mainly about?
(A) Misprints in a catalog
(B) Images on a Web site
(C) A product launch
(D) A customer complaint

中譯 此對話主要討論什麼事？
(A) 型錄上的印刷錯誤
(B) 網站上的圖片
(C) 產品發表會
(D) 客訴

51 What does the woman mention about a project?
(A) It doesn't have enough workers.
(B) It has been canceled.
(C) It needs a budget adjustment.
(D) It is still in progress.

中譯 女子提到某專案的什麼事？
(A) 員工不夠。
(B) 專案已經取消。
(C) 需要調整預算。
(D) 還在進行中。

52 What does the man plan to do next week?
(A) Assess a service
(B) Replace some images
(C) Assign a new task
(D) Repair some equipment

中譯 男子打算下週做什麼事？
(A) 評鑑某服務
(B) 更換圖片
(C) 分配新工作
(D) 維修一些設備

Questions 53-55 refer to the following conversation with three speakers. 美M 英W 美W 三人對話

M Hello. My name is Martin Hardy. ⑬ **I was here yesterday for a dental appointment, and I accidentally left my credit card behind.**
W1 Do you know who found it?
M Yes, ⑭ **it was Ms. Michaels. She left a message on my phone this morning saying it was here.**
W1 Just a moment, sir. Ms. Michaels? Mr. Hardy is here.
W2 Oh, hello, Mr. Hardy. I'm glad we were able to get in touch with you.
M Yes, I'm very lucky. Thank you for finding my card.
W2 No problem. I have it here, but ⑮ **I'll need to see a photo ID to give it back to you.**
M ⑮ **Of course.**

男：哈囉，我是馬丁・哈迪。⑬ **我昨天來這邊看牙齒，然後不小心把信用卡忘在這裡了。**
女1：你知道是誰找到的嗎
男：知道，⑭ **是麥克斯小姐。她今天早上留語音訊息給我，說信用卡在這兒。**
女1：先生，等一下喔。麥克斯小姐？哈迪先生過來了。
女2：喔，哈囉，哈迪先生。很高興能夠聯絡到你。
男：對啊，我很幸運。感謝你找到我的信用卡。
女2：沒問題。信用卡在這裡，但⑮ **我還是需要看過有照片的身分證件才能還給你。**
男：⑮ 沒問題。

字彙 leave behind 遺落

53 Why is the man visiting the business?
(A) To have a dental checkup
(B) To get a receipt
(C) To pick up an item
(D) To schedule an appointment

中譯 男子為什麼要到這個執業場所？
(A) 檢查牙齒
(B) 拿收據
(C) 取回某物品
(D) 安排約診

54 What did Ms. Michaels do in the morning?
(A) Processed a credit card payment
(B) Noticed a billing error
(C) Filled out some paperwork
(D) Left a telephone message

中譯 麥克斯小姐早上做了什麼事？
(A) 處理信用卡帳款
(B) 發現帳單上的錯誤
(C) 處理文書工作
(D) 留語音訊息

55 What will the man most likely do next?
(A) Speak to a dentist
(B) Confirm a schedule
(C) Show an ID card
(D) Go to an exam room

中譯 男子接下來最有可能做什麼事？
(A) 跟牙醫師談話
(B) 確認行程
(C) 出示身分證
(D) 去檢查室

Questions 56-58 refer to the following conversation. 英W 美M 對話

W Hi. My name is Sienna Talbot. I bought a rug from your store earlier this week, and it was supposed to be delivered yesterday. ⑯ **I'm wondering what's going on with my order.**
M I'm sorry about the delay, ma'am. Someone should have contacted you.

女：嗨，我叫席亞娜・泰伯特。我本週稍早在你們店裡買了一張地毯，本來應該昨天就要送到。⑯ **我想知道我的訂單發生什麼狀況。**
男：小姐，很抱歉延誤了，應該要有人聯絡您才對。

W Oh, so then you're aware of the problem?

M Yes. Unfortunately, ⑰ **there was some kind of trouble with our delivery truck's engine.** It's being repaired now.

W So what should I do?

M Our delivery schedule will be back on track soon, so ⑱ **I suggest waiting another twenty-four hours.** You'll almost certainly have your item by then.

W All right. I guess I have no choice.

女：喔，所以你們有發現這個問題？

男：是的。很不幸地，⑰ **我們的配送貨車引擎出了問題。**現在還在維修。

女：那我該怎麼辦？

男：我們的配送行程很快會回到正軌，⑱ **我建議您再等 24 小時，**到時候您應該就能收到了。

女：好吧。我想我沒得選。

字彙 **back on track** 回到正軌

56 What is the purpose of the call?
(A) To complain about a damaged item
(B) To apologize for a delay
(C) To check on the status of an order
(D) To inquire about a discount

中譯 這通電話的目的是什麼？
(A) 抱怨受損的物品
(B) 為某延誤情況道歉
(C) 了解訂單的狀態
(D) 詢問折扣

57 According to the man, what has caused a problem?
(A) An engine malfunction
(B) A computer error
(C) An employee's absence
(D) A major storm

中譯 根據男子的說法，什麼原因造成此問題？
(A) 引擎故障
(B) 電腦錯誤
(C) 員工曠職
(D) 嚴重的暴風雨

58 What does the man recommend doing?
(A) Checking information online
(B) Calling back later
(C) Waiting another day
(D) Providing a tracking number

中譯 男子建議做什麼事？
(A) 上網查看資訊
(B) 晚點回撥電話
(C) 再等一天
(D) 提供追蹤號碼

Questions 59-61 refer to the following conversation. 澳M 美W 對話

M Good morning. ⑲ **I'd like to check out of room 304. Here is my keycard.** And is it possible for me to leave my car here for the day? I've got some business at the Woodbridge Convention Center before flying out this evening.

W Unfortunately, ⑳ **our parking lot is for guests only,** so your pass is not valid after you check out.

M ㉑ **Couldn't you allow it just this once?** It would be a hassle to move my car.

W I know it's a strict policy, especially when we still have space in the lot. But I can't help you. ㉑ **I don't make those decisions.**

男：早安。⑲ **304 房要退房，這是我的房卡。**我今天是不是可以把車子先停在這邊？今天傍晚搭機離開前，我還要到木橋會議中心辦點事。

女：不好意思，⑳ **我們的停車場僅供房客使用，**所以您退房後，通行證就會失效。

男：㉑ **難道不能通融這一次嗎？**還要移車很麻煩。

女：我知道這規定很嚴格，尤其是現在還有車位的情況下。但我真的幫不了您。㉑ **這不是我能決定的。**

字彙 **check out** 退房 **fly out** 搭機離開 **pass** 通行證 **valid** 有效的 **hassle** 麻煩 **strict** 嚴格的

59 Where most likely are the speakers?
(A) At an airport
(B) In a public library
(C) At a convention center
(D) In a hotel lobby

中譯 談話者最有可能在哪裡？
(A) 機場
(B) 公共圖書館
(C) 會議中心
(D) 飯店大廳

60 What does the woman mention about the parking lot?
(A) It is restricted to guests.
(B) It is currently full.
(C) It is under construction.
(D) It is closed in the evenings.

中譯 女子針對停車場提到了什麼資訊？
(A) 僅限房客使用。
(B) 目前客滿。
(C) 在施工中。
(D) 夜間會關閉。

61 What does the woman imply when she says, "I can't help you"?
(A) She does not know the directions to a place.
(B) She is not allowed to make exceptions.
(C) She has trouble making recommendations.
(D) She cannot explain the policy's details.

中譯 女子說：「我真的幫不了您」時，是什麼意思？
(A) 她不知道去某地的方向。
(B) 她沒有給特例的權限。
(C) 她不太會給建議。
(D) 她無法解釋政策細節。

Questions 62-64 refer to the following conversation and seating chart. 美 對話和座位表

W ⓺② **Welcome to the Lyndale Theater. I hope you enjoy Andrew Livonia's concert this evening. May I see your ticket?**

M Of course. Here you are. I'm really looking forward to the show. The critics have been giving it excellent reviews.

W Yes, we're pleased about that. But it looks like you're at the wrong entrance for your section, sir. ⑥③ **This entrance is for Section C, but your seat is on the other side. You need to go to Door 4.**

M Oh, I see. ⑥④ **I guess I'd better text my friend.** She's sitting with me and will probably try to come in this way too.

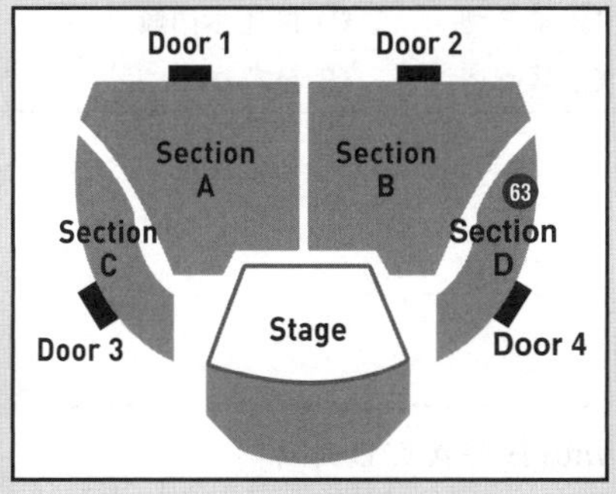

女： ⑥② **歡迎來到林黛爾劇院。希望大家今晚都能開心欣賞安德魯・李沃尼亞的音樂會。我可以看一下您的門票嗎？**

男： 沒問題，在這裡。我真的很期待這場表演。樂評都給很棒的評價。

女： 是的，我們感到很開心。但是先生您的座位區不是走這個入口。⑥③ **這個入口是往 C 區，您的座位在另一側，請您到 4 號入口。**

男： 喔，我了解了。⑥④ **我想我最好傳簡訊給我朋友。**她坐我旁邊，可能也會跑到這一側。

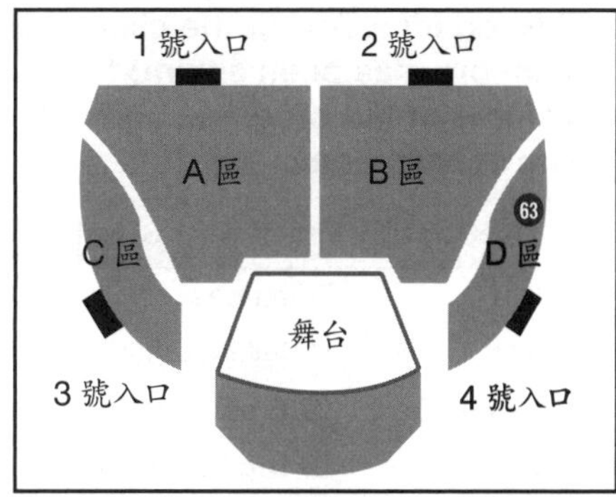

字彙 critic （尤指電影、書籍和音樂等的）評論家 review 評價 section 區 text 傳簡訊

62 Who most likely is the woman?
(A) A theater employee
(B) A media critic
(C) A musical performer
(D) A stage manager

中譯 女子最有可能是什麼身分？
(A) 劇院員工
(B) 媒體評論家
(C) 音樂演奏家
(D) 舞台監督

63 Look at the graphic. In which section will the man probably sit?
(A) Section A
(B) Section B
(C) Section C
(D) Section D

中譯 請看圖示。男子最有可能坐在哪一區？
(A) A 區
(B) B 區
(C) C 區
(D) D 區

64 What will the man most likely do next?
(A) Send a message
(B) Give the woman his seat
(C) Exchange a ticket
(D) Wait for a friend outside

中譯 男子接下來最有可能做什麼事？
(A) 傳送訊息
(B) 把自己的座位讓給女子
(C) 交換門票
(D) 在外面等朋友

Questions 65-67 refer to the following conversation and schedule. 美W 澳M 對話和行程表

W Richard, the head of the city's planning department called me this morning, and he informed me that ⑥⑤ **we need a permit to build the fence at the Crowley Street property.**

M We've built fences for clients before without a permit.

W Yes, but ⑥⑤ **this one will be over eight feet tall, so the regulations are different.** It'll take about a week to get the permit.

M Okay. ⑥⑥ **Since we were supposed to work on the fence next week, let's switch that task with the following week's so we don't get behind schedule.**

W ⑥⑥ **Good idea.** And ⑥⑦ **the client, Ms. Kenmore, has been asking for some pictures of the progress so far. I'll take care of that today.**

778 Crowley Street: Work Schedule	
Week 1	Trim trees
Week 2	Install irrigation system
⑥⑥ **Week 3**	⑥⑥ **Erect wooden fence**
⑥⑥ **Week 4**	⑥⑥ **Dig flower bed**

女：理查，本市規劃署主管今天早上打給我，他說⑥⑤ **我們需要許可證，才能搭建科洛利街房產的圍籬。**

男：我們以前在沒有許可證的情況下，就已經幫客戶搭過圍籬了啊。

女：對，但是⑥⑤ **這次的圍籬高度會超過八英尺，所以法規不同。**大概要一週才能拿到許可證。

男：好吧。⑥⑥ **既然我們下週才開始處理圍籬，我們就把這件事和再下一週的事對調，這樣我們進度才不會落後。**

女：⑥⑥ **好主意。**還有⑥⑦ **客戶肯摩爾小姐一直跟我們要目前進度的照片。我今天會處理好。**

科洛利街 778 號 工作行程表	
第一週	修剪樹木
第二週	裝設灌溉系統
⑥⑥ **第三週**	⑥⑥ **搭建木圍籬**
⑥⑥ **第四週**	⑥⑥ **挖花床**

字彙 inform 告知　property 房產　regulation 法規　switch A with B 將 A 與 B 對調

65 What does the woman mention about the permit?
(A) It has already been approved by the city.
(B) It is required because of the fence's height.
(C) It will take several weeks to process.
(D) It will be valid for eight months.

中譯 女子提到許可證的什麼事？
(A) 市政府已經核准。
(B) 因為圍籬的高度而需要有許可證。
(C) 需要幾週的處理時間。
(D) 效期是八個月。

66 Look at the graphic. What will the speakers do next week?
(A) Trim trees
(B) Install an irrigation system
(C) Erect a wooden fence
(D) Dig a flower bed

中譯 請看圖表。說話者下週要做什麼事？
(A) 修剪樹木
(B) 裝設灌溉系統
(C) 搭建木圍籬
(D) 挖花床

67 What will the woman send to Ms. Kenmore?
(A) A set of photographs
(B) An updated schedule
(C) A final bill
(D) A list of materials

中譯 女子會傳什麼給肯摩爾小姐？
(A) 一組照片
(B) 更新過的行程表
(C) 尾款帳單
(D) 材料清單

Questions 68-70 refer to the following conversation and chart. 美 對話和圖表

M Ms. Peterson, 68 **I'm sure you heard the news about last night's awards ceremony. Unfortunately, our company did not win the prestigious Horton Prize.**

W Yes, it was a disappointment. I was just looking over the market share figures since I was so surprised about the company that was chosen as the winner.

M Well, 69 **they may only have the third-largest market share, but they've been making a name for themselves since Jesse Dominguez, the new CEO, took over.**

W Right. 70 **That could be a problem for us if some of our clients want to switch to their firm.**

M Yes. We have to find a way to market ourselves better.

W Let's bring this up at the next meeting.

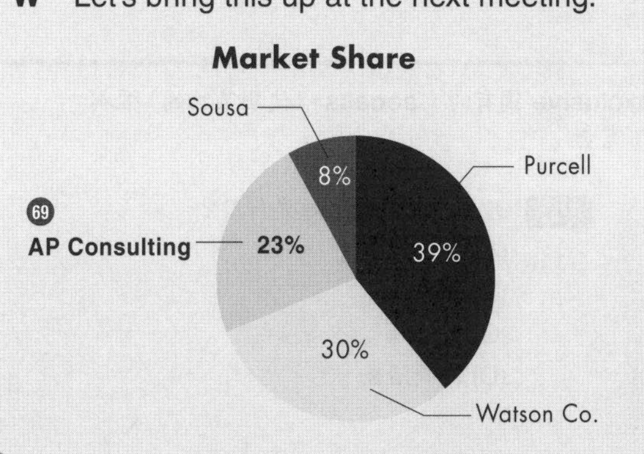

男：彼特森小姐，68 **我想你已經聽說昨晚頒獎典禮的消息。很可惜，我們公司沒能贏得頗具聲望的霍頓獎。**

女：是啊，讓人失望。我剛正在查看市占率數據，因為我對於獲獎公司被選上感到驚訝。

男：是這樣的，69 **他們的市占率也許只排第三，但是自從傑西．多明戈茲接任新任執行長後，他們就一直在打響名號。**

女：好吧。70 **如果我們的部分客戶想改和他們公司合作，對我們來說就會是個問題。**

男：對，我們必須有更好的行銷策略。

女：我們下次開會就討論這件事吧。

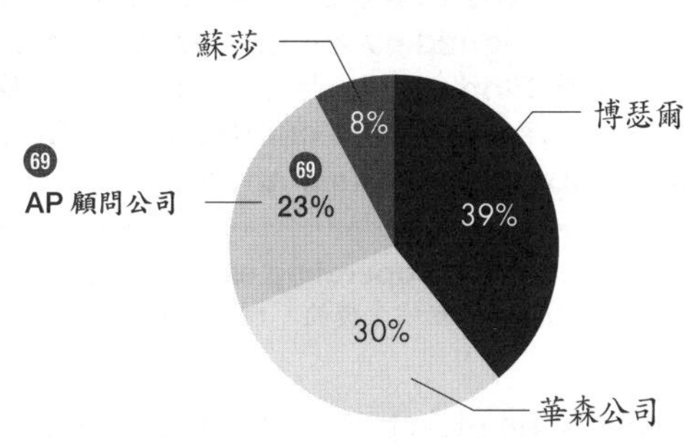

字彙 prestigious 有聲望的　market share 市占率　make a name for oneself 打響自己的名號
take over 接管　market 行銷

68 What does the man say happened yesterday?
(A) A budget proposal was submitted.
(B) A new branch opened.
(C) A marketing campaign was launched.
(D) An award was presented.

中譯 男子說昨天發生什麼事？
(A) 已提交預算案。
(B) 新的分公司開幕。
(C) 已推出行銷廣告。
(D) 已頒發某獎項。

69 Look at the graphic. Which company recently changed its CEO?
(A) Purcell
(B) Watson Co.
(C) AP Consulting
(D) Sousa

中譯 請看圖示。哪一家公司最近換了執行長？
(A) 博瑟爾
(B) 華森公司
(C) AP 顧問公司
(D) 蘇莎

70 What is the woman concerned about?
(A) Losing customers to a competitor
(B) Spending too much on marketing
(C) Failing to keep up with demand
(D) Having dissatisfied staff members

中譯 女子擔心什麼事？
(A) 顧客流失到競爭對手那裡
(B) 花太多行銷費用
(C) 無法跟上需求量
(D) 職員心懷不滿

PART 4

08

Questions 71-73 refer to the following radio broadcast. 美M 電臺廣播

Good morning. You're listening to *Culture Hour* with Benjamin Feldom. ⓻ **First up in culture news is the Alvarado Art Museum's upcoming gala. Everyone is invited to the gala, which is being organized to raise funds for operating expenses.** Your ticket gives you exclusive access to an after-hours banquet in the main hall. ⓼ **And the first fifty guests to register will also be given a free poster signed by famous artist Boris Nodova.** ⓽ **Find out more by listening to the interview with museum curator Alicia Coleman, coming up next on this station.**

早安，您現在收聽的是班傑明・費爾頓主持的《文化時光》。⓻ **第一個文化新聞是阿爾瓦拉多美術館即將到來的盛會。此活動的目的在於募集營運開銷所需的資金，而且所有人都能參加。**持入場券可執行長參與活動後的宴會，地點位於主廳。⓼ **前 50 名登記的來賓，可免費獲得知名藝術家波瑞斯・諾德瓦的簽名海報。** ⓽ **想了解更多活動訊息請繼續收聽，本臺將接著訪問美術館館長艾莉西亞・柯爾曼。**

字彙 gala 慶典、盛會　operating expense 營運開銷　exclusive 獨有的　access （使用某物的）權利
after-hours 活動結束後的　register 報名　station 電臺

71 What is the main topic of the broadcast?
(A) A museum tour
(B) An art contest
(C) A painting lesson
(D) A fundraiser

中譯 此廣播節目的主題是什麼？
(A) 博物館導覽
(B) 美術比賽
(C) 繪畫課
(D) 募款活動

72 How can participants receive a free gift?
(A) By adding their names to a mailing list
(B) By making a regular donation
(C) By being one of the first fifty people to enroll
(D) By purchasing more than one ticket

中譯 參加者該如何獲得免費禮物？
(A) 將自己的名字加到郵寄清單
(B) 藉由定期捐款
(C) 只要是前 50 名報名的人都可以拿到
(D) 購買超過一張的入場券

73 What does the speaker encourage listeners to do?
(A) Call the radio station
(B) Contact Ms. Coleman
(C) Listen to a program
(D) Visit a Web site

中譯 說話者鼓勵聽者做什麼事？
(A) 打電話給電臺
(B) 聯絡柯爾曼小姐
(C) 收聽某節目
(D) 造訪某網站

Questions 74-76 refer to the following announcement. 美W 宣告

May I have your attention, please? This announcement is for passengers traveling to Manchester. ⓻⓸ **The departure track has changed, so you should now board at platform 6, not 3.** ⓻⓹ **You will have to exit the area and present your ticket again at the platform 6 entrance,** so please have your ticket ready. You need to take the stairs to get to platform 6, so ⓻⓺ **those who require assistance in transporting their bags can speak to a staff member.** They can be found throughout the area and can be easily identified by their orange vests.

大家請注意。請前往曼徹斯特的旅客留意此公告。⓻⓸ **發車軌道已變更，請大家現在前往第 6 月臺搭車，而非第 3 月臺。** ⓻⓹ **您必須離開本區域，並至第 6 月臺入口再次出示車票，**所以請將車票準備好。您需要走樓梯前往第 6 月臺，因此 ⓻⓺ **需要協助搬運行李的人，可請站務人員幫忙。**車站各處都有我們同仁，他們身穿橘色背心，十分容易辨認。

字彙 departure 出發、離站　assistance 協助　transport 搬運　identify 辨認

74 Where most likely does the speaker work?
(A) At a taxi company
(B) At an airport
(C) At a train station
(D) At a travel agency

中譯 說話者最有可能在哪裡工作？
(A) 計程車公司
(B) 機場
(C) 火車站
(D) 旅行社

75 What will listeners be asked to do?
(A) Show a receipt
(B) Take their seats
(C) Wait for further instructions
(D) Present their tickets

中譯 聽者被要求做什麼事？
(A) 出示收據
(B) 坐到自己的座位
(C) 等候進一步指示
(D) 出示車票

76 What does the speaker say that employees will do?
(A) Issue new tickets
(B) Help to move luggage
(C) Update safety procedures
(D) Hang up some notices

中譯 說話者表示員工會做什麼事？
(A) 發新車票
(B) 協助搬運行李
(C) 更新安全程序
(D) 掛起公告

Questions 77-79 refer to the following telephone message. 美M 電話留言

Hi, Mr. Shaw. This is Henry calling. ⑰ ⑱ **I got your message saying that you'd like me to set up new displays for the windows of our department store. It's no problem for me to do this.** We've had the same ones for quite a while. Tourist season is starting soon, so ⑱ **we'd better get ready.** Since I'll be coming in early, ⑲ **please text me the six-digit code for the side door.** Thanks!

嗨，肖先生，我是亨利。⑰ ⑱ **我收到你的訊息，你希望我幫我們百貨公司的櫥窗設置新的展示內容。沒問題，我接受這工作。**畢竟現在的展示已經用很久了。觀光季即將開始，因此 ⑱ **我們最好趕快準備。**既然我會提早進公司，⑲ **請再把六位數的側門密碼傳訊給我。**感謝！

字彙 set up 設置　tourist season 觀光季　digit 數字　code 代碼

77 Why is the speaker calling?

(A) To accept a task
(B) To handle a complaint
(C) To show appreciation
(D) To leave early

中譯 說話者為什麼打電話？

(A) 為了接受某工作
(B) 為了處理客訴
(C) 為了表達感激
(D) 為了提早離開

78 What does the speaker imply when he says, "Tourist season is starting soon"?

(A) He is concerned about being short-staffed.
(B) He doesn't understand why profits are low.
(C) He agrees with the listener's suggestion.
(D) He thinks the store should advertise more frequently.

中譯 當說話者說：「觀光季即將開始」是什麼意思？

(A) 他擔心人手不足。
(B) 他不了解利潤低的原因。
(C) 他同意聽者的提議。
(D) 他覺得百貨公司應該更常打廣告。

79 What does the speaker ask for?

(A) An access code
(B) A floor plan
(C) An authorization form
(D) A colleague's phone number

中譯 說話者要求什麼？

(A) 門禁密碼
(B) 樓層平面圖
(C) 授權表
(D) 同仁的電話號碼

Questions 80-82 refer to the following telephone message 美M 電話留言

⑳ **Hello, this is Walter Freeman from Practon Middle School. I volunteered as a tutor at your library this past year.** It was an incredibly rewarding experience. ㉑ **However, I was just offered a job at a school in a different state and cannot participate in your program for the upcoming school year.** It truly saddens me to say this. I realize that finding a replacement on such short notice is difficult. So I would like to help you in any way I can. ㉒ **Please e-mail me your advertising flyer so that I may distribute it to my former colleagues.** I am sure some of them would be interested in helping out.

⑳ **哈囉，我是派瑞克頓中學的華特 ‧ 費里曼。我過去一年來在你們的圖書館擔任志工講師。**這真的是獲益良多的經驗。㉑ **不過，我剛被其他州的學校錄用，因此即將開學的這個學年就無法參加你們的計畫了。**我真的深感抱歉，我也知道這麼臨時才通知，你們很難找到接替的人。因此，我想盡可能提供協助。㉒ **請將你們的廣告傳單傳到我的電子信箱，我就可以發給前同事們。**我確定有些同事會有興趣協助。

字彙 tutor 輔導教師　rewarding 獲益良多的　sadden 使難過　replacement 接替者　on short notice 臨時通知　distribute 分發

80 Who most likely is the speaker?
(A) A librarian (B) A personnel manager
(C) A marketer **(D) A teacher**

中譯 說話者最有可能是什麼身分？
(A) 圖書館員 (B) 人事部經理
(C) 行銷人員 **(D) 教師**

81 Why does the speaker say, "It truly saddens me to say this"?
(A) To express his regret
(B) To emphasize his disagreement
(C) To reject an application
(D) To show his mood change

中譯 說話者為什麼說：「我真的深感抱歉」？
(A) 表達他的遺憾
(B) 強調他不認同
(C) 拒絕某申請
(D) 表現心境的轉變

82 What does the speaker ask the listener to do?
(A) Volunteer for a charity
(B) Provide a document
(C) Recommend a worker
(D) Lead a new program

中譯 說話者請聽者做什麼事？
(A) 當慈善團體的志工
(B) 提供文件
(C) 推薦工作者
(D) 主導新計畫

Questions 83-85 refer to the following excerpt from a meeting. 美M 會議節錄

83 **I regret to inform you that our CEO, Michael Hoskins, has decided to step down.** Mr. Hoskins is responsible for the enormous growth of our company, 84 **helping us to become the top producer of hybrid cars in the country.** We will miss him greatly. As board members, you will be expected to select a replacement. To assist you with this task, 85 **Ms. Melville has already put together a list of current staff members who may be qualified enough to take on the role.**

83 **我很遺憾的通知大家，執行長麥可・霍斯金斯已決定卸任。**霍斯金斯先生對我們公司的大幅成長貢獻良多，84 **他協助我們成為國內頂尖的油電混合車製造廠。**我們會非常想念他。各位身為董事會成員，需要選出接替人員。為了協助大家執行此任務，85 **梅維爾小姐已經編列好一份現有員工名單，他們可能有足夠資格擔任這個職位。**

字彙 step down 離職　enormous 龐大的　put together 彙整　qualified 合格的

83 What is the purpose of the meeting?
(A) To report on a competitor's plan
(B) To announce a leadership change
(C) To explain a new company policy
(D) To congratulate the listeners on an award

中譯 此會議的目的是什麼？
(A) 回報競爭對手的計畫
(B) 宣布領導階層的異動
(C) 說明新的公司政策
(D) 恭喜聽者得獎

84 What kind of company do the listeners most likely work for?
(A) An energy plant
(B) A vehicle manufacturer
(C) A communications company
(D) A construction firm

中譯 聽者最有可能在哪一種公司工作？
(A) 能源廠
(B) 汽車製造廠
(C) 通訊公司
(D) 建設公司

85 According to the speaker, what has Ms. Melville done?
(A) Ordered replacement parts
(B) Received an award
(C) Analyzed a competitor
(D) Prepared an employee list

中譯 根據說話者的說法，梅維爾小姐做了什麼事？
(A) 訂購替換零件
(B) 獲頒獎項
(C) 分析某競爭對手
(D) 準備員工名單

Questions 86-88 refer to the following introduction. 美W 行前介紹

Hello, everybody! ⑧⑥ **Welcome to the tour of the B&U facilities. Today you'll learn about the production process of our popular line of bicycles from start to finish.** You'll watch our technicians and machines cutting the aluminum frame, assembling the parts, adding tires, and more. You'll even see the testing process in action. Once we've gone through the entire process, ⑧⑦ **you'll get to meet Gustav Palmer, one of our senior engineers who helps to design new products for our line.** He'll answer your questions in detail. Now, before we get started, I just want to remind you all that, for safety reasons, ⑧⑧ **you must not wander off by yourselves.**

哈囉，大家好！⑧⑥ **歡迎參觀 B&U 廠區。今天大家將了解我們熱門腳踏車系列產品的製程始末。**大家將看到技師與機器切割鋁架、組裝零件、加裝輪胎等過程，甚至可看到檢驗流程。一旦我們完成整個流程，⑧⑦ **就可見到協助為本系列設計新產品的資深工程師古斯塔夫・帕爾默。**他會詳細回答大家的問題。現在，在開始之前，基於安全因素，我想先提醒大家，⑧⑧ **請勿自行遊蕩。**

字彙 facility（有特定用途的）場所　technician 技師　in action 進行中　go through 瀏覽　wander off 閒逛

86 Where is the introduction taking place?
(A) At a manufacturing plant
(B) At an auto repair shop
(C) At a construction site
(D) At a convention center

中譯 此說明在哪裡發生？
(A) 製造廠
(B) 修車廠
(C) 工地
(D) 會議中心

87 Who is Gustav Palmer?
(A) A business owner　**(B) An engineer**
(C) A reporter　(D) A physician

中譯 古斯塔夫・帕爾默的身分是什麼？
(A) 公司老闆　**(B) 工程師**
(C) 記者　(D) 醫師

88 What does the speaker ask the listeners to do?
(A) Suggest ideas for a design
(B) Wear protective gear
(C) Refrain from taking pictures
(D) Stay together as a group

中譯 說話者要求聽者做什麼事？
(A) 提出設計的點子
(B) 穿戴防護裝備
(C) 避免拍照
(D) 團體行動

Questions 89-91 refer to the following excerpt from a meeting. 英W 會議節錄

Good afternoon, everyone. ⑧⑨ **Thank you for coming to support our efforts to launch an adult literacy program here in Selby.** Registration for our first session is higher than expected, so we're looking forward to getting started. We had planned on conducting the session at the public library, but unfortunately, ⑨⓪ **its conference room is closed following damage from yesterday's storm. I'm worried about what we're going to do without a venue.** ⑨① **If you know of any sites that might be free, please e-mail me. I'll need to know the size of the building, where it is, and how many people it can accommodate.** Thank you.

大家午安，⑧⑨ **感謝大家前來支持我們在塞爾比推出的成人識讀課程。**第一堂課的報名人數超乎預期，所以我們很期待開始這項課程。我們本來打算在公共圖書館開課，但可惜的是，⑨⓪ **圖書館會議室因為昨天的暴風雨而受損關閉。我擔心沒場地可用該怎麼辦。**⑨① **如果大家知道任何可能免費的場地，請寫電子郵件給我。我需要知道建築的大小、地點、還有可容納的人數。**謝謝大家。

字彙 literacy 讀寫能力 registration 報名 venue 場地 accommodate 容納

89 What is the speaker mainly discussing?
(A) An educational program
(B) A registration fee
(C) A library fundraiser
(D) A community picnic

中譯 說話者主要在討論什麼？
(A) 教育課程
(B) 報名費
(C) 圖書館募款活動
(D) 社區野餐活動

90 Why is the speaker concerned?
(A) There is a shortage of funding.
(B) A meeting space is not available.
(C) Bad weather is expected soon.
(D) Interest in a project has declined.

中譯 說話者為什麼感到擔憂？
(A) 資金短缺。
(B) 某會議空間無法使用。
(C) 預計天氣很快會變差。
(D) 大家對某專案的興趣下滑。

91 What does the speaker ask the listeners to do?
(A) Register for an event
(B) Send her property information
(C) Meet in front of a building
(D) Make a financial donation

中譯 說話者要求聽者做什麼事？
(A) 報名某活動
(B) 傳場地資料給她
(C) 在大樓前見面
(D) 進行財務捐款

Questions 92-94 refer to the following announcement. 澳M 宣告

Good morning. ⑨② **It's wonderful to see so many people here for our hospital's free annual health screening. You'll be given a complete checkup by me or one of my colleagues.** We are also happy to answer any questions about specific concerns you may have. Although it's not required, ⑨③ **there is a survey form to fill out regarding amenities you'd like to see at the hospital.** This is really valuable information. ⑨③ **Without it, we have difficulty knowing our areas of weakness.** ⑨④ **Please remember to bring your coat, handbag, and other belongings with you when you come into the exam room.** We won't be monitoring this area, so it's best not to leave them unattended.

早安。⑨② **看到這麼多人來我們醫院進行免費的每年健康篩檢，真的太棒了。我和我的同仁會幫大家做完善的檢查。**我們也很樂於回答任何您可能想問的特定健康問題。雖然非硬性規定，⑨③ **但我們有問卷表可以讓大家填寫，希望在醫院看到哪些設施。**這是非常寶貴的資訊。⑨③ **如果沒有這些反饋，我們很難知道自己哪些部分該改進。**⑨④ **當你前往檢查室時，請記得攜帶您的外套、手提包和其他個人物品。**此區域沒有人員監管，所以東西最好隨身攜帶。

字彙 screening 篩檢　amenity 設施　weakness 弱點　belongings 個人物品　unattended 無人看守的

92 Who most likely is the speaker?
(A) A security guard
(B) A college lecturer
(C) A tour guide
(D) A medical professional

中譯 說話者最有可能是什麼身分？
(A) 警衛
(B) 大學講師
(C) 導遊
(D) 專業醫護人員

93 What does the speaker mean when he says, "This is really valuable information"?
(A) He encourages the listeners to complete a survey.
(B) He is concerned that some documents will get lost.
(C) He wants some data to be carefully protected.
(D) He is pleased that so much information has been gathered.

中譯 說話者說：「這是非常寶貴的資訊」是什麼意思？
(A) 他鼓勵聽者完成問卷。
(B) 他擔心有些文件會遺失。
(C) 他想要某些資料能被妥善保護。
(D) 他很開心收集到許多資訊。

94 What are the listeners reminded to do?
(A) Keep their personal items with them
(B) Call later for some test results
(C) Be ready to present an ID card
(D) Fill out a registration form in advance

中譯 聽者被提醒做什麼事？
(A) 隨身攜帶自己的個人物品
(B) 晚點打電話來了解檢驗結果
(C) 準備好出示身分證
(D) 事先填好報名表

Questions 95-97 refer to the following telephone message and order from. 美M 電話留言和訂單

Good morning, Ms. Segura. This is Jason from Summertime Landscaping. ⓽⓹ **I wanted to check a quantity on the order you placed.** Um . . . ⓽⓺ **There seem to be too many rose bushes for the size of your property.** Please call me back at 555-5928 to let me know how many you need. I'll be doing some planting at a customer's house this afternoon, so it would be better to call before lunch, if possible. ⓽⓻ **If I'm not here, just ask for Phillip. He can write down your comments and leave them on my desk.**

Customer: Faye Segura **Order number:** 1223389	
Description	**Quantity**
Daffodil bulbs	35
Tulip bulbs	30
⓽⓺ **Rose bushes**	**15**
Lavender bushes	6

早安，賽古拉小姐，我是夏日造景公司的傑森。⓽⓹ **我想確認一下您訂單上的數量。**嗯……⓽⓺ **以您的房屋大小來說，玫瑰灌木叢的數量似乎過多。**請回撥 555-5928 給我，跟我說您需要的數量。我今天下午會到顧客家施作植栽工務，所以可以的話，午餐前打給我比較好。⓽⓻ **如果我不在，請您找菲利浦。他會寫下您的意見並放在我桌上。**

顧客：菲・賽古拉 **訂單編號：**1223389	
說明	**數量**
水仙花球莖	35
鬱金香球莖	30
⓽⓺ **玫瑰灌木叢**	**15**
鬱金香灌木叢	6

字彙 quantity 數量　place an order 下訂單　bush 灌木叢　planting 植栽

95 What is the purpose of the call?
(A) To change an appointment
(B) To verify an order
(C) To notify of a delivery error
(D) To request a payment

中譯 此通電話的目的是什麼？
(A) 更改預約時間
(B) 確認訂單
(C) 通知貨運錯誤
(D) 要求付款

96 Look at the graphic. Which quantity does the speaker refer to?
(A) 35 (B) 30
(C) 15 (D) 6

中譯 請看圖表。說話者指的是哪個數量？
(A) 35 (B) 30
(C) 15 (D) 6

97 What does the speaker say about Phillip?
(A) He can issue a refund.
(B) He can take a message.
(C) He can design a garden.
(D) He can pick up some plants.

中譯 說話者提到菲利浦會做什麼事？
(A) 他可以辦理退款。
(B) 他可以記下留言。
(C) 他可以設計花園。
(D) 他可以去領取一些植物。

08

Questions 98-100 refer to the following excerpt from a meeting and chart. 美W 會議節錄和圖表

Here at Florence Inc., ⑱ **we're dedicated to maintaining a pleasant work environment for our staff as well as providing customers with the insurance they need.** That's why we asked for your suggestions at last week's meeting. You'll see on this chart the most popular ones. The managers have already started reassessing the company dress code, and we'll have more news on that in May. ⑲ **Then in June, we'll consider the second-most-common suggestion.** Also, although we can't provide free lunches like some of you suggested, ⑳ **I'm pleased to say there's coffee and doughnuts in the staff lounge today, so help yourselves.**

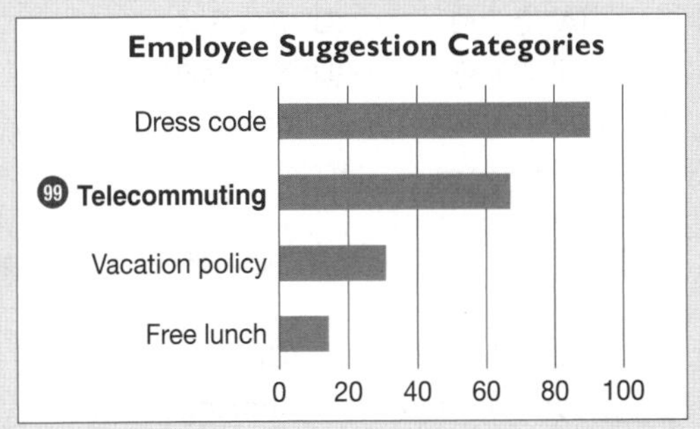

在佛羅倫斯公司，⑱ **我們致力為職員維護愉快的工作環境，同時提供顧客所需的保險。**這也是為什麼我們上週開會時請大家提出建議。大家可從此圖表看得出來最受歡迎的提議。經理們已經開始重新評估公司的服裝規範，五月的時候會有更多消息。⑲ **到六月時，我們會考慮第二熱門的建議。**此外，儘管我們無法如你們建議的那樣提供免費午餐，⑳ **但我很開心宣布，今天職員休息室裡有咖啡和甜甜圈，請大家自行取用。**

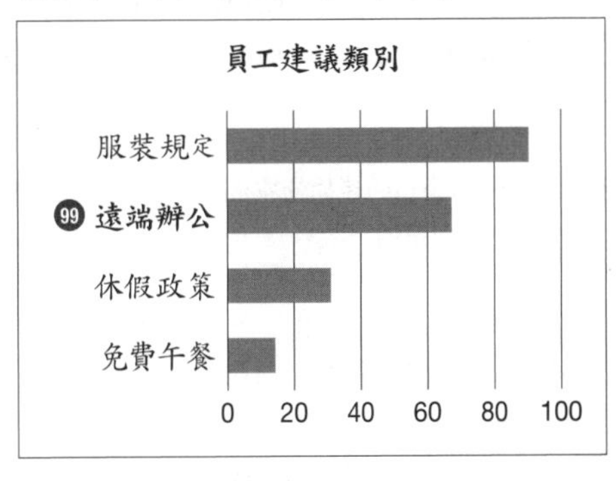

字彙 be dedicated to 致力於　reassess 重新評估

98 Where do the listeners most likely work?
(A) At an insurance company
(B) At a law firm
(C) At a magazine publisher
(D) At an environmental agency

中譯 聽者最有可能在哪裡工作？
(A) 保險公司
(B) 法律事務所
(C) 雜誌出版社
(D) 環境機構

99 Look at the graphic. What topic will the company address in June?
(A) Dress code **(B) Telecommuting**
(C) Vacation policy (D) Free lunch

中譯 請看圖表。該公司六月會處理什麼主題？
(A) 服裝規範 **(B) 遠端辦公**
(C) 休假政策 (D) 免費午餐

100 According to the speaker, what is available in the staff lounge today?
(A) A policy explanation
(B) Some survey forms
(C) Some refreshments
(D) A customer list

中譯 根據說話者的說法，今天的職員休息室有什麼？
(A) 政策說明
(B) 問卷表
(C) 點心飲料
(D) 顧客名單

PART 5

人稱代名詞——主格

101 大多數參加會議的人確認他們學到了很有用的資訊。
(A) 他們的東西 (B) 他們的
(C) 他們 **(D) 他們**

字彙 **attendee** 參加者 **conference** 會議

填入名詞+動名詞 vs 名詞

102 是否能可靠地滿足配送需求，是所有快遞業者很重視的部分。
(A) 依賴 (B) 依賴 (C) 可依賴的 **(D) 可靠度**

字彙 **reliability** 可靠度 **meet** 滿足 **courier** 快遞

不定代名詞 one

103 凱勒汽車公司的迷你油電混合車，是國內販售的同型車中最平價的一款。
(A) 如此
(B)（代名詞用法）一款
(C)（關係代名詞用法）……的事物
(D) 每個

字彙 **automotive** 汽車 **affordable** 平價的

動詞 change

104 愛默森鐵路公司為了省錢而想要更換保險公司。
(A) 涵蓋 (B) 浮現 **(C) 更改** (D) 取得

介系詞 along

105 馬拉松的參加者會沿著尼斯河跑步，並於柳木公園完成比賽。
(A) 沿著 (B) 到……之上 (C) 分離 (D) 除非

字彙 **participant** 參加者

不定詞to——副詞作用

106 齊普利家電公司新出的乾衣機，能自動感應衣物是否烘乾。
(A) 感應 (B) 感應 (C) 感應 (D) 感應

字彙 **appliance** 家電

副詞 barely

107 外燴人員對顧客幾乎沒拿海鮮開胃菜感到驚訝。
(A) 方便地 (B) 明顯地
(C) 幾乎沒有地 (D) 稍微地

字彙 **caterer** 外燴人員 **appetizer** 開胃菜

形容詞 imperative

108 冬裝的旺季快到了，所以當務之急是要盡快幫博卡分店找到新店長。
(A) 急迫的 (B) 有回應的
(C) 獨有的 (D) 有說服力的

字彙 **peak season** 旺季 **branch** 分店；分公司

連接詞 vs 介系詞

109 27 號高速公路新增車道的工程，因為建材短缺而延誤。
(A) 因為 (B) 因為 (C) 以免 (D) 因此

字彙 **construction** 工程 **shortage** 短缺

名詞 enrollment

110 社區中心官員很開心課程報名率已經增加 15%。
(A) 說明 **(B) 報名** (C) 存貨 (D) 態度

字彙 **community center** 社區中心 **official** 官員

連接詞 provided that

111 只要讀者有先取得圖書館主任的特殊許可，即可將參考書帶離圖書館。
(A) 否則 (B) 因此 (C) 儘管 **(D) 只要**
字彙 patron 主顧 reference book 參考書 permission 許可 head 負責人

填入形容詞——主詞補語

112 裝設好售票機後，車站就能接待更多乘客。
(A) 可能的 (B) 可能性
(C) 可能地 (D) 可能性
字彙 ticketing 售票 install 裝設

副詞 regularly

113 杜威特通信公司會定期為員工提供客服教育訓練，因此已建立服務卓越的名聲。
(A) 定期地 (B) 堅定地
(C) 近期地 (D) 迅速地
字彙 build a reputation 建立聲望 excellence 卓越

填入副詞——修飾形容詞

114 根據規定，我們會向直接涉及此事的人更新訊息。
(A) 更直接 **(B) 直接地**
(C) 直接的 (D) 直率
字彙 in compliance with 遵循…… regulation 法規

慣用片語 a wealth of

115 捷隆製藥公司所維護的研究資料庫，能為醫師提供豐富的資訊。
(A) 品質 (B) 相似性 **(C) 豐富** (D) 提及
字彙 pharmaceutical 製藥的 physician 醫師

填入形容詞+分詞

116 一旦交易完成後，要求此筆轉帳的人就會收到確認款項存入的訊息。
(A) 確認 (B) 確認 (C) 已確認 (D) 確認
字彙 transaction 交易 transfer 轉帳

連接詞 now that

117 林肯先生因為加入飛行常客計畫，於是一直搭乘同一家航空公司。
(A) 以便 (B) 即使 (C) 除非 **(D) 因為**
字彙 frequent flyer 飛行常客

填入動詞+主動語態

118 霍華先生洗車後，上了一層薄蠟以保持表面光亮。
(A) 塗抹 (B) 塗抹 (C) 被塗抹 **(D) 塗抹了**
字彙 apply 塗 coat 層

介系詞 in

119 梅森小姐在預測時，忘了將貨幣匯率的波動納入考量。
(A) 經常 **(B) 在……方面**
(C) 最後 (D) 在……上面
字彙 fluctuation 變動 currency rate 貨幣匯率 projection 預測

填入副詞——修飾形容詞

120 因為佛萊契手機公司類似的手機方案令人混淆，許多潛在顧客因此卻步。
(A) 令人混淆 **(B) 令人混淆地**
(C) 困惑 (D) 困惑的
字彙 potential 潛在的 discouraged 卻步的

填入名詞+名詞 signature

121 程小姐在合約裡加上簽名，以茲作為協議見證人。
(A) 已簽名 (B) 簽名 **(C) 簽名** (D) 簽名
字彙 witness 見證人 agreement 協議

不定代名詞 another

122 如果你遺失或損壞登機證，請跟登機門人員說一聲，他可以幫忙確認並再列印一張。
(A) 另一張 (B) 彼此 (C) 他人 (D) 互相
字彙 boarding pass 登機證 gate 登機門

動詞 specify

123 員工必須明確指出需要維修的裝置型號。
(A) 強化 **(B) 指明** (C) 整合 (D) 證明

介系詞 throughout

124 露西・柏曼八年的職業游泳選手生涯裡，創下許多游泳紀錄。
(A) 在……之上 (B) 關於
(C) 整個 (D) ……的
字彙 set a record 創紀錄

動名詞+被動語態

125 迪亞茲小姐開會遲到，因此她坐在後面以免被注意到。
(A) 注意到 **(B) 被注意到**
(C) 注意 (D) 已注意

填入形容詞+分詞

126 市鎮的獨立日遊行開始時，會先由新上任的民選市長發表簡短演說。
(A) 被選上 (B) 選舉 (C) 選舉 (D) 選出
字彙 Independence Day 獨立日 commence 開始

形容詞 ambitious

127 卡拉・史坦頓是個有抱負的企業家，她的新創事業迅速拓展至全國。

(A) 尷尬的　(B) 可接受的

(C) 有抱負的　(D) 擔心的

字彙 entrepreneur 企業家　launch 推出　start-up 新創事業　expand 拓展

副詞 markedly

128 維維可揚聲器的音質，與市場上其他揚聲器相比明顯優秀許多，但很多人買不起。

(A) 明顯地　(B) 分別地

(C) 固執地　(D) 可容許地

字彙 superior 優秀　on the market 市場上　afford 負擔得起

關係代名詞

129 禮堂裡的前兩排座位特別保留給 VIP 來賓，他們多為演講人。

(A) 之所以 ......　(B) 事實上

(C) 他們多數人　(D) 相反的

字彙 row 排　auditorium 禮堂　reserve 保留　presenter 演講人

形容詞 enjoyable

130 此導覽行程的許多參加者都很開心發現，原來了解本市歷史可以這麼愉快。

(A) 大量的　(B) 應負責任的

(C) 樂在其中的　(D) 可轉讓的

PART 6

Questions 131-134 refer to the following advertisement. 廣告

During the first week of July, Twinkle Jewelry will hold a special event to celebrate its first anniversary. For one week only, get two items, and we ------- (131.) you for only one. For example, if you buy one necklace and one bracelet, you'll pay for the cheaper item only! You can choose any two items you like from our wide ------- (132.) of jewelry. This offer applies to all of our products! ------- (133.), there is no limit to the number of times a person can benefit from it. However, jewelry will be given out on a first come, first served basis while supplies last. ------- (134.). The event starts on July 1.

閃耀珠寶公司將於七月的第一週，舉辦特殊活動來歡慶一週年。僅限一週時間，凡購買兩件商品，我們只 ⑬¹ **收取一件的費用**。假如您購買一條項鍊和一條手鍊，僅需支付金額較低的品項！您可從我們眾多珠寶 ⑬² **選項**裡選出任意兩件商品。此優惠適用於全商品！ ⑬³ **此外**，本優惠不限每人購買次數。不過，我們會以購買順序出貨珠寶，賣完為止。 ⑬⁴ **因此請儘早光臨，確保您不會錯過這個機會**。活動將從 7 月 1 日開始。

字彙 a wide selection 廣泛的選項　apply to 適用於　give out 出貨　on a first come, first served basis 先來後到的順序

填入動詞——未來式+主動語態

131 **(A) will charge**　(B) will be charged

(C) were charging　(D) have been charging

中譯 **(A) 將收費**　(B) 將被收費

(C) 被收費中　(D) 已經被收費中

填入名詞——形容詞+名詞

132 (A) select　(B) selects

(C) selection　(D) selected

中譯 (A) 選取　(B) 選取

(C) 可供挑選的東西　(D) 已選取

連接副詞 in addition

133 **(A) In addition** (B) As a result
(C) Therefore (D) Accordingly

中譯 **(A) 此外** (B) 結果
(C) 因此 (D) 相應地

選出合適的句子

134 (A) That is why we have agreed to refund your purchase.
(B) So come early to make sure you don't miss out.
(C) We will set the items you request aside for you.
(D) Please complete your payment as soon as possible.

中譯 (A) 這就是我們已經同意退款給您的原因。
(B) 因此請儘早光臨，確保您不會錯過這個機會。
(C) 我們會預留您要求的品項。
(D) 請您盡快付款完成。

Questions 135-138 refer to the following notice. 告示

Public Seminar with Nora Devons

Thursday, May 14, 7 P.M.

Nora Devons, a prominent ------- (135.) of eliminating homelessness in Fredrick City, will be presenting a two-hour seminar at the Renner Convention Center. Ms. Devons is the president of the Association of Social Workers, a group with over three hundred members. She ------- (136.) efforts to support the homeless community for the past eight years. During the seminar, she will tell the audience about the seriousness of the homeless problem. ------- (137.) .

The talk is open to audience members of all ages, and there is no entrance fee. ------- (138.) , donations will be collected at the door to support the Marigold Homeless Shelter. For more information, visit www.assocofsw.org.

諾拉・迪馮斯的公開講座

5 月 14 日 星期四 晚上七點

以終止費德烈克市無家者問題的知名 135 **倡議者**諾拉・迪馮斯，將於瑞納會議中心主講兩小時的講座。迪馮斯小姐是「社工協會」的會長，該協會擁有超過三百名的成員。她過去八年來，136 **持續帶領**協會努力支援無家者社群。在此講座裡，她會告訴聽眾無家者問題的嚴重性，137 **亦將提及解決辦法。**

此講座開放所有年齡層的聽眾參加，而且無需入場費。138 **不過**，會場門口會收取支援金盞花無家者收容所的捐款。如需了解更多資訊，請至 www.assocofsw.org。

字彙 **prominent** 著名的 **eliminate** 去除 **association** 協會 **shelter** 收容所

名詞 advocate

135 (A) founder **(B) advocate**
(C) candidate (D) prosecutor

中譯 (A) 創辦人 **(B) 倡議者**
(C) 候選人 (D) 檢察官

現在完成式

136 (A) had been leading **(B) has led**
(C) is leading (D) will lead

中譯 (A) 過去一直領導 **(B) 一直領導**
(C) 正在領導 (D) 將領導

選出合適的句子

137 **(A) She will also mention ways to help resolve it.**
(B) The audience asked questions during the break.
(C) At that time, she served as a city council member.
(D) She plans to return to Grayson University to earn a master's degree.

中譯 **(A) 亦將提及解決辦法。**
(B) 聽眾已於休息時間提問問題。
(C) 她當時是市議員。
(D) 她打算回到葛瑞森大學取得碩士學歷。

連接副詞 however

138 (A) Accordingly (B) Specifically
(C) Apparently **(D) However**

中譯 (A) 相應地 (B) 尤其是
(C) 明顯地 **(D) 不過**

Questions 139-142 refer to the following e-mail. 電子郵件

To: Natasha Seymour <nseymour@vicivenues.com>
From: Robert Thornton <r.thornton@hvelectronics.net>
Date: October 3
Subject: Event at Boulevard Hall

Dear Ms. Seymour,

I am part of a committee that is in charge of ------- **139.** a retirement dinner for one of my coworkers at HV Electronics. Several of your venues ------- **140.**, but Boulevard Hall received the most support. This was due to ------- **141.** modern facilities and proximity to our office in Blakeley Towers.

This will be our first time holding an event at Boulevard Hall. Could you confirm which dates are available in November? We prefer November 20, so we hope that evening is still free. ------- **142.**.

Sincerely,

Robert Thornton

收件人：娜塔莎・席莫爾 <nseymour@vicivenues.com>
寄件人：羅伯特・索恩頓 <r.thornton@hvelectronics.net>
日期：10 月 3 日
主旨：大道廳的活動

親愛的席莫爾小姐：

我是負責幫我 HV 電子公司同事 ⑬⑨ **安排**退休晚宴的委員之一。⑭⓪ 我們**考量過**你們的不少場地，不過大家最喜歡大道廳。這是因為大道廳 ⑭① **它的**現代化設施，且離我們布萊克利大樓的辦公室比較近。

這是我們第一次在大道廳舉辦活動。可否請你確認一下，11 月哪些日期有空檔？我們偏好 11 月 20 日，希望這天晚上仍可預訂。⑭② **如果不能，我們也有想好其他備案。**

敬祝一切順心
羅伯特・索恩頓

字彙 **committee** 委員會 **retirement** 退休 **electronics** 電子用品 **proximity** 鄰近

動詞 arrange

139 (A) inspiring **(B) arranging**
(C) contributing (D) visiting

中譯 (A) 啟發 **(B) 安排**
(C) 貢獻 (D) 造訪

填入動詞——主動語態+過去式

140 (A) will be considered
(B) had considered
(C) were considered
(D) were considering

中譯 (A) 將被考量
(B) 已經考量
(C) 已被考量
(D) 已考量中

所有格

141 (A) their (B) it
(C) its (D) them

中譯 (A) 他們的 (B) 它
(C) 它的 (D) 他們

選出合適的句子

142 (A) We think you will be impressed with the spacious room.
(B) Even so, many people can walk from the office.
(C) This fee is within our estimated budget.
(D) If not, we have a few other possibilities in mind.

中譯 (A) 我們認為你會對寬敞的空間感到印象深刻。
(B) 即使如此，許多人還是可以從辦公室走過去。
(C) 此費用在我們估計的預算內。
(D) 如果不能，我們也有想好其他備案。

Questions 143-146 refer to the following e-mail. 電子郵件

To: Travel Times <info@traveltimes-magazine.com>
From: Christopher Venn <c.venn@frequenx.com>
Subject: Subscription #28571
Date: September 3

To Whom It May Concern:

I currently have a subscription to *Travel Times* magazine which is valid until the end of February. I'm wondering ------- (143.) it is possible to change the mailing address before the next issue comes out. ------- (144.). I'm currently receiving the magazine at work, but the new manager ------- (145.) that we no longer have personal mail delivered there. ------- (146.) residential address is 798 Trelawney Way, Phoenix, AZ 85010. If there is a fee associated with this change, please e-mail me.

Thank you,

Christopher Venn

收件人：旅遊時光 <info@traveltimes-magazine.com>
寄件人：克里斯多夫・范恩 <c.venn@frequenx.com>
主旨：#28571 的訂閱
日期：9 月 3 日

敬啟者：

我目前訂閱的《旅遊時光》雜誌，將於二月底到期。我在想我 143 **是否**可以在下一期發行前，就更改郵寄地址。144 **我無法在你們的網站上，找到有關的任何資訊。**我目前的收件地址是公司，但新經理 145 **要求**我們不能再把個人郵件寄到公司。146 **我的**住家地址是 85010 亞利桑那州鳳凰城，崔羅尼大道 798 號。如果此異動會產生費用，請用電子郵件告知我。

謝謝你們
克里斯多夫・范恩

字彙 **subscription** 訂閱 **valid** 有效的 **come out** 發行、推出 **residential** 居住的

名詞子句連接詞 if

143 (A) what **(B) if**
(C) while (D) for

中譯 (A) ……的 **(B) 是否**
(C) 正當 …… (D) 為了……

選出合適的句子

144 (A) The information on Spain was particularly interesting.
(B) The monthly bill had charged me for two subscriptions.
(C) I couldn't find any information about doing this through your Web site.
(D) I appreciate your printing the article I submitted.

中譯 (A) 有關西班牙的資訊格外有趣。
(B) 每月帳單收取了我兩份訂閱的費用。
(C) 我無法在你們的網站上，找到有關的任何資訊。
(D) 我很感激你們刊出我投稿的文章。

動詞 request

145 **(A) requested** (B) facilitated
(C) acknowledged (D) canceled

中譯 **(A) 要求** (B) 促進
(C) 認可 (D) 取消

所有格

146 (A) Your (B) Its
(C) Each **(D) My**

中譯 (A) 你的 (B) 它的
(C) 每個 **(D) 我的**

PART 7

Questions 147-148 refer to the following notice. 告示

Warm Hands Warm Hearts (WHWH) ⑭⑦ **is seeking new members for Melville's local group,** which knits mittens and gloves to donate to the homeless. Our next meeting will be on Saturday, November 2, from 1 P.M. to 4 P.M. at the Lindale Coffee Shop. To get there, take subway line 5 to Kingstown Arena Station and use exit 5.

Participants should bring their own yarn and knitting needles. In addition, we would like a variety of colors and yarn types, ⑭⑧ **so please let us know what you plan to bring for your project by commenting in the forum at warmhandswh.org/forum.**

「暖手暖心」(WHWH) ⑭⑦ **在為梅維爾當地團體找尋新成員，**此團體會織連指和五指手套，以捐給無家者。我們下次聚會的時間是 11 月 2 日星期六，下午一點至四點，地點是林戴爾咖啡店。可以搭地鐵五號線到金士頓體育館站，然後走五號出口即可抵達。

請參加者攜帶自己的毛線和棒針。此外，我們希望能有各種顏色和不同種類的毛線，⑭⑧ **因此請在 warmhandswh.org/forum 的論壇留言，讓我們知道您會攜帶哪種毛線。**

字彙 knit 打毛線 mitten 連指手套 the homeless 無家者 yarn 毛線 knitting needle 棒針

出處問題

147 Where most likely would the notice be found?
(A) In a product catalog
(B) On a public bulletin board
(C) On a subway ticket receipt
(D) In a craft instruction book

中譯 最有可能在哪裡看到此告示？
(A) 產品型錄
(B) 公共布告欄
(C) 地鐵車票收據
(D) 手工藝說明手冊

確認特定資訊問題

148 According to the notice, why should people visit the Web site?
(A) To view photos of past projects
(B) To confirm registration for an event
(C) To request instructions by e-mail
(D) To report their choices of materials

中譯 根據告示內容，為什麼要大家去這個網站？
(A) 看過去活動的照片
(B) 確認報名某活動
(C) 以電子郵件索取說明資料
(D) 回報自己所選的材料

Questions 149-150 refer to the following invoice. 帳單

Wallace Tools

Invoice Date: October 25
Invoice Number: 8395
Name: Dean Monette
Address: 805 Carriage Drive, Arlington Heights, IL 60005
Contact Number: 555-6950

One-week Rental: $49.99
[Contents]
Hadron-360 electric drill
149D **Plastic carrying case**
149B **Charging device for unit battery**
149C **One-week insurance coverage (policy information printout)**
Tax and Shipping: $8.95
Total: $58.94

Payment has been received in full for the above service. 150 **If you would like to keep the item longer, please call us at 555-2900.** 149A **The device's user manual can be downloaded from our Web site at www.wallacetools.net.**

華勒斯工具

帳單日期：10月25日
帳單號碼：8395
姓名：狄恩・孟奈特
地址：60005伊利諾州阿靈頓高地，馬車大道805號
聯絡電話：555-6950

一週租金：$49.99
[明細]
哈頓360電鑽
149D **塑膠隨身包**
149B **電池所需的充電裝置**
149C **一週保險費(會有紙本保單資料)**
稅金和運費：$8.95
總金額：$58.94

上述服務已經收到全額款項。150 **如果您希望延長租用時間，請打555-2900通知我們。** 149A **您可至我們的網站www.wallacetools.net下載設備使用說明書。**

字彙 invoice 帳單　rental 租用的　coverage 保險範圍　printout 紙本資料　user manual 使用說明書

Not / True 問題

149 What was NOT sent with the rental item?
(A) A user manual
(B) A battery charger
(C) Insurance details
(D) A portable container

中譯 何者不會跟此租用物品一起寄出？
(A) 使用說明書
(B) 電池充電器
(C) 保險詳細資料
(D) 攜帶式收納袋

確認特定資訊問題

150 Why should Mr. Monette call the number provided?
(A) To give feedback about a service
(B) To make a payment
(C) To request instructions
(D) To extend a rental period

中譯 孟奈特先生為何會需要打電話？
(A) 反饋某服務
(B) 付款
(C) 索取說明書
(D) 延長租期

Questions 151-152 refer to the following article. 文章

BEIJING (July 5)—The price of raw silk is on the rise again after hitting a four-year low last quarter. This is in part due to trends in China and India, the world's largest producers of silk. ⓯ **Silk suppliers have been accumulating large quantities of the product at cheap prices and storing it rather than putting it on the market. This has led to an increase in price,** which is expected to continue for the next few quarters. Clothing producers have enjoyed the low price of silk, but now that a higher cost of raw materials is projected, the fabric is much less attractive. As a result, (152) **many such producers are designing clothing made from man-made fabric, such as nylon and rayon, to avoid the unpredictability of the silk market.**

北京訊(7月5日)——生絲的價格在上一季創下四年來新低後，終於再度爬升。部分原因來自全球最大宗蠶絲生產地——中國和印度的趨勢。(151) **蠶絲供應商一直以低價囤積大量產品，而非釋放到市場。因此導致價格增加，**預計此情況會延續至未來幾季。服飾生產商以往樂享蠶絲的低價格，但在市場已預見原物料成本上漲的情況下，絲質布料變得不那麼吸引人了。因此，(152) **許多此類生產商開始設計人造布料所製成的服飾，例如尼龍和嫘縈，來避免蠶絲市場難以預測的變化。**

字彙 raw silk 生絲　on the rise 爬升的　hit a low 創新低的　in part 部分　accumulate 累積　fabric 布料　man-made 人造的　unpredictability 難以預測性

確認特定資訊問題

151 According to the article, what has affected the price of silk?

(A) Some dealers are stocking up on the material.
(B) The currency value in China and India has dropped.
(C) Production has increased in efficiency.
(D) Customers are starting to prefer other fabrics.

中譯 根據文章的說法，什麼原因影響了蠶絲價格？

(A) 有些經銷商在囤積此原料。
(B) 中國和印度的貨幣貶值。
(C) 生產效率增加。
(D) 顧客開始偏好其他布料。

確認特定資訊問題

152 How are clothing manufacturers dealing with a change?

(A) By negotiating directly with suppliers
(B) By developing products with alternative materials
(C) By purchasing supplies in bulk
(D) By changing the way goods are advertised

 服飾製造商如何應對此變化？

(A) 直接和供應商協商
(B) 以替代性的原料來開發產品
(C) 大量購買庫存
(D) 改變廣告商品的方式

Questions 153-155 refer to the following e-mail. 電子郵件

To: Nina Ezell <n.ezell@prime-cleaning.net>
From: Akash Badal <a.badal@prime-cleaning.net>
Date: April 4
Subject: Cleaning services

收件人：妮娜・伊席爾 <n.ezell@prime-cleaning.net>
寄件人：阿卡希・巴戴爾 <a.badal@prime-cleaning.net>
日期：4月4日
主旨：清潔服務

Dear Nina,

I am writing to you regarding the professional cleaning services that we will provide for Gilbert & Associates starting from April 10. I was looking over the contract that you wanted me to review, ⑮³ **but I'm afraid we can't sign it in its current form because the wrong address was used.** ⑮⁴ **I know you met with a Gilbert & Associates representative on April 1 to discuss the contract terms. However, that person should have told you that they were going to relocate their offices two days later.** The contract should reflect the new building's address. Since you're the one who has been handling this client, ⑮⁵ **I think it would be best for you to call them to find out the exact new address.** We should send the signed version by courier tomorrow, ⑮⁵ **so please take care of this today so we don't get behind schedule on the paperwork.**

Sincerely,

Akash

親愛的妮娜：

我寫信給妳的目的，是要討論我們將從 4 月 10 日開始向吉伯特公司提供的專業清潔服務。我正在看妳要我審核的合約，⑮³ **但恐怕我們無法簽訂現行版本，因為地址寫錯了。** ⑮⁴ **我知道妳 4 月 1 日有和吉伯特公司的代表人員開會討論合約條款。不過，該人員應該已經告訴妳，他們兩天後要搬遷辦公室。**合約應該要寫出新大樓的地址才對。既然一直是妳負責與此客戶接洽，⑮⁵ **我想由妳聯絡他們來確認新的地址最好。**我們明天就該把簽好的合約交給快遞，⑮⁵ **所以請今天處理好這件事，文書作業的進度就不會落後了。**

敬祝一切順心，

阿卡希

字彙 associate 合夥　representative 代表人員　terms 條款　relocate 搬遷　reflect 對應、反映出　behind schedule 進度落後　paperwork 文書作業

目的問題

153 Why did Mr. Badal send the e-mail?

(A) To recommend a business
(B) To change a cleaning schedule
(C) To send an updated contract
(D) To point out an error

中譯 巴戴爾先生為什麼要傳送此電子郵件？

(A) 推薦某公司
(B) 更改清潔行程
(C) 傳送已更新的合約
(D) 指出某錯誤

確認特定資訊問題

154 When did Gilbert & Associates move to a new building?

(A) March 28　(B) March 30
(C) April 1　**(D) April 3**

中譯 吉伯特公司什麼時候要搬到新大樓？

(A) 3 月 28 日　(B) 3 月 30 日
(C) 4 月 1 日　**(D) 4 月 3 日**

確認特定資訊問題

155 What should Ms. Ezell do by the end of the day?

(A) Negotiate some contract terms
(B) Contact the Gilbert & Associates office
(C) Send Mr. Badal a client recommendation
(D) Mail some documents to Prime Cleaning

中譯 伊席爾小姐下班前應該要做什麼？

(A) 協商合約條款
(B) 聯絡吉伯特公司
(C) 向巴戴爾先生傳送想推薦的客戶資料
(D) 將文件郵寄給一流清潔公司

Questions 156-157 refer to the following text-message chain. 簡訊串

Donald Graham [9:12 A.M.]
156 I've e-mailed you the estimate from the interior designer for remodeling our lobby.

Wei Lu [9:14 A.M.]
It's more expensive than I was expecting, especially since our lawyers don't even use that area much.

Donald Graham [9:15 A.M.]
Yes, it's slightly over budget, but I think it's worth it.

Wei Lu [9:16 A.M.]
Do you? It doesn't even include the cost of furniture.

Donald Graham [9:18 A.M.]
157 You have to understand that the lobby is the first thing people see when they arrive. It's essential that they have a good opinion of our business right from the start.

Wei Lu [9:19 A.M.]
You have a point. I guess it will give people more confidence in our services.

唐諾・葛拉漢 [早上 9:12]
156 我已經把室內設計師重新整修我們大廳的估價，寄到你的電子信箱了。

盧薇 [早上 9:14]
比我預計的還要貴，尤其是我們的律師根本不常用到那個區域。

唐諾・葛拉漢 [早上 9:15]
是啊，有點超出預算，但我覺得值得。

盧薇 [早上 9:16]
真的嗎？估價甚至沒有包含家具的費用。

唐諾・葛拉漢 [早上 9:18]
157 你要知道，大廳是大家到這之後所看見的第一個地方。讓客戶從一開始就對我們公司產生良好印象是很重要的。

盧薇 [早上 9:19]
你說的有道理。我想這個形象會讓大家對我們的服務更有信心。

字彙 estimate 估價　slightly 有一點　budget 預算　essential 必需的
have a good opinion of 對……有良好印象

主題問題

156 What are the writers mainly discussing?
(A) Hotel accommodations
(B) Budget limits
(C) Renovation costs
(D) Customer reviews

中譯 簡訊串裡的人主要在討論什麼事？
(A) 飯店住宿
(B) 預算限制
(C) 裝修費用
(D) 顧客評價

掌握意圖問題

157 At 9:19 A.M., what does Ms. Lu most likely mean when she writes, "You have a point"?
(A) Attracting new customers is not easy.
(B) The business should be careful about spending.
(C) Making a good impression is important.
(D) The lobby needs to be expanded soon.

中譯 早上9點19分，盧小姐的訊息「你說的有道理」，最有可能是什麼意思？
(A) 吸引新顧客並不容易。
(B) 公司應該謹慎花費。
(C) 給人良好的印象很重要。
(D) 大廳必須盡快擴建。

Questions 158-160 refer to the following article. 文章

NEW YORK (September 10)—Paula Frederick is known for her trendy and sophisticated fashions both on and off the runway. In addition to her retail business, ⓯⓼ **she has created award-winning costumes for a number of films, most recently the sci-fi blockbuster *Golden Galaxy*.** Now Ms. Frederick is lending her talents to a new project—designing warm-up uniforms and performance outfits for the national ice skating team. The team will wear them at the International Ice Skating Tournament, which will take place from January 3 to January 16.

159 **Ms. Frederick was offered the project after meeting the team's coach, Vince Oliero, at an anniversary event for Charlotte Reeves, whose fashion house was Ms. Frederick's first employer after she graduated from design school.** When Mr. Oliero mentioned that the team needed to update its look, the idea for the project was born.

Industry insiders are interested to see how Ms. Frederick's elaborate style will translate to the sports world. "I'm looking forward to the challenge," 160 **Ms. Frederick said at the debut event for *Golden Galaxy* earlier this week.** "With the film, I was able to work with over-the-top designs and lavish embellishments. With my new project, I'll have limited fabric options and will need to prioritize comfort and practicality." 160 ***Golden Galaxy* producer Liam Hart, who accompanied Ms. Frederick to the event,** also commented on the project, saying that he was certain Ms. Frederick's limitless creativity would help to make it a success.

Fans of Ms. Frederick's work can see *Golden Galaxy* costumes on the big screen and on her Web site. However, to see the uniforms they'll have to watch the tournament in person or live on television.

紐約訊(9月10日)——寶拉・費德瑞克以她流行又精緻的伸展台與日常時裝聞名。除了零售事業以外,158 **她亦為為眾多電影設計戲服,獲獎無數。最近的作品就是賣座科幻片《黃金銀河系》。**費德瑞克小姐現在又將才華延伸至新專案,為國家溜冰隊設計熱身服和比賽服。溜冰隊將於1月3日至1月16日的國際溜冰錦標賽穿上她的設計。

159 **費德瑞克小姐與溜冰隊教練文斯・奧利若,在夏綠蒂・李維斯的週年活動見面時,受邀進行此隊服設計專案。而李維斯的時裝品牌,則是費德瑞克小姐從設計學院畢業後的第一份工作。**當奧利若先生提到溜冰隊必需更新服裝時,雙方即產生合作的想法。

業界人士均對於費德瑞克小姐的細膩風格會如何轉化到體壇很感興趣。160 **費德瑞克小姐這週稍早在《黃金銀河系》首映會上表示:**「我很期待這項挑戰。透過這部電影,我得以運用前衛設計和華麗的裝飾。至於我的新專案,布料選擇比較有限,我需要優先考量舒適度和實用性。」160 **陪同費德瑞克小姐參加首映的《黃金銀河系》製作人李恩・哈特,**亦對新專案表示看法。他確信費德瑞克小姐的無窮創意一定能成功呈現作品。

喜愛費德瑞克小姐作品的粉絲,可從大銀幕和她的網站上欣賞到《黃金銀河系》的戲服。不過,如果是想欣賞隊服,就得親自到場或看錦標賽的電視直播了。

字彙 sophisticated 精緻的　fashion house 時裝品牌　insider 內行人　elaborate 精心、細膩的　translate 轉化　over-the-top 前衛的　lavish 華麗的　embellishment 裝飾　prioritize 以……為優先

Not / True 問題

158 What is true about the *Golden Galaxy* costumes?
(A) They were Ms. Frederick's first project.
(B) They are practical and comfortable.
(C) They received an award.
(D) They are available for sale online.

中譯 關於《黃金銀河系》的戲服,以下說明何者為真?
(A) 是費德瑞克小姐第一次負責的專案。
(B) 實用又舒適。
(C) 獲得獎項肯定。
(D) 可在網路上購得。

推論問題

159 Who most likely is Ms. Reeves?
(A) An ice skating coach
(B) A fashion designer
(C) A film producer
(D) A professional athlete

中譯 李維斯小姐最有可能是什麼身分？
(A) 溜冰教練
(B) 時裝設計師
(C) 電影製作人
(D) 專業運動員

推論問題

160 What is suggested about Mr. Hart?
(A) He has worked with Ms. Frederick on several projects.
(B) He recently attended a movie premiere.
(C) He met Ms. Frederick at an anniversary party.
(D) He knows Ms. Reeves personally.

中譯 可從文中得知哈特先生的什麼資訊？
(A) 他已經和費德瑞克小姐合作過幾項專案。
(B) 他最近參加電影首映會。
(C) 他在某週年慶派對認識費德瑞克小姐。
(D) 他私下認識李維斯小姐。

Questions 161-163 refer to the following letter. 信函

March 8
Store Manager Shawn Boyd
Outdoors Plus, Soulard Branch
1009 Ash Avenue
Saint Louis, MO 63146

Dear Mr. Boyd,

As you know, 161 **Camping Sphere Inc. is introducing a new lightweight backpack to its product line. For the entire months of April and May, we will hold a special promotion, offering the product at 30% off its suggested retail price.** We'll start advertising the sale two weeks in advance. The official launch date will be April 1, 162 **and there will be a special launch event at the McKinley Heights branch.** I know you also applied to hold the event at the Soulard branch, 162 **but we decided to go with a store that had already been in charge of large-scale events such as this.** 163 **I will visit your store next week to drop off the displays for the new backpacks.** These stands should be placed in a prominent area, 163 **and I can advise you on the arrangement at that time.**

Sincerely,
Justin Dawson
Justin Dawson

3月8日
63146 密蘇里州聖路易市
艾許大道 1009 號
正宇戶外用品公司 紹萊德分店
店長 肖恩・博伊德 啟

親愛的博伊德先生：

如你所知，161 **露營星球公司目前的產品線正推出新款的輕型背包。整個四月和五月，我們都會有特殊促銷活動，新款背包的零售定價會打七折優惠。**我們會提早兩週廣告此活動。正式上市日期是 4 月 1 日，162 **而麥金利高地分店會舉辦特殊上市活動。**我知道你也有申請在紹萊德分店舉辦活動，162 **但我們決定由已經舉辦過此類大型活動經驗的分店來負責。**163 **我下週會去你的分店，給你新背包的展示素材。**這些立牌應該要放在顯眼的區域，163 **我到時候會建議你擺放的方式。**

敬祝一切順心，
賈斯汀・道森

字彙 lightweight 輕型的　in advance 事先　large-scale 大規模的　drop off 帶……去某處
prominent 顯著的　arrangement 擺放方式

確認特定資訊問題

161 How long will the discount on the new product be offered?
(A) One week (B) Two weeks
(C) One month **(D) Two months**

中譯 新產品提供折扣的期間有多久？
(A) 一週 (B) 兩週
(C) 一個月 **(D) 兩個月**

確認特定資訊問題

162 According to the letter, why was the McKinley Heights branch selected for an event?
(A) It needs the most improvement in its sales figures.
(B) Its employees have hosted similar events.
(C) It is the company's largest store.
(D) Its customers voted to hold the event there.

中譯 根據信件內容，麥金利高地分店為什麼獲選為活動舉辦場地？
(A) 銷售數據的改善空間最大。
(B) 員工已舉辦過類似活動。
(C) 是該公司規模最大的分店。
(D) 由顧客投票表決在那裡舉辦活動。

接下來要進行之事的問題

163 What will happen next week?
(A) A branch manager will print out some promotional material.
(B) Mr. Dawson will recommend some display strategies.
(C) A store will start selling a new line of backpacks.
(D) Mr. Boyd will oversee a product launch event.

中譯 下週會發生什麼事？
(A) 分店店長會印出一些促銷素材。
(B) 道森先生會建議一些展示策略。
(C) 某店會開始銷售新的背包系列。
(D) 博伊德先生將監督產品上市活動。

Questions 164-167 refer to the following online chat discussion. 網路聊天

Clara Starnes 1:09 P.M.
Hi. **164 I'm going to write about the Lafayette Art Museum for my next exhibit review. I know you've all been there before. Do you have any advice for me?**

Radha Pai 1:18 P.M.
The size of the collection is enormous, so you need to plan ahead to see everything.

Clara Starnes 1:42 P.M.
I've heard that visitors aren't allowed to take pictures in some sections of the museum.

Joyce Garza 1:46 P.M.
You're right, Clara. Photos are not permitted in some sections, but signs are prominently displayed to inform visitors.

克萊拉・史塔恩斯 下午 1:09
嗨，**164 我下一篇的展覽評論會寫拉法葉美術館。我知道大家都曾去過，有什麼建議嗎？**

蕾哈・派 下午 1:18
館藏量很龐大，所以你需要事先規劃，才有辦法看完所有東西。

克萊拉・史塔恩斯 下午 1:42
我聽說館內有些區域不讓參觀者拍照。

喬伊斯・加薩 下午 1:46
沒錯，克萊拉。雖然有些區域不許拍照，但是會有清楚張貼的告示來告知參觀者。

Clara Starnes 1:59 P.M.
⑯⑤ I assume it's really busy on weekends, so I think I'll go on a weekday. Which day is best?

克萊拉・史塔恩斯 下午 1:59
⑯⑤ 我猜週末會很多人，所以我想我會平日去。哪一天去最好？

Joyce Garza 2:16 P.M.
It's always packed. But in my experience, **⑯⑤ Tuesday is the best day to go if you don't want to be around a lot of tourists and school groups.**

喬伊斯・加薩 下午 2:16
人潮一直都很多。但以我的經驗，**⑯⑤ 如果你不想跟很多遊客和學校團體擠，星期二是最好的日子。**

Clara Starnes 2:25 P.M.
⑯⑤ Then I think I'll go there on Tuesday.

克萊拉・史塔恩斯 下午 2:25
⑯⑤ 那我想我會星期二去。

Alyssa Verdi 2:37 P.M.
⑯⑥ You can get information about their regulations from the Web site, information desk, and signs posted throughout the museum.

愛麗莎・佛迪 下午 2:37
⑯⑥ 你可以從他們的網站、服務台和館內隨處可見的告示，得知他們相關規定的資訊。

Radha Pai 2:51 P.M.
⑯⑥ Right. Lafayette is better than the place I visited last week, Timber Museum. Timber Museum should follow its example.

蕾哈・派 下午 2:51
⑯⑥ 沒錯。拉法葉比我上週參觀過的提姆波爾博物館還棒。提姆波爾博物館應該以他們為榜樣。

Alyssa Verdi 2:55 P.M.
⑯⑦ If you plan on going more than once, it's worth signing up for a membership. It costs $20 for a one-year membership, but you save $7 each time you visit.

愛麗莎・佛迪 下午 2:55
⑯⑦ 如果你打算去很多次，註冊會員就很划算。一年的會員費用是 20 美元，但每次參觀就會省下 7 美元。

Clara Starnes 3:39 P.M.
I appreciate your advice, everyone.

克萊拉・史塔恩斯 下午 3:39
很感激大家給的建議。

字彙 **collection** 館藏 **enormous** 龐大的 **plan ahead** 事先計劃 **sign up for** 註冊

確認特定資訊問題

164 What does Ms. Starnes ask for?
(A) Recommendations for tourist sites
(B) Tips for visiting a place
(C) Advice for opening an exhibit
(D) Explanation about a schedule

中譯 史塔恩斯小姐問了什麼事？
(A) 請大家推薦觀光景點
(B) 某處的參訪建議
(C) 開展覽的建議
(D) 請大家解說某行程

確認特定資訊問題

165 Why does Ms. Starnes decide to make a visit on Tuesday?
(A) Because she wants to avoid the crowds.
(B) Because she can listen to a special lecture.
(C) Because the entrance fee is discounted.
(D) Because a guided tour is being offered.

中譯 史塔恩斯小姐為什麼決定星期二去參觀？
(A) 因為她想避開人潮。
(B) 因為可以去聽特殊的演講。
(C) 因為門票有打折。
(D) 因為有導覽服務。

掌握意圖問題

166 At 2:51 P.M., what does Ms. Pai most likely mean when she writes, "Timber Museum should follow its example"?
(A) The attendance at Timber Museum has gone down significantly.
(B) The entrance fee at Timber Museum is too expensive for tourists.
(C) The policies at Timber Museum are not clearly explained.
(D) The collection at Timber Museum is not very big.

中譯 下午 2:51，派小姐的訊息「提姆波爾博物館應該以他們為榜樣」最有可能是什麼意思？
(A) 提姆波爾博物館的參觀人次大幅下降。
(B) 提姆波爾博物館的門票對觀光客而言太貴。
(C) 提姆波爾博物館未清楚說明政策。
(D) 提姆波爾博物館的館藏沒有很豐富。

推論問題

167 What does Ms. Verdi imply about a membership?
(A) It should be purchased online.
(B) It should be renewed annually.
(C) It offers a $20 discount each year.
(D) It allows members to buy a two-day pass.

中譯 佛迪小姐傳達了哪些會員相關資訊？
(A) 應上網購買。
(B) 應每年更新。
(C) 每年提供 20 美元的折扣。
(D) 可讓會員購買兩日通行證。

Questions 168-171 refer to the following e-mail. 電子郵件

To: Aida Mazzanti <a.mazzanti@smindustries.net>
From: Li Zhang <zhangli@metrorealty99.com>
Date: June 10
Subject: From Metro Realty

Dear Ms. Mazzanti,

Thank you for meeting with me last week to tour some of the apartments available through our firm. ⓰⓲ **Please note that the apartments in Elliot Tower and the one in Geo Suites have been rented.** —[1]—. ⓰⓲ ⓰⓳ **The two-bedroom apartment in the HSW Building is still available.** I know this is larger than what you wanted. —[2]—. However, ⓰⓳ **it's in the Arleta neighborhood, so you'd be able to walk to your office.** —[3]—. The current tenant is moving out on June 20, so you can move in on June 21. If you are interested, ⓱⓪ **I can send you a lease agreement, which should be signed and returned no later than June 14.** ⓱⓵ **At that time, we will collect a $200 holding fee.** —[4]—. This apartment is in a popular building, so I hope to hear from you soon so that you don't miss your chance.

Sincerely,

Li Zhang

收件人：艾達・馬尚堤 <a.mazzanti@smindustries.net>
寄件人：張立 <zhangli@metrorealty99.com>
日期：6 月 10 日
主旨：大都會房仲

親愛的馬尚堤小姐：

感謝您上週和我見面，一起參觀了我們事務所負責的部分公寓。168 **請注意一下，艾略特大樓和吉歐套房的公寓都已經被租走了。** 168 169 **現在還有 HSW 大樓的兩房公寓。**我知道這個大小超過您的需求。但是 169 **位於阿勒塔區，走路就能到您公司。**目前的租客將於 6 月 20 日搬出去，所以您可以在 6 月 21 日搬進來。如果您感興趣，170 **我可以傳租約協議書給您，請您簽名後，在 6 月 14 日前回傳。** 171 **到時候，我們會收取 200 美元的訂金。**此外，您搬進去的時候，會需要支付一個月租金金額的押金。此公寓所在的大樓很搶手，因此我希望您盡快回覆，以免錯失機會。

敬祝一切順心，
張立

字彙 realty 房仲業　lease agreement 租約協議書　holding fee 訂金

目的問題

168 Why did Mr. Zhang send the e-mail?
(A) To accept a suggestion
(B) To schedule a tour
(C) To send a housing contract
(D) To update property information

中譯 張先生為什麼傳送這封電子郵件？
(A) 以便接受某提議
(B) 以便安排賞屋
(C) 以便傳送租約
(D) 以便更新房產資訊

推論問題

169 What is suggested in the e-mail?
(A) Ms. Mazzanti prefers a two-bedroom home.
(B) Mr. Zhang will meet Ms. Mazzanti at her office.
(C) Ms. Mazzanti's workplace is located in Arleta.
(D) Metro Realty is gathering survey information.

中譯 可從電子郵件裡了解到什麼資訊？
(A) 馬尚堤小姐偏好兩房的住家。
(B) 張先生會到馬尚堤小姐公司見她。
(C) 馬尚堤小姐的公司位在阿勒塔區。
(D) 大都會房仲公司正在收集問卷調查的資料。

確認特定資訊問題

170 According to Mr. Zhang, by when should Ms. Mazzanti submit some paperwork?
(A) June 10 **(B) June 14**
(C) June 20 (D) June 21

中譯 根據張先生的說法，馬尚堤小姐什麼時間以前要交出某文件？
(A) 6 月 10 日 **(B) 6 月 14 日**
(C) 6 月 20 日 (D) 6 月 21 日

尋找句子位置問題

171 In which of the positions marked [1], [2], [3], and [4] does the following sentence best belong?
"Additionally, you will be expected to pay a deposit equal to one month's rent when you move in."
(A) [1] (B) [2]
(C) [3] **(D) [4]**

中譯 此句子「此外，您搬進去的時候，會需要支付一個月租金金額的押金」，最適合放在 [1]、[2]、[3]、[4] 哪一個位置？
(A) [1] (B) [2]
(C) [3] **(D) [4]**

Questions 172-175 refer to the following article. 文章

Cleanup Begins on Carriage Lake *By Jeremy Trigg*

September 9—172 **Plans for an extensive cleanup project at Carriage Lake are finally underway after the city encountered several obstacles.** — [1] —. Talks regarding the need to improve the lake's condition began earlier this year, and it didn't take long to gather the public support needed. The city opened the project up for bids from companies in late March. — [2] —. 175 **Fortunately, the second round of bids resulted in a suitable contract agreement with Morris Enterprises.**

馬車湖開始清淤作業 *傑瑞米．特瑞格 撰*

9 月 9 日訊——172 **市政府歷經重重阻礙後，馬車湖的大規模清理計畫終於展開。**政府今年初已開始討論改善此湖狀況的需求，且很快獲得大眾支持。市政府自三月底，就將此計畫公開給各公司招標。卻沒有一間潛在公司能在所提的預算內，完成如此規模的清理作業。175 **幸好，第二回的招標已與莫里斯企業達成合適的簽約協議。**

The work, which began last week, involves removing contaminated soil from the bottom of the lake. — [3] —. Crews from Morris Enterprises are using a Preston-680 hydraulic dredge to remove the sediment. This equipment has a pump that is 24 inches in diameter, and Morris Enterprises bought it to replace its Caramillo-55, which would not have been powerful enough for this project.

"While Carriage Lake used to be a major draw for boating and fishing enthusiasts, 174B **attendance figures have been on a downward trend for years,"** said city councilperson Jane Clifton. 173 **"This project is costing taxpayers tens of millions of dollars, but the finished result will attract tourists, and the revenue they bring along with them. When you take the environmental impact into account as well, it's a win-win situation for everyone."**

Once the work is completed, mercury levels in the water are expected to be reduced by as much as 97%. — [4] —. Because of that, 174A **officials will once again permit swimming in the lake, which hasn't been the case for decades.** 174D **The city will also build an outdoor stage at the site, which will host music concerts, awards ceremonies, and more.** To follow the progress of the cleanup, visit www.carriagelakecleanup.org.

上週開始的清理作業，在於清除湖底受汙染的泥土。莫里斯企業的工班採用普瑞斯頓-680液壓清淤船來清除淤泥。該設備的幫浦直徑為24吋，莫里斯企業購入它來取代卡拉米洛-55，因為此機型的動力不足以應付此作業。

市議員珍・克里夫頓表示：「雖然馬車湖曾是吸引划船與釣魚愛好者的主要勝地，174B **但是到訪人數年年每況愈下。** 173 **此計畫雖然花了納稅人數千萬元，但成果將吸引觀光客，同時帶來收益。在一併考量環境影響的因素下，這對每個人來說都是雙贏。」**

一旦完工，湖水裡的水銀量預計可減少高達97%。正因如此，174A **官員將再度允許民眾在湖裡游泳，這是數十年以來被禁止的。** 174D **市政府也會在此建造戶外舞台，並舉辦音樂會和頒獎典禮等活動。**如需追蹤清理作業的進度，請至 www.carriagelakecleanup.org。

字彙 **extensive** 廣泛的 **underway** 進行中的 **bid** 投標、出價 **contaminated** 受汙染的 **hydraulic** 液壓的 **dredge** 挖泥船 **sediment** 淤泥 **draw** 吸引人的事物 **downward trend** 每況愈下 **revenue** 收益

主題問題

172 What is the article mainly about?

(A) A project's progress
(B) A machine's availability
(C) A change in policy
(D) A tourism trend

中譯 此文章主題為何？

(A) 某計畫的進度
(B) 某機器的可用性
(C) 政策異動
(D) 觀光業趨勢

推論問題

173 What does Ms. Clifton most likely think about the project?

(A) It should have been started earlier in the year.
(B) The people handling it do not have enough experience.
(C) It will benefit the community despite its high costs.
(D) The final cost should be paid by boaters and fishermen.

中譯 克里夫頓小姐對於此計畫的想法最接近以下何者？

(A) 今年初就該開始了。
(B) 處理的人員沒有足夠經驗。
(C) 儘管處理所費不貲，但能有益社區。
(D) 最終的費用應由划船與釣魚人士支付。

Not / True 問題

174 What is NOT true about Carriage Lake?
(A) It is currently unsuitable for swimming.
(B) Its number of visitors has been steadily declining.
(C) It is the main source of drinking water in the town.
(D) It will be the site of an outdoor performance area.

中譯 關於馬車湖的敘述，何者為非？
(A) 目前不適合游泳。
(B) 遊客人數一直穩定下滑。
(C) 是市鎮的主要飲用水來源。
(D) 將成為戶外表演場地。

尋找句子位置問題

175 In which of the positions marked [1], [2], [3], and [4] does the following sentence best belong?
"None of the prospective businesses could complete the scope of the work within the proposed budget."
(A) [1] **(B) [2]**
(C) [3] (D) [4]

中譯 此句子「卻沒有一間潛在公司能在所提的預算內，完成如此規模的清理作業」放在 [1]、[2]、[3]、[4] 哪一個位置最適當？
(A) [1] **(B) [2]**
(C) [3] (D) [4]

Questions 176-180 refer to the following letter and survey. 信函與問卷調查

July 3 Anne Stein 414 Fulton Street Winchester, KY 40391	7 月 3 日 40391 肯塔基州溫徹斯特市 福爾頓街 414 號 安・史坦 啟
Dear Ms. Stein,	親愛的史坦小姐：
177 **You recently booked a vehicle rental through the Trivo Rentals mobile phone app.** We appreciate your business and 176 **would like to get your feedback on the enclosed form about the rental in order to improve our services further.** We conduct research such as this regularly because we 178 **find** that it is the best way to understand our customers.	177 **您近期透過崔佛租車公司的手機 app 預約租車。**我們感謝您的惠顧，176 **希望您可以在隨附表格上填寫租車反饋，協助我們進一步改善服務品質。**我們會定期進行此類調查，因為我們 178 **認為**這是了解顧客的最佳辦法。
179-1 **We hope you will also introduce us to a friend who might be interested in our service. If you do so,** your friend will receive a voucher by e-mail for 10 percent off any rental, 179-1 **and you will be given a voucher for a free GPS rental for the next time you rent from us.**	179-1 **如有可能對我們服務感興趣的朋友，也希望您能推薦我們。如果您有推薦，**您的朋友將可收到適用任何車款的九折電子禮券，179-1 **您則可獲得下次租車時可免費租用 GPS 導航的兌換券。**
Thank you for your participation!	謝謝您的參與！
The Trivo Rentals Team	崔佛租車公司團隊

字彙 enclose 隨附 conduct 進行 voucher 禮券

Trivo Rentals

Thank you for taking the time to complete this survey. Your opinion matters to us!
Name: Anne Stein
Most Recent Rental Date: June 25
Rental Location: Winchester
Duration of Rental: 1 week

1. How often do you use Trivo Rentals and why?
My personal vehicle is a van, so a few times a year I rent a fuel-efficient car to go on business trips out of state.

2. Why did you choose Trivo Rentals?
It's great that Trivo Rentals keeps costs down by using cars that are a few years old, rather than brand-new ones. 180 **What really sets the company apart is that it sends a representative to my home to give me a ride to the Trivo Rentals office. This is very convenient** because I can't drive there myself without creating a parking issue.

3. How can we improve our services?
I think the added charges for insurance and extra services should be explained more clearly up front.

4. 179-2 **Would you like to recommend our services to a friend or family member? (Y) / N**
Name: Cliff Bower
E-mail Address: c.bower@ferrel.com

崔佛租車公司

感謝您撥冗完成此問卷，我們十分重視您的意見！
姓名：安・史坦
最近租車日期：6月25日
租車地點：溫徹斯特
租用期間：一週

1. 您多久使用一次崔佛租車公司服務？為什麼？
我自己的車是廂型車，所以我一年會有幾次需要租用省油的車型，去其他州出差。

2. 您為何選擇崔佛租車公司？
崔佛租車公司的據點以有幾年車齡的車來維持低價，而非新車，這點很棒。180 **而讓這家公司與眾不同的是，他們會派遣員工來我家，載我去崔佛租車公司。這是很方便的服務，**因為我如果自己開車過去，就會有停車的問題。

3. 我們可以如何改善服務？
保險和額外服務的附加費用，應該事先更清楚說明。

4. 179-2 **您會向親友推薦我們的服務嗎？**
(是)／否
姓名：克里夫・包爾
電子信箱：c.bower@ferrel.com

字彙 **duration** 期間 **fuel-efficient** 省油 **up front** 事先

目的問題

176 What is the purpose of the letter?
(A) To request information about a customer's experience
(B) To gather feedback about a new product
(C) To thank a customer for their opinion
(D) To ask for some research results

中譯 此信函的目的是什麼？
(A) 請求顧客提供使用經驗的資訊
(B) 收集顧客對新品的反饋
(C) 感謝顧客提供意見
(D) 詢問研究成果

推論問題

177 What is implied about Trivo Rentals?
(A) It provides special packages to business professionals.
(B) It operates branches across the country.
(C) It offers a wide variety of insurance options.
(D) It has a smartphone application for reservations.

中譯 可從文中得知崔佛租車公司的什麼資訊？
(A) 向商業專業人士提供特殊套裝方案。
(B) 全國都有分公司。
(C) 提供各種保險選擇。
(D) 可讓顧客透過智慧型手機 app 預約。

同義詞問題

178 In the letter, the word "find" in paragraph 1, line 3, is closest in meaning to
(A) suggest (B) discover
(C) believe (D) acquire

中譯 在信函中，第 1 段第 3 行的「find」，意義最接近以下何者？
(A) 提議 (B) 發現
(C) 相信 (D) 獲得

兩則引文連結問題__Not / True問題

179 What is true about Ms. Stein?
(A) She can collect reward points for her rental.
(B) She will be e-mailed a coupon for 10% off.
(C) She will be entered into a drawing for a GPS device.
(D) She can receive a free equipment rental.

中譯 關於史坦小姐，以下何者為真？
(A) 她可以因為租車而獲得獎勵點數。
(B) 她會透過電郵收到九折的電子折價券。
(C) 她能參加導航裝置的抽獎活動。
(D) 她可以免費租用設備。

確認特定資訊問題

180 What is one thing that Ms. Stein likes about Trivo Rentals?
(A) Its convenient location
(B) Its brand-new vehicles
(C) Its cheap insurance
(D) Its pick-up service

中譯 史坦小姐喜歡崔佛租車公司的哪一點？
(A) 地點方便 (B) 全新的車款
(C) 保險便宜 **(D) 接送服務**

Questions 181-185 refer to the following memo and schedule. 備忘錄與行程表

To: Cervantes Incorporated Staff
From: Armando Dixon, General Manager
Subject: For your immediate attention
Attachment: Inventory Schedule

February 23

Following last year's merger, we are still downsizing our staff and looking for ways to cut overhead costs. As a result, 181 182 **we will be moving our offices next month from the Rinehart Building to the Werner Building, which has a lower rental fee.** Those of you who drive will be pleased to know 182 **that the Werner Building has an underground parking lot for employees only, just like our current building does.**

We have hired a professional moving company, Guerra Co., 183 **whose crew will visit our building on Friday, March 17.** You do not need to report to work on that day. Prior to the move, employees will assist with taking inventory of the company's furniture, equipment, and supplies according to the attached schedule. 184-2 **The head of HR will supply boxes, tape, and labels for you to gather your personal belongings.**

收件人： 瑟凡提斯公司職員
寄件人： 總經理 阿曼度・狄克森
主旨： 請大家即刻注意
附檔： 盤點行程表

2 月 23 日

因為去年合併案的緣故，我們還在精簡人力與尋找降低日常開銷的方法。因此，181 182 **我們下個月會從萊恩哈特大樓搬遷至租金較低的維納大樓。**開車的同仁會很高興知道，182 **華納大樓設有一個僅供員工使用的地下停車場，就像我們現在的大樓一樣。**

我們已經僱用專業的葛拉搬家公司，183 **其團隊會在 3 月 17 日週五來我們大樓。**大家當天不需要上班。搬遷之前，員工需要依據隨附行程表，協助公司盤點家具、辦公設備與用品。184-2 **人資主管會供應紙箱、膠帶和標籤，讓大家整理自己的個人物品。**

字彙 incorporated 公司的 attachment 附檔 merger 合併 downsize 縮減 overhead 營運費用的 report to work 上班 take inventory 盤點

Inventory Schedule

DATE	LOCATION	DEPARTMENT	MANAGER
Monday, March 13	2nd Floor	Accounting	Naoto Kodama
185 **Tuesday, March 14**	**3rd Floor**	Sales	Troy Concord
		Marketing	**Jesse Mateo ***
Wednesday, March 15	4th Floor	184-1 **Human Resources**	**Alana Templeton**
		R&D	Kamal Bakshi
Thursday, March 16	1st Floor	Administration	Joan Pafford

* 185 **As Jesse Mateo will be absent that week, Joan Pafford from administration will fill in for him on his department's assigned day.**

盤點行程表

日期	地點	部門	經理
3 月 13 日星期一	二樓	會計部	兒玉直人
185 **3 月 14 日星期二**	**三樓**	業務部	特洛伊・康克爾德
		行銷部	**傑西・馬提歐 ***
3 月 15 日星期三	四樓	184-1 **人資部**	**阿拉娜・譚普頓**
		研發部	卡默爾・巴克西
3 月 16 日星期四	一樓	行政部	瓊恩・帕菲德

* 185 **由於傑西・馬提歐當週缺席，因此行政部的瓊恩・帕菲德會代替他進行該部門指派日的工作。**

字彙 R&D (research and development) 研發部門 administration 行政 fill in for 代替 assign 指派

目的問題

181 Why did Mr. Dixon send the memo?
(A) To announce a company merger
(B) To explain a relocation procedure
(C) To give an update on a construction project
(D) To ask employees to reduce spending

中譯 狄克森先生為什麼要傳送此備忘錄?
(A) 宣布公司的合併案
(B) 說明搬遷程序
(C) 更新工程專案
(D) 要求員工減少開支

Not / True 問題

182 What is indicated about the Rinehart Building?
(A) It has a private parking area.
(B) It will become the Cervantes Incorporated headquarters.
(C) It will be torn down in March.
(D) It is larger than the Werner Building.

中譯 文中暗示了萊恩哈特大樓的什麼資訊?
(A) 有私人停車場。
(B) 將成為瑟凡提斯公司的總部。
(C) 三月會被拆除。
(D) 比維納大樓大。

推論問題

183 What is implied about Cervantes Incorporated's employees?
(A) They will be reassigned to different departments.
(B) They should work from home temporarily.
(C) They will be given a day off in March.
(D) They should report inventory problems to Mr. Dixon.

中譯 可從文中得知瑟凡提斯公司員工的什麼資訊？
(A) 他們將被指派至不同部門。
(B) 他們應該會暫時在家工作。
(C) 他們三月分會放一天假。
(D) 他們應該向狄克森先生回報盤點問題。

兩則引文連結問題＿推論問題

184 What is suggested about Ms. Templeton?
(A) She took a tour of the Werner Building.
(B) She works on the third floor.
(C) She made a suggestion to Mr. Dixon.
(D) She will distribute packing supplies.

中譯 可從文中得知譚普頓小姐的什麼資訊？
(A) 她已經去看過維納大樓。
(B) 她在三樓工作。
(C) 她已向狄克森先生建議某事。
(D) 她會發放打包用品。

接下來要進行之事的問題

185 What is scheduled to happen on March 14?
(A) A company will move to a new building.
(B) Ms. Pafford will assist a department that is not hers.
(C) Employees from Guerra Co. will visit the business.
(D) Mr. Concord will be absent from the office.

中譯 3月14日安排了什麼事？
(A) 某公司會搬到新大樓。
(B) 帕菲德小姐將協助非她管理的部門。
(C) 葛拉搬家公司的員工將前往此公司。
(D) 康克爾德先生會不在公司。

Questions 186-190 refer to the following flyer and e-mails. 傳單和電子郵件

Wednesday Night Documentary Screenings at Elsberry Hall

Elsberry Hall is pleased to bring you award-winning documentaries followed by a question-and-answer session with the special guests listed.

June 7: *Hourglass* / Running Time: 2 hrs 21 mins
Special Guest: Orlando Briggs (director)
This film 186 **explores how tourism has affected the small island of Kihoa over the past fifty years.**

June 14: *Powering the North* / Running Time: 2 hrs 18 mins Special Guest: Bruce Morrison (Can-Elec Vice President)
This film 186 **explores how Canadian energy company Can-Elec has adapted its business model since its inception decades ago.**

艾斯貝瑞劇院 週三紀錄片放映之夜

艾斯貝瑞劇院很開心能為大家播放獲獎的紀錄片，結束後還會有特別來賓的問答會。

6月7日：《沙漏》／電影時長：2小時21分鐘
特別來賓：奧蘭多・布里格斯（導演）
此電影 186 **探索觀光業對吉哈小島過去五十年的影響。**

6月14日：《電向北方》／電影時長：2小時18分鐘
特別來賓：布魯斯・莫瑞森（加電副總裁）
此電影 186 **探索加拿大能源公司「加電」數十年前創立以來，如何改變其商業模式。**

June 21: *In the Game* / Running Time: 2 hrs 5 mins
Special Guest: Shamba Metha (director)
186 **Watch the development of soccer from its humble beginnings in 19th-century England to becoming the world's most popular sport today.**

June 28: *Not for Sale* / Running Time: 1 hr 48 mins
Special Guest: Erin Hanson (director)
See how 186 **politician Benjamin Tribble's career has unfolded from his first election in 1982 to the present day.**

Book ahead for big savings! 187-2 **Buy your tickets within the month of May to get $5 off the entrance fee.**

6 月 21 日：《賽局》／電影時長：2 小時 5 分鐘
特別來賓：夏姆巴・梅薩（導演）
186 觀賞足球從 19 世紀英格蘭不起眼的起源，到成為現今世上最受歡迎運動的歷程。

6 月 28 日：《非賣品》／電影時長：1 小時 48 分鐘
特別來賓：艾琳・韓森（導演）
了解 186 政治人物班傑明・崔柏的事業，從 1982 年他第一次選舉開始，一直延續到今天

提早預訂以享超值價！187-2 五月底前購票，即可享有電影票減免 5 美元的折扣。

字彙 hourglass 沙漏　adapt 適應　inception 創立　unfold 展開

To: Elsberry Hall <bookings@elsberryhall.com>
From: Rosie Stiltner <r_stiltner@ravenpost.com>
Date: June 15, 10:33 A.M.
Subject: Tickets

To Whom It May Concern:

I attended last night's screening of *Powering the North*, and I found it to be both entertaining and informative. 188-2 **I'm wondering if there are still tickets available for *In the Game*. I already have one, but I'd like to buy three more, if possible.** 187-1 **I understand that the tickets would be $16 this time, instead of the $11 I paid in my original order.**

Sincerely,

Rosie Stiltner

收件人：艾斯貝瑞劇院 <bookings@elsberryhall.com>
寄件人：羅絲・史提納 <r_stiltner@ravenpost.com>
日期：6 月 15 日　早上 10 點 33 分
主旨：電影票

敬啟者：

我昨晚去參加《電向北方》的電影放映活動，我覺得娛樂效果和豐富知識兼備。188-2 我在想《賽局》還有沒有票。我已經有一張，但如果可以的話，我想再買三張。187-1 我也知道現在買票的話，票價會是 16 美元，不是我原本支付的 11 美元。

敬祝一切順心
羅絲・史提納

字彙 entertaining 娛樂的　informative 資訊豐富的　original 原本的

To: Rosie Stiltner <r_stiltner@ravenpost.com>
From: Elsberry Hall <bookings@elsberryhall.com>
Date: June 15, 1:41 P.M.
Subject: RE: Tickets

Dear Ms. Stiltner,

Elsberry Hall 189 **enjoys** a spacious seating area that can accommodate nearly five hundred people, 188-1 **so I'm pleased to inform you that we still have tickets available for the film you requested. However, you should note that the special guest for that date will be screenwriter Kevin Drummond, as the director cannot attend as planned.** If you still want the tickets

收件人：羅絲・史提納 <r_stiltner@ravenpost.com>
寄件人：艾斯貝瑞劇院 <bookings@elsberryhall.com>
日期：6 月 15 日　下午 1 點 41 分
主旨：關於：電影票

親愛的史提納小姐：

艾斯貝瑞劇院 189 坐擁可容納將近五百人的寬敞座位空間，188-1 因此我很高興的通知您，您所詢問的電影仍可購票。不過，請您留意一下，當天的特別來賓會是編劇凱文・卓蒙德，因為導演無法如期出席。如果在此異動狀態

despite this change, ⑲⓪ **you will have to call our box office at 555-3866 to give us your credit card details again,** as we do not save information from previous transactions.

Sincerely,

Miles Rahn

Customer Service Agent, Elsberry Hall

下，您仍想購票，⑲⓪ **請您撥打 555-3866 聯絡票務人員，並請再給我們您的信用卡詳細資料，**因為我們並未保留上次交易的資料。

敬祝一切順心，

邁爾斯・拉恩

艾斯貝瑞劇院　客服人員

字彙 spacious 寬敞的　accommodate 容納　screenwriter 編劇

確認特定資訊問題

186 What characteristic is shared by all of the films?

(A) They last longer than two hours.

(B) They explore a subject over time.

(C) They focus on business-related matters.

(D) They are made by well-known directors.

中譯 所有的電影都有什麼共同點？

(A) 電影時長都超過兩小時。

(B) 均以從古至今的發展來探索某主題。

(C) 均著重於商業相關的事。

(D) 均由知名導演所執導。

三則引文連結問題＿推論問題

187 What is implied about Ms. Stiltner?

(A) She wants to exchange her tickets for a different film.

(B) She created a documentary film on her own.

(C) She booked her original ticket before June 1.

(D) She signed up for a theater membership program.

中譯 可從文中得知史提納小姐的什麼資訊？

(A) 她想換不同電影的電影票。

(B) 她自己有拍紀錄片。

(C) 她原本的電影票是在 6 月 1 日前訂的。

(D) 她加入劇院的會員計畫。

三則引文連結問題＿確認特定資訊問題

188 Which film's special guest has changed?

(A) *Hourglass*　(B) *Powering the North*

(C) *In the Game*　(D) *Not for Sale*

中譯 哪部電影的特別來賓改變了？

(A)《沙漏》　(B)《電向北方》

(C)《賽局》　(D)《非賣品》

同義詞問題

189 In the second e-mail, the word "enjoys" in paragraph 1, line 1, is closest in meaning to

(A) experiences　**(B) possesses**

(C) appreciates　(D) welcomes

中譯 在第二封電子郵件裡，第 1 段第 1 行的「enjoys」，其意義最接近以下何者？

(A) 體驗　**(B) 擁有**

(C) 感激　(D) 歡迎

確認特定資訊問題

190 According to Mr. Rahn, why should Ms. Stiltner call the box office?

(A) To verify a change

(B) To get an updated schedule

(C) To cancel a purchase

(D) To provide payment information

中譯 根據拉恩先生的說法，史提納小姐為何需要聯絡票務人員？

(A) 以確認某異動

(B) 以取得更新後的時間表

(C) 以取消某訂單

(D) 以提供付款資料

Questions 191-195 refer to the following article, Web page, and online review. 文章、網頁和網路評價

McCabe Home Appliances to Trim Its Product Line

August 27— 191 **McCabe Home Appliances plans to halt production of its PrimeAir-60 air purifier sometime in September, and stores carrying the product will sell it until it is sold out.** Consumers who currently have the PrimeAir-60 are encouraged to stock up on filters, as the filters made for other McCabe air purifiers are a different shape and cannot be accommodated by the device.

A spokesperson for McCabe Home Appliances commented that the decision was made in order to focus on better-selling products. The PrimeAir-60 192 **accounts for** less than two percent of the company's revenue, so decision-makers at McCabe believed it was time to start promoting other designs. 194-2 **In addition, the majority of customers who did purchase the device complained about its loud operation.** For a complete listing of McCabe Home Appliances' products, visit www.mccabehomeapp.com.

麥卡貝家電公司縮減產品線

8 月 27 日——191 **麥卡貝家電公司預計 9 月左右停產「PrimeAir-60 空氣清淨機」，有此商品的門市會繼續銷售至售罄為止。**我們鼓勵目前擁有 PrimeAir-60 的消費者，可添購濾網，因為其他麥卡貝空氣清淨機的濾網形狀不同，無法與此機型相容。

麥卡貝家電公司的發言人表示，做出此決定是想著重在更熱賣的產品。PrimeAir-60 192 **占**公司收益不到 2%，因此麥卡貝的決策者認為，是時候推廣其他設計的機種了。194-2 **此外，大多數購買此款清淨機的顧客，均抱怨運轉聲音過大。**如需了解麥卡貝家電公司的完整產品清單，請至 www.mccabehomeapp.com。

字彙 trim 縮減　halt 停止　air purifier 空氣清淨機　stock up on 囤積某物　account for （在數量上）占　majority 多數的

www.mccabehomeapp.com

Home ≫ Catalog ≫ Sale Items ≫ Clearance

The following items are on sale until all items are sold.
Updated October 1

PrimeAir-60 ADD TO CART
Regular Price: $169.99
Clearance Price: $75.99

PrimeAir-60 is an air purifier that can be used in rooms up to 1,500 cubic feet. It has low energy usage and operates more efficiently than most air purifiers on the market today. Regular use of the PrimeAir-60 can reduce the presence of bacteria, viruses, and allergens in your home. The device is highly recommended for allergy sufferers and those with respiratory problems. The filter can be cleaned by hand and reused up to ten times.

PrimeAir-60 Replacement Filters 3-Pack ADD TO CART
Regular Price: $59.99
Clearance Price: $39.99

www.mccabehomeapp.com

首頁 >> 型錄 >> 出售商品 >> 出清活動

以下商品均為特惠價至售罄為止。
10 月 1 日更新

PrimeAir-60 加入購物車
原價：$169.99
出清價：$75.99

PrimeAir-60 空氣清淨機可用於 1500 立方英尺大小的空間。省電高效能，比現今市面上的多數空氣清淨機更有效率。定期使用 PrimeAir-60，可減少家中的細菌、病毒和過敏原。我們大力推薦給受過敏所苦和有呼吸道問題的人使用。濾網可手洗，並可重複使用至多十次。

PrimeAir-60 替換濾網三入組 加入購物車
原價：$59.99　出清價：$39.99

(195-2) **PrimeAir-60 Replacement Filters 5-Pack** ADD TO CART
Regular Price: $89.99
Clearance Price: $55.99

(193) All orders, including those containing clearance items, qualify for free delivery from October 1 to October 31.

(195-2) PrimeAir-60 加入購物車
替換濾網五入組
原價：$89.99 出清價：$55.99

(193) 包括出清商品在內的所有訂單，自10月1日至10月31日均可享有免運優惠。

字彙 clearance 出清 cubic foot 立方英尺 allergen 過敏原 respiratory 呼吸道的 replacement 替換

www.mccabehomeapp.com

Home ≫ Reviews ≫ PrimeAir-60

Written by: Olivia Densmore
Posted: October 5

I will be sad to see this product go. I bought mine last year and have enjoyed using it constantly since then. (194-1) **I understand that the company has to take action on the most common complaint, but I've never experienced that problem.** Even though the filters can be hand-washed and reused, (195-1) **I bought a 5-pack from the clearance sale today so I could ensure the use of the device for a long time.**

www.mccabehomeapp.com

首頁 >> 評價 >> PrimeAir-60

發文者：奧莉維亞・丹斯摩
發文日期：10月5日

這項產品停產真是讓我難過。我去年購入，從那時起就一直很愛用。(194-1) **我了解公司必須針對最常見的客訴採取行動，但我從來沒有遇過這個問題。**即便濾網可以手洗並重複使用，(195-1) **我今天還是從出清優惠區買了五入組，才能確保可以長久使用此裝置。**

目的問題

191 What is the purpose of the article?
(A) To promote a new product in the line
(B) To notify consumers of a product recall
(C) To commemorate a company achievement
(D) To report the discontinuation of a product

中譯 此文章的目的是什麼？
(A) 促銷系列新品
(B) 通知消費者需召回某產品
(C) 紀念公司成就
(D) 通知產品停產的消息

同義詞問題

192 In the article, the phrase "accounts for" in paragraph 2, line 2, is closest in meaning to
(A) uses **(B) represents**
(C) happens (D) explains

中譯 文章第2段第2行裡的片語「accounts for」，意義最接近下列何者？
(A) 使用 **(B) 相當於**
(C) 發生 (D) 說明

確認特定資訊問題

193 According to the Web page, what can customers receive in October?
(A) An extended warranty
(B) Free replacement filters
(C) An updated catalog
(D) Complimentary shipping

中譯 根據網頁的內容，顧客十月會獲得什麼福利？
(A) 延長保固
(B) 免費的替換濾網
(C) 更新後的型錄
(D) 免運費

三則引文連結問題__推論問題

194 What does Ms. Densmore imply about the PrimeAir-60?
(A) She uses it during the daytime only.
(B) She will replace it with a newer model.
(C) She does not think it was too noisy.
(D) She made a complaint about it to the company.

中譯 可看出丹斯摩小姐對 PrimeAir-60 有何看法？
(A) 她只有白天使用。
(B) 她會以較新機型替換此機型。
(C) 她不覺得此機型很吵。
(D) 她有向此公司客訴過。

三則引文連結問題__推論問題

195 What is most likely true about Ms. Densmore?
(A) She bought the PrimeAir-60 for $75.99.
(B) Her living room is less than 1,500 cubic feet.
(C) She spent $55.99 on replacement filters.
(D) Her purchase was delivered by express mail.

中譯 以下關於丹斯摩小姐的描述，何者為真？
(A) 她購買的 PrimeAir-60 價格是 $75.99。
(B) 她的客廳小於 1500 立方英尺。
(C) 她花了 $55.99 購買濾網組。
(D) 她購買的商品是以快遞配送。

Questions 196-200 refer to the following announcement, memo, and e-mail. 公告、備忘錄和電子郵件

Volunteers Needed

Richmond Public Library provides essential educational services to the community, and we are looking for volunteers to assist us with our programs. 196C **You must be at least eighteen years old** 196A **and be available for a minimum of four hours a week.** To apply as a volunteer, fill out a form at the front desk by March 20. 196B **Please note that all volunteers must go to an orientation workshop at the library before they can begin volunteering.** With help from members of the community, we can 197 **reach** more people and help them to attain their literacy goals. 198-1 **We hope to get at least thirty new volunteers for our programs,** so please encourage your family and friends to volunteer as well.

招募志工

理奇蒙公共圖書館向社區提供必要的教育服務，我們目前想招募志工來協助我們的各項課程。196C **您務必年滿 18 歲，** 196A **且一週至少服務四小時。**如欲申請擔任志工，請在 3 月 20 日以前到櫃台填表。196B **請注意，所有志工在開始執勤前，一定要參加圖書館舉辦的職前訓練工作坊。**在社區成員的協助下，我們可 197 **觸及**更多人，並幫助他們達到自己的讀寫目標。198-1 **我們希望能至少招募到 30 位新志工，**因此請鼓勵您的親友一起加入志工行列。

字彙 minimum 最小值 literacy 識讀能力、讀寫能力

MEMO

To employees,

Thank you, everyone, for taking the time out of your busy schedules to train our new library volunteers. 198-2 **The training session will be held on April 7, starting at 1 P.M.** There will be two hours of general library information followed by overviews of individual projects (30 minutes each) by the head of each program as below. 199 **At the end of the orientation, volunteers will be given a form on which they can indicate which programs they would like to assist with.** I cannot guarantee that all volunteers will be matched with their first choice, but I will do my best.

Program Coordinators:

- Silvano Marchesi, Adult Literacy
- Walter Vance, Children's Storytime
- 200-2 **Elizabeth Lancaster, Homework Help**
- Hariti Nayak, Early Readers

198-2 **We didn't quite make our recruitment goal. However, I'm still pleased with the group's size.** I will send a list of the volunteers later this week.

備忘錄

致全體員工：

感謝大家在忙碌行程裡，撥冗訓練我們圖書館的新進志工。198-2 **訓練課程將於4月7日下午一點開始。**會有兩小時的圖書館資訊總論，還有由下文所列每個企畫案負責人，所主講的個別課程概述（每段介紹30分鐘）。199 **職前訓練說明會結束時，我們會給志工填表，來了解他們想協助的課程。**我無法保證所有志工都能媒合到自己的首選，但我會盡力而為。

課程統籌人員：

- 成人識讀：席瓦諾・馬切斯
- 兒童故事時間：瓦特・范斯
- 200-2 **作業輔導：伊莉莎白・蘭卡斯特**
- 學齡前閱讀活動：哈瑞提・納亞克

198-2 **雖然我們沒有達到招募目標，我還是對於志工數量感到開心。**我會在本週稍晚寄出志工名單。

字彙 guarantee 保證　match with 媒合、配對　coordinator 統籌者　recruitment 招募

To: Miriam Jarmillo <m.jarmillo@richmondpl.org>
From: Wen Lang <w.lang@richmondpl.org>
Date: April 29
Subject: Programs Update

Dear Ms. Jarmillo,
I'd like to give you an update on how the library programs are going. The new volunteers are settling into their roles nicely, and we've had a lot of positive feedback from the people participating in the programs. 200-1 **Because of the high demand for the Homework Help program, especially among middle school students, the director of that program plans to find a few more volunteers.** I am tracking the weekly participation of each program and will have more detailed figures for you next month.

All the best,

Wen Lang
Richmond Public Library Program Coordinator

收件人：米瑞姆・賈米洛 <m.jarmillo@richmondpl.org>
寄件人：郎文 <w.lang@richmondpl.org>
日期：4月29日
主旨：課程更新

親愛的賈米洛小姐：
我想向您更新一下圖書館課程目前的進度。新志工均對職務適應良好，也從參加課程的民眾那邊得到很多正面反饋。200-1 **由於「作業輔導」課程的高需求量，尤其是中學生的部分，因此該課程主任打算再多找幾位志工。**我有記錄每項課程的每週參加狀況，下個月將可向您提供更詳細的數字。

敬祝一切安好

郎文
理奇蒙公共圖書館課程統籌人員

字彙 settle into 適應

Not / True 問題

196 What is NOT expected from volunteers?
(A) Working over a certain number of weekly hours
(B) Attending an on-site training session
(C) Meeting a minimum age requirement
(D) Submitting a letter of recommendation

中譯 志工不須進行何事？
(A) 每週需要工作超過特定工時。
(B) 參加現場訓練計畫
(C) 符合最低年齡要求
(D) 提交推薦信

同義詞問題

197 In the announcement, the word "reach" in paragraph 1, line 5, is closest in meaning to
(A) equal (B) stretch
(C) achieve **(D) approach**

中譯 公告中，第 1 段第 5 行的「reach」一字，意義最接近以下何者？
(A) 等於 (B) 伸展
(C) 達到 **(D) 接近**

三則引文連結問題__推論問題

198 What is suggested about the April 7 training session?
(A) It lasted for two hours in total.
(B) It assessed the volunteers' literacy.
(C) It had fewer than thirty participants.
(D) It got positive feedback from the volunteers.

中譯 可從文中得知 4 月 7 日訓練課程的什麼資訊？
(A) 總共會持續兩小時。
(B) 會評鑑志工的讀寫能力。
(C) 參加者少於 30 人。
(D) 志工均給予正面回饋。

確認特定資訊問題

199 Why will volunteers fill out a form at the training session?
(A) To express their preferences
(B) To rate the speakers' performances
(C) To confirm their schedules
(D) To suggest new programs

中譯 志工為什麼要在訓練課程期間填表？
(A) 表明自己想協助的計畫
(B) 評分講者的表現
(C) 確認自己的行程
(D) 建議新課程

三則引文連結問題__確認特定資訊問題

200 Who plans to recruit more volunteers?
(A) Mr. Marchesi
(B) Mr. Vance
(C) Ms. Lancaster
(D) Ms. Nayak

中譯 誰打算招募更多志工？
(A) 馬切斯先生
(B) 范斯先生
(C) 蘭卡斯特小姐
(D) 納亞克小姐

Actual Test 3

PART 1 09

1 **(A) She's pouring an ingredient into a bowl.**
美M
(B) She's tying an apron around her waist.
(C) She's mixing some food with a spoon.
(D) She's cleaning a kitchen counter.

(A) 她正把食材倒進碗裡。
(B) 她正把圍裙繫在腰上
(C) 她正用湯勺攪拌食物。
(D) 她正在清理廚房的流理台。

字彙 ingredient 材料，成分　apron 圍裙
kitchen counter 廚房流理台

2 (A) A lecturer is walking towards a projector screen.
英W
(B) Audience members are listening to a speaker.
(C) Some chairs are being arranged in an auditorium.
(D) Some papers are being distributed to people.

(A) 講師正走向投影螢幕。
(B) 聽眾正在聽演講者說話。
(C) 有人正在觀眾席擺放椅子。
(D) 有人正在分發文件給大家。

字彙 lecturer 演講者，講師　auditorium 觀眾席
distribute 分發

3 (A) They are typing on a keyboard.
美M
(B) The woman is pointing at a computer monitor.
(C) They are examining some documents.
(D) The man is writing on a clipboard.

(A) 他們正在鍵盤上打字。
(B) 女子正用手指著電腦螢幕。
(C) 他們正在查看某些文件。
(D) 男子正在寫字板上寫字。

字彙 clipboard 附有紙夾的寫字板

4 (A) He's hanging a painting on a building.
澳M
(B) He's closing the windows of a house.
(C) A ladder is placed against a wall.
(D) A bucket is being emptied onto the ground.

(A) 他正把一幅畫掛到建築物上。
(B) 他正在關屋子的窗戶。
(C) 梯子靠著牆擺放。
(D) 有人正把水桶往地上倒。

5 (A) Some umbrellas are being opened.
美W
(B) Some tables are located in front of some buildings.
(C) An open space is crowded with pedestrians.
(D) A section of a plaza is being paved.

(A) 有人正把遮陽傘撐開來。
(B) 桌子就在建築物前。
(C) 空地上擠滿了行人。
(D) 廣場一隅正在鋪設地面。

字彙 pedestrian 行人　plaza 廣場　pave 鋪(地面)

6 (A) A boat is arriving at the dock.
英W
(B) Luggage is being unloaded.
(C) Passengers are buying tickets.
(D) A walkway has been set up.

(A) 一艘船正抵達碼頭。
(B) 有人正把行李卸下來。
(C) 乘客正在買船票。
(D) 已經搭好了一條通道。

字彙 dock 碼頭　unload 卸下　walkway 步行通道

PART 2 10

7 What's the venue for the concert?
美M
(A) April 2.
英W
(B) March Hall.
(C) A piano recital.

音樂會的場地在哪？
(A) 4 月 2 日。
(B) 行軍廳。
(C) 鋼琴獨奏會。

字彙 venue 地點，場所　recital 獨奏會

8 Should I record the speech?
澳M (A) Twenty-five questions in total.
美W (B) The recent elections.
(C) Yes, if possible.

我應該把演講錄下來嗎？
(A) 總共 25 個問題。
(B) 最近的選舉。
(C) 是的，如果可以的話。

字彙 speech 演講 recent 最近的 election 選舉

9 Where do we store the client files?
美 **(A) There's a cabinet near the back door.**
(B) I have a meeting with him tomorrow.
(C) In alphabetical order.

我們都把客戶的檔案放哪兒？
(A) 後門附近有個檔案櫃。
(B) 我明天要跟他開會。
(C) 按照字母順序排列。

字彙 client 客戶 alphabetical 按字母排序的

10 It looks like it's going to rain.
美 (A) Why did you bring an umbrella?
(B) The forecast said it would.
(C) No, this lane is closed.

看樣子快要下雨了。
(A) 你為什麼帶著傘？
(B) 天氣預報說會下雨。
(C) 不是，這條車道被封閉了。

字彙 forecast 天氣預報 lane 車道

11 When was the last time you talked to Mark?
英W (A) Of course I did.
美M **(B) Three days ago.**
(C) We talked for two hours.

你上一次跟馬克說話是什麼時候？
(A) 我當然有。
(B) 三天前。
(C) 我們說了兩個小時。

12 Who is the guest speaker on today's show?
美 (A) It was a great performance.
(B) A best-selling author.
(C) It starts at 10 A.M.

今天節目的特別來賓是誰？
(A) 這場演出很精彩。
(B) 一位暢銷書作家。
(C) 上午十點開始。

13 How do I enter the parking garage after hours?
澳M
美W **(A) The security director can give you a pass.**
(B) Is there a fee to do so?
(C) It has room for three hundred cars.

下班後我要怎麼進入停車場？
(A) 保全主管會給你一張通行證。
(B) 這麼做要收費嗎？
(C) 可容納 300 輛汽車的空間。

字彙 after hours 在正常營業時間之外，下班後

14 Should we cancel the employee picnic or
美 just postpone it?
(A) Larry will bring food.
(B) To let the entire staff relax.
(C) There's time to do it next week.

我們是否應該取消員工野餐活動，還是延期就好？
(A) 賴瑞會帶食物來。
(B) 要讓全體員工放鬆一下。
(C) 下個星期有時間進行。

字彙 postpone 延期

15 Our profits increased dramatically last year,
美W didn't they?
英W (A) I hope they will.
(B) No. They were about the same.
(C) That doesn't sound profitable.

我們去年的盈利大幅增加，對吧？
(A) 希望如此。
(B) 並沒有，差不多一樣。
(C) 聽起來無利可圖。

字彙 profit 利潤，盈利 dramatically 大幅地
profitable 有盈利的

16 Are you sure you can pick me up from the
美 airport?
(A) Yeah, I don't have anything to do that day.
(B) I'm landing at 6:55 P.M. in Detroit.
(C) Probably by taxi.

你確定你可以到機場接我？
(A) 確定啊，我那天沒有什麼事要做。
(B) 我會於晚上 6:55 在底特律降落。
(C) 可能搭計程車吧。

字彙 land 降落

17 Why are there signs all over the building?
英W 澳M
(A) They are likely to sign the sales contract.
(B) For the new employees.
(C) The construction work is going smoothly.

為什麼大樓裡到處都有告示牌？
(A) 他們很有可能會簽銷售合約。
(B) 給新進員工看的。
(C) 工程目前進行得很順利。

字彙 construction 營建工程 smoothly 順利地

18 Didn't the organizers change the program?
美
(A) No, they decided to keep the original.
(B) Someone on the IT team.
(C) It's a charitable organization.

主辦單位不是改動節目了嗎？
(A) 沒有啊，他們決定維持原樣。
(B) 資訊科技部的某個員工。
(C) 這是一個慈善機構。

字彙 organizer 組織者，籌辦者 original 原件，原型

19 The art museum closes early on Mondays, doesn't it?
美W 澳M
(A) It just opened last month.
(B) Tuesday works better for me.
(C) Yes. We should hurry.

美術館星期一都比較早閉館，對不對？
(A) 上個月才開放參觀。
(B) 星期二我比較方便。
(C) 對，我們得加快腳步。

20 How did you get Ms. Brandon's business card?
美
(A) I met her at a networking event.
(B) Any form of photo ID will be okay.
(C) Turn right at the next intersection.

你是怎麼拿到布蘭登小姐的名片的？
(A) 我在一場社交場合上見過她。
(B) 有附照片的身分證件皆可。
(C) 在下個十字路口右轉。

字彙 business card 名片 networking 社交
intersection 十字路口

21 I'm not sure which color scheme to use for the Web site.
美M 英W
(A) Just click on "log in" in the top right corner.
(B) Didn't you register online?
(C) I personally prefer the blue version.

我不知道網站要用哪種色系。
(A) 點擊右上角的「登入」即可。
(B) 你沒有上網註冊嗎？
(C) 我個人更喜歡藍色版本。

字彙 color scheme 配色 register 登記

22 Can't you stay a little longer?
美W 澳M
(A) The shorter one would be better.
(B) I have a doctor's appointment.
(C) Yes, you can if you want.

你就不能多待一會兒嗎？
(A) 短一點的更好。
(B) 我和醫生有約診。
(C) 是的，你想要的話你可以做。

23 Which newspaper do you get your news from?
美
(A) Your subscription expires on May 20.
(B) A huge company merger.
(C) I usually listen to the radio.

你都看哪一家報紙的新聞？
(A) 您的訂閱將在 5 月 20 日到期。
(B) 一個大型的企業併購案。
(C) 我通常都是聽收音機廣播。

字彙 subscription 訂閱（費） expire 到期
merger （公司等的）合併

24 Where will the festival be held?
英W 美M
(A) At Willowbrook Park.
(B) Local artists and musicians will attend.
(C) Sometime next month.

節慶將在何處舉行？
(A) 在柳溪公園。
(B) 本地藝術家與音樂家都會參加。
(C) 下個月的某一天。

25 Have you reserved the venue for Mr. Allen's retirement party?
美W 澳M
(A) The new restaurant that opened last week.
(B) I'm still searching for a place.
(C) He's retiring at the end of May.

你已經預約好艾倫先生退休歡送會的場地了嗎？
(A) 上週才開幕的那家新餐廳。
(B) 我還在找場地。
(C) 他五月底就要退休了。

字彙 reserve 預約，預訂
retirement 退休（生活），退職　retire 退休

26 When does the conference end?
美 **(A) I haven't seen the schedule.**
(B) Why don't you come with me?
(C) It's at Carlton Center.
研討會什麼時候結束？
(A) 我還沒有看到時程表。
(B) 跟我一起去怎麼樣？
(C) 是在卡爾頓中心。

字彙 conference 會議，研討會

27 I can't refill this prescription without a doctor's note, can I?
英W 美M
(A) She works at Lakewood Hospital.
(B) Sorry, it's against our policy.
(C) I hope you feel better soon.
沒有醫生證明，我就不能重領這張處方箋的藥，對嗎？
(A) 她在湖木醫院工作。
(B) 抱歉，這是違反規定的。
(C) 祝你早日康復。

字彙 (re)fill a prescription 按處方箋（再）領藥
policy 政策

28 Why did the customer return the shirt?
美 (A) How much does it cost?
(B) Actually, she just exchanged it.
(C) At the counter over there.
那位顧客為什麼要退回襯衫呢？
(A) 那件要多少錢？
(B) 她其實只是來換貨。
(C) 在那邊的收銀台。

字彙 exchange 更換

29 Could you make fifty copies of this flyer?
澳M **(A) I was just about to leave.**
美M (B) My flight has been delayed.
(C) Thank you. That should be enough.
這張傳單可以請你印五十份嗎？
(A) 我正要離開。
(B) 我的班機延誤了。
(C) 謝謝你。這樣就夠了。

字彙 make a copy of 影印……　flyer （廣告）傳單
flight 航班

30 Who is in charge of the hiring process?
美W (A) The payment has been processed.
澳M (B) Interviews start next week.
(C) I thought you were.
僱用流程是誰負責的？
(A) 款項已經處理好了。
(B) 下週開始面試。
(C) 我以為是你負責的。

31 Did the tenant renew his lease?
美M (A) Because the rent is too high.
英W (B) It's due on the fifth of each month.
(C) He hasn't decided yet.
承租人是否要續租？
(A) 因為租金太高了。
(B) 每個月的五號付款。
(C) 他還沒有決定。

字彙 tenant 租客　renew 更新，延長（合約等）
lease 租約　due 到期的

PART 3

Questions 32-34 refer to the following conversation. 英W 美M 對話

W Hello, this is Dr. Martha Collins. ㉜ **I'm a history professor,** and I would like to bring two of my classes to your museum next month.

M Hello, Dr. Collins. We would be happy to welcome you and your students. ㉝ **Which day would you like to visit?**

W A Wednesday or Friday morning would be best for us.

M Fridays are usually quite busy. However, if you come on a Wednesday, we can let you in some of the rooms that are normally closed to the public. So how about Wednesday, May 4?

W That sounds good. ㉞ **I'll call again next week to let you know exactly how many we will be.**

女：你好，我是瑪莎・柯林斯博士。㉜ **我是一名歷史學教授**，下個月我想帶兩個班級的學生到你們博物館參觀。

男：柯林斯博士妳好。我們衷心歡迎您與您的學生前來。㉝ **您想要在星期幾參觀？**

女：對我們來說，星期三或星期五上午最好。

男：星期五通常人潮眾多。不過，要是你們星期三來的話，我們可以讓各位參觀一些通常不對外開放的展覽室。那麼，5月4日星期三怎麼樣？

女：聽起來不錯。㉞ **我下個星期會再打電話告訴你們確切人數。**

32 Where most likely does the woman work?
(A) At a hospital **(B) At a university**
(C) At a museum (D) At a restaurant

中譯 女子最有可能在哪裡工作？
(A) 在醫院 **(B) 在大學**
(C) 在博物館 (D) 在餐廳

33 What does the man ask about?
(A) How much a service costs
(B) What classes are being taught
(C) Which day is convenient
(D) How busy a location is

中譯 男子詢問了什麼？
(A) 某服務的費用
(B) 有教授哪些課程
(C) 星期幾方便前來
(D) 場所有多麼繁忙

34 What information will the woman provide next week?
(A) A business's opening hours
(B) A detailed schedule
(C) The topic of a lecture
(D) The number of visitors

中譯 女子下週會提供什麼資訊？
(A) 機構的營業時間
(B) 詳細的時間表
(C) 演講的主題
(D) 參觀者的人數

Questions 35-37 refer to the following conversation. 美 對話

M Hello, Ms. Rooney. This is Jason Trapper from Becca Industries. ㉟ **You spoke to my assistant a couple of weeks ago about a proposal for the merger of our two companies. I was wondering if we could meet in person to talk about it.**

男：魯尼女士妳好。我是貝卡工業的傑森・特拉珀。㉟ **幾個星期前，妳跟我的助理談過，提議要將我們兩家公司合併。不知道我們能不能當面談談這件事。**

W Hello, Mr. Trapper. I think that's a good idea. Unfortunately, ㉟ **I am at a convention all of this week.** However, I can make time any day next week.

M That's fine. I have thought about your offer, and ㊲ **I just want to discuss a few details in your proposal so we can reach an agreement.** Tuesday at 10 A.M. is the best time for me.

女： 特拉珀先生你好。我覺得這是個好主意。很可惜的是，㊱ **我這週都要參加會議。**不過，我下週可以擠出一天來。

男： 那好。我考慮過妳的提議，㊲ **我只是要討論妳提案裡的幾個細節，那麼我們就能達成協議。**我最方便的時間是週二上午十點。

字彙 proposal 建議　convention 大會　make time 挪出時間

35 Who most likely is the man?
(A) A manager's assistant
(B) An applicant for a grant
(C) The director of a company
(D) The keynote speaker at a convention

中譯 男子最有可能是誰？
(A) 經理的助理
(B) 補助金申請人
(C) 公司管理者
(D) 大會主講人

36 What is the woman doing this week?
(A) Writing up a proposal
(B) Attending a conference
(C) Interviewing candidates
(D) Training at a new company

中譯 女子這週都要做什麼事？
(A) 撰寫提案
(B) 參加會議
(C) 面試求職者
(D) 在新公司培訓

37 Why does the man want to meet the woman?
(A) To negotiate a deal
(B) To prepare a presentation
(C) To discuss a job opportunity
(D) To introduce a coworker

中譯 男子為什麼想跟女子見面？
(A) 協商交易
(B) 準備簡報
(C) 討論就業機會
(D) 介紹同事

Questions 38-40 refer to the following conversation with three speakers. 美W 英W 澳M 三人對話

W1 Hello. ㊳ **I'd like a haircut. I'm also thinking about dyeing my hair,** but I'm not sure.

W2 Okay. Well, how about taking a look at our colors? Jack! Can you bring the color catalog over, please?

M Here it is. Our most popular color right now for your hair type is this strawberry blond.

W1 That is a nice color. How much does dyeing cost?

M ㊴ **It would be $70.**

W2 Not for her. It's your first time here, right? ㊴ **Newcomers pay only $40 for their first dyeing.**

W1 Oh, that's a really good price! Let's do it!

M Great! ㊵ **If you come over here, I'll start your shampoo.**

女 1： 嗨，㊳ **我想要剪頭髮，我也在考慮染髮，**但還沒確定。

女 2： 好的。嗯，您要不要看一下我們染髮劑的顏色？傑克！可以請你把染髮色卡拿過來嗎？

男： 在這裡。以您的髮型來說，最受歡迎的是這種草莓金。

女 1： 這顏色不錯。染頭髮要多少錢？

男： ㊴ **要 70 美元。**

女 2： 她不用啦。這是您第一次來我們髮廊消費，對嗎？㊴ **新客戶首次染髮只要付 40 美元就好。**

女 1： 哦，這價格我可以！就這麼辦吧！

男： 好極了！㊵ **請到這邊來，我開始幫您洗頭。**

38 Where most likely are the speakers?
(A) At a clothing shop
(B) At a grocery store
(C) At a beauty salon
(D) At a paint retailer

中譯 說話者最有可能在什麼地方？
(A) 在服飾店
(B) 在食品雜貨店
(C) 在美髮沙龍
(D) 在油漆零售店

39 What do first-time customers receive?
(A) A discount
(B) A free item
(C) A gift certificate
(D) A membership card

中譯 首次消費的顧客會得到什麼？
(A) 折扣
(B) 贈品
(C) 禮券
(D) 會員卡

40 What will the man most likely do next?
(A) Make a purchase **(B) Wash some hair**
(C) Choose a color (D) Provide a refund

中譯 男子接下來最有可能做什麼？
(A) 進行購物 **(B) 洗頭髮**
(C) 挑選顏色 (D) 提供退款

Questions 41-43 refer to the following conversation. 美 對話

M Hello. I recently purchased an item from your Parson branch, and ❹❶ **I'd like to talk about an issue I have with your policy.**
W Yes, sir. What is the problem?
M ❹❷ **I bought a lawn mower. But when I got home, it wouldn't start.**
W I'm sorry to hear that. Did you try to return it?
M Of course. However, the manager told me I could not return it because it was on sale when I bought it.
W They must have misunderstood our policy. We accept returns for defective items, even if they were on sale. I'm very sorry about this, sir. ❹❸ **I will contact the Parson branch manager immediately.** Someone will call you back shortly.

男：你好。我最近在你們的帕爾森店買了一樣東西，然後 ❹❶ **我想要談談貴公司政策的一個問題。**
女：好的，先生。請問是什麼樣的問題？
男：❹❷ **我買了一台割草機，可是拿回家後卻無法發動。**
女：很遺憾聽到您這麼說。您有拿回來辦理退貨嗎？
男：當然有，可是經理說我是在特賣的時候買的，所以不能退貨。
女：他們肯定誤解了公司的政策。我們接受任何瑕疵品的退貨，即使是特賣品也一樣。先生，發生這樣的事，我真的很抱歉。❹❸ **我會立即聯絡帕爾森店的經理**，稍後將會有人回電給您。

字彙 **lawn mower** 割草機 **misunderstand** 誤會 **defective** 有瑕疵的

41 Why is the man calling?
(A) To complain about a rule
(B) To place an order
(C) To explain a service
(D) To ask about a price

中譯 男子為何打了這通電話？
(A) 抱怨某項規定
(B) 下訂單
(C) 說明一項服務
(D) 詢問價格

42 What problem does the man mention about the lawn mower?
(A) It wasn't delivered on time.
(B) It doesn't work properly.
(C) It is the wrong model.
(D) It was incorrectly priced.

中譯 男子說割草機有什麼問題？
(A) 沒準時送達。
(B) 運作不良。
(C) 型號錯誤。
(D) 標價錯誤。

43 What does the woman say she will do?
(A) Contact a manager
(B) Issue a refund
(C) Organize a sales event
(D) Repair a device

中譯 女子說她會做什麼？
(A) 聯繫經理
(B) 退還款項
(C) 籌辦特賣會
(D) 維修器具

Questions 44-46 refer to the following conversation with three speakers. 美W 澳M 美M 三人對話

W Hi, Charles and Walter. How was the cruise?
M1 It was amazing. I really recommend Gulliver Travel's cruises.
W ㊹ ㊺ **I'm actually thinking about going on one with Blue Green Travel.** You know, we get a discount with them for working at this company.
M2 I know, but Blue Green's customer service has a terrible reputation. ㊺ **So we went with Gulliver Travel instead. We'd rather pay more and not deal with bad service.**
W Oh, really? I should read the reviews.
M1 Yes, you should. ㊺ **I think Gulliver Travel is worth the extra money.** Anyway, I'm guessing we have a lot of work to do.
W We do. ㊻ **While you were away, Fiona quit.** So we have to cover for her.
M2 That's a surprise. I hope we find a replacement soon.

女： 嗨，查爾斯、華特。郵輪之旅好玩嗎？
男1： 令人驚嘆不已。我非常推薦格列佛旅行社的郵輪行程。
女： ㊹ ㊺ **我其實在考慮參加布魯格林旅行社的郵輪行程。**要知道，我們在這家公司工作，是可以拿到折扣的。
男2： 我知道，可是布魯格林客服的名聲很差。㊺ **我們這才選了格列佛旅行社。我們寧可多付一點錢，也不想跟糟糕的服務打交道。**
女： 喔，真的嗎？我應該要看看評價的。
男1： 對，你真的該看。㊺ **我認為格列佛旅行社值得我們多花些錢。**不管怎樣，我猜我們現在有很多工作要做吧。
女： 是沒錯。㊻ **你們休假期間，費歐娜離職了。**所以我們得接手她的工作。
男2： 這倒是個令人意外的消息，希望我們很快就可以找到她的接替人選。

字彙 cruise 乘船遊覽 reputation 名聲 cover for 接替……的工作 replacement 接替者

44 What does the woman say she plans to do?
(A) Go on a cruise
(B) Write a negative review
(C) Work some extra hours
(D) Resign from her position

中譯 女子說她打算做什麼？
(A) 去搭船旅行
(B) 寫負評
(C) 加班
(D) 辭職

45 What do the men imply about Gulliver Travel?
(A) It has poor customer service.
(B) It offers discounts to its employees.
(C) It has the cheapest cruises on the market.
(D) It is more expensive than Blue Green Travel.

中譯 關於格列佛旅行社，兩名男子暗示了什麼？
(A) 客戶服務做得很差。
(B) 自家員工可享折扣。
(C) 市面上最便宜的郵輪之旅。
(D) 比布魯格林旅行社還貴。

46 According to the woman, what happened at the company while the men were away?
(A) A coworker left her job.
(B) A customer made a complaint.
(C) A new person was hired.
(D) A survey was conducted.

中譯 據女子所說，兩名男子休假時，公司裡發生了什麼事？
(A) 有個同事離職了。
(B) 有個顧客提出客訴。
(C) 聘僱了一名新人。
(D) 進行了一項調查。

Questions 47-49 refer to the following conversation. 美 對話

W Hi, Danny. I wanted to show you these. ㊼ **They are two possible designs for the new juice cartons. What do you think?**	女：嗨，丹尼。我想給你看看這些東西。㊼ **新款果汁盒的兩種可能設計，你怎麼看？**
M I like the first one because it has nice colors. But... Um... The font is strange. It's too large, and it looks a bit silly.	男：我喜歡第一款設計，因為顏色好看，就是……嗯……字體怪怪的，太大了，而且看起來有點呆。
W I agree. ㊽ **I think the designers obviously wanted to appeal to children.**	女：我同意。㊽ **我認為設計師顯然想要吸引孩子們的注意。**
M Well, ㊽ **that is our target demographic.** But they went a little too far.	男：嗯，㊽ **那是我們產品的目標客群，**但他們做得太過頭了。
W Right. Even if we are selling to kids, the parents are the ones ultimately making the purchase decision. ㊾ **So I'll tell the designers we'd like the first design with a different font.**	女：沒錯。就算是賣給小孩，最後還是父母決定是否購買。㊾ **那我就跟設計師說，我們想用第一款設計，但不一樣的字體。**

字彙 carton 紙盒　font 字體，字型　obviously 顯然　demographic （顧客）族群　go too far 做得過火　ultimately 最後

47 What are the speakers mainly discussing?
(A) An article's contents
(B) A course's difficulty
(C) A product's packaging
(D) A beverage's price

中譯 說話者們主要在討論什麼？
(A) 文章內容
(B) 課程難易度
(C) 產品包裝
(D) 飲品價格

48 Why does the man say, "they went a little too far"?
(A) He finds a design childish.
(B) He thinks a product is expensive.
(C) He wants to relocate a branch.
(D) He disagrees with a policy.

中譯 男子為何說：「他們做得有點太超過了」？
(A) 他覺得設計很幼稚。
(B) 他認為產品很貴。
(C) 他想將分公司遷址。
(D) 他不同意某項政策。

49 What does the woman say she will do?
(A) Return an item
(B) Report a choice
(C) Create an advertisement
(D) Contact some customers

中譯 女子說她會做什麼？
(A) 退回商品
(B) 回報選擇
(C) 製作廣告
(D) 聯繫顧客

Questions 50-52 refer to the following conversation. 美M 英W 對話

M Hey, ㊿ **I heard you're transferring to another department.** Is that true? Where are you going?	男：嘿，㊿ **聽說妳要轉調到別的部門。**這是真的嗎？妳要去哪裡？
W Yeah. ㊿ **I'm going to be working in customer service.** 51 **I'm looking forward to interacting with our customers face-to-face.**	女：對啊。㊿ **我以後會在客服部工作。** 51 **我很期待能跟我們的顧客面對面互動。**
M Really? To me, that sounds so stressful. I prefer working in the back. I would hate to listen to complaints all day.	男：真的嗎？我會覺得壓力好大。我更喜歡做後勤的工作。我很不喜歡整天聽別人抱怨。

W Well, it's not all complaints. You get some positive feedback as well. But to be honest, I am a little bit nervous.	女：嗯，也不全都是抱怨啦，也會有一些正面的回饋啊。但是說實話，我也是有點緊張。
M Oh, 52 **you should talk to Marty.** He's worked in customer service for years. 52 **I'm sure he'll have some great tips.**	男：哦，52 **那妳得跟瑪堤聊聊。**他在客服部工作好幾年了，52 **肯定會有一些很棒的建議。**

字彙 transfer 調動　interact 互動　complaint 抱怨

50 What are the speakers mainly discussing?
(A) A new opening
(B) A job change
(C) A customer complaint
(D) An office layout

中譯 說話者主要在討論什麼問題？
(A) 新的職缺
(B) 職務變更
(C) 顧客客訴
(D) 辦公室格局

51 What does the woman say she is looking forward to?
(A) Talking to people directly
(B) Working with the man
(C) Reading some reviews
(D) Joining a new company

中譯 女子說她很期待能做什麼？
(A) 與人直接交談
(B) 與男子共事
(C) 看一些評價
(D) 進入新公司

52 What does the man suggest the woman do?
(A) File a complaint
(B) Consult a coworker
(C) Find a different job
(D) Provide some advice

中譯 男子提議女子應做什麼？
(A) 提出客訴
(B) 諮詢同事
(C) 找其他工作
(D) 提供建議

Questions 53-55 refer to the following conversation. 澳M 美W 對話

M 53 **Jeremy Billings has agreed to come to our bookstore on August 8. He will be signing copies of his bestseller, *The Confession*.**	男：53 **傑瑞米・比林斯已經答應8月8日來我們的書店，替自己的暢銷書《懺悔》舉辦簽書會。**
W Oh, that's great news. I think it will be a big event. It's a really popular book these days.	女：噢，這真是個好消息。我想這會是一場盛大的活動，這本書最近很受歡迎。
M Yes. I expect a lot of people will come. So we need to prepare the space to make it an ideal venue for a large crowd.	男：對啊，我預期會有很多人來，所以我們需要把場地準備好，才能理想地容納大批群眾。
W Right. There will be a long line. Perhaps 54 **we can rearrange the shelves in the children's section to make some room for people to line up.**	女：沒錯，一定會大排長龍。也許 54 **我們可以重新安排童書區的書架，騰出讓顧客排隊的地方。**
M Good idea. 55 **I'll start working on designing a flyer to publicize the event.**	男：好主意。55 **我會開始著手設計活動的宣傳單。**

字彙 ideal 理想的　rearrange 重新安排　line up 排隊　publicize 宣傳

53 What will happen on August 8?
(A) A business will be relocated.
(B) An author will be interviewed.
(C) A contract will be signed.
(D) A book signing will be held.

中譯 8月8日將會發生什麼事？
(A) 公司將搬遷。
(B) 作家將接受採訪。
(C) 將簽署一份合約。
(D) 將舉辦一場簽書會。

54 What does the woman suggest doing?
(A) Putting away some items
(B) Registering for an event
(C) Waiting in line
(D) Moving some furniture

中譯 女子建議做什麼？
(A) 收起一些物品
(B) 報名參加活動
(C) 排隊等候
(D) 移動家具

55 What does the man say he will do?
(A) Prepare an advertisement
(B) Reserve some tickets
(C) Write a summary
(D) Visit a venue

中譯 男子說他會做什麼？
(A) 準備廣告
(B) 預訂門票
(C) 撰寫摘要
(D) 參觀場地

Questions 56-58 refer to the following conversation. 美 對話

W Hi, Michael. ⑯ **I've just signed up for the Haya Corp. healthcare conference.** Are you going?
M Yes, I plan on going. It will be an interesting conference.
W Actually, I heard they're looking for more presenters. ⑰ **You should send in the study you did last month.** People would be interested in hearing about it.
M Um … Maybe I will. I'm not sure I have time, though. I've got a deadline coming up. What about the review you did on healthcare companies? That could be an interesting topic.
W I'm afraid ⑱ **that review is not relevant anymore. I did it six months ago, and two of the companies I wrote about have shut down since then.**

女：嗨，麥克。⑯ **我剛報名參加哈亞企業的醫療保健研討會。**你也會去嗎？
男：會，我打算去，那會是一場很有意思的研討會。
女：老實說，我聽說他們還在找發表人。⑰ **你應該把你上個月做的研究寄過去，**大家對這個主題會很有興趣。
男：呃……或許吧，但是我不確定我有沒有空，因為有個截止日期快到了。妳之前寫的醫療保健公司的評鑑報告怎麼樣？那會是個很有趣的主題。
女：恐怕 ⑱ **那個評鑑報告已經不適用了。我是六個月前寫的，而且後來有兩家公司就倒閉了。**

字彙 **sign up for** 報名參加　**presenter** 發表人　**relevant** 相關的　**shut down** 歇業

56 What has the woman recently done?
(A) Attended a lecture series
(B) Registered for an event
(C) Reviewed a research study
(D) Given a presentation

中譯 女子最近做了什麼事？
(A) 參加系列講座
(B) 報名某活動
(C) 寫研究報告
(D) 發表簡報

57 What does the woman think the man should do?
(A) Meet a speaker (B) Extend a deadline
(C) Submit a study (D) Choose a topic

中譯 女子認為男子應該做什麼事？
(A) 跟演講者見面 (B) 延長期限
(C) 遞交研究報告 (D) 選擇主題

58 What does the woman imply about a review she wrote?
(A) It is outdated.
(B) It will be published soon.
(C) It took a long time to make.
(D) It was presented at a conference.

中譯 女子暗示自己寫的評鑑報告怎麼樣？
(A) 資訊過時了。
(B) 即將刊載。
(C) 花了很長時間才完成。
(D) 曾在研討會上發表過。

Questions 59-61 refer to the following conversation. 美M 英W 對話

M Hello. 59 **Before I start the checkup, do you feel any pain anywhere?**
W 59 60 **Sometimes my teeth in the bottom right feel sensitive.** But overall, there is no specific problem.
M 60 **Do they feel like that all of the time?**
W No, not all of the time. Drinking cold water causes it.
M I see. Let me take a look. Um... well, you do have a cavity. It's a small one, but that is probably what is causing the problem. You're going to need a filling.
W Oh. Does that mean I should brush more often?
M Not necessarily. But 61 **I recommend staying away from sugary drinks.**

男：妳好，59 **在我開始檢查之前，你有感覺哪個地方會痛嗎？**
女：59 60 **我右下排的牙齒有時很敏感，**但是總的來說，沒有什麼特別症狀。
男：60 **妳一直都有這種感覺嗎？**
女：不，並非總是如此，喝冷水的時候才會。
男：我明白了。我看看。嗯，妳的確蛀牙了，蛀得不多，但可能是造成問題的原因。妳得要補牙了。
女：噢，這表示我應該要更勤快刷牙囉？
男：也不見得，但是 61 **我建議不要喝含糖飲料。**

字彙 **cavity** 蛀牙 **filling** （補牙用的）填料 **necessarily** 必然地 **sugary** 含糖的

59 Who most likely is the man?
(A) A secretary **(B) A dentist**
(C) A plumber (D) A nutritionist

中譯 男子最有可能是什麼人？
(A) 祕書 **(B) 牙醫**
(C) 水電工 (D) 營養師

60 Why does the woman say, "Drinking cold water causes it"?
(A) To suggest a possible treatment
(B) To describe a healthy habit
(C) To give details about her diet
(D) To explain when a problem occurs

中譯 為什麼女子會說：「喝冷水的時候就會這樣」？
(A) 建議可能的療法
(B) 描述健康習慣
(C) 說明她的飲食情況
(D) 解釋症狀何時發生

61 What does the man recommend the woman do?
(A) Follow a personal hygiene routine
(B) Make an appointment with a doctor
(C) Avoid drinking sweet beverages
(D) Take some time off from work

中譯 男子建議女子做什麼事？
(A) 遵循個人衛生習慣
(B) 跟醫生約時間看診
(C) 避免喝甜的飲料
(D) 請假一段時間

Questions 62-64 refer to the following conversation and schedule. 美 對話和時間表

M ❻❷ **Did you read the e-mail Mr. Porter just sent? The company is building another store in Weston.**

W I just saw that. And ❻❸ **it looks like they're looking for someone to be the manager there. Are you going to go for it?**

M ❻❸ **I'm not sure.** It's a great opportunity, but I don't know if I'd enjoy being a manager.

W I think you should see what the job would be and make a final decision later. They have the interview hours listed here.

M You're right. Well, ❻❹ **it looks like there's only one time slot I can sign up for since I work Monday through Friday until 4 P.M.**

Interview Hours

Time Slot	Day	Time
1	Monday	3:00 P.M.
2	Wednesday	10:30 A.M.
❻❸ **3**	**Wednesday**	**5:00 P.M.**
4	Friday	1:45 P.M.

男：❻❷ **你看到波特先生剛寄來的電子郵件了嗎？公司要在威仕頓再開一間店。**

女：我剛剛看到了，而且 ❻❸ **看起來公司在找人去當那家店的經理。你要不要去爭取一下？**

男：❻❸ **我不知道。**這是一個很好的機會，但我不知道我是否喜歡當店經理。

女：我認為你應該先了解一下工作內容，然後再做最後決定。這裡列出了面試的時間。

男：你說的沒錯。嗯，❻❹ **看來我只有一個時段能填，因為我週一到週五都要上班到下午四點。**

面試時間

時段	星期	時間
1	星期一	下午 3:00
2	星期三	上午 10:30
❻❸ **3**	**星期三**	**下午 5:00**
4	星期五	下午 1:45

字彙 **go for** 努力爭取 **opportunity** 機會 **time slot** 時間段

62 What was announced in an e-mail?
(A) An employee has been promoted.
(B) A new branch is opening.
(C) A deadline has been extended.
(D) A company is relocating.

中譯 電子郵件裡宣布了什麼事？
(A) 有員工升職了。
(B) 新分店即將開幕。
(C) 有個截止日期延後了。
(D) 公司即將搬遷。

63 What is the man hesitating to do?
(A) Accept an offer
(B) Apply for a position
(C) Choose a candidate
(D) Talk to a supervisor

中譯 男子在猶豫是否要做什麼？
(A) 接受某個工作邀約
(B) 應聘某個職位
(C) 揀選應徵者
(D) 與主管談話

64 Look at the graphic. Which time slot is the man able to attend?
(A) Time Slot 1 (B) Time Slot 2
(C) Time Slot 3 (D) Time Slot 4

中譯 請看圖表。男子能面試的是哪一個時段？
(A) 時段 1 (B) 時段 2
(C) 時段 3 (D) 時段 4

Questions 65-67 refer to the following conversation and menu. 美W 澳M 對話和菜單

W I'd like a small double latte, please. 65 **And what kinds of pastries do you have?**

M Well, 66 **if you order a coffee from the special menu, you can get a free snack with it.** Here is the special menu.

W That's right. I forgot about that menu. Let's see… 66 **I'll get a special then, please, with a mocha instead.**

M Okay. That will be $3.50 please.

W 67 **It's a shame you close so early.**

M 67 **Actually, we changed our hours. We're open until 11 P.M. tonight.**

W Oh! I had no idea. 67 **What a nice surprise!**

~ Special Menu ~

Each drink on the special menu comes with a free pastry!

black coffee	→	croissant	$2.50
single latte	→	éclair	$3.00
66 **mocha**	→	**Danish**	**$3.50**
cappuccino	→	cinnamon roll	$3.50

女：請給我一杯有雙份濃縮咖啡的小杯拿鐵。65 **你們有哪些糕點？**

男：嗯，66 **如果您是點特餐的咖啡，就可以免費享用一份點心。**這是特餐的菜單。

女：啊，對了，我都忘了還有特餐。我看看……66 **那我要一份摩卡咖啡的特餐。**

男：好的，一共是 3.5 美元。

女：67 **可惜你們這麼早就要打烊了。**

男：67 **其實，我們的營業時間改了，我們今晚會營業到 11 點。**

女：哦！我都不知道。67 **這真是個令人意外的好消息！**

~ 特餐 ~

特餐飲料皆附贈一份糕點！

黑咖啡	→	可頌	$2.50
單份濃縮拿鐵	→	閃電泡芙	$3.00
66 **摩卡**	→	**丹麥麵包**	**$3.50**
卡布奇諾	→	肉桂捲	$3.50

65 What does the woman ask about?

(A) What food is available

(B) How much an item costs

(C) Which coffee is best

(D) Where a menu is located

中譯 女子問了什麼問題？

(A) 供應哪些食物 (B) 某品項的價格

(C) 哪種咖啡最好喝 (D) 菜單的位置

66 Look at the graphic. Which pastry will the woman get?

(A) A croissant (B) An éclair

(C) A Danish (D) A cinnamon roll

中譯 請看圖表。女子會拿到哪一種糕點？

(A) 可頌 (B) 閃電泡芙

(C) 丹麥麵包 (D) 肉桂捲

67 Why is the woman surprised?

(A) The prices have been lowered.

(B) The shop closes late.

(C) The menu options have changed.

(D) The coffee is strong.

中譯 女子為什麼感到驚訝？

(A) 降價了。

(B) 店家很晚才打烊。

(C) 菜單的品項換了。

(D) 咖啡很濃。

Questions 68-70 refer to the following conversation and list. 美 對話和清單

W Hey, Ryan. If we're taking the train to the symposium next weekend, we should reserve tickets now.

M I'd rather rent a car. ⑱ **I know taking the train there sounds cheaper, but getting around while we're there will be less of a hassle if we have a car.**

W Okay. As long as you don't mind driving, I'm fine with that. Hold on one second . . . Um . . . Okay . . . I found a list of vehicles.

M Well, ⑲ **I can't drive manual. And we need a vehicle that can carry seven passengers.**

W ⑲ **There's a van that fits those criteria. I'll reserve it.**

M ⑳ **What's the total price going to be for three days?**

	Maximum passengers	Transmission
Vehicle 1	5	Manual
Vehicle 2	5	Automatic
Vehicle 3	8	Manual
⑲ **Vehicle 4**	**8**	**Automatic**

女：嘿，萊恩，如果我們要搭火車去參加下週末舉辦的專題討論，那我們現在就得要訂票了。

男：我偏好租車。⑱ **我知道搭火車去好像比較便宜，但是如果我們有車，在那四處移動也比較方便。**

女：好吧。只要你不介意開車，我沒意見。等等……有了，我找到車子的目錄了。

男：哦，⑲ **我不會開手排車，還有我們需要一輛七人座的車。**

女：⑲ **有一輛廂型車符合這些條件，我來訂這輛。**

男：⑳ **租三天總共要多少錢？**

	最大載客量	變速器
車輛 1	5	手排
車輛 2	5	自排
車輛 3	8	手排
⑲ **車輛 4**	**8**	**自排**

字彙 symposium 專題討論會　hassle 麻煩　drive manual 開手排車　criterion 標準（複數為 criteria）

68 Why does the man prefer renting a car to taking the train?
(A) It is cheaper.
(B) It is more convenient.
(C) It is faster.
(D) It is more reliable.

中譯 男子為什麼寧可租車，也不想搭火車？
(A) 比較便宜。
(B) 比較方便。
(C) 比較快速。
(D) 比較可靠。

69 Look at the graphic. Which vehicle will the woman most likely reserve?
(A) Vehicle 1　(B) Vehicle 2
(C) Vehicle 3　**(D) Vehicle 4**

中譯 請看圖表。女子最有可能會訂哪一輛車？
(A) 車輛 1　(B) 車輛 2
(C) 車輛 3　**(D) 車輛 4**

70 What does the man ask the woman?
(A) Where they will park
(B) How many people will drive
(C) How much the rental will cost
(D) When they should leave

中譯 男子問女子什麼問題？
(A) 車子要停哪
(B) 有多少人開車
(C) 車輛租金多少
(D) 他們何時啟程

Questions 71-73 refer to the following excerpt from a meeting. 英W 會議摘錄

71 I've called this meeting because our newest clothing line is not performing well. Staff at our retail stores reported that customers often grab the dresses off the shelves to try them on but rarely buy them. Many return them, too. The design is visually appealing, but customers complain that the dresses are itchy and too tight in the shoulders. Thus, **72 I think we need to concentrate more on making our items pleasant to wear rather than just attractive to look at.** To start with, **73 here are the fabrics used by some of our competitors. Let's talk about the advantages and disadvantages of each.**

71 由於我們最新服飾系列的銷售表現不佳，所以我召開了本次的會議。我們零售店的員工回報，顧客時常從貨架上拿了衣服試穿，卻沒什麼人買，還有很多人辦理退貨。衣服的設計在視覺上很吸引人，但是顧客抱怨穿了會讓皮膚發癢，而且肩膀部分太緊了。因此，**72 我認為比起讓衣服看起來賞心悅目，我們更應該關注穿著的舒適度。**首先，**73 這裡有些競爭對手們所使用的布料。我們來說說各自的優缺點。**

字彙 call a meeting 召開會議　retail store 零售店　visually 在視覺上　itchy 發癢的　fabric 布料

71 What industry does the speaker work in?
(A) Entertainment
(B) Fashion
(C) Automobile
(D) Marketing

中譯 說話者從事哪一行業？
(A) 娛樂
(B) 時尚
(C) 汽車
(D) 行銷

72 According to the speaker, what should the company focus on?
(A) More comfortable products
(B) Better customer service
(C) More competitive prices
(D) Safer designs

中譯 根據說話者所言，公司應該注重什麼？
(A) 更舒適的產品
(B) 更好的客戶服務
(C) 更有競爭力的價格
(D) 更安全的設計

73 What will the listeners most likely do next?
(A) Look at some designs
(B) Test-drive some vehicles
(C) Try on some clothes
(D) Review some materials

中譯 聽眾接下來最有可能會做什麼事？
(A) 查看設計
(B) 試駕車輛
(C) 試穿衣服
(D) 檢視原料

Questions 74-76 refer to the following telephone message. 美M 電話留言

Hello. **74 This is Adam Hayes from Corco Legal Group.** We were pleased with your interview last week, and **74 we'd like to offer you a job as a legal consultant.** First, however, I want to make sure you are able to start work on August 15 at the latest. During your interview, you had mentioned that you would prefer to start in September. Unfortunately, because of some urgent cases we have, **75 the start date is not negotiable.** We hope you understand and are still interested in the position despite the tight time frame. **76 Please call me back and let me know whether you wish to accept our offer.**

您好，**74 我是科爾科法律集團的亞當・海耶斯。**我們對上週與您進行的面試感到滿意，因而 **74 想聘請您擔任公司的法律顧問一職。**不過，首先我想確認您最晚能夠在 8 月 15 日開始上班。您在面試的時候提到您希望在 9 月到職。很遺憾，我們有幾件緊急的訴訟案，**75 所以到職的日期是無法更動的。**希望您諒解，並且在時間緊迫的情況下，仍對這個職位感興趣。**76 請您回電並告知您是否願意接受這份工作。**

字彙 consultant 顧問　case 案件　negotiable 可協商的　time frame 時間範圍

74 What type of business does the speaker work for?
(A) An insurance company
(B) A real estate agency
(C) A law firm
(D) An accounting business

中譯 說話者在什麼類型的公司工作？
(A) 保險公司
(B) 房地產仲介公司
(C) 法律事務所
(D) 會計事務所

75 What does the speaker mention about the position?
(A) Its salary can be negotiated.
(B) Its location has been changed.
(C) Its start date is fixed.
(D) Its duties require advanced skills.

中譯 說話者提到什麼與該職位有關的事？
(A) 薪資可以討論。
(B) 上班地點已變更。
(C) 到職日期固定。
(D) 工作需要高階技能。

76 What is the listener asked to do?
(A) Come in for an interview
(B) Return a phone call
(C) Submit a job application
(D) Modify a schedule

中譯 聽到留言的人要做什麼？
(A) 去面試
(B) 回覆電話
(C) 送交求職申請表
(D) 更改日程安排

Questions 77-79 refer to the following excerpt from a meeting. 美W 會議摘錄

Before we end this meeting, ⑰ **I'd like to remind you that several part-timers will start working full-time next week. That means that all of the files for those employees must be updated by Friday, including their benefits packages.** If you're not sure which package a person qualifies for, ⑱ **consult the document I sent you last week. It lists each person's department and status.** It is important that no mistake is made. Finally, ⑲ **remember our staff meeting on Wednesday.** Several department heads will be attending to give us information about new positions. ⑰ ⑲ **Please familiarize yourselves with the job descriptions we currently have for each position before then.**

在我們結束這場會議之前，⑰ **我想要提醒各位，下週有好幾位兼職員工將轉成全職員工，代表這些員工的檔案都要在星期五前更新完成，包括他們的福利待遇。**如果你們不確定某員工享有哪項福利待遇，⑱ **可以看一下我上週寄給你們的文件，上面列出了每個員工的部門與職位。**檔案內容不可有誤，這一點很重要。最後，⑲ **切記職員會議是在星期三舉行。**屆時幾個部門的主管都會出席，跟我們說說新職位的情況。⑰ ⑲ **請大家在那之前熟悉我們目前每個職位的工作內容。**

字彙 benefits package 福利待遇　consult 查閱

77 What department do the listeners most likely work in?
(A) Human resources
(B) Marketing
(C) Accounting
(D) Customer service

中譯 聽眾最有可能在哪個部門工作？
(A) 人力資源
(B) 市場行銷
(C) 會計
(D) 客戶服務

78 What can listeners find in the document the speaker sent last week?
(A) Contract terms
(B) Benefit options
(C) Employee information
(D) Required qualifications

中譯 聽眾可在說話者上週寄出的文件裡找到什麼資訊?
(A) 合約條款
(B) 員工福利
(C) 員工資料
(D) 所需資格

79 What should listeners do by Wednesday?
(A) Read about some occupations
(B) Review job applications
(C) Advertise a job opening
(D) Update a Web site

中譯 聽眾在下週三前應做什麼事?
(A) 閱讀職務資訊
(B) 審核求職申請表
(C) 刊登徵才廣告
(D) 更新網站資料

Questions 80-82 refer to the following telephone message. 澳M 電話留言

12

Hello, ⑧⓪ **this is Jonas Bolder calling from Valaca Systems regarding the workshop you will be leading next week. We want to make sure everything is ready.** ⑧① **I've confirmed with each person that will be attending.** The total is fourteen. We've reserved a room equipped with a projector and a whiteboard. If you need anything else, please let us know. ⑧② **I was also wondering whether you need a ride from the airport. We'd be happy to call a limo service so that you don't have to worry about finding your way to our office.** I look forward to hearing back from you.

您好,⑧⓪ **我是瓦拉卡系統公司的喬納斯・博爾德,事關您下週主持的研討會。我們想要確認一切都準備好了。**⑧① **我已經跟每位與會者確認過了,**總共 14 人。我們預訂配備了投影機與白板的會議室。如果您還需要什麼東西,請告知我們。
⑧② **我還想知道您是否需要機場接機服務。我們很樂意幫您安排禮車接送,這樣您就不用擔心如何前往我們公司。**靜候您的回覆。

字彙 ride (乘車的)行程 limo 禮車 (= limousine)

80 What is the speaker preparing for?
(A) Hosting an event
(B) Entering a contest
(C) Moving to a new location
(D) Installing new equipment

中譯 說話者在準備什麼?
(A) 主辦活動
(B) 參加比賽
(C) 搬遷到新址
(D) 安裝新設備

81 Why does the speaker say, "The total is fourteen"?
(A) To request a payment
(B) To report the number of participants
(C) To explain a policy
(D) To provide the number of lectures

中譯 說話者為何說:「總共 14 人」?
(A) 要求付款
(B) 告知與會人數
(C) 說明政策
(D) 提供課堂數

82 What does the speaker offer to do?
(A) Apply a discount
(B) Arrange a pickup
(C) Postpone a meeting
(D) Send directions

中譯 說話者主動提議做什麼?
(A) 使用折扣
(B) 安排接送
(C) 延後開會的時間
(D) 寄送交通指南

Questions 83-85 refer to the following talk. 美W 談話

Hello, everyone. ⑧③ ⑧⑤ **The second Stella's Kitchen has finally opened its doors in Chesterfield.** Colin Boyle will be the manager at this new restaurant. Mr. Boyle is a graduate of Millaty School of Culinary Arts, where he specialized in Italian cuisine. In addition, ⑧④ **he recently obtained a master's in business administration,** and is thus perfect for this job. The combination of his cooking knowledge and corporate know-how makes me confident that the Chesterfield branch will be highly successful. He will be joining us later today to watch how things are run here. He'll be here around 4 P.M. ⑧⑤ **Right now, he is visiting the facilities of the new location.**

大家好，⑧③ ⑧⑤ **史黛拉廚房二號店終於在切斯特菲爾德開業了。**科林・博伊爾將擔任這家新餐廳的經理。博伊爾先生畢業自米拉提廚藝學院，專研義大利料理。此外，⑧④ **他最近還拿到了商業管理的碩士學位，**因此完美契合這份工作。我相信，在他的烹飪知識與商務知識兩相結合下，切斯特菲爾德分店一定會大獲成功。他稍後就會加入我們，了解一下運作情形。他下午四點左右會到這裡。⑧⑤ **此刻，他正在參觀新分店的設施。**

字彙 graduate （大學）畢業生　culinary art 廚藝　cuisine 料理　master's 碩士學位（= master's degree）

83 According to the speaker, what recently happened?
(A) A branch was opened.
(B) Two companies merged.
(C) A product was launched.
(D) A restaurant changed its menu.

中譯 根據說話者所言，最近發生了什麼事？
(A) 有家分店開幕了。
(B) 兩家公司合併了。
(C) 有項產品上市了。
(D) 有家餐廳換菜單了。

84 What did Mr. Boyle study in graduate school?
(A) Cooking
(B) Business administration
(C) Italian
(D) Art

中譯 博伊爾先生在研究所學習什麼？
(A) 烹飪
(B) 商業管理
(C) 義大利語
(D) 美術

85 What is Mr. Boyle currently doing?
(A) Touring a restaurant
(B) Designing a menu
(C) Ordering some food
(D) Attending a class

中譯 博伊爾先生目前正在做什麼？
(A) 巡視餐廳
(B) 設計菜單
(C) 點餐
(D) 上課

Questions 86-88 refer to the following recorded message. 英W 語音留言

⑧⑥ **You have reached Hannon Telecom.** Thank you for contacting us. ⑧⑥ ⑧⑦ **We have received a number of calls regarding slow Internet connections in the past few hours.** We are working on fixing the issue and trust that the problem will be resolved soon. Internet speed should be back to normal for all customers by this evening. However, ⑧⑧ **if you are unable to connect to the Internet at all, please press 0 to explain the issue to the next available customer service representative.**

⑧⑥ **這裡是漢能電信公司，**感謝您來電與我們聯繫。⑧⑥ ⑧⑦ **本公司過去幾個小時內接到了數通電話，都與網路連線速度緩慢有關。**我們正在努力解決這個問題，相信問題很快就能順利排除。所有客戶的網速今晚應該就能恢復正常。不過，⑧⑧ **如果您完全無法連網的話，請按「0」向下一位接電話的客服人員說明問題。**

字彙 connection 連接　fix 維修，解決（問題）　resolve 解決（問題或困難）

86 What type of business has the caller reached?
(A) A communications provider
(B) An electronics manufacturer
(C) A Web design company
(D) A device repair shop

中譯 來電者打電話到什麼類型的公司？
(A) 通訊服務供應商
(B) 電子產品製造商
(C) 網頁設計公司
(D) 器材維修行

87 What problem does the speaker mention?
(A) A service is slow.
(B) A machine is defective.
(C) A delivery is delayed.
(D) A Web site is down.

中譯 說話者提到什麼問題？
(A) 服務很緩慢。
(B) 機器有瑕疵。
(C) 送貨延誤了。
(D) 網站癱瘓了。

88 Why should callers press 0?
(A) To upgrade a plan
(B) To report an issue
(C) To cancel an order
(D) To request a refund

中譯 來電者為什麼要按「0」？
(A) 升級方案
(B) 告知問題
(C) 取消訂單
(D) 要求退款

Questions 89-91 refer to the following talk. 美M 談話

❽❾ **Welcome to F&U Manufacturer. We are excited to start working with you.** Before we begin, ❾⓿ **let's go over some of our general safety guidelines.** First, you must wear a hard hat at all times. This includes when you are on break. As long as you are on factory premises, you must not be seen without a hard hat. ❾❶ **Please also wear safety glasses when you are doing work, no matter what the task is.** We work in close proximity to one another. ❾❶ **Even if you're not doing anything threatening to the eyes, the person next to you might be.** Finally, although they close automatically, always check that doors are shut properly.

❽❾ **歡迎來到 F&U 製造廠，我們都很高興能與各位共事。**在開始之前，❾⓿ **我們先來看看幾個一般性的安全準則。**首先，要隨時戴著安全帽，包括在休息的時候。只要在工廠裡，就不能被人看到你沒戴安全帽。❾❶ **還有，無論是做什麼工作，工作時請戴上護目鏡。**大家都緊挨著彼此工作，❾❶ **所以即便你做的事對眼睛無害，但你身邊的同事可能不然。**最後，雖然門會自動關上，但都還是要檢查門是否關好。

字彙 manufacturer 製造商　hard hat 安全帽　premises （複數）場所，地點　in close proximity to 接近

89 Who most likely are the listeners?
(A) Visiting clients
(B) Retired employees
(C) Branch managers
(D) New workers

中譯 聽眾最有可能是什麼身分？
(A) 來訪客戶
(B) 退休員工
(C) 分店經理
(D) 新進員工

90 What is the purpose of the talk?
(A) To outline some rules
(B) To announce break times
(C) To introduce a new manager
(D) To assess a performance

中譯 本次談話的目的為何？
(A) 簡單說明規則
(B) 宣布休息時間
(C) 介紹新任經理
(D) 評估工作表現

91 Why does the speaker say, "We work in close proximity to one another"?
(A) To justify a policy
(B) To provide directions
(C) To explain a layout
(D) To demand respect

中譯 說話者為什麼說：「大家都緊挨著彼此工作」？
(A) 證明政策的正當性
(B) 提供交通路線指南
(C) 說明格局佈置
(D) 要求尊重

Questions 92-94 refer to the following excerpt from a meeting. 美W 會議摘錄

Next on the agenda, I'd like to let you know that ㉒ **next week I'm going to be interviewing people for our graphic design team.** We are not a well-known company, so ㉓ **I know that some of you were concerned that the applicant pool for the job opening wouldn't be large enough.** Well, I'm pleased to say that it was twice what we expected. Now, ㉔ **I'll need some of you to give up your desks to allow applicants to do a computer-based exercise as part of the interview. Timothy will be asking you about this,** so if you're able to work from a laptop, or if you'll be out of the office next week, please talk to him.

接著是議程表的下一個事項，我想通知大家，㉒ **下個星期我將為平面設計部面試員工。**我們公司不是什麼知名企業，所以 ㉓ **我知道你們當中有些人擔心來應徵這個職缺的人數不夠多。**嗯，我很高興地說，人數是我們預期的兩倍。現在，㉔ **我需要你們中的幾位同事，把自己的桌子讓給應徵者進行電腦實作，這是面試的一環。提摩西會去問你們，**所以如果你能用筆電工作，或是下個星期不在辦公室的，請跟他說。

字彙 agenda 議程　pool（為了共同的活動或工作所需的）一群人

92 Who most likely will the speaker interview next week?
(A) Computer repair technicians
(B) Sales executives
(C) Graphic designers
(D) Laboratory researchers

中譯 說話者下週最有可能會面試什麼人？
(A) 電腦維修技師
(B) 業務主管
(C) 平面設計人員
(D) 實驗室研究員

93 What does the speaker mean when she says, "it was twice what we expected"?
(A) A job opening got many applicants.
(B) A company's market share grew significantly.
(C) A candidate requested a larger salary.
(D) A hiring process took longer than planned.

中譯 說話者說：「人數是我們預期的兩倍」，其言下之意為何？
(A) 有很多人來應徵職缺。
(B) 公司的市占率大幅增長。
(C) 應徵者要求更高的薪資。
(D) 聘僱過程比預計的還要長。

94 According to the speaker, what will Timothy do?
(A) Reserve a conference room for an interview
(B) Review the résumés of applicants
(C) Create a vacation schedule for the team
(D) Find volunteers to give up their workspaces

中譯 根據說話者所言，提摩西會做什麼事？
(A) 預約要進行面試的會議室
(B) 審核應徵者的履歷
(C) 為部門制定休假時間表
(D) 尋找自願讓出辦公座位的人

Questions 95-97 to the following radio broadcast and map. 澳M 電臺廣播與地圖

Good morning. You're listening to *Melville Traffic News*. 95 **The new department store at the intersection of Cane Street and First Avenue is still under construction,** making the area particularly dangerous and congested. 96 **Although the project was supposed to be finished last night, the end date has been pushed back another week due to budget issues.** The projected end date is now October 12. Until then, we recommend taking a detour on Pearson Road. Despite the disturbance, 97 **the annual arts and crafts market will still be held on Chestnut Street this afternoon.** Come check out some amazing items by local artists.

Pearson Road
Building A
Building B
95 Building C
Building D
95 First Avenue
Chestnut Street
95 Cane Street

早安，您正在收聽《梅爾維爾交通新聞》。95 **位於凱恩街與第一大道交叉口的新百貨公司仍在施工，**使得該區特別危險，交通也非常壅塞。96 **該項工程原本預計要在昨晚完工，但礙於預算問題，完工日期延宕一週。**目前預計於 10 月 12 日完工。在那之前，我們建議改道皮爾森路。儘管交通紊亂，97 **一年一度的手工藝品市集今天下午還是會在栗樹街舉行。**大家一起來看看當地藝術家令人讚嘆的創作吧。

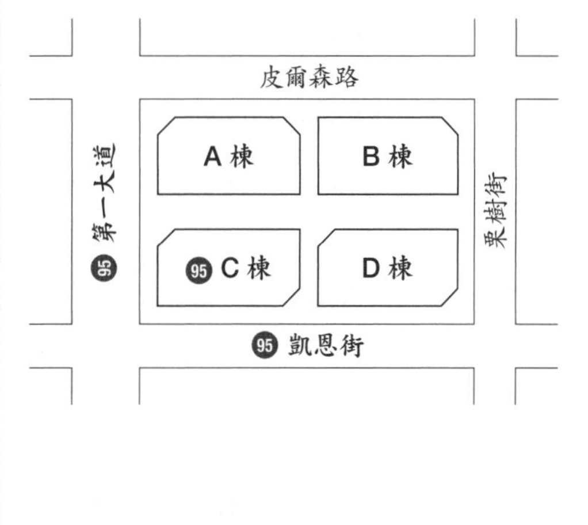

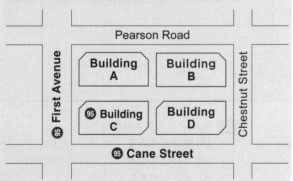

字彙 **under construction** 施工中　**congested** 擁擠的　**push back** 推遲　**take a detour** 繞道
disturbance 紛亂　**arts and crafts** 手工藝品

95 Look at the graphic. Which building is under construction?
(A) Building A　(B) Building B
(C) Building C　(D) Building D

中譯 請看圖表。哪一棟建築正在施工？
(A) A 棟　(B) B 棟
(C) C 棟　(D) D 棟

96 What has caused a delay in the construction project?
(A) Insufficient materials
(B) A car accident
(C) Weather conditions
(D) Financial problems

中譯 導致建案延誤的原因為何？
(A) 建材不足
(B) 車禍
(C) 天氣狀況
(D) 財務問題

97 What will take place this afternoon?
(A) A grand opening
(B) A sales event
(C) An anniversary party
(D) An artisan fair

中譯 今天下午會發生什麼事？
(A) 盛大開幕活動
(B) 促銷活動
(C) 週年紀念派對
(D) 手工藝市集

Questions 98-100 refer to the following introduction and list. 美W 行前介紹與清單

Good afternoon, everyone. 98 **My name is Fannie Willis, and I'm the head of the quality control team here at Nexxon Manufacturing.** 99 **I'll be giving you a tour of our facilities so that you understand our production process before making an investment in our company.** We make a wide range of furniture using various materials, and you will see each type today. 100 **We'll spend about twenty minutes in each section except for where we're producing metal items. That area is very hot, so we'll only stay there for ten minutes.** Please wear your safety gear at all times, and feel free to ask questions throughout the tour.

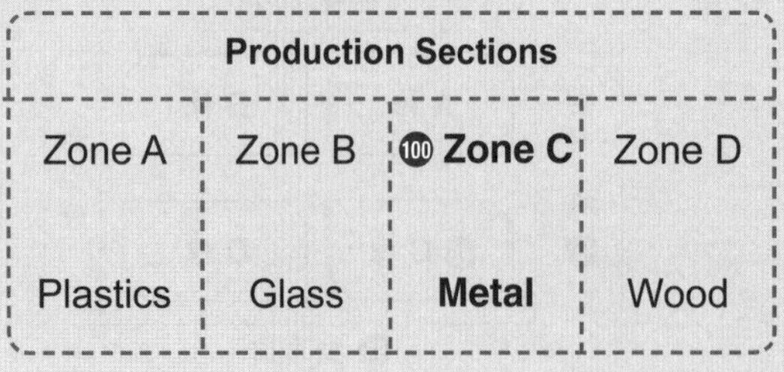

Production Sections			
Zone A	Zone B	100 **Zone C**	Zone D
Plastics	Glass	**Metal**	Wood

大家午安，98 **我叫范妮・威利斯，我是奈克森製造廠品管部的主管。** 99 **為了讓各位在投資我們公司之前，能了解我們的生產過程，我現在要帶大家參觀工廠的設施。**我們使用多種原料來製作各式各樣的家具，而今天你們都將會一一看到。100 **我們預計在每一區待 20 分鐘左右，除了生產金屬製品的那區，因為太熱了，因此我們只會在那裡待 10 分鐘。**請隨時隨地穿戴好安全裝備，參觀過程中也歡迎隨時提問。

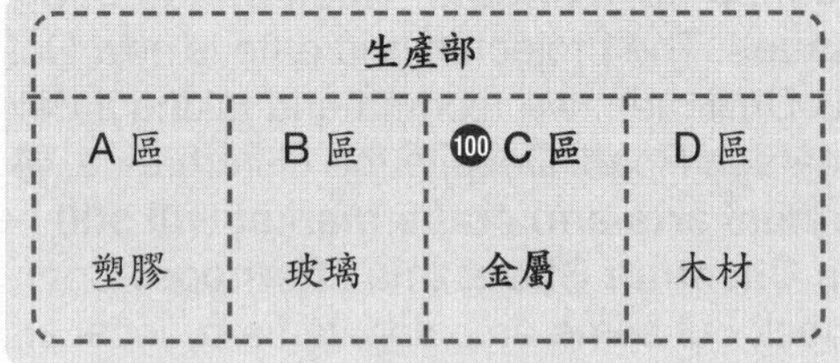

生產部			
A 區	B 區	100 C 區	D 區
塑膠	玻璃	**金屬**	木材

98 What is the speaker in charge of doing?
(A) Assuring the quality of goods
(B) Overseeing the hiring process
(C) Promoting the company's products
(D) Repairing production equipment

中譯 說話者是負責做什麼的？
(A) 確保產品品質
(B) 監督招聘流程
(C) 宣傳公司產品
(D) 維修生產設備

99 Who most likely are the listeners?
(A) Safety inspectors
(B) New employees
(C) Potential investors
(D) Department managers

中譯 聽眾最有可能是什麼人？
(A) 安檢人員
(B) 新進員工
(C) 潛在投資者
(D) 部門主管

100 Look at the graphic. In which area will the listeners spend the shortest amount of time?
(A) Zone A (B) Zone B
(C) Zone C (D) Zone D

中譯 請看圖表。聽眾在哪一區待的時間最短？
(A) A 區 (B) B 區
(C) C 區 (D) D 區

PART 5

對等連接詞 or

101 您可以提前買好5月11日演唱會的票，亦可現場購票。
(A) 為了 (B) 所以 **(C) 或者** (D) 也不
字彙 in advance 事先

填入名詞+人物名詞 vs 事物名詞

102 布莉琪・柯爾曼在課堂上提供了法庭上常用的外來術語翻譯。
(A) 翻譯 (B) 翻譯了 (C) 譯者 **(D) 翻譯**
字彙 translation 翻譯 term 術語

介系詞 by

103 馬格斯電子公司的儀器大多都是由海外工廠生產的。
(A) 被…… (B) 關於 (C) 經過 (D) 沿著
字彙 electronics（複數）電子器材 device 設備 manufacture 生產；製造

反身代名詞——強調用法

104 組長太忙了，沒辦法親自去機場接科爾考特的執行長。
(A) 她 (B) 她 (C) 她的 **(D) 親自**

形容詞 primary

105 本次會議的主要目的就是審核我們的安全程序。
(A) 主要的 (B) 嚴格的
(C) 豐富的 (D) 及時的
字彙 safety procedure 安全措施

填入副詞——修飾動詞

106 儘管彼得・博特蘭有練習，但針對面試官的提問，準備得還是不夠充分。
(A) 足夠 (B) 充足 (C) 足夠的 **(D) 充分地**
字彙 sufficiently 充分地

動詞 communicate

107 馬庫斯先生在去墨西哥出差前學了西班牙文，這樣就能跟當地人溝通。
(A) 陳述 **(B) 溝通** (C) 預約 (D) 理解

數量形容詞 every

108 每位與會者都會拿到一個文件夾，裡面有議程表以及每位演講者的額外資訊。
(A) 每一個 (B) 很少的
(C) 好幾個 (D) 全部
字彙 attendee 出席者 program（活動）時間表 note 補充資料

名詞 development

109 各科學領域近期的發展使得人類的預期壽命突然增加。
(A) 發展 (B) 版本 (C) 時間軸 (D) 範圍
字彙 life expectancy 預期壽命

填入形容詞——限定詞+形容詞+名詞

110 曼德女士在原來的晚宴賓客名單上增加了6個名字，預期的用餐人數因而來到了23人。
(A) 起源 (B) 起源於
(C) 原先的 (D) 起初
字彙 bring A up to B 使（總數）達到

動詞 unveil

111 薇薇時尚公司的春季系列皮革手提包，在上個星期的時裝秀首次推出。
(A) 諮詢 (B) 緩解 (C) 嘗試 **(D) 首次推出**
字彙 line 產品系列 leather 皮革 runway 伸展台

未來進行式

112 志工將於下週六上午11點在大樓大廳集合，為募款活動做準備。
(A) 聚集了 (B) 已聚集
(C) 將會聚集 (D) 將會一直聚集
字彙 gather 聚集 fundraising 募款

所有格代名詞

113 由於我的行程表比你的更有彈性，我們隨時可以約你方便的時間見面。
(A) 你 (B) 你自己
(C) 你的 **(D) 你的（行程表）**
字彙 flexible 彈性的

填入名詞+動名詞 vs 名詞

114 吉布森百貨公司把裝了免費試用品的小袋子分送給顧客，感謝他們前來參加盛大的開幕活動。
(A) 出席 **(B) 出席** (C) 出席者 (D) 出席
字彙 hand out 分發 grand opening 隆重開幕

介系詞 of

115 搭乘頭等艙的旅客每人最多可以託運三件行李。
(A) 在……上面 (B) 超出
(C) ……的 (D) 朝，向
字彙 check in 託運（行李） maximum 最大量 suitcase 行李

名詞 compliance

116 員工應始終嚴格遵守公司規定。
(A) 應用 **(B) 遵守** (C) 管理 (D) 更正
字彙 at all times 一直；始終

關係代名詞主格

117 請由位於沙加緬度街的北門進出本大樓。
(A) ……的人　(B) ……那樣的
(C) ……的地方　**(D) ……的那個**

填入副詞——修飾數字

118 根據新聞主播的報導，該病毒在短短幾分鐘內就感染了大約一萬台電腦。
(A) 大約的　**(B) 大約**　(C) 接近　(D) 近似值

字彙 infect 感染　approximately 大約；大概

形容詞 diverse

119 富魯科斯服飾公司計劃製作一系列的廣告，吸引不同類型的客群。
(A) 各式各樣的　(B) 正確的
(C) 尋常的　(D) 描述的

字彙 appeal to 吸引　clientele 顧客群

慣用片語 would rather A than B

120 本項研究顯示，客戶寧願在網路上買東西，也不願去店裡試穿。
(A) 進一步　(B) 也許　**(C) 寧願**　(D) 錯誤地

動詞 emerge

121 多家工廠排放有害氣體的事最近被揭露了，此事已成為公司一大問題。
(A) 成為　**(B) 成為**　(C) 造成　(D) 引起

字彙 revelation 揭發　emission 排放

填入名詞＋動名詞 vs 名詞

122 有鑒於該市的城市布局錯綜複雜，想要選出波特維爾分店位置並不容易。
(A) 選擇　(B) 選擇　(C) 選擇　(D) 選擇

字彙 location 位置　complex 複雜的　layout 布局

填入名詞

123 餐廳經理跟員工一起研究食品安全法規，為每個月一次的檢查做準備。
(A) 控管　(B) 控管　**(C) 法規**　(D) 控管

字彙 inspection 檢查

形容詞 detailed

124 請至總統候選人安・拉瑟普的競選網站，查看她對經濟計畫的詳細說明。
(A) 重複的　(B) 客製化的
(C) 已證實的　**(D) 詳細的**

字彙 presidential candidate 總統候選人
economic 經濟的　campaign 競選活動

被動語態

125 想要拿到退貨商品的全額退款，就必須向收銀員出示購買收據。
(A) 出示了　(B) 已出示
(C) 就會出示　**(D) 必須出示**

字彙 full refund 全額退款　receipt 收據

填入形容詞＋形容詞 vs 分詞

126 艾爾格超市提供有競爭力的價格，因此成為該地區最成功的雜貨店之一。
(A) 競爭　(B) 競爭
(C) 有競爭力的　(D) 競爭地

連接詞 vs 介系詞

127 艾比蓋兒・霍斯金斯獲頒市政府感謝狀，感謝她為提高教育水準所做的努力。
(A) 為了　(B) 進入　(C) 因為　(D) 在……的時候

字彙 certificate of appreciation 感謝狀
educational standards 教育水準

副詞 slightly

128 雖然瑪莉亞燒烤店離市中心僅稍近一點，但是該店的生意卻比普里馬韋拉燒烤店好很多。
(A) 稍微地　(B) 壓倒性地
(C) 小心地　(D) 流行地

不定詞 to——副詞用法

129 設計師用了新款軟體來設計大會的宣傳手冊。
(A) 設計　(B) 將設計　**(C) 來設計**　(D) 設計了

字彙 brochure 小冊子　convention 大會

名詞 shortcomings

130 儘管艾米・波爾福特的學歷有缺陷，但由於她的實習經歷，管理高層還是決定要聘僱她。
(A) 成就　**(B) 短處**　(C) 提交　(D) 資格

字彙 management 管理（層）
educational background 學歷

Questions 131-134 refer to the following e-mail. 電子郵件

To: Margaret Keeble <m_keeble@tysoncomm.com>
From: Juan Torres <j_torres@tysoncomm.com>
Date: November 18
Subject: Keep up the good work!

Dear Ms. Keeble,

I would like to thank you for handling the situation when Ms. Ferona came to our office upset because of a billing error. It is not always easy to know what to do in these situations, but the way you handled it was -------**131.**. Pleasing our clients is an important part of the job. -------**132.**, we can't give them everything they demand. This would have a detrimental effect on our finances. By explaining the reason for the error in a calm manner, you resolved the conflict quickly. -------**133.**. The other managers and I agree that you deserve -------**134.** from your hard work. Therefore, you will be given an extra day of paid vacation.

Congratulations!

Juan Torres
Office Manager, Tyson Communications

收件人：瑪格麗特・基博
<m_keeble@tysoncomm.com>
寄件人：胡安・托雷斯
<j_torres@tysoncomm.com>
日期：11 月 18 日
主旨：請繼續努力！

親愛的基博女士：

我要感謝妳處理費柔娜女士一事，她那時因帳單錯誤而氣沖沖地來到我們公司。碰到這種情況，知道如何處理並不容易，但是妳處理的方式很 131 **恰當**。讓客戶滿意是工作很重要的一環。132 **即便如此**，我們也不能對客戶有求必應，這可能會對我們的財務有不好的影響。妳以冷靜的態度向客戶說明出錯的原因，從而迅速地解決了衝突，133 **此舉亦為我們的基層員工樹立一個很好的榜樣**。我跟其他經理都認為，妳工作勤奮努力，理應 134 **獲得獎勵**。因此，我們將多給妳一天帶薪休假。

恭喜！

胡安・托雷斯
人事總務專員 泰森通訊公司

字彙 **detrimental** 有害的 **resolve** 解決（問題） **conflict** 衝突 **deserve** 應得 **benefit from** 受益於

形容詞 appropriate

131 (A) feasible **(B) appropriate** (C) steady (D) affordable

中譯 (A) 可行的 **(B) 恰當的** (C) 穩定的 (D) 負擔得起的

連接副詞 nonetheless

132 (A) In addition (B) Even if **(C) Nonetheless** (D) For instance

中譯 (A) 此外 (B) 即使 **(C) 儘管如此** (D) 例如

選出合適的句子

133 (A) Ms. Ferona will oversee this area from now on.
(B) We have already reprinted your new bill showing the change.
(C) It was also a good example to set for our junior staff members.
(D) The company will upgrade its billing software soon.

中譯 (A) 從現在起，費柔娜女士將會管理這一區。
(B) 我們已為您重印新帳單，上面顯示出此項異動。
(C) 此舉亦為我們的基層員工樹立一個很好的榜樣。
(D) 公司不久將會升級其帳務軟體。

不定詞 to——名詞用法

134 (A) to benefit
(B) will benefit
(C) being benefits
(D) it benefitted

中譯 **(A) 使得益** (B) 將得益
(C) 有利益 (D) 它得益

解析 空格是動詞 **deserve** 的受詞。在脈絡上，表示「有資格領賞」較自然，故正解為 **(A)**。「**deserve to do**」的意思是「有值得……的資格」，請記得這是常見用法。

Questions 135-138 refer to the following article. 文章

March 16, Narton—A new library ------- (135.) in the center of the small town of Narton will be opening its doors next month. The Narton Library will hold a collection of books, magazines, and videos on all topics. In addition, it will offer free Internet access, host regular events, and provide various workshops to ------- (136.) the community. "I think this library will be extremely helpful," indicated ------- (137.) resident Samuel Prendy. "Narton is isolated in a remote location, and it is difficult for us to stay up-to-date on all the latest information." Mayor Brenkel is scheduled to give a speech at the opening ceremony on April 2. ------- (138.). For more information about it, check Narton's official Web site.

3 月 16 日，納頓訊——135 **位於**納頓小鎮中心的新圖書館將於下個月正式啟用。納頓圖書館將有各主題的書報雜誌及影音光碟等館藏。此外，為 136 **服務**鄉親，該圖書館將會提供免費的上網服務，定期舉辦活動，以及辦理各式各樣的專題研討會。「我認為這個圖書館會大有助益」，137 **當地**居民塞繆・普蘭迪表示，「納頓地處遙遠的偏鄉地帶，我們很難掌握到最新資訊。」市長布倫克爾計劃在 4 月 2 日的揭幕儀式上發表演說，138 **敬邀大家參與此一盛會**。如欲了解更多資訊，請至納頓的官方網站查看。

字彙 **extremely** 極端地；非常 **resident** 居民 **isolated** 孤立的 **remote** 偏僻的 **up-to-date** 最新的

填入形容詞＋分詞

135 (A) will be located (B) locating
(C) is located **(D) located**

中譯 (A) 將位於 (B) 位於
(C) 就位於 **(D) 位於**

動詞 serve

136 **(A) serve** (B) organize
(C) request (D) visit

中譯 **(A) 服務** (B) 組織
(C) 要求 (D) 參觀

形容詞 local

137 (A) expert (B) dependent
(C) local (D) active

中譯 (A) 專業的 (B) 依賴的
(C) 當地的 (D) 積極的

選出合適的句子

138 **(A) All are invited to attend this event.**
(B) It will be announced on that day.
(C) You can pick up your books at that time.
(D) He was elected with a large majority.

中譯 **(A) 敬邀大家參與此一盛會。**
(B) 此事將在當日宣布。
(C) 屆時您可領取您的書。
(D) 他取得大多數的票數當選。

Questions 139-142 refer to the following notice. 公告

As you know, the company donates to the F&Y homeless shelter every year. This year, instead of money, we have decided to donate various goods that the shelter is in need of. You'll see bins at the entrance of each department head's office. Employees are -------(139.) to place items in good condition into these bins. When a bin is -------(140.), it will be picked up by PR staff and taken to the shelter. A list of acceptable items will be posted in the staff lounge. -------(141.). In particular, note that although clothing is welcome, certain -------(142.) are not accepted due to common allergies and limited washing options. Thank you in advance for your donations.

如大家所知，公司每年都會捐錢給 F&Y 無家者收容所。今年，我們決定不捐錢，改捐收容所需要的各類物資。各部門主管辦公室的門口都放了儲物箱。我們 139 **鼓勵**各位將狀況良好的物品放進箱子裡。箱子 140 **裝滿**後，將會由公關部員工拿去給收容所。收容所可接受的物品清單會張貼在員工休息室。141 **在往箱子裡放任何物品前，請先仔細查看此清單。**特別要注意的是，雖然他們很歡迎大家捐贈衣物，但是由於常見的過敏反應及有限的洗滌方法，某些 142 **材質**的衣物不接受捐贈。先感謝各位的愛心。

字彙 **homeless shelter** 無家者收容所 **bin** 儲物容器 **donation** 捐贈（物）

被動語態

139 (A) encouragement (B) encourage (C) encouraging **(D) encouraged**

中譯 (A) 鼓勵 (B) 鼓勵 (C) 鼓勵 **(D) 鼓勵**

形容詞 full

140 (A) open **(B) full** (C) finished (D) consumed

中譯 (A) 開著的 **(B) 裝滿的** (C) 完成的 (D) 消費的

選出合適的句子

141 **(A) Please consult it carefully before placing anything in a bin.**
(B) You may take anything that seems necessary to you.
(C) However, entrance is restricted to upper management only.
(D) If you agree with the terms, you may sign below.

中譯 **(A) 在往箱子裡放任何物品前，請先仔細查看此清單。**
(B) 你可以拿走任何你覺得需要的東西。
(C) 然而，入口僅限管理高層使用。
(D) 如果你同意這些條款，就在下方簽名。

名詞 material

142 (A) methods (B) amounts **(C) materials** (D) payments

中譯 (A) 方法 (B) 數量 **(C) 材質** (D) 付款

Questions 143-146 refer to the following letter. 信函

September 14
Sterling Murray
25 Morocco Drive
Newtown, PA 18777

Dear Mr. Murray,

It is our pleasure to award you first place in the Graper Scientific Research Competition for your paper entitled "Quality Control in Pharmaceuticals: Testing Three Methods." The study you conducted and your findings were fascinating. -------. (143.) We trust that the rest of the readers in the scientific community will find your work -------. (144.) In addition, you ------- (145.) $2,500 for further research. We hope that this will help in your future endeavors. Congratulations, and thank you for your ------- (146.) to the field of medicine.

Sincerely,

Richard Nelson
Director, Graper Science

18777 賓夕凡尼亞州
紐頓市摩洛哥路 25 號
斯特林・穆雷
9 月 14 日

親愛的穆雷先生：

我們很榮幸將第一名頒發給您以〈藥物品質管制：檢驗三方法〉為題，發表在「格雷珀科學研究競賽」的論文。您進行的這場研究及發現十分地吸引人。143 **您的論文將刊登在下個月的《格雷珀科學新知》上**。我們相信，科學界其他讀者也會認為您的研究 144 **深具啟發性**。此外，您 145 **將獲得** 2500 美元的獎金，以進行後續的研究。我們希望這對您未來的研究有所助益。恭喜，並感謝您對醫藥界的 146 **貢獻**。

誠摯地，

格雷珀科學期刊 董事長
理查・尼爾森

字彙 entitle 名叫（稱） conduct 執行 finding （一般複數）調查、研究的結果 inspirational 啟發靈感的 grant 授與 endeavor 努力，嘗試

選出合適的句子

143 (A) We highly recommend that you read this study.
(B) Many contestants have entered the competition.
(C) However, most of the information was already well-known.
(D) Your article will appear in next month's *Graper Science News*.

中譯 (A) 我們強烈建議您閱讀此項研究。
(B) 許多參賽者都參加了這場比賽。
(C) 然而，大部分資訊已是眾所週知。
(D) 您的論文將刊登在下個月的《格雷珀科學新知》上。

填入形容詞──受詞補語

144 (A) inspires (B) inspire
(C) inspirational (D) inspiration

中譯 (A) 靈感 (B) 靈感
(C) 啟發靈感的 (D) 啟發靈感的……

未來式＋被動語態

145 (A) will grant
(B) would have been granted
(C) would have granted
(D) will be granted

中譯 (A) 將授與
(B) 應該會被授與
(C) 應該會授與
(D) 將被授與

名詞 contribution

146 (A) distinction (B) survey
(C) contribution (D) knowledge

中譯 (A) 差異 (B) 調查
(C) 貢獻 (D) 知識

PART 7

Questions 147-148 refer to the following e-mail. 電子郵件

To: Veronica Tessier <v.tessier@greatinterior.com>
From: Lucy Bracker <l.bracker@memail.net>
Subject: Sample Pictures
Date: January 18

Dear Ms. Tessier,

147 **Thank you for sending pictures of possible layouts for our living room.** It is helpful to see pictures of various colors and textures put together to get an idea of how things would look. 148 **I am having trouble opening the last picture you sent, however.** It seems to be in a different format from the others, and my computer doesn't seem to be able to read it. Could you send it again in the same format as the others?

Thank you very much.

Sincerely,

Lucy Bracker

收件人：薇若妮卡・特西耶 <v.tessier@greatinterior.com>
寄件人：露西・卜拉格 <l.bracker@memail.net>
主旨：樣品圖片
日期：1月18日

特西耶小姐妳好：

147 **謝謝妳寄來我們客廳可能的配置圖。**看到各種顏色跟質感的擺設放在一起的圖片，就能了解大概會是什麼樣子，這對我們很有幫助。148 **不過，我無法開啟妳寄來的上一張圖片。**檔案的格式似乎和其他圖片不一樣，且我的電腦無法讀取。妳能不能用跟其他照片一樣的格式再寄一次呢？

非常謝謝妳。

露西・卜拉格 敬上

字彙 **texture** 質感 **format** 格式

推論問題

147 Who most likely is Ms. Tessier?
(A) A professional photographer
(B) An interior designer
(C) An IT expert
(D) An art gallery owner

中譯 特西耶小姐最有可能是什麼人？
(A) 專業攝影師
(B) 室內設計師
(C) 資訊專家
(D) 畫廊老闆

確認特定資訊問題

148 What problem is Ms. Bracker having?
(A) She doesn't have enough space.
(B) She doesn't like the color combinations.
(C) She is unable to view a file.
(D) She didn't receive an e-mail.

中譯 卜拉格小姐碰上什麼問題？
(A) 她沒有足夠的空間。
(B) 她不喜歡顏色的組合。
(C) 她無法查看某個檔案。
(D) 她沒收到電子郵件。

Questions 149-150 refer to the following calendar. 月曆

Mercer Real Estate New Employee Orientation Schedule

AUGUST						
Sunday	Monday	Tuesday	Wednesday	Thursday	Friday	Saturday
	1	2	3	149 **4** **OR**	5	6
7	8	9	10	11	12	13
14	15	16	17	18	19	20
21	22	23	150 **24** **DA**	25	150 **26** **PRO**	27
28	29 **FFD**	30	31			

OR: First day of orientation. Walk-through of premises
DA: Individual department assignments announced
PRO: Pictures taken and creation of Web site profiles
FFD: First full day compensated as a full-time employee

墨舍房地產新進員工培訓時間表

八月						
週日	週一	週二	週三	週四	週五	週六
	1	2	3	149 4 OR	5	6
7	8	9	10	11	12	13
14	15	16	17	18	19	20
21	22	23	150 24 DA	25	150 26 PRO	27
28	29 FFD	30	31			

OR: 入職培訓第一天，參觀公司
DA: 宣布個別分配到的部門
PRO: 拍攝照片及網站建檔
FFD: 作為正式員工支薪的第一個工作日

字彙 **real estate** 房地產　**walk-through** 參觀　**premises**（複數）營業場所　**assignment** 分配，指派
compensate 支付報酬

確認特定資訊問題

149 On which day will employees tour the facilities?

(A) August 4　(B) August 24
(C) August 26　(D) August 29

中譯 員工將在哪一天參觀設施？
(A) 8 月 4 日　(B) 8 月 24 日
(C) 8 月 26 日　(D) 8 月 29 日

Not / True 問題

150 What is indicated about the company's Web site pictures?

(A) They are required for finding one's department.
(B) They must be submitted on the first day of work.
(C) They are taken after departments have been assigned.
(D) They should be brought to work by employees on August 26.

中譯 關於公司網站的照片，何者為真？
(A) 要有照片才能找到自己的部門。
(B) 工作的第一天就要繳交照片。
(C) 照片是在分配部門後拍攝的。
(D) 員工應於 8 月 26 日帶照片去公司。

Questions 151-152 refer to the following text-message chain. 訊息串

Jimmie Kristof [3:08 P.M.]
Rebecca, have you made arrangements for going to the conference next Monday?

Rebecca Pauly [3:09 P.M.]
151 **I thought the company was taking care of that. Aren't they providing a bus for us?**

Jimmie Kristof [3:10 P.M.]
151 **No. They decided not to after all.** So most people are taking the subway or driving.

Rebecca Pauly [3:13 P.M.]
Then I guess I'll drive. There aren't any subway stations near my place. But I've never been to that venue. I have no idea how to get there.

Jimmie Kristof [3:14 P.M.]
Well, that's why I contacted you. 152 **I was wondering if you'd like me to pick you up.**

Rebecca Pauly [3:15 P.M.]
That would be much easier for me. Are you sure you don't mind?

Jimmie Kristof [3:17 P.M.]
Of course not. Your house is on my way. And I've been to that hall many times before.

吉米・克里斯托弗 [下午 3:08]
瑞貝卡，下週一要去參加大會的事妳都安排好了嗎？

瑞貝卡・波莉 [下午 3:09]
151 **我以為公司會負責處理這件事。公司不是會讓我們搭巴士嗎？**

吉米・克里斯托弗 [下午 3:10]
151 **不，公司最後決定不這麼做了。**所以員工大多會搭地鐵或開車去。

瑞貝卡・波莉 [下午 3:13]
那我想我會開車吧，我家附近一個地鐵站都沒有。但是我從來沒去過那個地方，完全不知道要怎麼去那裡。

吉米・克里斯托弗 [下午 3:14]
嗯，這就是我跟妳聯繫的原因。152 **我想知道妳需不需要我去載妳。**

瑞貝卡・波莉 [下午 3:15]
對我來說，那樣輕鬆多了。真的沒關係嗎？

吉米・克里斯托弗 [下午 3:17]
當然。妳家正好順路，而且我以前去過那會場很多次了。

字彙 **make arrangements for** 為……做出安排

Not / True 問題

151 What is indicated about the writers' company?
(A) It is not handling transportation for employees.
(B) It has offices located near a subway station.
(C) It is organizing an event for its employees.
(D) It is moving to a new location.

中譯 關於傳訊者的公司，何者為真？
(A) 公司不負責員工的交通。
(B) 地鐵站附近有辦公室。
(C) 公司正為員工籌辦活動。
(D) 公司將搬遷到新的地點。

掌握意圖問題

152 At 3:15 p.m., what does Ms. Pauly mean when she writes, "That would be much easier for me"?
(A) She prefers to go by bus.
(B) She would like Mr. Kristof to drive her.
(C) She can pick up Mr. Kristof at the conference.
(D) She doesn't mind taking the subway.

中譯 在下午 3:15，波莉小姐寫道：「對我來說，那樣輕鬆多了」，其意為何？
(A) 她更喜歡搭巴士去。
(B) 她想讓克里斯托弗先生開車載她。
(C) 她可以去會場接克里斯托弗先生。
(D) 她不介意搭地鐵。

Questions 153-155 refer to the following advertisement. 廣告

CLARENCE CO.

153 Clarence Co. provides the best service in the area for businesses that are relocating. We provide a variety of options so that your transition to the new location is as smooth as possible.

If you sign up for our deluxe package, we will provide the following services:

- Unlimited plastic crates for packing belongings
- Packing of large equipment and furniture
- Special packing by our IT experts for your computers and other electronics
- Loading and unloading of all items
- **154 Special clean-up service from our sister company, Sparkly Clean**

155 Call us today at 553-0295 to schedule a time for us to come take a look at your facilities. We will provide a free estimate for our services.

克拉倫斯公司

153 克拉倫斯公司為本地即將搬遷的企業，提供最優質的服務。我們有多種方案供您選擇，讓您儘可能順利地搬遷到新址。

若您選擇豪華方案，我們將提供以下服務：

- 無限量供應打包行李的塑膠籃
- 大型設備及辦公家具的打包
- 本公司的資訊專家會親自打包貴公司的電腦與電子設備
- 全品項的裝載與卸貨服務
- **154 由本公司姐妹公司「閃耀清潔公司」提供的特殊清潔服務**

155 今天就撥打 553-0295，與我們預約到貴公司場勘的時間，我們將為您免費報價。

字彙 relocate 搬遷　transition 過渡時期　belongings 行李　estimate 預估

確認特定資訊問題

153 What kind of company is Clarence Co.?
(A) A machinery manufacturer
(B) A delivery service
(C) A moving company
(D) A marketing consultant

中譯 克拉倫斯公司是一家什麼樣的公司？
(A) 機械製造廠
(B) 貨運公司
(C) 搬家公司
(D) 行銷諮詢公司

Not / True 問題

154 What is indicated about Clarence Co.?
(A) It partners with a cleaning company.
(B) It can fix broken devices.
(C) It has branches in several locations.
(D) It is currently offering free upgrades.

中譯 關於克拉倫斯公司，何者為真？
(A) 與清潔公司有合作關係。
(B) 可維修故障的儀器。
(C) 在數個地點有分公司。
(D) 現正提供免費升級服務。

確認特定資訊問題

155 What can customers learn if they have a consultation?
(A) How to set up some equipment
(B) How much they will have to pay
(C) Where to relocate their business
(D) When a delivery will be made

中譯 如果客戶接受諮詢服務，他們會知道什麼資訊？
(A) 設備的安裝方式
(B) 需支付的費用
(C) 公司搬遷的地點
(D) 貨物送達的時間

Questions 156-158 refer to the following online review. 線上評論

Hotel Review: Bashiva Hotel, 1882 Hummingbird Way

Rating: ★★★★☆
Name: Stella Manning
Date(s) of stay: January 18–20
Room type: Regular Single Room

I stayed at Bashiva Hotel for two nights. I was on a business trip to meet some clients. Bashiva Hotel was ideal for my purposes. The rooms are comfortable, and the breakfast buffet is nice and well worth the price. — [1] —. Most importantly, despite being in a busy area of the city, I didn't hear much noise at night.

156 I chose this hotel because of its proximity to the downtown area. 157 It was convenient for finding restaurants and getting to my meetings. — [2] —. 157 I was supposed to catch a train early in the afternoon. I asked the front desk to call a taxi. I had to wait about fifteen minutes for it to arrive. — [3] —. Then, although the hotel staff said it would take about twenty minutes to get to the train station, it took closer to forty-five minutes. — [4] —. Fortunately, I managed to make it on time for my train because I had left early. **158 However, all of this hassle could have been avoided had there been a bus from the hotel. The hotel already offers rides to and from the airport, but I think many of its guests come by train. Offering rides to the station as well would be very helpful.**

飯店評價：巴希瓦飯店，蜂鳥路 1882 號

評分：★★★★☆
姓名：史黛拉．曼寧
住房日期：1 月 18 至 20 日　**房型：**普通單人房

我在巴希瓦飯店住了兩個晚上，我是去出差拜訪客戶的。以我住房的目的來說，巴希瓦飯店是理想合適的住所。客房很舒適，自助早餐也很不錯，簡直物超所值，相當划算。最重要的是，儘管地處本市繁華地帶，晚上其實聽不太到什麼噪音。

156 我當初會選擇這家飯店，也是看上它的地點臨近鬧區。157 從這裡找餐廳、前往開會都很方便。我唯一碰到的問題是在我要離開飯店時發生的。**157 我原本要搭下午稍早的火車，我請櫃檯幫我叫計程車，我等了大約 15 分鐘計程車才來。然後，雖然飯店的櫃檯人員說，去火車站大約只要 20 分鐘，但我們花了將近 45 分鐘才到。**幸好我出發得早，這才趕上火車。**158** 然而，要是有從飯店發車的接駁巴士，這一切麻煩事便可避免了。飯店已提供往來機場的接駁車服務，但我認為有許多住客都是搭火車來的，如果飯店還可提供到火車站的接駁服務，會很有幫助的。

字彙 proximity to 臨近　hassle 麻煩，困難

Not / True 問題

156 What does Ms. Manning indicate about the hotel?
(A) It provides free breakfast.
(B) It is very noisy during the night.
(C) It is located near the city center.
(D) It is twenty minutes away from an airport.

中譯 關於曼寧女士提到的飯店，何者為真？
(A) 有提供免費早餐。
(B) 晚上很吵。
(C) 位於市中心附近。
(D) 離機場 20 分鐘的路程。

尋找句子位置問題

157 In which of the positions marked [1], [2], [3], and [4] does the following sentence best belong?
"The only issue I had was when I was leaving."
(A) [1] **(B) [2]**
(C) [3] (D) [4]

中譯 下列句子最適合出現在 [1]、[2]、[3]、[4] 的哪個位置中？
「我唯一碰到的問題是在我要離開飯店時發生的。」
(A) [1] **(B) [2]**
(C) [3] (D) [4]

確認特定資訊問題

158 What does Ms. Manning want the hotel to do?

(A) Add a shuttle service

(B) Adjust a timetable

(C) Clean its facilities

(D) Hire more staff

中譯 曼寧女士希望飯店做什麼？

(A) 增加接駁服務

(B) 調整時間表

(C) 清掃設施

(D) 聘僱更多員工

Questions 159-160 refer to the following notice. 公告

www.mimonaartgallery.net/home

The Mimona Art Gallery Web site is under construction. (159) **We anticipate that it will be up and running on November 1. Information about the first exhibits will be posted on this site one week before the gallery opens on November 21.** More detailed information about upcoming events will be available once the gallery is open.

In the meantime, (160) **please contact Eliza Rogers by calling 555-2937 or e-mailing elizarogers@mimonaartgallery.net for information about exhibiting your work.**

www.mimonaartgallery.net/home

米莫納美術館的網站正在創建中，(159) **預計於11月1日正式上線營運。首場展覽的相關資訊將於11月21日美術館開館的前一週，在本官網公布。**俟美術館開館後，本網站將提供近期活動的更多詳細資訊。

在此期間，(160) **如欲了解展出您作品的詳細資訊，請撥打555-2937或寄電子郵件到elizarogers@mimonaartgallery.net與伊莱莎・羅傑斯聯繫。**

字彙 anticipate 預期　be up and running 開始營運的　exhibit 展覽；展品

目的問題

159 What is the purpose of the notice?

(A) To request reviews of an exhibit

(B) To announce the opening of a gallery

(C) To advertise artwork available for sale

(D) To provide a timeline for a new Web page

中譯 本公告的目的為何？

(A) 要求寫展覽的評論

(B) 為了宣布美術館開幕

(C) 為了廣告可販售的藝術品

(D) 為提供新網頁的時間表

確認特定資訊問題

160 Why should Eliza Rogers be contacted?

(A) To make an appointment for a visit

(B) To purchase a work of art

(C) To ask about displaying artwork

(D) To register for an event

中譯 為什麼要聯繫伊萊莎・羅傑斯？

(A) 為了預約參觀時間

(B) 為了購買藝術作品

(C) 為了詢問作品參展的相關資訊

(D) 為了報名參加活動

Questions 161-163 refer to the following e-mail. 電子郵件

To: Brandon Mosher <bmosher@trupal.biz>
From: Karen Pesco <kpesco@trupal.biz>
Date: March 31
Subject: Tax Forms

Dear Mr. Mosher,

161 **I am currently going over your tax documents.** However, it has come to my attention that you worked at another company for two months last year. Although this is just a short period of time, 162 **your previous income must be taken into account and stated when submitting tax forms.** While companies submit the necessary declarations when the employee leaves, it appears that your previous place of employment has not. I would be happy to take care of this for you, but for that, 163 **I need information about your compensation at your last job. If you could provide the two pay stubs you received for those two months,** I will gladly adjust your documents for the tax year.

Let me know if you have any questions.

Sincerely,

Karen Pesco

收件人：布蘭登・瑪舍 <bmosher@trupal.biz>
寄件人：凱倫・佩斯科 <kpesco@trupal.biz>
日期：3月31日
主旨：納稅申報表

瑪舍先生您好：

161 **我目前正在查看您的稅務文件。**不過，我注意到您去年曾在另一家公司工作了兩個月。雖然只是很短的一段時間，162 **但之前的收入還是得申報，並在繳交納稅申報表時予以說明。**員工離職時，公司會提出必要的申報文件，但您之前任職的那家公司似乎沒有做到。我很樂意為您處理此事，但 163 **我需要了解一下您上一份工作的薪資資訊。若您能提供那兩個月的薪資單，**我很樂意為您調整本年度的稅務文件。

若您有任何疑問，請不吝告知。

凱倫・佩斯科 敬上

字彙 **declaration** 申報(單)　**compensation** 薪酬　**pay stub** 薪資條(= **payslip**)

推理問題

161 In what department does Ms. Pesco most likely work?
(A) Accounting
(B) Marketing
(C) Customer service
(D) Research and Development

中譯 佩斯科女士最有可能是在什麼部門工作？
(A) 會計
(B) 行銷
(C) 客服
(D) 研發

確認特定資訊問題

162 What problem does Ms. Pesco mention?
(A) Some income must be declared.
(B) A payment has been rejected.
(C) A tax rate has increased.
(D) Lots of employees have quit.

中譯 佩斯科女士提到了什麼問題？
(A) 部分收入必須申報。
(B) 一筆付款被拒絕。
(C) 稅率提高了。
(D) 許多員工都辭職了。

確認特定資訊問題

163 What does Ms. Pesco ask Mr. Mosher for?
(A) A job description
(B) Salary records
(C) Proof of employment
(D) Tax schedules

中譯 佩斯科女士跟瑪舍先生要什麼東西？
(A) 職務內容說明
(B) 薪資紀錄
(C) 任職證明
(D) 稅率表

Questions 164-167 refer to the following online chat discussion. 網路聊天

Clyde Mortensen [10:40 A.M.]
Hi, Jennifer and Henry. 164 **I want to get started on the design for the April issue's cover. Do you know who we are interviewing for the main article?**

Jennifer Sydnor [10:41 A.M.]
165 **It's going to be Jeff Blasio, a chef from an upcoming cooking show.** I'll be writing that article, actually. I'm interviewing him next Tuesday.

Henry Tessor [10:42 A.M.]
And I'm the photographer for this one. 166 **So I'll be there on Tuesday as well to do the photo shoot of Mr. Blasio.**

Clyde Mortensen [10:44 A.M.]
Oh, let me know when you're done. It would help to know what topics will be covered in the article and what the pictures will look like.

Jennifer Sydnor [10:45 A.M.]
How about we all meet on Wednesday? Henry, you can show us your pictures, and I can tell you both about the interview.

Clyde Mortensen [10:47 A.M.]
That works for me. 167 **I think the covers work best when the designers collaborate with the writers and photographers.**

Henry Tessor [10:48 A.M.]
I couldn't agree more. Wednesday works for me too. Morning or afternoon? I can meet at any time.

Clyde Mortensen [10:49 A.M.]
The morning would be much better for me. Let's say at ten.

Jennifer Sydnor [10:50 A.M.]
Ten is good. I'll see you two then.

克萊德．莫天森 [上午 10:40]
嗨，珍妮佛、亨利，164 **我想開始著手進行四月號的封面設計。你們知道我們的焦點人物要採訪誰嗎？**

珍妮佛．西德諾 [上午 10:41]
165 **會是傑夫．布拉席歐吧，一檔即將播出的料理節目的廚師。**其實，那篇文章是我主筆，我下週二會去採訪他。

亨利．特索爾 [上午 10:42]
我是這個採訪的攝影記者，166 **所以週二我也會去那裡幫布拉席歐拍照。**

克萊德．莫天森 [上午 10:44]
哦，採訪結束後跟我說一下。如果能先知道報導涵蓋的主題和照片的內容，對封面設計會很有幫助。

珍妮佛．西德諾 [上午 10:45]
大家週三來碰個面怎麼樣？亨利，你可以給我們看你拍的照片，而我可以跟你們兩位說一下採訪的內容。

克萊德．莫天森 [上午 10:47]
我可以。167 **我認為設計師要跟執筆者以及攝影記者合作，才能設計出效果最佳的封面。**

亨利．特索爾 [上午 10:48]
我完全同意。我週三也可以。早上還是下午？我隨時都可以碰面。

克萊德．莫天森 [上午 10:49]
對我來說早上會比較好，那就十點吧。

珍妮佛．西德諾 [上午 10:50]
十點不錯。兩位到時候見啦。

字彙 **issue**（報章雜誌的）期　**photo shoot** 攝影　**collaborate with** 與……合作

推理問題

164 Where do the writers most likely work?
(A) At a photo studio
(B) At a restaurant
(C) At a design firm
(D) At a magazine publisher

中譯 這些傳訊者最有可能是在哪裡工作？
(A) 在照相館
(B) 在餐廳
(C) 在設計公司
(D) 在雜誌社

Not / True 問題

165 What is indicated about Mr. Blasio?
(A) He owns a popular restaurant.
(B) He will be on television.
(C) He writes for a magazine.
(D) He applied for a new job.

中譯 關於布拉席歐先生，何者為真？
(A) 他擁有一間很受歡迎的餐廳。
(B) 他會上電視。
(C) 他為雜誌撰寫文章。
(D) 他應徵了一份新工作。

接下來要進行之事的問題

166 What will Mr. Tessor do on Tuesday?
(A) Create an advertisement
(B) Take some pictures
(C) Write an article
(D) Choose a menu

中譯 特索爾先生週二會做什麼事？
(A) 製作廣告
(B) 拍攝照片
(C) 撰寫文章
(D) 選擇菜單

掌握意圖問題

167 At 10:48 a.m., what does Mr. Tessor most likely mean when he writes, "I couldn't agree more"?
(A) He doesn't like the design of one of the projects.
(B) He believes pictures are the most important element.
(C) He thinks people from different departments should work together.
(D) He isn't sure what topics will be covered in the interview.

中譯 在上午 10:48 時，特索爾先生寫道：「我完全同意」，其意最有可能為何？
(A) 他不喜歡其中一項專案的設計。
(B) 他認為照片是最重要的元素。
(C) 他覺得不同部門的員工應一起合作。
(D) 他不太清楚採訪會涉及哪些主題。

Questions 168-171 refer to the following article. 文章

Broken Pearls to Be Performed at the Marina Theater

January 21—*Broken Pearls,* a play in three acts, will be performed at the Marina Theater in Dresdon on February 13, 14, and 15. The script was written by Maria Deluz, who also directed the play. ⑯⑧ **It will be the Marina Theater's first modern-era play.** — [1] —.

⑯⑨ **Because of a limited marketing budget and a rather low-profile cast, the premiere, which was at the Golden Volcano Theater in Henryville, did not attract a large audience.** However, the performance received such good reviews that the troupe was encouraged to start a tour of the region and perform at various local venues. — [2] —. ⑰⓪ **What sent the play's popularity skyrocketing was one review in particular, by notorious critic Joshua Corbett.** Mr. Corbett, who is known for his strict and often scathing reviews, called *Broken Pearls* "a jewel of modern theater" in a long-form article. ⑰⓪ **Thus, the play suddenly went from obscure piece to famous work.** — [3] —.

《碎珠》將於濱海劇院演出

1月21日——三幕劇《碎珠》將於2月13、14和15日在德勒斯敦的濱海劇院演出。該劇由瑪麗亞・德魯茲編劇，她亦執導了該劇。⑯⑧ **這將是首部在濱海劇院登場的現代劇。**

⑯⑨ **由於該劇團的行銷預算有限，再加上這部劇的演員陣容知名度不高，在亨利維爾的金火山劇院舉行的首演並未吸引大批觀眾。**然而，該劇演出後佳評如潮，劇團因而受到鼓舞，開始在該區各地的劇院巡迴演出。⑰⓪ **特別是其中一篇劇評，由大名鼎鼎的評論家喬書亞・科貝特所寫，使得該劇一夕爆紅。**科貝特先生向來以嚴格、通常可說是毒舌的劇評而著稱，他在一篇長評中說《碎珠》是「現代戲劇的瑰寶」，⑰⓪ **於是《碎珠》從名不見經傳一躍成為聲名鵲起的劇作。**

"We never expected *Broken Pearls* to become such a hit," lead actor Jeremy Moriah explained. "It is all very exciting. I look forward to performing at new venues. ⓱ **I hope to even travel overseas for a show someday."** — [4] —. ⓱ **Indeed, several venues around Europe have contacted production manager Isabelle Morton about possible future events.**

男主角傑瑞米・莫里亞解釋說：「我們無法想像《碎珠》會突然變得這麼火紅。這一切都令人感到振奮。我很期待在新地點演出。⓱ **我甚至希望有一天能到國外演出。**」這個夢想可能剛剛已經成真。⓱ **事實上，歐洲已有數家劇院跟劇團製作經理伊莎貝爾・莫頓聯繫未來可能的演出場次。**

字彙 low-profile 不顯眼的　cast 卡司、演出陣容　premiere 首映　troupe 劇團　skyrocketing 飆升的　notorious 惡名昭彰的　scathing 嚴厲的　obscure 鮮為人知的

推論問題

168 What is implied about the Marina Theater?

(A) It usually shows performances of older works.
(B) It has already hosted *Broken Pearls* several times.
(C) It has become Dresdon's most popular theater.
(D) It received a lot of negative reviews in the past.

中譯 關於濱海劇院，文中暗示了什麼？

(A) 通常演出較古典的作品。
(B)《碎珠》已於此演出好幾次。
(C) 已成為德勒斯敦最紅的劇院。
(D) 過去收到許多負面的評價。

Not / True 問題

169 What is indicated about the play's troupe?

(A) It spent a lot of money on advertising.
(B) It is composed of little-known actors.
(C) It is used to performing in renowned venues.
(D) It has performed in a variety of countries.

中譯 關於該劇劇團，文中指出什麼？

(A) 曾砸大錢打廣告。
(B) 其演員知名度皆不高。
(C) 常在知名劇院演出。
(D) 曾在多個國家巡迴演出。

確認特定資訊問題

170 According to the article, who contributed the most to the play's popularity?

(A) Maria Deluz
(B) Joshua Corbett
(C) Jeremy Moriah
(D) Isabelle Morton

中譯 根據本文，誰對該劇的知名度貢獻最大？

(A) 瑪麗亞・德魯茲
(B) 喬書亞・科貝特
(C) 傑瑞米・莫里亞
(D) 伊莎貝爾・莫頓

尋找句子位置問題

171 In which of the positions marked [1], [2], [3], and [4] does the following sentence best belong?
"This dream might just become a reality."

(A) [1]　(B) [2]
(C) [3]　**(D) [4]**

中譯 下列句子最適合出現在 [1]、[2]、[3]、[4] 的哪個位置中？
「這個夢想可能剛剛已經成真。」

(A) [1]　(B) [2]
(C) [3]　**(D) [4]**

Questions 172-175 refer to the following information. 資訊

Langda Goods Terms and Conditions

172 **Thank you for choosing Langda Goods to carry your luggage on your next trip. All Langda luggage is covered by our one-year warranty.** Please inspect your parcel carefully upon receiving it. 173A **If any part of the product is damaged, do not throw away any part of the product or its packaging.** 173B **Immediately inform the delivery company.** They will pick up the damaged goods 173C **and provide you with a claim form to fill out and a claim number.** 174 **You may then follow the progress of your request on our Web site.** 173D **It may take up to three weeks to review a claim.**

175 **A replacement will be sent to the customer if any of the following cases is reported within one year of purchase:**

- 175 **Flaws in workmanship or material**
- Tearing of the material
- Broken part
- Wearing of the wheels
- Color fading

Please note that in case of the following events, the customer is fully liable for the article and is entitled to no compensation:

- Unreasonable usage
- Staining
- Loss or theft

蘭達商品使用條款及細則

172 **感謝您選擇蘭達商品，作為您下次出遊的行李箱。本公司全品項行李箱均享有一年的保固。**收到包裹後請仔細檢查商品。173A **若產品有任何部件受損，應保持產品和包裝完整。**173B **立即通知貨運公司。**他們會取走損壞的商品，173C **並提供需要顧客填寫的賠償申請表以及一組賠償編號。**174 **之後，顧客便可在本公司官網上追蹤賠償進度。**173D **賠償的審查可能會長達三週。**

175 **若商品於購買後一年內出現下列任何一種情況，我們都將為您換貨：**

- 175 **製作工藝上或材質上的瑕疵**
- 材質撕裂
- 部件破損
- 輪子磨損
- 褪色

請注意，如發生以下情況，顧客需自付全責且無權要求賠償：

- 不合理的使用方式
- 污損
- 遺失或遭竊

字彙 terms and conditions 條款及細則　cover 給……保險　warranty 保固　claim form 賠償申請表　progress 進度　flaw 瑕疵　workmanship 工藝　be liable for 對……負責的　be entitled to do 有權做……的

推論問題

172 What is suggested about the recipients of the information?

(A) They have tried to return an item.
(B) They have recently purchased some luggage.
(C) They have just signed a contract with Langda Goods.
(D) They have posted a negative review of Langda Goods.

中譯 關於本資訊接收者，何者為真？
(A) 他們試圖退回商品。
(B) 他們最近買了行李箱。
(C) 他們剛與蘭達商品簽約。
(D) 他們對蘭達商品發表負評。

Not / True 問題

173 What does Langda Goods ask customers NOT to do if they receive a damaged item?

(A) Discard broken parts

(B) Notify the deliverer

(C) Complete a document

(D) Wait for a response

中譯 若顧客收到損壞的產品，蘭達商品要求他們不要做什麼？

(A) 丟棄破損部件

(B) 通知貨運公司

(C) 填寫文件

(D) 等待回覆

確認特定資訊問題

174 What can customers do on the Langda Goods Web site?

(A) Request faster delivery service

(B) Fill out a complaint form

(C) Check the status of a claim

(D) Extend the warranty of an item

中譯 顧客可在蘭達商品的官網上做什麼？

(A) 要求加快送貨服務

(B) 填寫客訴表

(C) 查看索賠狀態

(D) 延長產品保固期限

確認特定資訊問題

175 In which case can a customer get a replacement?

(A) If the item is stolen.

(B) If the product has defects.

(C) If the material becomes stained.

(D) If the luggage is overused.

中譯 在什麼樣的情況下，顧客可以換貨？

(A) 若產品遭竊。

(B) 若產品有瑕疵。

(C) 若材質出現污漬。

(D) 若行李箱被過度使用。

Questions 176-180 refer to the following flyer and form. 宣傳單與表格

Arnett Co.

Arnett Co. has been providing high-quality services for the past five years. From May 1 to October 31, 176 **we're here to help you keep your yard and garden in excellent condition. We can provide mowing, tree-trimming, and weeding on a weekly or biweekly basis.** If you are interested in having trees, flowers, or bushes planted, 177 **we can get you a discount with our partners at the Pineway Greenhouse, a reliable local business.**

We have lots of returning customers every season, 178B **but slots are still available even if you've never used our services before.** 178A **Please note that we do not serve corporate properties.** If you'd like advice about the best way to care for your yard, 178D **we'll send one of our technicians to your home for aconsultation**

阿爾內特公司

阿爾內特公司這五年來一直為客戶提供高品質的服務。從5月1日起至10月31日止，176 **本公司要幫助各位將庭院和花園維持在絕佳的狀態。我們可以每週或隔週提供割草、修剪樹木以及除雜草等服務。**若您對種植花草樹木或灌木叢感興趣，177 **我們可透過合作夥伴暨本地可靠商家「松路溫室」給您折扣。**

我們每季都有很多回頭客，178B **但即使您以前未曾使用本公司的服務，也仍然有可預約的時段。** 178A **請注意，本公司不服務企業場所。**若您想取得照料貴府庭院最佳方法的建議，178D **本公司可派遣一名技術人員到府免費諮詢。**本公司基本服務（僅割草與清潔）的

at no charge. **178C The monthly charge*** for our basic service (mowing and cleanup only) is $425 for weekly visits or $250 for biweekly visits.

180-2 There is also a premium service (the basic service plus weeding, bush trimming, and fertilizer treatments) for $675 for weekly visits or $450 for biweekly visits. Call us today at 555-5588.

* **178C Applies to standard lots only. For oversized lots, please call to inquire about our rates.**

178C 月費為 425 美元，每週到府服務一次；或是 250 美元，隔週到府服務一次。**180-2 另有尊榮服務（基本服務加上除雜草、修剪灌木與施肥）可供選擇，其月費為 675 美元，每週到府服務一次；或是 450 美元，隔週到府服務一次。**現在就撥打 555-5588 預約服務。

* **178C 本報價僅適用於標準範圍的土地，若是超過標準範圍，請您來電詢價。**

字彙 biweekly 兩週一次的 reliable 可靠的 slot 時段 corporate 公司的 consultation 諮詢 at no charge 免費 fertilizer 肥料 lot 一塊地

Arnett Co. – New Customer Information

179 Customer: Vickie Warnick

Property: 226 Sunburst Drive, Portland, OR 97221

Lot Type: Standard

* **179 Equipment: Lawnmower (model: Duncan-440)**

Type of Service requested: [ ] Basic

180-1 [X] Premium

[ ] Weekly

180-1 [X] Biweekly

Start Date of Service: June 2

Consultation Date: May 26

Property Assessed by: Robert Cass

* **179 If the customer prefers to use his/her own equipment, list the type and model name above.**

阿爾內特公司——新客戶資料

179 客戶姓名：維琪・瓦尼克

服務地點：97221 奧勒岡州波特蘭旭輝路 226 號

土地類型：標準

* **179 設備：割草機（型號：鄧肯 -440）**

所需服務類型：【 】基本 **180-1 【X】尊榮**

【 】每週 **180-1 【X】隔週**

服務開始日期：6 月 2 日

客戶諮詢日期：5 月 26 日

土地評估人：羅伯特・卡司

* **179 若客戶希望使用自己的設備，請在上面列出設備種類與型號名稱。**

字彙 assess 評估

目的問題

176 What is the purpose of the flyer?

(A) To announce a change in ownership

(B) To promote a gardening care business

(C) To advertise a sales event

(D) To introduce a new service

中譯 這張傳單的目的為何？

(A) 宣布經營權變更

(B) 促銷庭園養護業務

(C) 促銷活動打廣告

(D) 引進一項新服務

Not / True 問題

177 What is indicated about Arnett Co.?

(A) It collaborates with a greenhouse.

(B) It accepts bookings by e-mail.

(C) It sells several varieties of plants and flowers.

(D) It offers services year-round.

中譯 關於阿爾內特公司，可由文中得知什麼？

(A) 與一家溫室合作。

(B) 接受以電子郵件預約。

(C) 販售多種植物和花卉。

(D) 全年都有提供服務。

Not / True 問題

178 What is NOT mentioned about Arnett Co.?
(A) It only caters to residential properties.
(B) It is not currently accepting new customers.
(C) It has different prices for standard and oversized lots.
(D) It offers a free consultation.

中譯 關於阿爾內特公司，文中並未提到什麼？
(A) 僅提供住宅庭園養護服務。
(B) 目前不接受新客戶。
(C) 標準庭園與超大庭園的收費不同。
(D) 提供免費諮詢服務。

推論問題

179 What is suggested about Ms. Warnick?
(A) She will receive a discount for the first month.
(B) She wants her own equipment to be used.
(C) She was referred to Arnett Co. by a friend.
(D) She has a property that is larger than average.

中譯 關於瓦尼克女士，文中暗示了什麼？
(A) 第一個月的月費有折扣。
(B) 她希望使用自己的設備。
(C) 朋友把阿爾內特公司轉介給她。
(D) 她的房產比一般的還要大。

兩則引文連結問題_確認特定資訊問題

180 How much will Ms. Warnick be charged per month?
(A) $250 (B) $425
(C) $450 (D) $675

中譯 瓦尼克女士每個月要付多少錢？
(A) 250 美元 (B) 425 美元
(C) 450 美元 (D) 675 美元

Questions 181-185 refer to the following e-mails. 電子郵件

To: Gladwell Finance <info@gladwellfinance.com>
From: Keith Angulo <k.angulo@irvinemail.net>
Date: November 17
Subject: Transfer issue

To Whom It May Concern:

I tried to send money to my cousin in Vancouver using your online money transfer service. I applied a $5 credit toward the fees, which I got from signing up for your newsletter. He was able to pick up the cash at the Vancouver branch. However, after the transaction was completed, I noticed that I had been charged the full amount for the transfer fee. 181 **I looked over my account history to make sure I hadn't already used the credit,** and I confirmed that I hadn't. However, the credit is no longer listed on my account. 182-2 **Please let me know why there was a problem with this transaction, request #45960, and what can be done to resolve it.**

Thank you,

Keith Angulo

收件者：戈拉德維爾金融公司
<info@gladwellfinance.com>
寄件者：基斯・安古羅
<k.angulo@irvinemail.net>
日期：11 月 17 日
主旨：轉帳問題

敬啟者：

我試著用貴公司的線上轉帳服務，把錢轉給我在溫哥華的表弟。我用了訂閱你們電子報時獲得的五美元抵用金來折抵匯費。他在溫哥華分行領了現金。然而，在交易完成後，我發現被要求支付全額的匯費。181 **我查看了帳戶明細，想確認我之前是否已使用抵用金，**結果的確沒有使用，但我也找不到帳戶裡的這筆抵用金。182-2 **請讓我知道編號 45960 號的交易為何會出現問題，以及你們會如何解決。**

謝謝。

基斯・安古羅

字彙 **money transfer** 轉帳；匯款　**credit** 折抵金　**transaction** 交易

To: Keith Angulo <k.angulo@irvinemail.net>
From: Gladwell Finance <info@gladwellfinance.com>
Date: November 18
Subject: RE: Transfer issue

Dear Mr. Angulo,

On behalf of Gladwell Finance, I would like to apologize for the inconvenience you experienced. 182-1 **You did not mention the date that you sent the funds, but I was able to find it by using the number you provided.** We were experiencing some problems when our internal server 183 **went down** for a brief period on November 16, and this affected some customers. I have reissued you a credit of $5 to make up for the discount you should have gotten. My manager, Patrick Ogden, has also given me authorization to issue you a further $10 credit due to your inconvenience. This credit can be used toward our processing fees. 184 **You can verify that these amounts have been credited to you by clicking on the My Balance link after logging into your online account.** You can use the credit anytime at your discretion. 185 **Should you have any further problems, you can call 555-3940, extension 31, rather than our customer service hotline. That way, you can get straight through to me.**

Sincerely,

Brielle Stewart

收件者：基斯・安古羅 <k.angulo@irvinemail.net>
寄件者：戈拉德維爾金融公司 <info@gladwellfinance.com>
日期：11 月 18 日
主旨：關於：匯款問題

親愛的安古羅先生：

本人謹代表戈拉德維爾金融公司，為您遭遇的不便向您致歉。182-1 **您信中並未提到您匯出款項的日期，但我透過您提供的交易號碼找到該筆交易。**11 月 16 日，我們公司內部伺服器 183 **故障**，並遭遇一些問題，進而影響一些客戶。我重發了五美元抵用金，彌補您本應享有的折扣。因造成您的不便，我的主管派翠克・歐葛登也授權我，給您另外發一筆十美元的抵用金。這筆抵用金可折抵我們的手續費。184 **您登入網路帳號後，可以點擊「我的餘額」的連結，確認抵用金已經入帳。**您可隨時酌情使用抵用金。185 **若您有任何後續問題，您可以改撥 555-3940，分機 31，而非客戶服務專線，此便可直接與我聯繫了。**

誠摯地，
布里爾・斯圖爾特

字彙 **internal** 內部的　**go down** 當機　**make up for** 彌補　**authorization** 授權　**balance** 餘額　**at one's discretion** 由某人自行決定　**hotline** 熱線電話

確認特定資訊問題

181 What did Mr. Angulo do before contacting Gladwell Finance?
(A) He heard about the problem from his cousin.
(B) He received an invoice in the mail.
(C) He checked his past transactions
(D) He reviewed his credit card bill.

中譯 安古羅先生在聯絡戈拉德維爾金融公司之前做了什麼事？
(A) 他從他表弟那裡聽到了這個問題。
(B) 他收到了郵寄來的帳單。
(C) 他檢查了過去的交易紀錄。
(D) 他查看了自己的信用卡帳單。

兩則引文連結問題＿確認特定資訊問題

182 What did Ms. Stewart use to look into Mr. Angulo's complaint?
(A) His transaction code
(B) His account number
(C) His request date
(D) His credit balance

中譯 斯圖爾特小姐用什麼來調查安古羅先生的客訴？
(A) 他的交易代碼
(B) 他的帳戶號碼
(C) 他要求的日期
(D) 他的抵用金餘額

同義詞問題

183 In the second e-mail, the phrase "went down" in paragraph 1, line 3, is closest in meaning to
(A) deflated **(B) malfunctioned**
(C) decreased (D) lost

中譯 在第二封電子郵件中，第 1 段第 3 行的「went down」一詞，意思最接近下列何者？
(A) 洩氣 **(B) 故障**
(C) 減少 (D) 遺失

確認特定資訊問題

184 How can Mr. Angulo confirm that a credit was received?
(A) By reviewing an online page
(B) By checking a printed receipt
(C) By requesting a paper statement
(D) By e-mailing Ms. Stewart's manager

中譯 安古羅先生要如何確認已收到抵用金？
(A) 查看網頁
(B) 檢查列印出來的收據
(C) 要求提供紙本對帳單
(D) 寄電子郵件給斯圖爾特小姐的主管

確認特定資訊問題

185 What is Mr. Angulo told to do if he has more issues?
(A) Call a customer service hotline
(B) Request a contract termination
(C) File a formal complaint online
(D) Contact Ms. Stewart directly

中譯 若安古羅先生有其他的問題，他被指示要怎麼做？
(A) 撥打客服專線
(B) 要求終止合約
(C) 上網提出正式客訴
(D) 直接與斯圖爾特小姐聯繫

Questions 186-190 refer to the following summary, flyer, and review. 摘要、傳單與評論

Portrait Pro

186 ***Portrait Pro* is a four-part series for people who have already mastered the basics of oil on canvas and want to move on to more advanced methods of painting.** In these videos, renowned designer Gloria Hutton guides you through four steps to take your painting skills to the next level. 187-2 **In the first tutorial, you will learn how to choose the best brushes for various types of projects.** The second video focuses on several advanced techniques. Third, you will create a portrait based on a provided model. 190-2 **Finally, you will learn how to paint your own ideas instead of using a model.** The videos are available for download from all major Web sites.

專業肖像畫

186 **「專業肖像畫」是一門分為四部分的系列課程，適合有油畫基礎，嫻熟在畫布上作畫，並想繼續學習進階畫法的人。**在這些影片中，著名的設計師葛洛莉雅・赫頓會透過四個階段的教程來指導您，讓您的繪畫技巧更上一層樓。187-2 **在第一個教程中，您將學會如何為不同種類的專案選擇最適合的畫筆。**第二個影片則重點介紹幾種進階的繪畫技巧。第三個影片中，您將根據所提供的範本來繪製一幅肖像畫。190-2 **最後，您將學會如何在沒有範本的情況下，畫出自己的想法。**這些教學影片皆可從各大網站下載。

字彙 **portrait** 肖像畫 **master** 精通 **oil** 油畫顏料 **advanced** 進階的 **renowned** 著名的 **tutorial** 教程

187-1 **Special Seminar at Hacksburg Museum of Arts and Crafts**

187-1 **On October 30,** come to the Hacksburg Museum of Arts and Crafts for a special master class on painting. 187-1 **Artist Gloria Hutton will be giving a lecture based on the first video of her recently released four-part series, *Portrait Pro*.**

Gloria Hutton is a prominent painter who created hundreds of breathtaking works that have been displayed in museums and festivals worldwide. Her natural talent has allowed Ms. Hutton to make a living off of her art early on, so money was not the motivation for making the videos. 188 **But she was receiving repeated requests for tips and private lessons and didn't have time to give regular classes. So she finally decided to release her tutorial series,** which immediately became a bestseller.

Time: October 30, 3:00 P.M.
Place: Hacksburg Museum of Arts and Crafts, Shalandra Room
Fee: $35.00

Seating is limited for this event. Please register in advance by calling 555-8874.

187-1 哈克斯堡工藝藝術博物館專題研討會

187-1 **10月30日**到哈克斯堡工藝藝術博物館來上一堂別開生面的大師繪畫課吧。187-1 **藝術家葛洛莉雅・赫頓最近推出了「專業肖像畫」系列課程四部曲，她將以第一部教學影片為基礎進行演講。**

葛洛莉雅・赫頓是一名傑出的畫家，她創作了數百件令人歎為觀止的畫作，並在世界各地的博物館與藝術節上展出。赫頓女士在繪畫上的天賦才華，讓她很早就能夠靠自己的手藝謀生，所以錢並非是她製作這些影片的動機。188 **不過，她還是不斷收到詢問繪畫訣竅與私人家教的要求，而她又無暇開設常規課程。所以最後她決定推出系列教學課程，**且該課程一推出便十分暢銷。

時間：10月30日下午3點
地點：哈克斯堡工藝藝術博物館　沙蘭德廳
費用：35美元

本場活動座位有限，請事先致電555-8874報名參加，以免向隅。

字彙 release 發布　prominent 傑出的　motivation 動機　register 報名

Portrait Pro

Review by Margaret Jones

I highly recommend the *Portrait Pro* series to anyone passionate about art. I've been painting for several years now, and I thought all I could do to improve was to keep practicing. I never thought I'd learn so much simply by watching some videos. However, I've improved my skills tenfold by 189 **following** Ms. Hutton's tutorials. She manages to explain complicated techniques in simple terms, and I was amazed by what I could accomplish by the time I finished watching these.

190-1 **The only complaint I have is with the video about creating a project from scratch without referring to anything. I've watched that video dozens of times** and still can't understand what Ms. Hutton is saying. However, because the three other videos were so helpful, I still think this series is worth the purchase.

專業肖像畫
評論者：瑪格麗特・瓊斯

我向所有的藝術愛好者強力推薦「專業肖像畫」的課程。我已經畫畫好幾年了，我以為只能靠不斷練習來進步。我從沒想到光是看幾部影片，就能學到這麼多。然而，我只是 189 **遵循**赫頓女士的教學影片，繪畫技巧就提升了十倍。她會想辦法用簡單的話來說明複雜的繪畫技巧。在我看完教學影片後，我對自己的繪畫能力感到驚訝不已。

190-1 **我唯一的不滿就是，要在沒有任何範本可參考的情形下，從無到有自行創作的那部影片。我看了好幾十遍，**仍然無法理解赫頓女士在說什麼。不過，因為前三部影片對我的幫助很大，所以我依然認為這個系列課程很值得購買。

字彙 tenfold 十倍的　from scratch 從頭做起

確認特定資訊問題

186 According to the summary, who is the intended audience for the series?
(A) Professional artists with expert skills
(B) Beginners who never painted before
(C) People with experience in painting
(D) Collectors looking for artwork

中譯 根據摘要內容，這個系列課程的目標受眾是誰？
(A) 具有專業技能的職業畫家
(B) 沒有繪畫經驗的初學者
(C) 有繪畫經驗的人
(D) 尋找藝術品的收藏家

三則引文連結問題＿確認特定資訊問題

187 What will attendants do at the seminar on October 30?
(A) Participate in filming a video
(B) Learn how to select utensils
(C) Create a portrait
(D) Practice some brushstrokes

中譯 在 10 月 30 日舉行的研討會上，與會者將會做什麼？
(A) 參與影片的拍攝
(B) 學習如何挑選器具
(C) 繪製一幅肖像畫
(D) 練習繪畫筆法

確認特定資訊問題

188 According to the flyer, why did Ms. Hutton create the series?
(A) She needed more income.
(B) She wanted to advertise her classes.
(C) She was often asked for advice.
(D) She enjoyed her teaching experience.

中譯 根據傳單內容，赫頓女士為什麼要製作教學影片？
(A) 她需要更多收入。
(B) 她想幫自己的課程打廣告。
(C) 經常有人向她請教。
(D) 她有過愉快的教學經驗。

同義詞問題

189 In the review, the word "following" in paragraph 1, line 4, is closest in meaning to
(A) modifying (B) coming after
(C) using (D) testing

中譯 在評論中，第 1 段第 4 行的「following」一字，意思最接近下列何者？
(A) 修改 (B) 跟隨
(C) 使用 (D) 測試

三則引文連結問題＿確認特定資訊問題

190 Which video of the *Portrait Pro* series does Ms. Jones say she watched many times?
(A) The first (B) The second
(C) The third **(D) The fourth**

中譯 「專業肖像畫」系列課程中，瓊斯小姐說哪一部影片她看了很多遍？
(A) 第一部 (B) 第二部
(C) 第三部 **(D) 第四部**

Questions 191-195 refer to the following advertisement, e-mail, and text message. 廣告、電子郵件和簡訊

Divine Delights Caterer

For the best service in the area and the highest-quality food, choose Divine Delights Caterer! ⑲¹ **Summer is over, and our fall premium menus are here!** See our Web site www. divinedelightscaterer.com for beverages and many other types of menus.

天饗餐飲公司

想要享受本地最好的服務、最高品質的食物，就選擇天饗餐飲公司！191 **夏季已經結束，現為您獻上秋季豪華菜單！**欲知酒水飲料與許多不同類型的菜單內容，請至本公司官網 www. divinedelightscaterer.com 查詢。

Premium Menu 1 ($50 per person)	Premium Menu 2 ($75 per person)
	Includes one glass of wine
Appetizer (choose one)	**Appetizer (choose one)**
☐ Pumpkin soup	☐ Onion soup
☐ Caesar salad	☐ Cobb salad
195-2 **Main dish (choose one)**	**Main dish (choose one)**
☐ **Parmesan chicken**	☐ Beef tenderloin
☐ **Broccoli cream pasta**	☐ Stuffed mushrooms
Dessert	**Dessert**
Apple pie	Blueberry crumble

** Prices include service.* 193-2 ***Reservations for premium menus must be made at least one month in advance.*** *A minimum of twenty people are required.* 195-2 ***Only one type of premium menu is possible per event.*** *Please indicate each guest's dish preference at the time of reservation.*

豪華套餐 1（每人 50 美元）	豪華套餐 2（每人 75 美元）
	內含一杯紅酒
開胃菜（二選一）	開胃菜（二選一）
☐ 南瓜湯	☐ 洋蔥湯
☐ 凱撒沙拉	☐ 科布沙拉
195-2 主菜（二選一）	主菜（二選一）
☐ **帕瑪森起司雞肉**	☐ 菲力牛排
☐ **奶油綠花椰義大利麵**	☐ 鑲蘑菇
甜點	甜點
蘋果派	藍莓奶酥派

價格已含服務費。* 193-2 ***豪華套餐須至少提前一個月訂位，* *且用餐人數不得低於 20 人。* 195-2 ***每場活動僅提供一種豪華套餐。*** *請於訂位時一併告知每名賓客的飲食喜好。*

字彙 appetizer 開胃菜　tenderloin 里脊肉，嫩腰肉　stuffed 有填料的　reservation 預約
preference 偏好，偏愛

From: Rooter, Phil <prooter@glypha.com>
To: Stacker, Lindsay <lstacker@glypha.com>
Date: September 15
Subject: Corporate Dinner

Hi. 192 **I think your suggestion of holding a corporate dinner to celebrate the merger of Glypha Corp. and Baller Inc. is an excellent idea.** 193-1 **You mentioned October 20 as a possible date. I've checked with everyone, and it seems to be a good day to hold the event.** As requested, I've attached a flyer for a catering company I told you about. I know we want to have a nice meal, so I think we should get a premium menu. But I'm not sure what our budget is. Let me know which one you think would be best. I will then pass the menu around the office so that everyone can select their dish choices.

寄件人：菲爾・魯特 <prooter@glypha.com>
收件人：林賽・斯塔克 <lstacker@glypha.com>
日期：9 月 15 日
主旨：公司晚宴

嗨，192 **你建議辦個公司晚宴來慶祝葛呂發與伯樂兩家公司合併，我覺得這個提議好極了。** 193-1 **你提到可行的日期是 10 月 20 日。我跟大家確認過了，這天似乎是個辦活動的好日子。**按照你的要求，我附上了之前跟你說的外燴公司的傳單。我知道我們都想好好吃一頓，所以我認為我們應該訂豪華套餐。不過我不清楚我們的預算是多少。請告訴我你認為哪一種最適合，然後我會讓同仁傳閱菜單 ，讓大家選擇自己想吃的菜餚。

字彙 merger（公司）合併　pass . . . around 分發，傳閱

From: Tracy Meloy
To: Phil Rooter

Since Stephanie is out on vacation this week, I chose her dish preferences for her for the corporate dinner. 195-1 **I told you that she and I would both be having the same thing.** However, 194 195-1 **I just found out that she is a vegetarian, so could you switch her selection to the broccoli cream pasta?** Sorry about the change.

發信人：崔西・梅洛伊
收信人：菲爾・魯特

由於史蒂芬妮這個星期去度假了，所以我幫她選了公司晚宴的菜餚。195-1 **我之前跟你說，我們兩個人會點一樣的餐點。**但是，194 195-1 **我剛剛發現她吃素，所以可以把她的主菜換成奶油綠花椰義大利麵嗎？**很抱歉跟你改單。

推論問題

191 What is suggested about Divine Delights Caterer?
(A) It is closed in the winter and spring.
(B) It adapts its menus to the seasons.
(C) It offers only two types of menus.
(D) It has an online reservation system.

中譯 關於天饗餐飲公司，文中暗示了什麼？
(A) 冬春兩季不營業。
(B) 隨季節調整菜單。
(C) 僅提供兩種菜單。
(D) 有線上訂位系統。

確認特定資訊問題

192 What is the purpose of the planned event?
(A) To congratulate a colleague
(B) To celebrate a successful quarter
(C) To impress a potential client
(D) To mark a new partnership

中譯 規劃這場活動的目的為何？
(A) 為了祝賀同事
(B) 為了慶祝成功的季度
(C) 為了讓潛在客戶印象深刻
(D) 為了標誌新的夥伴關係

三則引文連結問題＿推論問題

193 When should Glypha Corp. make the catering reservation by?
(A) September 15 **(B) September 20**
(C) October 15 (D) October 20

中譯 葛呂發公司應在哪天之前訂位？
(A) 9 月 15 日 **(B) 9 月 20 日**
(C) 10 月 15 日 (D) 10 月 20 日

確認特定資訊問題

194 What is Mr. Rooter asked to do?
(A) Postpone a vacation
(B) Modify a meal choice
(C) Reschedule an event
(D) Add a guest to an attendance list

中譯 魯特先生被要求做什麼？
(A) 延後假期
(B) 修改餐點選擇
(C) 重新安排活動日期
(D) 在出席名單上增加一名賓客

三則引文連結問題＿推論問題

195 What main dish will Ms. Meloy most likely have at the corporate dinner?
(A) Parmesan chicken
(B) Broccoli cream pasta
(C) Beef tenderloin
(D) Stuffed mushrooms

中譯 梅洛伊小姐在公司晚宴上最有可能吃到的主菜是什麼？
(A) 帕瑪森起司雞肉
(B) 奶油綠花椰義大利麵
(C) 菲力牛排
(D) 鑲蘑菇

Questions 196-200 refer to the following Web pages and e-mails. 網頁與電子郵件

www.kikilafabrics.com/about

HOME	ABOUT	PRODUCTS	CLEARANCE	CART

196 **Kikila Fabrics is famous for having the widest selection of fabrics.** You can find any texture and color you need for all of your projects right here on our site.

199-3 **Make sure you check out the CLEARANCE page, where all items are 50 percent off.** There, you'll find the best value for your money. In addition, if you order more than 10 meters of any fabric, you are eligible for free delivery.

Fabric is cut to the size indicated in the order form. Please check your measurements carefully as we do not grant returns or exchanges if you entered the wrong numbers.

www.kikilafabrics.com/about

首頁	企業介紹	產品	出清特賣區	購物車

196 **綺綺拉織品公司，素來以提供種類最多樣的布料而知名。**所有您所需的織品，無論是什麼樣的質地與顏色，都可以在我們的網站上找到。

199-3 **請務必查看「出清特賣區」，該區所有品項一律半價出售。**在此，您可找到最物超所值的商品。此外，若您訂購超過 10 公尺的織物，便可享有免費送貨到府的服務。

布料是按照訂購單上標示的尺寸進行裁剪。請仔細檢查您欲購買的尺寸，若您輸入的數字有誤，本公司將無法予以退款或換貨。

字彙 **clearance**（貨物的）出清特價 **fabric** 織物 **be eligible for** 有資格的 **measurement** 尺寸

www.kikilafabrics.com/clearance

HOME	ABOUT	PRODUCTS	CLEARANCE	CART

199-2 SEPTEMBER CLEARANCE ITEMS

197 Flannel – print

Available prints: owls, cats, bears
Description: This single layer flannel is wonderful for quilts and children's apparel.
197 **Washing: machine wash/tumble dry**
Price: $9.50 per meter

Wool Blend

Available colors: green, red
Description: This is the perfect material for coats, jackets, blankets, and other winter favorites.
Washing: machine wash cold/tumble dry low; Note: do NOT iron
Price: $12.00 per meter

198-2 199-2 Faux leather

Available colors: brown, black
Description: This heavyweight imitation leather is great for luxurious pillows and other home decor elements.
Washing: wipe down with damp rag
Price: $6.00 per meter

www.kikilafabrics.com/clearance

首頁	企業介紹	產品	出清特賣區	購物車

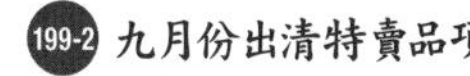

199-2 九月份出清特賣品項

197 法蘭絨（印花）

可選擇圖樣：貓頭鷹、貓咪、熊
產品描述：這種單層法蘭絨非常適合做成被子和兒童服飾。
197 **洗滌方式：可機洗 / 可烘乾**
價格：每米 9.5 美元

羊毛混紡

可選擇顏色：綠色、紅色
產品描述：這是製作大衣、夾克、毛毯與其他冬季服裝的完美布料。
洗滌方式：以冷水機洗 / 以低溫烘乾；〔注意〕請勿熨燙
價格：每米 12 美元

198-2 199-2 合成皮革

可選擇顏色：咖啡色、黑色
產品描述：這種厚重的人造皮革適合用於製成奢華的枕頭和其他家居裝飾品。
洗滌方式：以濕布擦拭即可
價格：每米 6 美元

字彙 **layer** 層 **apparel**（商店賣的）服裝 **heavyweight** 厚重的 **imitation** 人造的 **luxurious** 豪華的 **decor** 裝飾品 **damp** 略濕的 **rag** 抹布

To: Frances Olsen <folsen@pozmail.net>
From: Kikila Fabrics <cs@kikilafabrics.com>
Subject: Order Number 201483
Date: September 21

Dear Mr. Olsen,

We have received your request to exchange the faux leather you purchased. 198-1 199-1 **Please accept our sincerest apologies for sending you the wrong color. We have verified your original order and confirmed that you had in fact requested black. Your order of 6 meters of faux leather in black has been shipped.** You can expect to receive it by Friday afternoon. 200 **In addition, we've included 5 meters of red wool blend as an apology.** It can be easily combined with the faux leather to create a variety of winter apparel.

As for the material we originally sent, we kindly request that you send it back to us and we will refund you for its shipping.

Thank you for your patience and understanding.

Sincerely,

Kikila Fabrics

收件者：弗朗西斯・奧爾森 <folsen@pozmail.net>
寄件者：綺綺拉織品公司 <cs@kikilafabrics.com>
主旨：訂單編號 201483
日期：9月21日

奧爾森先生您好：

我們收到了您欲更換所購之合成皮革的要求。198-1 199-1 **對於寄給您的商品顏色有誤一事，請接受我們最誠摯的歉意。我們已核對您原本的訂單，確認了您實際要求的顏色是黑色。您所訂購之六米黑色合成皮革業已出貨，**預計於本週五下午到貨。200 **此外，為表歉意，我們隨貨附上五米的紅色羊毛混紡布料。**它可與合成皮革輕鬆搭配，製作出各式各樣的冬季服飾。

至於先前寄給您的商品，我們懇請您將其寄回本公司，我們會將運費退還給您。

感謝您的耐心與諒解。

綺綺拉織品公司 敬上

字彙 verify 核實　combine with 與……結合

確認特定資訊問題

196 According to the first Web page, what is Kikila Fabrics known for?
(A) Its low prices
(B) Its fast delivery
(C) Its variety of items
(D) Its return policy

中譯 根據第一個網頁的內容，綺綺拉織品公司以什麼而聞名？
(A) 價格低廉
(B) 快速到貨
(C) 商品種類繁多
(D) 退貨政策

確認特定資訊問題

197 How should the flannel material be washed?
(A) By wiping it with a wet piece of cloth
(B) By taking it to a dry cleaner
(C) By putting it in a washing machine
(D) By using cold water only

中譯 法蘭絨的布料應該如何洗滌？
(A) 用濕布擦拭
(B) 送去乾洗店
(C) 放進洗衣機洗
(D) 僅用冷水清洗

三則引文連結問題__確認特定資訊問題

198 What color material did Mr. Olsen originally receive?
(A) Green
(B) Red
(C) Black
(D) Brown

中譯 奧爾森先生最初收到的商品是什麼顏色？
(A) 綠色
(B) 紅色
(C) 黑色
(D) 咖啡色

三則引文連結問題__推論問題

199 What is implied about Mr. Olsen?
(A) He received a discount on his purchase.
(B) He provided the wrong measurements.
(C) He tried to exchange some apparel.
(D) He did not pay a delivery fee for his order.

中譯 關於奧爾森先生，文中暗示了什麼？
(A) 他購買的商品有打折。
(B) 他提供的尺寸錯誤。
(C) 他買的衣服要換貨。
(D) 他沒有付訂單的運費。

確認特定資訊問題

200 What does Kikila Fabrics offer as an apology to Mr. Olsen?
(A) Complimentary fabric
(B) A refund for his purchase
(C) An article of winter clothing
(D) Free shipping on a future order

中譯 綺綺拉織品公司為表歉意，主動提供了什麼給奧爾森先生？
(A) 免費的織物
(B) 所購商品退費
(C) 一件冬季服飾
(D) 下個訂單免運費

Actual Test 4

PART 1 (13)

1 **(A) A man is wearing an apron.**
英W (B) A man is drinking from a cup.
(C) A man is filling a pot with coffee.
(D) A man is making a copy.

(A) 男子身上穿著一件圍裙。
(B) 男子正在喝杯子裡的飲料。
(C) 男子正往壺裡倒咖啡。
(D) 男子正在影印。

字彙 apron 圍裙　make a copy 複印

---

2 (A) They are painting a wall.
美W (B) A woman is piling up cardboard boxes.
(C) They are taking some measurements.
(D) A man is putting a backpack next to a broom.

(A) 他們正在粉刷牆面。
(B) 女子正在堆紙箱。
(C) 他們正在量尺寸。
(D) 男子正把背包放在掃帚旁。

字彙 cardboard 硬紙板
take measurements 測量　broom 掃帚

---

3 (A) People are resting on a bench.
美M (B) A man is running beside a lake.
(C) A woman is taking off a jacket.
(D) People are looking at each other.

(A) 人們正坐在長椅上休息。
(B) 男子正在湖邊跑步。
(C) 女子正把夾克脫下。
(D) 他們正看著對方。

---

4 (A) Some bicycles have been left on a path.
英W (B) Cyclists are riding on a busy highway.
(C) Some people are resting on the grass.
(D) A bike lane runs alongside a field.

(A) 有人把自行車留在小路上。
(B) 自行車騎士騎在車多的高速公路上。
(C) 有些人在草地上休息。
(D) 田邊有條自行車專用道。

字彙 bike lane 腳踏車專用道
alongside 在……旁邊

---

5 (A) A woman is writing on a notepad.
澳M (B) A woman is gazing at a sheet of paper.
(C) A document is being stapled.
(D) A laptop has been placed on the desk.

(A) 女子正在記事本上寫字。
(B) 女子正盯著一張紙。
(C) 有人正在用訂書機裝訂文件。
(D) 桌上已放著一台筆電。

字彙 gaze at 凝視，注視　staple 用訂書機裝訂

---

6 **(A) Several cars are parked in a row.**
美M (B) Snow is being shoveled off the rooftops.
(C) Windows of the houses are being closed.
(D) The road is blocked by a traffic jam.

(A) 好幾輛汽車停成一排。
(B) 有人正在鏟屋頂上的積雪。
(C) 有人正在關屋子的窗戶。
(D) 這條路交通壅塞寸步難行。

字彙 in a row 排成一列　shovel 鏟起

PART 2 (14)

7 Who will pick up Mr. Mitchell from the airport?
美W 澳M
(A) At 3:55 P.M.
(B) I'm free this afternoon.
(C) It was delayed.

誰會去機場接米契爾先生？
(A) 下午 3 點 55 分。
(B) 我下午有空。
(C) 它誤點了。

---

8 Did you enjoy the test drive?
美 (A) I hope you pass the test.
(B) Yes. I like this car a lot.
(C) You can park over there.

您還滿意這次的試駕嗎？
(A) 我希望你能通過考試。
(B) 是的。我很喜歡這輛車。
(C) 你可以把車停那邊。

字彙 test drive 試駕

9 Have you seen the training manual?
美M 英W
(A) I don't know who took it.
(B) Here's the updated train schedule.
(C) It was written over a year ago.

你有看到培訓手冊嗎？
(A) 我不知道是誰拿走了。
(B) 這是最新的火車時刻表。
(C) 那是一年多前寫的。

字彙 training 訓練　manual 手冊

10 How far is the museum from here?
美
(A) I've been there once.
(B) Because it's further than expected.
(C) It's about a thirty-minute bus ride away.

博物館離這裡有多遠？
(A) 我曾去過一次。
(B) 因為比預期的要遠。
(C) 坐公車約 30 分鐘。

字彙 ride 車程　away （距此）……遠

11 Who replaced the printer cartridge?
澳M 美M
(A) The new intern did.
(B) It's out of ink.
(C) I placed it on the desk downstairs.

是誰換了印表機的墨水匣？
(A) 是新來的實習生換的。
(B) 沒墨水了。
(C) 我把它放在樓下的桌上了。

12 A plumber will stop by between one and three this afternoon.
英W 美M
(A) No problem. I'll be here.
(B) It took about two hours.
(C) I'll stop it now.

水管工人今天下午 1 點到 3 點之間會過來。
(A) 沒問題。我會在這裡。
(B) 大約花了兩個小時。
(C) 我現在就把它停下來。

字彙 plumber 水管工人　stop by 過來一趟

13 Would you be willing to fill in for Eric when he's on vacation?
美
(A) He's leaving this Friday.
(B) Yes, I can do that.
(C) He can work for me.

艾瑞克去度假的時候，你願意代他的班嗎？
(A) 他這個星期五出發。
(B) 可以，我能代班。
(C) 他可以為我工作。

字彙 fill in for 代替

14 Why isn't the image displaying properly?
美
(A) It's in the wrong format.
(B) On the top left corner of the page.
(C) Plays are more interesting than movies.

為什麼圖片沒有正常顯示？
(A) 格式不對。
(B) 在這頁的左上角。
(C) 話劇比電影更有趣。

字彙 display 顯示　properly 正確地　format 格式

15 How would you like to serve the food?
英W 美M
(A) We can just do a buffet.
(B) I'm in the mood for pasta.
(C) Yes, I'm already hungry.

你們想要如何供餐？
(A) 我們可以直接用自助式的。
(B) 我想吃義大利麵。
(C) 對，我已經餓了。

字彙 in the mood for 想要……

16 I'd like to know the library's hours.
美
(A) You can check out three books at a time.
(B) It opens every day from nine to seven.
(C) Yes, it will take just a few hours.

我想知道圖書館的開放時間。
(A) 你一次可以借三本書。
(B) 每天從 9 點開放到 7 點。
(C) 是的，只需要幾個小時。

字彙 check out （在圖書館）登記借（書）

17 Why are you wearing a suit and tie?
美W 澳M
(A) The pants are a little long.
(B) From the new shopping center.
(C) I have a job interview this afternoon.

你為什麼穿西裝打領帶？
(A) 西裝褲有點長。
(B) 從新開的購物中心。
(C) 我今天下午有場工作面試。

---

18 Is rent due at the beginning or the end of the month?
英W 美W
(A) I don't think I can meet that deadline.
(B) It should be paid a month in advance.
(C) I lent him some money last month.

租金是月初還是月底支付？
(A) 我想我無法如期完成了。
(B) 應該提前一個月支付。
(C) 我上個月借給他一些錢。

字彙 due 應支付的　meet 達到，完成
deadline 截止日期

---

19 When will the venue for the conference be announced?
美
(A) Definitely before the weekend.
(B) At the Coral Convention Center.
(C) Mr. Rose is the first speaker.

會議地點什麼時候公布？
(A) 肯定是在週末之前。
(B) 在珊瑚會議中心。
(C) 羅斯先生是第一位講者。

字彙 venue 場地　conference 會議
announce 公布　definitely 肯定地

---

20 Are you able to handle the negotiations on your own?
美
(A) They asked for more time to decide.
(B) We cannot sign this agreement.
(C) It would be nice to have some help.

你能獨自處理那場談判嗎？
(A) 他們要求多點時間來做決定。
(B) 我們不能簽這份協議。
(C) 如果有人幫忙的話，那就太好了。

字彙 analysis 分析報告（複數為 analyses）
sales figure 銷售額

---

21 I don't know who to give these reports to.
英W 美M
(A) They'll be done by five o'clock.
(B) They are analyses of our sales figures.
(C) Ms. Davis usually takes care of them.

我不知道該把這些報告交給誰。
(A) 報告五點前會完成。
(B) 這些是銷售額的分析報告。
(C) 通常是戴維斯女士負責處理的。

字彙 analysis 分析報告（複數為 analyses）
sales figure 銷售額

---

22 Which department do you work for?
澳M 英W
(A) No. I'm still looking for a job.
(B) Research and development.
(C) I bought it at Lloyd's Department Store.

你在哪個部門工作？
(A) 沒有，我還在找工作。
(B) 研發部。
(C) 我在勞埃德百貨公司買的。

字彙 research and development 研究發展（= R&D 研發）

---

23 Where did the author get the inspiration for her first novel?
美
(A) I usually read mysteries.
(B) This article doesn't say.
(C) She finished it last year.

這個作者寫第一本小說的靈感來自何處？
(A) 我一般都是看推理小說。
(B) 這篇報導並沒有說。
(C) 她去年完成的。

解析 本題詢問作者從何處獲得小說的靈感，表示這篇報導並未提及，委婉表示不知道的 **(B)** 為正解。

字彙 inspiration 靈感　mystery 推理劇；懸疑作品

---

24 There aren't enough chairs for everyone, are there?
澳M 美W
(A) No, but Ms. Zoey is getting some right now.
(B) He's the chair of the budget committee.
(C) Most people, but not everyone.

椅子的數量不夠大家坐，對吧？
(A) 對，不過柔伊小姐正在拿。
(B) 他是預算委員會的主席。
(C) 大多數人，但不是全部

字彙 budget 預算　committee 委員會

---

25 Do you know if the swimming pool offers classes?
美
(A) Only in the summer.
(B) I'm preparing for a triathlon.
(C) The fitness center is completed.

你知道游泳池是否有開課嗎？
(A) 只有在夏天。
(B) 我正在準備三鐵的比賽。
(C) 健身中心完工了。

字彙 triathlon 鐵人三項

26 I forgot to get you a copy of the brochure.
英W (A) It has a nice design.
美M (B) The photocopier is out of service.
(C) It's okay. I've already got one.

我忘了幫你拿一本手冊。
(A) 設計感不錯。
(B) 影印機不能用了。
(C) 沒關係,我已經有一本了。

字彙 brochure 手冊 photocopier 影印機
out of service 停止使用,故障

27 Aren't we supposed to turn left here?
美 (A) Yes, there are a few left.
(B) He'll be here in a minute.
(C) The map says to keep going.

這裡是不是該左轉?
(A) 是的,還剩下幾個。
(B) 他馬上就到了。
(C) 地圖上說一直走。

28 Can you print out these graphs so I can view them later?
美W (A) They're probably still in the cabinet.
澳M **(B) The printer is malfunctioning.**
(C) I'm curious about your views on the topic.

你能把這些圖表印出來,方便我之後看嗎?
(A) 可能還在櫃子裡。
(B) 印表機故障了。
(C) 我好奇你對這個主題的看法。

字彙 malfunction 故障,失靈

29 Where can I renew my subscription?
美 **(A) There's a link in the weekly e-mail.**
(B) It expires in February.
(C) Memberships start at $12.99 a month.

那裡可以辦理續訂?
(A) 每週發送的電子郵件裡就有連結。
(B) 二月分到期。
(C) 會員費每月 12.99 美元起。

字彙 renew 延長……的期限
subscription 訂閱(費) expire 到期
membership 會費

30 Which folder did you save the file in?
英W (A) Try restarting the computer.
美M **(B) Which file do you mean?**
(C) Under the pile of documents.

你把檔案存到哪個資料夾了?
(A) 電腦重新開機看看。
(B) 你說的是哪個檔案?
(C) 在那堆文件下面。

31 When will the store restock its shoe section?
美W (A) Sneakers are on sale.
澳M **(B) I don't work here.**
(C) I'm sorry, but they're out of stock.

這家店的鞋類區什麼時候會補貨?
(A) 運動鞋正在特賣中。
(B) 我不是這裡的員工。
(C) 抱歉,都沒庫存了。

字彙 restock 重新進貨 out of stock 缺貨

PART 3 15

Questions 32-34 refer to the following conversation. 美 對話

W Hi. ㉜ **I need a new desktop computer.** ㉝ **I heard you're offering 20 percent off some of your items this week. Is that right?**

M ㉝ **Yes, that is correct. But the ones on the top shelf are not on sale.** Those are full price.

W Oh, that's a shame. I was looking at the Raven-XT over there. Is there any way I can get a discount? I've bought many items from this store and have been a member for years.

M Ah, then, ㉞ **let me see your membership card. I'll take a look at your past purchases.** You might be eligible to trade some points for a discount.

女：嗨，㉜ **我需要一台新的桌上型電腦。** ㉝ **聽說你們這個星期部分商品提供八折的優惠，是這樣嗎？**

男：㉝ **是的，沒錯。但是架上最上層的商品沒有打折，**那些都是原價。

女：哦，好可惜啊。我剛剛在看那邊的渡鴉 XT 系列。請問有什麼辦法可以拿到折扣嗎？我在你們店裡買了很多東西，幾年來都是會員。

男：啊，那麼，㉞ **讓我看一下您的會員卡，查一下您過去的消費情況，**或許您可用積點來換取折扣。

字彙 shame 可惜；遺憾 trade A for B 以 A 換 B

32 What does the woman want to buy?
(A) A card (B) A desk
(C) A computer (D) A shelf

中譯 女子想要買什麼？
(A) 一張卡片 (B) 一張桌子
(C) 一部電腦 (D) 一個架子

33 What does the man say about the items?
(A) Not all of them are discounted.
(B) Most of them are out of stock.
(C) Many of them are outdated.
(D) Some of them are mislabeled.

中譯 男子說了什麼跟商品有關的事？
(A) 並非所有的商品都有打折。
(B) 大部分的商品都沒有存貨了。
(C) 許多商品都已過時了。
(D) 部分商品的標籤貼錯了。

34 What will the man most likely do next?
(A) Verify a product's price
(B) Speak to a manager
(C) Check an account history
(D) Print out a coupon

中譯 男子接下來最有可能做什麼？
(A) 核對產品的價格
(B) 跟經理談話
(C) 查看顧客的消費紀錄
(D) 印出優惠券

Questions 35-37 refer to the following conversation. 美W 澳M 對話

W Hello, Mr. Robbins. This is Samantha Kelly. ㉟ **Would it be okay for me to come in at ten instead of nine today? I could stay late tonight.**

M Good morning, Ms. Kelly. The company is rather strict with work hours. ㊱ **As you know, our most important work is done in the morning.**

女：羅賓斯先生您好，我是薩曼莎・凱利。㉟ **我今天可以從 9 點改為 10 點上班嗎？我今晚可以待比較晚。**

男：早安，凱利小姐。公司對工時的要求相當嚴格。㊱ **你知道的，我們最重要的工作都是在上午完成的。**

W Yes, I understand. Unfortunately, I had a dentist appointment at eight, but he is running behind schedule. It's difficult to get appointments with this doctor, so I was hoping it would be okay to be late just this once.	女：是的，我理解。遺憾的是，我跟牙醫預約了 8 點看牙齒，只是現在他的看診進度落後。這個醫生很不好預約，所以我希望就這一次可以晚點上班。
M I see. Well, to be honest, things are slow this week, so it should be fine just for today. ㊲ **I'll let the department head know about your situation.**	男：我明白了。好吧，說實話，這個星期生意清淡，事情不多，所以只有今天的話應該沒關係。㊲ **我會跟部門主管說你的情況。**

字彙 behind schedule 進度落後的

35 What is the purpose of the woman's call?
(A) To make an appointment
(B) To extend a deadline
(C) To report some test results
(D) To change work hours

中譯 女子打這通電話的目的為何？
(A) 進行預約
(B) 延長截止日期
(C) 報告測試結果
(D) 變更工作時間

15

36 What does the man mention about the company?
(A) Its workers' shift schedules are flexible.
(B) Its major tasks are done before noon.
(C) Its medical office isn't open in the morning.
(D) Its productivity is particularly high this week.

中譯 關於這家公司，男子提到了什麼？
(A) 員工的輪值時間很彈性。
(B) 重要工作會在中午前完成。
(C) 公司的醫療診所上午沒有營業。
(D) 這週的生產力特別高。

37 What does the man say he will do?
(A) Inform a manager of a change
(B) Reduce the workload for employees
(C) Postpone a dental checkup
(D) Promote the woman to a higher position

中譯 男子說他會做什麼？
(A) 通知主管有異動
(B) 減少員工的工作量
(C) 將牙科檢查延後
(D) 將女子升職

Questions 38-40 refer to the following conversation. 美 對話

M Hello, Ms. Rivers. ㊳ **This is Jason Best, calling to let you know that your passport is ready.** You may pick it up at City Hall.	男：里弗斯小姐您好。㊳ **我叫傑森・貝斯特，我打來通知您的護照已經好了。**您可以到市政府領回。
W Thank you. However, I live quite far from City Hall. Would it be possible to have it mailed to my address?	女：謝謝您。不過，我住在離市政府很遠的地方，能把它郵寄到我的住處嗎？
M I'm sorry, but you must pick it up in person. ㊴ **I have to see another form of photo ID to release the passport.**	男：很抱歉，您得親自來領回。㊴ **我必須看過其他有照片的證件後，才能發護照給您。**
W I see. Well, then, I will pick it up tomorrow. ㊵ **I wouldn't be able to make it to City Hall today before you close. It takes me at least an hour and a half to get there.**	女：了解。那好吧，我明天就去領回。㊵ **我沒辦法在你們今天下班前趕到市政府。我到那裡至少要一個半小時。**
M That's fine. I will see you tomorrow.	男：沒關係。明天見。

字彙 in person 親自　release 發放　make it 及時抵達

38 Why is the man calling?
(A) To schedule the delivery of an item
(B) To notify of a document's availability
(C) To update his personal information
(D) To request directions to a location

中譯 男子為什麼打這通電話？
(A) 安排運送物品
(B) 通知文件準備就緒
(C) 更新他的個人資訊
(D) 要求到某地的路線指引

39 What does the man say is required?
(A) Picture identification
(B) Contact information
(C) A local mailing address
(D) A payment receipt

中譯 男子說還需要什麼東西？
(A) 附照片的證件
(B) 聯絡方式
(C) 本地的郵寄地址
(D) 付款收據

40 Why can't the woman meet the man today?
(A) She forgot her passport.
(B) She didn't make an appointment.
(C) She is stuck in traffic.
(D) She lives too far away.

中譯 為什麼女子今天無法跟男子見面？
(A) 她忘了帶護照。
(B) 她沒有預約。
(C) 她塞在車陣中。
(D) 她住得太遠了。

Questions 41-43 refer to the following conversation with three speakers. 美M 英W 澳M 三人對話

M1 Hello, ㊶ **I'm here to return some books.**
W Okay… Um… ㊶ **It says you still have one book due tomorrow.**
M1 Right. Unfortunately, I left it on a train and can't return it by tomorrow. Is it possible to renew it?
W Well, you've already extended the due date once. Hold on. ㊷ **Mr. Clayton? Can we make an exception for this man?**
M2 Um… Are you sure you will find the book and be able to return it?
M1 I've contacted the train station. They said they have it. I can pick it up and bring it to you on Friday.
M2 I understand your situation, but we cannot renew the item. ㊸ **You will have to pay a late fee on Friday.**

男 1： 你好，㊶ **我來還幾本書。**
女： 好的…… 嗯……㊶ **上面顯示說你還有一本書明天到期。**
男 1： 沒錯。遺憾的是，我把它留在火車上了，明天之前還不了。我可以續借嗎？
女： 嗯，你已經續借過一次了。請等一下。㊷ **克雷頓先生？我們可以為這位先生破例一次嗎？**
男 2： 嗯……你確定你能找到書並歸還嗎？
男 1： 我已經聯絡過火車站了。他們說書在他們那邊。我星期五可以去把書拿回來還。
男 2： 我理解你的情況，但是我們沒辦法幫你續借這本書。㊸ **你星期五得付逾期費用。**

字彙 **extend** 延長 **due date** 到期日 **make an exception** 破例 **renew** 延長……的期限

41 Where most likely is the conversation taking place?
(A) At a train station
(B) At a bookstore
(C) At a print shop
(D) At a library

中譯 這段對話最有可能是在哪裡發生的？
(A) 在火車站
(B) 在書店
(C) 在影印店
(D) 在圖書館

42 What does the woman ask Mr. Clayton?
(A) Where a facility is located
(B) Whether an exception can be made
(C) How a process should be executed
(D) How much an item costs

中譯 女子問了克雷頓先生什麼問題？
(A) 設備的位置
(B) 是否可以破例
(C) 該如何執行程序
(D) 物品的價格多少

43 What will need to be paid on Friday?
(A) An overdue fine
(B) A transportation fee
(C) A lost item charge
(D) A luggage delivery bill

中譯 星期五要支付的是什麼費用？
(A) 逾期費
(B) 交通費
(C) 物品遺失費
(D) 行李運送帳單

Questions 44-46 refer to the following conversation. 美 對話

W Todd, ㊹ **did you finish writing the program notes for next week's concert?** The pianists want to see them before we give them out to the audience.
M Yes, I did. I was just going to send them to you. Here, you can check them right now if you'd like.
W They look nice. I like the design. ㊺ **But it seems like a piece is missing from the timetable on the first page.** The Beethoven sonata, right before intermission.
M You're right! How is that possible? ㊻ **I know I put it in there, and I checked the program twice this morning.** Anyway, I'll fix that right away.

女：陶德，㊹ **下週演奏會要用的節目簡介你做完了嗎？**在我們發給觀眾前，鋼琴演奏家們希望能先看過。
男：做完了。我正要寄給你。在這裡，你要的話，現在就可以檢查一下。
女：看起來很不錯。我喜歡這個設計，㊺ **但是第一頁的時間表好像漏掉了一首曲子**，中場休息前的貝多芬奏鳴曲。
男：沒錯！怎麼會這樣？㊻ **我明明把它放進去了，而且今天早上還檢查了兩遍。**總之，我會馬上去改。

字彙 **program note** 節目簡介 **intermission** （音樂會等）幕間休息，中場休息

44 What are the speakers mainly talking about?
(A) An audience review
(B) A musician's performance
(C) An advertisement design
(D) An informational handout

中譯 對話者主要在討論什麼？
(A) 觀眾的評論
(B) 音樂家的演奏
(C) 廣告設計
(D) 文宣資料

45 What problem does the woman mention?
(A) A show's break time is too short.
(B) A piece of music was poorly interpreted.
(C) An entertainer is running late.
(D) A schedule printout is incomplete.

中譯 女子提到的問題是什麼？
(A) 演出的休息時間過短。
(B) 音樂作品的詮釋很糟糕。
(C) 有個表演者遲到了。
(D) 時間表的資料不完整。

46 What does the man mean when he says, "How is that possible"?
(A) He doesn't understand how to do a task.
(B) He wants the woman to explain a change.
(C) He is surprised to notice an error.
(D) He disagrees with the woman's statement.

中譯 當男子說：「怎麼會這樣」時，其意為何？
(A) 他不知道要怎麼進行這項任務。
(B) 他希望女子說明某項異動。
(C) 他察覺到錯誤後非常吃驚。
(D) 他不同意女子的說法。

Questions 47-49 refer to the following conversation. 美M 英W 對話

M Hello, ㊼ **I'm calling about the apartment on Delaware Avenue. Is it still available for rent?**

W ㊼ **I'm sorry, I found a tenant just this morning. However, I have a similar property that is available.** It's the same size and goes for the same price. If you want, you can come by and see it tomorrow.

M ㊽ **What area is it in? Is it also close to Clarkston Station?** I need to take the subway every day.

W Yes, it is very close to the station. Are you familiar with Acorn Drive? It's only a five-minute walk away. ㊾ **I'll send you a map right now.**

男：你好，㊼ **我是打來詢問德拉瓦大道那間公寓，請問現在還有在出租嗎？**

女：㊼ **很抱歉，我今天早上才剛找到租客。不過，我有另一間類似的房子要出租。**大小跟價格都跟這間一樣。如果你要的話，明天可以過來看一看。

男：㊽ **那間公寓在哪一區？也靠近克拉克斯頓站嗎？**我每天都得搭地鐵。

女：對，離車站非常近。橡實路你熟嗎？走路只要五分鐘的距離。㊾ **我現在把地圖發給你。**

字彙 tenant 承租人　go for 適用於

47 What most likely is the woman's job?
(A) Subway ticket vendor
(B) Interior designer
(C) Real estate agent
(D) Taxi driver

中譯 女子最有可能是做什麼的？
(A) 地鐵售票員
(B) 室內設計師
(C) 房地產仲介
(D) 計程車司機

48 What does the man ask about?
(A) A meeting time
(B) A place's location
(C) Property values
(D) Ticket prices

中譯 男子問了什麼問題？
(A) 見面的時間
(B) 地點的位置
(C) 房地產的價值
(D) 票價

49 What will the woman most likely do next?
(A) Find a property for the man
(B) Help the man locate a place
(C) Drive the man to a station
(D) Send a document to the man

中譯 女子接下來最有可能會做什麼？
(A) 幫男子找房子
(B) 幫男子找某個地點
(C) 開車載男子去車站
(D) 發送文件給男子

15

Questions 50-52 refer to the following conversation with three speakers. 美W 美M 英W 三人對話

W1 Good afternoon, Maria and Clyde. Welcome to Cozy's. ㊿ **I'm going to show you several fireplaces today, but first, do you have anything special in mind?**

M ㊿ 51 **Well, we have a traditional house. So we are looking for a rustic style rather than something modern-looking.**

W2 We still want it to have modern features, though. 52 **The Windsor Gold model in your catalog looked like what we are looking for.**

W1 52 **That model is our most popular item.** However, before you decide, I can show you similar models that also have a wooden finish but are more energy-efficient.

M Yes, please. We would be happy to see everything you have.

W2 We are open to other suggestions as well.

女 1：瑪麗亞、克萊德，你們午安。歡迎來到科齊斯公司。㊿ **我今天準備了好幾個壁爐要給你們看，但是首先，你們打算找什麼特別的款式嗎？**

男：㊿ 51 **我們是傳統樣式的房子，所以比起現代化風格，我們更傾向於樸素一點的風格。**

女 2：但是我們還是希望具備現代化的功能。52 **貴公司產品目錄上有款叫「溫莎金」的，看起來正是我們要找的款式。**

女 1：52 **那款是本公司最熱門的產品。**但是在你們決定前，我可以給你們看一些類似的款式，同樣有木質飾面卻更節能的。

男：好的，麻煩你了。貴公司有的，我們都很樂意看看。

女 2：我們也樂意接受其他建議。

字彙 **fireplace** 壁爐　**rustic** 樸素的　**finish** （物體表面的）拋光，末道漆　**energy-efficient** 節約能源的

50 Where most likely is the conversation taking place?
(A) At a fire station
(B) At a real estate agency
(C) At a jewelry store
(D) At an interior designer's

中譯 這段對話最有可能是在哪裡進行的？
(A) 在消防局
(B) 在房屋仲介公司
(C) 在珠寶店
(D) 在室內設計公司

51 What characteristic do Maria and Clyde want?
(A) An old-fashioned appearance
(B) A contemporary look
(C) A traditional system
(D) A high energy production

中譯 瑪麗亞跟克萊德想要什麼特色？
(A) 老式的外觀
(B) 現代的外觀
(C) 傳統的系統
(D) 高能源生產

52 What is mentioned about the Windsor Gold?
(A) It has sold out.
(B) It's a customer favorite.
(C) It has a gold finish.
(D) It's in a modern style.

中譯 關於「溫莎金」，對話中提到了什麼？
(A) 已經售罄。
(B) 是客戶的最愛。
(C) 有上金色漆。
(D) 具現代風格。

Questions 53-55 refer to the following conversation. 美 對話

M Hello, I'm calling from Verano. ㊼㊽ **Ms. Vanessa Haley left us a message to ask for a reservation for tomorrow night at six thirty. I'm sorry, but we don't have any tables available at that time.** Would it be possible for your party to come at seven instead?

W Well, that's a little late for us. ㊽ **We're all coworkers, and we were planning on going out straight after work.**

M You are welcome to sit at the bar and even order some appetizers while you wait if you come early.

W That sounds nice actually. All right then. ㊾ **Put us down for seven.**

男：您好，這裡是維萊諾。㊼㊽ **凡妮莎・海莉女士留言說要訂明晚6點半的位子，但是很抱歉，那個時間都訂滿了。**請問您們一行人可以改到7點嗎？

女：嗯，那個時間對我們來說有點晚了。㊽ **我們都是同事，原本打算下班後就直接過去。**

男：如果您們提早到的話，歡迎到我們的吧台坐坐，甚至可以點些開胃菜邊吃邊等。

女：其實，聽起來還不錯。那好吧，㊾ **幫我們訂7點的位子吧。**

字彙 party 一群人　appetizer 開胃菜　put A down for B 為A預約B

53 Who most likely is the man?
(A) A hotel manager
(B) A restaurant worker
(C) A private caterer
(D) An event organizer

中譯 男子最有可能是什麼人？
(A) 飯店經理
(B) 餐廳工作人員
(C) 私人外燴公司
(D) 活動策劃人員

54 What does the woman plan on doing after work tomorrow?
(A) Going straight home
(B) Dining with colleagues
(C) Shopping for groceries
(D) Meeting her friends

中譯 女子打算明天下班後要做什麼？
(A) 直接回家
(B) 與同事一起吃飯
(C) 採買雜貨
(D) 跟朋友見面

55 What does the woman ask the man to do?
(A) Cancel her request
(B) Add items to her order
(C) Meet her at her office
(D) Make a reservation

中譯 女子要男子做什麼？
(A) 取消她的要求
(B) 加點餐點
(C) 到她辦公室會面
(D) 訂位

Questions 56-58 refer to the following conversation. 美W 澳M 對話

W Hi, Elliot! ㊿ **I'm trying to find your office, but I think I'm lost.** You said to turn left after the post office, but I don't see it.

M I'm sorry. I should have been clearer. 57 **I meant to say that you will see the post office right after you turn left.**

W Well, in that case, how do I know when to turn?

女：嗨，艾略特！㊿ **我試著找你的公司，可是我想我迷路了。**你叫我過了郵局後左轉，但是我沒看到郵局耶。

男：不好意思，我應該說得更清楚些。57 **我的意思是，你一左轉就會看到郵局。**

女：哦，那樣的話，我怎麼知道什麼時候要左轉？

M Just take the first left after the main intersection. **W** Ah, I'm going to have to turn back. **58 I crossed the main intersection a while ago.**	男：過了大十字路口後，在第一個路口左轉就行了。 女：啊，那我得迴轉了。**58 我不久前剛經過大十字路口。**

字彙 say to do (= tell someone to do) 叫（某人）做 intersection 十字路口

56 What is the purpose of the woman's call?
(A) To ask for directions
(B) To schedule a meeting
(C) To inquire about a package
(D) To report a missing item

中譯 女子打這通電話的目的為何？
(A) 請求路線指引
(B) 安排開會時間
(C) 查詢包裹情況
(D) 通報物品遺失

57 What does the man mean when he says, "I should have been clearer"?
(A) He needs to explain a new strategy.
(B) He thinks the woman went the wrong way.
(C) He is going to provide a status update.
(D) He is confused by the woman's statement.

中譯 當男子說：「我應該說得更清楚些」時，其意為何？
(A) 他需要說明新策略。
(B) 他認為女子走錯路。
(C) 他會提供最新情況。
(D) 女子說的話讓他很困惑。

58 What does the woman say about the intersection?
(A) She has already passed it.
(B) She used to work in an office near it.
(C) She doesn't know where it is.
(D) She has found a post office by it.

中譯 關於十字路口，女子說了什麼？
(A) 她已經經過那裡了。
(B) 她曾在那附近的公司工作。
(C) 她不知道十字路口在哪裡。
(D) 她看到那旁邊有個郵局。

Questions 59-61 refer to the following conversation. 美M 英W 對話

M 59 Thanks, Ms. Carson, for taking the time to answer my questions for the *Norville Tribune*. 60 Our subscribers love to read about how local businesses found success. **W** Well, **60 we decided to start offering more gluten-free options, and that strategy has helped us a great deal.** My pastry chef has come up with a lot of great ideas. **M** Appealing to a wider audience has certainly helped you to bring in business. What other plans do you have for the future? **W 61 We plan to host a cake decorating class for beginners next month right here at the bakery.**	男：**59 卡爾森女士，謝謝您抽空為《諾維爾論壇報》回答我的問題。60 本報讀者很愛看在地企業如何功成名就的故事。** 女：嗯，**60 我們之前決定開始提供更多無麩質產品的選項，這項策略對我們很有幫助。**我的糕餅師傅想出了很多很棒的點子。 男：吸引更廣大顧客群的注意肯定有助於招攬生意。您對未來還有什麼別的計畫嗎？ 女：**61 我們打算下個月在這家烘焙坊，為蛋糕裝飾初學者開一門課。**

字彙 subscriber 訂戶 option 選項 strategy 策略 appeal to 吸引

59 Who most likely is the man?
(A) A pastry chef
(B) A business consultant
(C) A newspaper reporter
(D) A fitness expert

中譯 男子的身分最有可能是？
(A) 糕餅師傅
(B) 商業顧問
(C) 報社記者
(D) 健身專家

60 What are the speakers mainly discussing?
(A) A business strategy
(B) A product launch
(C) A shortage of materials
(D) A training event

中譯 對話者主要在討論什麼？
(A) 商業策略
(B) 產品上市
(C) 材料短缺
(D) 培訓活動

61 What does the woman say will happen next month?
(A) Free refreshments will be served.
(B) A new location will be opened.
(C) A class will be offered.
(D) More employees will be hired.

中譯 女子說下個月會發生什麼事？
(A) 將免費供應茶點。
(B) 新分店即將開業。
(C) 將會開設課程。
(D) 將聘僱更多員工。

Questions 62-64 refer to the following conversation and schedule. 美 對話和時間表

W Nate, you're leaving already?
M Yes. I told Ms. Princeton yesterday that I had a train to catch this afternoon. ❻❷ **I'm going to Atlanta for a nutrition conference.**
W ❻❷❻❸ **Oh, you're going to the conference organized by the Healthy Ingredients Association? I thought it didn't start until tomorrow.**
M ❻❸ **That's right.** I am leaving today, because it starts early in the morning. So I want to stay in a hotel tonight and get a good night's sleep. There aren't any trains after six, though. ❻❹ **I'm going home to pick up my suit, then I'm taking the last train today.**
W I see. Well, I'd better let you go then.

WEEKDAY TRAIN SCHEDULE

Train Number	Destination	Departure Time	Arrival Time
105	Atlanta	6:20 A.M.	7:40 A.M.
207	Atlanta	10:30 A.M.	11:50 A.M.
482	Atlanta	2:20 P.M.	3:40 P.M.
❻❹ **553**	**Atlanta**	**5:50 P.M.**	**7:10 P.M.**

女：奈特，你已經要下班了？
男：對啊，我昨天跟普林斯頓女士說，我今天下午要趕火車。❻❷ **我要去亞特蘭大參加營養學研討會。**
女：❻❷❻❸ **哦，你要去健康食材協會主辦的研討會？我以為明天才開始。**
男：❻❸ **是沒錯。**我今天去，因為研討會明天一大早就開始了，所以今晚我想在飯店住一晚，然後好好地睡上一覺。不過，6 點過後就沒有車了。❻❹ **我現在要先回家拿西裝，然後坐今天的最後一班火車。**
女：原來如此。好吧，那我最好讓你下班了。

平日火車時間表

列車班次	終點站	發車時間	抵達時間
105	亞特蘭大	上午 6:20	上午 7:40
207	亞特蘭大	上午 10:30	上午 11:50
482	亞特蘭大	下午 2:20	下午 3:40
❻❹ 553	亞特蘭大	下午 5:50	下午 7:10

字彙 nutrition 營養 ingredient 食材 association 協會

62 What type of company do the speakers most likely work at?
(A) A travel agency
(B) A clothing store
(C) A transportation company
(D) A food producer

中譯 對話者最有可能在哪種類型的公司工作？
(A) 旅行社
(B) 服飾店
(C) 交通運輸公司
(D) 食物製造商

63 What will the man do tomorrow?
(A) Depart for Atlanta
(B) Attend an event
(C) Search for a hotel
(D) Leave the office early

中譯 男子明天要做什麼？
(A) 前往亞特蘭大
(B) 參加活動
(C) 找飯店
(D) 提早下班

64 Look at the graphic. Which train will the man most likely take?
(A) Train 105
(B) Train 207
(C) Train 482
(D) Train 553

中譯 請看圖表。男子最有可能搭哪一班火車？
(A) 105 車次列車
(B) 207 車次列車
(C) 482 車次列車
(D) 553 車次列車

Questions 65-67 refer to the following conversation and poster. 澳M 英W 對話和海報

M **65 I'm meeting with Theo Miller from the *Stroudville Herald* tomorrow to give an interview about our art contest.** He's planning to write an article about it.

W That's wonderful! We want as many people as possible to know about it. I think it'll be a great way for people to express their creativity, and they can also learn more about our museum.

M Exactly. We hope that people will take a look around the museum when they drop off their submissions. **66 Speaking of which, I still need a few people to collect the art on the last day of submissions.** Are you free?

W I'd love to help you out, but **67 I'm moving to a new apartment that week,** and I don't have a moment to spare.

Amateur Art Contest
Call for entries

66 Submission period: February 3–5
Awards Ceremony: February 7 at 6 P.M.
Show opens to the public: February 8
Show closes: February 20

Willow Art Museum

男： **65 我明天要跟《斯特勞德維爾先鋒報》的西奧・米勒見面，就美術大賽一事進行採訪。**他打算寫一篇相關報導。

女： 那真是太好啦！我們希望知道這個消息的人越多越好。我認為這是讓大家展現創造力的絕佳方式，還能讓大家更認識我們美術館。

男： 正是如此。我們希望大家過來交件的時候，能順便參觀一下美術館。**66 說到這，我還需要幾個人在交件的最後一天幫忙收件。**你有空嗎？

女： 我很想幫你的忙，但是 **67 那個星期我要搬到新的公寓，**抽不出時間來。

業餘美術大賽
作品徵集

66 收件期間：2 月 3 日至 2 月 5 日
頒獎典禮：2 月 7 日下午 6 點
作品展對外開放日期：2 月 8 日
展覽結束日期：2 月 20 日

威洛美術館

字彙 drop off 帶……到某處 submission 提交物 spare 抽出…… entry 參賽作品

65 What will the man do tomorrow?
(A) Write an article
(B) Meet with a reporter
(C) Tour a museum
(D) Purchase some artwork

中譯 男子明天要做什麼？
(A) 寫一篇文章
(B) 與記者見面
(C) 參觀美術館
(D) 採購藝術品

66 Look at the graphic. When does the man need extra help?
(A) February 3 **(B) February 5**
(C) February 7 (D) February 20

中譯 請看圖表。男子哪一天需要額外協助？
(A) 2 月 3 日 **(B) 2 月 5 日**
(C) 2 月 7 日 (D) 2 月 20 日

67 What does the woman say she will do?
(A) Move to a new home
(B) Submit an original painting
(C) Come to the museum early
(D) Create a registration form

中譯 女子說她會做什麼事？
(A) 搬到新家
(B) 繳交原創畫作
(C) 提早到美術館
(D) 製作報名表單

Questions 68-70 refer to the following conversation and floor plan. 美 對話和樓層圖

W Hello. ⑱ **Are there any seats left for tonight's performance?**
M ⑱ **Yes, there are. However, the only ones left are in the back of the room.**
W That's fine. I'll take one seat please.
M Okay. That'll be $15.50. And that includes the lecture before the performance.
W Oh, I heard about it. It's a talk by the first violinist, right?
M That's right. ⑲ **Mr. Rimple will give a brief introduction of tonight's program and the history of each piece.**
W That's wonderful! What time is it at?
M It's starting in just five minutes. You'd better hurry. ⑳ **It's in the room directly facing the entrance of the concert hall.**
W ⑳ **Okay.** Thank you very much!

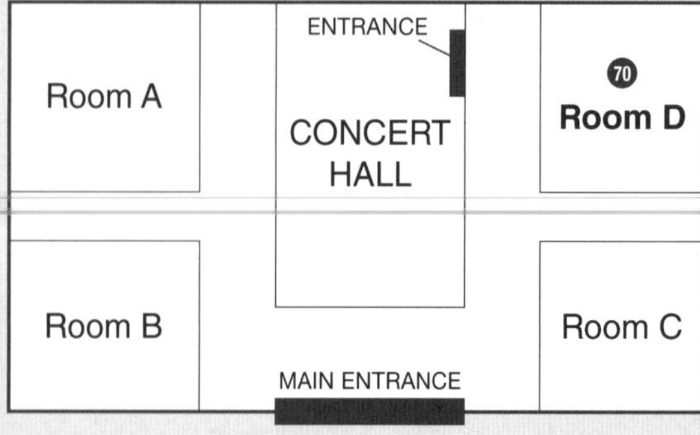

女： 哈囉，⑱ **請問今晚的演出還有座位嗎？**
男： ⑱ **是，有的。但是，只剩後面的座位。**
女： 沒關係，請給我一個座位。
男： 好的，費用是 15.5 美元，內含演出前的講座。
女： 哦，我聽說了。那是首席小提琴家的演講，對嗎？
男： 沒錯。⑲ **林普先生會簡單介紹一下今晚的節目以及每首曲子的歷史。**
女： 太棒了！幾點開始？
男： 還有五分鐘就開始了，您最好加緊腳步。⑳ **地點就在音樂廳入口處的正對面。**
女： ⑳ **好的。**非常謝謝你。

字彙 lecture 演講 brief 簡短的

68 Who most likely is the man?
(A) A conductor
(B) A musician
(C) A ticket agent
(D) An audience member

中譯 男子最有可能是什麼人？
(A) 指揮家
(B) 音樂家
(C) 售票員
(D) 觀眾

69 What does the man mention about the lecture?
(A) It costs extra to attend.
(B) It doesn't have any more seats available.
(C) It started a few minutes ago.
(D) It will be about tonight's music.

中譯 關於講座，男子提到了什麼？
(A) 要另外付費才能參加。
(B) 沒有多餘的座位了。
(C) 幾分鐘前開始的。
(D) 內容與今晚的音樂有關。

70 Look at the graphic. Where will the woman most likely go next?
(A) Room A (B) Room B
(C) Room C **(D) Room D**

中譯 請看圖表。女子接下來最有可能會去哪一廳？
(A) A 廳 (B) B 廳
(C) C 廳 **(D) D 廳**

PART 4 16

Questions 71-73 refer to the following introduction. 美M 介紹

Welcome to the Automatic Artifacts House. ⑪ **This month's special exhibit features clocks from around the world and from every time period since the Middle Ages.** ⑫ **At eleven thirty, I will show you the insides of a clock and disassemble it so that you may see how these fascinating machines work.** There is no better way to understand clockwork than by seeing how each piece fits together. ⑬ **And make sure you stay until noon. When the clocks strike twelve, look at the cuckoo clock.** It will play a beautiful song and give you a special show.

歡迎蒞臨自動文物館。⑪ **本月特展即將展出，自中世紀以來世界各地各時期的時鐘。**⑫ **在 11 點 30 分的時候，我會給大家看時鐘內部，把時鐘拆開來，這樣你們就能看到這些迷人的機械是如何運作的。**想要了解發條裝置，最好的辦法莫過於自己親眼看到每個零件是怎麼接合的。⑬ **還有，請務必要待到中午。當 12 點的鐘聲響起時，看一下咕咕鐘。**它會播放優美的音樂，為您獻上一場特別的演出。

字彙 artifact （有史學價值的）製品 disassemble 拆卸 clockwork 發條裝置 strike （鐘）敲響 cuckoo clock 布穀鳥自鳴鐘

71 Where is this talk most likely being heard?
(A) At a museum
(B) At a department store
(C) At a concert hall
(D) At a souvenir shop

中譯 最有可能在哪聽到這段談話？
(A) 在博物館
(B) 在百貨公司
(C) 在音樂廳
(D) 在紀念品店

72 What will the speaker do at eleven thirty?
(A) Host an auction
(B) Play a song
(C) Explain a device
(D) Start a guided tour

中譯 說話者 11 點 30 分會做什麼?
(A) 舉辦拍賣會
(B) 播放歌曲
(C) 解說裝置
(D) 開始導覽

73 What does the speaker recommend the listeners do at twelve o'clock?
(A) Meet with a specialist
(B) Attend a lecture
(C) Observe a specific item
(D) Exit the building

中譯 說話者建議聽眾在 12 點鐘時做什麼?
(A) 和專家會面
(B) 參加講座
(C) 觀察特定的物品
(D) 離開大樓

Questions 74-76 refer to the following excerpt from a meeting. 美W 會議摘錄

Thanks for being here, and ⑭ **I'm sorry we don't have chairs for everyone.** Some of our furniture is being repaired at the moment, so we have to get by with what we have. ⑮ **I wanted to meet with you to discuss our company's new dress code.** As you may have heard, we'll no longer wear uniforms, but employees should still be dressed in a professional manner. ⑯ **We're recording this meeting for those who cannot be here, so if you have questions, please write them down and pass them up to the front so I can read them into the microphone.**

感謝大家到場。⑭ **我很抱歉,不是每個人都有椅子坐。**因為有些家具目前還在修繕中,所以我們不得不將就一下現有的。⑮ **我想跟大家開會討論一下我們公司新的服裝規定。**你們可能已經聽說,我們以後不用穿制服了,但即便如此,員工的穿著打扮仍應符合專業。⑯ **我們會把這場會議錄下來,給那些無法到場的人聽,所以如果你們有疑問,請寫下並傳到前面來,我好對著麥克風唸出來。**

字彙 **get by with** 勉強應付 **dress code** 服裝規定

74 Why does the speaker apologize?
(A) There is a lack of seats.
(B) A machine malfunctioned.
(C) A meeting is starting late.
(D) A location has changed.

中譯 說話者為什麼道歉?
(A) 座位不夠。
(B) 機器故障了。
(C) 會議延後開始。
(D) 地點改變了。

75 What is the purpose of the meeting?
(A) To introduce an employee
(B) To select group members
(C) To explain a new policy
(D) To review a project's goals

中譯 本次會議的目的為何?
(A) 介紹員工
(B) 挑選組員
(C) 說明新政策
(D) 檢視專案目標

76 According to the speaker, why should the questions be written down?
(A) They should be reviewed by a supervisor.
(B) They will be read aloud for a recording.
(C) They need to be sorted by category.
(D) They are limited to one per person.

中譯 根據說話者所言,為什麼要把問題寫下來?
(A) 問題應先經主管審查。
(B) 大聲唸出問題才好錄音。
(C) 要針對問題進行分類。
(D) 每人限問一個問題。

Questions 77-79 refer to the following news report. 澳M 新聞報導

This is Brad Henderson reporting for *Channel 3 News* from the International Trade Expo. At this event, businesses are displaying everything from cosmetics to electronics. (77) **I'm here now at the Expeedo Sports booth checking out the company's new running shoes.** (78) **What really sets these shoes apart is how light they are.** (77) **This will definitely help long-distance runners to improve their race times.** But this is not the only interesting thing here. If you have a chance to visit the expo, (79) **you should try all of the various samples and items.** You can discover new things and try them out before you buy them.

我是《第三台新聞》的記者布萊德・亨德森，現在就在國際貿易博覽會為您進行報導。在這場活動中，企業一一展示了自家的產品，從化妝品到電子產品皆有。(77) **我現在在益佰鐸運動用品公司的攤位上，看他們新推出的跑步鞋。**(78) **真正讓這雙跑步鞋與眾不同的是，它們的重量很輕。**(77) **這肯定有助於長跑選手增進自己的跑步成績。**不過，這並非整場展覽唯一有看頭的地方。如果您有機會參觀這個博覽會，(79) **各種類型的樣品跟產品都要試用看看。**您會發現新穎的事物，還能在購買前試用一下。

字彙 **trade expo** 貿易博覽會 **cosmetics** 化妝品 **electronics** （複數）電子產品
set . . . apart 使……與眾不同

77 What kind of product does the report describe?
(A) Athletic shoes
(B) An electronic device
(C) Natural cosmetics
(D) A home appliance

中譯 記者描述的是什麼類型的產品？
(A) 運動鞋
(B) 電子器材
(C) 天然化妝品
(D) 家用電器

78 According to the speaker, what is special about the product?
(A) Its safety features
(B) Its recyclable materials
(C) Its compact size
(D) Its lightweight design

中譯 根據說話者所言，這項產品有何特別之處？
(A) 安全特性
(B) 可回收材料
(C) 體積小巧
(D) 輕量設計

79 What does the speaker recommend doing?
(A) Comparing prices
(B) Testing products
(C) Visiting a Web site
(D) Calling with questions

中譯 說話者建議做什麼？
(A) 比較價格
(B) 試用產品
(C) 瀏覽網站
(D) 致電諮詢

Questions 80-82 refer to the following talk. 英W 談話

(80) **On behalf of Monroe Beach Resort, I'd like to thank you all once again for attending this group interview.** You've all done a fantastic job answering our questions about your previous work experience. We now want to see how you think on your feet. (81) **I've prepared some common customer service scenarios that I want you to act out. I've just passed out the cards explaining the various situations.** You'll have some time to think because we're at a good stopping point now. (82) **Feel free to help yourself to some refreshments or take a quick stroll outside.** Let's meet back here in fifteen minutes to continue with the next session. See you then.

(80) **本人謹代表蒙羅海灘度假村，再次感謝各位參加這次的集體面試。**在回答先前工作經歷問題的這一環節，大家都表現得非常出色。現在我們想要看看各位隨機應變的能力怎麼樣。(81) **我準備了一些常見的客服情境，要讓各位演示一下。我剛才把寫有各種情境的卡片發給大家了。**你們會有時間思考，因為現在正好告一段落。(82) **你們可以隨意用點點心，或者是到外面去走一走。**我們15 分鐘後再回來這裡，繼續進行下一個環節。待會見。

字彙 on behalf of 代表（某人） previous 先前的 think on one's feet 思維敏捷 refreshments 茶點 take a stroll 散步

80 Who most likely are the listeners?
(A) Tour guides
(B) Job applicants
(C) Beach visitors
(D) Hotel guests

中譯 聽眾最有可能是誰？
(A) 導遊
(B) 求職者
(C) 海灘遊客
(D) 飯店住客

81 What are the listeners asked to do?
(A) Explain a problem
(B) Fill out a survey
(C) Find a partner
(D) Do a role-play activity

中譯 聽眾被要求做什麼？
(A) 解釋問題
(B) 填寫問卷
(C) 尋找搭檔
(D) 角色扮演

82 What will the listeners most likely do next?
(A) Pick up a handout
(B) Follow the speaker
(C) Take a break
(D) Sign up for a session

中譯 聽眾接下來最有可能會做什麼？
(A) 領取講義資料
(B) 跟隨說話者
(C) 休息一下
(D) 報名參加課程

Questions 83-85 refer to the following announcement. 英W 宣告

Your attention, please. ⓼③ **Due to the recent birth of a panda cub, we have a lot of visitors today.** In order to get people in as fast as possible, please queue up and be respectful. 84 **Do not cut in line.** This will only slow the process. There is a special line for those who wish to visit the pandas only. Proceed to this line only if you do not want to see any other animal. For safety purposes, we will not let anyone in after 3 P.M. instead of 5 P.M. today. 85 **Children who are not able to see the pandas today will receive a free stuffed animal as an apology.**

大家請注意，83 **因為最近有一隻貓熊寶寶出生了，所以我們今天會有很多遊客。**為了讓大家早點入場，請排隊並尊重他人，84 **切勿插隊。**那只會拖累大家的腳步。有一條專用道是給那些只想看貓熊的遊客使用。如果您只想看貓熊，不想看其他動物的話，請排這條隊伍。為了安全起見，今天下午 3 點後就不再開放入園，而不是 5 點。85 **今天沒看到貓熊的小朋友，將獲贈一隻動物造型的填充玩偶作為賠禮。**

字彙 cub 幼獸 queue up 排隊 cut in line 插隊 proceed 前往 stuffed animal 動物填充玩偶

83 Where is this announcement most likely being heard?
(A) At a grocery store (B) At an airport
(C) At a daycare center **(D) At a zoo**

中譯 我們最有可能在哪裡聽到這段宣告？
(A) 在雜貨店 (B) 在機場
(C) 在托兒所 **(D) 在動物園**

84 Why does the speaker say, "This will only slow the process"?
(A) To prevent rude behavior
(B) To clarify an estimate
(C) To encourage purchases
(D) To announce a delay

中譯 說話者為什麼說：「那只會拖累大家的腳步」？
(A) 為防止無禮行為
(B) 為說明估計
(C) 為鼓勵購買
(D) 為公布延遲

85 What does the speaker offer some young visitors?
(A) Priority seating
(B) Free entry
(C) A toy animal
(D) Photographs of animals

中譯 說話者提供什麼給部分年幼的遊客?
(A) 優先就座
(B) 免費入場
(C) 動物玩具
(D) 動物照片

Questions 86-88 refer to the following telephone message. 美W 電話留言

Hello. I'm calling about order number 81151. **86 87 I received a message saying that the book I ordered, *Agents and Foes*, is out of stock and that you will send it to me at a later date.** However, I need this item before April 16 because it is a birthday gift. **86 87 I saw that *The Grand Hope* is in stock according to your Web site, so could I get that book instead? 87 It is cheaper than my original order,** but rather than sending me a refund for the difference, **88 please just use an expedited delivery service.** Thank you for your time.

你好,我打這通電話是要詢問訂單編號 81151。**86 87 我收到一則簡訊,說我訂的書《特務與仇敵》沒有貨了,你們之後會再把書寄給我。**不過,我得在 4 月 16 日前拿到這本書,因為這是生日禮物。**86 87 我在你們的網站上看到《宏願》這本書還有存貨,那麼我可以換成這本書嗎? 87 這本書比我原先訂購的書還要便宜,**但是與其把差額退給我,**88 請你們改用急件的快遞寄給我吧。**謝謝您寶貴的時間。

字彙 be in stock 有存貨　expedite 加快

86 What is the purpose of the message?
(A) To modify an order
(B) To make an apology
(C) To explain a process
(D) To request a payment

中譯 這則留言的目的為何?
(A) 修改訂單
(B) 道歉
(C) 說明過程
(D) 要求付款

87 What is mentioned about *The Grand Hope*?
(A) It was written by a best-selling author.
(B) It is less expensive than *Agents and Foes*.
(C) It is currently out of stock.
(D) It was given as a birthday present.

中譯 關於《宏願》一書,留言中提到了什麼?
(A) 由暢銷作家所著。
(B) 售價比《特務與仇敵》低。
(C) 目前已經缺貨了。
(D) 已當作生日禮物送出。

88 What does the speaker ask the listener to do?
(A) Provide a refund
(B) Use a fast delivery service
(C) Update a Web site
(D) Return a phone call

中譯 說話者要收到留言的人做什麼?
(A) 提供退款
(B) 使用快遞服務
(C) 更新網站資訊
(D) 回覆電話

Questions 89-91 refer to the following talk. 美M 談話

Good morning, and thank you all for being a part of this customer panel. ⑧⑨ **Today I'll give you various flavors of our new soft drink. After you try each one,** I will record your comments. ⑨⓪ **Remember, some people in the group might have a widely different opinion from yours.** Don't pay attention to them. ⑨⓪ **We want you to share your thoughts freely, even if they're in disagreement.** ⑨① **Now, so that I can easily identify each of you, please make sure you're wearing the name badges I gave you before we begin.** Thanks.

早安，感謝各位成為客戶小組的一員。⑧⑨ **今天，我會給你們試喝許多種新口味的汽水，每喝完一種，**我就會記錄下你們的意見。⑨⓪ **切記，有些組員的意見可能與你的大不相同，**但請不要在意其他人說了什麼。⑨⓪ **即使大家意見分歧，我們希望你們能自在地分享自己的看法。** ⑨① **現在，為了能輕易地辨認各位，在我們開始前，請務必別上我發給你們的名牌。**謝謝。

字彙 panel 評鑑小組　soft drink 不含酒精的飲料；汽水　be in disagreement 意見不同　identify 認出

89 What task are the listeners expected to do?
(A) Taste some beverage samples
(B) Record some music performances
(C) Review some advertisements
(D) Assess some job candidates

中譯 聽眾要執行什麼樣的任務？
(A) 品嘗飲料樣品
(B) 錄製音樂表演
(C) 審核廣告內容
(D) 評估應徵者

90 What does the speaker imply when he says, "Don't pay attention to them"?
(A) The company wants independent opinions.
(B) Some handouts contain an error.
(C) The listeners were given the wrong instructions.
(D) Some employees will be monitoring the activity.

中譯 當說話者說：「不要在意其人說了什麼」時，其言下之意為何？
(A) 公司希望獲得獨立的觀點。
(B) 有些發放資料的內容有誤。
(C) 聽眾接收到的指示有誤。
(D) 有些員工會監控活動的進行。

91 What will the listeners most likely do next?
(A) Print some documents
(B) Write down questions
(C) Put on name tags
(D) Form small groups

中譯 聽眾接下來最有可能會做什麼？
(A) 列印文件
(B) 寫下問題
(C) 別上名牌
(D) 形成小組

Questions 92-94 refer to the following talk. 美W 談話

Ladies and gentlemen, ⑨② **tonight we are here to recognize the winner of this year's Best Young Novelist award: Justin Lawson.** Mr. Lawson's work, *Metallic Love*, has astonished critics who are all equally impressed by the beautiful writing and the intricate plot. *Metallic Love* is more than just another romance novel. The book makes powerful social statements while raising deep philosophical questions. ⑨③ **One thing is for sure—you will not be the same after reading this.** Trust me, ⑨③ **it will**

各位先生、各位女士，大家好。⑨② **今晚我們要在此表揚，本年度最佳青年小說家獎的得主：賈斯汀・勞森。**勞森先生的著作《金屬之戀》令文評家驚喜不已，他們都同樣被優美的文筆以及錯綜複雜的故事情節所折服。《金屬之戀》不僅僅是一本愛情小說。本書在傳達強而有力的社會論點時，也引出了深刻的哲學問題。⑨③ **有一點是肯定的——讀完這本書後，你將大不相同。**相信我，⑨③ **這本書會讓你重新思考一切。** ⑨④ **今天我非常**

make you rethink everything. 94 **It is a great honor for me to present Mr. Lawson with this prize today.** Please give him a warm welcome.

榮幸，能將這個獎項頒發給勞森先生。請大家熱烈鼓掌歡迎他。

字彙 recognize 表揚 astonish 使吃驚 critic 評論家 intricate 錯綜複雜的 plot 情節 statement 聲明，敘述 philosophical 哲學的

92 What is the purpose of the talk?
(A) To introduce an author
(B) To advertise a book
(C) To criticize an idea
(D) To request nominations

中譯 本談話的目的為何？
(A) 介紹作家
(B) 宣傳書籍
(C) 批評某個想法
(D) 要求提名

93 What does the speaker imply when she says, "Trust me"?
(A) She has read the book.
(B) She will write a novel.
(C) She plans on answering questions.
(D) She has won several awards.

中譯 當說話者：「相信我」時，其言下之意為何？
(A) 她已經讀過這本書了。
(B) 她會寫一本小說。
(C) 她打算回答問題。
(D) 她獲得數個獎項。

94 What will most likely happen next?
(A) A book will be signed.
(B) A passage will be read.
(C) Some questions will be asked.
(D) An award will be presented.

中譯 接下來最有可能發生什麼事？
(A) 有人會在書上簽名。
(B) 有人會讀一段文章。
(C) 會問幾個問題。
(D) 將頒發獎項。

Questions 95-97 refer to the following announcement and schedule. 澳M 宣告與行程表

Good morning, visitors! We thank you for coming to explore Emerald Park. Unfortunately, 95 96 **Sandra twisted her ankle yesterday and won't be able to give her tour today.** Those of you who were scheduled to tour the park with her can join Josh's group instead, since he doesn't have that many visitors signed up. We apologize for the inconvenience. Please meet your guide at the entrance of the park at least five minutes before your departure time. 97 **We would also like to kindly remind you that children under twelve must be accompanied by an adult at all times.** We have noticed several children running around alone. Thank you.

EMERALD PARK TOUR SCHEDULE

DEPARTURE TIME	GUIDE
11:00 A.M.	Cindy
96 **12:30 P.M.**	**Sandra**
2:00 P.M.	Josh
3:30 P.M.	Richard

各位來賓早安！感謝大家來探索翡翠公園。遺憾的是，95 96 **珊卓昨天扭傷腳踝，今天沒辦法為各位導覽解說。**原本預定與她一同參觀公園的遊客，可以改加入喬許那一團，因為那團的報名人數沒那麼多。造成您的不便，我們感到很抱歉。請您至少在出發前五分鐘，到公園入口處與您的導覽員會合。97 **再次溫馨提醒您，未滿 12 歲的孩童隨時都要由大人陪同。**我們注意到有好幾位小朋友自己一個人到處跑來跑去。謝謝您。

翡翠公園導覽時間表

啟程時間	導覽員
上午 11:00	辛蒂
96 **中午 12:30**	**珊卓**
下午 2:00	喬許
下午 3:30	理查

字彙 twist one's ankle 扭傷腳踝　inconvenience 不便　departure 出發，離開

95 Why has one of the tours been canceled?
(A) Weather conditions are unfavorable.
(B) An employee was injured.
(C) An area needs renovations.
(D) Not enough people registered.

中譯 其中有一場導覽活動被取消了，為什麼？
(A) 氣候不佳。
(B) 員工受傷。
(C) 有個區域要整修。
(D) 報名人數不足。

96 Look at the graphic. At what time was the canceled tour supposed to leave?
(A) At 11:00 A.M.　**(B) At 12:30 P.M.**
(C) At 2:00 P.M.　(D) At 3:30 P.M.

中譯 請看圖表。被取消的導覽活動原定何時出發？
(A) 上午 11 點　**(B) 中午 12 點半**
(C) 下午 2 點　(D) 下午 3 點半

97 What are the visitors prohibited from doing?
(A) Leaving children unattended
(B) Entering without a guide
(C) Running in the park
(D) Joining several tours

中譯 遊客禁止做什麼？
(A) 未看顧隨行孩童
(B) 無導覽員陪同下進入
(C) 在公園裡跑來跑去
(D) 參加多場導覽活動

Questions 98-100 refer to the following excerpt from a meeting and chart. 美W 會議摘錄與長條圖

Let's start by talking about our stock. We always seem to run out of the same kinds of candy. ⑱ **I believe we can significantly increase our profits by ordering more of our customer favorites each month.** So we have decided to adjust our orders and purchase more of the top-selling candy. However, ⑲ **we are going to buy less of our second most popular item.** I know this seems strange, but our supplier for that brand has raised prices by more than double, and it simply isn't as profitable for us anymore. ⑳ **I will now hand out the detailed outline of next month's order plan.**

我們先來談談庫存的問題。我們同一種類的糖果似乎總會賣到缺貨。⑱ **我認為我們每個月多訂一些顧客最喜歡的糖果，營收就會大幅增加。**因此我們決定要調整訂單數量，多買一些賣得最好的糖果，但 ⑲ **會少買一些第二暢銷的糖果。**我知道這聽起來很奇怪，但是那個品牌的供應商最近漲價的幅度已經超過一倍了，對我們來說，根本不再有什麼賺頭。⑳ **我現在把下個月訂購計畫的詳細綱要發給大家。**

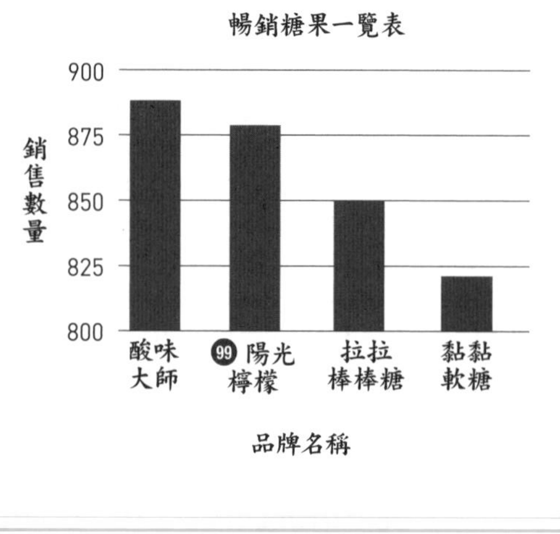

字彙 stock 存貨　significantly 顯著地　profit 利潤　adjust 調整　profitable 有利可圖的　outline 大綱

98 According to the speaker, how can the company increase profits?
(A) By selling a new product
(B) By changing suppliers
(C) By purchasing more goods
(D) By targeting different customers

中譯 根據說話者所言，公司如何增加營收？
(A) 銷售新產品
(B) 更換供應商
(C) 採購更多商品
(D) 鎖定不同的客群

99 Look at the graphic. What will the company buy less of?
(A) Master Sours **(B) Sunny Lemons**
(C) Lala Lollipops (D) Gooey Gummies

中譯 請看圖表。該公司將會減少採購哪樣商品？
(A) 酸味大師 **(B) 陽光檸檬**
(C) 拉拉棒棒糖 (D) 黏黏軟糖

100 What will the speaker most likely do next?
(A) Place an order
(B) Finalize a plan
(C) Give out documents
(D) Negotiate a price

中譯 說話者接下來最有可能做什麼？
(A) 下訂單 (B) 敲定計畫
(C) 分發文件 (D) 協商價格

PART 5

填入副詞──修飾動詞

101 安妮塔小姐總是透過烤餅乾義賣的方式，積極地參加募款活動。
(A) 積極 (B) 行事 **(C) 積極地** (D) 活動

字彙 participate in 參加 fundraiser 募款活動

慣用片語 be scheduled to do

102 市鎮節慶的遊行預定於明天下午 1 點開始。
(A) 預定 (B) 保留 (C) 考慮 (D) 慶祝

填入形容詞+形容詞 respective

103 門一打開，接待員就將觀眾帶到他們各自的座位。
(A) 各自的 (B) 尊敬
(C) 尊敬的 (D) 尊敬；關於

字彙 usher （尤指婚禮等正式場合或劇院的）接待員
show 帶領，引領

名詞 instructions

104 本店販售的家具皆附有簡單易懂的說明書，以便快速組裝家具。
(A) 估價 **(B) 說明書** (C) 舒適 (D) 退款

字彙 come with 與……一起供給的
easy-to-follow 簡單易懂的 assembly 組裝

填入名詞

105 夸博先生打電話給客服時，他得等 15 分鐘才得到答覆。
(A) 答案 (B) 回答 (C) 回答 (D) 答案

介系詞 for

106 在夏日度假酒店擔任禮賓員的一項必要條件，就是得精通至少兩種語言。
(A) 關於 (B) 透過 (C) 通過 **(D) 為了**

字彙 qualification 條件；資格
concierge （接待客人的）禮賓員

分詞構句

107 技師在維修電氣系統時必須關閉整棟大樓的電源。
(A) 維修 (B) 維修 **(C) 維修** (D) 維修

字彙 technician 技師 electrical 電的，與電有關的

動詞 demonstrate

108 這部影片示範了該軟體可以幫助企業整理資料的各種方式。
(A) 查詢 (B) 關注 (C) 結束 **(D) 展示**

解析 意義上，「關注」和「展示」較為適當。但是，若要使用 **(C)**「關注」之意，必須構成 focus on，故正解為 **(D)**。

所有格代名詞

109 推薦您的一個朋友加入我們健身房，我們就會提供優惠的會費。

(A) 您 (B) 您的 (C) 您自己 **(D) 您的**

字彙 recommend 推薦 membership fee 會員費

副詞 specifically

110 經理明確要求由妮可拉女士主導與信達公司的談判。

(A) 完全地 **(B) 明確地**
(C) 廣泛地 (D) 逐漸地

字彙 negotiation （常用複數）協商，談判

填入動詞＋主動語態

111 許多求職者已繳交應徵店員一職的申請書，所以需要時間來查看所有的申請。

(A) 要提交 (B) 被提交
(C) 提交 **(D) 已經提交**

字彙 candidate 求職者 application 申請書
sales associate 店員 go over 查看，仔細檢查

連接詞 vs 介系詞

112 沒有預約就不可能搭乘機場到飯店的接駁巴士。

(A) 除非 **(B) 沒有**
(C) 除……之外 (D) 除了……還有

字彙 shuttle bus 接駁巴士 reservation 預約

動名詞

113 莫斯先生表示有意參加工作坊來提升自己公開演說的技能。

(A) 參加了 (B) 參加 **(C) 參加** (D) 為參加

複合名詞 baggage allowance

114 這家航空公司的新政策是，國際航線每位乘客的行李限額將從一件行李箱增加到了兩件。

(A) 索取 (B) 參與 **(C) 限額** (D) 獲得

字彙 airline 航空公司 international flight 國際航線

所有格

115 孟瑟公共圖書館的讀者可上網續借書籍，從而避免逾期罰金。

(A) 他們的 (B) 他們的 (C) 他們 (D) 他們

字彙 patron 主顧 overdue fine 逾期罰金

片語動詞 benefit from

116 不僅資深員工，就連新進人員也將受益於薪資分級表的修訂。

(A) ……的 (B) 在……當中
(C) 從 (D) 對

字彙 revision 修改 pay scale 薪級表

連接詞 vs 介系詞

117 分店店長決定提早關店，好讓員工在暴風雪開始前回家。

(A) 以便 **(B) 在……之前**
(C) 提前 (D) 而不是

字彙 supervisor 管理人 snowstorm 暴風雪

副詞 still

118 雖然大會的日期與地點都已經選好了，但是日程表還有待最終定案。

(A) 仍然 (B) 最近 (C) 一旦 (D) 正是

字彙 convention 大會 finalize 定案

指示代名詞 those

119 同事們願意補貼油錢給那些自願開車載他們去年度野餐會的人。

(A) 他們 **(B) 那些** (C) 其他 (D) 任何人

字彙 offer 主動提出 annual 一年一度的，每年的

動詞 decline

120 黃金價格連續幾個月穩定上漲，但在六月底開始下跌了。

(A) 阻止 **(B) 下跌** (C) 花費 (D) 消除

字彙 steadily 逐漸地，穩定地

填入名詞——形容詞＋名詞

121 該工廠面對高污染程度的嚴厲批評，於是採取了保護周圍環境的措施。

(A) 批評的 (B) 批評 (C) 批評地 **(D) 批評**

字彙 criticism 批評 surrounding 周遭的

介系詞片語 based on

122 而今那家書店的網站更新後，常客便可根據自己的消費紀錄來獲得推薦書單。

(A) 代表 (B) 例如 **(C) 根據** (D) 儘管

字彙 recommendation 推薦

填入副詞——修飾動詞

123 雖然珍珠亮白牙膏獲得全國牙醫師的強力推薦，但消費者更喜歡該款牙膏的主要競爭對手。

(A) 強壯的 (B) 力量
(C) 最強壯的 **(D) 強烈地**

字彙 nationwide 全國範圍內的 competitor 競爭者

形容詞 equivalent

124 工程師必須有碩士學位或是同等工作經驗，才有望應聘高級管理人員的職缺。
(A) 故意的 (B) 盈利的
(C) 相等的 (D) 有系統的

字彙 master's degree 碩士學位
opening 空缺的職位

主動語態+單複數一致性

125 為了緩解市中心交通壅塞的問題，城市規劃師將把部分道路改成單行道。
(A) 已被改為 (B) 被改為
(C) 將改為 (D) 改為

字彙 alleviate 緩解 traffic congestion 交通壅塞
city planner 城市規劃師 convert 轉換
roadway 道路，公路

名詞 nomination

126 雖然最後的贏家會保密，但人才獎的最高提名人選將在頒獎典禮前兩週揭曉。
(A) 訂閱 (B) 信心 (C) 祝賀 **(D) 提名**

填入形容詞——副詞+形容詞

127 隨著面試的進行，丹尼・馬洛覺得他越來越有希望獲得這份會計工作。
(A) 希望 (B) 有希望地
(C) 有希望的 (D) 希望

從屬連接詞 whether

128 無論來賓打算出席活動與否，都應在月底前回覆邀請函。
(A) 要麼 **(B) 是否** (C) 因為 (D) 雖然

關係代名詞所有格 whose

129 主廚弗朗西斯・蓋爾斯開了一家餐廳，其菜單根據每天早上能買到的品質最好的魚和農產品而變化。
(A) ……那個 (B) 當……時
(C) ……的 (D) 當……的時候

字彙 produce 農產品

形容詞 selective

130 對於要讓誰參與制定公司目標的半年度會議，亨瑟公司的董事們是非常仔細篩選的。
(A) 仔細挑選的 (B) 知名的
(C) 易取得的 (D) 雄心勃勃的

字彙 biannual 一年兩次的

PART 6

Questions 131-134 refer to the following e-mail. 電子郵件

To: All members <memberlist@bettermegym.com> From: Dennis Primus <dprimus@bettermegym.com> Subject: New Weekend Hours Date: August 4 Dear members, Thank you to all who -------(131.) our survey to share ideas concerning Better Me Gym. We strive to keep our gym the most modern and convenient for our clients, so feedback such as yours is highly -------(132.) to us. While we cannot reply to each of you individually, we are happy to make changes to address the most common -------(133.). The first of these was about our closing times. Many of you complained about our short weekend hours. -------(134.). We hope that you will enjoy these added hours. See you at the gym! Dennis Primus Manager, Better Me Gym	收件者：全體會員 <memberlist@bettermegym.com> 寄件者：丹尼斯・普里茅斯 <dprimus@bettermegym.com> 主旨：週末營業時間更新 日期：8月4日 各位會員： 感謝所有 131 **填寫**問卷調查，並與我們分享您對善我健身中心看法的會員。我們努力為客戶提供最現代化、最便利的健身場地，因此您的意見回饋對我們而言是非常 132 **寶貴的**。雖然我們無法逐一回覆每一位會員，但是我們很樂意針對最多人 133 **要求的事項**做出改變。其中第一項就是關於本中心的閉館時間。許多會員曾抱怨我們週末的營業時間太短。134 **為此，我們決定每週六營業至晚間九點**。希望各位好好享受這額外的運動時間。 我們健身中心見！ 丹尼斯・普里茅斯 善我健身中心 經理

字彙 **strive to V** 努力……

填入動詞＋過去式

131 (A) completing (B) completes (C) are completing **(D) completed**

中譯 (A) 填寫中 (B) 填寫 (C) 正在填寫 **(D) 填寫完了**

填入形容詞——副詞＋形容詞

132 (A) values (B) value **(C) valuable** (D) valuing

中譯 (A) 價值 (B) 價值 **(C) 寶貴的** (D) 價值

名詞 demand

133 **(A) demands** (B) schedules (C) routines (D) patrons

中譯 **(A) 要求事項** (B) 時間表 (C) 例行公事 (D) 客戶

選出合適的句子

134 (A) Unfortunately, we cannot extend our hours of operation.
(B) In response, we have decided to stay open until 9 P.M. on Saturdays.
(C) Members are free to work out as many hours as they wish.
(D) These are described in detail in your gym membership contract.

中譯 (A) 很遺憾，我們無法延長營業時間。
(B) 為此，我們決定每週六營業至晚間九點。
(C) 會員可隨心所欲，想運動多久就運動多久。
(D) 這些在健身中心的會員合約裡都有詳細說明。

Questions 135-138 refer to the following advertisement. 廣告

Secure your house with Houseguard! Our -------(135.) security system has all the latest features you need to feel safe and comfortable in your own home. We will set up security cameras, motion sensors, and an alarm system that will cover all areas of your property. -------(136.), we will equip your home with our smart control robot, which constantly monitors your appliances to eliminate any danger. -------(137.). For example, should you leave the gas on when you leave, it will -------(138.) turn it off for you, thus preventing a potential fire. Make your home safer today! Visit www.houseguard.com today to schedule an installation.

讓房屋衛士來保衛您的家！我們 ⓭⓹ **最先進的**保全系統有最新的功能，讓您在自己的家中感到安全、舒適。我們將設置監視器、動作感應器以及警報系統，無死角保衛您的房屋。⓭⓺ **此外**，我們還會為您的房屋配備智慧控制機器人，它會持續監控家中的電器，排除任何危險。⓭⓻ **房屋衛士機器人能守護您的房屋。**例如，假使您忘了關瓦斯便外出，機器人會 ⓭⓼ **自動**替您關閉瓦斯，從而預防發生火災的可能。今天就讓您的家更安全吧！現在就到本公司官網 www.houseguard.com 安排安裝的時間。

字彙 constantly 不斷地　eliminate 消除　potential 潛在的　installation 安裝

形容詞 state-of-the-art

135 (A) second-hand　(B) ill-equipped
(C) out-of-date　**(D) state-of-the-art**

中譯 (A) 二手的　(B) 設備不良的
(C) 過時的　**(D) 最先進的**

連接副詞 in addition

136 (A) Therefore　(B) Nonetheless
(C) In addition　(D) On the other hand

中譯 (A) 因此　(B) 然而
(C) 此外　(D) 另一方面

選出合適的句子

137 (A) Indeed, burglaries have been on the rise lately.
(B) The Houseguard robot could save your house.
(C) There are many control systems to choose from.
(D) You can now cook amazing meals from your own kitchen.

中譯 (A) 的確，近來入室盜竊的案件不斷增加。
(B) 房屋衛士機器人能守護您的房屋。
(C) 有許多控制系統可供您選擇。
(D) 您現在可以在家中廚房煮出豐盛的菜餚。

填入副詞——修飾動詞

138 (A) automatic (B) automates
(C) automation **(D) automatically**

中譯 (A) 自動的 (B) 使自動化
(C) 自動化 **(D) 自動地**

Questions 139-142 refer to the following letter. 信函

November 25	11 月 25 日
Eric Closter 2957 Marisol Avenue Willows, PA 18765	艾瑞克·克洛斯特 18765 賓夕凡尼亞州威洛斯市 瑪麗索路 2957 號
Dear Mr. Closter,	克洛斯特先生您好：
We are writing to inform you that the latest payment for your subscription to *Monthly Talks* was declined. Thus, we were unable to process the transaction. -------. (139.) If you cannot determine the cause of the error after ------- (140.) all of your information, contact your bank.	我們寫信通知您，您最近一次為訂閱《月度會談》所支付的款項被拒絕了。因此，我們無法進行該筆交易。139 **問題可能出自於地址變更或卡片到期**。如果您在 140 **核對**過全部的資訊後，仍無法查出錯誤的原因，請您與您的銀行聯繫。
Since your payment did not go through, we have ------- (141.) shipment of the latest issue to your address. In order to receive the December issue, you must ------- (142.) provide valid payment information as we will be sending out the last issues soon.	由於您的款項未完成支付，我們 141 **取消**寄送最新一期期刊到府上。如果您想順利收到 12 月號，請 142 **立即**提供有效的付款資訊，因最請確認是否指：本期刊物寄送作業即將結束。
If you have any questions about your *Monthly Talks* subscription, please call us at 555-3548.	若您對訂閱《月度會談》有任何疑問，請致電 555-3548 與我們聯繫。
Sincerely, The *Monthly Talks* Staff	《月度會談》員工 謹上

字彙 **subscription** 訂閱（費） **decline** 拒絕 **transaction** 交易 **valid** 有效的

選出合適的句子

139 (A) However, we do not have the correct credit card information.
(B) A cancelation fee of $12.99 will be deducted from your account.
(C) Attached is a form for renewing your subscription to our magazine.
(D) This problem may be due to an address change or card expiration.

中譯 (A) 然而，我們沒有正確的信用卡資訊。
(B) 您的帳戶將會被扣除 12.99 美元的取消費。
(C) 附件是續訂本雜誌的表單。
(D) 問題可能出自於地址變更或卡片到期。

填入名詞+動名詞 vs 名詞

140 **(A) verifying** (B) verification (C) verify (D) verified

中譯 (A) 核對 (B) 核對 **(C) 核對** (D) 已核對

動詞 cancel

141 (A) timed (B) refunded **(C) canceled** (D) measured

中譯 (A) 計時了 (B) 退款了 **(C) 取消了** (D) 測量了

副詞 promptly

142 (A) incorrectly (B) surely **(C) promptly** (D) temporarily

中譯 (A) 錯誤地 (B) 肯定地 **(C) 立即地** (D) 暫時地

Questions 143-146 refer to the following article. 文章

Local Companies Commit to Change

BETHOS (January 22)— -------(143.). According to this potential contract, Frester Corp., Alphet Inc., and Proga Corp. would commit to limiting their factories' energy consumption and emission levels. Such changes could cost each company a large amount of money by slowing their production rates. -------(144.), the directors agreed that focusing on environmentally friendly methods would be beneficial in the long run. "If all three companies -------(145.) to the agreement, then no one will lose too much, and the environment will gain," argued a director of Frester Corp. -------(146.) of the sixteen directors volunteered any details about the logistics of the plan, but they did confirm that an agreement was reached and will be made public soon.

本地企業致力於改革

貝托斯訊(1月22日)——143 **三家大企業的董事昨日開會討論一項協議**。根據這項潛在的協議，佛萊斯特公司、阿爾普特公司以及普羅加公司將致力於限制旗下工廠的能源消耗以及汙染排放。這些變革會減緩各家企業的生產速度，從而導致巨額的損失。144 **儘管如此**，董事們一致認為，從長遠來看，注重環保的生產方法是有益的。「如果三家企業都 145 **遵守**協議，那麼大家都不會蒙受太大的損失，而環境則會獲得改善。」佛萊斯特公司的某位管理高層表示。16位管理高層中，146 **無人**主動透露該計畫的後勤細節，但是他們證實已經達成協議，很快將會公布。

字彙 consumption 消耗量　emission 排放(物)　beneficial 有益的　in the long run 最終，終究　logistics 後勤，組織工作

選出合適的句子

143 (A) A recent study shows that pollution levels in Bethos are at an all-time high.
(B) Several local companies are currently seeking to hire entry-level workers.
(C) The directors of three large companies met yesterday to discuss an agreement.
(D) Solar energy is just one example of renewable energy that is easy to harvest.

中譯 (A) 最近一項研究顯示，貝托斯的汙染程度達到歷史新高。
(B) 目前有幾家本地企業正試圖招聘基層員工。
(C) 三家大企業的董事昨日開會討論一項協議。
(D) 太陽能只是其中一例可輕易開發的再生能源。

連接副詞 nevertheless

144 (A) Furthermore **(B) Nevertheless**
(C) Similarly (D) Otherwise

中譯 (A) 此外 **(B) 儘管如此**
(C) 同樣地 (D) 否則

片語動詞 adhere to

145 (A) propose (B) follow
(C) compare **(D) adhere**

中譯 (A) 建議 (B) 遵循
(C) 比較 **(D) 遵守**

不定代名詞 none

146 (A) Those (B) Any
(C) None (D) Neither

中譯 (A) 那些（人） (B) 任何一（人）
(C) 沒有任何（人） (D) 兩者都（不）

PART 7

Questions 147-148 refer to the following receipt. 收據

Tina's Treasures

Date: 11/15
Member number: 194538838

---

147 Silk Tie	**$22.99**
Leather belt	**$39.99**
Linen shirt	**$45.00**
Subtotal	$107.98
Tax (6%)	$6.48
Total	$114.46
Cash	$120.00
Change	-$5.54

---

148 Member points earned	**110**
Total member points	**1,005**

Congratulations! 148 **You have reached more than one thousand member points and have earned this coupon:**

Good for $5.00 at Tina's Treasures
Coupon Code: A2225SG56

Find us online at www.tinastreasures.com, where you can browse our merchandise, write product reviews, and place orders. You can also sign up for our newsletter to receive special promotions by e-mail.

蒂娜的珍寶

日期：11/15
會員編號：194538838

---

147 絲質領帶	22.99 美元
真皮皮帶	39.99 美元
亞麻襯衫	45.00 美元
小計	107.98 美元
稅金（6%）	6.48 美元
合計	114.46 美元
現金	120.00 美元
找零	-5.54 美元

---

148 獲得會員點數	110
會員點數合計	1,005

恭喜您！148 **您的會員點數已累積超過1000點，因此可獲得以下優惠券：**

5 美元優惠券，適用於蒂娜的珍寶
優惠碼：A2225SG56

您可上網至本公司網站 www.tinastreasures.com 瀏覽商品資訊、寫產品評論以及訂購商品。您亦可訂閱本公司的電子報，透過電子郵件接收特別促銷的通知。

字彙 subtotal 小計　good for 能提供……　place an order 下訂單　promotion 促銷

推論問題

147 What kind of store most likely is Tina's Treasures?
(A) A fabrics distributor
(B) A clothing outlet
(C) A hardware store
(D) A jewelry shop

中譯 「蒂娜的珍寶」最有可能是哪種類型的商店？
(A) 織物經銷商
(B) 服飾專賣店
(C) 五金行
(D) 珠寶店

確認特定資訊問題

148 According to the receipt, how did the buyer receive a coupon?
(A) By winning a contest
(B) By reviewing a product
(C) By being a loyal customer
(D) By subscribing to a newsletter

中譯 根據收據內容，消費者如何獲得優惠券？
(A) 在比賽中得獎
(B) 寫產品的評價
(C) 成為忠實顧客
(D) 訂閱電子報

Questions 149-150 refer to the following text-message chain. 簡訊串

Laura Fisher [6:58 P.M.] Thomas, are you still at the office by any chance?	**蘿拉・費雪** [下午 6:58] 托馬斯，你會不會剛好還在辦公室啊？
Thomas Volpert [6:59 P.M.] Yes, I'm still here, but I was just about to leave for Jarrod's retirement party.	**托馬斯・弗爾佩特** [下午 6:59] 對，我還在，但我正要離開去參加賈羅德的退休歡送會。
Laura Fisher [7:00 P.M.] 149 150 **I was supposed to bring Jarrod's gift to the restaurant,** but I just noticed that I left it at the office. 150 **I'm almost at the restaurant already.**	**蘿拉・費雪** [下午 7:00] 149 150 **我本來要帶賈羅德的禮物去餐廳**，但是我剛發現我把它忘在辦公室裡了。150 **我已經快到餐廳了。**
Thomas Volpert [7:01 P.M.] No problem. Just tell me where it is, and I'll bring it.	**托馬斯・弗爾佩特** [下午 7:01] 沒問題。跟我說在哪，我會帶過去。
Laura Fisher [7:02 P.M.] Oh, that's such a relief. 149 **You'll see a box under my desk.** It's blue and black. It has a label from Galinda's Collection Shop on it.	**蘿拉・費雪** [下午 7:02] 啊，這下我可以放心了。149 **你會在我的桌子下面看到一個盒子。**藍黑相間的，上面貼著葛琳達精品店的標籤。
Thomas Volpert [7:03 P.M.] 149 **Okay, hold on. Let me check.**	**托馬斯・弗爾佩特** [下午 7:03] 149 **好，等等，我看一下。**
Thomas Volpert [7:07 P.M.] Got it. The invitation says seven thirty, right? 150 **I'd better get going.**	**托馬斯・弗爾佩特** [下午 7:07] 找到了。邀請函上面寫的是 7 點 30 分，對吧？ 150 **我得走了。**
Laura Fisher [7:08 P.M.] Yes. Thank you so much! You're a lifesaver.	**蘿拉・費雪** [下午 7:08] 對。非常謝謝你！你真是我的救星。

字彙 **by any chance** 碰巧，剛好　**lifesaver** 救星

掌握意圖問題

149 At 7:07 p.m., what does Mr. Volpert mean when he writes, "Got it"?

(A) He found the present.
(B) He understands the directions.
(C) He received a party invitation.
(D) He has a gift receipt.

中譯 在下午 7:07 時，弗爾佩特先生說：「找到了」，他是什麼意思？

(A) 他找到禮物了。
(B) 他聽懂指示了。
(C) 他收到了歡送會的邀請函。
(D) 他有一張禮物的收據。

推論問題

150 Where is Mr. Volpert most likely going next?

(A) To the office
(B) To Ms. Fisher's home
(C) To a restaurant
(D) To a store

中譯 弗爾佩特先生接下來最有可能會做什麼？

(A) 去辦公室
(B) 去費雪女士的家
(C) 去餐廳
(D) 去商店

Questions 151-152 refer to the following e-mail. 電子郵件

E-mail

To: Sooyeon Baek <baeksooyeon@harligen.net>
From: Gerald Finn <finngerald@harligen.net>
Date: January 18
Subject: Urgent

Dear Ms. Baek,

I need your help. ⓯151 **The foreman at the 171 Dutton Street property** has informed me that his team has nearly run out of the gravel for the water barrier. They need more as soon as possible not to fall behind schedule. 151 **I'll be away from the office the rest of the day performing safety checks at our other sites,** so I can't take care of this myself. 152 **Would you please call the supplier and ask for more gravel to be delivered?** The type we're using is listed in the database under that property's name. It should be easy to find.

Thank you!

Gerald Finn

電子郵件

收件者：白秀妍 <baeksooyeon@harligen.net>
寄件者：傑拉爾德・芬恩 <finngerald@harligen.net>
日期：1 月 18 日
主旨：緊急

親愛的白小姐：

我需要妳的協助。151 **達頓街 171 號建案現場的工頭**剛通知我，他們用來做防水層的砂石快要用完了。他們需要更多砂石，越快越好，以免工程的進度落後。151 **我今天接下來的時間都不在公司，要去別的工地進行安全檢查**，所以沒辦法親自處理這個問題。152 **可以麻煩妳打給供應商，請他們送更多砂石嗎？**我們目前使用的砂石種類就列在以該建案名稱命名的資料庫裡，應該很容易找到。

謝謝妳！

傑拉爾德・芬恩

字彙 **foreman** 工頭 **gravel** 砂礫 **water barrier** 防水層 **site** （建築的）工地

推論問題

151 For what kind of business does Mr. Finn most likely work?
(A) A construction company
(B) A manufacturing facility
(C) A hardware store
(D) A real estate firm

中譯 芬恩先生最有可能在什麼樣的公司工作？
(A) 建設公司
(B) 製造廠
(C) 五金行
(D) 房地產公司

尋找特定資訊問題

152 What is Ms. Baek asked to do?
(A) Meet a potential customer
(B) Place an order
(C) Update a database
(D) Pick up a delivery

中譯 白小姐被要求做什麼？
(A) 跟潛在客戶會面
(B) 下訂單
(C) 更新資料庫
(D) 取回包裹

Questions 153-154 refer to the following Web page. 網頁

https://www.tothecloudsclimbing.com/about

HOME	ABOUT	PRODUCTS	PARTNERSHIPS	CONTACT

153 **To the Clouds was established over fifteen years ago and has continuously strived to create the most innovative climbing gear and apparel around. Contact us today to become an official To the Clouds distributor.** 154C **We are one of the top-selling brands on the market, and you will want to have our products in your store to attract the climbing community.** By selling To the Clouds equipment, you will gain a reputation as a trustworthy store that sells excellent gear and apparel. Moreover, 154A **all of our products come with lifetime warranties to reassure customers that they are buying superior equipment.** And we supply high-quality posters, banners, and leaflets. 154D **Our merchandise is thus simple to market** and always sells out quickly.

https://www.tothecloudsclimbing.com/about

首頁	公司簡介	產品	合作夥伴	與我們聯繫

153 **「直上雲霄」成立逾15年，向來為製造最新穎的登山裝備與服飾而努力不懈。今天就與我們聯繫，成為本公司的官方經銷商吧。** 154C **我們是市面上最暢銷的品牌之一，您會希望在店裡販售我們的產品，以招徠熱愛登山的群體。**透過販售直上雲霄的裝備與服飾品，您將為自家商店贏得提供優質裝備與服裝的信譽。此外，154A **本公司產品皆提供終生保固，讓顧客放心，他們購買的是上等的裝備。**我們還會提供高品質的海報、橫幅及傳單。154D **我們的產品易於行銷，**而且總是很快就銷售一空。

字彙 **gear** 裝備 **apparel** （某一類的）服裝 **distributor** 經銷商 **reputation** 名聲 **warranty** 保證（書） **reassure** 使安心 **superior** 優越的 **leaflet** 傳單

確認特定資訊問題

153 Who should contact To the Clouds?
(A) Sporting goods retailers
(B) Professional athletes
(C) Climbing club leaders
(D) Equipment manufacturers

中譯 誰應該聯繫「直上雲霄」？
(A) 體育用品零售商
(B) 職業運動員
(C) 登山社社長
(D) 裝備製造業者

Not / True 問題

154 What is NOT mentioned about To the Clouds products?

(A) Their warranty doesn't expire.
(B) They are sold at affordable prices.
(C) They are popular among climbers.
(D) They are easy to advertise.

中譯 關於直上「直上雲霄」的產品，文中並未提到什麼？
(A) 永久保固。
(B) 價格便宜。
(C) 深受登山客喜愛。
(D) 容易宣傳。

Questions 155-157 refer to the following notice. 公告

Employee Notice: Annual Juny Fundraising Gala

The annual fundraising gala for Juny Children's Organization will be held at the Sarcona Convention Center on Sunday, April 30, from 6 P.M. to 8:30 P.M. Attendance for Dream Voyages employees is optional but strongly encouraged. As usual, our company will be sponsoring the event. ⑮ **However, instead of donating money as we have every other year, we are donating prizes for the raffle.** For those of you who have not been to this event before, please note the dress code.

Dress code
Men do not need to wear tuxedos but must wear dark-colored suits, with a white shirt and solid-color tie. Please avoid loud prints and patterns.

Acceptable attire for women includes long gowns and pantsuits. ⑯ **Please do not wear short-cut dresses.** If you decide to wear high heels, make sure you can comfortably stand in the shoes for a long period of time.

Prize donations
Dream Voyages will be donating one all-inclusive tour package to Europe, three vacation packages to resorts in Mexico, and ten weekend spa packages. ⑰ **Please note that anyone affiliated with Dream Voyages is not eligible to win any of these prizes.**

員工公告：朱尼年度募款晚會

朱尼兒童組織的年度募款晚會，將於 4 月 30 日星期日晚上 6 點至 8 點 30 分，於薩科納會議中心舉行。夢想旅程的員工可自由參加，但我們極力鼓勵各位參加。一如往常，公司將贊助此活動。⑮ **然而，今年將不會像以前那樣每兩年捐款一次，而是會捐出慈善抽獎活動的獎品。**未曾參加過本活動的員工，請注意服裝規定。

服裝規定
男士們不需穿燕尾服，但是必須穿深色西裝，搭配白色襯衫跟單色領帶。請避免過於招搖的印花及圖案。

女士們允許的服裝包括長禮服與褲裝。⑯ **請勿穿著短禮服。**若您要穿高跟鞋，請確保穿一雙長時間站著也很舒適的鞋。

獎品捐贈
夢想旅程將捐出費用全包的歐洲套裝行程一份、墨西哥休閒度假村的套裝行程三份，以及週末的溫泉 SPA 套裝行程十份。⑰ **請注意，所有夢想旅程關係人員皆無無法參加抽獎。**

字彙 fundraising 募款 gala 盛會，慶典 sponsor 贊助 raffle 慈善抽獎活動 loud 花俏的 attire (正式的)服裝 all-inclusive 全部包括的 affiliate with 與……相關的

確認特定資訊問題

155 What has Dream Voyages changed?

(A) Its dress code for employees
(B) Its contribution to the organization
(C) Its policy on attendance to the event
(D) Its type of rewards for customers

中譯 夢想旅程改變了什麼？
(A) 員工的服裝規定
(B) 給團體組織的捐贈
(C) 出席活動的規定
(D) 給客戶的獎品類型

Not / True 問題

156 What are women NOT allowed to wear?
(A) Dark-colored dresses
(B) High-heel shoes
(C) Long pants
(D) Short skirts

中譯 女士們不允許穿什麼？
(A) 深色禮服
(B) 高跟鞋
(C) 長褲
(D) 短裙

推論問題

157 What is suggested about the prizes donated by Dream Voyages?
(A) They may not be won by Dream Voyages employees.
(B) They do not include expenses related to plane tickets.
(C) They will be awarded to the best-performing workers.
(D) They are the most expensive gifts at the fundraiser.

中譯 關於夢想旅程捐贈的獎品，文中暗示了什麼？
(A) 夢想旅程的員工不能獲獎。
(B) 不包括機票相關費用。
(C) 將頒發給績效最好的員工。
(D) 是募款活動中最昂貴的獎項。

Questions 158-160 refer to the following e-mail. 電子郵件

To: Garfield, Anna
<annagarfield76@peoplesnet.com>
From: Customer Service
<cs@featherflights.com>
Date: July 12
Subject: Flight reservation – Action needed

Dear Anna Garfield,

158 **We are writing to inform you that payment for your flight to Los Angeles has not been processed. Please make a payment through our Web site in the amount of $636.88.** — [1] —. Your reservation will not be complete until this amount has been received. 158 159 **If payment is not submitted within twenty-four hours after the request was made, the seats will be forfeited.** — [2] —.

For your reference, you have requested two seats for a round-trip flight to Los Angeles departing from Austin on Saturday, August 7, at 3:20 P.M. and returning on Sunday, August 29, at 10:10 A.M. — [3] —.

收件人：安娜・加菲爾
<annagarfield76@peoplesnet.com>
寄件人：客戶服務部
<cs@featherflights.com>
日期：7 月 12 日
主旨：機票預訂——須採取行動

安娜・加菲爾您好：

158 **謹以此信通知您，您預訂飛往洛杉磯的航班費用尚未處理。請您至本公司官網支付總額 636.88 美元的款項。**在本公司收到這筆款項前，您的訂位程序仍未完成。158 159 **若您未能於訂位後 24 小時內付款，您的機位將會被取消。**如此一來，您將必須重新開始訂票的流程。

以下資訊供您參考，您預訂了 8 月 7 日星期六下午 3 點 20 分，從奧斯汀飛往洛杉磯的來回機票兩張，並於 8 月 29 日星期日上午 10 點 10 分返回。

⑯ **Please note that the price you were originally quoted for the tickets may no longer be available after today.** This is why we urge you to complete the reservation as soon as possible. If you require assistance, you may call our customer service line at 555-293-5892 between 9 A.M. and 5 P.M. on weekdays. — [4] —.

Thank you for choosing with Feather Flights. We look forward to serving you.

Regards,

The Feather Flights Customer Service Team

⑯ **請知悉，當初訂位的票價可能於今日後失效。**這就是為什麼我們籲請您儘速完成付款。若您需要協助，請於平日上午 9 時至下午 5 時撥打本公司的客服專線 555-293-5892。

感謝您選擇羽鴻航空，我們期待為您服務。

羽鴻航空客服部 敬上

字彙 forfeit 失去　reference 參考　quote 報價　urge 敦促

目的問題

158 What is the purpose of the e-mail?
(A) To confirm a reservation
(B) To explain a flight change
(C) To acknowledge a cancelation
(D) To notify a customer of a due payment

中譯 這封電子郵件的目的為何？
(A) 確認訂位
(B) 解釋航班異動
(C) 確認取消訂位
(D) 告知顧客有應付款項

尋找特定資訊問題

159 In which of the positions marked [1], [2], [3], and [4] does the following sentence best belong?
"Thus, you will have to start the reservation process again."
(A) [1]　**(B) [2]**
(C) [3]　(D) [4]

中譯 下列句子最適合放在 [1]、[2]、[3] 和 [4] 的哪個位置？
「如此一來，您將必須重新開始訂票的流程。」
(A) [1]　**(B) [2]**
(C) [3]　(D) [4]

Not / True 問題

160 What is indicated about the ticket price?
(A) It might change in the future.
(B) It is temporarily discounted.
(C) It includes only one way.
(D) It is payable only by phone.

中譯 關於機票價格，文中指出了什麼？
(A) 今後可能會變動。
(B) 暫時有打折。
(C) 只含單程。
(D) 只能通過電話付款。

Questions 161-164 refer to the following article. 文章

January 30— ⓰⓱ **After an unprecedented successful fourth quarter, it was rumored that Habbart Corp. would be giving large year-end bonuses to all of its employees.** — [1] —. 161 164 **Habbart Corp. spokesperson Mr. Bryan Caster announced that the company would instead be making a large donation to Enviro First, an environmental foundation.**

The revelation came as a surprise, as Habbart Corp. has a reputation for ignoring environmental issues. — [2] —. Controversy was especially intense after one of Habbart's plants had a small explosion that caused a chemical leak, contaminating a nearby river. 163 **Although the leak was quickly contained, local residents took to the streets to protest, denouncing the company's lack of care for ecological concerns.** — [3] —.

Yet Habbart Corp.'s latest decision seems to contradict those claims. Mr. Caster emphasized that the company took matters related to sustainable production very seriously. "We want to support and work in collaboration with organizations that fight to protect the environment," Mr. Caster declared. — [4] —. The total amount of the donation has not been revealed, but it is expected to be the largest one Enviro First has yet received. Mr. Caster insisted that all of Habbart Corp.'s extra profits would go to the organization.

1月30日——162 164 **哈伯特公司第四季的營收創下歷史新高後，便有傳聞說該公司將會發放豐厚的年終獎金給全體員工。**然而，該公司在昨日舉行的記者會上否認了此事。161 164 **哈伯特公司的發言人布萊恩・卡斯特宣布，該公司將捐贈一大筆錢給一家名為「環境至上」的環保基金會。**

此消息一出，眾人都感到非常訝異，因為哈伯特公司素來有忽視環境問題的惡名。尤其在哈伯特旗下的一間工廠因發生小爆炸，導致化學物質外洩，汙染了附近的河川之後，爭議格外激烈。163 **雖然外洩事件很快就獲得控制，但是當地的居民還是走上街頭抗議，譴責該公司對生態問題漠不關心。**

然而，哈伯特公司最近做出的這項決定似乎與這些說法相矛盾。卡斯特先生強調該公司非常重視與永續生產相關的事務。「我們想要支持那些為保護環境而奮鬥的團體，並且希望與之合作」，卡斯特先生明確表示。雖然該公司尚未公布捐款總額，但是預計將會是「環境至上」迄今收到的最大一筆捐款。卡斯特先生堅稱，哈伯特公司多的利潤都將捐給該團體。

字彙 unprecedented 前所未有的 revelation 暴露 controversy 爭議 contaminate 汙染 contain 阻止 denounce 譴責 ecological 生態的 contradict 發生矛盾 sustainable 永續的

目的問題

161 What is the purpose of the article?
(A) To criticize a corporation's approach to environmental issues
(B) To advocate stronger measures against natural disasters
(C) To announce a company's contribution to a nonprofit
(D) To report an accident that happened at a local factory

中譯 這篇文章的目的為何？
(A) 批評某公司對環境問題的做法
(B) 提倡採取更有力的措施來應對天災
(C) 公布某家公司對非營利組織的捐款
(D) 報導當地某家工廠發生的事故

Not / True 問題

162 What is indicated about Habbart Corp.?
(A) It is known for its environment-friendly methods.
(B) It will be giving extra compensation to its employees.
(C) It had an exceptionally profitable fourth quarter.
(D) It is planning on building a new plant near a river.

中譯 關於哈伯特公司，文中提到了什麼？
(A) 以採取環保的生產方式而聞名。
(B) 將發給員工額外的薪資報酬。
(C) 第四季的利潤特別高。
(D) 計畫在河川附近建造新的工廠。

確認特定資訊問題

163 According to the article, what caused people to protest against Habbart Corp.?
(A) Its neglect of the environment
(B) Its employee benefits packages
(C) Its frequent explosion accidents
(D) Its small charitable donations

中譯 根據文章，人們為何對哈伯特公司提出抗議？
(A) 對環境的忽視
(B) 員工的福利制度
(C) 頻繁發生爆炸事故
(D) 小額慈善捐款

尋找句子位置問題

164 In which of the positions marked [1], [2], [3], and [4] does the following sentence best belong?
"However, this was denied at a press conference held yesterday."
(A) [1] (B) [2]
(C) [3] (D) [4]

中譯 下列句子最適合放在 [1]、[2]、[3] 和 [4] 的哪個位置？
「然而，該公司在昨日舉行的記者會上否認了此事。」
(A) [1] (B) [2]
(C) [3] (D) [4]

Questions 165-167 refer to the following advertisement. 廣告

⑯⑤ **Boca Chocolates is seventy-five years old, and to celebrate, the factory will be opening its doors to the public for one week, from May 6 to May 12.** This is your chance to visit the premises and find out how Boca Chocolates makes its delicious sweets!

⑯⑤ **First, you will take a guided tour that will show you every step of the process from the bean to the box.** You will see our workers operating the machinery, and our chocolate artists decorating the final products.

After you learn all about how chocolate is made, you can taste special samples of upcoming products, enjoy our magical chocolate fountain, and purchase gift baskets at a discount. In addition, ⑯⑥ **every visitor will go home with a box of chocolates as a gift.**

For security purposes, ⑯⑦ **the number of visitors is limited, so make your reservation early!** Tours are $45 for adults, $30 for students, and $20 for children under twelve. ⑯⑦ **Call 555-9963 to schedule a time.**

⑯⑤ **博卡巧克力 75 歲了，為慶祝成立 75 週年，其工廠將於 5 月 6 日至 5 月 12 日對外開放一週。**這是大家參觀工廠的好機會，可以了解我們是如何製作出美味的巧克力！

⑯⑤ **首先，大家會在導覽員的帶領下，看到巧克力從可可果實到包裝成盒的每一個製程。**您會看到我們的員工操作機器，以及我們的巧克力設計師如何裝飾成品。

等你們了解了巧克力所有製程後，就可以試吃我們即將推出的新品，盡情享受我們神奇的巧克力噴泉，還能以優惠價格購買巧克力禮盒。此外，⑯⑥ **每位參觀者還可帶一盒巧克力回家。**

為了安全考量，⑯⑦ **參觀的人數有限，所以請儘早預約！**成人的參觀費用為 45 美元，學生 30 美元，未滿 12 歲孩童 20 美元。⑯⑦ **請致電 555-9963 安排參觀時間。**

字彙 premises （複數）廠區

主題問題

165 What is being advertised?
(A) A new kind of chocolate
(B) A special anniversary tour
(C) A sales event at a grocery store
(D) An innovative candy-making machine

中譯 這是什麼的廣告？
(A) 新種類的巧克力
(B) 週年紀念的特別導覽
(C) 雜貨店的促銷活動
(D) 創新的糖果製造機

確認特定資訊問題

166 What will be given out for free?
(A) Gift baskets (B) Fountains
(C) Decorations **(D) Boxes of sweets**

中譯 遊客將免費獲贈什麼？
(A) 禮品籃 (B) 噴泉
(C) 裝飾品 **(D) 盒裝巧克力**

確認特定資訊問題

167 What are readers encouraged to do?
(A) Reserve a time slot
(B) Place an order
(C) Taste a product
(D) Try a piece of equipment

中譯 文中鼓勵看到廣告的人做什麼？
(A) 預約時段
(B) 下訂單
(C) 品嘗產品
(D) 試用一件設備

Questions 168-171 refer to the following online chat discussion. 線上聊天

Selam Habte [4:26 P.M.] 168 **I know you two had to miss my announcements at the end of the weekly staff meeting,** so I wanted to fill you in.	瑟拉姆・哈布 [下午 4:26] 168 **我知道你們兩個錯過了我在每週員工會議結束時的通知**，所以我想給你們補充說明一下情況。
Anna Morgan [4:28 P.M.] Thanks. 168 **What did we miss?**	安娜・摩根 [下午 4:28] 謝謝。168 **我們錯過了什麼？**
Selam Habte [4:29 P.M.] 168 **Our company is going to release a new long-lasting lipstick.**	瑟拉姆・哈布 [下午 4:29] 168 **我們公司即將推出一款長效型的新口紅。**
Kikuyo Tsuruta [4:30 P.M.] That's great news. 169 **I'm glad the R&D department took my advice about adding another product to the line.**	鶴田菊陽 [下午 4:30] 這真是好消息。169 **我很高興研發部採納了我的建議，在產品線中新增了另一款產品。**
Anna Morgan [4:31 P.M.] When will we start advertising the new lipstick?	安娜・摩根 [下午 4:31] 我們何時開始宣傳新口紅？
Selam Habte [4:32 P.M.] Mr. Catteneo is putting together a marketing plan now.	瑟拉姆・哈布 [下午 4:32] 卡特尼奧先生現在正在制定行銷計畫。
Kikuyo Tsuruta [4:34 P.M.] 170 **Wouldn't this be a better job for a senior marketing executive?**	鶴田菊陽 [下午 4:34] 170 **這件事不是應該由資深行銷經理來負責嗎？**
Anna Morgan [4:35 P.M.] 170 **Yeah. Mr. Catteneo is new to our company and doesn't know much about our products.**	安娜・摩根 [下午 4:35] 170 **是啊，卡特尼奧先生才剛進公司沒多久，對我們的產品還不太熟悉。**
Selam Habte [4:39 P.M.] I realize that, 170 **but he has a marketing background in cosmetics.**	瑟拉姆・哈布 [下午 4:39] 我知道，170 **但是他有行銷化妝品的經驗。**
Anna Morgan [4:41 P.M.] I see. Well, it wouldn't hurt for him to see some of our previous work. 171 **I could send him a portfolio of previous projects.**	安娜・摩根 [下午 4:41] 我明白了。好吧，不妨讓他看看我們之前的作品。171 **我可以把過往專案的作品集寄給他。**

Kikuyo Tsuruta [4:42 P.M.]
And I'd be happy to review his work.

Selam Habte [4:43 P.M.]
I don't think that'll be necessary, Kikuyo, but ⑰ **I like your idea, Anna.**

Anna Morgan [4:44 P.M.]
⑰ **Okay. I'll do that now.**

鶴田菊陽 [下午 4:42]
我很樂意審查他的工作成果。

瑟拉姆・哈布 [下午 4:43]
菊陽，我覺得沒有這個必要，但是 ⑰ **我喜歡妳的辦法，安娜。**

安娜・摩根 [下午 4:44]
⑰ **那好，我現在就去做。**

字彙 fill . . . in 向……提供詳情　long-lasting 持久的　put together 擬定　executive 主管
have a background in 在……有專業背景

主題問題

168 What is mainly being discussed?
(A) A policy update
(B) A new client
(C) A schedule change
(D) A product launch

中譯 文中主要在討論什麼？
(A) 政策更新
(B) 新客戶
(C) 日程異動
(D) 產品上市

推論問題

169 What is implied about Ms. Tsuruta?
(A) She thinks the company needs to control spending.
(B) She made a suggestion about the company's goods.
(C) She asked Mr. Habte for some advice.
(D) She developed a new line of cosmetics.

中譯 關於鶴田小姐，文中暗示了什麼？
(A) 她認為公司需要控制開支。
(B) 她對公司的商品提出建議。
(C) 她向哈布先生請教一些問題。
(D) 她開發了新系列的化妝品。

掌握意圖問題

170 At 4:41 p.m., what does Ms. Morgan most likely mean when she writes, "I see"?
(A) Mr. Catteneo is too busy to work on a project.
(B) Mr. Catteneo cannot help Ms. Morgan with a problem.
(C) Mr. Catteneo has already reviewed a portfolio.
(D) Mr. Catteneo may be qualified for a task.

中譯 在下午 4:41 時，摩根小姐說：「我明白了」，最有可能是什麼意思？
(A) 卡特尼奧先生太忙了，沒時間做專案。
(B) 卡特尼奧先生沒辦法幫摩根小姐解決問題。
(C) 卡特尼奧先生已經檢查過作品集了。
(D) 卡特尼奧先生也許能勝任這項任務。

接下來要做的事問題

171 What will Ms. Morgan most likely do next?
(A) Review documents prepared by Mr. Catteneo
(B) Send information about previous projects
(C) Set up a meeting with Mr. Catteneo
(D) Recommend a new marketing director

中譯 摩根小姐接下來最有可能做什麼？
(A) 檢查卡特尼奧先生準備的文件
(B) 將之前專案的資料寄出
(C) 安排跟卡特尼奧先生開會
(D) 推薦新的行銷總監

Questions 172-175 refer to the following e-mail. 電子郵件

To: Katrina Simon <ksimon@presslerlibrary.org>
From: Nora Yales <nyales@presslerlibrary.org>
Date: November 30
Subject: Opening tomorrow

Dear Ms. Simon,

173 **I was told that you were willing to open the library in my place tomorrow morning and work my shift.** 172 **I wanted to send you a quick reminder to help you out with the opening procedure.** 173 **It's been a while since you last did this,** and there are several steps, so I thought it would be helpful.

174A **First, I wanted to make sure you know the code to disarm the alarm: 0358.** 174C **Remember to pick up the mail, including the newspapers. You can leave the mail on my desk.** Stamp the newspapers with the library stamp, and display them on the news shelf in the journals section. Make sure you take off yesterday's papers and classify them with the other past newspapers.

174D **The key to the cash register is in the top drawer of my desk. Double check that there is $48 in it to start the day.**

174B **After you turn on the lights on every floor, you should be ready to unlock the front doors.** The keys for that are in the key cabinet in my office.

The weather forecast says there will be a huge snowstorm, and since I live far away, I'd rather not drive in that weather, 175 **so I'm taking the whole day off and not leaving the house.** But if you run into any trouble or have any questions, feel free to call me. I will also be available to chat online if you need my advice.

I am very thankful that you live close enough to be able to walk to the library. Thank you for being willing to do this.

Good luck!

Nora Yales
Library Assistant

收件者：卡特麗娜・西蒙
<ksimon@presslerlibrary.org>
寄件者：諾拉・亞勒斯
<nyales@presslerlibrary.org>
日期：11 月 30 日
主旨：明天開館

親愛的西蒙小姐：

173 **我聽說妳願意明天早上替我去圖書館開館，並且值我的班。** 172 **我想給妳發個簡單的提醒信，協助你完成明天的開館程序。** 173 **因為距離妳上次開館已經有一段時間了，**而且有好幾個步驟，所以我想這會對妳有幫助。

174A **首先，我想要確認妳知道解除警報的密碼是 0358。** 174C **要記得拿郵件和報紙。妳可以把郵件放到我的桌子上。**先在報紙上蓋圖書館的章，然後拿去期刊區報紙架上陳列。務必把昨天的報紙取下，跟其他過期的報紙分類收好。

174D **收銀機的鑰匙在我桌子最上層的抽屜裡。請再次確認裡面是否有 48 美元的準備金，以便開始今天的工作。**

174B **把每一層樓的燈都打開後，就可以準備開正門。**大門的鑰匙就放在我辦公室的鑰匙保管櫃裡。

天氣預報說會有大規模的暴風雪，因為我住得很遠，我不想在這種天氣開車，175 **所以我會請整天的假，待在家裡不出門。**但是如果妳遇到什麼麻煩或有問題，隨時都可以打電話給我。如果妳需要任何建議，我也可以在線上聊天。

我很慶幸，妳住得夠近，可以走路去圖書館。謝謝妳願意幫這個忙。
祝好運！

諾拉・亞勒斯
圖書館助理

字彙 disarm 解除　journal 期刊，雜誌　classify 分類

目的問題

172 What is the purpose of the e-mail?
(A) To warn of weather conditions
(B) To recommend a schedule change
(C) To offer a position
(D) To outline a procedure

中譯 這封電子郵件的目的為何？
(A) 警告天氣情況
(B) 建議變更日程
(C) 提供一份工作
(D) 說明程序概要

推論問題

173 What is suggested about Ms. Simon?
(A) She has opened the library before.
(B) She will drive to work tomorrow.
(C) She reads the newspaper every day.
(D) She usually closes the library.

中譯 關於西蒙小姐的敘述，何者正確？
(A) 她曾為圖書館開館。
(B) 她明天會開車上班。
(C) 她每天都會看報紙。
(D) 她經常關閉圖書館。

Not / True 問題

174 What is NOT something Ms. Simon is expected to do?
(A) Disable a security system
(B) Open the front doors
(C) Read the mail
(D) Count money

中譯 下列何者不是西蒙小姐應該做的事？
(A) 解除安全系統
(B) 打開大門
(C) 看郵件
(D) 數錢

接下來要做的事問題

175 What will Ms. Yales do tomorrow?
(A) Retire from her job
(B) Drive Ms. Simon to work
(C) Stay home for the day
(D) Handle customer questions

中譯 亞勒斯小姐明天會做什麼？
(A) 辭去自己的職務
(B) 開車載西蒙小姐去上班
(C) 整天待在家裡
(D) 處理客戶提出的問題

Questions 176-180 refer to the following e-mail and voucher. 電子郵件和優惠券

To: Cage, Peter <pcage@jaysmail.net>
From: Topher, Edward <etopher@sapphireflowers.com>
Date: May 8
Subject: Free Voucher

Dear Mr. Cage,

176 177 **We are very sorry for the late delivery of your floral arrangement on May 5.** We understand that because of this delay, the celebration of your daughter's acceptance into Boston University was not as special as it could have been.

收件者：彼得・凱吉 <pcage@jaysmail.net>
寄件者：愛德華・托弗 <etopher@sapphireflowers.com>
日期：5月8日
主旨：免費優惠券

凱吉先生您好：

176 177 **對於您安排的花束在5月5日延誤送達一事，我們感到非常抱歉。**我們明白，因為花束延誤送達，令千金錄取波士頓大學的慶祝派對，便沒有如預期那樣特別。

⑰ **Unfortunately, we ran out of roses on that day and had failed to set some aside for your afternoon delivery. We placed another order, but since our supplier is located in Stratton, it took time to get the flowers.** We are in the process of switching to a more modern inventory management program, and we can ⑱ **assure** you that this kind of mistake will not happen again. We hope that you will continue to choose Sapphire Flowers for your future special occasions.

To express our regret, 180-1 **we are offering you a voucher for a complimentary bouquet of your choice to be delivered at any address in the area.** You will find it attached to this e-mail. Please print it and fill it out when you wish to order a delivery.

Sincerely,

Edward Topher
Sapphire Flowers

⑰ 遺憾的是，那天所有的玫瑰花都用完了，而我們又沒能為您預留下午要送的玫瑰。我們另外下了一筆訂單，但是由於我們的供應商位於斯特拉頓，需要些時間才能拿到花。本店正在轉換到更現代化的庫存管理程序，我們可以向您 ⑱ 保證不會再發生這樣的錯誤。我們希望您在今後的特殊場合繼續選擇青玉花卉。

為表歉意，180-1 **我們提供您一張免費花束券，您可以選擇送到本地的任何一個地址。**提貨券就在這封電子郵件的附件中。請您於訂購花束時，列印出來填寫。

愛德華・托弗 謹啟
青玉花卉

字彙 voucher 優惠券　floral arrangement 花束設計　inventory 庫存，存貨　assure 向……保證　occasion 特殊場合　complimentary 免費贈送的

~ Sapphire Flowers ~

Voucher Code: XS564813

180-2 **Good for one floral arrangement and its delivery within Jayville.**

Choose from the following selection:

☐ Classic Roses　■ Blue Bunch
☐ Dream Bouquet　☐ Spring Special

Delivery date: Monday, May 18
Delivery time: 10 A.M.
Address: ⑲ Janice Richards
Frontier Corp. finance department
514 Enterprise Drive

Message(Optional):
⑲ Dear Janice,

I am sad to see you go. ⑲ It was great working with you all these years. I hope you enjoy your new job in Bendertown!

Regards,
Peter Cage

青玉花卉

提貨券編號：XS564813

180-2 可兌換一組花束且於捷維爾市範圍內配送。

請在下列選項中勾選：

☐ 古典玫瑰　■ 藍色花束
☐ 夢幻捧花　☐ 春季特惠

送達日期：5 月 18 日星期一
送達時間：上午 10 點
地址：⑲ **珍妮絲・理查茲**
邊疆公司財務部
企業路 514 號

留言（非必須）：

⑲ **親愛的珍妮絲：**

很遺憾妳要離職了。⑲ **這些年與妳共事的日子很愉快。**希望妳喜歡本德鎮的新工作！

彼得・凱吉 謹啟

目的問題

176 What is the purpose of the e-mail?
(A) To notify of a delay
(B) To offer an apology
(C) To report a system error
(D) To congratulate a coworker

中譯 這封電子郵件的目的為何？
(A) 通知延遲到貨
(B) 表示歉意
(C) 通報系統錯誤
(D) 向同事道賀

確認特定資訊問題

177 What does Mr. Topher indicate happened on May 5?
(A) His store's inventory was mismanaged.
(B) His daughter was accepted into college.
(C) His supplier was replaced.
(D) His flowers were all delivered late.

中譯 托弗先生提到5月5日發生了什麼事？
(A) 他的店庫存管理不當。
(B) 他的女兒被大學錄取了。
(C) 他換了供應商。
(D) 他的花全都延誤送達。

同義詞問題

178 In the e-mail, the word "assure" in paragraph 2, line 4, is closest in meaning to
(A) convince (B) remind
(C) guarantee (D) compensate

中譯 在電子郵件中，第2段第4行的「assure」一字，意思最接近下列何者？
(A) 說服 (B) 提醒
(C) 保證 (D) 補償

推論問題

179 Who most likely is Janice Richards?
(A) Mr. Cage's colleague
(B) Mr. Topher's supervisor
(C) Mr. Cage's customer
(D) Mr. Topher's supplier

中譯 珍妮絲・理查茲最有可能的身分是？
(A) 凱吉先生的同事
(B) 托弗先生的主管
(C) 凱吉先生的客戶
(D) 托弗先生的供應商

兩則引文連結問題＿推論問題

180 Where most likely is Mr. Topher's store located?
(A) Boston (B) Stratton
(C) Jayville (D) Bendertown

中譯 托弗先生的花店最有可能位於何處？
(A) 波士頓 (B) 斯特拉頓
(C) 捷維爾 (D) 本德鎮

Questions 181-185 refer to the following letter and e-mail. 信函與電子郵件

July 31

Jerome Madison
2675 Chenoweth Drive
Nashville, TN 37214

Dear Mr. Madison,

I heard that you are searching for a new assistant manager for the marketing team. As you know, I have

7月31日

傑洛姆・麥迪遜
37214 田納西州納什維爾市
切諾威斯路 2675 號

麥迪遜先生您好：

聽說您正在為行銷部找新的副理。如您所知，我在伽馬汽車公司擔任了11年的設計部經

been the manager of Gamma Motors' design team for eleven years. 181 185-1 **Ms. Skye Armand started working on my team six years ago and has proven to be a strong asset.** 181 **She has informed me of her intention to apply for the position of assistant manager with the marketing team, and I offered to write a reference letter.**

I believe that Ms. Armand's transfer could be beneficial to the company. Her understanding of design strategies and how to appeal to customers is evident in her work, and this talent would be of high value in the marketing team. Moreover, her experience within Gamma Motors and her 182 **intimate** knowledge of its various models would contribute greatly to creating effective marketing campaigns. 184-2 **I know that you will soon be focusing on preparing for the launch of the new Gamma SUV 6.** 185-1 **Ms. Armand has been involved in several aspects of the vehicle's design, and I think she will have some great ideas about how to present it in its best light.**

If you have any questions about Ms. Armand's work, feel free to contact me.

Sincerely,

Melanie Yoder

Melanie Yoder, Design Manager

理。181 185-1 **斯凱・阿曼德女士於六年前加入設計部，並且證明自己是本部的強大資產。** 181 **她已經通知我，打算申請行銷部副理的職位，我便主動提出為她寫推薦信。**

我認為阿曼德女士的調職對公司有利。她對設計策略與吸引客戶方面的理解在她的工作過程中顯而易見，而這種才能在行銷部具有很高的價值。此外，她在伽馬汽車的經驗，以及她對各種車型的 182 **全盤**瞭解，對企劃有效的行銷活動大有助益。184-2 **我知道你們很快就會開始為新款伽馬 SUV 6 的推出做準備。** 185-1 **阿曼德女士參與了新車設計的許多層面，對於要如何盡顯新車的優勢，我認為她會有一些很棒的看法。**

若您對阿曼德女士的工作有任何疑問，請隨時與我聯繫。

梅蘭妮・約德
設計部經理

字彙 asset 資產　intention 意圖　evident 顯而易見的　intimate 精通的　aspect 方面

To: 185-2 **Marketing employees**
<marketingteam@gammamotors.com>
From: Jerome Madison
<jmadison@gammamotors.com>
Date: September 2
Subject: Marketing Campaign

184-1 **The campaign for our newest model has proven highly successful.** 183 **Our teaser video has been shared all over social media and has reached millions of views.** A reporter for a popular car magazine has even asked to interview one of our managers.

184-1 **Congratulations to everyone,** 185-2 **but especially to Ms. Armand. This was her first campaign, and we were able to come up with the best features to**

185-2 **收件人：行銷部員工**
<marketingteam@gammamotors.com>
寄件人：傑洛姆・麥迪遜
<jmadison@gammamotors.com>
日期：9 月 2 日
主旨：行銷活動

184-1 **事實證明，我們最新車款的促銷活動大成功。** 183 **新車的宣傳片在各大社群媒體被廣泛分享，影片觀看數達到了數百萬次。**甚至有知名汽車雜誌的記者要求採訪我們其中一位經理。

184-1 **恭喜各位，** 185-2 **特別是阿曼德女士。這是她第一個行銷活動，多虧了她在新車款設計開發的經驗，我們才能夠想到要在廣告中**

highlight in our advertisements thanks to her experience in developing its design. We already have a high number of test drive requests, and we expect the launch to be even more successful than our minivan's.

Regards,

Jerome Madison, Marketing Manager

突顯出的最佳特點。我們已經收到了大量的試駕請求，預計這次新車上市將會比之前的迷你廂型車更成功。

傑洛姆・麥迪遜 謹啟
行銷部經理

字彙 **highlight** 強調，突顯 **test drive** 試駕

目的問題

181 Why did Ms. Yoder write to Mr. Madison?
(A) To recommend a worker
(B) To submit her résumé
(C) To offer him a position
(D) To advertise a product

中譯 約德女士為什麼要寫信給麥迪遜先生？
(A) 推薦一名員工
(B) 提交自己的履歷
(C) 提供他一份工作
(D) 宣傳一項產品

同義詞問題

182 In the letter, the word "intimate" in paragraph 2, line 4, is closest in meaning to
(A) private **(B) detailed**
(C) objective (D) faithful

中譯 在信函中，第 2 段第 4 行的「intimate」一字，意思最接近下列何者？
(A) 私人的 **(B) 詳細的**
(C) 客觀的 (D) 忠實的

Not / True 問題

183 What is mentioned about the teaser video?
(A) Many people have watched it.
(B) It features a talk with a Gamma employee.
(C) It became a top-rated movie.
(D) It was released by Gamma's competitor.

中譯 關於宣傳片，文中提到了什麼？
(A) 許多人都曾看過。
(B) 內有伽馬員工的專訪。
(C) 成為最成功的的電影。
(D) 是由伽馬的對手發布的。

兩則引文連結問題＿確認特定資訊問題

184 What is Mr. Madison congratulating his team about?
(A) A minivan's advertisement
(B) An SUV's marketing
(C) A member's promotion
(D) A magazine's popularity

中譯 麥迪遜先生為什麼要向他的團隊道賀？
(A) 迷你廂型車的廣告宣傳
(B) 休旅車的行銷
(C) 組員的升遷
(D) 雜誌的人氣

兩則引文連結問題＿推論問題

185 What is suggested about Ms. Armand?
(A) She turned down a job offer.
(B) She has been promoted to manager.
(C) She recently switched teams.
(D) She wrote an article for a magazine.

中譯 關於阿曼德女士，文中暗示了什麼？
(A) 她拒絕了工作的邀約。
(B) 她已經晉升為經理。
(C) 她最近轉到別的部門。
(D) 她為雜誌寫報導文章。

Questions 186-190 refer to the following Web page, log sheet, and e-mail. 網頁、工作記錄表和電子郵件

Help Center

What can we help you with?

I have

☐ a Question ■ a Request/Problem ☐ a Comment

My Message to Fuchsia Foods:

I've been receiving Fuchsia Foods' organic food delivery boxes for three months now. I really enjoy receiving my package each afternoon, so 186 187-1 188-2 **I wish to upgrade my plan to the next level.** 187-1 188-2 **When you make the switch, please keep in mind that I am a vegetarian and continue to send me the packages that don't include meat or eggs.** If this change is possible, please bill me accordingly.

Thank you very much.

Sebastian Palmer

Do you expect a reply? If yes, please provide your e-mail address:

■ Yes ☐ No sebpalmer@yourmail.net

SUBMIT

Thank you for contacting us.
If you requested a reply, we will be in contact with you shortly regarding your inquiry.
If you have a question that requires immediate assistance, please call us at 352-555-2948.

客服中心

請問您需要什麼協助?

我有

☐疑問 ■要求 / 問題 ☐評論

留言給「富賀呷美食」的訊息:

我訂富賀呷美食的有機食品配送箱服務已有三個月。我喜歡每天下午都收到套餐,所以 186 187-1 188-2 我想將目前的方案升級。187-1 188-2 在切換方案時,請記得我吃素,同樣配送不含肉類跟蛋的套餐給我。如果可以進行變更,請按照相應的費用向我收費。

非常感謝您。

塞巴斯蒂安・帕默

您希望得到答覆嗎?

■是 ☐否

若您回答「是」,請提供您的電子郵件地址:

sebpalmer@yourmail.net

提交

感謝您與我們聯繫。
若您要求回覆,我們會儘快就您的詢問與您聯繫。
如果您有任何問題需要立即協助,請撥打我們的專線電話 352-555-2948。

字彙 organic 有機的 vegetarian 素食主義者 accordingly 相應地,照著

March 15 Deliveries

	Basic	Deluxe	187-2 **Basic vegetarian**	187-2 188-3 **Deluxe vegetarian**	Delivery Time
86 Tassen Road			✓		11:35 A.M.
15 Jordan Drive				✓	11:50 A.M.
56 Preston Avenue		✓			2:12 P.M.
188-3 **12 Mesca Street**				✓	**2:26 P.M.**

3 月 15 日配送表

	基本	豪華	187-2 基本素食	187-2 188-3 豪華素食	配送時間
塔森路 86 號			✓		上午 11:35
喬丹道 15 號				✓	上午 11:50
普雷斯頓大道 56 號		✓			下午 2:12
188-3 梅斯卡街 12 號				✓	下午 2:26

To: Sebastian Palmer <sebpalmer@yourmail.net>
From: Customer Service <cservice@fuchsiafoods.com>
Date: March 15
Subject: About your upgrade request

Dear Mr. Palmer,

This is to confirm that we have switched your package delivery plan. 188-1 **Your first package of the new plan was delivered this afternoon.** The credit card that we have on record for your account was billed accordingly.

Please note that we do not 189 **customarily** allow plan switches before the end of a month since we preschedule our orders ahead of time. However, 190 **another member asked to change to your original plan, so we were able to simply switch your two deliveries.** This was a lucky coincidence, but please note that if you wish to make future changes, you will have to wait until the end of a month to do so.

Thank you for your understanding, and enjoy your new food deliveries!

Sincerely,

Rebecca Lars
Customer Service Representative

收件者：塞巴斯蒂安・帕默
<sebpalmer@yourmail.net>
寄件者：客戶服務部
<cservice@fuchsiafoods.com>
日期：3月15日
主旨：關於您的升級要求

帕默先生您好：

此電子郵件是確認您的美食配送方案已經切換成功。188-1 **您新方案的首個套餐已於今日下午送達。**我們根據您帳戶登記的信用卡收取了相應的費用。

請知悉，本公司 189 **通常**不允許在月底前切換方案，因為我們都是提前安排好要配送的訂單。然而，190 **有另一名會員要求改成您原本的方案，所以我們能直接交換配送給兩位的套餐。**這是一個幸運的巧合，但是請注意，如果您之後要變更方案，就得等到月底了。

感謝您理解，並且好好享受新的美食方案！

瑞貝佳・拉爾斯 敬上
客戶服務部專員

字彙 **on record** 登記過的 **customarily** 通常，習慣上 **representative** 代表，專員

目的問題

186 Why did Mr. Palmer post on the Web page?
(A) To cancel an erroneous payment
(B) To ask for a non-vegetarian option
(C) To stop receiving packages
(D) To modify his current plan

中譯 帕默先生為什麼要在網頁上發布這則訊息？
(A) 取消付錯的款項
(B) 要求提供非素食選擇
(C) 不想再收到餐點
(D) 修改目前的方案

三則引文連結問題＿推論問題

187 What kind of package was Mr. Palmer originally receiving?
(A) Basic (B) Deluxe
(C) Basic vegetarian (D) Deluxe vegetarian

中譯 帕默先生起初收到的是那種類型的套餐？
(A) 基本 (B) 豪華
(C) 基本素食 (D) 豪華素食

三則引文連結問題＿推論問題

188 Where does Mr. Palmer most likely live?
(A) 86 Tassen Road
(B) 15 Jordan Drive
(C) 56 Preston Avenue
(D) 12 Mesca Street

中譯 帕默先生最有可能住在哪裡？
(A) 塔森路 86 號
(B) 喬丹道 15 號
(C) 普雷斯頓大道 56 號
(D) 梅斯卡街 12 號

同義詞問題

189 In the e-mail, in paragraph 2, line 1, the word "customarily" is closest in meaning to
(A) normally (B) fairly
(C) naturally (D) rarely

中譯 在電子郵件中，第 2 段第 1 行的「customarily」一字，意思最接近下列何者？
(A) 通常 (B) 相當
(C) 自然 (D) 很少

確認特定資訊問題

190 According to the e-mail, why was Mr. Palmer's request granted?
(A) He waited until the end of the month.
(B) He asked to switch in advance.
(C) Another customer requested a plan switch.
(D) The desired plan is more expensive.

中譯 根據電子郵件，為何帕默先生的要求會被批准？
(A) 他一直等到了月底。
(B) 他提前要求交換。
(C) 另一位顧客也要求切換方案。
(D) 他想要的方案比較貴。

Questions 191-195 refer to the following invitation, article, and text message. 邀請函、報導和簡訊

OFFICIAL INVITATION

191 **Dear Mr. Pratt,**

As a longtime investor of Barton Electronics, you are invited to Barton's Future and Progress Event on April 24. 192-1 **I will be making a major announcement that you do not want to miss.**

Date: April 24
Time: From 2 P.M. to 4 P.M.
Location: Falcon Room (third floor), Hiver Hotel
191 **Entrance: Free (must present this card)**

Looking forward to seeing you,

192-1 **Vin Vecino**

正式邀請函

191 **親愛的普拉特先生：**

您作為巴頓電子公司的長期投資人，敬邀您參加 4 月 24 日舉辦的「展望巴頓的未來與前景活動」。192-1 **屆時我將宣布一項重大消息，請您千萬不要錯過。**

日期：4 月 24 日
時間：下午 2 時至 4 時
地點：希佛酒店 獵鷹廳（三樓）
191 **入場費：免費（須出示本邀請函）**

期待與您見面。

192-1 **文・維西諾**

字彙 investor 投資人 electronics 電子產品 make an announcement 發表聲明

Barton Electronics' Upcoming Announcement

Barton Electronics will be holding a special event on April 24. The company is to make 192-2 **what its CEO called a "major announcement" in the invitations that were sent out.** It has since then been confirmed that Barton Electronics will be presenting a new device. Yet the type of device is still unconfirmed, and rumors have been flooding the Internet.

It all started when photos of a new laptop design were leaked on social media last week. However, the source of these leaks is unknown, and their authenticity has not been verified.

巴頓電子公司即將發布的公告

巴頓電子公司將於 4 月 24 日舉辦一場特別活動。該公司即將發表聲明，192-2 **即是其執行長在邀請函中所宣稱的「重大消息」。**此後，經證實巴頓電子公司將推出一款新設備。然而，這項設備的類型尚未確認，謠言卻已在網路上流傳開來。

一切肇因於上個星期，一款新型筆電設計的照片在社群媒體上曝光。不過，消息的來源不明，其真實性也尚未得到證實。

194-1 Mr. Vecino was also 193 caught on camera meeting with Ms. Beatrix Starling, the famous fitness expert who created a popular series of training videos. 194-1 Fitness trackers have recently seen a surge in popularity, so this meeting sparked rumors about a possible Barton fitness tracker. When asked about his reason for meeting with Ms. Starling, Mr. Vecino refused to comment.

Finally, it is likely that Barton Electronics will announce their new smartphone model. The company has released a new phone every year for the past four years, and their last model, the Barton 44, is close to a year old.

194-1 維西諾先生還曾被 193 拍到與碧翠絲・史達林會面。史達林女士是著名的健身專家，曾創作一系列受歡迎的健身影片。194-1 由於健身追蹤器近來人氣大增，因此兩人的會面引發了可能推出巴頓健身追蹤器的謠言。當被問及與史達林女士會面的原因時，維西諾先生拒絕發表評論。

最後，巴頓電子有可能會宣布推出新款的智慧型手機。這四年來，該公司每年都會推出一款新手機，而距離上一款的「巴頓 44」也將近一年了。

字彙 flood 充斥　leak 洩露　authenticity 真實性　surge 劇增　spark 引發

From: Vin Vecino
To: Steven Parker

194-2 Ms. Starling sent me a copy of the speech she intends to give. In it, she explains the advantages of the device's main features. Originally, we were going to have her present at the end, but I think it would be better if she went before we show the pictures of the device. 195 **So I've decided to save the pictures for last to build up anticipation.** I'll e-mail her speech to you now. Take a look at it and tell me if you agree.

發訊人：文・維西諾
收訊人：史蒂芬・帕克

194-2 史達林女生把她的演講稿寄給我了。她在其中解說了設備主要功能的優點。我們原本打算讓她在最後發表，但是我認為如果她先介紹，然後我們再展示產品的照片，效果會更好。195 **所以我決定把照片留到最後，以增加期待感。**我現在把她的演講稿用電郵發給你，你看一下，再告訴我你是否同意。

字彙 build up 逐漸增加　anticipation 期待

確認特定資訊問題

191 What is Mr. Pratt required to do for the event?
(A) Show the invitation
(B) Bring a device
(C) Reserve the room
(D) Prepare a presentation

中譯 普拉特先生要做什麼才能參加活動？
(A) 出示邀請函
(B) 攜帶某裝置
(C) 預訂房間
(D) 準備演講

三則引文連結問題＿確認特定資訊問題

192 Who is Vin Vecino?
(A) A special guest　**(B) A company CEO**
(C) A fitness expert　(D) A private investor

中譯 文・維西諾是什麼人？
(A) 特別嘉賓　**(B) 公司執行長**
(C) 健身專家　(D) 私人投資者

同義詞問題

193 In the article, the word "caught" in paragraph 3, line 1, is closest in meaning to
(A) recorded　(B) scheduled
(C) arrested　(D) expected

中譯 在新聞報導中，第 3 段第 1 行的「caught」一字，意思最接近下列何者？
(A) 錄影　(B) 安排
(C) 逮捕　(D) 期待

三則引文連結問題＿推論問題

194 What new device is Barton Electronics most likely launching?
(A) A smartphone (B) A camera
(C) A laptop **(D) A fitness tracker**

中譯 巴頓電子公司最有可能推出什麼樣的新設備？
(A) 智慧型手機 (B) 相機
(C) 筆電 **(D) 健身追蹤器**

確認特定資訊問題

195 When will people see pictures of the new device?
(A) Before the event
(B) At the start of the event
(C) At the end of the event
(D) After the event

中譯 來賓什麼時候會看到新款裝置的照片？
(A) 在活動開始前
(B) 活動一開始
(C) 活動的尾聲
(D) 在活動結束後

Questions 196-200 refer to the following advertisement, online form, and review.

廣告、線上表單和評論

Yula School Programs

Yula School provides the most comprehensive programs for event decorators. Learn how to design a space to create the best customized environment. 196C **Our programs take just one year to complete!** At Yula, you will take several core courses 196B **before moving on to your two specialty courses, which depend on the curriculum you choose. The specialty courses included in each curriculum are listed below.**

Curriculum A: Weddings and Showers
– Draping and Fabrics
– Using Plants and Trees

197-2 **Curriculum B: Private Holiday Celebrations**
– Choosing a Color Scheme
– 197-2 **Mood Creation with Lighting**

200-2 **Curriculum C: Corporate Events**
– Choosing a Color Scheme
– Creating a Stage

Curriculum D: Themed Children's Parties
– Balloon Sculptures
– Creating a Stage

* *The deadlines for applying are August 15 for the fall semester and November 15 for the spring semester.* 196A ***Submit a résumé, motivation letter, and letter of recommendation to admissions@yula.com to apply.***

尤拉學校課程

尤拉學校提供最全面的活動佈置課程方案。學員們在此學習如何設計空間，以打造最佳的客製環境。196C **本校的課程方案只需一年即可結業！**在尤拉，您將先修完幾門核心課程，196B **然後再學習兩門專業課程，而專業課程的內容則取決於您選擇怎樣的課程組別。以下列出每個課程所包含的專業課程組別。**

課程組別 A：婚禮和送禮派對
- 懸掛帷幕與紡織品
- 樹木與盆栽的使用

197-2 **課程組別 B：私人假期慶祝活動**
- 挑選配色方案
- 197-2 **用燈光營造氣氛**

200-2 **課程組別 C：企業活動**
- 挑選配色方案
- 舞臺設置

課程組別 D：兒童主題派對
- 造型氣球
- 舞臺設置

* 報名的截止日期為：秋季班為 8 月 15 日，春季班為 11 月 15 日。196A **如欲報名，請將履歷、動機信和推薦信一起寄到 admissions@yula.com。**

字彙 comprehensive 全面的 customize 客製 curriculum 課程 motivation letter 自薦信（= cover letter）

Questions & Comments

STUDENT
Jeremy Forester

I am in my last class to complete my Yula event decorator program. However, I was wondering if it would be possible to take one more class after this semester. 197-1 **My friend Kelly Leonard is in the Private Holiday Celebrations program, and she is really enjoying her current course, which is not offered in any other curriculum.** Is it possible to add just this class without following the entire curriculum? If so, how much would it cost?

SUBMIT

問題與評論

學生
傑若米・福斯特

我現在正在上最後一門課程，就完成我在尤拉的活動布置師課程。但是，我想知道這學期的課程結束後，是否能再上一門課？197-1 **我的朋友凱莉・李奧納德選擇了「私人假期慶祝活動」的課程，她很喜歡目前上的課，但是其他的課程組別都沒有這門課。**所以，能不能只增加這門課，而不是完整課程組別呢？如果可以的話，要花多少錢？

送出

Review: ★★★★★
Name: J. Forester

199 200-1 **Shortly after I completed the curriculum, I was contacted by a company to decorate their venue for a new product launch party.** Everyone was praising the decorations, and the company was so pleased with my work that they asked me to 198 **deal with** their tenth anniversary celebration. I never expected to be so quickly hired for such a big event. 199 **Thanks to all the hands-on experience I received at Yula School, everyone thought I'd been in the business for years!** Yula really prepares you well by giving you excellent tips and training you in everything you'll need for your decorating business. I highly recommend Yula to anyone who wants to become a professional decorator.

評價：★★★★★
姓名：J. 福斯特

199 200-1 **結業後不久，就有公司就跟我聯絡，要我去幫他們的新品發布會布置場地。**大家對布置讚不絕口，那家公司對我的表現非常滿意，還要我 198 **負責**他們公司十週年的慶祝活動。我從來沒想過這麼快就有人僱用我來替這麼大型的活動布置。199 **多虧了我在尤拉學校習得的所有實務經驗，大家都以為我已經在這一行工作很多年了！**尤拉學校提供卓越的指導和全方位培訓，真正為你的布置事業做好充分準備。我強烈推薦尤拉給任何想成為專業布置師的人。

字彙 anniversary 週年紀念　hands-on 實際操作的

Not / True 問題

196 What is NOT mentioned about Yula School's programs?
(A) How to submit an application
(B) What the specialty courses are
(C) How long a program lasts
(D) When each semester begins

中譯 關於尤拉學校的課程，並未提及下列何者？
(A) 報名表的繳交方式
(B) 專業課程的內容
(C) 課程持續的時間
(D) 每學期的開學日

三則引文連結問題＿確認特定資訊問題

197 Which class is Ms. Leonard currently taking?
(A) Draping and Fabrics
(B) Choosing a Color Scheme
(C) Mood Creation with Lighting
(D) Creating a Stage

中譯 李奧納德小姐目前正在上哪門課？
(A) 懸掛帷幕與紡織品
(B) 挑選配色方案
(C) 用燈光營造氣氛
(D) 舞臺布置

同義詞問題

198 In the review, the phrase "deal with" in paragraph 1, line 3, is closest in meaning to
(A) handle (B) touch
(C) inform (D) compensate

中譯 在評論中，第 1 段第 3 行的「deal with」一字，意思最接近下列何者？
(A) 處理 (B) 觸摸
(C) 通知 (D) 補償

推論問題

199 What is suggested about Mr. Forester?
(A) He has not worked as a decorator for very long.
(B) He now teaches courses at Yula School.
(C) He recently designed a new product.
(D) He will start a new program at Yula School.

中譯 關於福斯特先生的敘述，暗示了什麼？
(A) 他從事布置師的時間不長。
(B) 他現在在尤拉學校授課。
(C) 他最近設計了新產品。
(D) 他將在尤拉學校開始新的課程方案。

三則引文連結問題＿推論問題

200 Which curriculum did Mr. Forester most likely study?
(A) Curriculum A
(B) Curriculum B
(C) Curriculum C
(D) Curriculum D

中譯 下列何者最有可能是福斯特先生選的課程？
(A) 課程組別 A
(B) 課程組別 B
(C) 課程組別 C
(D) 課程組別 D

Actual Test 5

PART 1 

1 (A) He's standing by a stream.
美M **(B) He's looking at a map.**
(C) He's pointing at a mountain.
(D) He's putting on a backpack.

(A) 他正站在溪邊。
(B) 他正在看地圖。
(C) 他正指著一座山。
(D) 他正背起背包。

---

2 (A) A woman is paying for an item at a store.
美W **(B) A woman is carrying a basket on her arm.**
(C) A woman is displaying items for sale.
(D) A woman is cleaning some vegetables.

(A) 女子在商店裡付錢買東西。
(B) 女子手臂掛著一個籃子。
(C) 女子正把商品上架。
(D) 女子正在清洗蔬菜。

---

3 (A) A vehicle has stopped at an intersection.
美M (B) A man is parking a car on a road.
(C) Some boxes have been stacked in a truck.
(D) A man is kneeling down by a cart.

(A) 一輛車停在十字路口。
(B) 男子正把車停在馬路上。
(C) 一些箱子堆放在卡車裡。
(D) 男子正跪在手推車旁。

字彙 vehicle 車輛　intersection 十字路口
stack 堆疊　kneel down 跪下

---

4 (A) Some people are setting up furniture.
英W **(B) Some people are seated in the lobby.**
(C) One of the men is walking up the stairs.
(D) One of the women is moving a stool.

(A) 有些人正在擺放家具。
(B) 有些人正坐在大廳裡。
(C) 其中一名男子正走上樓。
(D) 其中一名女子正在搬凳子。

字彙 set up 擺放　stair 樓梯　stool 凳子

---

5 (A) The men are clearing a table.
美W (B) One of the men is holding a folder.
(C) The woman is handing out a document.
(D) One of the men is writing in a notebook.

(A) 男子們正在清理桌子。
(B) 其中一名男子拿著文件夾。
(C) 女子正把文件分給大家。
(D) 其中一名男子正在筆記本上寫字。

---

6 (A) A path is blocked by a crowd.
澳M (B) There are boats docked at a port.
(C) There's a bridge spanning a river.
(D) The benches are all occupied.

(A) 小路被一群人堵住了。
(B) 港口有船隻停泊。
(C) 一座橋橫跨於河流上方。
(D) 長椅都有人坐了。

字彙 dock 停泊　port 港口　span 橫跨
occupied 使用中的

PART 2 

7 Where is the list of updated mailing addresses?
美 (A) Yes, that's the right date.
(B) On Ms. Nelson's desk.
(C) For regular customers.

更新過的郵寄地址名單放哪兒了？
(A) 是的，日期正確。
(B) 在尼爾森小姐的桌上。
(C) 給常客的。

---

8 Who can answer my questions about the magazine's layout?
英W 美M (A) That explains it.
(B) One issue a month.
(C) The design team.

誰能回答我對雜誌版面的疑問？
(A) 那就說得通了。
(B) 一個月出一期。
(C) 設計部。

字彙 layout 版面編排；版面設計

9 When will the rest of the brochures for the trade expo be ready?
美
(A) It depends when the printer gets fixed.
(B) For the entire industry.
(C) I'm going to rest for a few minutes.

貿易博覽會剩下的簡介什麼時候會好？
(A) 這得看印表機什麼時候修好。
(B) 對整個產業來說。
(C) 我要休息幾分鐘

字彙 brochure 小冊子 trade expo 貿易博覽會

10 Are these refreshments for everyone?
美W 澳M
(A) They're for the candidates.
(B) It's very refreshing.
(C) Everyone must attend the training.

這些是給大家吃的茶點嗎？
(A) 那是給求職者吃的。
(B) 非常清涼提神。
(C) 所有人都必須參加培訓。

字彙 refreshments 茶點 candidate 求職者
refreshing 提神的

11 Why don't you make name tags for the attendees?
英W 美M
(A) The attendance was low.
(B) I'm Gerald Stevens.
(C) Sure, I'd be happy to.

你為什麼不幫參加者做名牌呢？
(A) 出席人數很少。
(B) 我是傑拉爾德·史蒂文斯。
(C) 沒問題，我很樂意。

字彙 attendee 出席者
attendance 出席人數

12 Isn't this bookshelf for user manuals only?
美
(A) No, we keep client files there too.
(B) If you can assemble it.
(C) We use them daily.

這個書架不是只放使用說明書嗎？
(A) 不是，也放客戶的檔案。
(B) 如果你能組裝起來的話。
(C) 我們每天都會用到。

字彙 user manual 使用說明書 assemble 組裝

13 Are you writing the survey, or is Clyde?
澳M 美M
(A) We're doing it together.
(B) More than a hundred respondents.
(C) By market research.

是你還是克萊德在寫問卷調查？
(A) 我們一起寫的。
(B) 超過 100 名受訪者。
(C) 透過市場調查。

字彙 respondent （問卷調查的）受訪者

14 Does this skin treatment produce fast results?
英W 澳M
(A) This time it's my treat.
(B) Sorry it took me so long.
(C) Not really, but it's still worth it.

這個皮膚療程很快就能見效嗎？
(A) 這次我請客。
(B) 抱歉，我花了這麼久的時間。
(C) 並沒有，但還是值得一試。

15 What's your opinion on this restaurant?
美
(A) Whenever you have time for a meal.
(B) I wish they had a delivery service.
(C) We need a recommendation.

你覺得這家餐廳怎麼樣？
(A) 只要你有時間吃飯的時候。
(B) 要是有外送服務就好了。
(C) 我們需要推薦。

字彙 recommendation 推薦

16 How can I make a donation to the animal shelter?
美
(A) No, it's closed for the day.
(B) Mostly stray cats and dogs.
(C) Mr. Frey is in charge of that.

怎麼捐錢給動物收容所？
(A) 不，今天沒開。
(B) 大部分是流浪的貓狗。
(C) 弗雷先生負責此事。

字彙 animal shelter 動物收容所 stray 流浪的

17 Household trash and recyclable items are collected every Wednesday, right?
英W 美M
(A) Look for the symbol on the package.
(B) Recycling is every other week.
(C) Yes, I have a collection.

家庭垃圾和資源回收物是在每週三丟，對嗎？
(A) 找找包裝上的標示。
(B) 回收是隔週收一次。
(C) 是的，我有收藏品。

字彙 household 家庭　recyclable 可回收利用的

18 Did you turn the air conditioner on?

美M (A) By pressing the red button.

英W **(B) Are you feeling cold?**

(C) Turn left at the next intersection.

你開冷氣了？

(A) 按紅色的按扭。

(B) 你覺得很冷嗎？

(C) 下個十字路口左轉。

19 How do I get a library card?

美W (A) A wide range of books.

澳M (B) For a week.

(C) Just fill out this form.

如何辦理圖書館的借書證？

(A) 書籍種類繁多。

(B) 要一個星期。

(C) 填這張表格就行了。

20 Could you help me carry this desk to the 美 fourth floor?

(A) Sorry. I hurt my back yesterday.

(B) Did you check the directory?

(C) The flowers haven't been delivered yet.

你能幫我把這張桌子搬到四樓嗎？

(A) 抱歉，我昨天傷到腰。

(B) 你查過樓層指南了嗎？

(C) 花卉還沒送到。

字彙 directory （大樓內的）樓層指南

21 Why was the meeting cut short?

澳M (A) Tomorrow afternoon at three.

英W (B) Only for a short period of time.

(C) There wasn't much to discuss.

會議怎麼提早結束了？

(A) 明天下午三點。

(B) 只有很短的一段時間。

(C) 要討論的事情不多。

字彙 cut short 提早結束（進行中的事）

22 When does the art auction begin?

美 (A) We enjoyed the exhibit.

(B) Paintings and sculptures.

(C) Check the invitation.

藝術品拍賣會什麼時候開始？

(A) 我們很喜歡這場展覽。

(B) 繪畫和雕塑。

(C) 看一下邀請函吧。

字彙 auction 拍賣　exhibit 展覽　sculpture 雕塑

23 The camera is out of focus.

澳M **(A) I'll try adjusting it.**

美W (B) From a new photo studio.

(C) I'm focusing on the presentation.

相機失焦了。

(A) 我來調整一下。

(B) 從新開的照相館。

(C) 我正全神貫注在簡報上。

字彙 out of focus 模糊不清的　adjust 調整

24 Who will oversee the merger negotiations?

美 (A) To gain more market share.

(B) That hasn't been determined yet.

(C) Sometime next month.

誰來監督合併案的協商？

(A) 為了提高市占率。

(B) 這還沒有確定。

(C) 下個月的某一天。

字彙 oversee 監督　merger 合併
negotiation 協商　market share 市占率

25 What computer did they buy as a

英W replacement?

美W **(A) Actually, I'm not sure.**

(B) Yes, that place is popular.

(C) Mine is brand-new.

他們買了什麼樣的電腦來替換？

(A) 說實話，我不太清楚。

(B) 對，那個地方非常受歡迎。

(C) 我的是全新的。

字彙 replacement 替換（品）　brand-new 全新的

26 How much did you spend on your business

澳M trip?

美W **(A) Didn't you get the receipts I sent you?**

(B) I just need to meet a few clients.

(C) Five days in Rome.

你這次出差花了多少錢？

(A) 你沒有收到我寄給你的收據嗎？

(B) 我只需要見幾個客戶而已。

(C) 在羅馬待五天。

27 We should wear gloves when using this

美 spray.

(A) Because my hands are cold.

(B) Spray it on the counter.

(C) It does contain some chemicals.

我們使用這種噴劑時應戴上手套。
(A) 因為我的手很冰冷。
(B) 把它噴到櫃檯上。
(C) 它確實含有化學成分。

字彙 counter 櫃檯　chemical 化學製品

---

28 Why hasn't the safety inspector arrived yet?
澳M (A) Before it passes the inspection.
美W **(B) He called to cancel.**
(C) We can put on the safety gear.

安檢人員怎麼還沒到？
(A) 在通過檢查之前。
(B) 他打電話說要取消。
(C) 我們可以穿上安全裝備。

字彙 inspector 檢查員　inspection 查驗
safety gear 安全裝備

---

29 Are the rates for the Layton Hotel affordable?
英W 美M
(A) Of course you can stay at my home.
(B) For at least three nights.
(C) Yes, they're not too expensive.

雷頓飯店的房價很親民嗎？
(A) 你當然可以住我家。
(B) 至少三個晚上。
(C) 對，不會太貴。

字彙 rate 費用　affordable 付得起的

---

30 Does your company handle residential or commercial cleaning?
美W 澳M
(A) Both are possible.
(B) Jeffrey can handle it.
(C) I saw the commercial on TV.

請問貴公司提供住宅還是企業的清潔服務？
(A) 兩者皆可。
(B) 傑佛瑞會處理。
(C) 我在電視廣告看到的。

字彙 residential 住宅的

---

31 I need to get an anniversary gift at the mall.
美M (A) Thanks for the thoughtful present.
英W **(B) You could just order one online.**
(C) We've been married ten years.

我得在購物中心買週年紀念日的禮物。
(A) 謝謝你送我這麼貼心的禮物。
(B) 你可以直接上網訂購啊。
(C) 我們已經結婚十年了。

字彙 anniversary 週年紀念　thoughtful 貼心的

PART 3 19

Questions 32-34 refer to the following conversation. 美 對話

W Hi, Mr. Carlson. ㉜ **You said you wanted to speak to me about the order I submitted for supplies?** Was there a problem with it?

M It's missing some data. You need to list the product code for each item that you're ordering. ㉝ **Here is a catalog with pictures of all the available items and their codes. You can keep it.**

W Thank you, and sorry about that. I wasn't sure how to complete the form because it was my first time doing it.

M I understand. ㉞ **It would probably be helpful for you to check out the example that's posted on the company Web site.** Then you can see exactly what to do.

女：嗨，卡爾森先生。㉜ **您說要找我談之前繳交的辦公用品訂購單。**是不是有什麼問題？

男：訂單上漏了一些資料。訂購品都要列出產品代碼。㉝ **這本目錄，上面有可訂購物的照片跟代碼，你留著吧。**

女：謝謝您，還有很抱歉。因為這是我第一次做這件事，所以不太清楚要怎麼填寫訂購單。

男：我明白。㉞ **去看看公司網站上發布的範本吧，可能會有幫助。**這樣你就確切知道該怎麼做了。

字彙 submit 提交　supplies （複數）用品

32 What are the speakers discussing?
(A) A product description
(B) A seating chart
(C) An entrance code
(D) A supplies order

中譯 說話者在討論什麼？
(A) 產品描述
(B) 座位表
(C) 門禁密碼
(D) 用品訂單

33 What does the man give the woman?
(A) A product catalog
(B) An ID badge
(C) A new form
(D) A training manual

中譯 男子給了女子什麼？
(A) 產品目錄
(B) 識別證
(C) 新的表單
(D) 教育手冊

34 What does the man recommend doing?
(A) Canceling an order
(B) Directing questions to a coworker
(C) Viewing an example online
(D) Getting approval in advance

中譯 男子建議做什麼？
(A) 取消訂單
(B) 向同事提問
(C) 上網看範例
(D) 事先得到批准

Questions 35-37 refer to the following conversation. 美W 澳M 對話

W Mr. Donovan, ㉟ **is everything ready for the product presentation for the marketing event?** Do you have all of the information you need?

女：多諾萬先生，㉟ **行銷活動的產品介紹你都做好準備了嗎？**你需要的資料也都有了嗎？

M Yes, I do. Thanks. ㊱ **But I'm wondering if you have time to put up some posters around the room.** I think it would be helpful to have images and statistics visible. ㉟ **It would help sell more products.**	男：有，我都有了。謝謝。㊱ **但是我想知道你是否有空在會議室裡張貼一些海報？**我認為將圖像和統計資料以視覺化呈現會很有幫助，㉟ **有助於賣出更多的產品。**
W Sure. ㊲ **But first I'd like to get the final count for how many people will be here.** That'll affect how I arrange the room.	女：當然有。㊲ **不過，首先我想知道最終會有多少人參加。**這會影響到會議室的安排。
M No problem. I'll e-mail you the participant list right away.	男：沒問題。我現在就把參加名單用電子郵件寄給妳。

字彙 statistics（複數）統計資料　visible 可見的　count 總數

35 Who most likely are the speakers?
(A) Salespeople (B) Researchers
(C) Lecturers (D) Photographers

中譯 說話者最有可能是什麼人？
(A) 銷售人員 (B) 研究人員
(C) 講師 (D) 攝影師

36 What does the man ask the woman to do?
(A) Contact a supplier right away
(B) Put some information on display
(C) Finish a project ahead of schedule
(D) Make some suggestions for improvements

中譯 男子要女子做什麼？
(A) 立即聯絡供應商
(B) 把資料展示給大家看
(C) 提前完成專案計畫
(D) 提出改進的建議

37 What does the woman say she wants to do?
(A) Check the inventory
(B) Adjust a fee
(C) Arrange a meeting
(D) Confirm the attendance

中譯 女子說她要做什麼？
(A) 檢查庫存
(B) 調整費用
(C) 安排會議
(D) 確認出席人數

Questions 38-40 refer to the following conversation. 美M 英W 對話

M Good morning, Evelyn. ㊳ **I was just reading over your report for the board meeting this afternoon, but I noticed that you left out the sales figures for the Fletcher branch.**	男：伊芙琳早安。㊳ **我剛剛仔細看了你為今天下午的董事會議所做的報告，不過我發現你漏了弗萊契分公司的銷售額。**
W Oh, no. Really? I've got the figures saved on my computer. ㊴ **How much would it be to get the report reprinted using the express service?**	女：噢，不。真的嗎？我有把銷售額都存在我的電腦裡。㊴ **如果用急件服務重印報告，需要花多少錢？**
M Probably around one hundred dollars. They'd need to redo the entire document since the pages are bound together.	男：可能要 100 美元左右。因為是裝訂成冊，所以他們需要重印整本報告。
W Hmm... In that case, ㊵ **how about I just print out supplementary pages using the printer here at the office?** It won't look as professional, but I'm sure the board members will understand our situation.	女：嗯……這樣的話，㊵ **要不我用公司的影印機來印增訂頁怎麼樣？**雖然看起來沒那麼專業，但是我相信董事會理解我們的情況。

字彙 board 董事會　express 快速的　bind 裝訂　supplementary 補充的

38 What problem does the man mention?
(A) A board member hasn't arrived yet.
(B) A sales promotion didn't go well.
(C) A document is missing some information.
(D) A branch is performing more poorly than expected.

中譯 男子提到什麼問題?
(A) 有位董事還沒有到。
(B) 促銷活動進行得不順利。
(C) 文件遺漏了某些資訊。
(D) 分公司業績不如預期。

39 What does the woman ask about?
(A) The topic of a report
(B) The cost of a service
(C) The number of board members
(D) The start time of a meeting

中譯 女子問了什麼樣的問題?
(A) 報告的主題
(B) 服務的費用
(C) 董事會成員人數
(D) 會議開始的時間

40 What does the woman suggest doing?
(A) Hiring a different printing service
(B) Contacting the Fletcher branch
(C) Changing the meeting date
(D) Completing a task on site

中譯 女子建議做什麼事?
(A) 另請別家印刷公司
(B) 與弗萊契分公司聯絡
(C) 更改開會的日期
(D) 當場完成工作

Questions 41-43 refer to the following conversation with three speakers. 澳M 美W 美M 三人對話

M1 Thanks for stopping by the store today, ma'am. Are you shopping for anything specific?
W **41 I'm in the market for a new smartphone** because my current one keeps having problems.
M1 All right. I mainly deal with our large appliances such as refrigerators, so let me check with my coworker. Barrett, this woman wants to replace her current phone.
M2 Hello, ma'am. We have quite a few models to choose from, but **42 I recommend the Stinson brand. Its products work well for years with the same level of performance.**
W That's not a brand I'm familiar with, actually.
M2 No problem. **43 I can show you the main features on this display model. It'll just take a moment of your time.**
W **43 All right. Thank you.**

男 1: 女士,歡迎今日光臨本店。您在找什麼特定的東西嗎?
女: **41 我想要買新的智慧型手機**,因為我現在用的這一支經常出問題。
男 1: 好的,我主要負責如冰箱等大型家電的銷售,所以我跟同事確認一下。巴瑞特,這位女士說想她想要換手機。
男 2: 女士您好。我們有好幾款手機供您挑選,但是 **42 我挺推薦史丁森這個品牌的,他們家的產品即使用了好幾年,效能還是一樣好。**
女: 其實我對這個品牌不太熟悉。
男 2: 沒問題。**43 我可以用這台展示機給您看一下主要功能,只會佔用您一點時間。**
女: **43 好吧,謝謝你。**

字彙 be in the market for 想要購買 appliance 家用電器

41 What is the woman interested in buying?
(A) A refrigerator
(B) A television
(C) A smartphone
(D) A software program

中譯 女子想購買什麼產品?
(A) 冰箱
(B) 電視
(C) 智慧型手機
(D) 軟體程式

42 Why does Barrett recommend the Stinson brand?
(A) It has the widest selection.
(B) It is currently on sale.
(C) It is the most popular brand.
(D) It has long-lasting products.

中譯 巴瑞特為什麼推薦史丁森這個品牌？
(A) 它可供挑選的款式最多。
(B) 它目前正在特價中。
(C) 它是最熱銷的品牌。
(D) 它的產品持久耐用。

43 What will the woman probably do next?
(A) Watch a demonstration
(B) Ask for a discount
(C) Extend a warranty
(D) Fill out a registration form

中譯 女子接下來可能會做什麼？
(A) 觀看展示
(B) 要求打折
(C) 延長保固
(D) 填寫報名表

Questions 44-46 refer to the following conversation. 美W 澳M 對話

19

W Hi, Justin. I saw that there's an interpersonal skills workshop coming up. ㊹ **Do you know how to sign up for it?**
M As far as I know, there's a form we need to fill out on the host company's Web site. It's explained in the promotional material, but ㊺ **I haven't had time to read through it. Liam is on vacation, so I'm trying to complete his expense report for him.**
W You shouldn't have to do that alone. ㊻ **I could look over part of it so we have time to find out more about the workshop together.**
M Thanks! I really appreciate that.

女：嗨，賈斯丁。我看到有個人際關係技能的工作坊馬上就要舉行了。㊹ **你知道怎麼報名嗎？**
男：就我所知，我們要到主辦公司的網站上填寫報名表。宣傳資料裡有說明，但是 ㊺ **我還沒有時間把它看完。因為利亞姆正在度假，我正試著幫他完成他的費用核銷報告。**
女：你不應該自己一個人做這件事。㊻ **我可以幫忙看其中的一部分，這樣我們就有時間一起了解工作坊的情況。**
男：謝謝！真的太感謝了。

字彙 **interpersonal** 人際的 **come up** 發生 **promotional** 宣傳的 **expense** 費用

44 What are the speakers mainly discussing?
(A) A hiring decision
(B) An employee evaluation
(C) A registration process
(D) A business trip

中譯 說話者主要在討論什麼？
(A) 聘僱決定
(B) 員工考核
(C) 報名程序
(D) 出差

45 Why was the man unable to read some materials?
(A) He had a problem with his computer.
(B) He recently returned from a vacation.
(C) He had to visit an important client.
(D) He was working on a coworker's task.

中譯 男子為什麼沒能閱讀資料？
(A) 他的電腦有問題。
(B) 他最近才剛度假回來。
(C) 他得去拜訪重要客戶。
(D) 他正在處理同事的工作。

46 What does the woman imply when she says, "You shouldn't have to do that alone"?
(A) She will help train the new employees.
(B) She can assign an extra task to Liam.
(C) She can help the man finish a report.
(D) She will speak to the man's supervisor.

中譯 當女子說：「你不應該自己一個人做這件事」，她的意思是什麼？
(A) 她會幫忙培訓新進員工。
(B) 她可以多分配工作給利亞姆。
(C) 她可以協助男子完成報告。
(D) 她會去跟男子的主管談談。

Questions 47-49 refer to the following conversation. 美 對話

M Amy Evans from AR Insurance just called. ㊼ **We're working on a few banners for her company,** and she said she'd like twelve instead of three.	男：AR 保險公司的艾米・埃文斯剛剛打電話來。㊼ **我們正在做她公司訂購的橫幅**，她說她想要十二幅，不是三幅。
W Twelve? That's great news, isn't it?	女：十二幅？這還真是個好消息，對吧？
M Well, ㊽ **we don't have that many in stock at the moment,** and we can't get more of the size she needs until next week.	男：嗯，㊽ **我們目前沒有那麼多存貨**，她要的尺寸要下個星期才會到貨。
W When was this order originally due?	女：這批訂單原本什麼時候要交貨？
M April 2, but ㊾ **I can ask Ms. Evans for more time.** She didn't seem to be in much of a hurry.	男：4月2日，但是 ㊾ **我可以請埃文斯女士給我們多一點時間**，她好像不是很急著要。
W ㊾ **Okay, that's a good idea.** Let me know what she says.	女：㊾ **好，這是個好辦法**。再告訴我她怎麼說。

字彙 banner 橫幅　in stock 有存貨（↔ out of stock 缺貨）

47 What kind of business do the speakers probably work for?
(A) A delivery service
(B) A printing company
(C) A clothing outlet
(D) An insurance agency

中譯 說話者可能在哪種公司工作？
(A) 快遞公司
(B) 印刷公司
(C) 服飾專賣店
(D) 保險公司

48 According to the man, what is the problem?
(A) There is a shortage of supplies.
(B) An order form contained an error.
(C) There are not enough workers.
(D) A client has made a complaint.

中譯 根據男子所言，發生了什麼問題？
(A) 物品供應短缺。
(B) 訂購單裡有個錯誤。
(C) 員工人手不足。
(D) 有客戶提出客訴。

49 What do the speakers decide to do?
(A) Work additional hours
(B) Purchase some equipment
(C) Cancel a project
(D) Request a deadline extension

中譯 說話者決定做什麼？
(A) 加班
(B) 採購設備
(C) 取消專案
(D) 要求延後交貨期限

Questions 50-52 refer to the following conversation. 英W 美M 對話

W Did you find everything you were looking for today?	女：您今天想買的東西都找到了嗎？
M Yes, thanks. ㊿ **I always love shopping at this store. There are so many items to choose from.** Oh, and ㊿① **I'd like to use this coupon, please.**	男：找到了，謝謝。㊿ **我一直都很喜歡在你們店裡買東西，有許多商品可供挑選**。哦，對了，51 **我想要使用這一張優惠券，謝謝**。
W 51 **I'm sorry, but you have to purchase at least fifty dollars' worth of goods to use this.** Maybe you can use it the next time you come in.	女：51 **很抱歉，但是您必須消費滿 50 美元才能使用這張優惠券**。或許您可以下次再使用。
M All right. And I've filled out this form for your loyalty program. 52 **Do I need to take it to the customer service desk?**	男：好吧。我已經填寫好會員的申請表了。52 **我需要把它拿去客戶服務台嗎？**
W I'll go there shortly. Don't worry about it.	女：我待會就會過去那裡。您不用擔心。

字彙 loyalty program 會員制度

50 What does the man say he likes about the store?
(A) Its wide selection
(B) Its friendly employees
(C) Its convenient hours
(D) Its member rewards

中譯 男子說他喜歡這家店的什麼？
(A) 可供挑選的商品眾多
(B) 員工很友善
(C) 便利的營業時間
(D) 會員獎勵

51 Why is the man unable to use his coupon?
(A) It has already expired.
(B) It has a minimum purchase amount.
(C) It is for a different store.
(D) It cannot be used with other offers.

中譯 男子為什麼無法使用優惠券？
(A) 已經過期了。
(B) 有最低消費金額限制。
(C) 適用於別家店。
(D) 無法與其他優惠合用。

52 What does the woman mean when she says, "I'll go there shortly"?
(A) She can drop off some paperwork for the man.
(B) She will help the man carry his items.
(C) She plans to take a break soon.
(D) She will try to find some merchandise for the man.

中譯 當女子說：「我待會就會過去那裡」，她的意思是什麼？
(A) 她會幫男子送文件。
(B) 她會幫男子拿商品。
(C) 她打算不久後休息一下。
(D) 她會試著幫男子找商品。

19

Questions 53-55 refer to the following conversation. 美 對話

M Good morning, Ms. Cummings. 53 **On behalf of Green Environmental Consulting,** I'd like to say how much of a pleasure it is to have the head of the county commission here.

W Thank you, Mr. Raja. 53 54 **I think your firm can give us the best advice for solving the pollution problem at Centennial Beach.**

M Yes, I'll walk you through a few options today. 54 **We'll focus both on removing trash and other waste from the shoreline as well as cleaning up the picnic facilities.** 55 **A lot of the work can be done by volunteers.**

W 55 **Well, I'm not sure we can get enough people for that.**

M Don't worry. Our preliminary research shows that plenty of residents are willing to share their time.

男：康明斯女士早安。53 **代表綠色環境諮詢公司**，我們很榮幸能請郡委員長來到這裡。

女：謝謝你，拉賈先生。53 54 **我認為貴公司能提供我們最好的建議，來解決森坦尼爾海灘的汙染問題。**

男：好的，今天我會詳細地為您說明幾個解決方案。54 **我們會著重在海岸線垃圾及其他廢棄物的清除，以及野餐設施的打掃這兩個部分。** 55 **有很多工作可以交由志工來完成。**

女：55 **嗯，我不確定我們能找到足夠的人手來做這些事。**

男：別擔心。根據我們的初步調查，許多居民都很願意撥空參加。

字彙 county 郡；縣 commission 考察團，委員會 walk A through B 詳細給……說明（某事物） preliminary 初步的

53 What field does the man most likely work in?
(A) Tourism **(B) Ecology**
(C) Construction (D) Agriculture

中譯 男子最有可能從事哪一行業？
(A) 觀光旅遊業 **(B) 生態環境業**
(C) 建設業 (D) 農業

54 What kind of project will the man explain?
(A) A local cleanup
(B) A building renovation
(C) A marketing campaign
(D) A company picnic

中譯 男子將說明什麼樣的專案？
(A) 地方清理
(B) 大樓翻修
(C) 行銷活動
(D) 公司野餐

55 What is the woman concerned about?
(A) Staying within a budget
(B) Getting official approval
(C) Finding enough volunteers
(D) Starting a study on time

中譯 女子在擔心什麼？
(A) 維持在預算內
(B) 獲得官方的批准
(C) 找到足夠的志工
(D) 準時開始一項研究

Questions 56-58 refer to the following conversation with three speakers. 英W 美M 美W 三人對話

W1 Good morning. ⑯ **I'd like to check out. Here is the keycard for my room.**	女1：早安。⑯ **我要辦理退房手續，這是我的房卡。**
M All right. Let's see … Ms. Brooks, everything for your room has been paid for, but ⑰ **you owe twenty dollars extra for the airport shuttle.**	男：好的，我看看……布魯克小姐，您房間的費用全都已經付清了，但是 ⑰ **還需支付機場巴士的 20 美元。**
W1 Can I pay that in cash?	女1：可以用現金支付嗎？
M Of course. I'll let Alexandra take care of that for you. Alexandra, could you process a cash payment for the shuttle for Ms. Brooks?	男：當然可以。我請亞莉珊德拉幫您處理一下。亞莉珊德拉，可以請你幫布魯克小姐處理一下巴士的現金款項嗎？
W2 Certainly. And the next shuttle departs in about fifteen minutes.	女2：沒問題，下一班巴士大約 15 分鐘後發車。
W1 Do I need a ticket?	女1：我需要買車票嗎？
W2 No, I'll just add your name to the passenger list. ⑱ **Do you need a receipt?**	女2：不用，我只需把您加上乘客名單就行了。⑱ **您需要收據嗎？**
W1 ⑱ **Yes, please.** I want to get reimbursed from my company.	女1：⑱ **要，麻煩你。**我要跟公司請款。

字彙 owe 欠（錢） payment 支付款項 reimburse 償還；補償

56 Where most likely is the conversation taking place?
(A) At a bus terminal (B) At an airport
(C) At a hotel (D) At a theater

中譯 這段對話最有可能是在哪裡發生的？
(A) 在公車總站 (B) 在機場
(C) 在飯店 (D) 在劇院

57 According to the man, what is the additional fee for?
(A) A transportation service
(B) A room upgrade
(C) A cancellation fee
(D) A deposit

中譯 根據男子所言，什麼需要額外付費？
(A) 交通運輸服務
(B) 房型升等
(C) 取消費
(D) 押金

58 What will Alexandra most likely give Ms. Brooks next?
(A) A ticket **(B) A receipt**
(C) A schedule (D) A business card

中譯 亞莉珊德拉接下來最有可能給布魯克小姐什麼？
(A) 車票 **(B) 收據**
(C) 時間表 (D) 名片

Questions 59-61 refer to the following conversation. 美 對話

19

W Fred, ⑲ **did you pick the venue for the party yet?** We only have a month left. We should reserve a place now.
M It's going to be at Mariano's Restaurant. But I haven't reserved it yet because I'm still not sure about the date. ⑲ **We had decided December 20, but many people can't make it that day.**
W Oh, it's true that many people are going on vacation at that time. ⑳ **Do you want me to send an e-mail asking if people would prefer the first week of December?**
M ⑳ **That would be great.** ㉑ **In the meantime, I'll start choosing what kind of food to order.** Mariano's will want to know what to prepare in advance.

女：弗瑞德，⑲ **公司聚會的場地你選好了嗎？**我們只剩下一個月了，現在應該要訂好位子了。
男：聚會的地點是馬里亞諾餐廳，但是我還沒有訂位，因為我還不確定聚會的日期。⑲ **我們之前決定好要辦在12月20日，但是那天有很多人來不能來。**
女：哦，確實有很多人要在那個時候去度假。⑳ **需要我發一封電子郵件給大家嗎？問他們要不要在12月的第一週進行？**
男：⑳ **那就太好了。**㉑ **同時，我會開始選擇要訂什麼餐點。**馬里亞諾餐廳會想知道他們需要提前做哪些準備。

字彙 **venue** 場所 **make it** 趕到，到達 **in advance** 提前，事先

59 What are the speakers mainly discussing?
(A) Vacation plans
(B) An opening celebration
(C) An end-of-year event
(D) A catering service

中譯 說話者主要在討論什麼？
(A) 度假計畫
(B) 開幕慶祝活動
(C) 年末活動
(D) 外燴服務

60 What will the woman ask her coworkers?
(A) What type of venue they want
(B) When their vacations are
(C) Who they plan to invite
(D) Which date they prefer

中譯 女子會問她的同事什麼問題？
(A) 他們想要的場地類型
(B) 他們休假的時間
(C) 他們打算邀請的人選
(D) 他們偏好的日期

61 What does the man say he will do next?
(A) Select menu items
(B) Reserve a restaurant
(C) Prepare a meal
(D) Contact guests

中譯 男子說他會做什麼？
(A) 選擇餐點
(B) 去度假
(C) 準備飯菜
(D) 聯絡賓客

Questions 62-64 refer to the following conversation and list. 澳M 美W 對話和清單

M Hi. This is Akash Bahri. Is it too late to change an order I placed this morning?

W Let's see, Mr. Bahri … No, it's okay. Your order hasn't been processed yet.

M Great. I originally wanted the Lancaster brand, but **62 63 now that I took a closer look at the catalog, I found one I like better—the Saldana brand.**

W All right. It's a bit more expensive than the Lancaster and Reiser brands, but getting the right color is the most important thing.

M I agree. I think I need two cans of it, but I'm worried it won't be enough.

W **64 If you tell me the length and width of your room's walls, I can calculate that for you.**

Dark Tan Shades

Brand	Product Code
Bridgeport	147
Lancaster	295
Reiser	466
63 Saldana	**803**

男：妳好，我是阿卡施・巴利。現在還來得及更改我早上下的訂單嗎？

女：我看一下哦，巴利先生……是的，還可以改，還沒處理到您的訂單。

男：太好了。我原先想要買蘭卡斯特牌的，但是 **62 63 我仔細看過目錄後，我發現我更喜歡薩爾達納牌。**

女：好的。這個牌子比蘭卡斯特牌跟雷瑟牌要貴一些，但是選對顏色是最重要的。

男：我同意。我認為我需要兩罐，但是我擔心會不夠用。

女：**64 如果您告訴我房間牆壁的長寬，我可以幫您計算一下。**

深棕褐色

品牌	產品代號
布里奇波特	147
蘭卡斯特	295
雷瑟	466
63 薩爾達納	803

字彙 place an order 下訂單　take a look at 看一看　length 長度　width 寬度　calculate 計算

62 Why did the man change his mind?
(A) He asked a colleague's opinion.
(B) He tested some free samples.
(C) He found a cheaper item.
(D) He reviewed a product catalog.

中譯 男子為什麼改變心意？
(A) 他徵詢了同事的意見。
(B) 他測了幾份試用品。
(C) 他找到更便宜的產品。
(D) 他再次看過產品目錄。

63 Look at the graphic. Which product will the man purchase?
(A) Product 147　(B) Product 295
(C) Product 466　**(D) Product 803**

中譯 請看圖表。男子會購買下列哪項產品？
(A) 產品 147　(B) 產品 295
(C) 產品 466　**(D) 產品 803**

64 What is the man asked to do?
(A) Call back again later
(B) Provide room measurements
(C) Update an order form online
(D) Return some unused goods

中譯 男子被要求做什麼？
(A) 稍後回電
(B) 提供房間的尺寸
(C) 上網更新訂購單
(D) 將未使用的商品退回

19

Questions 65-67 refer to the following conversation and price list. 美 對話和價目表

M Hello, this is Luke Hastings from Intergrowth Corp. ⑥⑤ **I'm in charge of making the arrangements for an upcoming conference.** We need someone to interpret English into Japanese.

W All right. Let me check if we have someone available. ⑥⑥ **When is your conference?**

M It's on November 3. ⑥⑦ **We need someone for the whole day, seven hours total.** It would be nice if the person had a background in science. There might be a bit of technical language.

W All right. We do have an interpreter who fits that profile. Mr. Yamura has a degree in chemistry and has a lot of experience interpreting for science conferences.

M Perfect. What are your rates?

INTERPRETATION RATES	
Number of Hours	**Price per Hour**
1 hour	$80
2-4 hours	$75
5-6 hours	$70
⑥⑦ **More than 6 hours**	**$65**

男：妳好，我是共生公司的盧克・海斯廷斯。⑥⑤ **我負責籌備一場即將舉行的研討會。**我們需要有人將英語口譯為日語。

女：好的，我看看有沒有可用的人選。⑥⑥ **請問研討會什麼時候舉行？**

男：在 11 月 3 日。⑥⑦ **我們需要有人整天待在會場，總共是 7 個小時。**如果這個人有科學方面的背景就更好了。可能會有一些術語。

女：好的。我們確實有一位符合該條件的口譯員。田村先生擁有化學學位，科學研討會的口譯經驗非常豐富。

男：非常好，你們的收費標準是什麼？

口譯收費標準	
時數	每小時價格
1 小時	80 美元
2-4 小時	75 美元
5-6 小時	70 美元
⑥⑦ 6 小時以上	65 美元

字彙 make arrangements for 為……做安排　interpret 口譯　technical 專門性的　fit 適合　profile 簡介，概況　chemistry 化學

65 Who most likely is the man?
(A) An event organizer
(B) A language specialist
(C) An information technology expert
(D) A chemistry professor

中譯 男子最有可能是什麼人？
(A) 活動策劃人
(B) 語言專家
(C) 資訊科技專家
(D) 化學教授

66 What information does the woman ask for?
(A) The date of the event
(B) The address of a venue
(C) The languages needed
(D) The registration fee

中譯 女子要求什麼資訊？
(A) 活動日期
(B) 場地地址
(C) 語言需求
(D) 報名費

67 Look at the graphic. How much will the man most likely pay per hour?
(A) $80　(B) $75
(C) $70　**(D) $65**

中譯 請看圖表。男子每小時最有可能支付多少錢？
(A) 80 美元　(B) 75 美元
(C) 70 美元　**(D) 65 美元**

Questions 68-70 refer to the following conversation and subway plan. 英W 美M 對話和地鐵路線圖

W You look a bit lost, sir. Can I help you with anything?

M I'm not sure I'm in the right place. ⑱ **I'm trying to get to the Sunnyvale Arena to see a soccer game,** but I think I got off the subway too early.

W You did. If you look at this map, ⑲ **you'll see that you're here at Irwin Station. You need to get back on the eastbound train and get off at the second stop from here.**

M ⑳ **Oh, no. Does that mean I need to pay for another ticket?**

W No. You can still use the one you have since you didn't leave the station.

女：先生，您看起來迷路了。我能幫您什麼忙嗎？

男：我不太確定我是否在正確的地方。⑱ **我想去桑尼維爾體育場看足球賽，**但我想我太早下車了。

女：確實如此。如果您看這張地圖，⑲ **您會發現您現在在歐文站。您得搭乘往東的列車，然後在第二個站下車。**

男：⑳ **喔，不會吧。這表示我還要再買一張車票嗎？**

女：不用，您還是可以用您那張車票，因為您沒有離站。

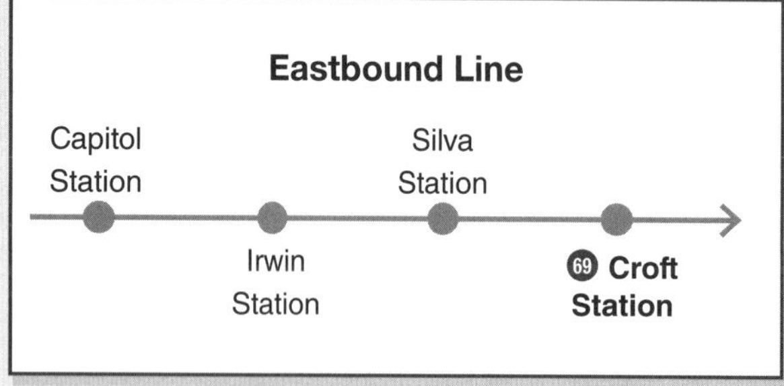

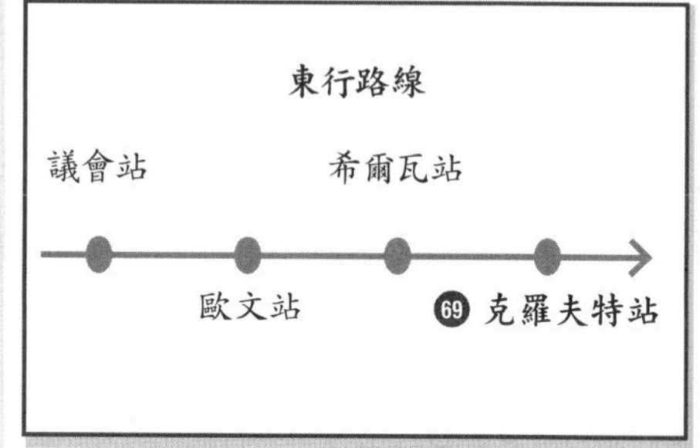

字彙 arena 體育場　eastbound 往東的，向東的

68 What does the man want to do?
(A) Find a sports facility
(B) Pick up a map
(C) Change a train ticket
(D) Get to a theater

中譯 男子想要做什麼？
(A) 尋找體育場館
(B) 索取地圖
(C) 更換火車票
(D) 去劇院

69 Look at the graphic. To which stop is the man told to go?
(A) Capitol Station　(B) Irwin Station
(C) Silva Station　**(D) Croft Station**

中譯 請看圖表。男子被告知應去哪一站？
(A) 議會站　(B) 歐文站
(C) 希爾瓦站　**(D) 克羅夫特站**

70 What is the man concerned about?
(A) Having to buy another ticket
(B) Moving his luggage by himself
(C) Missing the next train
(D) Walking through a crowded station

中譯 男子擔心什麼？
(A) 必須再買一張車票
(B) 獨自搬自己的行李
(C) 錯過下一班列車
(D) 穿過人潮擁擠的車站

Questions 71-73 refer to the following announcement. 美W 廣播

May I have your attention, please? Today we are holding a special sales event to commemorate our five-year anniversary. ⑪ **Power tools, paint, and more are on sale throughout the store.** In addition, ⑫ **one of our staff members will be demonstrating basic drilling techniques in our showroom in the west wing for the next thirty minutes.** And ⑬ **if you're interested in more do-it-yourself projects, visit our customer service counter to enroll in our next workshop for beginners on March 8.** Thank you for choosing Garcia's for all of your hardware needs.

各位來賓請注意，為慶祝成立五週年，本店今天舉辦了特賣活動。⑪ **電動工具、油漆及更多商品全店現正特價中。**此外，⑫ **在接下來的30分鐘，將有工作人員於西棟樓的展示廳裡，為各位示範鑽孔的基本技巧。**⑬ **對DIY課程有興趣的來賓，請至服務臺報名參加下一場我們在3月8日為初學者舉辦的工作坊。**感謝您選擇加西亞來滿足您對五金產品的各種需求。

字彙 commemorate 慶祝　power tool 電動工具　showroom 展示廳　wing （建築的）側廳，廂房　enroll in 報名參加　hardware 五金製品

71 Where most likely are the listeners?
(A) At a fashion show
(B) At an art institute
(C) At a hardware store
(D) At a community center

中譯 聽眾最有可能在哪裡？
(A) 在時尚秀上
(B) 在藝術學院
(C) 在五金行
(D) 在社區活動中心

72 According to the speaker, what can be found in the west wing?
(A) A promotional video
(B) A demonstration
(C) Some free samples
(D) Some paintings

中譯 根據說話者所言，可以在西棟樓看到什麼？
(A) 示範影片
(B) 一段演示
(C) 免費樣品
(D) 繪畫作品

73 What does the speaker encourage listeners to do?
(A) Enroll in a rewards program
(B) Share their feedback
(C) Make some suggestions
(D) Sign up for a workshop

中譯 說話者鼓勵聽眾做什麼？
(A) 加入會員獎勵制度
(B) 回饋意見分享
(C) 提出一些建議
(D) 報名參加工作坊

Questions 74-76 refer to the following telephone message. 澳M 電話留言

Hi, Ms. Griffin. ⑭ **This is Thomas Collins calling from Whitfield Inc., the company that manages the apartment building you live in.** ⑮ **I got your online request form saying that the water pressure in your bathroom suddenly became low. I can send a plumber today at 4 P.M.** One of our representatives can let the person in if you're not there. ⑯ **Please call me back if you want to change the time.** Otherwise, you can expect someone at 4. Thanks.

嗨，葛里芬小姐。⑭ **我是湯瑪斯・科林斯，從惠特菲爾德公司打來的，本公司管理您住的公寓大樓。**⑮ **我收到您在網路上填寫的報修申請表，上面說您浴室的水壓突然變小了。我可以派水電工於今天下午4點過去。**如果您不在家，我們的工作人員可以讓他進去。⑯ **如果您想要改時間，請回電給我。**不然，下午4點就會有人拜訪。謝謝。

字彙 plumber 水電工　representative 代表

74 Where most likely does the speaker work?
(A) At a construction company
(B) At a property management firm
(C) At an insurance agency
(D) At a plumbing company

中譯 說話者最有可能在哪裡工作？
(A) 在建設公司
(B) 在物業管理公司
(C) 在保險公司
(D) 在管道工程公司

75 What is the call mainly about?
(A) Arranging a repair
(B) Scheduling a tour
(C) Announcing renovations
(D) Signing a lease

中譯 這通電話的主要內容是什麼？
(A) 安排維修時間
(B) 排定參觀行程
(C) 告知翻修工程
(D) 簽署租賃契約

76 Why should the listener call the speaker back?
(A) To pay for a service
(B) To register a complaint
(C) To approve a charge
(D) To change an appointment

中譯 為何聽眾應回電給留言者？
(A) 支付某服務費用
(B) 進行客訴
(C) 批准收費
(D) 更改預約時間

Questions 77-79 refer to the following radio broadcast. 美W 電臺廣播

Good evening. You are listening to *Brush Stroke*. **⑦ Today's special guest is Jackie Galvani, whose paintings you can see at the Madison Gallery in Stoneville for the entire month of July.** In addition to her artwork, **⑱ Ms. Galvani will be talking about the art school she just opened for children with learning disabilities.** Ms. Galvani believes that practicing art can help students perform better in school. She will explain why, and she will also talk about how her innovative school is organized. **⑲ Give us a call at 555-2020 and tell us what you'd like us to ask Ms. Galvani.**

晚安，您正在收聽的是《筆觸》。**⑦ 今天的特別來賓是潔姬・加爾瓦尼，整個 7 月您都可以在斯通維爾的麥迪遜美術館裡看到她的畫展。**除了她的畫作外，**⑱ 加爾瓦尼女士還會談談她剛替學習障礙兒童開設的美術學校。**加爾瓦尼女士認為，練習美術能幫助孩子們在學校表現得更好。她會解釋原因，也會告訴我們她這所創新學校是如何建立。**⑲ 現在就來電 555-2020，告訴我們您希望我們問加爾瓦尼女士什麼問題。**

字彙 learning disability 學習障礙　innovative 創新的

77 Who is Jackie Galvani?
(A) A radio host　(B) A researcher
(C) A painter　(D) An art critic

中譯 誰是潔姬・加爾瓦尼？
(A) 電台主持人　(B) 研究人員
(C) 畫家　(D) 美術評論家

78 What did Ms. Galvani recently do?
(A) Started a school
(B) Gave a lecture
(C) Opened a gallery
(D) Reviewed a sculpture

中譯 加爾瓦尼女士最近做了什麼事？
(A) 創辦了一所學校
(B) 進行了一場演講
(C) 開了一間畫廊
(D) 評論了某雕塑作品

79 What does the speaker ask listeners to do?
(A) Register for a class
(B) Buy a painting
(C) Speak with the guest
(D) Submit questions

中譯 說話者要求聽眾做什麼?
(A) 報名課程
(B) 購買畫作
(C) 與來賓交談
(D) 提出問題

Questions 80-82 refer to the following advertisement. 英W 廣告

⑳

80 Are you tired of wasting time looking for new employees? Let us do the work for you! 81 Propool has helped hundreds of software companies find well-suited hires. Whether you need full-time staff, part-time staff, or unpaid interns, you can count on us to provide you with a list of IT professionals. We handle everything from the job posting to the preliminary interviews. We then set up final interviews for you to meet the potential candidates. All you have to do is choose the person you prefer. No more sorting through piles of résumés and reading cover letters. **82 Send us your job description now and find the perfect worker!**

80 您是否厭倦了花費大把時間尋找新員工?就讓我們代勞吧!81「專業人才庫」已幫助數百家軟體公司找到合適的員工。無論您需要全職員工、兼職員工,還是無薪實習生,都可仰賴我們為您提供一份資訊技術專業人士的名單。我們負責處理從發布徵人啟事到初步面試的所有事宜,然後安排您與潛在求職者進行最終面試。您只要從中挑選出您喜歡的人選,再也不需要篩選堆積如山的履歷表,也無需閱讀求職信了。**82 現在就把職務說明寄給我們,就能找到最完美的員工!**

字彙 well-suited 合適的　hire 新雇員　sort through 分類;整理

80 Who is this advertisement intended for?
(A) Job seekers
(B) Business owners
(C) New employees
(D) Interns

中譯 這則廣告是要給誰看的?
(A) 求職者
(B) 企業老闆
(C) 新進員工
(D) 實習生

81 What field does the speaker's company specialize in?
(A) Pharmaceuticals
(B) Journalism
(C) Fashion
(D) Computer science

中譯 說話者的公司專營哪一個領域?
(A) 製藥
(B) 新聞
(C) 時尚
(D) 電腦科學

82 What are listeners asked to send?
(A) A description of their facilities
(B) A selection of preferred candidates
(C) An explanation of their needs
(D) A list of interview questions

中譯 聽眾被要求寄出什麼?
(A) 對設施的描述
(B) 可供選擇的偏好求職者
(C) 對需求的說明
(D) 面試問題清單

Questions 83-85 refer to the following recorded message. 美M 預錄／答錄留言

Hello, you've reached the Britton Dental Clinic. ⑧③ **Our offices are currently closed for the summer holidays.** If this is a medical emergency, hang up now and call 911. If you wish to schedule an appointment, leave a message with your name, number, and time you'd like to come in. ⑧④ **If applicable, also tell us which dentist usually treats you.** Otherwise, tell us if you have a preferred dentist. Note that Dr. Doyle is fully booked until August 8. His next available appointments are on August 9. ⑧⑤ **We will reopen on Monday, July 30 at 8 A.M.** and resume regular hours. Dr. Howard, whose off day is Monday, will return on Tuesday, July 31.

您好，這裡是布里頓牙科診所。⑧③ **我們牙科目前因暑假而停診。**如果您是因緊急醫療情況而來電，請立即掛斷電話並撥打 119。如果是想要預約，請在留言中告知您的姓名、電話號碼以及希望的看診時間。⑧④ **如果有固定看診的牙醫師，也請告知我們。**如果沒有，請告訴我們您是否有偏好的牙醫師。請注意，道爾醫師 8 月 8 日前的預約都額滿了，他下一個可預約的時間是 8 月 9 日。⑧⑤ **本診所將於 7 月 30 日，星期一上午 8 點開診，**恢復正常門診時間。週一休診的霍華德醫師將於 7 月 31 日星期二看診。

字彙 emergency 緊急情況　hang up 掛斷電話　applicable 適用的　resume 恢復　regular hours 營業時間　off day 休息日

83 Why is the business closed?

(A) An emergency happened.

(B) Renovations are being made.

(C) A dentist recently retired.

(D) Workers are on vacation.

中譯 這個營業場所為什麼關閉了？

(A) 發生緊急情況。

(B) 正在進行裝修。

(C) 一名牙醫師最近退休了。

(D) 員工都在休假中。

84 What does the speaker imply when he says, "Otherwise, tell us if you have a preferred dentist"?

(A) New customers may choose a dentist.

(B) A new dentist will be hired.

(C) Patients can write reviews of their dentists.

(D) Regulars may select a new dentist.

中譯 當說話者說：「如果沒有，請告訴我們是否有偏好的牙醫師」，其言下之意為何？

(A) 新客戶可以選擇牙醫。

(B) 診所將會聘僱新的牙醫。

(C) 病人可以評價自己的牙醫。

(D) 常客可以選擇新的牙醫。

85 When will the clinic reopen?

(A) On July 30　(B) On July 31

(C) On August 8　(D) On August 9

中譯 診所何時重新開放？

(A) 7 月 30 日　(B) 7 月 31 日

(C) 8 月 8 日　(D) 8 月 9 日

Questions 86-88 refer to the following excerpt from a meeting. 美W 會議摘要

⑧⑥ **OK. First, let's talk about how things went on at the National Electronics Expo.** Our booth was well-positioned, and visitors showed a lot of interest in our new mini printer, the Kenosha-50. ⑧⑦ **We've just started offering a 10-year warranty instead of a 5-year one,** and that seems to be helping sales. There are still adjustments that need to be made, however. ⑧⑧ **The printer is intended to be portable,** but it's currently just under five hundred grams. ⑧⑧ **That's nearly four times the weight of an average cell phone.** I don't think consumers are going to find that characteristic attractive.

⑧⑥ **好。首先，我們要來談談這次參加全國電子博覽會發生的事。**我們攤位的位置很好，參展者對我們新推出的迷你印表機「肯諾夏-50」表現出極大的興趣。⑧⑦ **我們剛開始提供十年的保固，而不是五年的，**這似乎對銷售很有幫助。不過，仍有一些地方需要進行調整。⑧⑧ **這台印表機的設計初衷是便於攜帶，**但是目前它的重量僅略低於500公克，⑧⑧ **幾乎是一般手機重量的四倍。**我不認為消費者會覺得這個特點很有吸引力。

字彙 warranty (品質的)保固　portable 便攜的　characteristic 特性

86 Why did the speaker schedule the meeting?
(A) To give a demonstration of a product
(B) To make corrections to a sales report
(C) To provide information about an industry event
(D) To request volunteers for a trade fair booth

中譯 說話者為什麼要安排這場會議?
(A) 為了進行產品展示
(B) 為了修正銷售報告
(C) 為了提供產業活動的資訊
(D) 替貿易展的攤位徵求志工

87 What recently changed about the Kenosha-50?
(A) Its battery weight was reduced.
(B) Its warranty period was extended.
(C) Its processing speed was improved.
(D) Its screen size was increased.

中譯 關於肯諾夏-50,最近有什麼變化?
(A) 它的電池重量減輕了。
(B) 它的保固期延長了。
(C) 它的處理速度改善了。
(D) 它的螢幕變大了。

88 What does the speaker mean when she says, "it's currently just under five hundred grams"?
(A) The price is too high for the weight.
(B) A device does not meet the industry standard.
(C) Supplies are running out faster than expected.
(D) The product is inconvenient to carry around.

中譯 當說話者說:「目前它的重量僅略低於 500 公克」,她的意思是什麼?
(A) 以這重量來說,價格太高。
(B) 該設備不符合產業標準。
(C) 供應品的消耗速度比預期更快。
(D) 產品攜帶不便。

Questions 89-91 refer to the following talk. 澳M 談話

Good afternoon, ladies and gentlemen. ❽❾ **I'm pleased to introduce Nicholas Stroud for this special event at the Ellis Community Center. Mr. Stroud will be reading excerpts from his latest novel, *On the Banks of the Nile*.** It's about the history of the Egyptian people in that area, and it will be made into a movie later this year. ❾⓿ **The director of the movie was going to join us, but I'm sorry to say he's had a last-minute schedule change and won't be here.** ❾❶ **After the talk, Mr. Stroud will be signing copies of his book at the table near the east entrance. We don't have any for sale,** so I hope you brought your own.

各位先生、女士,大家午安。❽❾ **我很高興能在艾利斯社區活動中心舉辦的這場特別活動裡,為介紹大家尼可拉斯・斯特勞德。斯特勞德先生將朗讀他最新小說《尼羅河畔》裡面的幾段選文。**這本書講的是在尼羅河畔生活的埃及人的歷史故事,本書預計將於今年稍晚翻拍成電影。❾⓿ **我很遺憾地告訴各位,這部電影的導演原本要來到現場,但是他的行程臨時變動而無法到場。** ❾❶ **座談結束後,斯特勞德先生將在東門附近的桌子為他的新書簽名。**我們沒有書可供銷售,所以我希望大家都有帶自己的書來。

字彙 excerpt 摘錄　last-minute 最後一刻的

89 Who does the speaker introduce?
(A) An author (B) A history professor
(C) A director (D) A movie producer

中譯 說話者欲介紹的人是誰？
(A) 作家 (B) 歷史教授
(C) 導演 (D) 電影製片人

90 What does the speaker apologize for?
(A) A leaflet has an error.
(B) A presentation is delayed.
(C) A movie screening is canceled.
(D) A guest cannot come.

中譯 說話者為了什麼而道歉？
(A) 宣傳單內容有誤。
(B) 演講延後了。
(C) 電影放映取消了。
(D) 有位嘉賓無法前來。

91 What does the speaker imply when he says, "I hope you brought your own"?
(A) Items will not be available on site.
(B) Listeners need an entrance ticket for the talk.
(C) Mr. Stroud will answer some prepared questions.
(D) Listeners may suggest their own ideas.

中譯 說話者說：「我希望大家都有帶自己的書來」，其言下之意為何？
(A) 現場沒有書可賣。
(B) 聽眾需要入場券才能參加朗讀。
(C) 斯特勞德先生將回答準備好的問題。
(D) 聽眾可以提出自己的看法。

Questions 92-94 refer to the following excerpt from a meeting. 美M 會議摘錄

To start off today's meeting, ⑨② **I'd like to congratulate you all on your achievement. We've been trying to get Cornell Industries to sign a contract with us for a long time, and it finally happened!** The presentation by Mr. Monroe's team was a huge factor in our success. ⑨③ **What I found particularly impressive was the wide range of photos they used to support their points.** That really made it memorable. We're ready to approach more clients in this way, so ⑨④ **I'd like you to think of new companies who could use our services. I'll write them on the board as you shout them out.**

在今天會議的一開始，⑨② **我要恭喜大家的成就。長久以來，我們一直努力要和康乃爾工業公司簽訂合約，如今終於實現了！**門羅先生團隊的簡報是此事成功很重要的因素。⑨③ **其中讓我印象特別深刻的是，他們使用了各式各樣的照片來佐證他們的論點。**這真的令人難忘。我們準備如法炮製，以此方式來與客戶商談接洽。所以 ⑨④ **我想請大家想想，還有哪些新公司可能會使用我們的服務。你們一邊大聲說出來，我會把它寫在白板上。**

字彙 **achievement** 成就 **memorable** 令人難忘的 **approach** 接洽；找……商談

92 Why does the speaker congratulate the listeners?
(A) They improved their work efficiency.
(B) They exceeded a sales goal.
(C) They hired a hard-working employee.
(D) They attracted a new client.

中譯 說話者為什麼要跟聽眾道賀？
(A) 工作效率提高。
(B) 超過業績目標。
(C) 僱用到勤快的員工。
(D) 吸引到新客戶。

93 According to the speaker, what was the most impressive part of a presentation?
(A) Its simple explanations
(B) Its variety of photographs
(C) Its accompanying handout
(D) Its helpful charts

中譯 根據說話者所言，簡報上哪個部分最令人印象深刻？
(A) 簡潔的說明
(B) 各式各樣的照片
(C) 附帶的講義
(D) 有用的圖表

94 What will the speaker probably do next?
(A) Introduce a coworker
(B) Present some awards
(C) Write a list of companies
(D) Assign the listeners to teams

中譯 說話者接下來可能會做什麼？
(A) 介紹同事
(B) 頒發獎項
(C) 寫一份公司名單
(D) 將聽眾分配到各個小組

Questions 95-97 to the following announcement and boarding pass. 英W 廣播與登船證

Good morning, ladies and gentlemen waiting for the ferry to Bainbridge Island. Please remember that lockers are no longer available at this terminal, so ⑮ **you must hold onto your bags and personal items at all times,** both here at the terminal and on board the ferry. ⑯ **We'll begin boarding shortly, with vehicles boarding at eight fifty and walk-on passengers at nine o'clock.** We expect an on-time departure at nine twenty, and with this beautiful weather, our arrival should also be on time. ⑰ **Please stay in the boarding area, as we'll be presenting a short safety announcement in a few minutes.** Thank you.

Elliot Bay Ferries
Seattle → Bainbridge Island

Departure: 9:20 A.M.　Arrival: 10:10 A.M.

⑯ **Ticket Type: Walk-on Passenger**
Ticket Fee: $8.20

等待搭乘渡輪前往班布里奇島的女士和先生們，大家早安。請大家記住，碼頭不再提供置物櫃了，因此無論是在碼頭這裡還是在渡輪船上，⑮ **請大家務必隨身攜帶您的行李和個人物品。** ⑯ **我們馬上就會開始登船手續，車輛的登船時間為8點50分，而徒步乘客則是在9點整登船。**我們預計在9點20分準時出發，由於天氣晴朗，我們應該也會準時抵達。⑰ **請留在登船區，因為我們將在幾分鐘後進行一個簡短的安全須知宣導。**謝謝您。

艾略特灣渡輪
西雅圖 → 班布里奇島

開船時間：上午 9:20　抵達時間：上午 10:10

⑯ **船票類型：步行乘客**
票價：8.20 美元

字彙 **ferry** 渡輪　**hold onto** 保管　**walk-on** （有別於開車的）徒步搭船的

95 What does the speaker remind listeners to do?
(A) Direct questions to terminal employees
(B) Keep their belongings with them
(C) Check the departure dock
(D) Have their tickets ready

中譯 說話者提醒聽眾要做什麼？
(A) 向碼頭員工提問
(B) 隨身攜帶個人物品
(C) 確認出發的碼頭
(D) 準備好船票

96 Look at the graphic. When should the ticket holder board the ferry?
(A) At 8:50 A.M.　**(B) At 9:00 A.M.**
(C) At 9:20 A.M.　(D) At 10:10 A.M.

中譯 請看圖表。持票人應於何時登船？
(A) 上午 8:50　**(B) 上午 9:00**
(C) 上午 9:20　(D) 上午 10:10

97 What will be given to listeners soon?
(A) A ticket receipt　**(B) A safety briefing**
(C) A terminal map　(D) A seat assignment

中譯 聽眾很快就會接收到什麼？
(A) 船票收據　**(B) 安全須知**
(C) 碼頭地圖　(D) 座位分配表

Questions 98-100 refer to the following excerpt from a meeting and chart. 美M 會議摘要與圖表

98 **I'd like to give you all an update regarding the consulting advice provided by Audrey Gordon at Tuesday's meeting.** As some of you may know, 99 **Upton Inc. has gone bankrupt and will no longer supply cosmetics to our store.** We had considered adding a new brand to our inventory, but 100 **Ms. Gordon recommended that we start carrying more products by the most popular brand. So we'll do that as soon as possible, using the display cases that used to house Upton Inc.'s products.** You can see our average sales per brand on this chart. I'll be working with managers to place the necessary orders.

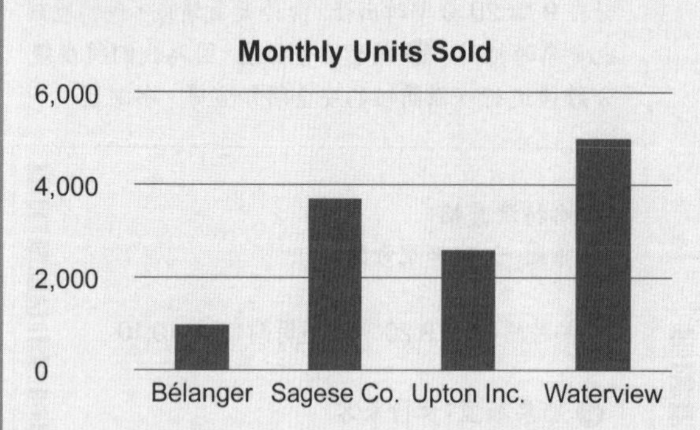

98 **關於奧黛莉・葛登在上週二的會議上提供的諮詢建議，我想要跟大家更新一下。**你們當中有些人可能知道，99 **烏普頓公司已經破產了，將不再提供化妝品給我們。**我們曾考慮在庫存裡加入一個新品牌，但是 100 **葛登小姐建議我們開始多銷售最高人氣品牌的產品。因此，我們會儘快照她所說的去做，直接使用過去放置烏普頓產品的貨架。**你們可以從這張圖表上看到，我們賣場各個品牌的平均銷量。我會跟主管們一起完成必要的訂單。

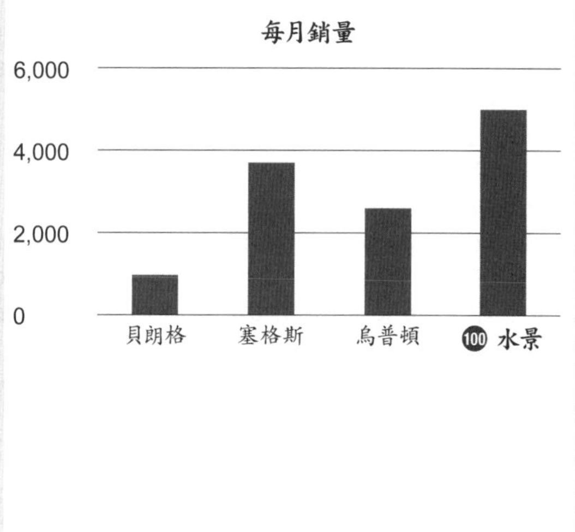

字彙 go bankrupt 破產　inventory 庫存（物品）　house 收納

98 What did the speaker do on Tuesday?
(A) Met with a consultant
(B) Tested product samples
(C) Checked the inventory
(D) Processed an order

中譯 說話者星期二做了什麼事？
(A) 跟顧問開會
(B) 測試產品樣品
(C) 確認庫存
(D) 處理訂單

99 What is causing a change in product supplies?
(A) A building expansion
(B) A business closure
(C) An inventory error
(D) A training event

中譯 產品供應發生異動的原因為何？
(A) 建物擴建
(B) 公司停業
(C) 庫存錯誤
(D) 培訓活動

100 Look at the graphic. Which brand will have more items added?
(A) Bélanger　(B) Sagese Co.
(C) Upton Inc.　**(D) Waterview**

中譯 請看圖表。下列哪個品牌會追加進貨？
(A) 貝朗格　(B) 塞格斯
(C) 烏普頓　**(D) 水景**

PART 5

所有格

101 韋克斯勒先生請他的團隊吃午餐，以此表示感謝。
(A) 他 (B) 他 **(C) 他的** (D) 他自己

字彙 appreciation 感謝，感激

連接詞 vs 介系詞

102 這三個月以來，石板健身房的會員人數增加為兩倍。
(A) 在……下面 (B) 在……的時候
(C) 在……之時 **(D) 在……期間**

填入名詞＋人物名詞 vs 事物名詞

103 那封寫給編輯的信是《國家園藝雜誌》的訂戶詹妮絲・李維寫的。
(A) 訂閱了 (B) 訂閱 **(C) 訂戶** (D) 訂閱費

字彙 subscriber 訂戶 gardening 園藝

副詞 soon

104 博塞爾製造公司不久將用現代化設備來精簡其生產線。
(A) 相當 **(B) 不久** (C) 其他 (D) 一直

字彙 streamline 簡化 production line 生產線

填入副詞——修飾介系詞片語

105 由於這家麵包店招徠了長期的投資者，該店的財務狀況良好。
(A) 財務 (B) 財務 (C) 財務的 **(D) 財務上**

字彙 bring in 引入 in good shape 狀況良好

名詞 addition

106 由於奔馳運動公司新增為兒童設計的新服飾系列，他們的銷量才得以增加。
(A) 送貨 (B) 建議 (C) 內容物 **(D) 新增**

字彙 athletics 體育運動

填入動詞＋被動語態

107 如果消費者在家自行組裝家具，他們可以省下一大筆錢。
(A) 組裝中 (B) 將被組裝
(C) 已經組裝 **(D) 被組裝**

字彙 consumer 消費者 component 零件
assemble 組裝

介系詞 through

108 自然愛好者喜歡在德比國家公園北部的樹林中遠足。
(A) 穿過 (B) 到……之上
(C) 關於 (D) 除了

字彙 enthusiast 愛好者 section 部分

填入名詞＋人物名詞 vs 事物名詞

109 在公司餐會上，坐在貴賓席的來賓包括了年度最佳員工的被提名人。
(A) 被提名的 (B) 提名 **(C) 被提名人** (D) 提名

字彙 banquet 宴會 nominee 被提名人
annual 年度的

慣用片語 be aware of

110 梅菲爾國際機場的保全人員必須知道旅客的相關法規。
(A) 警覺的 (B) 準確的
(C) 知道的 (D) 嚴格的

字彙 security guard 保全人員 regulation 規定

反身代名詞慣用法 by oneself

111 由於主管那天不在，所以行銷部的成員自己跟買家做了產品的簡報。
(A) 他們自己 (B) 他們
(C) 他們 (D) 他們的

主動語態＋單複數一致性

112 水貝公用事業公司已把網站上的資訊翻譯成西班牙文及中文，好讓更多顧客能夠了解。
(A) 被翻譯 (B) 已翻譯
(C) 已翻譯 (D) 被翻譯

字彙 utility （水、電等）公用事業

填入形容詞——形容詞＋名詞

113 現今的資訊技術部確實是公司有史以來最多元的部門。
(A) 多元地 (B) 多元化（經營）
(C) 多元的 (D) 使多元化

字彙 diverse 多元化的

副詞 almost

114 柯爾比女士得獎的暢銷書原稿差點被出版社退稿。
(A) 相當 (B) 附近 (C) 還沒有 **(D) 差點**

字彙 manuscript 手稿 publisher 出版商

人稱代名詞——主格

115 辛普森女士是卡羅來納州分公司業績最好的銷售員，她要求晉升為團隊主管。
(A) 她自己 **(B) 她** (C) 她 (D) 她的

字彙 branch 分公司 promote 晉升，升遷

動詞 accommodate

116 EZ 快遞公司將為其車隊再多買三輛廂型車，以因應對其服務日益增長的需求。
(A) 預測 **(B) 順應**
(C) 把……歸因於 (D) 造成

字彙 courier 快遞公司 fleet 車隊

填入副詞——修飾形容詞

117 遊客跟當地人都會去農民市集，因為那裡的農產品價格非常合理。

(A) 理由　(B) 合乎邏輯的

(C) 公道地　(D) 公道的

字彙 **reasonably priced** 定價合理的

介系詞 upon

118 抵達目的地後，飛機乘客們就到行李轉盤等待他們的行李。

(A) 沿著　**(B) 一……後立即**

(C) 不像　(D) 在……期間

字彙 **destination** 目的地　**belongings** 所有物
luggage carousel 行李轉盤

形容詞 essential

119 剛培訓的廚師忘了在湯裡加上兩種必要的食材，結果湯的味道不對。

(A) 必要的　(B) 固有的

(C) 相等的　(D) 可靠的

字彙 **ingredient** 食材　**turn out** 最後是，結果是

對等連接詞 so

120 該公司的形象建立在信任之上，因此員工在任何時候都應對顧客坦誠和誠實。

(A) 從不　**(B) 因此**　(C) 什麼　(D) 然後

字彙 **build A on B** 把 A 建立在 B 之上　**open** 坦誠

介系詞 before

121 沃恩先生希望在與他人討論細節之前先準備一個原型機的試驗機型。

(A) 即使如此　**(B) 在……之前**

(C) 以便　(D) 作為替代

字彙 **working model** 試驗機型　**prototype** 原型

名詞 reputation

122 拉沃拉餐廳幾乎總是座無虛席，向來以美食佳餚和優質服務而著稱。

(A) 澄清　(B) 聲明　(C) 承諾　**(D) 聲譽**

字彙 **be filled to capacity** 客滿的
earn a reputation 贏得聲譽

不定詞 to——副詞用法

123 這家百貨公司提供香水樣品，以便讓顧客試用。

(A) 到目前為止　(B) 由於……

(C) 為了　(D) 最重要的是

動詞 recruit

124 隨著擴建工程完成，林茨飯店將招聘更多工作人員以應付增加的客流量。

(A) 放棄　**(B) 招聘**　(C) 奉獻　(D) 委任

字彙 **expansion** 擴張　**volume** 數量

填入形容詞——主詞補語

125 這份報告初稿的品質令人無法接受，所以經理要求重寫。

(A) 接受　(B) 可接受地

(C) 可接受的　(D) 可接受性

字彙 **first draft** 初稿

名詞 proximity

126 由於英格拉姆中心鄰近幾條主要的高速公路，活動策劃人員因而選擇在此舉辦軟體大會。

(A) 宣傳　**(B) 鄰近**　(C) 規律性　(D) 地區

字彙 **convention** 大會

形容詞 extensive

127 卡帕迪亞博士在基因工程領域進行了大量的研究，是一位備受尊敬的生物學家。

(A) 備有家具的　**(B) 廣泛的**

(C) 易腐爛的　(D) 準時的

字彙 **conduct** 進行　**genetic engineering** 基因工程
biologist 生物學家

複合關係副詞 however

128 無論對員工的批評有多溫和，仍可能冒犯敏感的人。

(A) 或多或少　**(B) 無論……**

(C) 完全　(D) 很少

字彙 **criticism** 批評　**offense** 冒犯
sensitive 敏感的

副詞 efficiently

129 加百列・法爾肯發明了一套全自動系統，使製藥公司能夠更有效率地評估醫療檢查的準確度。

(A) 勉強地　(B) 不斷增加地

(C) 部分地　**(D) 有效率地**

字彙 **automated** 自動化的　**pharmaceutical** 製藥的
evaluate 評估　**accuracy** 準確度

名詞子句連接詞 whether

130 有些董事會成員質疑伍德沃斯先生是否有資格擔任這個職務。

(A) 兩者皆　(B) 除非　(C) 因為　**(D) 是否**

字彙 **board member** 董事會成員
qualification 資格條件　**position** 職務

PART 6

Questions 131-134 refer to the following advertisement. 廣告

Jacobs Interiors

Why move when you can just upgrade for a fraction of the cost? Our experienced designers have -------131. homes, offices, and even television studios! They will help you every step of the way, starting with the selection of materials. -------132.. Nevertheless, we are willing to get items imported or shipped to get you exactly what you want. We will also keep your safety in mind, as we have engineers inspect structures -------133. to the building's support system before making any changes. Visit our Web site at www.jacobsint.com to see photos of past projects and read testimonials about how we fulfilled customers' -------134..

雅各布室內裝修公司

如果只需要花很少的錢就能讓你的家煥然一新，何必要搬家呢？本公司經驗豐富的設計師已經 131 **改造**過許多家庭、公司行號，甚至電視台的攝影棚！他們會從材料的選擇開始，一步步協助您完成裝修。132 **我們會儘量使用在地的建材**。儘管如此，為了滿足您的需求，我們也樂意進口或運送材料。我們也將您的安全放在心上，因為在做任何變更之前，我們的工程師會對建物承重系統 133 **至關重要的**結構進行檢查。請至本公司官網 www.jacobsint.com 查看過去專案的照片，看看客戶的感言，了解一下我們是如何完成顧客 134 **訂單**吧。

字彙 **fraction** 小部分 **selection** 選擇 **inspect** 檢查 **structure** 構造 **vital to** 對……至關重要的 **testimonial** 感言，薦言

動詞 transform

131 (A) related **(B) transformed** (C) invested (D) toured

中譯 (A) 涉及了 **(B) 改造了** (C) 投資了 (D) 遊覽了

選出合適的句子

132 (A) The business offers a money-back guarantee on the work.
(B) Don't hesitate to share your project ideas with the designer.
(C) Some colors remain popular from year to year.
(D) We try to use locally sourced supplies as often as we can.

中譯 (A) 公司對其工程提供退款保證。
(B) 別猶豫，跟設計師分享您對專案的看法吧。
(C) 有些顏色是永不退流行的。
(D) 我們會儘量使用在地的建材。

填入形容詞

133 (A) vitally **(B) vital** (C) vitalize (D) vitality

中譯 (A) 極其 **(B) 至關重要的** (C) 振興 (D) 活力

名詞 order

134 **(A) orders** (B) relations (C) behaviors (D) forms

中譯 **(A) 訂單** (B) 關係 (C) 行為 (D) 表單

Questions 135-138 refer to the following memo. 備忘錄

To: All Haynes Airlines Ticket and Gate Agents
From: Crystal Lecuyer
Date: October 25

In preparation for the busy holiday travel season, we will be ------- (135.) two extra lines in our check-in area. We believe this will help us to reduce the long wait times for check-in.

Under this new plan, part-time workers will have additional shifts ------- (136.) January 5. You may also ------- (137.) to work at the gate, as boarding is an important factor in on-time departures. Your supervisors plan to set a schedule soon. ------- (138.).

Thank you for your hard work and cooperation.

收文人：海恩斯航空公司票務部及登機門的全體員工
發文人：克莉絲朵・勒古耶
日期：10 月 25 日

為準備迎接繁忙的旅遊度假季節，我們將在辦理登機手續的報到區多 135 **開**兩條通道。我們相信這將有助於縮短辦理登機手續的漫長等待時間。

根據這項新計畫，136 **到**明年 1 月 5 日**前**，兼職的工作人員將增加輪班的班次。你們也許會 137 **被分配到**登機門工作，因為登機是準時起飛與否的一個重要因素。你們的主管很快就會排出輪值表。138 **若時間安排上有衝突，請通知他們。**

感謝各位的辛勞與配合。

字彙 **check-in** 辦理登機手續　**shift** 輪班　**assign** 分派　**boarding** 登機

動詞 open

135 **(A) opening** (B) relocating (C) decorating (D) suspending

中譯 (A) 開設 (B) 搬遷 (C) 裝飾 (D) 暫停

介系詞 until

136 (A) within **(B) until** (C) during (D) following

中譯 (A) 在（某段時間）內 **(B) 直到** (C) 在……期間 (D) 在……之後

助動詞＋原形動詞

137 (A) assigning **(B) be assigned** (C) assigned (D) having assigned

中譯 (A) 分配中 **(B) 被分配** (C) 分配了 (D) 已分配

選出合適的句子

138 (A) Gate numbers should be posted as soon as possible.
(B) A copy of it is attached to this memo.
(C) Travelers are expected to request this service.
(D) Please notify them of any potential scheduling conflicts.

中譯 (A) 登機門的號碼會儘早公布。
(B) 本備忘錄附有一份輪值表。
(C) 預計旅客會要求這項服務。
(D) 若時間安排上有衝突，請通知他們。

Questions 139-142 refer to the following article. 報導

Golf Club to Raise Funds for Local Museum

HOLTONVILLE, August 7—The Holtonville Golf Club will hold its first-ever tournament at Greenway Golf Course to raise money for the Contemporary Art Museum. -------. (139.) Winners will take home a trophy as well as gift cards. The club hopes that participants will not only have a good time but will also become ------- (140.) informed about the importance of art in the community. -------, (141.) the event provides a great opportunity for young golfers to play in a friendly competition. All ------- (142.) from the event will go toward making urgent roof repairs at the museum.

高爾夫俱樂部為當地美術館募款

霍爾頓維爾市，8 月 7 日——霍爾頓維爾高爾夫俱樂部將在格林威高爾夫球場舉行首次的錦標賽，為當代美術館募款。139 **這場比賽的獎項將由本地企業捐贈**，而獲勝者則可將獎盃與禮品卡帶回家。該俱樂部希望參賽者不僅能玩得開心，還能 140 **充分**了解在地藝術的重要性。141 **此外**，這場活動還為年輕的高爾夫球手提供一個進行友誼賽的好機會。本活動所有的 142 **收益**將用來支付美術館屋頂緊急修繕工程的部分款項。

字彙 **raise funds** 募款 **golf course** 高爾夫球場 **contemporary** 當代的
go toward 用於支付……的部分款項

選出合適的句子

139 (A) The city's mayor praised organizers for their focus on the environment.
(B) Golf lessons are offered at the site throughout the summer months.
(C) The prizes for the competition will be announced at a later date.
(D) The competition will grant participants prizes donated by local businesses.

中譯 (A) 該市市長稱讚了主辦方對環境的關注。
(B) 整個夏天都將在現場提供高爾夫球課程。
(C) 比賽的獎品將在日後公布。
(D) 這場比賽的獎項將由本地企業捐贈。

填入副詞——修飾形容詞

140 (A) full (B) fullness
(C) fuller **(D) fully**

中譯 (A) 充滿的 (B) 充滿
(C) 更滿的 **(D) 充分地**

連接副詞 furthermore

141 (A) Otherwise (B) Thus
(C) Furthermore (D) In fact

中譯 (A) 否則 (B) 因此
(C) 此外 (D) 事實上

名詞 proceeds

142 (A) interest **(B) proceeds**
(C) materials (D) separation

中譯 (A) 利息 **(B) 收益**
(C) 材料 (D) 分離

Questions 143-146 refer to the following e-mail. 電子郵件

To: Pamela Rardin <p.rardin@montoyainc.net>
From: Aarom Communications <info@aaromcomm.com>
Date: September 4
Subject: Aarom-6 Phone

Dear Ms. Rardin,

Our records show that you recently made a ------- (143.) of an Aarom-6 smartphone from Aarom Communications. We are delighted to offer you our noise-canceling wireless headphones for just $89.99. ------- (144.). These headphones provide premium sound quality, a comfortable fit, and a long battery life.

If you are interested, please ------- (145.) to this e-mail no later than September 10 with your preferred mailing address. We will then make a charge to your Aarom customer account. ------- (146.) will appear on your monthly statement as "Aarom Headphones." We hope you will deal, and we look forward to serving you.

Sincerely,

Sharon Kearney
Customer Service Agent, Aarom Communications

收件人：帕梅拉・拉爾丁
<p.rardin@montoyainc.net>
寄件人：阿羅姆通訊公司
<info@aaromcomm.com>
日期：9 月 4 日
主旨：阿羅姆 6 手機

親愛的拉爾丁女士：

我們的紀錄顯示，您最近向阿羅姆通訊公司 143 **購買**了阿羅姆 6 的智慧型手機。我們很高興為您提供一款無線降噪耳機，價格僅 89.99 美元。144 **這個特價是已經打了七折的優惠價**。這款耳機的音質卓越，配戴起來舒適貼合，而且電池壽命長。

若您有意購買，請您最晚於 9 月 10 日之前 145 **回覆**本電郵，並提供您想要收件的地址。我們之後將從您的阿羅姆顧客帳戶中收費。146 **它**在您的電話費月結單上將會顯示為「阿羅姆耳機」。我們希望您能利用這個優惠，並期待為您服務。

誠摯地，

雪倫・科爾尼
阿羅姆通訊公司 客服專員

字彙 noise-canceling 降噪　statement 對帳單

名詞 purchase

143 (A) review　(B) repair
(C) purchase　(D) profit

中譯 (A) 評價　(B) 維修
(C) 購買　(D) 利潤

選出合適的句子

144 **(A) This special price reflects a thirty percent discount.**
(B) They come as a standard accessory at no extra charge.
(C) You can read more about this in your product warranty.
(D) We appreciate your notifying us of the issue promptly.

中譯 **(A) 這個特價是已經打了七折的優惠價。**
(B) 這些是標準配件，不另外收費。
(C) 您可在產品保證書裡讀到更多相關內容。
(D) 我們感謝您立即通知我們這個問題。

動詞 respond

145 **(A) respond** (B) subscribe
(C) disregard (D) feel free

中譯 **(A) 回覆** (B) 訂閱
(C) 忽略 (D) 隨意

代名詞 it

146 (A) Those (B) Few
(C) Another **(D) It**

中譯 (A) 那些 (B) 很少的
(C) 另一個 **(D) 它**

PART 7

Questions 147-148 refer to the following notice. 公告

Crestar Maintenance Project

From June 3 to July 18, we will be working on several maintenance projects on our network. This work may affect ⓮ **your departure time and/or journey duration.** ⓮ ⓮ **Signs are posted throughout the station to inform you of the changes to the timetable for each day.** ⓮ **Please be sure to view this posted information to ensure that you know what to expect.** Thank you for your patience.

柯斯達修繕工程

從6月3日至7月18日，本公司將會進行數項鐵路網的修繕工程，屆時可能會影響 ⓮ **您的班次發車時間以及(或者)行車時間。** ⓮ ⓮ **車站各處都會張貼告示，通知旅客當日時刻表的異動。** ⓮ **請各位旅客務必查看公告資訊，確保您預先掌握情況。**感謝您的耐心。

字彙 **maintenance** 維修 **network** 網路 **duration** 持續時間 **timetable** 時刻表

對象問題

147 For whom is the notice most likely intended?
(A) Safety inspectors
(B) Travel agents
(C) Construction workers
(D) Train passengers

中譯 這則公告最有可能是要給誰看的？
(A) 安全檢查人員
(B) 旅行社
(C) 建築工人
(D) 搭火車的乘客

確認特定資訊問題

148 What does the notice instruct people to do?
(A) Check an adjusted schedule
(B) Provide feedback about a service
(C) Report problems to the company
(D) Make a payment in advance

中譯 公告中指示旅客要做什麼？
(A) 查看調整後的時刻表
(B) 提供對某服務的意見回饋
(C) 向公司報告問題
(D) 預先付款

Questions 149-150 refer to the following invoice. 費用清單

Barrington Roofing

305 Acres Lane, Brentwood, TN 37027
(615) 555-8483

Customer: Leonard Harper
Property Site: 4651 Guevara Street, Brentwood, TN 37027

Description of Work: Replace roof on residential property

Original Quote	$7,500	**Issue Date**	May 3
Updated Quote	$6,300	**Issue Date**	May 7

Notes: ⓮⓽ **The original quote included the entire roof replacement process. Now the client will remove the old shingles before the project begins and handle their disposal separately.**

⓯⓪ **Start Date**	**May 15**	**End Date**	May 16
Deposit and first payment received			$300 on May 7

* ⓯⓪ **Half of the balance ($3,000) is due as a second payment on the first day of work.** The final payment is due one week after the completion of the work. Please note that payments must be made in accordance with this schedule regardless of weather delays.

巴林頓屋頂工程公司

37027 田納西州布蘭特伍德市
艾克斯街 305 號
(615) 555-8483

顧客姓名：李奧納多・哈柏
房屋地址：37027 田納西州布蘭特伍德市格瓦拉街 4651 號

施工內容：更換住宅屋頂

原始報價	7,500 美元	**報價日期**	5 月 3 日
最新報價	6,300 美元	**報價日期**	5 月 7 日

備註：⓮⓽ **原始報價為更換整個屋頂的工程，但如今客戶將於施工前自行拆除舊屋瓦並處理廢棄物。**

⓯⓪ **開工日期**	**5 月 15 日**	**完工日期**	5 月 16 日
收到訂金暨第一筆工程款			300 美元，5 月 7 日

* ⓯⓪ **第二筆工程款應於施工的第一日支付，金額為剩餘應付款的一半（3,000 美元）。**尾款應於完工後一週內支付。請注意，無論工程是否因天候因素延宕，款項都必須如期支付。

字彙 roofing 維修屋頂　quote 報價　shingle 屋瓦　disposal 清除　deposit 訂金　balance 餘款　in accordance with 依據

確認特定資訊問題

149 Why has a charge on the invoice been changed?
(A) The price of materials has increased.
(B) The customer presented a coupon.
(C) The permit had to be paid for separately.
(D) The customer will take care of some of the work.

中譯 為什麼收費單上的金額有變動？
(A) 建材價格上漲了。
(B) 客戶出示了優惠券。
(C) 許可證必須另外付費。
(D) 客戶將處理部分工程。

確認特定資訊問題

150 When should Mr. Harper make his second payment?
(A) On May 15　(B) On May 16
(C) On May 22　(D) On May 23

中譯 哈柏先生何時應支付第二筆工程款？
(A) 5 月 15 日　(B) 5 月 16 日
(C) 5 月 22 日　(D) 5 月 23 日

Questions 151-152 refer to the following text-message chain. 訊息串

Cynthia Spencer [11:13 A.M.] Hi, Ralph. ⑮¹ **You're away from the office today, right?**	**辛西婭・史賓塞 [上午 11:13]** 嗨，拉爾夫。151 你今天不會在辦公室，對嗎？
Ralph Wallace [11:16 A.M.] 151 **Yes. I'll be attending meetings with representatives from one of our largest accounts.** Why?	**拉爾夫・華勒斯 [上午 11:16]** 151 對，我要去跟公司最大客戶之一的代表開會。為什麼這麼問？
Cynthia Spencer [11:17 A.M.] 152 **I'm wondering if I could borrow your laptop just for today.** Mine isn't working, and the IT team doesn't have a replacement.	**辛西婭・史賓塞 [上午 11:17]** 152 想問能不能借你的筆電用，就今天一天。我的壞了，可是資訊科技部沒有備用機。
Ralph Wallace [11:18 A.M.] Of course. Just return it when you're done.	**拉爾夫・華勒斯 [上午 11:18]** 當然可以，用完歸還就行。
Cynthia Spencer [11:19 A.M.] I will. Thanks a lot! It's in the common department locker, right?	**辛西婭・史賓塞 [上午 11:19]** 我會的，多謝你啦！放在部門的公共儲物櫃裡，對吧？
Ralph Wallace [11:20 A.M.] Yes, it should be. And there isn't a password, so you should be fine.	**拉爾夫・華勒斯 [上午 11:20]** 是的，應該是。沒有設置密碼，所以妳應該沒問題。

字彙 representative 代表　account 客戶

確認特定資訊問題

151 What is Mr. Wallace doing today?
(A) Meeting some clients off-site
(B) Training some IT workers
(C) Setting up a meeting room
(D) Giving some customers a tour

中譯 華勒斯先生今天要做什麼？
(A) 外出見客戶
(B) 培訓資訊科技部員工
(C) 設置會議室
(D) 帶客戶參觀

意圖掌握問題

152 At 11:18 a.m., what does Mr. Wallace mean when he writes, "Of course"?
(A) He will call the IT team to make a request.
(B) He does not mind lending some equipment to Ms. Spencer.
(C) He can help repair Ms. Spencer's malfunctioning laptop.
(D) He will order a replacement item for Ms. Spencer.

中譯 在上午 11:18 時，華勒斯先生寫：「當然可以」，他的意思是？
(A) 他會打電話向資訊技術部提出要求。
(B) 他不介意把設備借給史賓塞小姐。
(C) 他可以幫史賓塞小姐修理壞掉的筆電。
(D) 他會幫史賓塞小姐訂購替換的筆電。

Questions 153-154 refer to the following memo. 備忘錄

To: All Osage Consulting Employees
From: Carla Watson, Branch Supervisor
Date: October 17
Subject: Employee break room

Now that the employee break room is open again following the renovations, we want to make sure that this area is kept clean and tidy for all who use it. 153 **Therefore, from now on, we are changing the policy on the usage of the refrigerator.** 154 **Whenever you put something in the refrigerator, it must have your name and the date marked on it clearly.** Every Friday afternoon, the refrigerator will be cleaned out, and items that have expired and those that do not have names on them will be thrown out. This will ensure that the refrigerator does not get too full and does not have any spoiled food in it. Thank you in advance for your cooperation.

受文者：奧薩奇顧問公司全體員工
發文者：卡拉・華森，分公司主管
日期：10 月 17 日
主旨：員工休息室

由於員工休息室在裝修後又重新開放了，我們希望確保這裡能保持乾淨整潔，以供大家利用。153 **因此，從現在開始，我們將改變冰箱的使用規定。** 154 **每次把物品放進冰箱時，都必須清楚地標示出姓名及日期。**每週五下午，我們都會清理冰箱，凡是過期或是上面沒有標示姓名的物品都會被扔掉。這將確保冰箱不會被塞得太滿，裡面也不會有變質的食物。在此預先感謝您的配合。

字彙 renovation 裝修　usage 使用　spoil （使食物）變質

目的問題

153 Why did Ms. Watson write the memo?
(A) To notify staff of a renovation
(B) To explain a break schedule
(C) To report a room closure
(D) To announce a new rule

中譯 華森女士為什麼要寫這個公告？
(A) 通知員工要進行裝修
(B) 解釋休息時間表
(C) 通報關閉某空間
(D) 宣布一項新規定

確認特定資訊問題

154 What are readers of the memo asked to do?
(A) Refrain from eating food in the office
(B) Empty the refrigerator every Friday
(C) Label their food and drink items
(D) Volunteer for a weekly cleanup job

中譯 備忘錄的讀者被要求做什麼？
(A) 避免在辦公室飲食
(B) 每週五清空冰箱
(C) 在自己的食物及飲料上貼標籤
(D) 自願負責每週清潔冰箱的工作

Questions 155-157 refer to the following Web page. 網頁

http://www.bloomfieldpublib.org/news

HOME	ABOUT	SERVICES	**NEWS**	SERACH

The Bloomfield Public Library is proud to be 155A **one of the venues for the city's first-ever Spring Literary Festival,** 155B **which runs from April 16 to 20.** 155D 157 **The event will feature talks all over the city from professional writers who have had their works published recently, including Jiang Li, Linda**

http://www.bloomfieldpublib.org/news

首頁	認識本館	各項服務	**最新消息**	搜尋

布盧姆菲爾德公共圖書館很榮幸成為 155A **本市第一屆春季文學節的會場之一，** 155B **於 4 月 16 日至 20 日舉行。** 155D 157 **本活動將在本市各地舉辦講座，主推最近有出版新書的專業作家，包括李健、琳達・艾奇遜、亞穆納・博斯以**

Atchison, Yamuna Bose, and Patrick Corona. ⓯⓰ Ms. Atchison's talk, which will be held at our library, is expected to be a particularly big draw, as her latest mystery novel, *Onward North*, has spent thirty weeks on the bestseller list. The book also took home the prestigious Larochelle Prize last month.

Tickets for the event can be purchased at the Bloomfield Community Center.

及派屈克・科羅納等人前來演講。156 157 艾奇遜小姐的講座將在本館舉行，預計會特別地吸引人，因為她最新出版的推理小說《向北而行》已連續 30 個星期蟬聯暢銷書排行榜，還在上個月獲得了享有盛譽的拉羅謝爾獎。

本活動門票可於布盧姆菲爾德活動中心購買。

字彙 run 舉行　draw 有吸引力的事物　prestigious 有聲望的

Not / True 問題

155 What is NOT true about the Spring Literary Festival?
(A) It has never been held before.
(B) It will last for less than a week.
(C) It includes an author awards ceremony.
(D) It will take place in several locations.

中譯 關於春季文學節，下列何者錯誤？
(A) 以前從未舉辦過。
(B) 為時不到一個星期。
(C) 包括作家的頒獎典禮。
(D) 將在多個地點舉行。

確認特定資訊問題

156 Who has recently won an award?
(A) Jiang Li
(B) Linda Atchison
(C) Yamuna Bose
(D) Patrick Corona

中譯 最近誰得獎了？
(A) 李健
(B) 琳達・艾奇遜
(C) 亞穆納・博斯
(D) 派屈克・科羅納

確認特定資訊問題

157 What is mentioned about Bloomfield Public Library?
(A) It will be closed in preparation for the festival.
(B) It organizes the literary festival every year.
(C) It will host a lecture by a professional writer.
(D) It is seeking volunteers to assist with the festival.

中譯 關於布盧姆菲爾德公共圖書館，文中提到了什麼？
(A) 將為準備文學節而休館。
(B) 每年都會舉辦文學節。
(C) 將主辦專業作家的講座。
(D) 正在徵求能協助文學節的志工。

Questions 158-160 refer to the following e-mail. 電子郵件

To: Gwen Landry <gwenlandry@milagrosinc.com>
From: Amanda Morgan <amanda@nsrmembers.org>
Date: July 29
Subject: Important Notice

收件人：葛溫・蘭德里 <gwenlandry@milagrosinc.com>
寄件人：阿曼達・摩根 <amanda@nsrmembers.org>
日期：7 月 29 日
主旨：重要通知

Dear Ms. Landry,

According to our records, ⑮⑧ **you have been a member of the National Society of Realtors for the past three years.** —[1]—. Thank you for your patronage, and we hope you are enjoying the benefits of being a part of this group.

We are currently holding our annual membership drive and would like to ask for your assistance. —[2]—. If you have friends or colleagues who would be suitable for our group, please have them complete the attached application form. 160 **This form has a special number so we can determine that the referral came from you.** —[3]—.

159C **For each member you refer, you will receive $10 off your monthly dues.** 159B **In addition, you will have a seat reserved for you in the VIP section at our annual conference.** —[4]—. 159A **We will also enter your name into a prize drawing for a five-day vacation in the Bahamas.**

If you have inquiries about recruitment, please feel free to e-mail me anytime.

Sincerely,

Amanda Morgan
Membership Services

蘭德里女士您好：

根據我們的紀錄，158 **您在這三年來一直是全國房地產經紀人協會的會員**。感謝您的支持，我們希望您享受身為協會會員的福利。

我們目前正在舉辦年度會員宣傳活動，想要請您給予協助。如果您的朋友或同事適合加入本協會，請讓他們填寫附件中的會員申請表。160 **這張申請表上有一組特殊號碼，這樣我們便能確定該人是經由您的推薦而來**。您可在申請書的頁底看到這組編號。

159C **您每推薦一名會員加入，每月會費便可減免 10 美元**。159B **此外，我們將為您在年度大會的貴賓區中預留一個座位**。159A **還可參加巴哈馬五日遊的抽獎**。

若您對會員的招募活動有任何疑問，請隨時發電子郵件給我。

阿曼達・摩根 敬上
會員服務部

字彙 realtor 房地產經紀人 patronage 惠顧 drive 宣傳運動 referral 被推薦人 recruitment 招募

推論問題

158 Who most likely is Ms. Landry?
(A) A group founder
(B) A real estate agent
(C) A homeowner
(D) A bank teller

中譯 蘭德里女士最有可能的身分是？
(A) 團體的創辦人
(B) 房地產經紀人
(C) 屋主
(D) 銀行櫃員

Not / True 問題

159 What is NOT an advantage of referring members?
(A) A chance to win a trip
(B) Priority seating at an event
(C) A reduction in membership fees
(D) Discounted tickets to a conference

中譯 下列何者並非推薦會員的好處？
(A) 有機會贏得一次旅行
(B) 活動中的優先座位
(C) 會員費有減免
(D) 大會門票有打折

尋找句子位置問題

160 In which of the positions marked [1], [2], [3], and [4] does the following sentence best belong?
"It can be found at the bottom of the page."
(A) [1] (B) [2]
(C) [3] (D) [4]

中譯 下列句子最適合放在 [1]、[2]、[3] 和 [4] 的哪個位置？
「您可在申請書的頁底看到這組編號。」
(A) [1] (B) [2]
(C) [3] (D) [4]

Questions 161-163 refer to the following letter. 信函

Aiden Holt
739 Kessler Way
Syracuse, NY 13202

Dear Mr. Holt,

161 162 We hope you have enjoyed the free one-month trial of our Premium Sports Package.
161 162 Your access to the four international football channels, two basketball channels, and two mixed sports channels will end on April 30 if you take no further action. **161 To make sure you don't miss any of the sports coverage you love, sign up for a one-year subscription to the Premium Sports Package,** which will add just $7.95 to your monthly bill. You can do so by changing the settings on your online account with Chapman Cable through our Web site. There you can also check your user agreement for details about how to add or discontinue premium packages.

163 Enclosed you will also find a postage-paid postcard, on which you can share your suggestions, ideas, and complaints. We'd love to hear how you are finding your Chapman Cable experience so far.

Warmest regards,

The Chapman Cable Accounts Team

艾登・霍爾特
13202 紐約州雪城
凱斯勒街 739 號

親愛的霍爾特先生：

161 162 我們希望您對免費試用一個月的高級體育套餐感到滿意。如果您今後不採取任何措施，**161 162 您觀賞四個國際足球頻道、兩個籃球頻道，以及兩個綜合體育頻道的權限將於 4 月 30 日終止。161 為確保您不會錯過任何您喜歡的體育節目，請訂閱一年期的高級體育套餐，**而每月帳單只會增加 7.95 美元。您可以透過本公司官網，變更您在查普曼有線電視的網路帳號的設定即可，您還可在此查看您的用戶合約條款，了解如何增加或終止訂閱高級套餐的詳細資訊。

163 隨函附上一張郵資已付的明信片，您可藉此與我們分享您的建議、想法與客訴。我們很想聽聽到目前為止您對使用查普曼有線電視的感受。

致上最溫暖的問候

查普曼有線電視客戶部

字彙 **trial** 試用 **coverage** 新聞報導 **access** 使用之權利 **subscription** 訂閱 **enclose** 附上 **agreement** 合約 **postage-paid** 郵資已付的

目的問題

161 What is the purpose of the letter?
(A) To encourage a customer to continue a service
(B) To announce which channels will be added next month
(C) To introduce a new package of sports channels
(D) To remind a customer to make a payment on his account

中譯 這份信函的目的為何？
(A) 鼓勵顧客繼續訂閱服務
(B) 宣布下個月將增加哪些頻道
(C) 介紹體育頻道的新套餐方案
(D) 提醒顧客在其帳戶付款

確認特定資訊問題

162 What will happen on April 30?
(A) A free trial will expire.
(B) A sports event will take place.
(C) A discount will be applied.
(D) An online account will be disabled.

中譯 4 月 30 日會發生什麼事?
(A) 免費試用即將到期。
(B) 將舉行體育活動。
(C) 將適用某優惠。
(D) 網路帳號將失效。

確認特定資訊問題

163 What is enclosed with the letter?
(A) A discount coupon
(B) A broadcast schedule
(C) An updated user agreement
(D) A comment card

中譯 隨信附上了什麼?
(A) 優惠券
(B) 節目時間表
(C) 更新的用戶條款
(D) 客戶意見卡

Questions 164-167 refer to the following online chat discussion. 網路聊天室

Latika Nair [1:23 P.M.]
Renovations on our office will not start next week as planned.

Chet Matthews [1:25 P.M.]
I heard that the company we were supposed to use went out of business unexpectedly.

Latika Nair [1:26 P.M.]
Right. 164 **So I'm looking for another construction firm, preferably one endorsed by someone I know. Any ideas?**

Diane Perdue [1:27 P.M.]
165 166 **I was very pleased with the work done by Norris Construction at my house last year.**

Chet Matthews [1:28 P.M.]
165 166 **But that business was sold to another person last month, so the quality might not be the same.**

Diane Perdue [1:29 P.M.]
166 **I didn't know that.** We'd better not take any chances.

Chet Matthews [1:30 P.M.]
The dental clinic across the street recently had its interior redesigned, and it looks great.

Latika Nair [1:31 P.M.]
167 **We should try to find out the address and contact number of their contractor.**

Motoshi Tenno [1:32 P.M.]
167 **I actually have an appointment there on Friday, so I'll do that during my visit.**

拉提卡・奈爾 [下午 1:23]
我們辦公室的修繕工程無法照計劃於下週展開了。

切特・馬修斯 [下午 1:25]
我聽說我們本來要僱用的那家公司突然歇業了。

拉提卡・奈爾 [下午 1:26]
沒錯。164 **所以我正在找其他建設公司,最好是由我認識的人推薦的。有什麼建議嗎?**

黛安・普度 [下午 1:27]
165 166 **我非常滿意諾里斯建設公司去年在我家進行的工程。**

切特・馬修斯 [下午 1:28]
165 166 **但是那家公司上個月就賣掉了,所以施工品質可能會不一樣哦。**

黛安・普度 [下午 1:29]
166 **我不知道這件事。**我們最好不要冒任何的風險。

切特・馬修斯 [下午 1:30]
對面牙醫診所最近室內重新裝潢,看起來還不錯。

拉提卡・奈爾 [下午 1:31]
167 **我們應該想辦法找出他們承包商的地址和聯絡電話。**

天野元志 [下午 1:32]
167 **其實,我星期五有預約看牙,我去的時候會順便打聽一下。**

字彙 preferably 最好是　endorse 擔保　contractor 承包商

目的問題

164 Why did Ms. Nair start the online chat?
(A) To get a business recommendation
(B) To introduce a new contractor
(C) To review some contract terms
(D) To approve a renovation schedule

中譯 奈爾小姐為什麼開始在網路上聊天?
(A) 找到推薦的商家
(B) 介紹新的承包商
(C) 審查合約條款
(D) 批准翻修時間表

Not / True 問題

165 What is indicated about Norris Construction?
(A) It was endorsed by a dental clinic.
(B) It canceled a contract unexpectedly.
(C) It is under new ownership.
(D) It has lower prices than its competitors.

中譯 關於諾里斯建設,文中說了什麼?
(A) 有牙醫診所的認可。
(B) 突然取消合約。
(C) 有了新的老闆。
(D) 開價比競爭對手低。

意圖掌握問題

166 At 1:29 p.m., what does Ms. Perdue most likely mean when she writes, "We'd better not take any chances"?
(A) She wants to retract her suggestion.
(B) She thinks they should do a safety check.
(C) She plans to do further research.
(D) She needs more time for a decision.

中譯 在下午 1:29 時,普度小姐寫:「我們最好不要冒任何的風險」,她最有可能是什麼意思?
(A) 她想要撤回她的提議。
(B) 她覺得他們應進行安全檢查。
(C) 她打算做進一步的調查。
(D) 她需要更多的時間來做決定。

接下來要做的事問題

167 What will Mr. Tenno do on Friday?
(A) Contact Norris Construction
(B) Gather information about a business
(C) Reschedule an appointment
(D) Visit a new contractor

中譯 天野先生週五會做什麼?
(A) 聯絡諾里斯建設公司
(B) 蒐集某家公司的資料
(C) 重新預約時間
(D) 拜訪新的承包商

Questions 168-171 refer to the following e-mail. 電子郵件

To: Gregory Pearlman <g.pearlman@oakway.com>
From: Tibbs Inc. <inquiries@tibbsinc.com>
Date: August 26
Subject: RE: Inquiry

Dear Mr. Pearlman,

⑯⑧ **I received your message about your recent participation in our sightseeing boat ride around Nieves Bay.** I've checked our lost-and-found box, and there are indeed a few men's watches in there, one of which might be yours. ⑯⑨ **Unfortunately, I cannot**

收件人:格雷戈里・柏爾曼 <g.pearlman@oakway.com>
寄件人:提普斯公司 <inquiries@tibbsinc.com>
日期:8 月 26 日
主旨:關於:詢問

親愛的柏爾曼先生:

⑯⑧ **我收到了您的來信,內容關於您最近乘坐本公司的觀光船遊覽尼夫斯灣。**我查看過公司失物招領處的箱子,裡面確實有幾支男士手錶,其中一支可能是您的。⑯⑨ **可惜根據公**

provide you with a photograph of these items as requested, as our company regulations do not allow it. To claim a lost item, you should come to our office at the harbor and give a description of the item. ⓱⓪ **If possible, showing the ticket from your boat ride will make the process faster.** That's because we will be able to determine exactly which boat you were on, and our found items are cataloged by date and boat.

There is no need to book an appointment in advance. Simply stop by during our office hours, which are 9 A.M. to 6 P.M. daily. Please note that we are a seasonal business, and the season is wrapping up at the end of the month. ⓱① **Therefore, you only have a few days to visit us before the office closes for the low season, so please do so if you can, as returning your item will become a lot more complicated after that.**

Sincerely,

Lucy Wooldridge

Administrative Assistant, Tibbs Inc.

司規定，**我無法如您所要求的提供這些物品的照片。**如欲認領您的遺失物，您須至本公司位於港灣的辦公室並描述該物品。⓱⓪ **如果可以的話，出示您的船票會加快這個過程。**這是因為我們能藉此確定您當時搭乘的確切船隻，而本公司的遺失物品都是按照日期及船隻編入目錄的。

您不需要提前預約，只需在我們的營業時間內（每天上午 9 點至下午 6 點）直接來辦公室就行了。請注意，本公司的營業時間會隨著季節而變化，而本季即將在這個月底結束。⓱① **因此，在辦公室因淡季而關閉之前，只剩下幾天的時間，所以如果您方便的話，請儘早過來，因為在那之後，取回遺失物的程序會變得複雜許多。**

誠摯地，

露西・伍德里奇

提普斯公司 行政助理

字彙 wrap up 結束　low season 淡季　administrative 行政的

推論問題

168 What kind of service does Tibbs Inc. most likely provide?

(A) Event photography

(B) Swimming lessons

(C) Group tours

(D) Hotel bookings

中譯 提普斯公司最有可能提供什麼樣的服務？

(A) 活動拍攝

(B) 游泳課

(C) 團體遊覽

(D) 飯店訂房

確認特定資訊問題

169 Why was Ms. Wooldridge unable to send Mr. Pearlman a picture?

(A) A Web site is not working.

(B) It is against company policy.

(C) Some equipment is missing.

(D) The image needs to be edited.

中譯 伍德里奇小姐為什麼不能將照片寄給柏爾曼先生？

(A) 網站無法使用。

(B) 違反公司規定。

(C) 設備不見了。

(D) 圖像需要編輯。

確認特定資訊問題

170 According to the e-mail, how can Mr. Pearlman expedite a process?

(A) By avoiding the peak times

(B) By paying an additional fee

(C) By booking an appointment

(D) By presenting a ticket

中譯 根據電子郵件的內容，柏爾曼先生如何才能加快這個過程？

(A) 避開尖峰時間

(B) 支付額外費用

(C) 進行預約

(D) 出示船票

確認特定資訊問題

171 What does Ms. Wooldridge recommend doing?
(A) Purchasing a season pass
(B) Contacting her manager
(C) E-mailing a description
(D) Taking action quickly

中譯 伍德里奇小姐建議做什麼？
(A) 購買季票
(B) 聯絡她的經理
(C) 以電子郵件傳送物品描述
(D) 迅速採取行動

Questions 172-175 refer to the following article. 報導

Investment at GT Communications

March 3—GT Communications has confirmed its plans to invest heavily in technology for its facilities. ⑰② **Customers have shifted away from landlines, which previously made up GT Communications' entire business, and started using mobile phone networks and the Internet. Therefore, the company is adapting its business model by changing its infrastructure.** — [1] —.

⑰③ **The smallest of the company's facilities—located in Nashville—already received the new machines so that the plan could be tried out on a small scale before rolling out the changes companywide.** — [2] —. GT Communications is taking measures to ensure that its staff members are not negatively affected by the upgrades. ⑰⑤ **"During the transition at Nashville, we looked for areas where we could retrain our people instead of laying them off," said company spokesperson Katherine Coyle.** "— [3] —. ⑰⑤ **We expect similar figures at the rest of our facilities."**

GT Communications is now ready for Phase 2 of its transition, which is installing the state-of-the-art equipment at all sites. — [4] —. ⑰④ **The work will begin with the Detroit site later this year, followed by the Kansas City branch early next year, and the Houston branch late next year. Once all of the upgrades have been completed, the final site will be open for public tours so that people can see the operations for themselves.**

GT 電信通訊公司的投資案

3 月 3 日——GT 電信通訊公司證實其將在設備技術上挹注大量資金。⑰② **消費者紛紛從市話(此前曾是 GT 電信通訊公司的全部業務)，轉而開始使用行動電話與網際網路。因此，該公司正在透過改變其基礎建設來調整其經營模式。**

⑰③ **GT 電信通訊公司規模最小的工廠就位於納什維爾，該廠已經拿到新機器，因此得以在公司全面實施新計畫之前，先進行小規模的試驗。**GT 電信通訊公司正在採取措施，以確保員工不會因此次升級受到負面影響。⑰⑤ **「在納什維爾廠的轉型時期，我們找到了可以重新培訓員工的領域，而不是直接解僱他們」，公司的發言人凱薩琳・科伊爾說，**「於是，我們就保住了該廠百分之 90 的員工。⑰⑤ **我們希望其他工廠也能有類似的數字」。**

GT 電信通訊公司現在已經準備好迎接第二階段的轉型，亦即在所有工廠安裝最先進的設備。⑰④ **這項作業將於今年稍晚從底特律廠開始，爾後分別是明年年初的堪薩斯市廠，以及明年稍晚的休士頓廠。一旦所有的工廠都升級完成後，最後完成的工廠將會開放大眾參觀，讓大家可以親自看到營運狀況。**

字彙 **shift** 轉換　**landline** 固網電話　**infrastructure** 基礎設施　**roll out** 推出　**transition** 轉變，過渡
phase 階段　**state-of-the-art** 最先進的

確認特定資訊問題

172 According to the article, what caused GT Communications to transform its business plan?
(A) A new government regulation
(B) A complaint from the workforce
(C) A change in consumer behavior
(D) An increase in shareholders

中譯 根據報導的內容，造成 GT 電信通訊公司變更其事業計畫的原因為何？
(A) 政府的新法規
(B) 全體員工的抱怨
(C) 消費者行為的改變
(D) 股東人數的增加

Not / True 問題

173 What is mentioned about the company's facility in Nashville?
(A) It was used as a testing site.
(B) It received a technology award.
(C) It is the first factory opened by GT Communications.
(D) It was the meeting place of investors.

中譯 關於納什維爾廠，文中提到了什麼？
(A) 被用來作為試驗場地。
(B) 曾榮獲技術獎。
(C) 是 GT 電信通訊公司開設的第一家工廠。
(D) 是投資者們的會議場所。

確認特定資訊問題

174 Where does GT Communications plan to offer public tours of a site?
(A) Nashville (B) Detroit
(C) Kansas City **(D) Houston**

中譯 GT 電信通訊公司打算讓大眾現場參觀的工廠在哪？
(A) 納什維爾 (B) 底特律
(C) 堪薩斯市 **(D) 休士頓**

尋找句子位置問題

175 In which of the positions marked [1], [2], [3], and [4] does the following sentence best belong?
"We were thus able to keep ninety percent of staff members at that location."
(A) [1] (B) [2]
(C) [3] (D) [4]

中譯 下列句子最適合放在 [1]、[2]、[3] 和 [4] 的哪個位置？
「於是，我們就保住了該廠百分之 90 的員工。」
(A) [1] (B) [2]
(C) [3] (D) [4]

Questions 176-180 refer to the following information and e-mail. 資訊與電子郵件

⑯ Four intense workshops are being made available to employees of HTT Corp. Employees must choose one of the four courses below. **⑰ Each course comprises three three-hour sessions unless otherwise specified. The sessions will be held on Fridays (March 14, 21, and 28) from 2 P.M. to 5 P.M.**

Exchange Rates Risk Management

☐ Instructor: Frederic Masker
This course will look closely at how exchange rates affect markets, explain how predictions are made, and go over the best strategies for investing in an international context. This course has one additional two-hour session on April 4.

⑯ HTT 公司將為員工舉辦四場密集的專題研討會。員工必須從以下四門課程中擇一參加。**⑰ 除特別註明外，每門課程包括三堂三個小時的講座。講座將於每週五（3 月 14 日、21 日和 28 日）下午 2 點至 5 點舉行。**

匯率風險管理

☐講師：弗雷德里克・麥斯克
本課程將仔細研究匯率對市場的影響，並解釋如何預測，並介紹在國際背景下投資的最佳策略。本課程在 4 月 4 日另有一堂兩小時的講座。

179-2 **International Capital Flows**

□ **Instructor: Lydia Benson**
This course will explain how capital flows globally, introduce a few key relationships among countries, and go over the major effects of these flows on the global economy.

Multinational Corporations

□ 177 **Instructor: Sylvia Glazkova**
This course will introduce three major multinational corporations and give an in-depth analysis of their functioning and budget management.

178 **Case Studies**

□ **Instructor: Trenton Blair**
This hands-on course will have students work in groups to analyze a case and determine the best strategy for the sample corporation to take. Each group will present their findings in the last session.

179-2 國際資本流動

□講師：莉迪亞・本森
本課程將解釋全球資本流動的方式，介紹一些國家間的重要關係，並討論資本流動對全球經濟的主要影響。

跨國企業

□ 177 講師：席薇亞・格拉斯科娃
本課程將介紹三大跨國企業，並深入分析它們的運作與預算管理。

178 個案研究

□講師：特倫頓・布萊爾
這門實踐課程會讓學生分組分析某個案例，並為案例公司找到最佳的策略。每個小組將在最後一堂課上台報告他們的研究結果。

字彙 **comprise** 組成 **exchange rate** 匯率 **context** 背景，環境 **capital flow** 資本流動 **in-depth** 徹底的，深入的 **case study** 個案研究

To: Linda Kay <lindakay@httcorp.com>
From: Peter Moreno <petermoreno@httcorp.com>
Subject: Friday Afternoon
180D **Date: Thursday, March 27**

Dear Ms. Kay,

179-1 180A **Ms. Benson has changed the last session for the workshop from tomorrow to next Tuesday.** 179-1 180D **I am thus free to work tomorrow afternoon.** However, I was wondering if it would be acceptable for me to watch the presentations from Mr. Blair's class. 180B **Several coworkers taking that course have told me about their work, and I am highly interested in seeing the results.** Of course, if I am needed in the office at that time, I will be available to work.

Thank you for your consideration.

Sincerely,

Peter Moreno
Budget Analyst, HTT Corp.

收件者：琳達・凱
<lindakay@httcorp.com>
寄件者：彼得・莫雷諾
<petermoreno@httcorp.com>
主旨：星期五下午
180D **日期：3 月 27 日星期四**

凱女士您好：

179-1 180A **本森女士將明天專題研討會的最後一堂課改到下週二，** 179-1 180D **所以我明天下午就可以工作了。**不過，我想知道我能不能去看一下布萊爾先生課堂上的報告。180B **有幾個選這門課的同事跟我說報告的事，我很想看看他們的研究結果。**當然，如果到時候辦公室需要我的話，我也可以工作。

感謝您給予考慮。

彼得・莫雷諾 敬上
HTT 公司 預算分析員

字彙 **analyst** 分析員

出處問題

176 Where will the information most likely appear?
(A) In a brochure
(B) On a bulletin board
(C) In a magazine
(D) On a flyer

中譯 上述資訊最有可能出現在什麼地方？
(A) 在小冊子裡
(B) 在布告欄上
(C) 在雜誌裡
(D) 在宣傳單上

確認特定資訊問題

177 When will Ms. Glazkova's last class be held?
(A) March 14 (B) March 21
(C) March 28 (D) April 4

中譯 格拉斯科娃女士的最後一堂課將在何時舉行？
(A) 3 月 14 日 (B) 3 月 21 日
(C) 3 月 28 日 (D) 4 月 4 日

確認特定資訊問題

178 Which instructor will have students collaborate on a project?
(A) Frederic Masker
(B) Lydia Benson
(C) Sylvia Glazkova
(D) Trenton Blair

中譯 下列哪一位講師會讓學生合作做一項專題研究？
(A) 弗雷德里克・麥斯克
(B) 莉迪亞・本森
(C) 席薇亞・格拉斯科娃
(D) 特倫頓・布萊爾

兩則引文連結問題＿確認特定資訊問題

179 Which course has Mr. Moreno been attending?
(A) Exchange Rates Risk Management
(B) International Capital Flows
(C) Multinational Corporations
(D) Case Studies

中譯 莫雷諾先生參加的是哪一門課程？
(A) 匯率風險管理
(B) 國際資本流動
(C) 跨國企業
(D) 個案研究

Not / True 問題

180 What is NOT true about Mr. Moreno?
(A) He has already attended several classes.
(B) He wants to see his coworkers' projects.
(C) He is scheduled to give a presentation.
(D) He is able to come to the office on Friday.

中譯 關於莫雷諾先生，下列何者錯誤？
(A) 他已經上過幾堂課了。
(B) 他想看他同事的專題研究。
(C) 他被安排上台報告。
(D) 他星期五可以到辦公室。

Questions 181-185 refer to the following memo and schedule. 備忘錄與時間表

To: MMH Law Firm Employees
From: Tamara Caudill, Attorney
Subject: Re: Building for Sale

April 16

As discussed in the weekly meeting, the owner of Midland Tower will put the building up for sale next month, and we will relocate our offices. Aldridge Co., the realtor handling the sale of the building, would like professionals to take photos for the property listing on its Web site. 181 183 **This photo shoot will take place on April 24 and will be carried out in all parts of the building.** I have attached a schedule with the offices that are going to be photographed. In preparation for the photographers' visit, all items must be cleared from your desk except your computer and phone. 182 **We will provide plastic bins for you, and you should put your items in them for the short duration of the shoot.** 184-1 **A maintenance worker will visit you ten minutes before your appointed time to collect these bins with a cart.** Furniture might be rearranged in your office, but it will be returned to its original placement before you get back. 183 **The entire process will take about twenty minutes maximum, during which time you can take a break in the staff lounge. This does not count toward your usual daily break time.**

Thank you for your cooperation, and we apologize for any inconvenience this may cause.

[Attachment: Final Schedule]

受文者：MMH 法律事務所員工
發文者：塔瑪拉・高第爾 律師
主旨：關於：大樓出售

4 月 16 日

正如我們在每週會議上討論的，「米蘭辦公大樓」的所有權人將於下個月出售本棟大樓，而我們公司將會搬遷。阿爾德里奇公司負責處理本大樓的銷售事宜，想請專業攝影師來拍照，然後放到他們網站的待售房屋清單上。181 183 **拍攝工作將於 4 月 24 日進行，範圍為整棟大樓。**我已經附上一份時間表，其中列出即將被拍攝的辦公室。為了在攝影師來訪時做好準備，桌上除了電腦跟電話以外的所有物品都要清空。182 **公司會提供塑膠收納箱給您，供您在短暫的拍攝期間存放物品。**184-1 **維修人員會在您指定拍攝時間的 10 分鐘前，帶著手推車到您的辦公室蒐集收納箱。**您辦公室裡的家具可能會重新擺設，但是在您回到辦公室前會恢復原狀。183 **整個拍攝過程最多需要 20 分鐘，在拍攝期間，您可以到員工休息室休息。這不會計入您平常的每日休息時間。**

感謝您的合作，造成您任何的不便，我們深表歉意。

【附件：最終時間表】

字彙 relocate 搬遷　count toward 計入

Aldridge Co. Schedule: 184-2 185 **April 24**

TIME	OFFICE	OCCUPANT(S)
9:00 A.M.	201	Harriet Duncan
9:20 A.M.	185 **202**	**Ranjan Singh**
9:40 A.M.	203	Dale Mumford, Michael Bellamy
184-2 **10:00 A.M.**	**204**	**Shirley Swain**
10:20 A.M.	205	Brandon Parra, Huan Ren

185 **Brandon Parra will handle room 202 because the occupant won't be in the office that day.**

阿爾德里奇公司時間表： 184-2 185 **4 月 24 日**

時間	辦公室	使用者(們)
上午 9:00	201	哈莉雅・鄧肯
上午 9:20	185 **202**	**蘭詹・辛格**
上午 9:40	203	戴爾・蒙福德，邁克爾・貝勒米
184-2 **上午 10:00**	204	**雪莉・斯韋恩**
上午 10:20	205	布蘭登・帕拉，胡安・任

185 **布蘭登・帕拉將負責處理 202 辦公室，因為使用者當天不在辦公室裡。**

字彙 occupant 佔用者，使用者

目的問題

181 What is the purpose of the memo?
(A) To introduce a new building owner to employees
(B) To explain how an office relocation will occur
(C) To distribute a schedule for a renovation project
(D) To announce a plan for photographing a building

中譯 此備忘錄的目的為何？
(A) 向員工介紹大樓的新主人
(B) 解釋公司如何進行搬遷
(C) 分發翻修工程的時間表
(D) 宣布大樓的拍攝計畫

確認特定資訊問題

182 What does Ms. Caudill advise the memo recipients to do?
(A) Direct their questions to Aldridge Co.
(B) Use containers to temporarily move items
(C) Contact her regarding their availability on April 24
(D) Leave their personal belongings at home

中譯 高第爾女士建議本通知的收文者做什麼？
(A) 向阿爾德里奇公司提問
(B) 使用收納箱來臨時搬運物品
(C) 與她聯繫，告知 4 月 24 日是否有空
(D) 將個人物品放在家裡

確認特定資訊問題

183 What can the memo recipients do on April 24?
(A) Take an additional break
(B) Work part of the day from home
(C) Leave work early
(D) Have an extended lunchtime

中譯 本備忘錄的受文者在4月24日這天能做什麼？
(A) 可以多休息一會兒
(B) 部分時間在家工作
(C) 提早下班
(D) 有延長的午餐時間

兩則引文連結問題＿確認特定資訊問題

184 At what time will a maintenance worker arrive at Ms. Swain's office on April 24?
(A) 9:40 A.M. **(B) 9:50 A.M.**
(C) 10:00 A.M. (D) 10:10 A.M.

中譯 4 月 24 日維修人員幾點會到斯韋恩女士的辦公室？
(A) 上午 9:40 **(B) 上午 9:50**
(C) 上午 10:00 (D) 上午 10:10

推論問題

185 What is implied about Mr. Singh?
(A) He will move to office 203.
(B) He shares an office with Mr. Parra.
(C) He will be absent on April 24.
(D) He requested a change in the schedule.

中譯 關於辛格先生，文中暗示了什麼？
(A) 他會搬到 203 辦公室。
(B) 他跟帕拉先生共用一間辦公室。
(C) 他 4 月 24 日不在辦公室。
(D) 他要求變更時間表。

Questions 186-190 refer to the following product description, online review, and online response. 產品說明、網路評價與線上回覆

The Bag of the Future: Zimmer-40

The Zimmer-40 will revolutionize the way you think about backpacks. 186B **It features a fold-out solar panel that can be used to charge your personal electronics.** The advanced battery ensures that you always have the power you need on the go. 186A **The outer section is fully resistant to water, so your devices are always protected.** 186C **In addition, all plastic parts on the backpack come from recycled plastic.**

The Zimmer is sold at department stores and sporting goods outlets. 187-2 **Sign up for our monthly newsletter at the time of purchase to get a free second battery.**

未來的背包：奇默-40

奇默-40將顛覆你對背包的看法。186B **他配備可折疊的太陽能板，可為您的個人電子產品充電。**這款最先進的電池，能隨時提供您所需的電力。186A **背包外層完全防水，所以您的電子設備始終受到保護。**186C **此外，背包的塑膠零件全都來自回收塑料。**

奇默在各大百貨公司以及體育用品專賣店皆有販售。187-2 **購買本產品時，請註冊接收本公司的每月電子報，即可免費獲得第二個電池。**

字彙 revolutionize 徹底改變　fold-out 可摺疊的　solar panel 太陽能板　on the go 隨時隨地

www.ucanreview.net/customer_reviews/accessories

Brand: Zimmer	**Item:** Zimmer-40
Reviewer: Tyson Quintero	**Post Type:** New

After researching several technology-enabled backpacks on the market, I selected the Zimmer-40 because of Zimmer's solid reputation. The color of the bag was darker than it appeared in the catalog, but that wasn't a problem for me. I'm impressed with how long the battery holds its charge, 187-1 **and I'm glad to have the second free one.** 189-1 **The only thing that disappointed me was that my 15-inch laptop does not fit inside the bag.** Despite this, I highly recommend this product, 188 **and I intend to buy it as a gift for several friends.**

www.ucanreview.net/customer_reviews/accessories

品牌：奇默	品項：奇默-40
評價人：泰森・金特羅	發布類型：新發布

在研究了市面上幾款有科技功能的背包之後，我選擇了奇默-40，因為該品牌有著良好聲譽。這款背包顏色比目錄上看到的要再深一些，但這對我來說不是問題。令我刮目相看的是電池的續航時間，187-1 **我也很高興有免費的第二個電池。**189-1 **唯一令我失望的是，我的15吋筆電放不進背包裡。**儘管如此，我還是強烈推薦這款背包，188 **我也打算買來當禮物送給幾個朋友。**

字彙 technology-enabled 由科技驅動的　solid 可靠的

www.ucanreview.net/customer_reviews/accessories

Brand: Zimmer	**Item:** Zimmer-40
Reviewer: Phillip Sandoval	**Post Type:** Reply

As a Zimmer customer service agent, I'm sorry you were not completely satisfied with your purchase. 189-2 **Based on your needs, you might want to consider the**

www.ucanreview.net/customer_reviews/accessories

品牌：奇默	品項：奇默 -40
評論人：飛利浦・桑多瓦	發布類型：回覆

身為奇默的客服專員，我很遺憾您對所購買的產品並非完全滿意。189-2 **根據您的需求，您或許可以考慮奇默-40B。**這款背包內部有個特

Zimmer-40B. It has a special charging compartment on the inside that can accommodate up to a 17-inch laptop. It has the same gel-filled shoulder straps as the Zimmer-40, so you can still wear it comfortably even if it is loaded with heavy items. Since you already have the Zimmer-40, there isn't any (190) **point** in buying a new battery because the same one can be used in all of our bags. I hope this resolves your issue.

殊的充電隔間，最大可容納17吋的筆電。它跟奇默-40一樣，都是凝膠填充背帶，所以即使裡面裝滿重物，背著它也很輕鬆。既然您已經有奇默-40，那麼買新電池就沒有任何 (190) **意義**了，因為同一款電池可以相容於我們所有的背包。我希望這有助解決您的問題。

字彙 compartment 隔間　accommodate 容納　load 裝載　resolve 解決

Not / True 問題

186 What is NOT indicated about the Zimmer-40?
(A) It has a waterproof exterior.
(B) It makes use of renewable energy.
(C) It is partially made from recycled materials.
(D) It is light enough to use during sports.

中譯 關於奇默-40，下列哪個說法不正確？
(A) 其外部可防水。
(B) 它利用可再生能源。
(C) 部分是由回收材料製成的。
(D) 它夠輕，可於運動時使用。

三則引文連結問題__推論問題

187 What can be inferred about Mr. Quintero?
(A) He will receive monthly updates from Zimmer.
(B) He purchased the bag at a department store.
(C) He doesn't like the color of the bag.
(D) He mainly uses the bag for outdoor activities.

中譯 關於金特羅先生，我們可以推論出什麼？
(A) 他每個月都會收到奇默的最新消息。
(B) 他在百貨公司買了這個背包。
(C) 他不喜歡這個背包的顏色。
(D) 他主要用這個背包進行戶外活動。

推論問題

188 What is suggested in the online review?
(A) Zimmer is a relatively new company.
(B) Mr. Quintero plans to purchase more bags.
(C) Zimmer sells a line of laptop computers.
(D) Mr. Quintero noticed some damage on his bag.

中譯 網路評價暗示了什麼？
(A) 奇默是一家相對較新的公司。
(B) 金特羅先生打算買更多的包包。
(C) 奇默販售筆電系列產品。
(D) 金特羅先生注意到他的背包有些損壞。

三則引文連結問題__確認特定資訊問題

189 Why does Mr. Sandoval recommend the Zimmer-40B to Mr. Quintero?
(A) It is the only bag with gel-filled straps.
(B) It can charge items more quickly.
(C) It has a larger carrying capacity.
(D) It is more durable than the Zimmer-40.

中譯 為什麼桑多瓦先生向金特羅先生推薦奇默-40B？
(A) 它是唯一有凝膠填充背帶的背包。
(B) 它可以更快速地給物品充電。
(C) 它的置物空間更大。
(D) 它比奇默 -40 更耐用。

同義詞問題

190 In the online response, the word "point" in paragraph 1, line 6, is closest in meaning to
(A) opinion **(B) reason**
(C) aspect (D) spot

中譯 在線上回覆中，第 1 段第 6 行的「point」一字，意思最接近下列何者？
(A) 意見 **(B) 理由**
(C) 層面 (D) 地點

Questions 191-195 refer to the following e-mails and information. 電子郵件與資訊

To: Kimberly Garrett <kgarrett@saezinc.net>
From: Marietta Convention Center <info@mariettacc.com>
Date: February 19
Subject: Information

Dear Ms. Garrett,

193-2 **Thank you for taking a tour of the Marietta Convention Center on February 18.** I hope you enjoyed viewing our technology-enabled facilities, including the expansion of the west wing. Based on your description of the banquet your company plans to hold, I believe we would be the perfect site. 191 **Each room comes equipped with a stage, which could be used to present awards to your art instructors and give speeches**, and there are a variety of amenities to suit your needs. Furthermore, I can confirm that we currently have no reservations booked for your desired date of March 31. Attached, please find the detailed information you requested about each room. If you would like to make a booking, or if you have any further questions, do not hesitate to contact me at 555-6677, extension 21. I hope to hear from you soon.

Sincerely,

Ralph Shelby

Guest Services Representative, Marietta Convention Center

收件人：金柏莉・葛瑞特 <kgarrett@saezinc.net>
寄件人：瑪麗埃塔會議中心 <info@mariettacc.com>
日期：2 月 19 日
主旨：資訊

親愛的葛瑞特小姐：

193-2 **感謝您於 2 月 18 日蒞臨參觀瑪麗埃塔會議中心**，希望您對所參觀的科技化設施（包括擴建後的西側廳）感到滿意。根據您對貴公司計劃舉辦宴會的描述，我相信本會議中心是最理想的場所。191 **每間宴會廳都有舞臺，可供貴公司進行美術教師的頒獎活動與發表演說**，還有各式各樣的便利設施可以滿足貴公司的需求。此外，我可以確認貴公司活動預定的 3 月 31 日這天，目前尚無人預約。隨信附上您所要求的每間宴會廳的詳細資訊。若您想要預約或是還有其他問題，請不要猶豫，隨時可撥打 555-6677 轉分機 21 與我聯繫。靜候您的佳音。

誠摯地

拉爾夫・謝爾比
瑪麗埃塔會議中心 客服專員

字彙 **wing** （常指增建的）側廳 **amenity** （常用複數）便利設施 **extension** 分機

Marietta Convention Center Room Descriptions

Daisy Room-Maximum Capacity: 50 / Rental Fee: $2,600
4 x 8 m stage, podium, projector, pull-down video screen

Sunflower Room-Maximum Capacity: 50 / Rental Fee: $2,900
4 x 8 m stage, podium, projector, pull-down video screen, 192 **exterior doorway to garden**

195-2 **Peony Room-Maximum Capacity: 100 / Rental Fee: $3,500**
6 x 10 m stage, podium, projector, flat-screen built-in television, full-service bar

Orchid Room-Maximum Capacity: 100 / Rental Fee: $4,800
6 x 12 m stage, podium, projector, flat-screen built-in television, full-service bar, view of Lochmere Bay
Various seating arrangements are available. Guests may use south or west parking lot for a nominal fee.

瑪麗埃塔會議中心 宴會廳簡介

雛菊廳——最大容納人數：50 人 / 場租：2,600 美元
4 x 8 公尺的舞臺、講臺、投影機和下拉式投影螢幕

葵花廳——最大容納人數：50 人 / 場租：2,900 美元
4 x 8 公尺的舞臺、講臺、投影機、下拉式投影螢幕和 192 通往花園的外門

195-2 牡丹廳——最大容納人數：100 人 / 場租：3,500 美元
6 x 10 公尺的舞臺、講臺、投影機、嵌入式平面電視和服務周全的酒吧

蘭花廳——最大容納人數：100 人 / 場租：4,800 美元
6 x 12 公尺的舞臺、講臺、投影機、嵌入式平面電視、服務周全的酒吧和洛克米爾灣海景有多種的座位安排可供選擇。賓客僅需支付極少費用便可使用南面或西面的停車場。

字彙 pull-down 下拉的 built-in 嵌入的 nominal （金額）微小的

E-MAIL MESSAGE

To: Amina Jeffries, 194 **Dean McGraw**, Kimberly Garrett, Bai Tan
From: Amil Rao
Date: February 20
Subject: Banquet plans

Hi Everyone,

It seems like we are making progress on our committee's plans for the upcoming banquet for our staff and their families. 193-1 **Thank you, Kimberly, for taking over the Marietta Convention Center visit for me, since I had to fly to Toronto that day for an unexpected business matter.** 194 **I'm still waiting for the reports from the rest of you regarding the caterers you were assigned to research.** Please e-mail that information to me by Thursday afternoon.

As for the venue options, 195-1 **I'd love our ninety guests to be able to overlook Lochmere Bay as they dine, but I don't think this will be feasible, given our limited budget. Instead, I think it would be best to rent the cheaper room that fits our size needs.** We can discuss this further at Friday's meeting. See you then!

Amil

電子郵件訊息

收件人：阿米娜・傑弗里斯、194 迪安・麥格勞、金柏莉・葛瑞特、白潭
寄件人：阿米爾・拉奧
日期：2 月 20 日
主旨：宴會規劃

大家好：

看來我們的委員會在即將為員工及其家屬舉辦的宴會規劃上有了進展。193-1 金柏莉，謝謝妳代替我去參觀瑪麗埃塔會議中心，因為那天我得飛去多倫多處理生意上的突發事件。194 其他被指派調查外燴餐飲公司的人，我還在等你們的報告。請你們在週四下午前把資料以電子郵件寄給我。

至於場地的選擇，195-1 我希望我們的 90 名賓客用餐時能遠眺洛克米爾灣，但是考慮到有限的預算，我認為這不太可行。作為替代，我認為最好租一間比較便宜而又符合我們人數規模的宴會廳。我們可以在週五開會的時候進一步討論這個問題。咱們到時見！

阿米爾

字彙 feasible 切實可行的

推論問題

191 Where does Ms. Garrett most likely work?
(A) At a technology company
(B) At a fitness center
(C) At an art institute
(D) At a performance venue

中譯 葛瑞特小姐最有可能在哪裡工作？
(A) 在科技公司
(B) 在健身房
(C) 在美術學院
(D) 在表演場所

Not / True 問題

192 Which room amenity is indicated in the information?
(A) Special lighting for the stage area
(B) A view of the city skyline
(C) Complimentary parking for guests
(D) Access to an outdoor space

中譯 宴會廳的簡介裡提到下列哪項便利設施？
(A) 舞臺區的特殊照明
(B) 城市天際線的景觀
(C) 提供賓客免費停車
(D) 可以使用戶外空間

三則引文連結問題＿推論問題

193 What is implied about Mr. Rao?
(A) He joined the committee at the last minute.
(B) He visited several meeting venues.
(C) He wrote a review of a caterer.
(D) He took a business trip on February 18.

中譯 關於拉奧先生，文中暗示了什麼？
(A) 他到最後一刻才加入委員會。
(B) 他參觀了幾個會議地點。
(C) 他寫了對外燴承辦公司的評論。
(D) 他在 2 月 18 日出差。

推論問題

194 What can be inferred about Mr. McGraw?
(A) He is in charge of the committee's budget.
(B) He is gathering information about caterers.
(C) He is unable to attend Friday's meeting.
(D) He visited the Marietta Convention Center.

中譯 關於麥格勞先生，我們可以推論出什麼？
(A) 他負責委員會的預算。
(B) 他正在蒐集外燴公司的資訊。
(C) 他無法參加星期五的會議。
(D) 他參觀了瑪麗埃塔會議中心。

三則引文連結問題＿推論問題

195 Which room would Mr. Rao most likely want to rent?
(A) Daisy Room
(B) Sunflower Room
(C) Peony Room
(D) Orchid Room

中譯 拉奧先生最有可能會租下哪一間宴會廳？
(A) 雛菊廳
(B) 葵花廳
(C) 牡丹廳
(D) 蘭花廳

Questions 196-200 refer to the following article, Web page, and review. 文章、網頁及評論

Theater Fundraiser a Success

Last night's charity banquet to raise funds for the Gilcrest Theater was 196 **deemed** a remarkable success by event planners, who reported proceeds of nearly $12,000, approximately $2,000 over the goal. 197 **The money will be used for the installation of a cutting-edge sound system in the theater,** which will serve as a much-needed replacement for the outdated system currently being used.

The work will be completed just in time for the Regional Film Festival, of which the Gilcrest Theater is a hosting site. While the facility usually presents live theater performances, it is equipped with a large projection screen for movies. Other theaters across the region will also participate, 198-1 **but Gilcrest Theater has the highest seating capacity among them,** more than double that of the second-largest one, Corinth Theater.

Tickets for the film festival go on sale next week. Movie fans can take in intense dramas by critically acclaimed directors. Or for those looking for something light, there are plenty of films with comedic writing.

劇院募款活動圓滿成功

活動策劃者 196 **認為**昨晚的慈善晚宴成效斐然，一共為吉爾克雷斯特劇院籌措了近 12,000 美元的捐款，約比目標金額多出 2,000 美元左右。197 **這筆錢將用來為劇院安裝最先進的音響系統**，以取代目前使用中的老舊系統，這是劇院迫切需要的。

這項工程將在地區電影節前及時完成，而吉爾克雷斯特劇院則是電影節的主辦場地。雖然劇院平常都是現場的戲劇表演，但這裡也配備了用來播放電影的大型投影螢幕。本地的其他劇院也將參與，198-1 **但是吉爾克雷斯特劇院是其中座位最多的劇院**，是第二大劇院柯林斯劇院的兩倍以上。

電影節的入場券下週開始販售。影迷可以看到由廣受好評的導演所拍攝的緊張劇情片，或是對那些想要看點輕鬆小品的人來說，有許多電影都具喜劇風格。

字彙 proceeds 收入　cutting-edge 先進的　seating capacity 座位數量　take in 去觀看，觀賞　critically acclaimed 廣受好評的

www.regionalfilmfestival.com/schedule

HOME	ABOUT	**SCHEDULE**	SEATING	DIRECTION

Regional Film Festival

Thursday, September 6	Friday, September 7	**Saturday, September 8**	Sunday, September 9

Venue / Phone Number	Film	Start Time	
200-2 **24th Street Theater / 555–4102**	***Underground***	7:00 P.M.	[More Info]

www.regionalfilmfestival.com/schedule

首頁	簡介	**時刻表**	座位	交通路線

地區電影節

9月6日 星期四	9月7日 星期五	**9月8日 星期六**	9月9日 星期日

場地 / 電話號碼	影片名稱	播映時間	
200-2 **第 24 街劇院 / 555-4102**	《地下》	晚上 7:00	[詳細資訊]

Corinth Theater / 555–0578	*A Summer's Day*	7:30 P.M.	[More Info]
198-2 **Gilcrest Theater / 555–5855**	***The Tale of Marco***	**7:05 P.M.**	[More Info]
Palacios Theater / 555–9360	*Wilson's Army*	8:10 P.M.	[More Info]

199 **Customers should select the seat number and row when purchasing tickets, so please review the map of the venue's seating sections, downloadable at www.regionalfilmfestival.com/seating, before calling to order tickets.** This will speed up the ordering process.

柯林斯劇院 / 555-0578	《盛夏之日》	晚上 7:30	[詳細資訊]
198-2 **吉爾克雷斯特劇院 / 555-5855**	**《馬可傳奇》**	**晚上 7:05**	[詳細資訊]
帕拉西奧斯劇院 / 555-9360	《威爾遜軍團》	晚上 8:10	[詳細資訊]

199 **顧客購票時應一併選擇座位號碼與排數，因此在打電話訂票前，先行查看場地的座位圖（可至 www.regionalfilmfestival.com/seating 下載）**，此舉將加快訂票的過程。

***Underground:* Best Thriller of the Year**

****

By Casey Ashton

If you're looking for a thriller that will keep you guessing until the very end, 200-1 **look no further than *Underground*, the latest masterpiece by director Mia Camacho. I recently saw it at the Regional Film Festival,** and I was extremely impressed with the character development, intriguing plot, and fantastic acting. This film is a must-see!

《地下》：今年最佳驚悚電影

****

凱西・阿什頓 撰

如果你正在找一部直到結尾都充滿懸疑的驚悚片，200-1 **那就直接選擇導演米亞・卡瑪丘的最新力作《地下》就對了。這是我最近在地區電影節上看到的電影**，我對電影裡的角色塑造、引人入勝的情節，以及精彩絕倫的演技印象深刻。這是一部不容錯過的電影！

字彙 **thriller** 驚悚電影 **very** 最後的 **masterpiece** 傑作 **intriguing** 引人入勝的

同義詞問題

196 In the article, the word "deemed" in paragraph 1, line 2, is closest in meaning to
(A) considered (B) expected
(C) admired (D) caused

中譯 在文章中，第 1 段第 2 行的「deemed」一字，意思最接近下列何者？
(A) 認為 (B) 期待
(C) 欽佩 (D) 造成

確認特定資訊問題

197 How will the raised funds be used at Gilcrest Theater?
(A) To launch an advertising campaign
(B) To purchase a projection screen
(C) To upgrade an outdated Web site
(D) To install new audio equipment

中譯 吉爾克雷斯特劇院將如何使用募集來的資金？
(A) 展開廣告宣傳活動
(B) 購買投影螢幕
(C) 升級過時的網站
(D) 安裝新的音響設備

三則引文連結問題__確認特定資訊問題

198 When will the largest theater start its screening event on September 8?
(A) At 7:00 P.M.
(B) At 7:05 P.M.
(C) At 7:30 P.M.
(D) At 8:10 P.M.

中譯 9 月 8 日，規模最大的劇院將於何時開始放映影片？
(A) 晚上 7:00
(B) 晚上 7:05
(C) 晚上 7:30
(D) 晚上 8:10

確認特定資訊問題

199 What are ticket purchasers advised to do?
(A) Download a digital receipt
(B) Check a seating chart in advance
(C) Read some online movie reviews
(D) Receive tickets by express mail

中譯 網頁中建議購票者做什麼？
(A) 下載電子收據
(B) 提前查看座位表
(C) 閱讀網路上的影評
(D) 透過快遞收到入場券

三則引文連結問題__確認特定資訊問題

200 Where did Mr. Ashton watch a film?
(A) 24th Street Theater
(B) Corinth Theater
(C) Gilcrest Theater
(D) Palacios Theater

中譯 阿什頓先生是在哪裡看電影的？
(A) 第 24 街劇院
(B) 柯林斯劇院
(C) 吉爾克雷斯特劇院
(D) 帕拉西奧斯劇院

核心字彙表

Actual Test 1

PART 1

pour 傾倒
water 澆水
pile 堆放
put away 收拾……
fold 折疊
position 放置
stack 疊放
arrange 排列
wait in line 排隊
instrument 樂器
copy 副本
store 存放
place 擺放

PART 2

landlord 房東
property 房產
give a tour 帶領參觀
site 地點
sustainable 永續的
sign up 報名
give a ride 載某人一程
go on a business trip 出差
trim 修剪
lot 某種場地
leftover 剩餘的
promotional 促銷的
laboratory 實驗室
full-time position 全職職位
check （在機場）託運（行李）
streamline 簡化
copy （書報雜誌等的）一本，一份
take a day off 請假

> 例 If you need to take a day off, ask your manager for approval.
> 如需請假，請向管理人員申請批准。

video conference 視訊會議
turn in 繳交
portable 可攜帶的

PART 3

work from home 在家工作
be responsible for 為……負責
device 裝置
protective 保護的
from place to place 到處
patio 露臺
job opening 職缺
alert 通知
firm 事務所
individual 個體戶
focus A on B 著重在 A 方面進行 B
base 基礎
register 登記
in stock 有貨的
renovate 整修
be promoted to 被提拔為……

> 例 She was recently promoted to marketing director.
> 她最近被升遷為行銷總監。

accomplishment 成就
be pleased with 對……感到開心
business hours 營業時間
sell out 賣完
plan on 打算做某事
out-of-town 城外的；外地的
earn 獲得
regional 地區的
meet 達到
quota 配額；目標
work on 進行某事

PART 4

tourist site 觀光景點
workshop 工作坊
talented 才華洋溢的
identify 辨別
membership 會員資格
fitness 健康
special deal 特殊優惠
demand 需求量
inspect 視察
feel reassured 感到安心的
thorough 周全的
guidance 指引
knowledgeable 學識淵博的
operate 運作
current 目前的
essential 必需的
cover letter 求職信
résumé 履歷
short-staffed 人手短缺的
guarantee 保證
keep . . . up to date 讓……得知最新消息
trend 趨勢
harvest 收割
applicant 應試者
move on to 進行下一個……
annual 年度的
trade expo 貿易博覽會

PART 5

corporate 企業的；公司
structure 結構
manufacturing 製造業
access （使用某物的）權利
analyst 分析師
predict 預測
closure 歇業
restriction 限制
self-employed 自營作業者
carry out 執行

> 例 Soil samples were taken to carry out the testing to check for pollution.
> 已採集土壤樣本，好進行汙染檢測。

replacement 替換
setback 阻礙
assess 評估
favorable 有利的
condition 條件
result in 導致

> 例 The favorable market conditions resulted in more business investment.
> 良好的市場環境導致更多的商業投資。

built-in 內建的

PART 6

for one's convenience
為了某人方便

例 An order form is enclosed for your convenience.
附上訂購表以方便使用。

personalize 個人化
meet the needs 滿足需求
short notice 臨時通知
residential 居住的
from scratch 從零開始

例 We have to do the whole thing again from scratch.
我們得從頭開始重做這整件事。

existing 現有的
unwanted 不需要的
distracting 令人分心的

PART 7

launch 推出
attract 吸引
public relations 公關
prior to 在……之前
acknowledge 告知收到(信件等)
be eligible for 符合……資格
patronage 光臨;惠顧
warehouse 倉庫
overnight shipping 隔日送達
registration 登記;註冊
on a first-come, first-served basis 先到先得的

例 Spots will be assigned on a first-come, first-served basis.
場地將按照「先到先得」的原則進行分配。

grant 補助金
required 必要的
certification 證照
fit 適合
provider 供應商
on site 現場
overnight 過夜(的)
enter into a contract 簽訂合約
headquarters 總公司;總部
reimburse 補貼;償還
provided 前提是……
completion 完成
houseware 家庭用品
sluggish 遲滯的
respectively 分別
yield 產出
promising 有前景的
ongoing 持續的
date back to 時間追溯至

例 The college dates back to 1870s.
這所大學可追溯至 1870 年代。

fragile 脆弱的
unmatched 無人能比的

例 Our track record for dealing with fragile artifacts is unmatched.
我們在處理易碎文物方面的紀錄是無人能比的。

operation 運作
line up 契合
house 存放
come along 進展
promote 推廣
high-profile 能見度高的
register for 報名……
along with 邊進行……
fall through 失敗;落空
specialize in 專精於……
in-house 駐點的
affordably priced 平價的
compliment 讚賞
venue 場地
underway 進行中的
screening 篩檢
vendor 廠商
supplement 補充物
address 處理

例 Many issues were addressed at the meeting with board members.
董事會會議上討論了許多議題。

beneficial 有益的
transition 轉換
be concerned about 擔心……
knowledgeable 知識豐富的
circumstance 情況
submission 提交
initiative 倡議
carry 販售
high-end 高檔的
outgoing 即將離職的;外向的
expenditure 開銷
qualification 資格(證明)
list 列出
quarterly 每季的;每季地
misconception 誤解
head 帶領
high-ranking 高階的
chair 主席

Actual Test 2

PART 1

groceries 生活雜貨
stroll 漫步
on display 陳列,展示
put away 收拾
operate 操作
remove 卸下
hard hat 工程帽
install 裝設
unoccupied 空著的;閒置的

PART 2

depart 發車
recommend 推薦
book 訂房
plenty of 足夠的
promote 升遷
branch 分公司
vending machine 販賣機
unplug 拔掉插頭
electrical 電路的
reach 達到
fundraising 募款
charity 慈善
short 短缺的
restore 修復
sales figure 銷售數據
accurate 準確的
evaluation 評鑑

cover 處理；涵蓋
fill a prescription 領處方箋的藥
be out of town 在外地
present 主講
give a lecture 教課
renew 更新
release 發行
trade agreement 貿易協議書
take apart 拆卸
relief 安心
instructions 説明書
approve 核准
in transit 運輸途中
advanced 進階的
minor 輕微的
calculate 計算
cut back 縮減
notice 發現；注意

PART 3

flyer 傳單
discontinue 停止（生產等）
work overtime 加班
on schedule 準時到達
permit 許可證
lot （用於特定目的的）土地
assignment 工作
make a delivery 配送
make an adjustment 調整

例 I'd like to make an adjustment to the current policy.
我想調整一下目前的政策。

take part in 參加
get together with 聚在一起
oversee 監督
screen 審查；篩選
be out sick 請病假
under control 得到控制
leave behind 遺落；丟下
get in touch with 與……聯絡上
strict 嚴格的
look forward to 期待
property 房產
regulation 法規
switch A with B 將 A 與 B 對調
prestigious 有聲望的
bring up 提出

PART 4

raise funds 募款
operating expense 營運開銷
exclusive 獨有的；專用的
assistance 協助
transport 運輸
set up 設置

例 How many chairs need to be set up for the reception?
招待會要擺幾張椅子？

volunteer 自願
rewarding 獲益良多的
participate in 參加
replacement 接替者；替代品
on short notice 臨時通知
distribute 分發
step down 辭職
enormous 龐大的
put together 整理出
qualified 合格的
take on 接任
literacy 識字能力
registration 報名
venue 場地
accommodate 容納
screening 篩檢
specific 特定的
valuable 寶貴的
quantity 數量
place an order 下訂單
be dedicated to 致力於
pleasant 愉快的
provide A with B 向 A 提供 B
reassess 重新評估

PART 5

reliability 可靠度
demand 需求量
provider 供應者
appliance 家電
caterer 外燴業者
peak season 旺季
additional 額外的
shortage 短缺
community center 社區中心
patron 主顧
reference book 參考書
build a reputation 建立聲譽
in compliance with 遵循……
update 更新；新資訊
involved in 涉入……
pharmaceuticals 製藥的
physician 醫師
transaction 交易
transfer 轉帳
deposit 存款
take . . . into account 將……納入考量
make a projection 預測
potential 潛在的
discouraged 卻步的；沮喪的
confusingly 令人困惑地
boarding pass 登機證
agent 代理人；特務
verify 確認；證明
commence 開始
entrepreneur 企業家
launch 推出
start-up 新事業
expand 拓展
on the market 市場上
auditorium 禮堂
reserve 保留
presenter 演講人
on the contrary 相反的

PART 6

charge 收費
a wide selection of 多樣的

例 You can choose any two items you like from our wide selection of jewelry.
你可以從我們多樣的珠寶選擇任兩件你喜歡的物品。

offer （短期的）折扣
prominent 著名的
association 協會
donation 捐款；捐獻
shelter 收容所
retirement 退休
facility 設施
proximity 鄰近
subscription 訂閱
valid 有效的
come out 發行、推出

例 His new novel is coming out in October.
他最新的小說即將於十月發行。

residential address 住家地址
associated with 與……有關

PART 7

donate 捐贈
comment 留言
invoice 帳單
rental 租用的
unit 小機器；元件
coverage 保險（範圍）
policy 保單
printout 印出的資料
in full 全部地
on the rise 上升的
in part 一部分
supplier 供應商
accumulate 累積
project 預測
unpredictability 不可預測性
associate （生意）夥伴
representative 代表；代理人
relocate 搬遷
reflect 對應、反映出
paperwork 文書作業
estimate 估價
budget 預算
worth 值得
have a point 有道理
confidence 信心
sophisticated 精緻的
outfit 服裝
prioritize 以……為優先
accompany 陪伴
introduce 推出
large-scale 大規模的
drop off 送東西去某處
assume 假設
follow one's example
以某人為榜樣
sign up for 報名
realty 房仲業
lease agreement 租賃協議書
collect 收集
obstacle 障礙
bid 招標

contaminated 受汙染的
revenue 收益
conduct 進行
regularly 定期地
voucher 禮券
matter 要緊；有關係
set . . . apart 讓……與眾不同

例 Her creativity sets her apart from other candidates.
她的創意使她與其他候選人不同。

give sb. a ride 載某人
convenient 方便的
immediate 立即的
attachment 附件
downsize 縮減
underground 在地下（的）
report to work 上班
prior to ……之前
take inventory of 盤點

例 They took inventory of the company's furniture, equipment, and supplies.
他們盤點了公司的家具、設備和用品。

administration 行政；管理
absent 缺席的
humble 普通的；不起眼的
unfold 展開；打開
entertaining 使人愉快的
informative 資訊豐富的
spacious 寬敞的
trim 縮減
halt 停止
stock up on 大量購買；囤積
account for （在數量上）占
majority 多數的
operation 運作
clearance 出清特賣
qualify for 有資格……的

例 All orders qualify for free delivery from October 1 to October 31.
10 月 1 日到 10 月 31 日的所有訂單皆免運。

constantly 不斷地
minimum 最小值

attain 達到
overview 概述；概觀
indicate 表明；指出
coordinator 統籌者
track 記錄

Actual Test 3

PART 1

apron 圍裙
kitchen counter 廚房流理台
pedestrian 行人
section 路段；區域
plaza 廣場
pave 舖（地面）
luggage 行李
unload 卸下
walkway（尤指架高的）走道
lecturer 演講者；講師

PART 2

forecast （天氣）預報
lane 車道
best-selling 暢銷的
after hours 下班後；工作時間之後
pass 通行證
postpone 延期
dramatically 突然地；戲劇化地
profitable 有盈利的
organizer 組織者，籌辦者
original 原版；原件
charitable 慈善的
business card 名片
reserve 預約，預訂
retire 退休
make a copy of 複印
flight 航班
tenant 租戶；房客
lease 租約
due 應支付的；預計的

PART 3

normally 通常，一般
the public 大眾
assistant 助理，助手
proposal 提案，建議
convention 大會，會議
make time 挪出時間

reach an agreement 達成協議
dye 染色
lawn mower 割草機
misunderstand 誤解
defective 有瑕疵的
shortly 很快，不久
cruise 乘船遊覽
reputation 名聲
cover for 頂替，代理
font 字體，字型
appeal to 引起注意
target 對象；目標
demographic （顧客）族群
go too far 做得過火
ultimately 最終，最後
transfer 調動
look forward to V-ing 期待做（某事）
interact 互動，交流
stressful 壓力大的
complaint 抱怨，投訴
positive 建設性的；正向的
line up 排隊
publicize 宣傳
healthcare 醫療保健
presenter 演講人
send in 提交
relevant 相關的；切題的
shut down 歇業
checkup 身體檢查
sensitive 敏感的
overall 整體而言
necessarily 必然地
stay away from 遠離
symposium 專題討論會
get around 四處走走
hassle 麻煩
criterion 標準（複數為 criteria）

PART 4

call a meeting 召開會議
retail store 零售店
grab 抓取
rarely 很少
visually 在視覺上
appealing 吸引人的
itchy 發癢的
concentrate on 專注於
fabric 布料；織物
advantage 優點
legal 法律的
consultant 顧問
at the latest 最遲
case 訴訟案；官司
negotiable 可協商的
time frame 時間範圍
benefits package 福利待遇
consult 查閱；諮詢
status 狀態
lead 主持；領導
graduate （大學）畢業生
cuisine 料理
obtain 取得，獲得
business administration 商業管理
combination 結合
connection（事物間的）連接，聯結
resolve 解決（問題或困難等）
connect （使）連接
manufacturer 製造商
safety guideline 安全準則
safety glasses 護目鏡
task 工作；任務
threatening 威脅（性）的
agenda 議程
pool （為了共同活動或工作所需的）一群人
under construction 施工中
congested 壅塞的
project 工程；專案計畫
push back 推遲，拖延
take a detour 改道，繞道
disturbance 紛亂；干擾
make an investment 進行投資
except for 除了……以外（不包括所列舉人事物）
safety gear 安全裝備

PART 5

term 術語，專門名稱
manufacture 生產，製造
purpose 目的
safety procedure 安全措施，安全規定
business trip 出差
diner 用餐者，食客
line （商品的）種類，類別
leather 皮革
volunteer 自願參加者
gather 聚集，集合
flexible 彈性的，靈活的
grand opening 隆重開幕
passenger 乘客
check in 託運（行李）
maximum 最大限度，最大量
suitcase（旅行用的）行李箱
compliance 服從；遵守
strict 嚴格的
policy 政策；規定
clientele （總稱）顧客
complex 複雜的
layout 格局，設計
inspection 檢查
campaign 競選活動
full refund 全額退款
receipt 收據
present 出示；呈現
management 管理（層）
shortcomings 缺點

PART 6

keep up 繼續
manner 態度；方式
conflict 衝突；矛盾
benefit from 受益於
appropriate 合適的；恰當的
resident 居民
isolated 偏僻的；隔絕的
remote 遙遠的
up-to-date 最新的
in addition 此外；而且
in need of 需要

> 例 We're in need of people to help out with the beverage booths.
> 我們需要人來協助飲料攤位。

in particular 特別，尤其
material 布料；織物
entitle 命名為
inspirational 啟發靈感的
grant 授予
endeavor 努力；嘗試

PART 7

put together 組合，合併
have trouble V-ing 做……有困難
expert 專家
real estate 房地產，不動產
premises (用複數)營業場所
compensate 支付報酬；補償
make arrangements for 安排……

例 She will make all the arrangements for the company retreat next month.
她將為下個月的公司聯誼安排一切事宜。

after all 終究；畢竟
relocate 搬遷
transition 轉移，過渡時期
load 裝進
set up 安裝
ideal 理想的
manage to do 設法完成……
on time 準時
timetable 時間表
anticipate 預期
exhibit 展覽；展品
come to one's attention 引起某人的注意
take . . . into account 考慮，計入

例 You must take the environmental impact into account.
你必須把環境影響納入考量。

compensation 薪酬
declare 公布；聲明
collaborate with 與……合作
skyrocketing 飆升的，劇增的
notorious 惡名昭彰的
obscure 鮮為人知的
be composed of 由……組成
a variety of 各式各樣的
warranty 保固(書)
progress 進度
flaw 瑕疵，缺陷
in case of ……的情況下
be liable for 有責任，對……負責

例 You will be liable for any damage caused.
你將對造成的任何損害負責。

be entitled to V 有權，有……資格(做)
reliable 可靠的
at no charge 免費
apply to 適用於
temporary 暫時的
internal 內部的
make up for 彌補，補償
balance 餘額
at one's discretion 由某人自行決定
file a complaint 提出客訴
release 發布，推出
prominent 著名的；傑出的
limited 有限的
by the time 到……的時候
from scratch 從頭做起，從零開始
preference 偏好
apparel 服裝
luxurious 豪華的，奢華的
verify 查證，核實
as for 至於，關於

例 As for the flight, it is delayed for two hours.
關於航班，它延誤了兩個小時。

Actual Test 4

PART 1

fill A with B 用 B 填滿 A
pot 壺
make a copy 複印；備份
pile up 堆，疊
take measurements 測量(尺寸)
bike lane 腳踏車道
alongside 在……旁邊
gaze at 凝視，注視
place 放置
in a row 排成一列
rooftop 屋頂
traffic jam 交通阻塞，塞車

PART 2

delay 延誤，耽擱
test drive 試駕，試乘
manual 使用手冊；說明書
out of 用完；耗盡
plumber 水管工人
fill in for 代替，臨時補缺
display 顯示
properly 正確地
format 格式
serve 上菜；供應食物
in the mood for 想要……

例 I'm not in the mood for jokes.
我現在不想聽笑話。

check out (在圖書館)登記借(書)
at a time 每次
meet 完成
deadline 截止日期，最後期限
lend 借出
conference 會議
definitely 肯定
speaker 演講者
handle 處理
on one's own 獨自一人
analysis 分析報告
sales figure 銷售額
author 作者
inspiration 靈感
article 報導，文章
committee 委員會
offer 提供
complete 完成
out of service 停止使用，故障
in a minute 馬上，立即
print out (從電腦)列印出
malfunction 故障，失靈
pile 一堆，一疊
restock 補貨，重新進貨
section 區，部門
out of stock 缺貨

PART 3

shame 可惜；遺憾
trade A for B 以 A 換 B
come in 進來，到達
behind schedule 進度落後

in person 親自
make it 及時抵達

例 Mr. Li made it to the engineering conference on time.
李先生準時參加了工程會議。

extend 延長；使延期
due date 到期日
make an exception 破例；作為例外
contact 聯繫
late fee 逾期費
give out 分發
property 房地產
go for 適用於
come by 短暫拜訪；順道拜訪
feature 功能，特點
energy-efficient 節能的
suggestion 推薦，建議
coworker 同事
in that case 既然如此；那樣的話
intersection 十字路口
subscriber 訂戶；用戶
option 選擇，選項
strategy 策略
a great deal 大量；很多
come up with 想出，提出
bring in 帶來，增加
host 舉辦，主辦
nutrition 營養（學）
submission 提交；呈遞
speaking of which 說到這
spare 抽出，撥出（時間或金錢等）
entry 參賽作品；參賽
lecture 講座；課
brief 簡短的
directly 直接地
face 面對

PART 4

artifact （有史學價值的）製品、手工藝品
exhibit 展覽；展品
disassemble 拆卸，拆開
dress code 服裝規定
manner 方式，態度
trade expo 貿易博覽會
cosmetics 化妝用品
electronics （複數）電子產品
set . . . apart 使……與眾不同
previous 先前的
pass out 分發
refreshments 茶點，點心
take a stroll 散步
queue up 排隊
respectful 畢恭畢敬的；尊重的
cut in line 插隊
proceed 前往
apology 道歉，歉意
be in stock 有存貨
original 原先的，起初的
expedite 加速
panel 小組
flavor 口味
comment 評論
be in disagreement 看法不同
identify 辨認
recognize 表揚，認可
astonish 使吃驚
critic 評論家
intricate 錯綜複雜的
philosophical 哲學的
sign up 報名；申請
apologize for 為……致歉
be accompanied by 由……陪同，伴同
stock 存貨，庫存
run out of 用完，耗盡
adjust 調整
simply 完全地，簡直
profitable 有利可圖的
hand out 分發

例 I have to pick up the promotional materials that will be handed out to attendees.
我必須去拿即將分發給參加者的宣傳資料。

outline 大綱，概要

PART 5

fundraiser 募款活動
audience 觀眾
respective 各自的
come with 與……一起供給
assembly 組裝
instructions 說明書
fluent 流利的
qualification 條件，資格
demonstrate 示範
negotiation （常複數）協商，談判
submit 提交；呈遞
application 申請書，履歷表
sales associate 店員
go over 查看，仔細檢查
reservation 預約
baggage allowance 行李限額
patron 顧客；主顧
renew 延長……的期限
revision 修改
ahead of 在……之前
supervisor 經理；主管
steadily 逐漸地，穩定地
decline 減少；降低
in response to 為因應，回答

例 In response to consumer complaints, assembly instructions have been simplified.
因應消費者的抱怨，安裝說明已經簡化。

severe 嚴厲的；猛烈的
criticism 批評
concerning 關於
take measures 採取行動
on behalf of 代表
in spite of 儘管
now that 既然，由於
recommendation 推薦
competitor 競爭者
opening （職位的）空缺；機會
deliberate 故意的
traffic congestion 交通壅塞
convert 轉換，改變
reveal 揭露；透露
prominent 知名的
accessible 平易近人的
director 董事；主管
objective 目標

PART 6

survey 調查
strive to do 努力去做……
valuable 寶貴的，重要的
routine 例行公事
secure 保護；使安全

constantly 不斷地
eliminate 消除；擺脫
potential 潛在的，可能的
state-of-the-art 最先進的
inform 通知
subscription 訂閱（費）
transaction 交易
determine 找出；查明
verify 核對
go through 通過，完成
valid 有效的
attach 附上
expiration 過期
promptly 立即
be committed to 致力於

例 We are committed to maintaining the highest level of customer satisfaction.
我們致力於保持最高水準的客戶滿意度。

consumption 消耗量
beneficial 有益的
gain 獲益；得到改善

PART 7

subtotal 小計
promotion 促銷
newsletter （機構定期寄發的）簡報，通訊
subscribe 訂閱
by any chance 或許；萬一
real estate 房地產
distributor 經銷商
warranty 保證（書），保固（卡）
leaflet 傳單
retailer 零售商
equipment 設備；器材
sponsor 贊助
raffle 慈善抽獎活動
attire （尤指特定或正式的）服裝
be eligible to V 有資格（做）……

例 He is eligible to receive a higher salary.
他有資格獲得較高的薪水。

reference 參考，查閱
quote 報價
urge 敦促，強烈要求
unprecedented 前所未有的
revelation 被揭示的真相
controversy 爭議
intense 激烈的
sustainable 永續的
advocate 提倡；主張
exceptionally 卓越地；傑出地
premises （複數）廠區
senior 級別高的；資深的
executive 行政主管；經理
launch 發布；發表
procedure 程序
classify 分類
outline 大綱
voucher 優惠券
set . . . aside 撥出，留出（金錢或時間等）
inventory 庫存
assure 向……保證
complimentary 免費贈送的
asset 資產
intention 意圖
evident 顯而易見的
intimate 精通的，詳盡的
contribute to 有助於，做出貢獻
aspect 方面
accordingly 相應地
modify 修改；調整
source 來源
authenticity 真實性
comprehensive 全面的
curriculum 課程
hands-on 實際操作的，親身實踐的

Actual Test 5

PART 1

intersection 十字路口
stack 堆疊
kneel down 跪下
set up 擺放
hand out 分發
dock 停泊，靠岸
port 港口
occupied 使用中的

PART 2

update 更新
regular customer 常客，老客戶
issue （報紙期刊的）期，號
depend 取決於
industry 產業，行業
candidate 申請者；候選人
refreshing 提神的
attendee 出席者
attendance 出席人數
user manual 使用說明書
assemble 組裝
respondent 回答者
market research 市場調查
treatment 治療
produce 發生，產生
treat 請客，招待
make a donation 捐款；捐贈
stray 流浪的
household 家庭
recyclable 可回收的
fill out a form 填寫表格
directory （大樓內的）樓層介紹
auction 拍賣
sculpture 雕塑
invitation 邀請函
out of focus 失焦，沒對焦的
adjust 調整
focus on 把焦點對準；注意力集中於……
oversee 監督
merger 合併
negotiation 協商
market share 市占率
replacement 替換（品）
brand-new 全新的
counter 櫃檯
contain 含有
inspector 檢查員
safety gear 安全裝備
rate 費用，價格
affordable 付得起的；便宜的
handle 處理
residential 住宅的

PART 3

submit 提交
supplies （複數）用品，物資

available 可獲得的
post 發布，張貼（公告）
put up 張貼，掛起
statistics （複數）統計資料
count 總數
participant 參加者
board 董事會
leave out 遺漏
sales figure 銷售數字
express 快速的
bind 裝訂
supplementary 補充的，附加的
stop by 短暫停留，順道拜訪
specific 具體的，特定的
deal with 負責，處理
quite a few 相當多的
be familiar with 對……很熟悉
feature 功能，特性
interpersonal 人際的
as far as 就……而言
promotional 宣傳的，推廣的
expense 費用
look over 費用
appreciate 感謝，感激
insurance 保險
work on 從事；修理
in stock 有存貨
at the moment 目前，現在
due 到期的

例 When is the quarterly report due?
季度報告的截止日期是什麼時候？

loyalty program 忠誠系統；酬賓方案
on behalf of 代表
environmental 環境的
commission 委員會
plenty of 充裕的，大量的
resident 居民
owe 欠（錢）
process 處理
reimburse 報銷；償還
reserve 預約，預訂
in the meantime 在此期間，與此同時
in advance 提前，事先
length 長度
width 寬度

make arrangements for 為……做安排

例 Please make your own arrangements for accommodation.
請自行安排住宿。

interpret 口譯
fit 適合；勝任
profile 簡介，概況
arena 體育館

PART 4

commemorate 紀念、慶祝
throughout 遍及，到處
demonstrate 示範，展示
enroll in 報名參加
representative 代表，負責職員
innovative 創新的
well-suited 合適的，適合的
hire 新雇員；新入職者
count on 指望，依靠
job posting 招聘啟示，職缺公告
potential 潛在的，可能的
job description 職務描述；工作說明
reach （透過電話）聯繫
emergency 緊急情況
hang up 掛斷電話
schedule an appointment 預訂
applicable 適用的
fully booked 額滿的；客滿的；訂滿的
resume 恢復
regular hours 正常辦公時間，營業時間
offer 提供
warranty （品質的）保固
intend to do 打算（做）……
average 普通的，平常的
characteristic 特性，特徵
attractive 有吸引力的
excerpt 摘錄，節選
last-minute 最後一刻的；臨時的
entrance 入口處
achievement 成就
sign a contract 簽約
factor 因素

impressive 令人印象深刻的
support 支持
memorable 令人難忘的
approach 方法
hold onto 緊緊抓住
on board 在船（火車或飛機）上

例 You can bring two pieces of luggage on board the train.
你可以攜帶兩件行李上火車。

on-time 準時的
announcement 廣播，公告
regarding 關於
inventory 庫存；物品清單

PART 5

appreciation 感謝，感激
subscriber 訂戶
production line 生產線
long-term 長期的
addition 增加；添加
athletics 體育運動
component 零件；成分
enthusiast 熱衷……的人；愛好者
banquet 宴席，宴會
nominee 被提名人
be aware of 意識到……

例 Everybody is aware of the hazards of smoking.
每個人都意識到吸煙的危害。

regulation 法規；條例
precise 準確的，精確的
indeed 的確，確實
diverse 多元化的
reject 拒絕；排斥
courier 快遞公司
fleet 車隊；機群
reasonably priced 定價合理的
destination 目的地，終點
belongings 行李；所有物
luggage carousel 行李轉盤
ingredient 食材
at all times 隨時，無時無刻
expansion 擴張，擴大
volume 數量；總額
reputation 名聲；名氣
field 領域；範圍
cause 造成，引起

sensitive 敏感的
efficiently 有效地
be filled to capacity 客滿的

例 The theater was filled to capacity for the opening of the new play.
這場新劇開演時，劇院座無虛席。

above all 最重要的是；首先
proximity 接近；鄰近
major 主要的；重大的
extensive 廣泛的
pharmaceutical 製藥的
evaluate 評估
accuracy 準確度
a number of 一些，許多
board member 董事會成員
qualification 資格條件

PART 6

selection 選擇
inspect 檢查
vital to 對……至關重要的
fulfill 履行，實現
transform 徹底改變；轉換
check-in 辦理登機手續
urgent 緊急的
no later than 不晚於

例 Please submit all expense reports no later than February 15.
請在 2 月 15 日之前繳交所有費用報告。

shift 輪班
assign 分派
raise funds 募款
contemporary 當代的

PART 7

maintenance 維護；保養
affect 影響
duration 持續時間
property 房地產
quote 報價
disposal 清除；處理
balance 餘款；結餘
inform A of B 通知某人(A)某事(B)

例 The store sent an e-mail to customers informing them of the upcoming holiday sale.
這家店向顧客發送了一封電子郵件，通知他們即將到來的假日特賣。

regardless of 無論……；不管……
representative 代表
account 客戶
renovation 整修；翻新
from now on 從現在起
break room 休息室
expire 過期
spoil （食物等）變壞，腐敗
prestigious 有聲望的
patronage 惠顧
drive 宣傳活動
suitable 適宜的，合適的
referral 被推薦人；轉介
enter 報名……；安排……參加
drawing 抽獎；抽籤
inquiry 詢問；調查
recruitment 招募
enclose 隨信（或包裹）附上
go out of business 歇業
preferably 更好地；最好是
endorse 認可；支持；擔保
take a chance 冒險
contractor 承包商
lost-and-found 失物招領處
claim 認領；索取
description 描述；形容
wrap up 完成，結束

例 Let's wrap up the marketing meeting.
讓我們完成這場行銷會議。

complicated 複雜的
administrative 行政的；管理的
previously 之前，先前
adapt 調整；適應
transition 過渡；轉變
lay off 解僱，裁員
phase 階段，時期
operation 運作；實施
comprise 包括，組成
specify 明確指出，具體說明
in-depth 徹底的，深入的
take place 發生

maximum 最大量；最大限度
wing （常指後來增建的）側廳，翼部
amenity （常複數）便利設施
suit 滿足，符合
extension 分機
make progress 取得進展
overlook 眺望，俯瞰
feasible 切實可行的，可能的
remarkable 非凡的；非常奇特的
proceeds 收入
cutting-edge 先進的，尖端的

例 The company provides cutting-edge software for artificial intelligence.
這家公司提供最先進的人工智慧軟體。

outdated 過時的；老舊的
in time 及時

Answer Sheet

TOEIC TEST 1

LISTENING SECTION

1 Ⓐ Ⓑ Ⓒ Ⓓ
2 Ⓐ Ⓑ Ⓒ Ⓓ
3 Ⓐ Ⓑ Ⓒ Ⓓ
4 Ⓐ Ⓑ Ⓒ Ⓓ
5 Ⓐ Ⓑ Ⓒ Ⓓ
6 Ⓐ Ⓑ Ⓒ Ⓓ
7 Ⓐ Ⓑ Ⓒ Ⓓ
8 Ⓐ Ⓑ Ⓒ Ⓓ
9 Ⓐ Ⓑ Ⓒ Ⓓ
10 Ⓐ Ⓑ Ⓒ Ⓓ
11 Ⓐ Ⓑ Ⓒ Ⓓ
12 Ⓐ Ⓑ Ⓒ Ⓓ
13 Ⓐ Ⓑ Ⓒ Ⓓ
14 Ⓐ Ⓑ Ⓒ Ⓓ
15 Ⓐ Ⓑ Ⓒ Ⓓ
16 Ⓐ Ⓑ Ⓒ Ⓓ
17 Ⓐ Ⓑ Ⓒ Ⓓ
18 Ⓐ Ⓑ Ⓒ Ⓓ
19 Ⓐ Ⓑ Ⓒ Ⓓ
20 Ⓐ Ⓑ Ⓒ Ⓓ
21 Ⓐ Ⓑ Ⓒ Ⓓ
22 Ⓐ Ⓑ Ⓒ Ⓓ
23 Ⓐ Ⓑ Ⓒ Ⓓ
24 Ⓐ Ⓑ Ⓒ Ⓓ
25 Ⓐ Ⓑ Ⓒ Ⓓ
26 Ⓐ Ⓑ Ⓒ Ⓓ
27 Ⓐ Ⓑ Ⓒ Ⓓ
28 Ⓐ Ⓑ Ⓒ Ⓓ
29 Ⓐ Ⓑ Ⓒ Ⓓ
30 Ⓐ Ⓑ Ⓒ Ⓓ
31 Ⓐ Ⓑ Ⓒ Ⓓ
32 Ⓐ Ⓑ Ⓒ Ⓓ
33 Ⓐ Ⓑ Ⓒ Ⓓ
34 Ⓐ Ⓑ Ⓒ Ⓓ
35 Ⓐ Ⓑ Ⓒ Ⓓ
36 Ⓐ Ⓑ Ⓒ Ⓓ
37 Ⓐ Ⓑ Ⓒ Ⓓ
38 Ⓐ Ⓑ Ⓒ Ⓓ
39 Ⓐ Ⓑ Ⓒ Ⓓ
40 Ⓐ Ⓑ Ⓒ Ⓓ
41 Ⓐ Ⓑ Ⓒ Ⓓ
42 Ⓐ Ⓑ Ⓒ Ⓓ
43 Ⓐ Ⓑ Ⓒ Ⓓ
44 Ⓐ Ⓑ Ⓒ Ⓓ
45 Ⓐ Ⓑ Ⓒ Ⓓ
46 Ⓐ Ⓑ Ⓒ Ⓓ
47 Ⓐ Ⓑ Ⓒ Ⓓ
48 Ⓐ Ⓑ Ⓒ Ⓓ
49 Ⓐ Ⓑ Ⓒ Ⓓ
50 Ⓐ Ⓑ Ⓒ Ⓓ
51 Ⓐ Ⓑ Ⓒ Ⓓ
52 Ⓐ Ⓑ Ⓒ Ⓓ
53 Ⓐ Ⓑ Ⓒ Ⓓ
54 Ⓐ Ⓑ Ⓒ Ⓓ
55 Ⓐ Ⓑ Ⓒ Ⓓ
56 Ⓐ Ⓑ Ⓒ Ⓓ
57 Ⓐ Ⓑ Ⓒ Ⓓ
58 Ⓐ Ⓑ Ⓒ Ⓓ
59 Ⓐ Ⓑ Ⓒ Ⓓ
60 Ⓐ Ⓑ Ⓒ Ⓓ
61 Ⓐ Ⓑ Ⓒ Ⓓ
62 Ⓐ Ⓑ Ⓒ Ⓓ
63 Ⓐ Ⓑ Ⓒ Ⓓ
64 Ⓐ Ⓑ Ⓒ Ⓓ
65 Ⓐ Ⓑ Ⓒ Ⓓ
66 Ⓐ Ⓑ Ⓒ Ⓓ
67 Ⓐ Ⓑ Ⓒ Ⓓ
68 Ⓐ Ⓑ Ⓒ Ⓓ
69 Ⓐ Ⓑ Ⓒ Ⓓ
70 Ⓐ Ⓑ Ⓒ Ⓓ
71 Ⓐ Ⓑ Ⓒ Ⓓ
72 Ⓐ Ⓑ Ⓒ Ⓓ
73 Ⓐ Ⓑ Ⓒ Ⓓ
74 Ⓐ Ⓑ Ⓒ Ⓓ
75 Ⓐ Ⓑ Ⓒ Ⓓ
76 Ⓐ Ⓑ Ⓒ Ⓓ
77 Ⓐ Ⓑ Ⓒ Ⓓ
78 Ⓐ Ⓑ Ⓒ Ⓓ
79 Ⓐ Ⓑ Ⓒ Ⓓ
80 Ⓐ Ⓑ Ⓒ Ⓓ
81 Ⓐ Ⓑ Ⓒ Ⓓ
82 Ⓐ Ⓑ Ⓒ Ⓓ
83 Ⓐ Ⓑ Ⓒ Ⓓ
84 Ⓐ Ⓑ Ⓒ Ⓓ
85 Ⓐ Ⓑ Ⓒ Ⓓ
86 Ⓐ Ⓑ Ⓒ Ⓓ
87 Ⓐ Ⓑ Ⓒ Ⓓ
88 Ⓐ Ⓑ Ⓒ Ⓓ
89 Ⓐ Ⓑ Ⓒ Ⓓ
90 Ⓐ Ⓑ Ⓒ Ⓓ
91 Ⓐ Ⓑ Ⓒ Ⓓ
92 Ⓐ Ⓑ Ⓒ Ⓓ
93 Ⓐ Ⓑ Ⓒ Ⓓ
94 Ⓐ Ⓑ Ⓒ Ⓓ
95 Ⓐ Ⓑ Ⓒ Ⓓ
96 Ⓐ Ⓑ Ⓒ Ⓓ
97 Ⓐ Ⓑ Ⓒ Ⓓ
98 Ⓐ Ⓑ Ⓒ Ⓓ
99 Ⓐ Ⓑ Ⓒ Ⓓ
100 Ⓐ Ⓑ Ⓒ Ⓓ

READING SECTION

101 Ⓐ Ⓑ Ⓒ Ⓓ
102 Ⓐ Ⓑ Ⓒ Ⓓ
103 Ⓐ Ⓑ Ⓒ Ⓓ
104 Ⓐ Ⓑ Ⓒ Ⓓ
105 Ⓐ Ⓑ Ⓒ Ⓓ
106 Ⓐ Ⓑ Ⓒ Ⓓ
107 Ⓐ Ⓑ Ⓒ Ⓓ
108 Ⓐ Ⓑ Ⓒ Ⓓ
109 Ⓐ Ⓑ Ⓒ Ⓓ
110 Ⓐ Ⓑ Ⓒ Ⓓ
111 Ⓐ Ⓑ Ⓒ Ⓓ
112 Ⓐ Ⓑ Ⓒ Ⓓ
113 Ⓐ Ⓑ Ⓒ Ⓓ
114 Ⓐ Ⓑ Ⓒ Ⓓ
115 Ⓐ Ⓑ Ⓒ Ⓓ
116 Ⓐ Ⓑ Ⓒ Ⓓ
117 Ⓐ Ⓑ Ⓒ Ⓓ
118 Ⓐ Ⓑ Ⓒ Ⓓ
119 Ⓐ Ⓑ Ⓒ Ⓓ
120 Ⓐ Ⓑ Ⓒ Ⓓ
121 Ⓐ Ⓑ Ⓒ Ⓓ
122 Ⓐ Ⓑ Ⓒ Ⓓ
123 Ⓐ Ⓑ Ⓒ Ⓓ
124 Ⓐ Ⓑ Ⓒ Ⓓ
125 Ⓐ Ⓑ Ⓒ Ⓓ
126 Ⓐ Ⓑ Ⓒ Ⓓ
127 Ⓐ Ⓑ Ⓒ Ⓓ
128 Ⓐ Ⓑ Ⓒ Ⓓ
129 Ⓐ Ⓑ Ⓒ Ⓓ
130 Ⓐ Ⓑ Ⓒ Ⓓ
131 Ⓐ Ⓑ Ⓒ Ⓓ
132 Ⓐ Ⓑ Ⓒ Ⓓ
133 Ⓐ Ⓑ Ⓒ Ⓓ
134 Ⓐ Ⓑ Ⓒ Ⓓ
135 Ⓐ Ⓑ Ⓒ Ⓓ
136 Ⓐ Ⓑ Ⓒ Ⓓ
137 Ⓐ Ⓑ Ⓒ Ⓓ
138 Ⓐ Ⓑ Ⓒ Ⓓ
139 Ⓐ Ⓑ Ⓒ Ⓓ
140 Ⓐ Ⓑ Ⓒ Ⓓ
141 Ⓐ Ⓑ Ⓒ Ⓓ
142 Ⓐ Ⓑ Ⓒ Ⓓ
143 Ⓐ Ⓑ Ⓒ Ⓓ
144 Ⓐ Ⓑ Ⓒ Ⓓ
145 Ⓐ Ⓑ Ⓒ Ⓓ
146 Ⓐ Ⓑ Ⓒ Ⓓ
147 Ⓐ Ⓑ Ⓒ Ⓓ
148 Ⓐ Ⓑ Ⓒ Ⓓ
149 Ⓐ Ⓑ Ⓒ Ⓓ
150 Ⓐ Ⓑ Ⓒ Ⓓ
151 Ⓐ Ⓑ Ⓒ Ⓓ
152 Ⓐ Ⓑ Ⓒ Ⓓ
153 Ⓐ Ⓑ Ⓒ Ⓓ
154 Ⓐ Ⓑ Ⓒ Ⓓ
155 Ⓐ Ⓑ Ⓒ Ⓓ
156 Ⓐ Ⓑ Ⓒ Ⓓ
157 Ⓐ Ⓑ Ⓒ Ⓓ
158 Ⓐ Ⓑ Ⓒ Ⓓ
159 Ⓐ Ⓑ Ⓒ Ⓓ
160 Ⓐ Ⓑ Ⓒ Ⓓ
161 Ⓐ Ⓑ Ⓒ Ⓓ
162 Ⓐ Ⓑ Ⓒ Ⓓ
163 Ⓐ Ⓑ Ⓒ Ⓓ
164 Ⓐ Ⓑ Ⓒ Ⓓ
165 Ⓐ Ⓑ Ⓒ Ⓓ
166 Ⓐ Ⓑ Ⓒ Ⓓ
167 Ⓐ Ⓑ Ⓒ Ⓓ
168 Ⓐ Ⓑ Ⓒ Ⓓ
169 Ⓐ Ⓑ Ⓒ Ⓓ
170 Ⓐ Ⓑ Ⓒ Ⓓ
171 Ⓐ Ⓑ Ⓒ Ⓓ
172 Ⓐ Ⓑ Ⓒ Ⓓ
173 Ⓐ Ⓑ Ⓒ Ⓓ
174 Ⓐ Ⓑ Ⓒ Ⓓ
175 Ⓐ Ⓑ Ⓒ Ⓓ
176 Ⓐ Ⓑ Ⓒ Ⓓ
177 Ⓐ Ⓑ Ⓒ Ⓓ
178 Ⓐ Ⓑ Ⓒ Ⓓ
179 Ⓐ Ⓑ Ⓒ Ⓓ
180 Ⓐ Ⓑ Ⓒ Ⓓ
181 Ⓐ Ⓑ Ⓒ Ⓓ
182 Ⓐ Ⓑ Ⓒ Ⓓ
183 Ⓐ Ⓑ Ⓒ Ⓓ
184 Ⓐ Ⓑ Ⓒ Ⓓ
185 Ⓐ Ⓑ Ⓒ Ⓓ
186 Ⓐ Ⓑ Ⓒ Ⓓ
187 Ⓐ Ⓑ Ⓒ Ⓓ
188 Ⓐ Ⓑ Ⓒ Ⓓ
189 Ⓐ Ⓑ Ⓒ Ⓓ
190 Ⓐ Ⓑ Ⓒ Ⓓ
191 Ⓐ Ⓑ Ⓒ Ⓓ
192 Ⓐ Ⓑ Ⓒ Ⓓ
193 Ⓐ Ⓑ Ⓒ Ⓓ
194 Ⓐ Ⓑ Ⓒ Ⓓ
195 Ⓐ Ⓑ Ⓒ Ⓓ
196 Ⓐ Ⓑ Ⓒ Ⓓ
197 Ⓐ Ⓑ Ⓒ Ⓓ
198 Ⓐ Ⓑ Ⓒ Ⓓ
199 Ⓐ Ⓑ Ⓒ Ⓓ
200 Ⓐ Ⓑ Ⓒ Ⓓ

Answer Sheet

TOEIC TEST 2

LISTENING SECTION

1	Ⓐ Ⓑ Ⓒ Ⓓ	11	Ⓐ Ⓑ Ⓒ Ⓓ	21	Ⓐ Ⓑ Ⓒ Ⓓ	31	Ⓐ Ⓑ Ⓒ Ⓓ	41	Ⓐ Ⓑ Ⓒ Ⓓ	51	Ⓐ Ⓑ Ⓒ Ⓓ	61	Ⓐ Ⓑ Ⓒ Ⓓ	71	Ⓐ Ⓑ Ⓒ Ⓓ	81	Ⓐ Ⓑ Ⓒ Ⓓ	91	Ⓐ Ⓑ Ⓒ Ⓓ
2	Ⓐ Ⓑ Ⓒ Ⓓ	12	Ⓐ Ⓑ Ⓒ Ⓓ	22	Ⓐ Ⓑ Ⓒ Ⓓ	32	Ⓐ Ⓑ Ⓒ Ⓓ	42	Ⓐ Ⓑ Ⓒ Ⓓ	52	Ⓐ Ⓑ Ⓒ Ⓓ	62	Ⓐ Ⓑ Ⓒ Ⓓ	72	Ⓐ Ⓑ Ⓒ Ⓓ	82	Ⓐ Ⓑ Ⓒ Ⓓ	92	Ⓐ Ⓑ Ⓒ Ⓓ
3	Ⓐ Ⓑ Ⓒ Ⓓ	13	Ⓐ Ⓑ Ⓒ Ⓓ	23	Ⓐ Ⓑ Ⓒ Ⓓ	33	Ⓐ Ⓑ Ⓒ Ⓓ	43	Ⓐ Ⓑ Ⓒ Ⓓ	53	Ⓐ Ⓑ Ⓒ Ⓓ	63	Ⓐ Ⓑ Ⓒ Ⓓ	73	Ⓐ Ⓑ Ⓒ Ⓓ	83	Ⓐ Ⓑ Ⓒ Ⓓ	93	Ⓐ Ⓑ Ⓒ Ⓓ
4	Ⓐ Ⓑ Ⓒ Ⓓ	14	Ⓐ Ⓑ Ⓒ Ⓓ	24	Ⓐ Ⓑ Ⓒ Ⓓ	34	Ⓐ Ⓑ Ⓒ Ⓓ	44	Ⓐ Ⓑ Ⓒ Ⓓ	54	Ⓐ Ⓑ Ⓒ Ⓓ	64	Ⓐ Ⓑ Ⓒ Ⓓ	74	Ⓐ Ⓑ Ⓒ Ⓓ	84	Ⓐ Ⓑ Ⓒ Ⓓ	94	Ⓐ Ⓑ Ⓒ Ⓓ
5	Ⓐ Ⓑ Ⓒ Ⓓ	15	Ⓐ Ⓑ Ⓒ Ⓓ	25	Ⓐ Ⓑ Ⓒ Ⓓ	35	Ⓐ Ⓑ Ⓒ Ⓓ	45	Ⓐ Ⓑ Ⓒ Ⓓ	55	Ⓐ Ⓑ Ⓒ Ⓓ	65	Ⓐ Ⓑ Ⓒ Ⓓ	75	Ⓐ Ⓑ Ⓒ Ⓓ	85	Ⓐ Ⓑ Ⓒ Ⓓ	95	Ⓐ Ⓑ Ⓒ Ⓓ
6	Ⓐ Ⓑ Ⓒ Ⓓ	16	Ⓐ Ⓑ Ⓒ Ⓓ	26	Ⓐ Ⓑ Ⓒ Ⓓ	36	Ⓐ Ⓑ Ⓒ Ⓓ	46	Ⓐ Ⓑ Ⓒ Ⓓ	56	Ⓐ Ⓑ Ⓒ Ⓓ	66	Ⓐ Ⓑ Ⓒ Ⓓ	76	Ⓐ Ⓑ Ⓒ Ⓓ	86	Ⓐ Ⓑ Ⓒ Ⓓ	96	Ⓐ Ⓑ Ⓒ Ⓓ
7	Ⓐ Ⓑ Ⓒ Ⓓ	17	Ⓐ Ⓑ Ⓒ Ⓓ	27	Ⓐ Ⓑ Ⓒ Ⓓ	37	Ⓐ Ⓑ Ⓒ Ⓓ	47	Ⓐ Ⓑ Ⓒ Ⓓ	57	Ⓐ Ⓑ Ⓒ Ⓓ	67	Ⓐ Ⓑ Ⓒ Ⓓ	77	Ⓐ Ⓑ Ⓒ Ⓓ	87	Ⓐ Ⓑ Ⓒ Ⓓ	97	Ⓐ Ⓑ Ⓒ Ⓓ
8	Ⓐ Ⓑ Ⓒ Ⓓ	18	Ⓐ Ⓑ Ⓒ Ⓓ	28	Ⓐ Ⓑ Ⓒ Ⓓ	38	Ⓐ Ⓑ Ⓒ Ⓓ	48	Ⓐ Ⓑ Ⓒ Ⓓ	58	Ⓐ Ⓑ Ⓒ Ⓓ	68	Ⓐ Ⓑ Ⓒ Ⓓ	78	Ⓐ Ⓑ Ⓒ Ⓓ	88	Ⓐ Ⓑ Ⓒ Ⓓ	98	Ⓐ Ⓑ Ⓒ Ⓓ
9	Ⓐ Ⓑ Ⓒ Ⓓ	19	Ⓐ Ⓑ Ⓒ Ⓓ	29	Ⓐ Ⓑ Ⓒ Ⓓ	39	Ⓐ Ⓑ Ⓒ Ⓓ	49	Ⓐ Ⓑ Ⓒ Ⓓ	59	Ⓐ Ⓑ Ⓒ Ⓓ	69	Ⓐ Ⓑ Ⓒ Ⓓ	79	Ⓐ Ⓑ Ⓒ Ⓓ	89	Ⓐ Ⓑ Ⓒ Ⓓ	99	Ⓐ Ⓑ Ⓒ Ⓓ
10	Ⓐ Ⓑ Ⓒ Ⓓ	20	Ⓐ Ⓑ Ⓒ Ⓓ	30	Ⓐ Ⓑ Ⓒ Ⓓ	40	Ⓐ Ⓑ Ⓒ Ⓓ	50	Ⓐ Ⓑ Ⓒ Ⓓ	60	Ⓐ Ⓑ Ⓒ Ⓓ	70	Ⓐ Ⓑ Ⓒ Ⓓ	80	Ⓐ Ⓑ Ⓒ Ⓓ	90	Ⓐ Ⓑ Ⓒ Ⓓ	100	Ⓐ Ⓑ Ⓒ Ⓓ

READING SECTION

101	Ⓐ Ⓑ Ⓒ Ⓓ	111	Ⓐ Ⓑ Ⓒ Ⓓ	121	Ⓐ Ⓑ Ⓒ Ⓓ	131	Ⓐ Ⓑ Ⓒ Ⓓ	141	Ⓐ Ⓑ Ⓒ Ⓓ	151	Ⓐ Ⓑ Ⓒ Ⓓ	161	Ⓐ Ⓑ Ⓒ Ⓓ	171	Ⓐ Ⓑ Ⓒ Ⓓ	181	Ⓐ Ⓑ Ⓒ Ⓓ	191	Ⓐ Ⓑ Ⓒ Ⓓ
102	Ⓐ Ⓑ Ⓒ Ⓓ	112	Ⓐ Ⓑ Ⓒ Ⓓ	122	Ⓐ Ⓑ Ⓒ Ⓓ	132	Ⓐ Ⓑ Ⓒ Ⓓ	142	Ⓐ Ⓑ Ⓒ Ⓓ	152	Ⓐ Ⓑ Ⓒ Ⓓ	162	Ⓐ Ⓑ Ⓒ Ⓓ	172	Ⓐ Ⓑ Ⓒ Ⓓ	182	Ⓐ Ⓑ Ⓒ Ⓓ	192	Ⓐ Ⓑ Ⓒ Ⓓ
103	Ⓐ Ⓑ Ⓒ Ⓓ	113	Ⓐ Ⓑ Ⓒ Ⓓ	123	Ⓐ Ⓑ Ⓒ Ⓓ	133	Ⓐ Ⓑ Ⓒ Ⓓ	143	Ⓐ Ⓑ Ⓒ Ⓓ	153	Ⓐ Ⓑ Ⓒ Ⓓ	163	Ⓐ Ⓑ Ⓒ Ⓓ	173	Ⓐ Ⓑ Ⓒ Ⓓ	183	Ⓐ Ⓑ Ⓒ Ⓓ	193	Ⓐ Ⓑ Ⓒ Ⓓ
104	Ⓐ Ⓑ Ⓒ Ⓓ	114	Ⓐ Ⓑ Ⓒ Ⓓ	124	Ⓐ Ⓑ Ⓒ Ⓓ	134	Ⓐ Ⓑ Ⓒ Ⓓ	144	Ⓐ Ⓑ Ⓒ Ⓓ	154	Ⓐ Ⓑ Ⓒ Ⓓ	164	Ⓐ Ⓑ Ⓒ Ⓓ	174	Ⓐ Ⓑ Ⓒ Ⓓ	184	Ⓐ Ⓑ Ⓒ Ⓓ	194	Ⓐ Ⓑ Ⓒ Ⓓ
105	Ⓐ Ⓑ Ⓒ Ⓓ	115	Ⓐ Ⓑ Ⓒ Ⓓ	125	Ⓐ Ⓑ Ⓒ Ⓓ	135	Ⓐ Ⓑ Ⓒ Ⓓ	145	Ⓐ Ⓑ Ⓒ Ⓓ	155	Ⓐ Ⓑ Ⓒ Ⓓ	165	Ⓐ Ⓑ Ⓒ Ⓓ	175	Ⓐ Ⓑ Ⓒ Ⓓ	185	Ⓐ Ⓑ Ⓒ Ⓓ	195	Ⓐ Ⓑ Ⓒ Ⓓ
106	Ⓐ Ⓑ Ⓒ Ⓓ	116	Ⓐ Ⓑ Ⓒ Ⓓ	126	Ⓐ Ⓑ Ⓒ Ⓓ	136	Ⓐ Ⓑ Ⓒ Ⓓ	146	Ⓐ Ⓑ Ⓒ Ⓓ	156	Ⓐ Ⓑ Ⓒ Ⓓ	166	Ⓐ Ⓑ Ⓒ Ⓓ	176	Ⓐ Ⓑ Ⓒ Ⓓ	186	Ⓐ Ⓑ Ⓒ Ⓓ	196	Ⓐ Ⓑ Ⓒ Ⓓ
107	Ⓐ Ⓑ Ⓒ Ⓓ	117	Ⓐ Ⓑ Ⓒ Ⓓ	127	Ⓐ Ⓑ Ⓒ Ⓓ	137	Ⓐ Ⓑ Ⓒ Ⓓ	147	Ⓐ Ⓑ Ⓒ Ⓓ	157	Ⓐ Ⓑ Ⓒ Ⓓ	167	Ⓐ Ⓑ Ⓒ Ⓓ	177	Ⓐ Ⓑ Ⓒ Ⓓ	187	Ⓐ Ⓑ Ⓒ Ⓓ	197	Ⓐ Ⓑ Ⓒ Ⓓ
108	Ⓐ Ⓑ Ⓒ Ⓓ	118	Ⓐ Ⓑ Ⓒ Ⓓ	128	Ⓐ Ⓑ Ⓒ Ⓓ	138	Ⓐ Ⓑ Ⓒ Ⓓ	148	Ⓐ Ⓑ Ⓒ Ⓓ	158	Ⓐ Ⓑ Ⓒ Ⓓ	168	Ⓐ Ⓑ Ⓒ Ⓓ	178	Ⓐ Ⓑ Ⓒ Ⓓ	188	Ⓐ Ⓑ Ⓒ Ⓓ	198	Ⓐ Ⓑ Ⓒ Ⓓ
109	Ⓐ Ⓑ Ⓒ Ⓓ	119	Ⓐ Ⓑ Ⓒ Ⓓ	129	Ⓐ Ⓑ Ⓒ Ⓓ	139	Ⓐ Ⓑ Ⓒ Ⓓ	149	Ⓐ Ⓑ Ⓒ Ⓓ	159	Ⓐ Ⓑ Ⓒ Ⓓ	169	Ⓐ Ⓑ Ⓒ Ⓓ	179	Ⓐ Ⓑ Ⓒ Ⓓ	189	Ⓐ Ⓑ Ⓒ Ⓓ	199	Ⓐ Ⓑ Ⓒ Ⓓ
110	Ⓐ Ⓑ Ⓒ Ⓓ	120	Ⓐ Ⓑ Ⓒ Ⓓ	130	Ⓐ Ⓑ Ⓒ Ⓓ	140	Ⓐ Ⓑ Ⓒ Ⓓ	150	Ⓐ Ⓑ Ⓒ Ⓓ	160	Ⓐ Ⓑ Ⓒ Ⓓ	170	Ⓐ Ⓑ Ⓒ Ⓓ	180	Ⓐ Ⓑ Ⓒ Ⓓ	190	Ⓐ Ⓑ Ⓒ Ⓓ	200	Ⓐ Ⓑ Ⓒ Ⓓ

Answer Sheet

TOEIC TEST 3

LISTENING SECTION

No.	Answer	No.	Answer	No.	Answer	No.	Answer	No.	Answer
1	Ⓐ Ⓑ Ⓒ Ⓓ	11	Ⓐ Ⓑ Ⓒ Ⓓ	21	Ⓐ Ⓑ Ⓒ Ⓓ	31	Ⓐ Ⓑ Ⓒ Ⓓ	41	Ⓐ Ⓑ Ⓒ Ⓓ
2	Ⓐ Ⓑ Ⓒ Ⓓ	12	Ⓐ Ⓑ Ⓒ Ⓓ	22	Ⓐ Ⓑ Ⓒ Ⓓ	32	Ⓐ Ⓑ Ⓒ Ⓓ	42	Ⓐ Ⓑ Ⓒ Ⓓ
3	Ⓐ Ⓑ Ⓒ Ⓓ	13	Ⓐ Ⓑ Ⓒ Ⓓ	23	Ⓐ Ⓑ Ⓒ Ⓓ	33	Ⓐ Ⓑ Ⓒ Ⓓ	43	Ⓐ Ⓑ Ⓒ Ⓓ
4	Ⓐ Ⓑ Ⓒ Ⓓ	14	Ⓐ Ⓑ Ⓒ Ⓓ	24	Ⓐ Ⓑ Ⓒ Ⓓ	34	Ⓐ Ⓑ Ⓒ Ⓓ	44	Ⓐ Ⓑ Ⓒ Ⓓ
5	Ⓐ Ⓑ Ⓒ Ⓓ	15	Ⓐ Ⓑ Ⓒ Ⓓ	25	Ⓐ Ⓑ Ⓒ Ⓓ	35	Ⓐ Ⓑ Ⓒ Ⓓ	45	Ⓐ Ⓑ Ⓒ Ⓓ
6	Ⓐ Ⓑ Ⓒ Ⓓ	16	Ⓐ Ⓑ Ⓒ Ⓓ	26	Ⓐ Ⓑ Ⓒ Ⓓ	36	Ⓐ Ⓑ Ⓒ Ⓓ	46	Ⓐ Ⓑ Ⓒ Ⓓ
7	Ⓐ Ⓑ Ⓒ Ⓓ	17	Ⓐ Ⓑ Ⓒ Ⓓ	27	Ⓐ Ⓑ Ⓒ Ⓓ	37	Ⓐ Ⓑ Ⓒ Ⓓ	47	Ⓐ Ⓑ Ⓒ Ⓓ
8	Ⓐ Ⓑ Ⓒ Ⓓ	18	Ⓐ Ⓑ Ⓒ Ⓓ	28	Ⓐ Ⓑ Ⓒ Ⓓ	38	Ⓐ Ⓑ Ⓒ Ⓓ	48	Ⓐ Ⓑ Ⓒ Ⓓ
9	Ⓐ Ⓑ Ⓒ Ⓓ	19	Ⓐ Ⓑ Ⓒ Ⓓ	29	Ⓐ Ⓑ Ⓒ Ⓓ	39	Ⓐ Ⓑ Ⓒ Ⓓ	49	Ⓐ Ⓑ Ⓒ Ⓓ
10	Ⓐ Ⓑ Ⓒ Ⓓ	20	Ⓐ Ⓑ Ⓒ Ⓓ	30	Ⓐ Ⓑ Ⓒ Ⓓ	40	Ⓐ Ⓑ Ⓒ Ⓓ	50	Ⓐ Ⓑ Ⓒ Ⓓ

No.	Answer	No.	Answer	No.	Answer	No.	Answer	No.	Answer
51	Ⓐ Ⓑ Ⓒ Ⓓ	61	Ⓐ Ⓑ Ⓒ Ⓓ	71	Ⓐ Ⓑ Ⓒ Ⓓ	81	Ⓐ Ⓑ Ⓒ Ⓓ	91	Ⓐ Ⓑ Ⓒ Ⓓ
52	Ⓐ Ⓑ Ⓒ Ⓓ	62	Ⓐ Ⓑ Ⓒ Ⓓ	72	Ⓐ Ⓑ Ⓒ Ⓓ	82	Ⓐ Ⓑ Ⓒ Ⓓ	92	Ⓐ Ⓑ Ⓒ Ⓓ
53	Ⓐ Ⓑ Ⓒ Ⓓ	63	Ⓐ Ⓑ Ⓒ Ⓓ	73	Ⓐ Ⓑ Ⓒ Ⓓ	83	Ⓐ Ⓑ Ⓒ Ⓓ	93	Ⓐ Ⓑ Ⓒ Ⓓ
54	Ⓐ Ⓑ Ⓒ Ⓓ	64	Ⓐ Ⓑ Ⓒ Ⓓ	74	Ⓐ Ⓑ Ⓒ Ⓓ	84	Ⓐ Ⓑ Ⓒ Ⓓ	94	Ⓐ Ⓑ Ⓒ Ⓓ
55	Ⓐ Ⓑ Ⓒ Ⓓ	65	Ⓐ Ⓑ Ⓒ Ⓓ	75	Ⓐ Ⓑ Ⓒ Ⓓ	85	Ⓐ Ⓑ Ⓒ Ⓓ	95	Ⓐ Ⓑ Ⓒ Ⓓ
56	Ⓐ Ⓑ Ⓒ Ⓓ	66	Ⓐ Ⓑ Ⓒ Ⓓ	76	Ⓐ Ⓑ Ⓒ Ⓓ	86	Ⓐ Ⓑ Ⓒ Ⓓ	96	Ⓐ Ⓑ Ⓒ Ⓓ
57	Ⓐ Ⓑ Ⓒ Ⓓ	67	Ⓐ Ⓑ Ⓒ Ⓓ	77	Ⓐ Ⓑ Ⓒ Ⓓ	87	Ⓐ Ⓑ Ⓒ Ⓓ	97	Ⓐ Ⓑ Ⓒ Ⓓ
58	Ⓐ Ⓑ Ⓒ Ⓓ	68	Ⓐ Ⓑ Ⓒ Ⓓ	78	Ⓐ Ⓑ Ⓒ Ⓓ	88	Ⓐ Ⓑ Ⓒ Ⓓ	98	Ⓐ Ⓑ Ⓒ Ⓓ
59	Ⓐ Ⓑ Ⓒ Ⓓ	69	Ⓐ Ⓑ Ⓒ Ⓓ	79	Ⓐ Ⓑ Ⓒ Ⓓ	89	Ⓐ Ⓑ Ⓒ Ⓓ	99	Ⓐ Ⓑ Ⓒ Ⓓ
60	Ⓐ Ⓑ Ⓒ Ⓓ	70	Ⓐ Ⓑ Ⓒ Ⓓ	80	Ⓐ Ⓑ Ⓒ Ⓓ	90	Ⓐ Ⓑ Ⓒ Ⓓ	100	Ⓐ Ⓑ Ⓒ Ⓓ

READING SECTION

No.	Answer	No.	Answer	No.	Answer	No.	Answer	No.	Answer
101	Ⓐ Ⓑ Ⓒ Ⓓ	111	Ⓐ Ⓑ Ⓒ Ⓓ	121	Ⓐ Ⓑ Ⓒ Ⓓ	131	Ⓐ Ⓑ Ⓒ Ⓓ	141	Ⓐ Ⓑ Ⓒ Ⓓ
102	Ⓐ Ⓑ Ⓒ Ⓓ	112	Ⓐ Ⓑ Ⓒ Ⓓ	122	Ⓐ Ⓑ Ⓒ Ⓓ	132	Ⓐ Ⓑ Ⓒ Ⓓ	142	Ⓐ Ⓑ Ⓒ Ⓓ
103	Ⓐ Ⓑ Ⓒ Ⓓ	113	Ⓐ Ⓑ Ⓒ Ⓓ	123	Ⓐ Ⓑ Ⓒ Ⓓ	133	Ⓐ Ⓑ Ⓒ Ⓓ	143	Ⓐ Ⓑ Ⓒ Ⓓ
104	Ⓐ Ⓑ Ⓒ Ⓓ	114	Ⓐ Ⓑ Ⓒ Ⓓ	124	Ⓐ Ⓑ Ⓒ Ⓓ	134	Ⓐ Ⓑ Ⓒ Ⓓ	144	Ⓐ Ⓑ Ⓒ Ⓓ
105	Ⓐ Ⓑ Ⓒ Ⓓ	115	Ⓐ Ⓑ Ⓒ Ⓓ	125	Ⓐ Ⓑ Ⓒ Ⓓ	135	Ⓐ Ⓑ Ⓒ Ⓓ	145	Ⓐ Ⓑ Ⓒ Ⓓ
106	Ⓐ Ⓑ Ⓒ Ⓓ	116	Ⓐ Ⓑ Ⓒ Ⓓ	126	Ⓐ Ⓑ Ⓒ Ⓓ	136	Ⓐ Ⓑ Ⓒ Ⓓ	146	Ⓐ Ⓑ Ⓒ Ⓓ
107	Ⓐ Ⓑ Ⓒ Ⓓ	117	Ⓐ Ⓑ Ⓒ Ⓓ	127	Ⓐ Ⓑ Ⓒ Ⓓ	137	Ⓐ Ⓑ Ⓒ Ⓓ	147	Ⓐ Ⓑ Ⓒ Ⓓ
108	Ⓐ Ⓑ Ⓒ Ⓓ	118	Ⓐ Ⓑ Ⓒ Ⓓ	128	Ⓐ Ⓑ Ⓒ Ⓓ	138	Ⓐ Ⓑ Ⓒ Ⓓ	148	Ⓐ Ⓑ Ⓒ Ⓓ
109	Ⓐ Ⓑ Ⓒ Ⓓ	119	Ⓐ Ⓑ Ⓒ Ⓓ	129	Ⓐ Ⓑ Ⓒ Ⓓ	139	Ⓐ Ⓑ Ⓒ Ⓓ	149	Ⓐ Ⓑ Ⓒ Ⓓ
110	Ⓐ Ⓑ Ⓒ Ⓓ	120	Ⓐ Ⓑ Ⓒ Ⓓ	130	Ⓐ Ⓑ Ⓒ Ⓓ	140	Ⓐ Ⓑ Ⓒ Ⓓ	150	Ⓐ Ⓑ Ⓒ Ⓓ

No.	Answer	No.	Answer	No.	Answer	No.	Answer	No.	Answer
151	Ⓐ Ⓑ Ⓒ Ⓓ	161	Ⓐ Ⓑ Ⓒ Ⓓ	171	Ⓐ Ⓑ Ⓒ Ⓓ	181	Ⓐ Ⓑ Ⓒ Ⓓ	191	Ⓐ Ⓑ Ⓒ Ⓓ
152	Ⓐ Ⓑ Ⓒ Ⓓ	162	Ⓐ Ⓑ Ⓒ Ⓓ	172	Ⓐ Ⓑ Ⓒ Ⓓ	182	Ⓐ Ⓑ Ⓒ Ⓓ	192	Ⓐ Ⓑ Ⓒ Ⓓ
153	Ⓐ Ⓑ Ⓒ Ⓓ	163	Ⓐ Ⓑ Ⓒ Ⓓ	173	Ⓐ Ⓑ Ⓒ Ⓓ	183	Ⓐ Ⓑ Ⓒ Ⓓ	193	Ⓐ Ⓑ Ⓒ Ⓓ
154	Ⓐ Ⓑ Ⓒ Ⓓ	164	Ⓐ Ⓑ Ⓒ Ⓓ	174	Ⓐ Ⓑ Ⓒ Ⓓ	184	Ⓐ Ⓑ Ⓒ Ⓓ	194	Ⓐ Ⓑ Ⓒ Ⓓ
155	Ⓐ Ⓑ Ⓒ Ⓓ	165	Ⓐ Ⓑ Ⓒ Ⓓ	175	Ⓐ Ⓑ Ⓒ Ⓓ	185	Ⓐ Ⓑ Ⓒ Ⓓ	195	Ⓐ Ⓑ Ⓒ Ⓓ
156	Ⓐ Ⓑ Ⓒ Ⓓ	166	Ⓐ Ⓑ Ⓒ Ⓓ	176	Ⓐ Ⓑ Ⓒ Ⓓ	186	Ⓐ Ⓑ Ⓒ Ⓓ	196	Ⓐ Ⓑ Ⓒ Ⓓ
157	Ⓐ Ⓑ Ⓒ Ⓓ	167	Ⓐ Ⓑ Ⓒ Ⓓ	177	Ⓐ Ⓑ Ⓒ Ⓓ	187	Ⓐ Ⓑ Ⓒ Ⓓ	197	Ⓐ Ⓑ Ⓒ Ⓓ
158	Ⓐ Ⓑ Ⓒ Ⓓ	168	Ⓐ Ⓑ Ⓒ Ⓓ	178	Ⓐ Ⓑ Ⓒ Ⓓ	188	Ⓐ Ⓑ Ⓒ Ⓓ	198	Ⓐ Ⓑ Ⓒ Ⓓ
159	Ⓐ Ⓑ Ⓒ Ⓓ	169	Ⓐ Ⓑ Ⓒ Ⓓ	179	Ⓐ Ⓑ Ⓒ Ⓓ	189	Ⓐ Ⓑ Ⓒ Ⓓ	199	Ⓐ Ⓑ Ⓒ Ⓓ
160	Ⓐ Ⓑ Ⓒ Ⓓ	170	Ⓐ Ⓑ Ⓒ Ⓓ	180	Ⓐ Ⓑ Ⓒ Ⓓ	190	Ⓐ Ⓑ Ⓒ Ⓓ	200	Ⓐ Ⓑ Ⓒ Ⓓ

Answer Sheet

TOEIC TEST 4

LISTENING SECTION

No.	Answer	No.	Answer	No.	Answer	No.	Answer	No.	Answer	No.	Answer	No.	Answer	No.	Answer	No.	Answer	No.	Answer
1	Ⓐ Ⓑ Ⓒ Ⓓ	11	Ⓐ Ⓑ Ⓒ Ⓓ	21	Ⓐ Ⓑ Ⓒ Ⓓ	31	Ⓐ Ⓑ Ⓒ Ⓓ	41	Ⓐ Ⓑ Ⓒ Ⓓ	51	Ⓐ Ⓑ Ⓒ Ⓓ	61	Ⓐ Ⓑ Ⓒ Ⓓ	71	Ⓐ Ⓑ Ⓒ Ⓓ	81	Ⓐ Ⓑ Ⓒ Ⓓ	91	Ⓐ Ⓑ Ⓒ Ⓓ
2	Ⓐ Ⓑ Ⓒ Ⓓ	12	Ⓐ Ⓑ Ⓒ Ⓓ	22	Ⓐ Ⓑ Ⓒ Ⓓ	32	Ⓐ Ⓑ Ⓒ Ⓓ	42	Ⓐ Ⓑ Ⓒ Ⓓ	52	Ⓐ Ⓑ Ⓒ Ⓓ	62	Ⓐ Ⓑ Ⓒ Ⓓ	72	Ⓐ Ⓑ Ⓒ Ⓓ	82	Ⓐ Ⓑ Ⓒ Ⓓ	92	Ⓐ Ⓑ Ⓒ Ⓓ
3	Ⓐ Ⓑ Ⓒ Ⓓ	13	Ⓐ Ⓑ Ⓒ Ⓓ	23	Ⓐ Ⓑ Ⓒ Ⓓ	33	Ⓐ Ⓑ Ⓒ Ⓓ	43	Ⓐ Ⓑ Ⓒ Ⓓ	53	Ⓐ Ⓑ Ⓒ Ⓓ	63	Ⓐ Ⓑ Ⓒ Ⓓ	73	Ⓐ Ⓑ Ⓒ Ⓓ	83	Ⓐ Ⓑ Ⓒ Ⓓ	93	Ⓐ Ⓑ Ⓒ Ⓓ
4	Ⓐ Ⓑ Ⓒ Ⓓ	14	Ⓐ Ⓑ Ⓒ Ⓓ	24	Ⓐ Ⓑ Ⓒ Ⓓ	34	Ⓐ Ⓑ Ⓒ Ⓓ	44	Ⓐ Ⓑ Ⓒ Ⓓ	54	Ⓐ Ⓑ Ⓒ Ⓓ	64	Ⓐ Ⓑ Ⓒ Ⓓ	74	Ⓐ Ⓑ Ⓒ Ⓓ	84	Ⓐ Ⓑ Ⓒ Ⓓ	94	Ⓐ Ⓑ Ⓒ Ⓓ
5	Ⓐ Ⓑ Ⓒ Ⓓ	15	Ⓐ Ⓑ Ⓒ Ⓓ	25	Ⓐ Ⓑ Ⓒ Ⓓ	35	Ⓐ Ⓑ Ⓒ Ⓓ	45	Ⓐ Ⓑ Ⓒ Ⓓ	55	Ⓐ Ⓑ Ⓒ Ⓓ	65	Ⓐ Ⓑ Ⓒ Ⓓ	75	Ⓐ Ⓑ Ⓒ Ⓓ	85	Ⓐ Ⓑ Ⓒ Ⓓ	95	Ⓐ Ⓑ Ⓒ Ⓓ
6	Ⓐ Ⓑ Ⓒ Ⓓ	16	Ⓐ Ⓑ Ⓒ Ⓓ	26	Ⓐ Ⓑ Ⓒ Ⓓ	36	Ⓐ Ⓑ Ⓒ Ⓓ	46	Ⓐ Ⓑ Ⓒ Ⓓ	56	Ⓐ Ⓑ Ⓒ Ⓓ	66	Ⓐ Ⓑ Ⓒ Ⓓ	76	Ⓐ Ⓑ Ⓒ Ⓓ	86	Ⓐ Ⓑ Ⓒ Ⓓ	96	Ⓐ Ⓑ Ⓒ Ⓓ
7	Ⓐ Ⓑ Ⓒ Ⓓ	17	Ⓐ Ⓑ Ⓒ Ⓓ	27	Ⓐ Ⓑ Ⓒ Ⓓ	37	Ⓐ Ⓑ Ⓒ Ⓓ	47	Ⓐ Ⓑ Ⓒ Ⓓ	57	Ⓐ Ⓑ Ⓒ Ⓓ	67	Ⓐ Ⓑ Ⓒ Ⓓ	77	Ⓐ Ⓑ Ⓒ Ⓓ	87	Ⓐ Ⓑ Ⓒ Ⓓ	97	Ⓐ Ⓑ Ⓒ Ⓓ
8	Ⓐ Ⓑ Ⓒ Ⓓ	18	Ⓐ Ⓑ Ⓒ Ⓓ	28	Ⓐ Ⓑ Ⓒ Ⓓ	38	Ⓐ Ⓑ Ⓒ Ⓓ	48	Ⓐ Ⓑ Ⓒ Ⓓ	58	Ⓐ Ⓑ Ⓒ Ⓓ	68	Ⓐ Ⓑ Ⓒ Ⓓ	78	Ⓐ Ⓑ Ⓒ Ⓓ	88	Ⓐ Ⓑ Ⓒ Ⓓ	98	Ⓐ Ⓑ Ⓒ Ⓓ
9	Ⓐ Ⓑ Ⓒ Ⓓ	19	Ⓐ Ⓑ Ⓒ Ⓓ	29	Ⓐ Ⓑ Ⓒ Ⓓ	39	Ⓐ Ⓑ Ⓒ Ⓓ	49	Ⓐ Ⓑ Ⓒ Ⓓ	59	Ⓐ Ⓑ Ⓒ Ⓓ	69	Ⓐ Ⓑ Ⓒ Ⓓ	79	Ⓐ Ⓑ Ⓒ Ⓓ	89	Ⓐ Ⓑ Ⓒ Ⓓ	99	Ⓐ Ⓑ Ⓒ Ⓓ
10	Ⓐ Ⓑ Ⓒ Ⓓ	20	Ⓐ Ⓑ Ⓒ Ⓓ	30	Ⓐ Ⓑ Ⓒ Ⓓ	40	Ⓐ Ⓑ Ⓒ Ⓓ	50	Ⓐ Ⓑ Ⓒ Ⓓ	60	Ⓐ Ⓑ Ⓒ Ⓓ	70	Ⓐ Ⓑ Ⓒ Ⓓ	80	Ⓐ Ⓑ Ⓒ Ⓓ	90	Ⓐ Ⓑ Ⓒ Ⓓ	100	Ⓐ Ⓑ Ⓒ Ⓓ

READING SECTION

No.	Answer	No.	Answer	No.	Answer	No.	Answer	No.	Answer	No.	Answer	No.	Answer	No.	Answer	No.	Answer	No.	Answer
101	Ⓐ Ⓑ Ⓒ Ⓓ	111	Ⓐ Ⓑ Ⓒ Ⓓ	121	Ⓐ Ⓑ Ⓒ Ⓓ	131	Ⓐ Ⓑ Ⓒ Ⓓ	141	Ⓐ Ⓑ Ⓒ Ⓓ	151	Ⓐ Ⓑ Ⓒ Ⓓ	161	Ⓐ Ⓑ Ⓒ Ⓓ	171	Ⓐ Ⓑ Ⓒ Ⓓ	181	Ⓐ Ⓑ Ⓒ Ⓓ	191	Ⓐ Ⓑ Ⓒ Ⓓ
102	Ⓐ Ⓑ Ⓒ Ⓓ	112	Ⓐ Ⓑ Ⓒ Ⓓ	122	Ⓐ Ⓑ Ⓒ Ⓓ	132	Ⓐ Ⓑ Ⓒ Ⓓ	142	Ⓐ Ⓑ Ⓒ Ⓓ	152	Ⓐ Ⓑ Ⓒ Ⓓ	162	Ⓐ Ⓑ Ⓒ Ⓓ	172	Ⓐ Ⓑ Ⓒ Ⓓ	182	Ⓐ Ⓑ Ⓒ Ⓓ	192	Ⓐ Ⓑ Ⓒ Ⓓ
103	Ⓐ Ⓑ Ⓒ Ⓓ	113	Ⓐ Ⓑ Ⓒ Ⓓ	123	Ⓐ Ⓑ Ⓒ Ⓓ	133	Ⓐ Ⓑ Ⓒ Ⓓ	143	Ⓐ Ⓑ Ⓒ Ⓓ	153	Ⓐ Ⓑ Ⓒ Ⓓ	163	Ⓐ Ⓑ Ⓒ Ⓓ	173	Ⓐ Ⓑ Ⓒ Ⓓ	183	Ⓐ Ⓑ Ⓒ Ⓓ	193	Ⓐ Ⓑ Ⓒ Ⓓ
104	Ⓐ Ⓑ Ⓒ Ⓓ	114	Ⓐ Ⓑ Ⓒ Ⓓ	124	Ⓐ Ⓑ Ⓒ Ⓓ	134	Ⓐ Ⓑ Ⓒ Ⓓ	144	Ⓐ Ⓑ Ⓒ Ⓓ	154	Ⓐ Ⓑ Ⓒ Ⓓ	164	Ⓐ Ⓑ Ⓒ Ⓓ	174	Ⓐ Ⓑ Ⓒ Ⓓ	184	Ⓐ Ⓑ Ⓒ Ⓓ	194	Ⓐ Ⓑ Ⓒ Ⓓ
105	Ⓐ Ⓑ Ⓒ Ⓓ	115	Ⓐ Ⓑ Ⓒ Ⓓ	125	Ⓐ Ⓑ Ⓒ Ⓓ	135	Ⓐ Ⓑ Ⓒ Ⓓ	145	Ⓐ Ⓑ Ⓒ Ⓓ	155	Ⓐ Ⓑ Ⓒ Ⓓ	165	Ⓐ Ⓑ Ⓒ Ⓓ	175	Ⓐ Ⓑ Ⓒ Ⓓ	185	Ⓐ Ⓑ Ⓒ Ⓓ	195	Ⓐ Ⓑ Ⓒ Ⓓ
106	Ⓐ Ⓑ Ⓒ Ⓓ	116	Ⓐ Ⓑ Ⓒ Ⓓ	126	Ⓐ Ⓑ Ⓒ Ⓓ	136	Ⓐ Ⓑ Ⓒ Ⓓ	146	Ⓐ Ⓑ Ⓒ Ⓓ	156	Ⓐ Ⓑ Ⓒ Ⓓ	166	Ⓐ Ⓑ Ⓒ Ⓓ	176	Ⓐ Ⓑ Ⓒ Ⓓ	186	Ⓐ Ⓑ Ⓒ Ⓓ	196	Ⓐ Ⓑ Ⓒ Ⓓ
107	Ⓐ Ⓑ Ⓒ Ⓓ	117	Ⓐ Ⓑ Ⓒ Ⓓ	127	Ⓐ Ⓑ Ⓒ Ⓓ	137	Ⓐ Ⓑ Ⓒ Ⓓ	147	Ⓐ Ⓑ Ⓒ Ⓓ	157	Ⓐ Ⓑ Ⓒ Ⓓ	167	Ⓐ Ⓑ Ⓒ Ⓓ	177	Ⓐ Ⓑ Ⓒ Ⓓ	187	Ⓐ Ⓑ Ⓒ Ⓓ	197	Ⓐ Ⓑ Ⓒ Ⓓ
108	Ⓐ Ⓑ Ⓒ Ⓓ	118	Ⓐ Ⓑ Ⓒ Ⓓ	128	Ⓐ Ⓑ Ⓒ Ⓓ	138	Ⓐ Ⓑ Ⓒ Ⓓ	148	Ⓐ Ⓑ Ⓒ Ⓓ	158	Ⓐ Ⓑ Ⓒ Ⓓ	168	Ⓐ Ⓑ Ⓒ Ⓓ	178	Ⓐ Ⓑ Ⓒ Ⓓ	188	Ⓐ Ⓑ Ⓒ Ⓓ	198	Ⓐ Ⓑ Ⓒ Ⓓ
109	Ⓐ Ⓑ Ⓒ Ⓓ	119	Ⓐ Ⓑ Ⓒ Ⓓ	129	Ⓐ Ⓑ Ⓒ Ⓓ	139	Ⓐ Ⓑ Ⓒ Ⓓ	149	Ⓐ Ⓑ Ⓒ Ⓓ	159	Ⓐ Ⓑ Ⓒ Ⓓ	169	Ⓐ Ⓑ Ⓒ Ⓓ	179	Ⓐ Ⓑ Ⓒ Ⓓ	189	Ⓐ Ⓑ Ⓒ Ⓓ	199	Ⓐ Ⓑ Ⓒ Ⓓ
110	Ⓐ Ⓑ Ⓒ Ⓓ	120	Ⓐ Ⓑ Ⓒ Ⓓ	130	Ⓐ Ⓑ Ⓒ Ⓓ	140	Ⓐ Ⓑ Ⓒ Ⓓ	150	Ⓐ Ⓑ Ⓒ Ⓓ	160	Ⓐ Ⓑ Ⓒ Ⓓ	170	Ⓐ Ⓑ Ⓒ Ⓓ	180	Ⓐ Ⓑ Ⓒ Ⓓ	190	Ⓐ Ⓑ Ⓒ Ⓓ	200	Ⓐ Ⓑ Ⓒ Ⓓ

Answer Sheet

TOEIC TEST 5

LISTENING SECTION

1 Ⓐ Ⓑ Ⓒ Ⓓ
2 Ⓐ Ⓑ Ⓒ Ⓓ
3 Ⓐ Ⓑ Ⓒ Ⓓ
4 Ⓐ Ⓑ Ⓒ Ⓓ
5 Ⓐ Ⓑ Ⓒ Ⓓ
6 Ⓐ Ⓑ Ⓒ Ⓓ
7 Ⓐ Ⓑ Ⓒ Ⓓ
8 Ⓐ Ⓑ Ⓒ Ⓓ
9 Ⓐ Ⓑ Ⓒ Ⓓ
10 Ⓐ Ⓑ Ⓒ Ⓓ
11 Ⓐ Ⓑ Ⓒ Ⓓ
12 Ⓐ Ⓑ Ⓒ Ⓓ
13 Ⓐ Ⓑ Ⓒ Ⓓ
14 Ⓐ Ⓑ Ⓒ Ⓓ
15 Ⓐ Ⓑ Ⓒ Ⓓ
16 Ⓐ Ⓑ Ⓒ Ⓓ
17 Ⓐ Ⓑ Ⓒ Ⓓ
18 Ⓐ Ⓑ Ⓒ Ⓓ
19 Ⓐ Ⓑ Ⓒ Ⓓ
20 Ⓐ Ⓑ Ⓒ Ⓓ
21 Ⓐ Ⓑ Ⓒ Ⓓ
22 Ⓐ Ⓑ Ⓒ Ⓓ
23 Ⓐ Ⓑ Ⓒ Ⓓ
24 Ⓐ Ⓑ Ⓒ Ⓓ
25 Ⓐ Ⓑ Ⓒ Ⓓ
26 Ⓐ Ⓑ Ⓒ Ⓓ
27 Ⓐ Ⓑ Ⓒ Ⓓ
28 Ⓐ Ⓑ Ⓒ Ⓓ
29 Ⓐ Ⓑ Ⓒ Ⓓ
30 Ⓐ Ⓑ Ⓒ Ⓓ
31 Ⓐ Ⓑ Ⓒ Ⓓ
32 Ⓐ Ⓑ Ⓒ Ⓓ
33 Ⓐ Ⓑ Ⓒ Ⓓ
34 Ⓐ Ⓑ Ⓒ Ⓓ
35 Ⓐ Ⓑ Ⓒ Ⓓ
36 Ⓐ Ⓑ Ⓒ Ⓓ
37 Ⓐ Ⓑ Ⓒ Ⓓ
38 Ⓐ Ⓑ Ⓒ Ⓓ
39 Ⓐ Ⓑ Ⓒ Ⓓ
40 Ⓐ Ⓑ Ⓒ Ⓓ
41 Ⓐ Ⓑ Ⓒ Ⓓ
42 Ⓐ Ⓑ Ⓒ Ⓓ
43 Ⓐ Ⓑ Ⓒ Ⓓ
44 Ⓐ Ⓑ Ⓒ Ⓓ
45 Ⓐ Ⓑ Ⓒ Ⓓ
46 Ⓐ Ⓑ Ⓒ Ⓓ
47 Ⓐ Ⓑ Ⓒ Ⓓ
48 Ⓐ Ⓑ Ⓒ Ⓓ
49 Ⓐ Ⓑ Ⓒ Ⓓ
50 Ⓐ Ⓑ Ⓒ Ⓓ
51 Ⓐ Ⓑ Ⓒ Ⓓ
52 Ⓐ Ⓑ Ⓒ Ⓓ
53 Ⓐ Ⓑ Ⓒ Ⓓ
54 Ⓐ Ⓑ Ⓒ Ⓓ
55 Ⓐ Ⓑ Ⓒ Ⓓ
56 Ⓐ Ⓑ Ⓒ Ⓓ
57 Ⓐ Ⓑ Ⓒ Ⓓ
58 Ⓐ Ⓑ Ⓒ Ⓓ
59 Ⓐ Ⓑ Ⓒ Ⓓ
60 Ⓐ Ⓑ Ⓒ Ⓓ
61 Ⓐ Ⓑ Ⓒ Ⓓ
62 Ⓐ Ⓑ Ⓒ Ⓓ
63 Ⓐ Ⓑ Ⓒ Ⓓ
64 Ⓐ Ⓑ Ⓒ Ⓓ
65 Ⓐ Ⓑ Ⓒ Ⓓ
66 Ⓐ Ⓑ Ⓒ Ⓓ
67 Ⓐ Ⓑ Ⓒ Ⓓ
68 Ⓐ Ⓑ Ⓒ Ⓓ
69 Ⓐ Ⓑ Ⓒ Ⓓ
70 Ⓐ Ⓑ Ⓒ Ⓓ
71 Ⓐ Ⓑ Ⓒ Ⓓ
72 Ⓐ Ⓑ Ⓒ Ⓓ
73 Ⓐ Ⓑ Ⓒ Ⓓ
74 Ⓐ Ⓑ Ⓒ Ⓓ
75 Ⓐ Ⓑ Ⓒ Ⓓ
76 Ⓐ Ⓑ Ⓒ Ⓓ
77 Ⓐ Ⓑ Ⓒ Ⓓ
78 Ⓐ Ⓑ Ⓒ Ⓓ
79 Ⓐ Ⓑ Ⓒ Ⓓ
80 Ⓐ Ⓑ Ⓒ Ⓓ
81 Ⓐ Ⓑ Ⓒ Ⓓ
82 Ⓐ Ⓑ Ⓒ Ⓓ
83 Ⓐ Ⓑ Ⓒ Ⓓ
84 Ⓐ Ⓑ Ⓒ Ⓓ
85 Ⓐ Ⓑ Ⓒ Ⓓ
86 Ⓐ Ⓑ Ⓒ Ⓓ
87 Ⓐ Ⓑ Ⓒ Ⓓ
88 Ⓐ Ⓑ Ⓒ Ⓓ
89 Ⓐ Ⓑ Ⓒ Ⓓ
90 Ⓐ Ⓑ Ⓒ Ⓓ
91 Ⓐ Ⓑ Ⓒ Ⓓ
92 Ⓐ Ⓑ Ⓒ Ⓓ
93 Ⓐ Ⓑ Ⓒ Ⓓ
94 Ⓐ Ⓑ Ⓒ Ⓓ
95 Ⓐ Ⓑ Ⓒ Ⓓ
96 Ⓐ Ⓑ Ⓒ Ⓓ
97 Ⓐ Ⓑ Ⓒ Ⓓ
98 Ⓐ Ⓑ Ⓒ Ⓓ
99 Ⓐ Ⓑ Ⓒ Ⓓ
100 Ⓐ Ⓑ Ⓒ Ⓓ

READING SECTION

101 Ⓐ Ⓑ Ⓒ Ⓓ
102 Ⓐ Ⓑ Ⓒ Ⓓ
103 Ⓐ Ⓑ Ⓒ Ⓓ
104 Ⓐ Ⓑ Ⓒ Ⓓ
105 Ⓐ Ⓑ Ⓒ Ⓓ
106 Ⓐ Ⓑ Ⓒ Ⓓ
107 Ⓐ Ⓑ Ⓒ Ⓓ
108 Ⓐ Ⓑ Ⓒ Ⓓ
109 Ⓐ Ⓑ Ⓒ Ⓓ
110 Ⓐ Ⓑ Ⓒ Ⓓ
111 Ⓐ Ⓑ Ⓒ Ⓓ
112 Ⓐ Ⓑ Ⓒ Ⓓ
113 Ⓐ Ⓑ Ⓒ Ⓓ
114 Ⓐ Ⓑ Ⓒ Ⓓ
115 Ⓐ Ⓑ Ⓒ Ⓓ
116 Ⓐ Ⓑ Ⓒ Ⓓ
117 Ⓐ Ⓑ Ⓒ Ⓓ
118 Ⓐ Ⓑ Ⓒ Ⓓ
119 Ⓐ Ⓑ Ⓒ Ⓓ
120 Ⓐ Ⓑ Ⓒ Ⓓ
121 Ⓐ Ⓑ Ⓒ Ⓓ
122 Ⓐ Ⓑ Ⓒ Ⓓ
123 Ⓐ Ⓑ Ⓒ Ⓓ
124 Ⓐ Ⓑ Ⓒ Ⓓ
125 Ⓐ Ⓑ Ⓒ Ⓓ
126 Ⓐ Ⓑ Ⓒ Ⓓ
127 Ⓐ Ⓑ Ⓒ Ⓓ
128 Ⓐ Ⓑ Ⓒ Ⓓ
129 Ⓐ Ⓑ Ⓒ Ⓓ
130 Ⓐ Ⓑ Ⓒ Ⓓ
131 Ⓐ Ⓑ Ⓒ Ⓓ
132 Ⓐ Ⓑ Ⓒ Ⓓ
133 Ⓐ Ⓑ Ⓒ Ⓓ
134 Ⓐ Ⓑ Ⓒ Ⓓ
135 Ⓐ Ⓑ Ⓒ Ⓓ
136 Ⓐ Ⓑ Ⓒ Ⓓ
137 Ⓐ Ⓑ Ⓒ Ⓓ
138 Ⓐ Ⓑ Ⓒ Ⓓ
139 Ⓐ Ⓑ Ⓒ Ⓓ
140 Ⓐ Ⓑ Ⓒ Ⓓ
141 Ⓐ Ⓑ Ⓒ Ⓓ
142 Ⓐ Ⓑ Ⓒ Ⓓ
143 Ⓐ Ⓑ Ⓒ Ⓓ
144 Ⓐ Ⓑ Ⓒ Ⓓ
145 Ⓐ Ⓑ Ⓒ Ⓓ
146 Ⓐ Ⓑ Ⓒ Ⓓ
147 Ⓐ Ⓑ Ⓒ Ⓓ
148 Ⓐ Ⓑ Ⓒ Ⓓ
149 Ⓐ Ⓑ Ⓒ Ⓓ
150 Ⓐ Ⓑ Ⓒ Ⓓ
151 Ⓐ Ⓑ Ⓒ Ⓓ
152 Ⓐ Ⓑ Ⓒ Ⓓ
153 Ⓐ Ⓑ Ⓒ Ⓓ
154 Ⓐ Ⓑ Ⓒ Ⓓ
155 Ⓐ Ⓑ Ⓒ Ⓓ
156 Ⓐ Ⓑ Ⓒ Ⓓ
157 Ⓐ Ⓑ Ⓒ Ⓓ
158 Ⓐ Ⓑ Ⓒ Ⓓ
159 Ⓐ Ⓑ Ⓒ Ⓓ
160 Ⓐ Ⓑ Ⓒ Ⓓ
161 Ⓐ Ⓑ Ⓒ Ⓓ
162 Ⓐ Ⓑ Ⓒ Ⓓ
163 Ⓐ Ⓑ Ⓒ Ⓓ
164 Ⓐ Ⓑ Ⓒ Ⓓ
165 Ⓐ Ⓑ Ⓒ Ⓓ
166 Ⓐ Ⓑ Ⓒ Ⓓ
167 Ⓐ Ⓑ Ⓒ Ⓓ
168 Ⓐ Ⓑ Ⓒ Ⓓ
169 Ⓐ Ⓑ Ⓒ Ⓓ
170 Ⓐ Ⓑ Ⓒ Ⓓ
171 Ⓐ Ⓑ Ⓒ Ⓓ
172 Ⓐ Ⓑ Ⓒ Ⓓ
173 Ⓐ Ⓑ Ⓒ Ⓓ
174 Ⓐ Ⓑ Ⓒ Ⓓ
175 Ⓐ Ⓑ Ⓒ Ⓓ
176 Ⓐ Ⓑ Ⓒ Ⓓ
177 Ⓐ Ⓑ Ⓒ Ⓓ
178 Ⓐ Ⓑ Ⓒ Ⓓ
179 Ⓐ Ⓑ Ⓒ Ⓓ
180 Ⓐ Ⓑ Ⓒ Ⓓ
181 Ⓐ Ⓑ Ⓒ Ⓓ
182 Ⓐ Ⓑ Ⓒ Ⓓ
183 Ⓐ Ⓑ Ⓒ Ⓓ
184 Ⓐ Ⓑ Ⓒ Ⓓ
185 Ⓐ Ⓑ Ⓒ Ⓓ
186 Ⓐ Ⓑ Ⓒ Ⓓ
187 Ⓐ Ⓑ Ⓒ Ⓓ
188 Ⓐ Ⓑ Ⓒ Ⓓ
189 Ⓐ Ⓑ Ⓒ Ⓓ
190 Ⓐ Ⓑ Ⓒ Ⓓ
191 Ⓐ Ⓑ Ⓒ Ⓓ
192 Ⓐ Ⓑ Ⓒ Ⓓ
193 Ⓐ Ⓑ Ⓒ Ⓓ
194 Ⓐ Ⓑ Ⓒ Ⓓ
195 Ⓐ Ⓑ Ⓒ Ⓓ
196 Ⓐ Ⓑ Ⓒ Ⓓ
197 Ⓐ Ⓑ Ⓒ Ⓓ
198 Ⓐ Ⓑ Ⓒ Ⓓ
199 Ⓐ Ⓑ Ⓒ Ⓓ
200 Ⓐ Ⓑ Ⓒ Ⓓ

Answer Key

Actual Test 1

1 (B)	2 (A)	3 (C)	4 (C)	5 (D)
6 (D)	7 (B)	8 (A)	9 (A)	10 (B)
11 (C)	12 (B)	13 (C)	14 (A)	15 (B)
16 (C)	17 (C)	18 (B)	19 (A)	20 (B)
21 (A)	22 (C)	23 (B)	24 (B)	25 (A)
26 (B)	27 (C)	28 (C)	29 (A)	30 (C)
31 (A)	32 (C)	33 (A)	34 (A)	35 (B)
36 (D)	37 (C)	38 (D)	39 (D)	40 (A)
41 (C)	42 (A)	43 (D)	44 (B)	45 (B)
46 (D)	47 (D)	48 (A)	49 (D)	50 (D)
51 (C)	52 (A)	53 (C)	54 (B)	55 (B)
56 (B)	57 (D)	58 (A)	59 (A)	60 (C)
61 (D)	62 (B)	63 (B)	64 (C)	65 (A)
66 (D)	67 (C)	68 (C)	69 (B)	70 (A)
71 (A)	72 (A)	73 (C)	74 (C)	75 (D)
76 (D)	77 (D)	78 (A)	79 (B)	80 (B)
81 (C)	82 (B)	83 (A)	84 (D)	85 (C)
86 (D)	87 (B)	88 (A)	89 (D)	90 (A)
91 (C)	92 (B)	93 (D)	94 (C)	95 (C)
96 (D)	97 (B)	98 (A)	99 (D)	100 (D)

101 (D)	102 (B)	103 (A)	104 (A)	105 (D)
106 (C)	107 (B)	108 (A)	109 (D)	110 (D)
111 (A)	112 (A)	113 (C)	114 (B)	115 (A)
116 (B)	117 (C)	118 (B)	119 (D)	120 (C)
121 (A)	122 (B)	123 (B)	124 (C)	125 (A)
126 (D)	127 (B)	128 (C)	129 (C)	130 (D)
131 (D)	132 (A)	133 (D)	134 (B)	135 (C)
136 (C)	137 (B)	138 (A)	139 (B)	140 (C)
141 (D)	142 (B)	143 (B)	144 (D)	145 (B)
146 (A)	147 (A)	148 (B)	149 (B)	150 (D)
151 (C)	152 (D)	153 (D)	154 (D)	155 (D)
156 (B)	157 (A)	158 (C)	159 (A)	160 (C)
161 (D)	162 (B)	163 (C)	164 (B)	165 (B)
166 (C)	167 (B)	168 (D)	169 (D)	170 (A)
171 (B)	172 (D)	173 (C)	174 (D)	175 (B)
176 (A)	177 (C)	178 (C)	179 (D)	180 (B)
181 (D)	182 (B)	183 (D)	184 (A)	185 (C)
186 (A)	187 (D)	188 (C)	189 (B)	190 (C)
191 (D)	192 (B)	193 (A)	194 (C)	195 (C)
196 (C)	197 (B)	198 (C)	199 (A)	200 (D)

Actual Test 2

1 (B)	2 (C)	3 (B)	4 (A)	5 (C)
6 (D)	7 (B)	8 (C)	9 (A)	10 (C)
11 (B)	12 (A)	13 (A)	14 (C)	15 (B)
16 (A)	17 (C)	18 (B)	19 (A)	20 (C)
21 (A)	22 (C)	23 (C)	24 (B)	25 (B)
26 (A)	27 (C)	28 (B)	29 (C)	30 (B)
31 (C)	32 (C)	33 (B)	34 (B)	35 (C)
36 (A)	37 (D)	38 (D)	39 (D)	40 (B)
41 (C)	42 (A)	43 (C)	44 (D)	45 (C)
46 (A)	47 (C)	48 (A)	49 (B)	50 (B)
51 (D)	52 (A)	53 (C)	54 (D)	55 (C)
56 (C)	57 (A)	58 (C)	59 (D)	60 (A)
61 (B)	62 (A)	63 (D)	64 (A)	65 (B)
66 (D)	67 (A)	68 (D)	69 (C)	70 (A)
71 (D)	72 (C)	73 (C)	74 (C)	75 (D)
76 (B)	77 (A)	78 (C)	79 (A)	80 (D)
81 (A)	82 (B)	83 (B)	84 (B)	85 (D)
86 (A)	87 (B)	88 (D)	89 (A)	90 (B)
91 (B)	92 (D)	93 (A)	94 (A)	95 (B)
96 (C)	97 (B)	98 (A)	99 (B)	100 (C)

101 (D)	102 (D)	103 (B)	104 (C)	105 (A)
106 (A)	107 (C)	108 (A)	109 (A)	110 (B)
111 (D)	112 (A)	113 (A)	114 (B)	115 (C)
116 (A)	117 (D)	118 (D)	119 (B)	120 (B)
121 (C)	122 (A)	123 (B)	124 (C)	125 (B)
126 (A)	127 (C)	128 (A)	129 (C)	130 (C)
131 (A)	132 (C)	133 (A)	134 (B)	135 (B)
136 (B)	137 (A)	138 (D)	139 (B)	140 (C)
141 (C)	142 (D)	143 (B)	144 (C)	145 (A)
146 (D)	147 (B)	148 (D)	149 (A)	150 (D)
151 (A)	152 (B)	153 (D)	154 (D)	155 (B)
156 (C)	157 (C)	158 (C)	159 (B)	160 (B)
161 (D)	162 (B)	163 (B)	164 (B)	165 (A)
166 (C)	167 (B)	168 (D)	169 (C)	170 (B)
171 (D)	172 (A)	173 (C)	174 (C)	175 (B)
176 (A)	177 (D)	178 (C)	179 (D)	180 (D)
181 (B)	182 (A)	183 (C)	184 (D)	185 (B)
186 (B)	187 (C)	188 (C)	189 (B)	190 (D)
191 (D)	192 (B)	193 (D)	194 (C)	195 (C)
196 (D)	197 (D)	198 (C)	199 (A)	200 (C)

Actual Test 3

01 (A)	02 (B)	03 (C)	04 (C)	05 (B)
06 (D)	07 (B)	08 (C)	09 (A)	10 (B)
11 (B)	12 (B)	13 (A)	14 (C)	15 (B)
16 (A)	17 (B)	18 (A)	19 (C)	20 (A)
21 (C)	22 (B)	23 (C)	24 (A)	25 (B)
26 (A)	27 (B)	28 (B)	29 (A)	30 (C)
31 (C)	32 (B)	33 (C)	34 (D)	35 (C)
36 (B)	37 (A)	38 (C)	39 (A)	40 (B)
41 (A)	42 (B)	43 (A)	44 (A)	45 (D)
46 (A)	47 (C)	48 (A)	49 (B)	50 (B)
51 (A)	52 (B)	53 (D)	54 (D)	55 (A)
56 (B)	57 (C)	58 (A)	59 (B)	60 (D)
61 (C)	62 (B)	63 (B)	64 (C)	65 (A)
66 (C)	67 (B)	68 (B)	69 (D)	70 (C)
71 (B)	72 (A)	73 (D)	74 (C)	75 (C)
76 (B)	77 (A)	78 (C)	79 (A)	80 (A)
81 (B)	82 (B)	83 (A)	84 (B)	85 (A)
86 (A)	87 (A)	88 (B)	89 (D)	90 (A)
91 (A)	92 (C)	93 (A)	94 (D)	95 (C)
96 (D)	97 (D)	98 (A)	99 (C)	100 (C)

101 (C)	102 (D)	103 (A)	104 (D)	105 (A)
106 (D)	107 (B)	108 (A)	109 (A)	110 (C)
111 (D)	112 (C)	113 (D)	114 (B)	115 (C)
116 (B)	117 (D)	118 (B)	119 (A)	120 (C)
121 (B)	122 (A)	123 (C)	124 (D)	125 (D)
126 (C)	127 (A)	128 (A)	129 (C)	130 (B)
131 (B)	132 (C)	133 (C)	134 (A)	135 (D)
136 (A)	137 (C)	138 (A)	139 (D)	140 (B)
141 (A)	142 (C)	143 (D)	144 (C)	145 (D)
146 (C)	147 (B)	148 (C)	149 (A)	150 (C)
151 (A)	152 (B)	153 (C)	154 (A)	155 (B)
156 (C)	157 (B)	158 (A)	159 (D)	160 (C)
161 (A)	162 (A)	163 (B)	164 (D)	165 (B)
166 (B)	167 (C)	168 (A)	169 (B)	170 (B)
171 (D)	172 (B)	173 (A)	174 (C)	175 (B)
176 (B)	177 (A)	178 (B)	179 (B)	180 (C)
181 (C)	182 (A)	183 (B)	184 (A)	185 (D)
186 (C)	187 (B)	188 (C)	189 (C)	190 (D)
191 (B)	192 (D)	193 (B)	194 (B)	195 (A)
196 (C)	197 (C)	198 (D)	199 (A)	200 (A)

Actual Test 4

01 (A)	02 (C)	03 (D)	04 (D)	05 (D)
06 (A)	07 (B)	08 (B)	09 (A)	10 (C)
11 (A)	12 (A)	13 (B)	14 (A)	15 (A)
16 (B)	17 (C)	18 (B)	19 (A)	20 (C)
21 (C)	22 (B)	23 (B)	24 (A)	25 (A)
26 (C)	27 (C)	28 (B)	29 (A)	30 (B)
31 (B)	32 (C)	33 (A)	34 (C)	35 (D)
36 (B)	37 (A)	38 (B)	39 (A)	40 (D)
41 (D)	42 (B)	43 (A)	44 (D)	45 (D)
46 (C)	47 (C)	48 (B)	49 (D)	50 (D)
51 (A)	52 (B)	53 (B)	54 (B)	55 (D)
56 (A)	57 (B)	58 (A)	59 (C)	60 (A)
61 (C)	62 (D)	63 (B)	64 (D)	65 (B)
66 (B)	67 (A)	68 (C)	69 (D)	70 (D)
71 (A)	72 (C)	73 (C)	74 (A)	75 (C)
76 (B)	77 (A)	78 (D)	79 (B)	80 (B)
81 (D)	82 (C)	83 (D)	84 (A)	85 (C)
86 (A)	87 (B)	88 (B)	89 (A)	90 (A)
91 (C)	92 (A)	93 (A)	94 (D)	95 (B)
96 (B)	97 (A)	98 (C)	99 (B)	100 (C)

101 (C)	102 (A)	103 (A)	104 (B)	105 (A)
106 (D)	107 (C)	108 (D)	109 (D)	110 (B)
111 (D)	112 (B)	113 (C)	114 (C)	115 (A)
116 (C)	117 (B)	118 (A)	119 (B)	120 (B)
121 (D)	122 (C)	123 (D)	124 (C)	125 (C)
126 (D)	127 (C)	128 (B)	129 (C)	130 (A)
131 (D)	132 (C)	133 (A)	134 (B)	135 (D)
136 (C)	137 (B)	138 (D)	139 (D)	140 (A)
141 (C)	142 (C)	143 (C)	144 (B)	145 (D)
146 (C)	147 (B)	148 (C)	149 (A)	150 (C)
151 (A)	152 (B)	153 (A)	154 (B)	155 (B)
156 (D)	157 (A)	158 (D)	159 (B)	160 (A)
161 (C)	162 (C)	163 (A)	164 (A)	165 (B)
166 (D)	167 (A)	168 (D)	169 (B)	170 (D)
171 (B)	172 (D)	173 (A)	174 (C)	175 (C)
176 (B)	177 (A)	178 (C)	179 (A)	180 (C)
181 (A)	182 (B)	183 (A)	184 (B)	185 (C)
186 (D)	187 (C)	188 (D)	189 (A)	190 (C)
191 (A)	192 (B)	193 (A)	194 (D)	195 (C)
196 (D)	197 (C)	198 (A)	199 (A)	200 (C)

Actual Test 5

01 (B)	02 (B)	03 (C)	04 (B)	05 (D)
06 (C)	07 (B)	08 (C)	09 (A)	10 (A)
11 (C)	12 (A)	13 (A)	14 (C)	15 (B)
16 (C)	17 (B)	18 (B)	19 (C)	20 (A)
21 (C)	22 (C)	23 (A)	24 (B)	25 (A)
26 (A)	27 (C)	28 (B)	29 (C)	30 (A)
31 (B)	32 (D)	33 (A)	34 (C)	35 (A)
36 (B)	37 (D)	38 (C)	39 (B)	40 (D)
41 (C)	42 (D)	43 (A)	44 (C)	45 (D)
46 (C)	47 (B)	48 (A)	49 (D)	50 (A)
51 (B)	52 (A)	53 (B)	54 (A)	55 (C)
56 (C)	57 (A)	58 (B)	59 (C)	60 (D)
61 (A)	62 (D)	63 (D)	64 (B)	65 (A)
66 (A)	67 (D)	68 (A)	69 (D)	70 (A)
71 (C)	72 (B)	73 (D)	74 (B)	75 (A)
76 (D)	77 (C)	78 (A)	79 (D)	80 (B)
81 (D)	82 (C)	83 (D)	84 (A)	85 (A)
86 (C)	87 (B)	88 (D)	89 (A)	90 (D)
91 (A)	92 (D)	93 (B)	94 (C)	95 (B)
96 (B)	97 (B)	98 (A)	99 (B)	100 (D)

101 (C)	102 (D)	103 (C)	104 (B)	105 (D)
106 (D)	107 (D)	108 (A)	109 (C)	110 (C)
111 (A)	112 (C)	113 (C)	114 (D)	115 (B)
116 (B)	117 (C)	118 (B)	119 (A)	120 (B)
121 (B)	122 (D)	123 (C)	124 (B)	125 (C)
126 (B)	127 (B)	128 (B)	129 (D)	130 (D)
131 (B)	132 (D)	133 (B)	134 (A)	135 (A)
136 (B)	137 (B)	138 (D)	139 (D)	140 (D)
141 (C)	142 (B)	143 (C)	144 (A)	145 (A)
146 (D)	147 (D)	148 (A)	149 (D)	150 (A)
151 (A)	152 (B)	153 (D)	154 (C)	155 (C)
156 (B)	157 (C)	158 (B)	159 (D)	160 (C)
161 (A)	162 (A)	163 (D)	164 (A)	165 (C)
166 (A)	167 (B)	168 (C)	169 (B)	170 (D)
171 (D)	172 (C)	173 (A)	174 (D)	175 (C)
176 (B)	177 (C)	178 (D)	179 (B)	180 (C)
181 (D)	182 (B)	183 (A)	184 (B)	185 (C)
186 (D)	187 (A)	188 (B)	189 (C)	190 (B)
191 (C)	192 (D)	193 (D)	194 (B)	195 (C)
196 (A)	197 (D)	198 (B)	199 (B)	200 (A)

分數換算表

本分數換算表是為了換算教材中收錄之五回份量的測驗分數而製成。完成各回測驗後，試著預估看看自己的預期分數區間吧！

LISTENING RAW SCORE（答對題數）	LISTENING SCALED SCORE（換算分數）
96-100	475-495
91-95	435-495
86-90	405-475
81-85	370-450
76-80	345-420
71-75	320-390
66-70	290-360
61-65	265-335
56-60	235-310
51-55	210-280
46-50	180-255
41-45	155-230
36-40	125-205
31-35	105-175
26-30	85-145
21-25	60-115
16-20	30-90
11-15	5-70
6-10	5-60
1-5	5-50
0	5

READING RAW SCORE（答對題數）	READING SCALED SCORE（換算分數）
96-100	460-495
91-95	425-490
86-90	395-465
81-85	370-440
76-80	335-415
71-75	310-390
66-70	280-365
61-65	250-335
56-60	220-305
51-55	195-270
46-50	165-240
41-45	140-215
36-40	115-180
31-35	95-145
26-30	75-120
21-25	60-95
16-20	45-75
11-15	30-55
6-10	10-40
1-5	5-30
0	5

註：上述表格僅供參考，實際計分以官方分數為準。